~~~~~~~~~~~~~~~~~~~~~~~~~~

ALMOST HUMAN

⌁ THE SECOND TRILOGY ⌁

VOLUME 3

DESTINED FOR DIVINITY

BY

MELANIE NOWAK

~~~~~~~~~~~~~~~~~~~~~~~~~~

*ALMOST HUMAN - The First Series was originally published as a trilogy of novels, now broken into novellas as an alternate format. The story is told in a serial succession - not stand-alone books. Each novella is meant to be read in order, as the story unfolds chronologically. Each series will be contained enough to be read on its own, with a certain amount of main storyline closure with the last novella, but there will also be some story-ties leading from one series into the next.

If you enjoy this book, please take a moment to leave a review online, on your favorite book review website! Questions and comments can be directed to: WoodWitchDame@aol.com

You can join author/reader discussions about the series, and get updates on upcoming book releases for this series on the author's web site at:

www.MelanieNowak.com

Copyright 2015, 2018
Melanie Nowak, WoodWitchDame Publications
Cover Artwork, Book formatting/Editing: Melanie Nowak

DESTINED FOR DIVINITY
ISBN: 1-944303-00-6
ISBN-13: 978-1944303006

~~~~~~~~~~~~~~~~~~~~~~~~~~~~~~~~~~~

A Special Thanks to

~~~

My Mom & Step-Dad, Adele and David Weitzel
who have always given their love and support

~~~

My dearly departed brother, John,
who is loved, and missed each day

~~~

And to my wonderful and loving husband,
Scott,
and our sons, William & Eric,

who had patience when I was obsessed with writing,
gave me never-ending confidence and inspiration,
and for whom I am forever grateful
and blessed to have in my life.
I love you dearly.

~~~~~~~~~~~~~~~~~~~~~~~~~~~~~~~~~~~

ALMOST HUMAN was originally published as a series of novels, now also broken into novellas as an alternate format. These are not stand-alone books - they are meant to be read in order, as the story unfolds chronologically.

ALMOST HUMAN ∽ THE SECOND TRILOGY

VOLUME 3 ∽ DESTINED FOR DIVINITY

Contents

Part 3: Vicious Survival

Part 4: Divining Destiny

Part 1

Home of the Bloodthirsty

Chapter 1 - Welcome to paradise

Sindy

Kana Susamiş Icin Ev
Montauk, Long Island, New York
An evening in late May

The scent of blood filled the room, tantalizingly sharp, masculine and beckoning. Sindy swiped her long black hair back behind her shoulder as she stood over the United One, watching as the vampire greedily drank all the blood that could be pulled from their human victim, as quickly as the small punctures in the man's neck would allow. Sindy had vetoed the vampire's plea to inflict a larger wound. It would be too difficult for Sindy to monitor, and too risky for the victim. The guy needed to live through this drink, or they would all regret it. *How is it, that I am stuck babysitting the blood-thirst of the United One...again?*

This was turning out to be one hell of an evening. It had started out as a simple 'girl's night out'. Sindy and Alyson had gone to listen to a band at a bar, and take a few nice, carefully moderated drinks from a couple of unsuspecting humans while they were there. Sindy had seduced some blood out of a few guys without them being any the wiser, but Allie couldn't handle that level of finesse. She was the United One, a vampire with the combined powers of all breeds, and she had a powerful thirst to match. She needed Sindy to help keep her drinking in check. Usually it wasn't a problem, but tonight had been anything but 'usual'.

Allie had chosen to sample the blood of the lead guitarist in the band they'd come to see. Through a combination of bad luck and bad company, Sindy hadn't monitored things as closely as she should have, Allie had not been as careful as she might have been, and Zach, the guitarist, had not lived through it.

Such an empowering, yet frightening feeling, to stand over a lifeless corpse, and know that not only could you cause such a state, you could bring the body back to some semblance of life if you chose. The responsibility, the weight of that, was something Sindy felt now more than ever, because when she had stood over Zach's dead, lifeless body, and Allie had begged her to bring him back, Sindy had done it.

Sindy had found Zach sprawled out on the couch in his tour bus, head back, lips slightly parted, eyes glazed over white, staring dead at the ceiling and seeing nothing...he was gone. Sindy's brief impression of him in life, had been that of a cocky, raunchy, scoundrel of a musician. Although insulting, annoying, and totally not her type, she still had to admit that he was a good looking guy.

Zach was a tall, handsome man, of slim build, with dark brown hair that he kept fairly long for maximum effect while head banging on stage. His facial hair had been trimmed to leave only a tuft of a goatee and a thin outline of his chin that accentuated his great cheekbones. He wore heavy black eyeliner as stage make-up, but he was anything but feminine. The rumbling growl in his voice and the mischievous sparkle in his eye as he'd grabbed Allie's ass had definitely been masculine. By the mildly obscene gestures he'd made towards her with his tongue while on stage, and the way he'd eyed Sindy upon their introduction, it was clear that he'd be more than happy to party with them both.

Too bad for Zach, the night hadn't been nearly as much fun as he'd imagined. The idiot had decided to shoot up before Allie went in to join him and steal a drink of his blood. When she'd bitten him, her venom had reacted badly with the drugs in his system, and had stopped his heart. Allie had been panicked and distraught, and Sindy was stuck cleaning up the mess. The guy was kind of a jerk, but seeing him lying there like that, she had to feel bad for him.

Alyson would have changed him herself, turning him into a vampire to try to ease her guilt over his death, but Sindy had forbidden Allie to do it, and forced her to comply by promising to step in and do it herself. It was more of a sacrifice than anyone would ever know, a threefold loss for Sindy.

In bringing Zach over to an existence as one of the undead, Sindy was not only losing a part of herself to be forever bound to this stranger, she could be losing the love and respect of Cain, the only man who had ever truly believed in her. To boot, she was giving up a shot at an easy ticket into the elite vampire compound of *Kana Susamiş Için Ev.*

The United One was considered a valuable commodity to the head of the compound, Coven Master Arif. Although Arif had originally wanted Sindy to bring him Allie, it must be her powerful blood he was after, and if Allie had turned Zach, he would also become a United One. Sindy should

2

be rewarded for his capture just as well, without having to directly betray Alyson.

But did she really want to align herself with Arif, working to unravel the careful boundaries that Cain, Mattie and Allie had set in order to protect the world from such power? Letting Allie change him would have accomplished something Cain had been trying so hard to prevent, and as much as Sindy had originally thought she'd wanted to please Arif, she just couldn't bring herself to allow it.

So why had Sindy changed him? Because on top of her secret, complicated dealings with Arif, and adding unexpected guilt to the equation, Alyson thought of her as a real friend. Allie had been counting on her to help, and no one had ever shown such faith and trust in her over something so important before. How could she let Allie down? How could she dash hopeful expectations and prove herself to be no better than the untrustworthy trash that others often accused her of being? She was better than that, wasn't she?

So, she had drained herself to gaunt depletion, using every last drop of blood she could spare to bring Zach back from the dead. She'd promised Cain that she would make no more new vampires, and without a full explanation she wasn't entirely ready or willing to give, she might lose him over this…but she might not, and she had done right by Alyson, which felt unexpectedly good inside.

Arif would not benefit, and unless she was ready to hand over the United One to him, he wouldn't grant her residence at *Kana Susamiş Için Ev,* but Sindy was beginning to think Arif wasn't someone she should be assisting anyway. He hadn't been truthful with her about his reasons for interest in Allie, and his power, which she had originally viewed as admirable, was now seeming little more than a manifestation of unattractive greed and callous manipulation. Perhaps his vampire compound also wasn't quite the utopia she had once believed it to be.

She had turned her back on it, and changed Zach, so that Allie wouldn't have to, but it hadn't quite solved things as she'd hoped it would. Allie felt better, her conscience eased of its murderous guilt, but that was because Allie didn't yet know what a miscalculation they'd made. Allie had left to return to Cain's estate with false explanations for Cain and her husband Mattie, to keep them from worrying. Allie didn't know that Sindy was now in some deep shit.

Zach had woken up, just as they'd hoped he would. It hadn't even taken very long, really. He had woken up almost right after Allie had left. Sindy had slipped out to steal a quick drink from the motel desk clerk.

Then she'd taken a little more from the guy in the room next door. Refueled and feeling much better, she noticed the psychic mark of a newly made vampire flare into existence.

Zach had returned from the dead. His mark looked very bright and strong. That was promising; it meant he was in decent shape. Sindy quickly extended the mental cloak she used to cover her own psychic mark, to hide Zach's as well, a useful new trick she'd learned from observing Arif's coven. As long as she was fairly close to him, she could keep him psychically invisible to other vampires. Hopefully he'd be capable of doing it himself before long, because his mark was damn bright and hard for her to cover while still tending to her own.

It took her a little time to extricate herself from the room of the guy next door, where she'd been exchanging some unseemly attention for a stealthy sampling of his blood, and get back to Zach, but luckily she could tell from his mark that he wasn't going anywhere. She returned to find the shower running in the bathroom. Apparently, he was capable and cognizant enough of his state to want to clean himself up; definitely a good sign.

One lucky thing about creating a vampire from a corpse, it spared them the pain. Zach's body had undergone its transformation before he had regained consciousness. She pitied housekeeping, because the bed he'd been on was so soiled, they'd have to throw away the mattress, but Sindy had known that was coming. His body would void itself of anything it didn't need during his change.

She'd stripped Zach of his clothing and laid it on the other bed, so he'd have something clean to wear when he revived. She'd also gone through his pockets, and his guitar case, which now rested in the corner. He didn't have much on him, not even a driver's license. All she'd found were guitar picks, keys, a pair of sunglasses, a pack of cigarettes and some books of matches with phone numbers scribbled on the inside covers. She'd dumped his stuff on the dresser, and gone out to seduce some blood out of the desk clerk before Zach had revived.

He'd woken up in a strange motel room, naked, alone, and lying in a bed of filth. The funny part was, he probably didn't even think it was odd. For a drug addict musician on the road, this was an average Sunday morning. He came out of the bathroom wearing only tattoo ink and a towel. He didn't seem distressed in the least. In fact, when he saw Sindy, a wide grin spread across his face.

He might recognize her from earlier in the evening, but probably couldn't remember much. If anything, he'd undoubtedly expected Allie to come through the door, because before he'd died, although Allie had seemed accommodating, Sindy hadn't given him any indication that he'd have a shot in hell with *her*.

Before getting into explanations, Sindy turned and opened the front window. "It smells like a barn in here," she muttered.

Zach chuckled with slight apology. "Yeah, I must have had a bad reaction to something earlier." He grabbed the bottom of the coverlet on the soiled bed and quickly pulled it up and tossed the end towards the head of the bed, to fold it over and cover the mess. "I'm feeling much better now though."

When Sindy turned from opening the window, Zach let his towel drop. Nice view…but she had other things on her mind. Besides the rush of annoyed impatience she felt over the act, she had an odd, disconcerting sense of déjà vu.

Years back, she'd been in a similar situation, with the roles reversed. She had been staying in a motel room, and Cain had come to visit her. In that instance, she'd been the one in the towel, and dropped it as he'd turned to face her, as Zach had just done. Much as Sindy felt now, Cain had been focused on more serious business, having no patience for her brash attempts at seduction. She hoped to God Cain hadn't viewed her then with the same disposition she was viewing Zach now, because her main reaction was amusement. Zach was making a total ass of himself.

He didn't even know her name, she'd been here for all of five minutes, and yet he thought the sight of him naked would be enough to win her over, in this room that smelled like crap? She already knew from stripping him earlier, that he had a body she wouldn't mind taking for a spin, but it wasn't quite enough to make her forget all else. Right now, all she could do was raise an eyebrow at his audacity.

Zach didn't seem to pick up on the fact that she wasn't flattered and pleased with his actions. He just smiled and nodded towards the clean bed, as though she was supposed to join him there. "As a matter of fact," he told her, "I feel fuckin' amazing."

Sindy laughed, making no move towards the bed. "I'll bet you do." Irritating as he was, she couldn't stop smiling. He looked good, healthy, aware and intelligent…well, at least as intelligent as he'd started out anyway…which might not be saying much, but he was using full sentences, which made him a marvel of wisdom compared to some of the other vampires she'd made. Her sacrifice had paid off for him. He thought she was smiling at his naked body though, and evidently found the thought very arousing.

He came towards her, his hand out to caress her face. She swiped it away, and he stroked her hair instead. "You are gorgeous. Are you here 'cause Sweet Cheeks didn't want you to join us on the bus?"

Even through his annoying fondling, she continued to grin. He was aware enough to remember some events from earlier in the evening, and he was even trying to use deductive reasoning to figure out why she would be here with him now. It was almost as though nothing had happened to him. Had this guy really been a dead body a few hours ago?

He was stroking her hair and trying to incite a reaction from her to build on the broad smile she couldn't wipe off her face. She hadn't bolted when he'd dropped his towel, so he seemed to have decided she thought it was a perfectly reasonable thing for him to do. He continued his questioning. "Did we… Were you here earlier? 'Cause my memory's a little hazy, but I can't believe I'd forget that."

She was amazed and pleased that his change had gone so well. Allie was going to be so relieved. However, it might make things more difficult for Sindy, because he was going to need a more thorough explanation than she'd had to give past protégés. "About earlier," she told him, as she gave him a little shove to sit down on the clean bed, "we need to talk."

He sat, and as she joined him, she tried to keep some space between them and ignore his nakedness, not to give any hint that his attention was welcome. He completely disregarded her body language though, scooching closer to her anyway.

He'd been looking at her boobs, enjoying the nice view her low cut top provided, but then his gaze was drawn to her throat, staring with such intensity and determination that undoubtedly his thirst was kicking in. He didn't understand the urges. He knew only that he wanted her…badly. "Actions speak louder than words," he whispered, leaning in and trying to kiss her.

She turned away. "Not this time. I really need to explain a few things." Undaunted by her refusal to kiss him, Zach began kissing the side of her throat instead. "Quit it and listen," she said, shrugging him off in annoyance. He was undeterred, and kept coming back for more.

The blood thirst was kicking in; it had to be. New vampires always woke up thirsty as hell, and the predatory vibe that was beginning to come off him was practically palpable. The vampire within was driving him to claim her, and he didn't know any better than to follow his urges. He thought he wanted sex, but instinct would take over soon enough to show him otherwise. Sindy thought about just pushing him off of her…but then decided that maybe he needed to learn how to take *no* for an answer, the hard way.

Just as she thought he might try for a bite, he paused and looked up at her with fascinated intrigue. "Do you feel that?"

She watched him for a moment, wondering if he might let her explain after all. She gave a slight nod with a smirk. "Oh, I feel it alright."

His eyes were still brown, but she was certain they'd be glazing over vampiric red at any moment…if he was lucky enough to have inherited that color from her. Her blood was pretty mixed, and so far, all of her past creations had turned out to have eyes of orange. She was hoping for red for him though, as he gazed at her with a smile. "What are we on, anyway?" he asked.

She chuckled. "It's called immortality. Let me tell you about it."

She could see she was losing him again. He thought she was naming a drug, and he didn't really care. He refused to try to control himself long enough for a conversation. "Later, let's just enjoy the ride." He dove back down to her throat for more kisses, wrapping his arms around her.

"I wouldn't do that if I were you," she warned, trying to shrug out of his grasp. He held her tightly and his words sent ticklish shivers over her skin as he mumbled against her throat.

"What's the matter babe? It'll be awesome, I swear."

Sindy chose to let actions speak louder than words, as Zach had suggested. She sat unresponsive as his kisses became more and more forceful, turning to sucking pulls on her skin that were sure to be soon followed by nips with his teeth. "Okay, I'll just wait for it…" she said with a quiet lilt of humor.

Zach tried to mumble a response, but then his urges overwhelmed him, and his fangs distended to try to pierce her throat, as she had known they would. The moment that happened, and the tips of his new fangs touched her skin, he cried out in agony and jumped back away from her to land on the floor.

"There you go," Sindy responded with a slight smile.

Sindy was marked. She had allowed Cain to bite her and drink her blood, laying claim to it as his alone. Now his strong venom was in her body, marking and protecting her from other vampires. When Zach's fangs tried to break her skin and taste that blood, it sent a blinding stab of pain through his temple, to warn him off another vampire's property. It had dropped him quicker and more surely than any defensive move Sindy could have made.

She watched him writhe in pain on the floor for a moment before commenting. What a baby. The pain should have been instant and sharp, but also should have disappeared almost immediately after he'd backed away from her. His fangs had likely retracted with the shock as well. "That's what you get for having no manners, dipshit. Now are you ready to listen?"

He glared up at her while holding a hand to the side of his head. "What the fuck did you do to me?" he asked in outrage.

"Things you aren't going to believe," she replied confidentially. After another second, she took pity on him and reached down to lend him a hand and pull him back up to the bed. "Come on, let's have that talk." He was hesitant to take her hand, worried she was somehow going to hurt him again. "Relax, as long as you behave yourself, you'll be fine."

He stood from the floor, shaken from his previous ambitions and eying her warily. She reached behind her to grab hold of his clothing, laid out for him on the bed earlier. "Why don't you put something on, stud? Not that you're bad to look at," she told him with a grudging grin, "but I've already had to seduce more than my share of guys tonight to get what I needed, and I am *not* in the mood."

He caught the clothing she tossed at him and began to get dressed. She gave him a nod and smile of thanks for his cooperation. "It's been a long night already," she told him, "and we have a serious discussion to get through before the sun comes up." They still had a couple of hours left, but there was no telling how he would take the news.

Complicated and convoluted as it seemed, the explanation itself didn't really take very long...but he didn't believe her. When he'd tried to bite her, his fangs had retracted with the pain, just as quickly as they had descended, and with his eyes closed and caught up in lustful anticipation, he hadn't even really noticed. He still didn't realize his body had gone through any changes. He thought he had passed out on drugs and been dumped here by his band, who had then sent Sindy in. He believed her story was some elaborate prank, initiated by one of his band-mates. Evidently, practical jokes were a favorite pass-time of theirs.

"I'm not a vampire," he insisted with a laugh. "I'm a Satan-worshipping rock star, but I'm not a vampire. I can see how you might confuse the two."

"Well, you can believe what you want about yourself," she told him, with a warm, throaty chuckle, "but I know what I am." It wasn't until she changed for him, showing him her vampire eyes, that he began to realize something was very wrong...and it wasn't funny.

He backed away from her with a start. "What the… How did you do that? Are those contacts or something?" Her eyes were glittering crimson, with long, thin, upright black pupils that were decidedly inhuman. It might have been a look that could be achieved with contact lenses, but not in the space of a blink. He realized that, and backed into the bathroom, quickly slamming the door…as if that could keep her out.

"Zach, I'm not here to hurt you. I'm here to help."

"Stay the fuck away from me, you freak!"

"Zach, you're going to need some instruction, trust me."

"This isn't funny anymore. Get out of here, and tell Rudy I've had enough of this crap."

"I don't even know Rudy. What I told you was the truth, Zach. I'm a vampire, and so are you. You've changed, and you need my help. If you don't believe me, just look in the mirror."

He didn't answer her, but he must have followed her suggestion, because after a moment, she heard startled exclamations and curses. Then came the crashing of smashed glass. That brought some more cursing, and then silence.

Zach opened the door and came out with a large shard of glass in his hand. "How come I'm not in the mirror? What is this, some kind of trick glass? You stay the hell away from me," he warned her.

Sindy had changed back to her human visage again. No need to upset him more than she already had. She stood with her hand on her hip, between Zach and the door, in case he tried to bolt. She let out a weary sigh, and nodded towards the broken mirror glass he carried. "All that's going to do is give you seven years of bad luck. You can't hurt me, Zach, and if I was going to do anything else to you, I would have already done it, don't you think?"

Zach looked at the long, sharp shard of glass in his hand, and then back at her. "I don't care what you are, if you come near me, I will cut you."

Sindy scoffed at the threat, and then walked slowly towards him. Better to get this stuff out of the way so he would listen. She stopped just shy of touching him, while he held the glass before her menacingly.

"Don't make me cut you, bitch," he warned.

She held out her hand for him to give it over. He looked at her as though she was crazy, and raised the glass higher, threateningly. "Go ahead," she invited. "Cut me." When he made no move, she nodded towards her hand, raising it a little higher in invitation. "Do it."

Rather than accept her challenge, he tossed the glass to the floor, and quickly pushed his way past to get away from her. "You're fucking crazy."

She laughed in relief. Nice to know the guy wasn't a sadistic creep. Even in fear and with invitation, he didn't really want to hurt her. Good sign. She picked up the glass and then called to him before he could go for the door. "Hey, Zach," She held up the glass for him to see, and then, holding out her other hand, palm up, brought it down as though she were going to stab herself with it.

Just before the glass cut her, she caused her hand to turn to mist. She did it slow enough for him to clearly see what had happened, even if he couldn't quite believe it. The glass passed right through. She held it there, with the misty particles of her hand swirling around it like disturbed dust, and she then reformed her hand around the glass. It felt very strange to have a foreign object impaled through the center of her hand, and her body wouldn't let her keep it there for long before trying to push it out, but it looked pretty cool for a momentary display. She let go and held up her hand to show him the glass sticking through the middle of it, and she then dissolved her hand into mist again. The glass fell to the carpet and Sindy was rewarded with a gasp of amazement from Zach. She smiled, pleased with herself. It was a damn impressive trick.

Sindy often transformed her entire body into mist. It was the first step in the process of shape-change into the form of a wolf or a bat, the rare and valuable talent bestowed upon her in conjunction with her red eyes. However, she had seen the vampire Kieran, who was a shade/vampire with green eyes and the ability to transform into mist, cause only parts of his body to become discorporate. It had intrigued her, so she had been experimenting to see if she could do the same. She couldn't remain in mist form indefinitely, as Kieran did, but she could change select parts of herself for just under a minute or so; just long enough for a display like she'd done with the glass. It had worked like a charm.

"You can't hurt me," she told Zach, as her hand reformed to its normal state once again, "and I'm not here to hurt you, but if you walk out that door, you're going to be a loose end that I can't let go." She let her fangs distend, just resting their tips on her bottom lip, lending an eerie and dangerous edge of supernatural predator to her beauty. "Don't make me chase you down, 'cause I can...easily, and you won't like it. Although *I* might," she added with a grin. His eyes widened and his hand froze as he'd been reaching to open the door. "You can avoid that unpleasant scenario if you just keep things calm and friendly-like. Sit down, shut up, and let me explain where we go from here, okay?"

She let him take in the sight of her fangs and her red vampire eyes for another moment, before she changed back and sat down on the bed. He watched her warily, trying to understand what he had seen. As he let his hand slip from the doorknob, she patted the bed next to her in invitation. Whether it was fear of her threat, or curiosity that got the better of him, he gave up his resistance and joined her, ready to listen.

"Do you really worship Satan?" she asked as he sat down, trying to keep his distance from her on the bed. He looked startled and worried by the question…as though she was going to profess that she was a minion of the Dark Lord herself.

After a second, he shook his head. "Not really. It just kind of goes with the image, you know? …Do you?" he added after a second of uncertainty.

She grinned. "Nope. I'm what you'd call independent."

He was very relieved. "How did you do that thing with your hand?"

"It's a neat trick, but we have more important things to talk about." She refused to get into anything complicated. She just went through the basics. She explained again how he had over-dosed on drugs and died, prompting her to change him into a vampire, to be like her. He seemed to believe what she told him about herself, but he still wouldn't accept that he was a vampire too. He stood from the bed, his hands out in disbelief. "Clearly, I'm not dead."

"Not anymore, thanks to me."

"Right, because you're a vampire. You and Sweet Cheeks are both vampires, and brought me back from the dead."

Sindy shook her head in impatient disgust. "Her name is Alyson, and she only drank from you, I brought you back."

"She drank my blood?" he asked with sarcastic disbelief. "From where?" He made a show of feeling his throat, which currently showed no sign of trauma.

Sindy sighed. "Why are you making this so difficult? You don't *seem* entirely stupid. I told you, we heal. I shared my blood with you, to bring you back from the dead, and it healed your body as it changed you into a vampire."

"If you girls are vampires, why didn't you just kill me and leave me dead?"

"I'm beginning to wonder," she mumbled. "We don't do that. We usually try *not* to kill people."

"You just said she drank my blood!"

"Yeah, a little taste. She didn't kill you. You took care of that all by yourself. I told you, you OD'd you moron."

He dismissed the idea. "That couldn't have happened. It was only the usual. I do it all the time."

"Well I guess that was your poor judgment, huh, dumbass? Allie only took a little bit of your blood, then she couldn't stomach anymore because you tasted like shit. It was the cocktail of crap that you pumped in there that killed you." He might not have died without Allie's venom added to the mix, but why should she take the blame for his death? The idiot probably would've killed himself with that stuff soon enough anyway.

He squinted at her and then the corner of his mouth turned upwards just a bit in a hint of a grin. "Okay, drugs are bad, thanks for the tip. You sound a little bitter. What'd you used to use?"

Sindy let out a huff of disdain. "You couldn't pay me to touch that stuff."

He raised his eyebrows and then nodded in understanding. "You knew someone then."

She squinted at him without answering. First, he treats her like some pathetic groupie sex-doll, now he thinks he knows about her emotional scars? "What I know," she told him, "is that that stuff will kill you."

He shrugged, recognizing her refusal to delve any deeper. "Fair enough. Say it did kill me."

"It did."

"You brought me back?"

"Allie begged me to. She couldn't do it herself and she felt bad for you."

He smiled. "*She* did? And what about you?"

"Me? I think you're a complete tool." He smirked at her mockingly, as though she was hiding affection for him or something. She gave him a look of disdain and shook her head. How did she wind up saddled with this guy? Finally, she chuckled. "But now you're *my* tool, so I hope you prove me wrong."

It took some settling down and coaxing, but she was finally able to get him to truly accept what she was. She showed him her fangs again, and then proved that they were the real deal with a demonstration. She bit him. She caught him off guard, lunging for his throat, and it only took a moment for her venom to calm his struggling and erase any uneasiness he felt.

It had to be the quickest and best high he'd had in a while, even taking into account his vast experience with such things. She only took a small taste, but what a taste it was! It may have been a while since she'd sampled vampire blood, but none of her past creations had ever tasted this good. Zach's blood was a compelling and unexpected delicacy. It took a decent amount of effort to keep herself in check.

When she finally pulled away, she eyed him with new appreciation. "You may have tasted like shit to Allie, but damn if you aren't my new favorite flavor!" It took some strong willpower not to go back for more. He looked dizzy and shocked over the incident, holding his hand up to his throat and trying to comprehend the fact that she truly had bitten him and drunk his blood, but he didn't complain. When she leaned back to meet his eyes, she knew he was putty in her hands.

Sindy tried to force herself to back off, before the urge to take more overwhelmed her. She wasn't really thirsty, and hadn't expected drinking from him to be so intoxicating; she had done it to be practical. It marked him so she could keep tabs on him until she was convinced he could be independent. Unable to resist taking one last taste, she came forward for a final lick from the wound at his throat.

His thirst was re-awakened by the act. She could feel it, almost as though his thoughts and desires were her own. As his head stopped swimming from the invasion of her toxin, she could practically feel the thirst building within him. It grew quickly. He needed blood, and if he didn't feed, the vampire within him would take over and get some for itself, whether he was ready or not.

He watched her with a desperate gaze, pleading for her to help him process what was happening to him and end his torment. It brought out a protectiveness from her deeper than she'd felt for her creations of the past, although she had no idea why. She took hold of him, trying to give him assurance that she could make things better. "Now it's your turn," she told him gently, as she bit her wrist. "You can't bite me. Remember that headache? You don't want that back. You can only take what I give you. You have to suck gently. Even though you might have the urge to bite, don't. But you are a vampire, Zach, and I'm going to give you a chance to use your own fangs soon enough, trust me."

"My own…" he couldn't finish his contemplation, because she offered him her wrist and the change over-took him as soon as he smelled her blood. His fangs distended, but he barely even noticed. As with most new vampires, his altered eyesight was immediately disconcerting. He blinked at her wrist with an exclamation of surprise, and reached out for her arm to steady himself.

"It's okay Zach. Your eyes have changed. You can see the warmth of the blood in me. I've just fed, so it should have a decent amount of heat to it. Just relax, you'll get used to it. Don't worry, your regular eyesight will come back after you've fed." She knew that sometimes the most upsetting thing was simply the thought that nothing would ever look the same again. Reassurance that the change was temporary usually calmed the new ones down and helped them deal.

The fear over his change had momentarily pushed thirst from his mind. She laid a hand on his back to try to comfort him; he was very shaken up. She could feel him un-tense a little at her touch, and she offered her wrist again, while still gently rubbing his back. He raised her arm slowly closer to his face and then looked up at her, grateful that she was being so supportive through this crazy ordeal.

She smiled, glad that she had a chance to mentor someone properly for a change. Admittedly, she hadn't done a great job with vampires she had made in the past. She met his eyes…and then jerked back from him. Zach was startled by her abrupt change in demeanor, but not nearly as startled as she was. She flinched away from him and fell off the edge of the bed. "What the fuck?" she muttered, as she hit the floor with a thump. "No! No way! This cannot be happening to me!"

"What? You did this to me! What's wrong with you?" Zach was very confused. She was freaking him out again.

Well, she couldn't help it. He was freaking her out too. Somehow, some way, she and Allie had really screwed up big time, because when he'd met her gaze, she had caught her first glimpse of Zach's vampire eyes…and they were white.

White? How the hell had they turned out white? Allie hadn't given him any blood. That's what Sindy had gone through all of this to prevent! "Your vampire eyes…they're white, and they damn well shouldn't be!"

Before she even had a chance to truly take in this new development, there was a knock on the motel room door; a knock accompanied by a mark… She didn't recognize the mark of the vampire at the door, but he wore Arif's signature. It was an emissary from the coven. Great, just what she needed to make this hellish evening complete.

What did they want? Arif's spy, Kieran, had witnessed Zach's death at Allie's hands. He must also know that Sindy had turned the guy into a vampire afterwards, but that shouldn't matter. He didn't know that Sindy had stopped Alyson from doing it. For all he knew, Allie had refused. There was no way in hell anyone could know that despite Sindy's precautions with Allie, the guy had turned out with white eyes anyway. *She* didn't even understand how that had happened!

It didn't matter how…Kieran had obviously managed to follow them, and reported their whereabouts. Now Arif had sent someone to meet with them. She had no idea why he'd done that, but one thing was certain, he didn't know that Zach had the white eyes of a United One, and she couldn't let him find out…not until she had decided what she wanted to do about it. She hadn't gone through all this trouble to be a friend to Allie and uphold Cain's plan for the United One, only to hand a white-eyed vamp over to Arif.

Zach was panicked, staring at the door in bewilderment. In his fear, he had reverted back to his human image again, but he could psychically see the other vampire's mark, and he didn't understand it. Sindy scrambled over to him and grabbed his hands with a force that made him turn away from the door and pay attention to her. "Zach," she hissed at him. "That is another vampire at the door. I don't know what this is about, but you have to trust me when I tell you that if you don't do *exactly* what I say, you are going to find yourself dead again before the sun comes up. Keep your mouth shut, and do not, no matter what, *do not let yourself change*. You cannot let them see your vampire eyes. Got it?" He didn't answer her, but seemed suitably impressed and willing to obey. It was possible he didn't even know *how* to reveal his vampire eyes voluntarily, but she didn't have time to explain.

Sindy rose and went to the door as the strange vampire knocked again. She had no choice but to answer. Arif did not know that she was having second thoughts about their arrangement, and once he realized she was being uncooperative she would be in some deep trouble. She was better off pretending that she was still in league with him.

She turned to Zach and gestured for him to stay put on the bed before she opened the door to meet their visitor. It was a nicely dressed man, in his thirties by appearance, although his mark showed him to be upwards of fifty. There was a large black sedan parked horizontal with the curb behind him, its door open to show that there was another man in the car waiting.

He didn't bother to introduce himself. "Arif wants to see you. Get in."

No wonder it wasn't Kieran at the door. Arif wasn't just sending her a message; he wanted to see her personally. After all this time, why did he want to see her *now*? Sindy tried to look more annoyed than alarmed as she answered. "I'm a little busy right now." She turned to indicate Zach, sitting frozen on the bed. "I just turned this guy. Let me get him settled first. I'll come tomorrow, at sunset."

The man didn't even bother to glance at Zach; he just stared through Sindy with a gaze that could cut glass. "Bring him. Arif wants to see you *now."* Sindy tried to protest, but he cut her off. "Do you need help getting him into the car?" He stared her down, almost daring her to answer.

She turned and went back into the room for Zach. She couldn't even risk trying to speak to him privately with the vampire standing at the door waiting for them. She simply glared at Zach desperately, hoping it would remind him that she had told him to obey her and say nothing.

She noticed his mirrored sunglasses sitting on the dresser and grabbed them. She put them on his face as she spoke. "Come on, Zach, we need to go for a ride." Luckily, it seemed he was still in a bit of shock over the whole ordeal, and rather than question her, or make a smart-ass remark, he followed her into the car without comment. He did however, have the presence of mind to grab the rest of his stuff, and take his guitar from its place leaning against the wall, on the way out. Good thing, because something told her they weren't coming back any time soon.

It was a long way to *Kana Susamiş İçin Ev,* but they were racing down the highway at break-neck speed and would surely be there before dawn. The inhabitants of the car were eerily silent for the trip. Zach began to squirm uneasily, but Sindy did her best to keep him still and quiet. The thirst must really be kicking in now. The poor guy hadn't had a chance to drink since his change. He was chain smoking the last of his cigarettes, but it wouldn't quell his thirst. He was starting to come unhinged, fidgeting, grunting and huffing in anxiousness with his need for blood. It drew an irritated glare from the driver. "What is his problem?"

"He's just been turned..." Sindy explained, "barely cold even. He needs to drink." She addressed the man in the passenger seat, who had collected them from the hotel. "I told you this was a bad time."

The driver seemed sympathetic, but the other man reacted with annoyance. "Well shut him up. He can have something when we get there."

One look at Zach, and she knew that if he had to wait, they were going to have a problem. How was she going to let him change in front of Arif to feed? She'd better take care of him here in the dark car as best as she could. Sindy plucked the cigarette from his hand and threw it out the open crack of the window. Ignoring his protest, she then shifted and brought her fangs to bear on her own wrist. The others watched her curiously, but she ignored them and put an arm around Zach, pulling him in close to the now bleeding wrist that she held against her bosom. He didn't need to further invitation. The smell of her blood drove him to clasp her wrist and greedily bring it to his lips.

He began to suck on it ferociously, impatient with the small amount he was getting. She wanted to remind him not to bite her, but he tried before she had the chance. He'd forgotten that he could not cross her mark, but was quickly reminded. He let out a howl of pain and a mumbled curse as his teeth punctured her skin. She grabbed him closer in a hug, stifling him into her chest as the vampires of the car gave her odd looks and chuckled.

"Don't bite," she whispered, "I know it's hard, but this is just to tide you over. I know what you're going through," she assured him. "I'll find you more as soon as we get there, I promise." He went back to sucking what blood he could get from her as she sat back and closed her eyes.

She was already beginning to feel a bit light headed. She'd bled herself gaunt earlier in making him, and had barely drunk enough to regain her strength before he was taking it from her again. She hoped she would be in a condition to think clearly when they got there, because once she heard why Arif was summoning her, she was definitely going to need to think on her feet.

Was she being really stupid in thinking that she would be able to hide Zach's eyes from everyone? If Arif was going to find out anyway, maybe she should just tell him; hand Zach over and take the credit for turning him in, to earn herself a place in the coven. She'd be granted residence at the compound for bringing in a United One, and there were worse things than living a life of vampiric luxury...even if she was committing herself to servitude under a master.

But she had turned Zach as a favor to Allie, as a display of loyalty towards their friendship. Allie would never forgive her if she let Zach be tossed into Arif's dungeon for her own gain. She didn't actually know what Arif would do with the guy, dungeon or otherwise, but it was a safe bet to think that it wouldn't be something good. Still...hiding Zach's eyes would be a trespass that would earn Sindy her own place in one of Arif's torture chambers for sure. Was hiding him worth the risk?

She desperately wished that she had never even gone out with Allie this evening. She could be in bed right now, back at Cain's estate, snuggling beneath the sheets in his loving embrace. What would Cain do in her place? Cain would never have displayed such sketchy integrity to get himself into this mess, but if he were in her position? She knew he'd keep Zach from Arif, without thought for his own personal sacrifice, just on the principle that such power shouldn't be allowed into corrupt hands. He'd protect Zach simply because it seemed the right thing to do.

She'd always held to the tenant that she was a woman worth Cain's affections, hadn't she? Maybe it was time to step up and prove it. She took a page from his book and prayed to God that Arif would not catch on to her duplicity. Being a vampire who used to pride herself on her lack of morals, and dedication to her own selfish ends, she doubted God would actually bother to listen to her requests, if there even *was* such a being as the Almighty, but she needed all the help she could get!

By the time they arrived at *Kana Susamış İçin Ev,* Sindy managed to muster up a sense of confidence that would allow her to conduct herself with the haughty arrogance Arif would expect from her. She could do this. She had to believe it, or he would feel her hesitant worry before she said a word.

She wrested her wrist back from Zach, despite his protests that he wasn't nearly finished drinking from her. "I need more," he cajoled in a desperate whisper.

"Well, I need to keep some myself. You're lucky you got what you did," she hissed back, as she nodded out the window for Zach to see that they had reached their destination.

They passed through a set of large iron gates, flanked by a set of guards, each with an alert and imposing Doberman Pinscher by their side. As the car entered the coven's home compound, the dogs watched, eerily silent. Sindy noticed that their eyes glowed oddly, even after the headlights moved off them. She got the sense that they weren't just…dogs. Great, as if the world didn't already harbor enough creepy things in the night. Now she had to worry about demon dogs?

Demons? The responsive thought drifted into her mind, in line with her own thinking, but certainly not her own. She realized almost immediately that it had to be Zach. It felt like him…his voice and tone, although there was no actual sound, just the thought in her mind. Along with his white eyes must have come the talent of telepathy. Finally, a surprise that could actually be useful! She didn't have the skill herself, but maybe she could help Zach hone his to their advantage.

*I don't know if they're demons, but I don't think they're just dogs…*she replied gently, hoping he would catch the thought. He might not even realize that they weren't speaking aloud. Allie had told her that telepathy could be like that sometimes, an unconscious thing.

When Zach didn't respond, she tried again. *Zach, can you hear me?* Now he sat up straighter to meet her gaze in confusion. Yes, he definitely heard her, and realized this was not normal. *You're reading my mind,* she explained. *No one else can hear us like this…I hope.* Actually, she had no idea if other vampires of Arif's coven were telepathic, but she knew Arif was, so they'd better not try this in his presence. She decided their psychic conversation had better be short and sweet.

Zach, listen carefully. I have to meet with the leader of this coven. His name is Arif and he is a very powerful vampire. Not all of us can read minds like you are now, but Arif can, so don't try it when he's around. In fact, you should try not to let him read your mind if you can help it. Try not to think about much of anything when he's around, okay?

The directive sounded pretty stupid even to her, but she wasn't sure how else to try to protect them. *Maybe you could just mentally recite song lyrics or something when he's around, to throw him off. It's important that these other vampires do not know what you are capable of. You're more powerful than them, than anyone, Zach, but we'll be totally outnumbered here. Most vampires can't do the things you'll be able to, so if we're going to fly under the radar, they need to believe you are nothing special.*

Zach seemed to be paying close attention, but she couldn't tell if he would obey her. He seemed too caught up in this new development to listen. *What can I do? I can read people's minds? That's awesome!*

Zach, will you please concentrate? This is important and we haven't got much time. Sindy had just realized something that was going to unravel everything if it wasn't immediately addressed. His mark; she was currently cloaking it from view, but she couldn't keep that up forever, especially if they were separated. Zach's mark was damn bright, and now she knew why. She needed to teach him to cover it up before it was seen, or someone would notice that Zach was more than he appeared.

Luckily, Allie had told her that she'd learned to hide her trace in record time. Even though it was a talent that had taken Sindy forever to figure out, it should be simple for Zach to master. She did her best to hurriedly explain the concept to him. It was difficult at first, considering the fact that he didn't even really understand what a mark was, but thankfully, he was smart enough to get the gist of what she wanted from him. He was able to read enough of it from her mind to figure it out before they reached their final destination.

Sindy let her own psychic shield slip away, while keeping his covered, so he could practice on her first. He was shaky, but managed to cover it after only a few tries. There wasn't time for her to wait for him to be more confident with it. The driver was parking the car and they'd be forced to get out and concentrate on other things. She hoped he could cover his own mark, one less thing for her to worry about. Tentatively, after a quick telepathic warning, she stopped hiding his mark for him. He was able to cover it before it even came fully into view. It seemed that the other vampires in the car didn't even notice. Sindy let out a sigh of relief. First hurdle of their charade down…but this was only the beginning.

19

Keep that mark covered, all the time. She instructed him, as the car was parked. *Can you do that? I know this is a lot to handle Zach, but you have to trust me. Our lives may depend on it.*

The driver had gotten out and was now holding the door open for her to do the same. "Ready to see the Master?"

She tried her best to put on a confident smile as she exited the vehicle. "Ready as I'll ever be."

~~~~~~~~~~~~~~~~~~~~~~~~~~~~~~~~

They entered the impressive manor, but before allowing her and Zach to be taken to Arif, the driver stopped their escort. "You should let them feed first."

The man looked aggravated by the delay, but Sindy gave the driver a very grateful smile for the consideration. "It won't take long," the driver continued. "Better a small delay, than to have a newbie lunging for the Master's concubines."

That was logic hard to argue with. "Fine," the man said. "You handle it then. I'll let the Master know that we've arrived and you'll bring our guests to see him shortly."

The driver didn't look thrilled to have the task given over to him, but Sindy lightly touched his arm as the other men left them. "Thank you. He really needs it."

The man was of a decent height, with broad shoulders but not an overly muscular build. He had straight, light brown hair and a kind face. He looked down at her with a piteous sigh. "Byron," he said, offering his name. "I can find you two donors and a place to drink, but you'd better be quick about it, and don't hurt them, I'll need them back."

Sindy nodded, although she wasn't sure how she was going to manage letting Zach drink while keeping him in check and not letting others observe them too closely. "Thanks. I'll keep a close eye on him."

Byron parked them in a small sitting room, and put a guard in the open doorway as he went to collect a pair of humans for them to feed from. Zach seemed too busy taking in the splendor of Arif's estate and smiling over the thought of being given fresh blood, to look at all concerned by their situation.

The guard was watching them too intently for Sindy to risk trying to speak with Zach anyway. Not that she even knew what to say. It wasn't much of a wait before Byron came back with a pair of humans in tow. He pulled Sindy out into the hallway for a quick private conference before letting the humans into the room with Zach. "I am doing you a big favor here," he informed her quietly.

Sindy looked over the pair. They were a man and a woman, both in their early twenties and obviously healthy, clean, and they were even attractive. "I can see that," Sindy replied with a smile as her eyes lingered on the man, who gave her a hesitant smile.

Byron took back her attention, sensing that she did not fully realize the extent of the favor. "They're both experienced with our coven, but currently unmarked, a pretty valuable acquisition around here. I could've just sent up something bottled, but you said he's new," he explained with a nod towards Zach, "so I thought you'd appreciate the opportunity for a learning experience. I happen to know that the Master's busy, so you should have time before you're brought to him. Just don't take too long, and whatever you do, don't hurt them or you'll be paying for it, and not with money. Can you handle him?"

On those conditions, she certainly hoped so. "Yeah, I've got it. Thanks. I owe you." She met his eyes, hoping he could see that she truly appreciated his help. Of course, it might have been easier just to give Zach blood from a bottle, eliminating the need for him to change and possibly let someone see his white eyes. However, she couldn't tell Byron that. Zach would be much more satisfied with fresh blood, and she was going to have to teach him drinking with control at some point. Better now, than later, possibly in front of Arif.

Byron instructed the humans to follow her into the room, and told Sindy he would be back to collect them in about twenty minutes. Byron even swung the door mostly closed for them, only leaving it open a crack for the guard's supervision.

Sindy observed for a moment, as the young woman took in Zach's appearance and looked very pleased with it, giving him a smile and a wink. The way Zach was eyeing her back, told Sindy she was going to have her hands full. Strict ground rules were definitely going to be in order. She took the woman by the arm and pulled her closer. "Don't even think about it," she told Zach. "She's mine." She gave the human man a quick glance and noted his disappointment. "Sorry, buddy. I hate to give you up, but I've got to play this smart. You're with him."

Zach was still eyeing the woman in Sindy's hold with an intense gaze. He lifted his guitar strap off, over his head, and put the instrument case down, without breaking eye contact with the girl. "No way," he demanded. "I'm ready for a drink and she is looking damn delicious."

Sindy snapped her fingers in front of his face for attention. "Zach, this is *not* negotiable. You don't even know what you're doing. If you let yourself get distracted playing touchy-feely, you're going to take too much. She'll end up dead and we'll end up in shackles!"

Zach didn't seem very concerned, but the woman stopped flirting and moved away from him pretty quickly to gesture towards the human man. "You should definitely drink from Frank. He's bigger," she nervously agreed, as Frank gave them each a worried glance.

Sindy let go of the woman to approach Frank. The last thing she needed was for the guy to back out on them or call for the guard to come in and help. "Relax. You've done this before, right?" The guy nodded warily. "So have I, for years. Zach is new to this, but I'll be right here and I won't let him get out of hand, I promise." She mouthed him a little kiss and he seemed willing to stay, however uneasy he might be.

She turned to Zach, who was beginning to look more and more predatory by the second. "I'll tell you what, how about a compromise?" she offered. "Start off with Frank. I know he's not necessarily your type, but you're going to bite him, not tongue him. He's a clean, strong, healthy looking guy. I can almost guarantee you that he's yummy as hell," she added, licking her lips. "If you take it slow, follow my directions and stop when you're told, I'll let you have some from…" Sindy turned and snapped her fingers towards the woman. "What's your name?"

The woman was backed into the corner, shoulders slumped, evidently trying to make herself seem unappealing. "Lisa."

"Zach, Lisa here will let you have a little nip, if you can prove yourself capable while drinking from Frank first. Fair enough?"

So it was settled, and in the interest of keeping things under control, Sindy was going thirsty. Disappointing, but she could handle it. Getting Zach fed and satisfied to keep quiet and follow orders was more important. She led him through the basics of controlled feeding and then let him bite the man's throat.

The scent of blood filled the room, tantalizingly sharp, masculine and beckoning. Sindy tried not to think about what she was missing, as she swiped her long black hair back behind her shoulder and stood over Zach. Sindy had barely regained the blood and strength she had lost in making Zach to begin with. Then she had fed Zach some more in the car…now the scent of blood and her view of Zach drinking from this hunk of a human were practically making her drool.

Zach began to slip in hiding his mark while so distracted, but Sindy was able to cover for him, while giving him a mental reminder. She watched as Zach greedily drank all the blood he could pull from his victim, as quickly as the small punctures in the man's neck would allow. Sindy had to stop him from inflicting a larger wound, so poor Frank could survive the drink. It was like over-seeing Allie's insatiable thirst all over again. Sindy impatiently shifted her weight. She would give him just a few more seconds before making him stop. *How is it, that I am stuck babysitting the blood-thirst of the United One...again?* she thought to herself irritably.

Luckily, she was able to intervene before Frank was in any difficulty. She pulled at Zach, and after only a few tugs, the vampire sat back with a bloody grin. "Pure, luscious perfection, and I want more," he informed her, giddy and anxious to move on to Lisa.

Now that his initial thirst had been sated, Sindy wasn't as worried over how he would handle drinking from Lisa, but she gave him a warning anyway. "Slow and gentle, baby."

Zach seemed in complete control, cloaking his mark and eying Lisa with a look of predatory desire. He moved towards the woman, who still seemed dubious, but observed that Frank was still alive. He was slumped down to the floor, deliriously high and sporting a stupid grin as a thin trickle of blood dried on his throat where he'd been bitten, but he'd be just fine.

Zach smiled and shushed any worries she might have. "Fragile as a flower," he agreed, licking his lips. "And I'm just a gentle bumble bee, buzzing by for a drink and then moving on to the next."

Lisa was delighted with his words, and rather than shrink away from his advance, she bravely bared her throat for him. Sindy ensured that he was indeed tender and careful as promised, although she felt an intruding voyeur as Zach whispered in the girl's ear of how much looked forward to sampling her flavor, which would undoubtedly be more intoxicating than anything Frank had provided. He then proceeded to tickle the woman's long, graceful neck with his tongue and thoroughly enchant her with kisses before piercing her skin.

The guy seemed to know what he was doing. Once he got down to business, she let him take a decent amount. That was preferable to having him complain about thirst while they were having an audience with Arif. Allie always seemed to be thirsty, and if Zach was anything like her, Sindy would have to give him all the blood she could to keep from raising suspicions.

Sindy was about to part Zach from Lisa's throat, when he began to mumble and groan, pushing the woman away. Lisa was fine, if a bit bewildered. Sindy caught Zach's shoulders, trying to figure out what was wrong. He held his head with his eyes clamped shut. "Why?" he muttered inexplicably.

"Why what? What's the matter?"

"Nothing. Nothing matters. It's done now. The future will overshadow the past. It's begun again, and nothing will stop it this time. That's all there is to know," he finally answered, with a strangely satisfied smile.

Sindy narrowed her gaze at him and wiped the blood from his goatee with her hand. The guy must be high as hell off the experience, because he sure wasn't making any sense. "What are you talking about?"

"The visions," he answered happily. "Did you see them? Do you know the story?" It was obvious to him by her blank stare that she no idea what he could be referring to. "It's alright. I know my place now. It's all good."

"Glad to hear it, because we're almost out of time." She momentarily worried that Lisa's blood had been laced with something to cause this weird behavior, but then ruled it out. Why would Byron give her a victim with tainted blood? It was presumably just Zach's way of trying to analyze the amazing experience. Musicians were strange. "Please don't go spouting stuff like that in front of Arif, okay? He'll have you locked in a box to be studied or something. The man loves a good project." Sindy retrieved Zach's sunglasses from where he'd discarded them on the chair, and slipped them back onto his face to help disguise his eyes, just in case. "Just keep your mark covered and play it cool…please?"

"Cool as a cucumber," he assured her with a teasing grin as the door opened. Their time was up.

Byron seemed very relieved when he came to collect the humans and they were both still conscious, with no complaints of mistreatment. In fact, Zach's venom seemed to have left them both in a state of intoxicated bliss. She had to help Byron get them standing and into the arms of the guards. She heard him tell them something about receiving payment as the guards escorted them out. Byron then took Zach and Sindy to the Master's office.

Sindy was a little surprised to find that Arif wasn't even there yet. "The Master will be joining you shortly," Byron told them. He then closed the door, leaving them to wait.

Sindy settled herself in a leather armchair before Arif's large mahogany desk. She directed Zach to sit in a smaller chair off to the side, hoping it would help keep him out of the main conversation. He leaned his guitar case against the wall, plopped himself down into the chair, and they waited.

After only a few minutes, Arif entered through a door behind his desk, in the back corner of the room. He looked rather imposing, despite his average height and build. The man wore his arrogance like a cloak over his finely tailored clothing. He always dressed in the flashiest of expensive materials, displaying his wealth through Armani suits, brightly colored silk shirts, and layers upon layers of jewelry. Stud earrings, Rolex watch, and rings on every finger, all adorned with diamonds and gems set in gold and platinum. Even the top few buttons of his shirt were open, so that he could reveal the expensive gold chains that lay beneath, against his chest.

In the past, she had known him to sometimes have his dark hair ironed to fall straight down his back, fully as long as her own, but tonight it had been moussed to enhance his natural flowing waves of curls. His thin mustache and beard had been trimmed to sharp angles that accentuated his jaw, and his burnt sienna skin had a warm glow, giving him the overall appearance of a vampire well-fed, pampered and polished to perfection.

He paused for a moment behind his chair before sitting, as though he expected his visitors to show some sign of respect towards him at his arrival. Sindy just sat in her chair with her long legs crossed, the short hemline of her tight dress giving him a nice view of her thighs to an almost indecent proportion.

Arif may be older and far more powerful than she was, but she hadn't been formally inducted into his coven yet, so he wasn't *her* master. What did he expect her to do, get up and bow, kiss his ring or something? Screw that. She wasn't looking to make him mad, but she wasn't planning to kiss his ass. She never had; to start now would just make him suspicious.

After a moment, he smiled and nodded his head towards her, seeming privately amused by her self-confidence. "Sindy my dear, your presence does enhance these surroundings. You look even lovelier than usual."

She smiled in response. Then Arif looked over at Zach, and was much less impressed by *his* presence. Zach was wearing the only clothing she'd had for him, his stage attire from his last gig; ripped black jeans, and a leather vest with no shirt, unrepentantly showing off his full sleeves of tattoo art and his nipple piercings. His eyes hidden behind his mirrored sunglasses, he lounged in his chair as though he owned it, and gave Arif a casual nod and grin.

Arif turned to Sindy with knitted brows, as though it would be beneath him to have to address Zach directly. "I see you have brought a friend," he observed with thinly veiled disdain.

Sindy turned a reprimanding gaze on Zach, who sat up straighter, not that it improved his casual appearance much. "That's just Zach. He's my latest spawn. Sorry, I couldn't leave him on his own, so I had to bring him, but he'll mind his manners. Feel free to ignore him."

"Aren't there other things you should be focusing on, besides creating younglings to mentor?"

She tilted her head with a slight nod, as though agreeing with him. "It was kind of a favor to Allie. I couldn't very well turn her down, could I?" She glanced over at Zach with a smile. "I'll just consider him collateral. Now she owes me."

Arif raised an eyebrow, and then took his seat behind the desk. "The musician," he said, pointing the finger towards Zach, as he recalled Kieran's last report, "the man the United One drank to death."

Sindy couldn't help but smirk at Zach's surprised reaction to the account. He still hadn't quite brought himself to believe what she had told him about his own death. Now Sindy smiled and concurred with Arif's knowledge. "That's the one. She was…kind of upset about it, being her first kill and all. You understand."

Actually, he didn't look as though he understood at all. The man undoubtedly reveled in his kills, and always had. "What I wish to understand, is why you did not use her guilt to drive her here, where she can drink her fill of human blood while being carefully monitored, and have no fear for endangering her victim's lives."

"I am…I will. I just haven't had a chance."

"Wouldn't such a tactic receive better results, if the death she felt guilt over was not up and walking around?"

Sindy opened her mouth for retort, but was not quick enough in producing an answer. Arif rose and put out a hand to stop her from finding a response. "Never mind, it's irrelevant now. I'm amending our agreement."

Sindy did not like the sound of that, but Arif smiled as though to assure her that she should be thrilled with his new proposal. "Your wish has been for me to grant you a place in my coven and residence here in this luxurious community. That is why you have done all of this." He made a gesture to encompass Zach as part of her work towards her goal. "Isn't that so?"

What could she do, but nod in agreement? "And you tell me that although it looked to be poor tactics to my view, this…Zach, was turned as a *favor* to our dear Alyson." Again, Sindy nodded tentatively. Arif grinned and became preoccupied for a moment. "Kieran confirms what you say," he informed her.

Arif must be in psychic contact with Kieran right now. He smiled and nodded. "Very good," Arif murmured, seeming to conclude his mental conference. "Here is what I will do for you," he said, turning his attention back to Sindy. "I shall grant your wish. You are to stay here as my guest, awaiting initiation into my esteemed coven."

Sindy froze in shock, trying not to let panic wash over her face. "But I'm not done," she protested. "I'm supposed to persuade Allie...and what about Zach?"

Arif gave a slight shake of his head, as though she shouldn't worry. "Zach is a new vampire in need of mentoring and safe-haven, is that not what Alyson expected from you, when she asked that you care for him? It makes perfect sense that you should bring him here to me. I cared for *you*, when you were unguided and alone, didn't I?"

Sindy couldn't help but open her mouth in outrage. She softened the tone of her response from the biting edge it might have had, but couldn't keep herself from saying her piece. "Actually, you pretty much told me *good luck*, and sent me out to live on the street. That's why I don't live here."

Arif narrowed his eyes that she would dare to dispute his version of events. "Alyson knows that I assisted you in your earlier troubles with Cain and in your pursuit of that young human boy, Benjamin. She will remember that I came to your aid, and that paints me in a favorable light for this situation, as someone a vampire can count on in times of need."

Alyson had been human then, and beneath Arif's notice, or he might have remembered that part of that *favorable* situation included Sindy's goons clubbing Allie in the back of the head. Clearly, he also hadn't bothered to learn that Ben was Allie's best friend when she was human, making Sindy's past pursuit to turn him against his will, anything *but* favorable from Allie's point of view.

Sindy could hardly keep herself from rolling her eyes, but Arif didn't seem to care. "Although your actions on my behalf have not thus far proved fruitful, I will reward your efforts. I wanted Alyson, and it was in exchange for her deliverance that I was prepared to reward you so well...but I believe it may be a benefit to induct you into my coven at this time despite your failure. You have not brought Alyson to me, but perhaps you can still be useful in persuading her to stay once she arrives. Don't worry about details. I'll have another fetch her here. You will rest the day, and then tomorrow evening we will prepare a proper ceremony welcoming you into my coven. I look forward to initiating you to become one of my own," he told her with a seductive grin.

Sure...now. When she'd begged him in the past, he'd turned her down. Now that she'd decided it might not be what she wanted after all...*now* he wanted to let her in; great.

This was just the sort of thing she had tried to protect herself from, when she had made the decision to let Cain into her heart, and show allegiance to him and his small coven of Mattie and Alyson by letting Cain mark her. The protection should hold, for now, but explaining it was going to be a delicate matter.

"Thank you. That's very generous of you." She tried to sound sincerely grateful. After all, this initiation was something she had asked him for many a time in the past. Now came the catch... "But, I'm afraid the ceremony will have to be postponed for a few weeks." She was quick to explain, answering his look of confused disapproval. "I'm honored, of course, but I'm just going to have to take a rain-check. I'm marked."

To her relief, Arif appeared more amused than angered. "By whom?" he asked with an arched brow. "This whelp?" He nodded at Zach, who had produced a guitar pick from somewhere, and was deftly maneuvering it between his fingers as though performing a magic trick. Zach looked up as he realized that Arif was talking about him, but thankfully, he didn't offer comment.

Arif chuckled. "Never fear. One such as he could never keep me from you. I am old and powerful. A mark from such a lesser vampire is but a nuisance that will hardly impede me. In but a night or two, I will overcome it. I shall take you under my protection and possess you fully my dear, as you have begged of me in the past. I shall be able to grant your deepest desires, as through your thoughts I come to know them as well as my own, and you may consider yourself of my family."

Having him in her head was a little more intimate than she'd had in mind...even when she had *wanted* to be accepted into his coven. She positively wasn't at all keen on letting him in now. Sindy was amazed that Kieran hadn't informed Arif already that she was marked by Cain, but after her initial showing of the mark to Mattie and Alyson, she had kept herself cloaked most of the time, so maybe he hadn't noticed. If he had, he hadn't thought it worth mentioning to Arif. Maybe he'd figured it would just tick Arif off, so he'd let it slide in the hopes that the mark would be gone by the time Sindy had audience with him.

She wasn't anxious to correct him, but it had to be done. She hoped the benefit of the time Cain's mark on her would buy, would be worth the wrath it would incur. "It's not Zach's bite. I'm afraid this is a mark that you're going to have to wait longer for."

Arif looked highly insulted that she was claiming her marker to be more powerful than he was, but he had to have guessed whom she was implying. He took on an air of supreme arrogance and disgust at the thought that she would force him to keep his venom from infiltrating her. She was quick to explain before he could speak accusations. "As part of my mission for you, it was important that I gain the trust of those closest to the United One; the people she looks to for guidance and advice. I'm marked by Cain."

Cain, the only vampire she knew of who could effectively protect her from Arif's venom, psychic will and control, through age and power. She had manipulated Cain into biting her, to show his love and commitment to her. Cain's intentions had been pure, although she still couldn't decide whether it was something she had wanted as an expression of her own feelings, or just to protect herself from Arif. Her only hope now, was that no matter her feelings, the protection would be effective to buy her time to figure her way out of this mess.

"Well, isn't that convenient for you?" Arif asked her in a whisper. If he could not bite her, he could not truly read her mind and divine her motives. But she could not let him believe *that* had been her incentive for the act.

"I never dared to hope that you'd be inducting me into to your coven so soon. I had to show Cain my faith in him, to gain his trust in guiding Allie. He and Mattie keep that girl on a short leash. She's not easy to win over, and Mattie doesn't like me much, but they do what Cain tells them, more or less. Once I had Cain's approval, they let me have time with Allie alone. I did what I had to."

"I see. It was a mutual show of trust then? And he is marked by you as well?" Arif asked with a smirk.

He knew damn well that Cain wasn't marked by her. How could he be? "You know he shares the mark of the coven with Mattie and Alyson. We've already agreed that I can't take part in that. It'd be a disaster to give Allie access to read my mind. That coven mark keeps me from Cain, but trust me, letting him mark me was a huge factor in gaining his trust. It cemented our relationship in his eyes, and erased his suspicions."

"Of course it did. Because a one-way mark, is the sign of a slave. Very good," he told her sarcastically. "He owns you now, and that makes you almost worthless to me."

Sindy sat up straighter in offense. "I'm not his slave! Cain isn't like that." Arif watched her in amusement, daring her to draw conclusions to how Cain's ways might be purer than his own. "He doesn't follow old rules," Sindy clarified. "You know he doesn't think of himself as a master of his coven. He doesn't have any kind of real hold over me. If anything, I lead him...by the heart. He's a trusting, sentimental fool. One act of submission on my part, and I've got him eating out of my hand."

"We shall see." Arif held up a hand to halt the discussion, as a look crossed his face that evidenced that he was in psychic conference with someone else for a moment. Then, looking rather pleased, he sat and leaned back in his chair as the office door opened and they were joined by another.

A very large and impressive bald man entered the room. He was huge and muscular, with skin the color of dark chocolate, and in Sindy's eyes, just as bitter-sweet, creamy and delicious. She knew that his name was Elric. She had seen him before and had always found him to be extremely sexy; dangerous, but with just a hint of kindness flashing in his big dark eyes now and then, beneath his imposing, stern countenance.

None of that kindness could be seen now though. In fact, he looked really pissed, but seemed to catch himself and disguise his expression when he noted that he and Arif were not alone in the office. He seemed caught off guard by Sindy's presence, an unexpected and very attractive delight to his eye, she could tell. He entered the office, observed its occupants and then, getting himself in check, tilted his head with a respectful nod of greeting to Arif.

Zach looked the guy up and down, and then went back to playing with his guitar pick, seeming to decide that he had no interest in whatever was going on here, and was better off ignored. Sindy hoped that he would be forgotten, as he sat fondling the pick and tapping out a tune quietly on his leg with his fingertips.

Arif had a sinisterly amused smile on his face as he greeted their new arrival. "Come in Elric, sit." Elric nodded a greeting to Sindy and sat next to her, taking the second leather chair before Arif's large mahogany desk as Arif continued his greeting. "I hope this impromptu meeting isn't too great an interruption. I know you're a busy man."

Sindy could tell that for some reason the comment rubbed Elric the wrong way, although he tried to hide it, and she couldn't imagine why the words would be grating to him. After a brief pause, Arif continued his introduction. "You remember Sindy. This is her new youngling, Zach. Kieran suggested that I have them brought in for a conference regarding our painfully slow progress with the United One."

Sindy felt a flash of annoyance at the mention of Kieran, but Elric perked up at the name. "And is Kieran joining us?" Elric asked.

"I'm afraid not. After arranging Sindy's transport, he went back to check on the United One with the intention of joining us after. However, he now feels that it would be more prudent for him to remain in surveillance. I would have Lorelei here, but she is currently still settling business in Albany, so it's just us."

Arif turned away from them and seemed suddenly interested in a spot on the far wall. The room was filled with an uncomfortable silence. Sindy shifted in her seat and tried to catch Elric's eye, questioning what was going on, but Elric just gave her a subtle shake of his head to show that she should be quiet and patient.

After another moment, the back door that Arif had used to enter the room opened again, and this time, they were joined by a beautiful young human woman, who very clearly wore Arif's mark. She had thick, dark, curly hair, and wore a dress constructed of draped and wrapped material of exquisite color and design. She looked as though she had stepped out of an *Arabian Nights* movie.

Arif spoke to her, as she stopped with her head bowed before him. "Marguerite, I have a guest in need of hospitality for a short while as I meet with these," he said, with a gesture towards Elric and Sindy. "Zach." The guitarist perked up at his name. Sindy noticed that his eyes were glued to the beautiful woman, although she couldn't tell whether lust or thirst was his strongest motivation. "You may go with Marguerite," Arif told him, "and I will send Sindy to collect you later."

Arif turned back to his concubine, who stood as the perfect embodiment of beauty and obedience. "Give him a tour of the grounds and then perhaps he would enjoy some refreshment from the bar."

The woman nodded humbly. Zach slid his mirrored shades down his nose a bit, to peer at the woman over their rim, and then broke into a broad grin. He looked like he thought he had just won the lottery. It was a good thing Sindy's heart no longer beat, because she would be having palpitations right about now. Arif was sending her newborn vampire off for a stroll with that gorgeous human woman unsupervised? Was he insane?

No, most likely he was testing Sindy's ability to create and mentor a vampire who possessed self-control. But she hadn't even had more than an hour alone with the guy! This could be a recipe for disaster. Even more probable, was that Arif was looking for Zach to screw up, so there would be an excuse for him to be detained as a prisoner, until Arif could figure out if Zach could be useful to him in manipulating Allie.

Sindy could only hope and pray that Zach had drunk enough blood to keep him thinking clearly, and he would realize the severity of the situation. "Behave yourself," she desperately muttered to him as he stood. "No fangs, and if you touch her, you're dust."

31

As Zach moved out from the chairs, the human woman, Marguerite, spoke quietly to Arif. "Master, if it pleases you, may I speak?"

Arif smiled at her fondly. "What troubles you my dear? I can assure you that you have nothing to fear from our guest."

Unbelievable! Arif didn't even know Zach's name ten minutes ago, and now he was assuring this woman that he was harmless? Marked or not, for all he knew, the woman could be murdered by Zach the moment they left the room! Sindy reminded herself never to trust *her* life in his hands.

The woman answered Arif with a saccharine smile that made Sindy's stomach turn. "Oh, I would never worry for my safety as long as I am yours, Master. I wondered only if I might have permission to speak with Elric."

"If you wish, you may speak."

Marguerite gave Elric a deep and graceful curtsy. "I never properly thanked you, sir, for your kindness and care, and for your role in bringing me to my master. I am eternally grateful."

Elric had brought the woman to Arif? Sindy wondered how that had come about, but was more concerned with sending Zach the strongest mental warnings possible, to try to impress on him that if he touched the woman inappropriately, he would truly die for it. He wouldn't even bother to glance in Sindy's direction, but she hoped he'd gotten the message.

The woman received an appreciative answer from Elric, and then gave an even deeper curtsy to her master, and led Zach from the room.

As soon as they closed the door, Arif became abruptly serious. "It seems that Sindy has been having a difficult time convincing the United One that joining us would be in her best interest," he informed Elric.

"I'm not having a difficult time," Sindy protested. "She's coming around. I just need a little longer to clinch the deal. You didn't have to swoop in and abduct me for an update. Kieran could have told you. Everything was coming along fine."

Arif gave her a cold stare. *You may not formally be my subject, but this is my domain. You are not to speak until directly addressed.*

His telepathic reprimand startled her. He could not read her thoughts against her will unless they shared blood, but he could still send to her, and if she allowed it, he could receive her response. She didn't bother to answer though. She just slumped back in her chair, mentally biting her tongue before she could make things worse.

Arif continued as though uninterrupted. "It has been over a year since my sire graced us with his presence, remarking on the fact that my many endeavors have our coven widespread and unfocused. He is right that I have perhaps been too patient, too trusting that my plans would come to fruition if I waited," he said with a pointed look at Sindy. "I think the time for waiting is done.

The situation is becoming more pressing for our dear Alyson, I'm afraid. She is losing control of her thirst, as I am sure our new friend Zach could attest. It would undoubtedly be best for all, if she was under my supervision."

"You don't believe that you will acquire the United One by force, do you?" Elric asked.

"No," Arif assured him. "It seems that inexperienced as she is, her powers of defense have come to her rather naturally. She has somehow thwarted every team I have sent against her. The small group I sent after her and her lover at Mardi Gras in New Orleans a few years back, were easily manipulated by her, and unable to properly carry out their directives. The pair that followed her to that wedding she attended were killed. Lorelei and her team were similarly ineffective. Direct measures do not seem the proper course. She is far too strong. She must be convinced to come to us of her own free will. If Sindy cannot accomplish this, perhaps there is someone else who can."

Sindy couldn't help but speak to defend herself, no matter what his stupid coven etiquette dictated. She still had the slim hope that he might let her go back to Cain's, if he thought it would get him closer to attaining Alyson. "If you would've just left me there, I told you I can do it. Let me go back." Arif's expression was annoyed and uncompromising. She softened her tone and tried to reason with him. "Allie's not an idiot. If she's going to be manipulated, it has to be slow and subtle. There are very few people that she trusts."

"And I do not think that you are one of them," Arif said, uninterested in entertaining her plea. "The young Mattie and the vampire Cain are her coven, and those are the only advisors she will listen to. Sindy, you wear Cain's mark. Evidently, you have become important to him during your stay. Perhaps you could persuade him that Alyson is safer with us. She clearly respects his wishes."

Sindy answered quickly. "Sure, I can do that." She would try to convince him that she could do anything, if it let her out of here.

Arif assessed her for a moment, and then reconsidered, "Forgive me, but I find you unconvincing of late." Arif sat back in his chair, his fingers steepled before him, tapping his chin as he considered something they weren't yet privy to. "Direct force will start a war that we will not win. Guile seems not to be working either. Perhaps what she needs at this point is simple incentive. The problem is that we are not in a position to strike a deal. If we want samples of her blood, we must sit her down and plainly draw up terms for a trade."

What did he want to trade? All Sindy could think of was Zach, but while she had turned Zach at Allie's request, he wasn't all that important to her. It would never work. Elric was also unconvinced that they had decent leverage. "We do not have anything that she wants."

"Precisely," Arif replied. "So tell me how we are going to rectify that." Elric offered no response. "Nothing?" Arif asked. "You are my senior guardsman and you have nothing to say? You cannot find me the piece for this puzzle?"

"Time, my lord. Let me consider it a while."

Arif was disgusted with the request. "We've wasted enough time. I already know the answer. Kieran supplied it to me over his last few reports. Sometimes it seems he is the only member of my coven of any true use to me.

There is something valued not only by the United One, but by Cain as well. Something she should be happy to trade for, and if she is not, Cain would surely convince her. Such a thing would be very useful to us, don't you think?"

Elric traded a confused glance with Sindy. "Very useful, sir. I will fetch it for you without fail."

Arif smiled. "Good. I'm sure you will."

"Tell me where to find this object, Master."

Arif answered with a tone of delighted malice. "Her name is Felicity."

Sindy tried not to let her feelings over the name show too clearly upon her face, but it didn't matter. What emotion had she to show but mute shock? She couldn't even say how she felt about the plan. Arif wasn't stupid. He knew Zach was not important enough to Allie to lure her, although, if Allie ever did visit, she would certainly recognize and feel sympathetic towards him, as her first kill.

The most obvious person close to Allie's heart was Mattie, but trying to gain him would be too risky. Not only was he a vampire capable of defending himself, but he was always near to Allie and under her protection.

Felicity, however, was a human with no current supernatural protection, whose safety would never be ignored by Allie or Cain. Even if Allie wanted to resist dealing with Arif, Cain wouldn't allow the situation to be ignored, and would insist on her cooperation. Felicity's safety was leverage too valuable for either Cain or Alyson to risk.

Meanwhile, Arif would also have Sindy and Zach here, waiting in the wings to be used as back-up in whatever manipulative way he could devise. Sindy had no idea how things would actually play out. Her ethics had been too murky to firmly align her with either side, which made her position rather precarious.

If she stayed, allowing herself to submit to Arif's coven, as originally intended, he might eventually learn of Zach's eyes, or one of the other millions of ways she hadn't been truthful with him, and punish her for it. If she tried to disengage herself from Arif to return to Cain, how was he going to forgive her, if Arif harmed Felicity? She wouldn't be able to deny her dealings with Arif. Being here while they plotted to take Felicity hostage made Sindy an accomplice.

The idea of Felicity suffering some indignity and a good scare, compliments of Arif, wasn't an entirely undesirable one. It might even be nice to get rid of her, and not feel that Felicity was always one step away from commanding Cain's attention and stealing back his heart...but even if the woman died, Cain probably wouldn't love her any less.

Felicity would always be just under the surface of his thoughts. If anything, her death would make him love her more, feeling that guilt should dictate the full attention of his pining heart. To think that Sindy might be connected to the cause of harm to Felicity, would forever tarnish her in Cain's eyes. She doubted Cain's sympathy for her could be stretched beyond that breaking point.

Besides, annoying as she was, Sindy wasn't looking to kill Felicity just for being competition. Sindy much preferred to leave the girl to her human life, little more than a fading memory for Cain. The possibility of her coming to harm would just bring him running to the rescue, no matter what the price of exchange.

She couldn't help but wonder what Cain would do if he knew that *Sindy* was being held here against her will... It didn't really matter, did it? No one was running to her rescue. She had put herself here by her own dealings, and she was going to have to get herself out.

Elric had seemed just as surprised as Sindy, to hear that he would be fetching a person rather than an object, but although he didn't seem happy with the realization, he did not object to it. Something told Sindy that the man had been ordered to do far worse things for his master, and at the moment, he looked as though he would do whatever it took to get Arif to ease up and leave him alone. Presumably, he had his own problems to worry about. Felicity would be just another human among the many here at *Kana Susamış İçin Ev.*

After letting them soak in the information for a moment, Arif smiled and continued with Elric's instructions. "Report back to me tomorrow at sunset and I will give you details. I'd like you to put together a team and begin planning as soon as possible. I have no more patience for sloppy tactics. I want this done right."

"I won't fail you, sir."

"I know you won't. I've been pondering your request to defer your favored human Latisha's departure from our community. Perhaps I was hasty in my judgment of the situation. There are certain liberties I might be willing to bestow, if this goes well…permanent residence perhaps? I'm sure you will not disappoint me."

The clear, deep gong of a bell sounded, reverberating through the window panes. Sindy was surprised by the sound, but neither of the men seemed alarmed.

Arif glanced at the expensive gold watch that he wore and then stood from his chair. Elric stood as well. Sindy eyed them curiously and then rose to join them. "That's the first bell," Arif announced, as though that explained anything. He held up a hand before them, instructing them to wait as he apparently had another mental conference with someone.

Elric turned to Sindy to quietly explain. "The first bell means thirty minutes until official sunrise. There'll be another fifteen-minute warning, and then the compound goes on curfew security lockdown. Any humans without clearance must get indoors before the third bell at dawn."

Dawn already? She'd hoped to get a better handle on her situation before the evening ended, but in some ways, it had already seemed one of the longest nights of her life. Even if she was stuck spending the day here, it'd be good to have rest and quiet to think things through. With any luck, Arif would allow her a bed and a small degree of privacy. She also desperately hoped they would reunite her with Zach for the day. The idea of him being off wandering the compound without her, had her fidgeting on the edge of panic, though she tried not to let it show.

Arif finished his telepathic conference. "Elric, I'm having Miss Sindy temporarily ensconced at Kieran's estate. He doesn't expect to return for a good amount of time yet, and the house could stand to have a vampire in residence."

He turned to address Sindy directly. She did her best to look grateful for the hospitality. She'd rather be back at Cain's, but staying at Kieran's sounded much better than other accommodations she had imagined he might offer. "There, you may reside as befitting a vampire of your exceptional skill," Arif told her, "and be reminded of why you so desperately craved that I grant you induction to my coven and permanent status here at *Kana Susamiş İçin Ev.*"

Was he looking to impress her, in case she might be having second thoughts? Well, if he wanted to show off the luxuries available here, she wouldn't mind staying for a while…except for the fact that she was going to have to spend her time keeping Zach and his white eyes from getting them both killed.

Arif came out from behind his desk to take her by the arm as he showed her and Elric to the door. "All of the humans in Kieran's harem are marked by him of course, so you will be unable to drink from them. However, as a vampire, you are inherently above their station, and as handmaidens they will implicitly obey any other requests you may have. Just don't abuse them," he added with a wink. "You don't want Kieran angry with you upon his return.

The kitchen will be stocked with stored blood, and Elric will see that you are given carte blanche at the commissary to quench your thirst as well. You will also have access to all of the amenities the community provides. I trust you will find the accommodations quite to your liking."

"What about Zach?" she asked nervously.

"Ah yes…Zach. I must admit, you seem to have improved your procreation skills since last we met. He looks to have retained his full faculties, although he is obviously of your making. His charming disposition is reminiscent of your own," Arif said with a smirk. She had to admit, the comment was deserved. She'd been rather rough around the edges when Arif had first met her. "Tell me," he asked, "has he been endowed with your splendidly rare red eyes as well?"

She shook her head, trying to look regretful. "No, I'm afraid not." It was the truth, and hopefully Arif's talent for reading people would confirm that. "I must have pretty mixed blood," she explained. "I've created almost a dozen vamps and none of them had red eyes."

Arif didn't seem surprised. He probably already knew that her past underlings had all had orange eyes. A lucky break for her, because it was also undoubtedly the reason he hadn't bothered to check out Zach's eyes for himself. "That is a pity, but to be expected. Your own red eyes were an unexpected anomaly. Yours is a strain of vampire breed that is normally secretive, keeping together in small, concealed covens. When one like you is found alone, it is usually the result of mixed blood that rarely breeds true. I haven't any need for a newborn such as Zach in my ranks, but he may prove useful with Alyson in times to come. He can stay with you at Kieran's for now. I'll see that Marguerite brings him there to meet you."

Sindy tried not to reveal her great relief to have Zach under her watchful eye. Arif wasn't even paying her attention anymore, as he doled out more instructions. "Elric, be sure to apprise the cadet in Kieran's service."

Elric nodded as Sindy took back Arif's attention to meet his eyes with a very sincere gaze of appreciation. Treated like a guest of rank, and allowed to stay together with Zach too? This was working out much better than she had hoped. This wasn't what she'd initially had in mind, but maybe she could work things to her advantage here after all. "Thank you. You're being very generous."

Arif was visibly pleased to see her recognize the hospitality, rather than act as brash as he sometimes knew her to be. "I am disappointed that you haven't served me better, but a vampire of your talents and experience could be granted a coveted rank in my Guard, if I were shown that you were worthy. Over the next few weeks, you will be given a taste of just how desirable such a rank can be.

When your mark from Cain fades, I will have you brought to me for proper initiation, and at that time, I will read the desires of your heart. Let us hope that I find you to be worthy indeed, so that you might stay here in the capacity to which you will quickly become accustomed and fond of."

Sindy couldn't help but notice the look of worried pity that Elric gave her at the words. It made her fiercely hope that if she couldn't avoid the exchange altogether, Arif found her worthy. Because clearly the alternative was something Elric did not want to see become of her. She refused to let her smile waver, as Arif took both of her hands into his own, and gave them a squeeze before raising one to his lips for a departing kiss.

"During your stay, be sure to acquaint yourself with the Common House, and all of its purposes. It will be best if you have a thorough understanding of our community before your initiation."

As he dropped her hands, she simply smiled and nodded, unsure of why he seemed to find his last directive somehow amusing. Elric took her elbow to guide her out as Arif nodded their dismissal and closed the door behind them.

"What's at the Common House?" she asked warily.

Elric guided her through the hallways and down the stairs to the front entrance as he answered. "You'll find out soon enough." As they came outside, Sindy noted that the sky was indeed showing signs of the coming dawn.

Elric gestured towards a sprawling one-story building across the way. The road circled around it in front of Arif's, and it seemed to have a few entrances. Many people were leaving the structure and rushing off into the development to get where they needed to be before the last bell.

"That's it there," Elric told her. "It's sort of a central meeting place. There's a blood bar there that you can go to, and the place has other uses as well, but we can talk about that some other time. Right now, we've got to get you settled over at Kieran's. I've got my own harem to attend to, and I'd like some time with them before I've got to prepare for this mission, if you don't mind," he added with an edge of impatience.

Sunrise was approaching quickly. They made their way down the steps and driveway, past the lawn and fountain. They reached the road in front of Arif's mansion as the fifteen-minute bell sounded. The general vicinity was teeming with the varied marks of humans belonging to the numerous vampires of the coven. There were too many to sort through and most of them began to scatter at the sound of the bell, hurrying to reach their destinations before curfew. Sindy glanced around, worriedly. Fifteen minutes until daybreak, and they still had to find Zach and get to Kieran's house? "Where's Kieran's; is it far?"

Elric didn't seem anxious at all. "Relax, it's right there." There was a decent amount of property surrounding Arif's estate, setting it far apart from the rest of the homes, but Elric pointed vaguely to the right, where a few very large, beautiful Victorian style houses could be seen, before the rows of attached townhouses began that ranged further out into the community.

As they approached the first house, Sindy truly began to appreciate how generous Arif was being, regarding her accommodations. She would be staying in style, rather than being stuck in a room in his basement as she had first assumed she might be. These homes were gorgeous! The more she saw, the more she realized that it was every bit as luxurious as other vampires had told her it would be. She was beginning to remember why she had wanted so badly to be accepted here in the first place. "Wow, that's it?" she asked. "It's beautiful."

"Actually, that's mine," Elric answered with a smirk. "Kieran's next door."

Comforting to know Elric wouldn't be far away. Not that she knew him well, but he was one of the few vampires here that she knew at all. As they reached the lawn of the house on the other side of Elric's, Sindy recognized Arif's mark on the woman Marguerite approaching from the Common House behind them. She turned to see the woman rushing to meet them, with Zach in tow; thank goodness.

Zach was taking his time, despite the lightness of the sky. The poor woman was practically dragging him to the porch. Sindy gave her a sympathetic look of thanks as she met them. "Everything okay?"

Marguerite nodded, without elaborating, but Zach broke into a broad grin as he joined them on the covered porch at the front door. "Better than okay, and feeling finer by the second. What is that tingly goodness? Is that coming from you?"

He moved a hand closer to Sindy, feeling her proximity through the mark from when she had bitten him. She swatted his hand away, but her touch on his skin just made him let out another expression of delight. She watched his eyes widen as he seemed to pull a quick explanation of her mark on him and its side effects from her mind. She rolled her eyes and mentally begged him not to embarrass her by being such a newbie. He just continued speaking in excitement. "This place is righteous! She says we're staying, is that right? I'm all for that!"

Marguerite addressed Elric, although she kept her eyes lowered towards the ground. "I have orders to deliver him into your care."

Elric gave her a tender smile. He seemed fond and almost protective of the woman. "Yes, I'll take him from here." Marguerite dipped her head with a brief nod and then seemed ready to leave, but Elric stopped her. "Marguerite…"

She paused, but he did not continue, instead waiting for her to raise her eyes to meet his before he spoke. "It's been good to see you again." She did not respond, although there may have been a hint of a smile in her eyes. "Latisha, your dance teacher, speaks kindly of you." Marguerite gave a small start of recognition at the name. "She's my Haseki," Elric explained. "I've asked after you. She says you're doing well."

"She's a good teacher," Marguerite answered.

"Yes, she is…and an amazing woman." Elric spoke the words with genuine feeling and authority. Sindy had no idea what a *Haseki* was, but Latisha was obviously someone very dear to his heart. If Arif was going to do something good for Latisha in return for Elric abducting Felicity, it seemed to Sindy that Elric would be willing to do it.

Marguerite also saw his devotion for Latisha, and seemed pleasantly surprised. It made Sindy wonder just what life was like here, from a human standpoint. Sindy assumed that to see Elric admit affection and respect for one of his humans was not a normal display. It confirmed her suspicions that the man was not nearly as stern as he usually appeared.

"She likes you a lot," Elric added with a smile.

"I like her too…" Marguerite answered hesitantly. "I have to go." She was visibly nervous that she would be late getting indoors by curfew. As if to prove her point, the final bell rang.

"I know," Elric answered. The woman gave Sindy and Zach a nod goodbye and turned to leave when Elric stopped her once more. "Marguerite…I'm sorry."

It was said with firm sincerity. Whatever he was sorry for, he meant it deeply. Marguerite held his gaze for a few moments, deciphering his words; taking them in and contemplating them before giving a response. "Don't be."

She turned and hurried off towards Arif's estate without another word. Sindy shifted uncomfortably as the first rays of sunlight began to peek over the horizon. Elric was a bit perplexed by Marguerite's response, but Sindy wasn't going to give him time to stand here thinking about it. "Can we go inside now?" she prompted. "It's about to get pretty crispy out here."

Elric opened the door and ushered them inside. A vampire sat at a small desk in the front entryway. Elric spoke to him as Zach and Sindy moved inside to take a look around. The house was spotless and beautifully appointed with marble tiled floors, cathedral ceilings and tasteful yet irrefutably expensive décor.

After a moment, the vampire at the door addressed an intercom, while Elric took Sindy and Zach aside. "That's Mick. He's the cadet currently assigned here. Basically, he keeps track of who comes and goes. This is the only open entrance. Each house has a cadet that clears the humans for departure for their classes and community service assignments. Everyone is always carefully accounted for, but you don't have to worry about that. Vampires have free rein of the facilities. You can come and go as you want. Just be sure to clear it with him if you plan to have a human accompany you anywhere."

A blonde human woman hurried down the stairs to meet them. She looked to be in her late thirties, lovely, but well past the blush of youth. She wore a short satin slip dress of deep rosy pink, and nothing beneath it, as her un-naturally large, firm breasts attested through the thin material as she bounced down the stairs. She composed herself at the foot of the staircase and greeted them with a formal bow of her head.

Elric addressed her almost impatiently. "It's Kym, isn't it?"

"Yes, sir," she answered obediently.

"Kym, this is the vampiress Sindy, a special guest of the Coven Master, and this is her young protégé, Zach. Coven Master Arif has granted that they stay here while Kieran is away."

He turned to Sindy, as Kym humbly inclined her head in greeting. "Kym is Kieran's Haseki. It's a term we use for a vampire's favorite human, and the head of their harem," Elric explained. "She is in charge of the humans here and coordinates all of their scheduling. Vampires of the compound always have a human assigned to them, rotating in 24-hour shifts, for feeding and companionship. You won't be drinking from Kieran's harem, but Kym will see to it that you have someone available to assist you at all times with anything else you might need. You can think of her as your concierge. I'm going to leave you in her capable hands."

With that, Elric left. Sindy and Zach found themselves with Kym, wondering if they should be giving instruction or receiving it. After a moment of silence, Kym acknowledged that they didn't have immediate directions for her, and took the initiative. "I'm sure you're eager to retire for the day. I can give you a tour of the house tomorrow evening, but for now why don't I take you upstairs and show you to your sleeping quarters?"

Sindy nodded, gratefully. Zach seemed a bit in awe of the situation, but Sindy knew that appealing as the accommodations seemed, they did not come without a price. She wasn't planning to let her guard down and enjoy things too much yet. A good day's rest and some time to think would be a welcome thing.

As they reached the top of the stairs, they came out into a small sitting room where there were six other girls waiting for them, formally assembled in a line. They ranged in age from barely legal to just under Kym's age, and all were very pretty, with curvy hourglass figures and wearing slip dresses identical to Kym's, in a variety of colors.

"Maybe you really did kill me," Zach turned to whisper to Sindy as they stopped before the girls, "because this is definitely my idea of heaven!"

Kym graciously waited for Zach to finish speaking, although she did not acknowledge the remark. "May I present the harem of the vampire Kieran. We are very honored to have you as our guests, and hope to please you as we do our master," she said, as the girls all dipped their heads to bow respectfully in unison. "As you are aware, you will each have one of us at your disposal at all times. We are all well versed in many aspects of social entertaining and personal assistance, to handle whatever you might need." From the way the women were eying Zach, they were going to be fighting over who got to handle those needs.

Kym turned to Sindy, to give her private comment. "Although there are no men in our harem, I may be able to arrange a loan of some from another household if you'd like. In the meantime, I can assure you that any of us can satisfactorily provide whatever personal services you might require."

Sindy furrowed her brow, unsure how to respond, as Zach elbowed her with a broad grin. "Did I ever thank you for pulling me into this? 'Cause I take back any shit I put you through. This is awesome! And if you're not gonna use your girl, can I have her? 'Cause I've got plenty for them to handle."

Sindy shot him an irate glance for his enthusiasm. "Down Fido." She turned back to Kym with a weary sigh. "I don't need any *servicing*. I just want a bed."

"Of course, Miss. Let me show you to Kieran's suite where you'll be staying. Will you be needing a second bedroom as well?"

Sindy spared Zach another quick glance. This wasn't going to make her very popular, but she and Zach needed some time alone so she could better acquaint him with what was really going on. Besides, she wasn't ready to trust him alone with humans yet…the last thing they needed was an unfortunate accident. "No, we're going to be sharing the bedroom."

That drew a few disappointed pouts from the girls and a very curious stare from Zach. "We are?" He broke into a big smile. "Well then, the more the merrier."

"Not today hotshot. You can play Hugh Hefner tomorrow. Today it's just you and me for some peace and quiet." He looked outraged, but she silenced him before he could truly protest. "Don't start with me. I'm your maker and I'm calling the shots. Got it?"

He stared at her for a moment, obviously disgruntled to have her reprimanding him in front of their audience, but he conceded with a little mocking bow. "Yes Ma'am." He tilted his head towards the women with a lopsided grin. "Sorry girls, she's kind of possessive. You understand."

Kym showed them into the master bedroom suite, a very large and tastefully appointed bedroom, which also included a sitting area and an adjoining bath. It was impeccably neat and looked as unused as a hotel suite. Kym then shut the door, leaving them alone. Zach immediately went to lounge on the King-sized bed with a sly expression. "Wanted me all to yourself for the day, huh?"

Sindy sat down on the bed to slip off her shoes. "Zach, I am almost too exhausted to even begin to explain to you the depths of the trouble we are in right now." She suddenly glanced around, realizing that the room could be bugged. Video didn't matter, because as vampires, they wouldn't show up on film, but sound could be captured. This was supposedly Kieran's personal bedroom, so she would expect it to be private, but they shouldn't take any chances. She met his eyes and did her best to send him her thoughts. *We can't stay here for long.*

He gave her a look of annoyed disbelief. "Are you kidding? I'm movin' in. I love this place!"

She gave him a fierce, stabbing glance not to say anything else aloud. He seemed to get the message, but clearly thought she was being ridiculous. *I thought that Arif guy was doing you a favor. Didn't you want to be here? Why wouldn't you want to be here?* he added with a chuckle.

It's complicated, she answered mentally, with a sigh.

There was a gentle knock on the door, bringing Sindy to full alertness, although Zach seemed mildly curious, rather than alarmed. "Come in," Sindy called.

It was Kym again, with clothing draped over her arm. "Forgive the interruption. I thought you might like a change of clothes for the day." She handed Sindy the clothing, an assortment of silk and satin nightgowns of varying colors and lengths. She then crossed to a dresser to open a drawer for Zach. "There are men's sleep clothes in here that you can use for the day if you'd like." She pointed to an intercom mounted on the wall by the bed. "If you need anything, just press that buzzer. Pleasant day," she told them, with a bow as she closed the door.

Zach laughed, tickled by the subservient service. "I'm gonna like it here. Maybe we should have them send in some stuff. You want some booze or something? Maybe some whipped cream?" he asked with a wink. He noted her stern expression. "Or maybe you'd just prefer a whip... Bet they've got all kinds of sex toys and stuff. Let's ask." He rolled over on the bed, towards the intercom.

Sindy dumped the nightgowns on a chair and shook her head in disgust. "Don't touch it. I just want us to have some quiet time alone." He still looked a little too hopeful after that statement. "And I'm not in the mood," she added firmly.

Zach made a face at her, accompanied by a snort of disgust. "So let me get this straight. You won't let the *willing* women in here with me, but I can't touch *you* either? Are you punishing me for something, or are you just a frigid bitch?"

Sindy let out a huff of a sigh as she mumbled to herself, "Why did I let myself get saddled with you? I'm such a sap. I should have just ditched you and lied to Allie; told her you never woke up. She wouldn't have known."

Zach didn't seem to take the insult too seriously. "Stop playing hard to get. You couldn't bring yourself to ditch me, not without trying out the goods first. I see the way you look at me."

Sindy raised her eyebrows in shock, and then squinted at him in irritation. "Hell, I could dust you now, and no one would be the wiser." She nodded her head towards the door, "You think they care if you disappear?"

"You can't kill me," Zach told her in cocky disbelief.

"Why not?" she asked with an amused grin. "I brought you back, what makes you think I can't take you out just as easy?"

After a faltering moment, Zach replied, "Because I'm more powerful than you, than anyone. You said so yourself."

Sindy chuckled. "And what are you going to do with that power, hot shot? You haven't got a clue." For effect, Sindy allowed herself to unsheathe her fangs and gaze into him with her crimson vampire eyes, mentally showing him brief flashes of visions of herself taking the form of a vicious wolf, just to remind him that she had tricks he couldn't even fathom yet. He definitely received the thoughts from her and was taken aback by them.

"You wouldn't even know how to kill me," she informed him. "Let's get something straight. You're enjoying this powerful, undead existence only by being in my good graces. You had better make damn sure that when you open your mouth, you aren't going to piss me off, or I might forget to be gracious, and you might find yourself a truly dead little pile of dirt on the floor, got it?" He contemplated her display, and nodded his head with some small measure of respect, although she was certain his obedience was sure to be short lived.

She gave him a smile. "You're going to keep your dick in your pants and quit complaining about it. I just think we should stick together, and I have other things on my mind right now."

"Sure, fine," he said with a return false smile, as he pulled off his boots. He then took off his vest, mumbling under his breath. "Prude."

Sindy couldn't help but let out a sharp bark of a laugh. "Wow. You don't know me, *at all*. Let me fill you in. They know me here, because this was my scene. I hadn't quite made it to this level yet, but I know what it's about," she said with a wave of her hand towards the door, where Kieran's harem waited at their beck and call. "I've had a harem of adoring slaves of my very own. I've done the group thing, hell, I've done things you probably haven't even thought of yet.

You want to call me a bitch? Go ahead, I admit, it'd be an accurate assessment. But a frigid prude? Buddy, if I don't want to have sex with you right now, you can believe that either I'm not in the mood, or you aren't as irresistible as you thought you were; your choice.

Between the guy I drank from during your band's set at the bar, and then the pimply faced motel clerk, and the slob next door to us that I needed to drink from after I made you, I've had enough jerks pawing at my body for one night."

"Triple play huh? Okay, I guess you're not a prude...by a long shot."

She gave him a withering glance. "I didn't actually have sex with them. I just let them get far enough so I could drink them."

"Tease."

She chuckled. "I left them all smiling...believe me."

"So, who makes *you* smile? That guy Cain?"

Apparently, he'd been paying attention to some of her discussion with Arif after all. Sindy narrowed her eyes and then stood from the bed. "None of your business. I'm your sire, not your girlfriend." She picked up the nightgowns off the chair and gestured towards the drawer Kym had left open for Zach. "Get dressed, I'll be out in a minute," she told him as she went into the bathroom to change.

She chose the longest of the satin nightgowns to put on. It was a deep shade of burgundy. She also took the opportunity to slim down her body a bit. She hadn't changed form since getting ready to go to the club with Allie before all of the night's chaos had begun. Earlier she had plumped up her breasts and hips a little, for an eye-catching, victim-attracting figure.

After spending over a decade as a willowy-slim teenager, it was still a pleasing novelty to shape-shift into an extra curvy figure for a change, but at the moment, she was better off keeping her body slim and supple, with just a few subtle touches of enhancement, allowing her to feel more like her sexy self, without looking like a walking invitation.

She knocked on the inside of the bathroom door before slowly opening it to re-enter the room. Zach didn't bother to answer, but after a moment, she came out anyway and saw that he was lying on the bed in a black pair of cotton pajama pants. Hopefully Zach's obedience would extend to allowing her to explain a few more things and then leaving her alone to get some rest.

Zach propped himself up by his elbows to a half sitting position and eyed her in the nightgown. He seemed a bit perplexed to notice that her body was not nearly as voluptuous as it had been when she'd left the room, but rather than remark on it, he patted the bed in invitation for her to join him.

With a weary sigh, she sat down on the bed next to him. "So…how are you holding up? You're certainly acting lively enough, but it's been a long night." She paused for a moment. "How are you even awake?" *Allie has white eyes like you, and she gets exhausted by the end of the night. She couldn't stay awake during the day if she wanted to. She conks out cold with the sunrise.* She explained silently, hoping to avoid giving a potential eavesdropper any vital intel.

Zach gave a little shrug. "I'm a little tired, but I've still got enough left in me to go the distance," he told her with a wink.

Sindy tilted her head, considering him as she remembered snippets of past conversation. *Cain said it was a gradual shift with Allie. Maybe it takes a while for all of your powers to emerge and drain your strength. Besides, you were literally dead a few hours ago, so maybe you've had all the rest you need for a while.*

Zach dismissed the thought, not wanting to dwell on the idea of being a corpse. "I'm fine. Never felt better."

Sindy smiled. "Got to admit, you are handling this pretty well. Being changed into a vampire is crazy enough. I'm sorry you got dragged away from your band and caught up in all of this hectic crap on top of it."

Zach smiled, and after a moment of concentration, let his fangs distend. He chuckled and ran his tongue over the sharp points. He kept his eyes closed, although whether he was worried over Sindy's warning not to display them, or was just put off by the disorientation of the new color spectrum, Sindy was unsure. "This is pretty wild," he admitted, retracting his fangs again. "But I can get used to it. If drinking blood always feels that good, I can get used to this fast."

"Yeah…" Sindy closed her own eyes with a shiver, remembering drinking from Zach back at the motel. No wonder his blood had tasted so good to her…Zach was a United One. Now she could understand why Mattie and Cain were so smitten over Allie. With blood of that caliber, Zach could quickly become her favorite addiction, no matter how annoying he was. "Drinking blood is good…which reminds me. You owe me some."

She eyed him with a suddenly predatory gaze that clearly unnerved him. Not that he hadn't enjoyed the venom high from her last bite, but she had lunged at him and pierced his throat with the quick skill of a viper strike before he'd even been able to prepare himself, and it had definitely rattled him a bit.

"Right. You…fed me…in the car. I was in pretty bad shape. Is it always like that when you don't get enough? I wasn't even sure what I needed, but I knew I needed something bad and it had me awful strung out; thanks."

"I gave up my human for you too," Sindy was quick to remind him. "Frank and Lisa…remember them?"

He couldn't hide the way the memory affected him. "That was something else," he admitted. "I'm lookin' forward to more of that. I guess you're pretty thirsty, after giving yours up for me. Why don't we see about bringing some of those girls in here?"

Sindy shook her head. "We can't drink from them. They're marked."

"Marked…" He obviously wasn't following her explanation. "What does that mean again?"

"Headaches."

That brought things into focus for him quickly enough. "Right. No thanks. Well, they had blood at the bar that girl brought me to. She even gave me a glass. Wasn't nearly as good as drinking from a person, but that'll fill you, right? We'll just have them bring some in."

She watched him steadily as he reached over and pressed the intercom button. It was answered immediately by a dulcet voice. "How may I be of service?"

"Could you, um…send up…something to drink?" Zach asked hesitantly.

Sindy couldn't help but chuckle. "You can ask for *blood*, Zach. They know what we are."

He gave her a sheepish shrug. "It sounds weird."

The lady on the intercom answered with a bit of amusement, having heard Sindy's comment. "Of course sir. I'll have some blood sent up immediately."

Zach smiled. "See, just like that. Tell me again why you think we should leave? Head dude seems to run a pretty slammin' place here. I could get used to livin' large vampire style."

"Yeah," Sindy acceded, "welcome to paradise." She gave Zach a sober stare to accompany her next thoughts. *I hope you don't mind living in indentured servitude.* Zach definitely caught the thought, but didn't understand her concern. She tried to explain. *I know the place seems great. I was drinkin' the Kool Aid myself not that long ago. It is great if you're just a run-of-the-mill vampire with ambitions of earning your way up the ladder to a mansion full of hotties of your very own. Problem is, we aren't exactly run-of-the-mill. We've got something the boss wants. You don't have the option of being some semi-anonymous underling. Arif gets one look at those white eyes of yours, and you're stuck being master's pet project, and God knows what he'll do with me if he finds out I gave them to you. We're only safe for the moment, because Arif is arrogant enough to think that he already knows everything.*

Zach was finally starting to look as unsettled about their situation as she felt. He had the sense to answer her telepathically, rather than aloud. *Wait, I thought you said the guy's a mind-reader? Won't he find out about my eyes just by reading our thoughts?*

Sindy shook her head, taking his hand in reassurance. *You shouldn't have to worry about that. He can only get into your head if you let him. You're more powerful than you realize, Zach. You should be able to block Arif from using his powers of telepathy...until he drinks your blood...or mine. Then we're both goners. That's why we can't stay. The only thing protecting you right now is the mark I gave you when I bit you back at the motel. It should be strong enough to keep him out of your head for a few weeks at least, longer if I do it again.*

Zach nodded in understanding. *And you're marked by that Cain dude, right?*

For another month anyway, so that's how long we have to plan our exit...if that long. At any time, he could ask to see your eyes, and I can't think of a good reason you could give him not to show them. You can't let anyone here see you in your vampire state, not even the humans. In fact, Allie always wears tinted glasses around other vamps. You'd better keep those sunglasses on as much as possible. You cannot let them see your eyes.

There was a soft knock on the door. Room service had arrived. Sindy called for them to come in. One of the girls entered with a small tray bearing a carafe and two goblets. She set it down on the end table next to the bed, and then bowed her way out of the room.

Sindy poured them each some blood. After handing Zach his, she downed hers in a single gulp, hoping it would clear her head. Zach only hesitated for a moment before drinking his in the same manner, followed by making a face of dissatisfaction. It was cow's blood and not nearly as good as human...but it would do. Zach settled on the bed, lying back and soaking in the situation. Finally, he telepathically asked, *Okay, so what's the plan?*

Sindy sat back down on the edge of the bed to keep herself from pacing, rigidly trying to keep her cool and figure out what they should do. Back when she had asked for residence at the compound, she'd thought she was such a player; clever and in control. What a fool she had been to get herself in over her head, assuming she knew all the angles. Of course, even if she had known about Arif's plans and the United One, she never would have counted on getting emotionally involved. At this point, turning in Allie, or even Zach, to save her own skin, just didn't seem an option.

Besides dealing with her own personal demons, Cain would forever hate her for it. She may never be able to work things out with him after this, but she wasn't ready to shut that door quite yet.

There had to be a way to extract herself and Zach, so they could escape Arif's coven and stay out of the whole thing. Maybe she could even get Cain to take them under his protection. She didn't have much right to expect anything from him, but hopefully he cared too much for her not to protect her, even if he didn't fully forgive her trespasses. Besides, if she went to him, warning him about Arif's plans for Felicity, and turning Zach over for training, that would have to count for something, wouldn't it? But she had to get them there first…

The plan is that we are going to secretly work on tapping into the mega amounts of power I know you have locked away in you, until we find something that can get us the hell out of here.

Zach raised an eyebrow at her in disbelief. *That's an awful lot of pressure on me. Only thing I'm good at is playing guitar. Well, that and pleasing the ladies.*

Sindy shook her head dismissively as she tried to decide what helpful abilities he could master quickly enough to be of use. *You'll learn. You have to.*

Zach shrugged it off and sat up to move close behind her and begin massaging her shoulders. *Why don't you stop worrying about all that stuff for now and just chill? We're not in immediate danger, right? The master guy said we could stay. Right now, he thinks you're his bitch, and as long as we play it cool, he's got no reason to change his mind. So put it aside and enjoy yourself.* "Tell you what, why don't you just lie back and relax?" he instructed her, as he gently turned and pushed her to recline on the bed with her head on the pillow. "I'll give you a nice rub down; clear your head and turn your body into a slick quivering sigh of satisfaction," he added, as he let his hands leave her shoulders to run intimately down the sides of her body to her thighs.

She opened her eyes to turn her head and stare at him with an arched brow and a smirk. He smiled and spread his hands in an attempt at innocence. "Simply offering use of my skills, no strings attached."

She shook her head with a weary sigh. "I used to say things like that, and I believed it too. But it turns out there are always strings, and I'm getting so tangled, I'm going to end up hanging myself with them."

Zach let his shoulders slump with a grunt of disdain. "That Cain guy, right? But you can't be too worried about being faithful, after your triple play earlier."

She made a face of distaste. "Messing with humans doesn't really count. It's just a means to a meal."

"So why wouldn't you mess around with *me* when I was human?"

"Because you weren't *my* meal."

"But now I count, because I'm a vampire, huh? Now I'd give you a guilty conscience. I get it, but I still think you need to unwind. Why don't we call some humans in here then? Let *them* rub you down and make you tremble. I'll just watch."

"Oh for Pete's sake, you're like a horny little teenage boy. I'm not going to get any peace at all with you in here, am I?"

"I'm the one who's not gettin' a piece."

"Zach, I can't let you inflict yourself on those poor girls out there. You're a new vampire, and evidently self-control isn't your thing."

Zach affected to be insulted. "I've got self-control. If I didn't, I would have jumped you by now."

She laughed. "And landed in a cloud of smoky mist," she said, waving a hand at him and momentarily turning her arm into a discorporate puff of smoke. "Good luck with that."

Zach couldn't help but be impressed by the display. Obviously, no one could touch Sindy unless she let them. "Okay, look. I can't really hurt those human girls anyway, can I? They're marked."

"It doesn't mean you *can't* hurt them, it's just a really strong deterrent. Bite them and you'll feel like your head's going to explode. You could hurt them some other way and drink their blood, but if you do, you can be sure that when Kieran gets back he'll take your head off for you."

"See? What better incentive for self-control is there? I'm not looking for any trouble, just a little fun; their blood is off limits. I won't bite them…but they can bite me, right?"

Sindy looked at him with amused disdain. "If that's what you're into… Fine, I'll make you a deal. I will send you out to spend the day in the bed of whatever lucky little trollop you choose, on one condition. You owe me blood, and I'm taking back my share." She knew she shouldn't leave him thirsty again, but his blood had tasted so damn good…she wanted more; needed it. Let him be the one to fill up on unsavory cow's blood.

Zach backed away from her, holding up his hands as though to ward her off. "Whoa, whoa, whoa… What do you think I called that in for?" he asked, gesturing towards the pitcher of blood on the table. "Drink up. It's all yours."

Sindy sat up, peering at him from beneath her lashes with a seductive leer. "What's the matter? You want the human girls to bite you, but I'm suddenly not your type?" she asked with a grin. "That," she said, pointing at the carafe, "is a poor substitute, and you know it. I want it back the way I gave it to you, straight from the vein." She only gave him a moment to consider it, before adding, "Or, you can spend the day sleeping in the bathtub, Romeo; your choice."

She unsheathed her fangs, giving him a start. He stopped backing away, but was still unnerved by the idea that she would attack him. She smiled. "I know I've got some quality-buzz venom for you, so it's not a bad deal…and to be honest, I'm asking like a lady, but if I really wanted to take it, you know you couldn't stop me. So why don't you get comfy here on the bed and show me some vein, before those sweet things out there turn in for the day without you?"

Eyeing her warily, Zach slowly moved back toward the bed, but wasn't quite ready to sit down as instructed. "Okay, okay, but you'll be gentle, right?"

She chuckled, rising toward him and snaking an arm around his shoulder. "Honey, your knees are gonna buckle from the high before you even know I've pierced the skin."

True to her threat, she dove for his throat and had him slouching in her arms before he could try and protest. She did give him a few seconds of venom injection, but then she couldn't wait any longer to sample and savor his blood.

As she took the first sucking pull, Zach's blood flowed into her mouth like liquid ecstasy unleashed. United One…yes she could definitely taste the difference. An overwhelming, complex and sensual blend of savory flavor, reminiscent of other vampires she had tasted, but yet so much more. It was as though the blood of every vamp she had ever sampled had been mixed and infused with a strong current of an intensely pleasurable essence she couldn't begin to describe or identify. She knew only that she wanted more…and more, and more.

Luckily, she had the presence of mind to realize that leaving poor Zach as a blood starved husk would not be good for anyone. She wasn't above taking a little more than she should, but once the initial tingling tremors of ecstasy subsided enough for thought, she was aware enough to retain some judgment on the matter. Sindy forced herself to retreat from his throat, licking her lips and leaving Zach sprawled across the bed.

She took a moment to collect herself from the dizzy haze of delight Zach's blood had induced. *After that, who needs sex?* she thought, looking down at his unconscious form with a sigh. She crossed to the intercom. If he had the power of all breeds in him, his body would heal him of her venom and allow him to awaken soon, despite his depletion. "Hello? I need a lucky gal Friday to come and collect prince charming. He's a little sleepy, and it turns out this bed isn't big enough for the two of us."

The woman on the other end didn't hesitate, although she sounded amused, considering it was a King-sized bed. "Yes Miss, right away."

"She might need some help. He's not fit to walk. And whoever's bed you put him in, had better want him there, because he's going to be feeling pretty feisty, and he's not going to be out for long. Stock up on the refreshments for him too, fair warning."

She glanced down at Zach one more time, before heading into the adjoining room to run a warm bath for herself before bed. That blood of his had her body singing with sensation, alive and tingling. "You wanted to make me quiver with satisfaction," she teased him as she left the room. "That'll do it."

Chapter 2
It's darkest before Dawn

Cain

A Park in Johnson City
Binghamton, New York
An evening in early June

Cain shifted, as unsatisfied by his view as he was with his limited success in taking his mind off Sindy's recent absence. She'd left him…just like that. He had finally opened his mind to the possibility of loving another, and allowed his fragile, bruised heart to believe he could draw out the tenderness in Sindy that she hid from the world…and she had just walked away.

They had finally become comfortable as a couple, and he had been sure that he felt cautious love beginning to blossom between them, but apparently that was only his own hopeful, romantic nature straining to replace the love he had lost with Felicity; a valiant effort, unrewarded.

Although others would see it as nothing more than confirmation of Sindy's fickle, self-serving nature, Cain knew better. There was a woman within Sindy who had been taught to fear love, and he suspected her disappearance was more for fright over her own feelings, than the absence of love, and displeasure over settling down with Cain.

Or maybe she *had* just gotten bored of him…

He needed to focus less on his own dark thoughts and personal situation, and more on his larger mission; get his head back in the game. He stood in the park, leaning against a tree in the warm spring breeze. He was watching a woman sitting on a bench not very far away. She was intently reading a book under the yellow glow of the streetlamp, which brightened the violet-blue twilight tones that were turning the surrounding park to true darkness.

She was a lovely young thing, in an understated sort of way. Her light brown hair was pulled back into a ponytail, a few strands having worked their way loose to fall forward and obscure her reading. Now and then, she would try to tuck them behind her ear, but they wouldn't stay for long. She sat crossed legged on the bench in a powder blue sweat suit and sneakers. She looked as though she could have been out jogging, and then sat to rest with the fall of darkness. She read with a quiet intensity, seemingly oblivious to the world around her, displaying an innocent sort of beauty that reminded him of Felicity... No, he couldn't start thinking of Felicity, not now. He had work to do.

The girl on the bench hadn't noticed Cain. She didn't seem to be observing her surroundings at all, although the park had pretty well cleared out with the nightfall. She appeared very vulnerable sitting there all alone and apparently unaware. Cain was about to go and speak to her about it, when someone else beat him to the approach.

It was a man that had come upon her, in his early thirties perhaps, and fairly good looking. Cain had been watching him too. He'd been in the park since Cain had gotten there. The man seemed to size up each person he saw, considering their potential not as a date, but as a victim. The way that he kept glancing around to see if he was being observed as he made his way closer to the girl, told Cain that his intentions were likely to be impure. Cain melted back against the tree, and escaped the man's wary gaze.

The young woman had not yet glanced up from her paperback. The park was quickly becoming deserted in the darkness and the man seemed pleased at the prospect of having her all to himself. He now came close enough to attempt to demand her attention. "Must be a good book," he remarked, noting her refusal to stop reading, despite his presence and the poor light.

She now observed him over the top edge of her novel, but didn't speak. The man tilted his head to see the cover of her book. "Vampires, huh? Are you one of those romantics, waiting for a dark, mysterious stranger to show up, all tortured and brooding, to tell you that you're the most beautiful thing he's ever seen, and give you an experience of unbridled passion?"

The phrase seemed practiced, and was spoken with a seductively joking air. The man undoubtedly thought himself charming. Cain hoped the words made the woman as nauseous as he felt. Unfortunately, after a moment, she smiled, seeming to find him amusing and worth her time. She arched an eyebrow as she answered with a cautious smile. "Something like that."

Now the man grinned too, encouraged by her tentative acceptance. "Well, I just might be able to fill that role," he told her, leaning closer. He continued in a teasing, conspiratorial whisper. "But I hope you won't be disappointed that I don't have any fangs."

She chuckled appreciatively at his humor, and put down her book. "That's okay, I brought my own."

Before the man could reply with more than a look of confusion, she lunged for him. The woman wrapped her arms around his neck and pulled him down to tear into his throat with a savage snarl, unworried for the damage she caused.

Cain had seen more than enough. He emerged from his place in the shadows, where he had blended with the darkness, and came up behind the struggling man. He ripped the victim away from the vampiress with a rough tug by his hold on the man's collar.

She was startled, having had not an inkling of awareness of Cain's presence. Her fingers still clutched at her victim's clothing, and she actually had the audacity to hiss at him, fangs bared and bathed in blood, as though that would frighten him. Very amateur of her, but he held back any sharp response to the gesture.

She was a vicious killer, but this was not what he had expected to find at the end of the trail of mangled bodies police had reported over the past few weeks in the area. He could see by her mark that she was barely a month undead. That most likely meant ignorance rather than maliciousness, a much preferred scenario. He swung the man behind him, to be held out of her reach.

Cain allowed his own mark to flare into psychic view, from beneath the mental cloak he had held it under. As he'd expected, this youngling had never seen a vampire as old as he was. His three and half centuries of experience gave the vampire presence within her automatic instinctual pause for respect, whether she consciously understood it or not. She was frightened of it…of him. Her bright orange eyes widened as they darted to observe the air about him and tried to comprehend what his aura could mean.

He continued to hold the human out of her reach. Although the unlucky fellow hung limply, from the combination of her narcotic vampire venom and dazed shock, Cain was quite certain that he was not in need of immediate attention, despite the wound she had given him. When the vampiress' thirst overcame her fear, and she bared her fangs at him again in protest, he raised his eyebrows in mock sympathy. "Oh, I'm sorry, were you not finished?" he asked facetiously.

She squinted at him and tried to make a grab for her victim. "Get your own," she told Cain, as he dragged the man a bit further back from reach.

The guy moaned as he began to come around. Both vampires ignored him as Cain shook his head over this girl's severe misguidance. "First of all," he said, giving the man in his grasp a cursory appraisal, "he doesn't seem at all appetizing in my opinion. And secondly, I couldn't bite him even if I wanted to. He is *your* victim, marked by your personal venom. You've made him unattainable for any other vampire to feed off of. Did you not know that? Have you been taught nothing?"

The man began to struggle as consciousness returned. Cain allowed him to stand, but did not give him his freedom yet. The man began frantically feeling the wound at his neck. "Is that blood? Am I bleeding? She bit me!" he exclaimed to Cain. "That crazy bitch bit me!"

The woman frowned, trying to process what Cain had told her, plainly having no idea what he was talking about. After only a moment, the sight and smell of the blood at her victim's throat drew her to move towards him a step, her lips parted in longing. She shook the dazed expression from her face when Cain moved to block her again. She swallowed back her thirst in annoyance, and gathered her courage to speak. Although she was still a bit frightened of him, her fangs remained bared. "If he's mine, then give him back."

The man was trying to disengage himself from Cain's hold with some affront, when he heard the woman's plea. He hadn't actually looked at her face to note her vampiric eyes and fangs, but was outraged all the same. "What the fuck? Get your hands off of me," he told Cain, although he couldn't work free of the vampire's strong hold, "before I call the cops on you freaks!"

Cain shifted into his feeding state, his eyes becoming a bright golden yellow, and his fangs extending to expose themselves between his slightly parted lips. The man stopped his struggling, frozen in terror. After ensuring that he wouldn't be interrupted, Cain went back to speaking to the young vampiress. "I'm not here to *steal* him. I'm here to save him from you."

"What?" she asked in outrage.

The man now realized that the woman looked every bit as inhuman as Cain, and he was in very dangerous territory. He tried to compose himself, attempting to address Cain in a rational, grateful manner, as his only hope of surviving the situation. "Thank you," he said, through thinly veiled fear of Cain's appearance.

"Not so fast," Cain said, as the man tried to pull away. "If I ever see you lurking about, seeking to accost another again, marked or not, I'll kill you myself."

The man shook his head. "I wasn't…" he began indignantly.

Cain narrowed his eyes. "Don't lie to me." He turned to the vampiress as though seeking counsel. "Perhaps I should just give him back, and let the lessons begin from there."

The man struggled for Cain's attention and forgiveness. "No, I'm sorry. You'll never see me out here again, I promise."

Cain met his eyes with a discriminating stare, knowing that his vampire visage commanded intimidating respect. He was sure to let his fangs show as he spoke. "I'm not chasing you away. You can go where you please. It makes no difference to me. I can easily find you, regardless. Just be sure to behave yourself and we'll have no quarrel. Understood?"

The man nodded emphatically. "Wonderful," Cain said, letting him go as he whispered, "I'll be watching." The man immediately took off running. Cain gave the vampiress a look warning her not to give chase, as her instincts were urging.

She did seem poised to run after him, but held herself in check as she watched with longing and disappointment until the man disappeared. When he was gone from view, she spoke. "Are you really going to watch him?"

Cain shook his head. "No need. He wouldn't dare cause any trouble after *that* warning." He consulted the air of confused awe she seemed to have over him. "I could if I wanted to though. So could you. Can you see him?"

She looked confused, but after a moment of interpretation, she finally consulted her psychic view of the surroundings. There were no other vampires in the area, or other victims either. The only marks to be seen were her own, Cain's, and that of the victim they had just let go. She noticed her new mark upon him and became alarmed. "Is that the guy I bit? Is he going to turn into a vampire now?"

Poor thing, she'd really been taught virtually nothing. Cain silently cursed her maker as he explained. "No, it takes far more than a bite to create another. His mark isn't like ours. Look carefully and you'll see the difference. He'll remain human. The mark only shows that he's been fed from. Do you see how it has a signature similar to your own? It shows that he was *your* victim. Other vampires can see that, and will know this territory is your hunting ground. Have you always drunk them to death? You've never left a victim alive before?" he asked her gently.

She didn't answer. She was gazing into his vampire eyes, seeming taken with the sight of them. He wondered if she had ever even seen another vampire. From her complete lack of knowledge, he would guess her maker had abandoned her before she had even awoken from her deadly slumber. She was truly alone.

Well, that was why he'd set the task for himself of seeking out such orphans. When he'd become aware of multiple deaths in the area, the bodies left practically bloodless and having suffered severe throat trauma, he knew it had to be a violent vampire needing to be taught discretion. However, he'd assumed it was a vampire fairly cognizant of what it was doing; one needing much convincing to change its ways, through either words or battle, as was usually the case. Dealing with the ignorance of a newborn would be a much easier endeavor.

He caused the vampire nature within himself to recede, allowing his eyes to turn blue again. The girl seemed delighted by the transformation. "Is that what I look like? Do my eyes do that too?"

He had to smile at her tenderly. The young woman he stood before was a feared serial killer, and yet she displayed such innocence. He could work with her. "Yes, although your eyes are more of an orange color." Too bad. This would go more quickly if her eyes had been red. Then he could have simply brought her to Khalon, master of the Crimson Coven, to be taught. Red eyes were very rare though, and orange was most common for this continent.

It would be an easier adjustment for her to learn from Cain directly anyway. Red-eyed vampires had such startling skills and the Crimson Coven lived very differently than anything she would be used to. Her own latent powers of weather manipulation went undiscovered and unnoticed by most of her breed. Cain could show her how to control herself as a vampire without even touching on more subtle skills. It would be good to get back to his set crusade to educate others, and not have to focus on his own life for a while.

"But you haven't answered my question," he reminded her gently. "Have all of your past victims died?"

She shrugged, her eyes lowered to the ground in guilt. At least she seemed to retain a conscience over it, even if she hadn't done anything to resolve the trespass. "That's what they do. I drink their blood. They can't live without it. We're vampires, right? That's how it is."

Cain gave a slight nod, to show that he understood that she didn't take delight in hurting others. She simply knew not what else to do. That's why he was here. She continued before he could offer comment. "Do you have any idea how long I've waited for a creep like him? I'm starving! I can't believe you just let him go. I have to kill *somebody*."

Cain shook his head with a sympathetic smile. "No, it doesn't have to be that way." She looked up at him skeptically, not yet daring to hope that he was speaking the truth. "That man," Cain said, with a nod in the general direction her victim had taken. "You drank from him, and yet he lives. He'll be a bit traumatized over the incident," he added with a grin, "but he'll be alright. Finesse can be learned in time, so that those you drink from suffer no real harm."

She still seemed reluctant to believe him. "But I need more. I hardly got any," she pleaded desperately. He knew it was true. She couldn't even seem to shift her eyes and retract her fangs. She was too badly in need of blood. "I'll just have to do it again. What's the point?"

"The point is, killing others so that you may live, is an unacceptable way in which to exist. Wouldn't you agree?" Again, she lowered her gaze in shame. He reached out to her. At first, she flinched away, as though he would harm her, but he moved slowly, pausing and then reaching for her hand again. After a moment of indecision, she let him take it to give it a squeeze of reassurance. "You can drink a little from two or three, and kill none. It takes time, and practice, but it is a worthy thing to learn so that lives may be spared. Are you willing to try?"

She didn't answer immediately. He knew her thirst must be intense; making her doubt her ability to follow his direction. Although reports of her murders had caught his attention, he'd done some research on the area, and it seemed that she wasn't killing as often as her hunger for nourishment should demand. There weren't nearly enough bodies and missing persons to suggest that amount of feeding, even if authorities hadn't discovered them all. She must be starving herself, fighting off the thirst until unable to stand it any longer, and then making a kill two or three times a week, rather than nightly. No wonder she was having a hard time believing him, once the need was that strong, control would seem impossible.

"There are other things I can teach you as well. Did you know that you don't even need to attack humans to feed?" Now he had her attention. She couldn't imagine what he was suggesting. "Animal blood would do just as well. You don't even have to hunt animals if you don't want to. They sell blood at the Oriental grocery down the road, and at most butcher shops as well. Wouldn't that be nice, to be able to buy yourself all that you need, and forgo all of this?" he asked, with a gesture to include her current hunting ground.

"Really?" she asked with enormous relief, clutching her stomach as though to soothe her hunger pains. "I could *buy* something that would make it stop?"

He nodded with a smile. "Come on," he said with a slight tug of his hold on her hand. "I'll take you right now and give you all that you can hold."

She let out a laugh that was almost tinged with tears for the simple but overwhelming relief at the idea that she could feel full and satisfied without killing someone for it. "You would do that? You want to help me?"

Cain gave her a nod of reassurance. "Everyone needs help now and then." He leaned in, and lowered his voice to a joking whisper, "Even us vampires."

"The only other vampire I've ever seen tried to kill me."

"Did they succeed?"

She looked at him oddly over the question. "No…he said I was in his territory and then he tried to run me out of the park."

Cain observed her for a moment in contemplation. "But you're still here."

"He's not," she replied steadily.

"What did you do?"

"I sucked him dry and chopped his head off."

Cain remained staring at her while he tried to merge that information with the visage of the vulnerable young woman that she presented. "Remind me not to judge a book by its cover," he observed quietly.

"He tried to kill me first."

"Indeed," he agreed bemusedly. "You've never met your maker then?"

Now she understood his inquiry about being killed. "No. I guess that could have been him, but he seemed surprised to see me. I don't think he knew me. Maybe the guy who made me got jumped by that psycho too. I hope so. I don't remember much. I woke up under the bushes over there," she said with a gesture vaguely to her right. "I'd been…attacked. It was dark when I came to. I didn't realize that I'd been out for two days. I thought it'd only been a few hours."

There was a trembling hitch in her voice as she chose to confide in him. Cain patiently waited for her through her stuttering pauses. "I was…half dressed, filthy dirty all over, and my shirt was ripped…but nothing hurt." She wouldn't meet his eyes and tried to finish her explanation without being emotional, but Cain could feel her degradation and distress all the same. "I found my pants in the bushes nearby, and I went home; back to my apartment."

Cain clenched his jaw in a grim scowl. The pity he felt was accompanied by burning anger over what some monster had put this poor girl through. Humiliation kept her gaze trained on the ground as she continued. "I didn't go to the police. I was going to, but I wanted to go home first, and then…I looked in the mirror."

"I'm so sorry," Cain told her sincerely, but she barely seemed to hear him. She was gazing at nothing as she relived the trauma in her mind.

"I thought I was crazy, or a ghost, or something. There was blood on my skin but not a single bruise or a scratch. I couldn't see myself in the mirror and I couldn't feel my heartbeat. I kept waiting for something to happen, like an angel of death was going to come and collect me, or some ethereal stairway would appear. I was solid though; whole, and conscious, dead or not. I took a shower, changed my clothes and then I just sat there all night, waiting…but nothing happened.

By the morning, I was famished. Nothing I had in the kitchen seemed appealing, so I thought I would go out to a diner or something. I'd have something to eat, collect my thoughts and then maybe go to the police station after all; let them try to figure out what was wrong with me. I tried to go out, but the sun hurt my eyes and it stung my skin. I only lasted a minute or two before it burned so bad that I had to run back inside. That's when the word *vampire* first entered my thoughts.

Crazy though, right? I mean, I thought I'd have to be crazy to really believe it. Vampires aren't supposed to be real. They're just scary, romantic fun for dumb girls like me, who like to daydream about mysterious bad boys." Her voice now became infused with quiet outrage, as she let anger replace the frightened confusion she had felt as a victim. "Even if they are real, they're supposed to charm you and drink your blood until you swoon. They're not supposed to knock you out, rape you and leave you for dead in the bushes."

"No," he answered quietly. The horrible injustice of it made him want to hold and protect her. He could see her anxiously recoiling from the thought of such invasive liberties taken with her body though, and felt that he should keep his distance. After all, he was still a stranger to her, and his attempt at comfort might simply feel like another trespass. "That should never happen to anyone. If I ever find your maker, you can be sure I'll tell him that, just before I turn him to dust."

His comment brought her full attention back to the present. She looked at him, slightly bewildered by the angered determination in his voice. She processed it for a moment. "So, real vampires aren't all horrible then, like the one who did this to me, or the one I killed in the park?"

"There are many horrible things in this world, real vampires surely being near the top of the list, but anyone who wields free will has the choice to be as they choose. Are you horrible?"

Her eyes widened, her lips slightly parted, before she dropped her gaze in shame. "Maybe I am. I've done some awful things."

"Yes, you have, but you can choose to put that behind you now. The kind of vampire you become is up to you. Do you think I am horrible?"

"No. You seem..." she shyly averted her eyes again with a smile. "You're more like what I'd want a vampire to be like."

"I wasn't always. I've done awful things too. But every night that we exist, is an opportunity. Every moment is a choice to either do things that make us proud of who we are, or are a confirmation that the humanity within us is dead, and we deserve to be nothing but dust. I'm not ready to be dust yet. I believe I can still do good in the world. That is why I go on. You need to make your own choices. Decide what it is that will make it worth the struggle for you to go on. It is a struggle, make no mistake, but I hope you will find that it is worth it."

She quietly pondered his statement before looking up at him with a new glimmer of hope in her eyes. "I don't *want* to hurt people, but...the thirst, it's like dry stinging needles in my throat that drive me crazy, and nothing makes it go away...until I kill. Everyone that walks by smells so good, and when they stand close, I can hear their hearts beating. I tried to fight it, but the temptation is just too strong to resist. I never wanted to kill anyone. I just want it to stop. Will you help me? Will animal blood really make it stop?"

"I know how hard it is, and you should know that no amount of help from anyone else will be enough, if you aren't willing to work for it yourself. But animal blood will make it easier. If you'll accept my advice, I'll teach you all that I can to help you succeed. Let's go get you something to drink."

She seemed grateful and eager to leave, but Cain stopped to gesture towards the bench. "Don't forget your book."

She barely glanced at it. "I've already read it dozens of times," she admitted sheepishly. "I kept hoping that somehow it would come true, because so far, the reality of being a vampire has been a big disappointment."

Cain hadn't bothered to read a vampire novel in decades, but had a fair idea of the current idolized representations going around. "I can imagine."

"But I guess they got some of it right after all, because you're like a hero walking right out of the pages!"

She squeezed his hand and he began to recognize the fawning adoration that she was emanating. He took back his hand and stopped walking for her to pay him strict attention. "I'm here to help, but I'm not a hero, and I am most definitely *not* the romantic lead in this story," he told her with a wave of his hand to indicate things between the two of them. "My name is Cain," he told her softly, "and I'm just helping where I can. I'm afraid my heart is unavailable, but I hope you'll accept me as a friend," he concluded with a hopeful smile.

She seemed disappointed, but amicable, and finally gave him a slight nod. "Are there others?" she asked after a moment. "Other vampires like you?"

"Like *us?*" he corrected her with a smile, for her to stop thinking of herself as one of the bad guys. "Yes, there are others," he assured her. "Although many are not the type you'd want to come across, there are some who will unquestionably be quite capable of playing your leading man if you'd like."

She gave him a sheepish grin. "Cool."

"What's your name?" he asked, as they continued walking.

"Dawn."

"Well, that's an unfortunate name for a vampire, isn't it?" he observed teasingly.

She laughed. "I've been having such a hard time figuring out what happened to me and what I should do, I never even thought about it."

"Well, not to worry, Dawn. Things will be better for you now, I promise.

~~~~~~~~~~~~~~~~~~~~~~~~~~~~~~~~

It turned out that the Asian market and the butcher shop were both closed already, but Cain had enough of his own supply to feed her back at his hotel room. Dawn was edgy and impatient as he heated it in the microwave, but was valiantly attempting to reign in her thirst and her doubts.

As soon as he handed her the mug, she began to gulp down its contents as though starved...which of course she was. However, the moment she finished, she licked her lips and seemed unsatisfied with the experience.

"Feel better?" Cain asked tentatively.

She was looking more dissatisfied with the beverage by the second. "Better? You think this is better?" she asked him in disbelief.

"Better than killing someone?" he clarified with an arched brow. "Yes."

She slouched back in her chair and inspected the remaining blood in her cup, as though offended by it. "This is disgusting."

"It's not disgusting," Cain disagreed wearily.

"Well, it ain't good," she insisted as she put down the cup and gave it a push away from her across the table.

"Want me to warm it up some more?"

"Won't help."

Cain gave her a disapproving look for her lack of compromise. "Alright," he said with a sigh, "so you don't like cow's blood."

"I'm not surprised," she informed him. "I'm a vegetarian." Cain could hardly help but let out a choked chuckle. "What?" She was annoyed that he might be mocking her.

"Nothing… Let's try pig's blood, it's a bit closer to human."

She made a face at him. "I have to drink pigs?"

"Better than *Long Pig,*" he replied snidely.

She didn't place the reference, still focused on her discontent with the idea. He ignored her resistance, going back to the refrigerator to prepare another mug from the small container of pig's blood he had left. She watched him skeptically. "Are you gonna try to tell me pigs taste like people?"

He put it in the microwave and then turned to answer her with a sigh. "No, not really, but we're a bit short on options here. I told you it wouldn't be easy. You get used to it though. It's not bad." He retrieved the cup, gave it a stir and handed it over. "Try this."

She took the cup, but as she brought it to her lips, she lowered it again without even taking a sip, as though the scent alone had repulsed her. "I'm not going to be able to do this."

"Yes you can."

She wrinkled her nose and then pouted, as though it was his fault. "Now I keep thinking of Wilbur…you know, from *Charlotte's Web.*"

Cain tried not to smirk at the comment. "I realize that you were a vegetarian, but people eat animals all the time, and even a vegan must admit that it's preferable to cannibalism."

"Animals are nicer than most people, as a general rule," she informed him with a smirk. He refused to relent, and after a moment, she obediently took another drink. Under his watchful gaze, she finished the whole mug, but she plainly wasn't happy. "I guess it's better than nothing."

Cain asked that she stay the day, if it didn't make her uncomfortable. He'd feel better being able to keep a close eye on her. The room had two beds, and she seemed amicable enough. He woke during the day, hearing her toss and turn. Just as he was wondering if he should try to wake and comfort her, she cried out and woke up on her own.

"Sorry," she said quietly, upon seeing that he was also awake. She seemed mortified. "I have nightmares... I was hoping maybe I wouldn't, with you here and all. Sorry I woke you."

Cain offered her a sympathetic smile. "I've had plenty myself. Don't give it another thought. They'll fade."

As the sun set the next evening, Cain was up and about before her, although she was also a surprisingly early riser for one so young. She respected the dangers of the sun, but wasn't so concerned as to worry over awakening before full darkness. "Trust me, waking up early is much better than risking more nightmares," she confided, sheepishly. From the little bar area in the corner of the room, Cain brought her the cup of blood that he had been preparing.

"The more we work to improve reality, the less hold the dreams will have over you." He assured her, as he handed her the mug. "Have faith. Things are going to be much better for you now. Do you believe that?" A small smile crept over her face as she nodded.

She accepted the mug and lost her smile almost immediately as the scent reached her nostrils. After a slight pause, she obediently began to drink it, but gave up after only a few swallows and handed it back to him. "I'm sorry, but I can't live on this stuff, all the time, forever. Didn't you say you could teach me how to drink from people *without* killing them? Let's do that."

He chuckled, shaking his head. "No one in the world has patience anymore. It's going to be a long time before you're ready for that, my dear. The time will come, but you really need to discipline yourself to drink what's more easily offered. Your body is rebelling against it at the moment because it knows what it's missing, but after a while you'll get used to it and it won't seem nearly so distasteful, really."

She rose from her chair, pacing in antsy discomfort. "I'm starving, and that is not going to be enough! The thirst is ripping me up inside. How do you stand it? I'm sorry. I know you're trying to help, but I'm never going to be able to control it like you do. I'm just wasting your time. I've got to go."

As though he would just let her walk out the door to go and kill someone. "You're not going anywhere."

She opened her mouth indignantly as he blocked the door. "What am I, your prisoner now?"

"No," he answered quietly, although he didn't move to let her out. "But I now consider you my friend. I vowed to help you, and if I let you go out and kill again, I'll have failed us both. I know this is difficult, but I promise that it will get better. I've helped dozens...in all probability hundreds of others to dominate their vampire natures, and I can teach you as well. Please trust me. I believe that you can resist killing, and I can help if you give me a chance."

She still seemed reluctant. He gave in a bit. "In time, I can teach you to drink from humans in small amounts, without hurting them," he offered, regaining her interest. "But if you're going to have the restraint to do that, you're going to have to learn to fill yourself with this first."

She took a deep breath and let it out slowly, contemplating his directive. Taking that as slight acceptance, he moved back to the counter and refilled her cup. She watched him silently, although he did see her eye the door once or twice, considering her options. Most likely, she didn't have anywhere better to go. He was pretty sure she'd stay.

Finally, he brought her another warm, full mug. "Come on, it's not that bad. If you can get yourself started with this, you can get even better animal blood outside of the city later. You may be averse to paying secret visits to nearby farms or hunting in the forest for animals, but you'll find their blood much more satisfying if you can get it fresh. Then, if you really need to, we can discuss gradually working your way back up to humans, but this is the first step."

He handed over the mug, but she barely spared it a glance. "Out of the city where? Your territory's not around here?"

"Territory is for hunters," he told her with slight reprimand. "I travel quite a bit, but home base is in a small town up further north. I don't care for cities; too crowded...and tempting." He interpreted her surprise. "Yes, even I still get tempted at times. Being an anonymous face in the crowd makes it far too easy to drink from humans compared to being in a small town.

Sometimes I hate small towns just for that reason, because I'm feeling weak and annoyed at the restraint of having to maintain a civilized image for myself, instead of being in a city where no one knows me or cares. But I'd rather battle my demons in a small town, than feel I've got permission to get away with something easily. In my experience, in most situations, easy is never good.

I travel wherever I feel I need to intervene, and I make do. You could learn to find yourself animal blood more to your liking around here. I can show you how, but when I'm on my own time, I prefer almost total isolation from humans, to be honest. A word of advice, try not to interact with humans very closely, or often. Even *if* you can manage not to view them as prey," he confided in her, "you start forming bonds, friendships, and that brings about a whole new set of problems."

"Like what?"

"Well, for starters, we need to be secretive by nature. Obvious rule of our kind, we cannot let humans know of our supernatural existence."

"Okay, that makes sense," she answered with a smirk. "Except you gave that dude in the park a nice show."

Cain laughed. "Well, I didn't say that I always follow my own rules, but I think over three centuries of experience has made me a fair judge of which actions pose a threat, and which are acceptable. He'll be no danger to us. However, when you reside in a small town and deal with the same people on a regular basis, hiding your nature becomes cumbersome and stressful. After a while, you get weary of all the lies, and the urge to share your secret becomes hard to resist."

She thought about that for a moment, possibly comparing his words to the scenarios posed in the many vampire novels she'd read. "Would it be so bad to tell someone? As long as they kept your secret and didn't try to kill you, I mean."

"No, it can be a great comfort, if you have someone who can truly understand and sympathize, but such confidential relationships are treacherous to maintain. They often lead to heartbreak," he informed her quietly.

She played her eyes over his face as she took this in. After a moment, she replied with a sympathetic smile. "Spoken like a man with a broken heart."

After avoiding her gaze during an awkward pause, Cain gestured towards the mug in her hand, still full. "Drink up."

"On one condition," she answered quietly. "When you leave the city, will you take me with you? I haven't got anyplace else to go. The last time I...drank...well, I guess I wasn't careful enough ditching the body, because the police already have my apartment staked out. I can't go back. It's been really hard to find a safe place to spend the day, 'cause I'm out of cash, and I don't know what to do. I know you've already got a girlfriend or whatever, but I'll mind my own business and I won't be any trouble. Just please don't leave me here."

Cain smiled at her eager insistence. "There'll be no more drinking from humans, until I think you can handle it safely, no matter how bad you think that tastes," he added with a gesture towards her cup.

She was eager to be accepted, but still seemed worried over her ability to manage his request. "You'll help me, right?"

He nodded in reassurance. "You can do it."

"No more people until further notice, I promise."

"Then you're welcome to join me. I'd the intention of inviting you all along. It's going to take some time and work to truly break the pattern of your thirst. I usually stay where I'm needed, but if there's nothing tying you here, we can spend the time more comfortably in controlled surroundings back at my estate."

"*Estate*, huh?"

"Well, there are some advantages to being immortal," he answered with a grin. "One thing I've learned as a vampire, about money and people; long term investments pay off." At least he hoped so…

In recent years he'd invested his time, energy and heart into mentoring the United One, and what had that earned him? Allie and Mattie had taken off on him. They would be back though, he was sure. He just hoped they returned before Allie managed to get herself into serious trouble, because he'd a feeling that trouble was something it wouldn't take her at all long to find.

Chapter 3 - A crack of the whip

Allie

Outside of a mini-mart
Somewhere Upstate New York
An evening in June

The rumbling roar of a motorcycle engine attracted Alyson's attention from the man she'd been watching make his way across the parking lot and into the mini-mart. It was foolish how her heart leapt for a moment at the sound, expecting joyful recognition of the rider. The bike was a Harley alright, but as it pulled into the lot, she could see that its rider was a much larger man than anyone she knew. Anyway, there was no shared coven mark upon him; he was human.

Her beloved friend Cain, vampire and mentor, was far from here. It had been about a week since she and Mattie had left him to have some time on their own, and it had been a bit longer than that since they had shared blood, but they still shared the mark of the coven. It wouldn't wear off for almost three weeks yet, and she would feel Cain if he were anywhere near. It wasn't him.

The biker was a hefty guy though…and when Allie was hunting, size mattered. The bigger the victim, the longer the drink, and a better chance the guy would survive her thirst. The last thing she needed right now was another accident.

She emerged from the shadows as the man cut his engine and removed his helmet. Wow, he was a big guy, and his long heavy beard could easily cause him to be mistaken for a guitarist from ZZ Top…or two…put together. Yeah, the guy was that big. How was she supposed to find his throat under there?

He didn't intimidate Allie in the least. Besides the fact that she was the United One – currently the most powerful vampire on the planet to her knowledge, with nothing to fear from a human of any size, she could also telepathically and empathically read the guy's thoughts and intentions. Despite his ominous appearance, he seemed decent enough, with no overt hostile tendencies. Good, she hated drinking from creeps.

Mattie always told her that it seemed backwards, like she should be seeking out bad guys to drink from. It felt icky to do that though, like she was sucking out their evil into herself. Why should she feel obligated to meet out vigilante justice? Besides, she didn't view blood drinking as a punishment. She didn't kill her victims, or even hurt them…well, just the once. She tried to be very careful. She usually just took a drink, and went on her way, leaving her victims slightly disoriented, but none the worse or the wiser for the experience.

She approached the biker as he dismounted the motorcycle and stowed his helmet. He barely even glanced at her until she stopped right in front of him, and then he looked very surprised to see that she wasn't giving him wide berth.

At barely 5'2", slight little Allie should be frightened of someone like him. The girl herself didn't look like much of a threat, even with the ends of her shoulder length platinum blonde hair dyed a bright punk pink. She wore a simple tee-shirt with jeans and sneakers. She'd been trying to appear approachable and non-threatening for her hunt.

Although dressing slutty and portraying a blonde bombshell might have drawn easier prey, with her husband Mattie looking on, it wasn't a part she was comfortable playing, so she had gone the simple route, planning to draw   someone in with a friendly demeanor. However, now that she had this particular prey in her sights, she wished she was wearing her leathers and boots. It would have made her sincere appreciation of his bike that much more believable.

The man squinted at her suspiciously, as she openly admired the motorcycle. "Nice wheels," she remarked with a smile.

"You ride?"

"Haven't got my own, but I know a quality hog when I see one."

Allie caught telepathic snippets of him envisioning her on the bike. He seemed more amused than aroused by the thought of her tiny little frame trying to straddle the large motorcycle and harness its power. She tried not to be insulted as he raised an eyebrow and cracked a smile.

Thoughts of any further response she might make were cut off by the rolling surge of thirst rumbling through her insides, and then settling in her stomach like a handful of swallowed razorblades. Blood, her body demanded. Fill me with the warm blood encased in the man before you, or I'll claw your insides to ribbons until you can focus on nothing else.

Alyson concentrated on the man with eerie intensity, as she commanded the thirst within her to be still and allow her to land her meal. Forget the small talk; it was time to get down to business. "I know you've got some fun, mocking response brewing in there for me, but I'm afraid I'm gonna have to cut you off and get right to the point."

The biker straightened, understandably taken aback, as Allie continued. "You see, Rick," she began, as the man was startled by her knowledge of his name, telepathically plucked from his mind. "I've got a problem, a problem that a big strapping guy like you can easily help me solve."

The guy put up his hands to back her off. "Whoa, wait a minute. Did Cliff send you to me? 'Cause I told him, I ain't that hard up for cash. I won't do those kinds of jobs."

"No, of course you wouldn't. You're a nice guy, aren't you Rick? I think you can help me out. Don't worry," she assured him, making her way around the bike, to move close and speak to him confidentially. "Nobody gets hurt. I promise."

Ten minutes later, she had him sitting on the ground behind the mini-mart. He was completely under her spell, first mesmerized by the power of thrall she had wielded with her white vampire eyes, and now intoxicated near to unconsciousness by the venom in her bite. He sat on the ground, his back against the building, with Allie curled up in his lap and suckling blood from his wrist.

So good...it felt so good to allow the vampire within to manifest and fulfill its desires, even if she *was* keeping it on a short leash. Darker urges tried to convince her that she should quench her thirst more quickly and deeply. The man was drugged into submission, she should take the opportunity to truly rip open his vein and let his strong heart pump blood into her mouth in spurting bursts, rather than meekly sucking thin streams through the holes her fangs had made. As it was, she'd already torn his skin a bit, rather than settle for neat and tiny punctures; but that would have to be enough. She wasn't going to rip the poor guy's arm beyond repair.

She could almost picture herself leaving his arm to slash his throat and let his blood poor over her face in glorious excess...but no. That was not acceptable. She allowed herself to take victims on the condition that they survive the encounter; the vampire within her was not to be fully unleashed to drive her to revel in a drink enjoyed for sport. This was enough. She blocked out further insidious suggestions from the subconscious entity within, and concentrated instead on the man's heartbeat. It was steady and strong. Good, she could continue feeding, as long as she kept her focus to ensure careful moderation.

Pushed to the background of control, her vampire nature kept psychic watch of her surroundings. A few humans could be seen, evidenced psychically by their life-forces, as they came and went from the convenience store, but they were oblivious to her dark deed behind the building, and posed no danger. Then the vampire within her became aware of the aura of another vampire approaching. It shouldn't matter though. This human victim was already thoroughly marked by her venom. He was undeniably hers. No other could take him from her.

Alarm was short-lived anyway, as the approaching vampire's presence brought with it the comforting tingle of ownership. This vampire was no threat; he was marked as a coven mate; her maker. The reassuring shiver of his closeness wrapped around her like a blanket of psychic security. Her vampire nature was convinced he was non-threatening, allowing Allie to continue feeding undisturbed.

Blood, so desperately needed and appreciated by her body, flowed into her mouth, filling her with power. It had been a long time since she had landed such a meal. Allie savored it as she kept an ever-watchful connection with the man's heartbeat. White noise buzzed about her awareness, but she tuned it out to focus on the all-important health of her victim.

Allie felt a tugging at her arm. Someone was trying to remove her from her place curled in her victim's lap. Someone wanted to end her feast, but there was still plenty more to drink before she would endanger his life. She shooed the annoyance away with a backward swipe of her hand.

Wind swirled about her, tugging at her hair and buffeting her body as she curled herself more tightly to be protected by the form of the unconscious man she drank from. She could feel waves of hostility flowing towards her, breaking upon her like the wrath of the ocean, as a booming crack of thunder sounded from the sky overhead. It was Mattie, she could feel him…and boy was he pissed.

Allie took a last swallow and then forced herself to disengage from her meal. She retracted her fangs and caused her vampire vision to recede, her human-blue eye coverings blinking back into place. She straightened, coming out from where she had been nestled against Rick's chest, under his hunched shoulders. She looked up, expecting to see Mattie standing over her in angry disapproval.

He wasn't there. He was nearby, she could feel him, but he wasn't standing over her as expected. She sat up further and swiped the hair from her face as the wind caused it to obscure her view. There he was.

Mattie was just standing up from a place on the ground, a few feet away, near the wall of the building. She couldn't help but smile at him, her handsome man. Young and robust, he'd been just shy of eighteen when he'd died, but physically he was every inch a mature man in Allie's estimation, and of course, by this time, chronologically he was almost twenty-eight. His copper gold hair had a fiery tinge to it in the glow of the street lamp that made him look really hot, but the expression on his face was more stormy than seductive. He glared at her as he brushed himself off and came closer. "Are you done?" he asked mockingly.

She furrowed her brow at his tone. What was his problem? He'd known she was out hunting for a drink. "No. Actually, I wasn't." Mattie looked away for a moment, his mouth open as though he couldn't believe her audacity, and wished he had an audience to share his outrage with.

"What?" she asked defensively. "I was being careful."

"Careful?" he repeated, facetiously. "You threw me at the God-damn wall!"

Allie stared at him in confusion, but then read the experience from his mind. It was true, she had. He had tried to interrupt her feeding, and she had backhanded him into the side of the building as easily as shooing away a fly. "Sorry," she offered weakly. "I was being careful for him," she explained, indicating the man in whose lap she sat. "Not so careful of you, I guess."

"Well you'd better learn to multi-task! If I was some human that had come along, you would have killed me! You can't just go charging through life like a bull in a china shop, Allie! Be aware and show a little restraint," Mattie implored her. "Restraint is sexy," he added, trying to sound persuasive.

"I'm not a bull! Restraint is sexy? Sure...when you aren't the one with thirst driving you to distraction and mega power flowing through you, trying to claw its way out...on my end, it's just a never-ending struggle. Look, I'm sorry you got tossed like that, but it wasn't me."

Now he arched an eyebrow, wanting to laugh, like a parent listening to a child with a face full of chocolate explain how they hadn't eaten any sweets. "No?"

"Not really," she insisted. "I mean, obviously it was me, but I wasn't aware. *I* didn't do it. I was on auto-pilot. It was the blood."

Her explanation didn't seem to be helping. If anything, he was looking more alarmed. Great, the last thing she needed was for him to think she was losing her mind...it wouldn't be the first time he'd had that concern.

"Mattie, you know those zombie things we see sometimes…the vampires that have no human mind left?" He nodded cautiously. "It's the vampire blood that controls them, all on its own. You and I, we still have our intelligence, so we're in control, but the vampire intelligence, it's still there too. It doesn't control us, it lets us be in charge…most of the time, but when I'm not paying attention, it's still aware. I was busy, so I guess it figured it should take charge and protect me from you. I didn't mean to hurt you. I didn't even realize. I'm sorry."

He just stood there for a minute, taking in what she had said. Mattie rarely gave in to his vampire urges. He didn't even drink from humans. He tried to ignore the fact that there was another consciousness within him, capable of actions he wouldn't necessarily approve of. Now he shook his head, shaking off the thought, and gestured towards the man Allie was still sitting entangled with. "You were drinking from him for a long time. I was afraid you were going to kill him."

Allie smiled and shook her head. "I told you, I was being careful. Here, see for yourself," she said, offering Mattie the man's wrist. "Check his pulse. He's only out because my venom threw him for a loop. He's fine."

Mattie seemed doubtful as he knelt next to her, taking the man's wrist into his hands to feel for a pulse as she had suggested. "See? He's a big strong guy Mattie, and clean too, no drugs or anything. I made sure." Allie continued to reassure him, but soon realized that Mattie wasn't even listening to her. He wasn't really checking Rick's pulse either. He was holding the man's wrist and staring at it while fighting an internal battle for control. He could smell the blood. He was still as stone, struggling. His eyes finally glazed over orange, losing the contest of will he had been waging with his thirst. Mattie dropped the man's wrist and backed away, disgusted by his own weakness.

Allie quickly climbed from Rick's lap to follow Mattie, trying to catch his gaze as he turned away. She moved in front of him, taking his arms and sending him currents of soothing understanding. "It's okay, Mattie. You need blood just like I do. There's no shame in wanting it. You know, human blood would make you stronger than anything from the butcher. Maybe you should drink from him." She noticed that he'd retracted his fangs, his vampire nature once again under strict control. "You'll just be drinking it from me later anyway," she added quietly.

He made a face and turned away again. "That's not why I drink from you."

"I know, I'm just saying…it's no big deal." She glanced back at Rick, still leaning peacefully against the building; his head slumped down onto his shoulder. "He's still got enough left to spare."

Mattie just shook his head and dropped his gaze. "Let's get out of here. Are you going to do something with him, or do you just leave them like that?"

Although she didn't hide her habits from him, Mattie had never actually watched her hunt before. "Na, I'll fix him up. Watch," she told him, as she went back to her victim. She took Rick's bloodied wrist in her hands. Mattie moved close enough to see, but still seemed to want to keep his distance, lest his urges resurface.

Allie used a finger to wipe away the blood that had pooled at the site of her bite, raising her finger to her lips to lick clean. She then unsheathed her fangs and bit her own finger, causing two drops of her own vampire blood to appear there. Now Mattie moved closer in concern. "What are you doing?"

"Ancient vampire secret," she replied with a smile. "Cain showed me." She wiped her own blood over the bite on her victim, letting her blood cover the ragged edges. After a moment, she squeezed her finger to coax out a few more drops onto the spot before bringing her finger back up to her mouth to clean.

The bite on Rick's arm began to heal before their eyes. The edges pulled closed and sealed themselves until there was nothing but a slightly raised red mark on his skin. Mattie's eyes were wide, but he seemed more worried than impressed. "Are you sure that's a good idea?"

"It's fine. Look, he'll never even remember what happened. By tomorrow, he'll be good as new."

"Yeah, with some blood from the United One in his veins! What happens if he ever gets turned into a vamp in the future? Won't he have white eyes?"

Allie smirked at him and dismissed it. "Relax. It was hardly any blood at all, just enough to fix him up. Besides, who's gonna turn him into a vampire? The chances are astronomical. Forget it."

"I guess," Mattie reluctantly agreed. "Let's go."

"Wait a sec. I'm not just leaving him on the ground, silly. He deserves better than that after his generosity, don't you think?" she asked with a smile. Mattie rolled his eyes as she knelt down again next to the guy. She gave him a light tap on the cheek and some mental nudging to bring him around. It took a few moments, but he finally dredged his way out of the spell she'd put him under. "Rick, come on buddy, stand up."

He focused on her and then she helped him slowly get to his feet. "What happened?" he asked groggily.

Allie let her eyes glaze over white and caught his attention with her hypnotizing gaze. "Nothing happened, you're just fine. You're going into the store now. You won't even remember me, and you won't notice any of the effects my drinking might have had on you. You're just out picking up some snacks."

He nodded agreeably. "Okay."

"Oh, and Rick, eighty days clean and sober is a really awesome accomplishment. Keep it up, buddy. You don't need that shit." Rick just nodded as she broke their gaze and turned him towards the entrance to the store with a slight shove. He wandered away, bewildered, but none the worse for the experience.

Allie turned to find Mattie watching her with arms crossed and a smile playing about his lips. "Now you're sending them off with self-help advice? Maybe you should've hypnotized him into dropping a few pounds too while you were at it," he suggested with a snort.

"Very funny. I like the idea of trying to give something back. I can read their minds, you know. If I know what's going on with them and how to help, a little encouragement never hurt anyone, right?"

Mattie grinned. "It's sweet."

She came closer and let him enfold her into his arms. "See, being a vampire doesn't have to be all bad, even when you drink from humans...which is something I still think you're going to have to give in to eventually, by the way." He didn't answer. Deep down, she was pretty sure that he knew she was right. He didn't *have* to give in, but it would make things easier for him, and strengthen his powers better than animal blood ever could. In all likelihood, he couldn't hold out forever anyway. He was made to drink from humans; it was inevitable.

"So, big and burly isn't your type," she teased. "Doesn't mean you have to go thirsty," she told him, eyeing a car that had just pulled into the lot. Three young women were in the vehicle, loud and laughing with each other. "I could snag one for you, hypnotize her right into your arms...it would be easy," Allie offered, as the girls got out of the car.

"No thanks," Mattie answered condescendingly.

Two of the girls went into the store, while the third stayed behind, leaning on the hood of the car to finish her cigarette. Allie smiled. "Look at that. She's waiting for you. I'll bring her over, and you can take a quick nip and be done before her friends even come back."

Wow, he actually considered it for a second before shooting her down. That was progress. Not that she really cared if he wanted to keep drinking butcher bought animal blood, but drinking stronger blood meant his vampiric skills would be stronger, and she felt better to know that they were both as powerful as possible. Besides, he was a vampire, same as she was, and it would be nice if he would embrace it as she did, rather than act as though it was some terrible affliction.

Mattie did reject the idea though, after a brief pause. "No. The fridge is stocked back at the RV. I'm good. Besides," he added indignantly, "I don't need you to hypnotize anyone for me, thank you very much. You know, I have managed to pick up a girl or two *without you* in my day."

Allie laughed and raised an eyebrow at his boast. "Oh really?"

"Not to drink," he clarified. Although the thought that she read as it surfaced in his mind was of a time that he *had* flirted with the idea of drinking from someone, before he had turned Allie to join him.

It was a beautiful woman in a bar. He had thought he would try sampling her blood, and so he had bought her a cocktail and seduced her into following him to a hotel. But in the end, after spending half the night talking to her, fending off her advances and trying to work up the nerve to drink her blood, he hadn't been able to go through with it. Sleeping with her would have just made the cravings for her blood worse, and made him feel sleazy about it, so he had sent her home.

"No, of course not to drink. So, what *did* you do with them?" she asked tauntingly. Mattie was usually fairly shy. While he was very good looking, and could be a wonderfully aggressive and amazing lover in their bed, she couldn't imagine he'd had very much experience with other women during the brief times that they were apart, especially if he was trying *not* to drink from people.

He squeezed his arms tighter around her waist. "Why don't we get out of here and I'll show you?" he whispered seductively.

"Oh, are you going to buy me a drink and then talk my ear off for hours?" she asked snarkily.

He narrowed his eyes and then gave her a light shove away from him. "Well, no, not if you're going to be snide about it. Then you can pay for your own drink," he teased in return.

They passed Rick's Harley as they made their way back through the parking lot to their motor-home parked at the far end. Allie trailed her fingers along the seat of the bike, thinking of Cain again. "Mattie, do you think we did the right thing, leaving Cain's?"

"Sure I do; don't you? I didn't like the idea of us being so easy to find…especially when we're not sure where Sindy's loyalties lie. Right now, the best thing for us is to have a little time off the radar."

"I guess…but I'll feel better after I've talked to Cain."

"Allie, he's fine. We've barely been gone a week."

"I know, but I worry, and I miss him. Maybe I should try to contact him."

Mattie slumped his shoulders with a sigh as he rested his hand on the door latch to their trailer. Rather than open the door, he turned to Allie wearily. "Well, this didn't last long, did it?"

"We just left him there."

Mattie held open the door for her. "We left a note. He'll be okay."

"It feels so wrong though," Allie insisted, as Mattie closed and locked the door behind them. Mattie didn't respond, but just made his way back into the bedroom, as Allie followed. "No offense hon, but I feel like we're incomplete without him. Don't you?" Mattie did not look sympathetic as he turned to sit on the bed. "We're a coven," she insisted, a plea for understanding.

"It's the mark. It makes you feel his absence more strongly. It'll fade."

Allie scrunched up her face in annoyance at his assessment. "It's not just the mark. Don't you have a heart?"

He gave her a lop-sided smile. "You've gotten pretty attached to him haven't you? The girl who hates everybody; you really love the guy."

"So do you. And I don't hate everybody; people just get on my nerves a lot. Cain's your best friend."

Mattie kicked off his shoes and lay back on the bed. "But it's different, what you feel. You two have a special bond."

Allie flopped herself down next to him in exasperation. "Oh my God. Is this going to be like the time when you accused me of loving Ben?" She could feel that he wasn't jealous in a romantic sense, but he did envy the emotional connection that she had with these other men in her life. "Yes, I love Ben, and I love Cain, and I love you, all in your own ways. I'm a regular emotional slut, aren't I? But they are like brothers to me. You are my man."

"I'm not jealous," he confirmed. "I know you love me, Allie. I'm your husband and your maker, and I'm secure in that. But you have to admit that your relationship with Cain is almost beyond brotherhood. You guys share something else…something…vampire. You see him as an equal to you, like I'll never be."

Allie sat up to take off her sneakers and jeans. "What? Don't be stupid."

"It's true, Allie, and you don't have to pretend that it's not. It's no secret that I'm not thrilled with being a vampire like you are. Cain's an elder, and he's strong. He's the closest thing to an equal that you've ever encountered."

"So? He's a good friend and I've learned a lot from him. It doesn't have to mean any more than that."

"No, but I know you can't hide out with me forever, Allie. I plan to enjoy this little vacation, but we can't just be oblivious to the fact that there are larger forces at work around us."

"What larger forces?"

Mattie shrugged. "Who knows? But Arif and his coven seem to believe you're a major player in some prophecy, and you know you've got an inherent authority over other vampires that no one else has. At some point, you're going to have to come out of this 'I'm nobody special' denial, and claim your power. The truth is, you have no equal, Allie, and that is the kind of power a person can't deny…or squander."

"Squander? What am I supposed to do with it?"

"I don't know, but some night, something will happen that you just can't stand by and watch, and when it does, you'll stand up to it. You'll have to, I know you. You're going to have to reveal your power over vampires everywhere, and use it to take your place as their leader in order to make things right. When you do, Cain will be there at your side."

Allie looked at him quizzically before giving him a shove on the shoulder. "Shut up. I've already told you that if I end up having to act as some kind of Queen, then you're my King; no one but you."

Mattie smiled. "I know, and I will be, always. But Cain will be more than just a supporter in the background like me; he always has been. He'll be your confidant, your advisor, your right-hand-man."

Allie laughed. "What are you, clairvoyant now? I thought you were the weatherman?"

"Predict the weather, predict the future, are they really all that different? I've got a really strong feeling about this. We both know the climate is going to change, and when the storm comes, there'll be no hiding from it."

Allie lay with her head next to his on her pillow. "Okay, say all that is true, would it be so bad?"

"No, if someone else is going to be at our side, I wouldn't want it to be anyone but Cain," Mattie admitted. "As much as I'd like to claim that it should be you and me alone forever, something in me knows you're right, that we need him. It seems right somehow, that it should be the three of us again. I just wanted you to know that I see it coming, and I can swallow it.

I won't deny that it's hard, knowing he shares so much with you. You guys have always seemed to have a special understanding of each other. It's not what you and I have, but it's still something intimate. I might grumble a little, but I can live with it. I was just hoping to have you all to myself for a little longer first."

Allie rolled towards him, resting her head on his shoulder. "There's still a few more weeks before our mark of the coven fades. I won't contact him yet, okay? He's probably still mad at me, anyway. We'll keep it just you and me; radio silence for a little longer. Whatever is going on with Cain, whatever happened when he went to see Sindy and Zach, they can handle it without us. I can wait. If things are destined to get crazy, let's soak up our private time while we can. I'm sure you can keep my mind on other things," she told him as her hand wandered over his body.

Mattie smirked at the invitation. "You sure just the two of us is enough for you? You won't get the urge to summon some company for a threesome?"

She couldn't hide the look of guilt that flashed over her face. Sharing blood with both Mattie *and* Cain together had certainly spawned a few fantasies...but luckily Mattie couldn't read *her* mind. Not that he couldn't guess, but at least it spared him the visual. She chuckled. "Oh my God, Cain would rather die. Just admitting that drinking my blood turned him on a little, nearly killed him."

Mattie gave her a droll look. "Did it? Well, you've already invited Fiona into our bed. Who else were you thinking? That guy Kieran seemed pretty into you...as a humble servant to the Queen," he reminded her with sarcastic resentment.

Mattie wasn't very amused any longer but Allie couldn't help but giggle, remembering when she had used her venom to put Arif's spy, Kieran, under her control. He had been a very willing and adoring slave during the brief time she'd spent pumping him for information. He'd made it obvious that he wouldn't have minded being pumped for more...

Mattie didn't think it was very funny anymore, though. "Na, I'm thinkin' three's a crowd. Besides, you know I don't go in for submissives," Allie assured him. She now wore only her panties and tee-shirt, although Matt was still dressed. She sat up and noticed him eying her bare legs. She could feel his desire for her building, along with his urge to prove to her that he alone was worth her affection.

Mattie gave her an almost evil grin. "No, you need a real man, one who can put you in your place now and then."

She smiled at his boast. "Oh ho…you think you're up for it?"

"You'd better believe it."

Allie grinned and pulled her shirt over her head, to be thrown to the floor. "Prove it, tough guy."

Mattie was more than willing to take her up on her invitation. He eagerly grabbed for her, obviously planning to hold her down on the bed, but Allie was too fast for him. Her supernatural speed kept her just ahead of his every move, making her impossible to catch, even in the confined space of their small bedroom.

After a few moments of exertion to no avail, Mattie finally wised up and switched tactics. He faked her out by mentally broadcasting plans to go in one direction, and then going the other way instead when she anticipated his move. She'd caught the surface thoughts from his mind without digging deeper and he'd fooled her. Now he caught and threw her down onto the bed, pinning her there with his firm grasp of her wrists and holding his body over her.

She had to admit, the rough rasping of denim from his jeans rubbing against her bare legs was kind of a turn on, but she wasn't ready to be defeated. Allie could easily throw him off her with her paranormal strength if she wanted, but she chose a route that would be more delicate to Mattie's ego. She dissolved her body into mist, escaping his hold and floating up to the ceiling. He was left lying on the bed over nothing but her bra and panties.

Mattie rolled over to look up at the ceiling where she had reformed, nude and floating just out of reach. "You're resorting to blatant cheating?" he asked her in feigned disgust. "If I had known we were playing dirty, I might have pulled out a trick or two of my own."

"I already know all of your tricks," she taunted, as he stripped off his clothing, visibly ready to make good on his threat.

He raised his eyebrows at her audacity. "You think so? Get your ass down onto this bed or I'll show you a new one."

Allie shimmied her shoulders, making her small breasts dance and sway mockingly. "Come and get me. You've got nothin'."

Allie laughed as he got up onto his knees on the bed and grabbed her waist to pull her down. She let him grab hold without truly avoiding him, and he pinned her to the bed as before, but she didn't plan to let him keep her there for long.

"Right, 'cause this worked so well for you last time," she teased. "How you gonna keep me?" As he kept his grasp firm on her wrists, she wiggled her fingers, letting them begin to dissipate, threatening to turn completely to mist again.

"Don't try it," he warned, pushing himself against her body, as though that would keep her in place.

Allie leaned up to give him a little kiss, and then let herself begin to dissolve out of his grasp. However, before she had completely turned to mist and disengaged herself from him, she suddenly felt a very startling and sharp shock of electricity run through her with an audible crackle. It was reminiscent of Mattie's deadly power of lightening, and quite frankly, it was scary as hell.

Allie lost the thread of what she was doing, halting her shape change, and she defaulted back to her human body again. She lay under Mattie on the bed, staring up at him wide eyed. She'd half expected him to be just as startled as she was, but he was just watching her for reaction.

"What the hell was that?" she asked shakily.

"I believe that was me putting you in your place," he replied with a confident smirk.

She stared at him in shock for a moment, still not sure what the hell he'd done. He hadn't actually struck her with lightning, had he? "Well, don't fry me to a crisp! Holy shit, Mattie!"

He cocked an eyebrow at her. "Are you scared of me?" he asked.

Allie considered his position for a moment. Strong as he may be, Mattie had never given her cause to doubt his prudent caution where her safety was concerned. Even when she had been human and he was a vampire, he'd always taken pride in the fact that she'd trusted him not to hurt her. Allie, on the other hand, had spent the last few years tapping into untold powers, and displaying strength and unpredictable skill. She wasn't exactly known for being careful. If anything, she wouldn't blame Mattie if *he* was frightened of *her* sometimes.

"No, I'm not scared of you. Never. Are you scared of me?"

He smiled that she had turned the question on him, and thought for a second before answering. "You've given me a few uneasy moments," he admitted with a little grin, "but no. I'm always scared *for* you, not *of* you."

"Good. I know you'd never really hurt me, just like I'd never hurt you," she told him with a loving smile. "But...damn, Mattie. That hurt!"

He laughed at her. "That was a baby shock. You've never scuffed your socks across the carpet before? It's just static electricity. Freaked you out, huh?"

She tugged a little at his hold on her wrists, a token struggle, but he wouldn't let them go. "Kinda," she admitted. "How'd you do that?"

"Dried out the air," he explained. "I can sort of gather the charge to me in the right conditions. Cool, isn't it?"

"You sneaky thing! You've been practicing that, haven't you?" she accused.

He smiled. "You're not the only one with tricks up your sleeve," he said, giving her forearm a little flick with his tongue, although she wasn't wearing any sleeves at the moment. "I've been working on some stuff. And now…I'll claim my reward," he said, dipping his lips down to steal some kisses upon her throat.

She wriggled at the ticklishness of it, but he quickly raised himself to meet her eyes. "Uh, uh-uh" he warned.

She flinched as she anticipated another shock, though none came. She knew he wouldn't really hurt her, but she couldn't help but feel nervous to disobey. He grinned at his power over her. "Sure you're not scared?" he asked again.

"Umm…let's just call it a healthy dose of respect," she answered.

He leaned back further to look at her in astonishment, with a little shake of his head. "Well, it's about fucking time. Can't say I like the implication though. You're supposed to respect me for being the man that I am, not because I can toast your ass if you step out of line!"

Allie couldn't help but chuckle. "I do. You know I do. What can I say? I guess I'm a girl who enjoys the thrill of a good crack of the whip now and then."

Mattie licked his lips, punctuated with an exploratory thrust of his hips against her. "Well, now that's something I can arrange."

~~~~~~~~~~~~~~~~~~~~~~~~~~~~~~~~

Allie awoke, and although she could feel the reassurance of Mattie's mark nearby, she was alone in the dark emptiness of the bedroom. That was one of the minor things she slightly resented about her metamorphosis. Since she had gained full use of her powers as the United One, fueled by human blood, try as she might, she simply could not awaken before the full darkness of night fell.

No more sleepy snuggling with Mattie as the sun set, cozy and quiet together before getting up to greet the night. No more rolling over in a dreamy haze during their slumber to find his strong form next to her, winding her legs about him and hugging him tight as she fell back to sleep;

nope, not anymore. She was as good as dead, completely comatose until not a trace of light was left in the sky, no exceptions. It was a small price to pay, and Mattie made up for it with his amorous attentions throughout their evenings together, but she still missed those little things.

Mattie woke with the sunset, sometimes even slightly before. He often came back to bed to greet her when she woke, but usually he was up and about. She couldn't blame him. She didn't expect him to spend the first two hours of his evening just lying in bed with her unconscious form, waiting for her to wake up…but it would be nice.

She'd picked up the habit of spending those first waking moments reaching out for telepathic company. Once she'd learned to control her telepathy, she hadn't used it much in an exploratory sense. She used it if speech was impractical for some reason, but she hadn't really played with it much, until recently.

Lately, when she woke up feeling alone and lonely, she'd stretch her psychic awareness to see what she could read from whoever happened to be nearby. They were always humans she didn't know, and nothing pertinent to her own existence, but it was an interesting distraction. She and Mattie tended to stay in sparsely populated areas, so there weren't usually many people around to read anyway.

After exhausting the local prospects, she would have the urge to move on to read more personal candidates for her attention. Cain was the first person who came to mind; he was off limits though. She had promised Mattie she wouldn't contact him yet, keeping their private time private. It was tough to resist though. She missed him. She could easily contact him without telling Mattie, but the guilt would be awful. She had done too many things behind Mattie's back in their relationship as it was. She had promised herself that she would respect his wishes from now on, even if she thought he was being silly or overly dramatic.

Still…if she didn't actually *contact* Cain, it wouldn't count, would it? She wouldn't read his thoughts, just take a quick peak, and let herself feel his emotions empathically, to check in on him and make herself feel a little better. She found him easily. They still shared their coven mark, making him as closely connected to her as another vampire could be. She lightly skimmed his surface thoughts to find he was at home in his kitchen, moving about in his nightly routine, making coffee and such.

Allie was a bit surprised to find him actually humming a snippet of song in a content and even chipper mood. She knew that he always kept the sorrow of lost love and anxiety for the future just beneath the surface of his exterior, so to find him in such good spirits was a pleasant surprise.

Cain felt fulfilled, as though he was serving a satisfying purpose. She knew he was still slightly worried about she and Mattie, but he was trusting them to be responsibly independent, and had allowed himself a break from worrying. It made Allie feel so much better, and far less guilty about not being in touch. She watched for a moment more as Cain prepared two mugs of blood, in preparation to share a meal with another. Things must have gone alright when he went to find Sindy then.

She didn't allow herself to try to read further, to learn what had happened to Zach. If he wasn't there, it was likely that he hadn't survived the transformation. She couldn't open up that door to guilt, self-loathing and worry for herself. She had killed Zach by accident, and then done what she could to rectify things. At this point, it was out of her hands. She would learn what had happened soon enough when she and Mattie finally did return to see Cain again. For now, it was enough to know that Cain was doing fine and well without them. She let go of the connection.

A quick check on Mattie proved that he was in the little living area of their trailer, watching Jimmy Fallon lose a lip sync battle. He had no idea that she was awake, or tenuously skirting the confines of her promise not to contact Cain. She would leave him to watch television as she played with her telepathy just a bit more.

Felicity was the next obvious choice; an easy read. She and Felicity had forged a bond of friendship that transcended the separation of physical space. She could read the girl from almost any distance, but they didn't have much in common these days. Allie would usually check in, feel that things were fine for her friend, who was busy with duties of homemaking and motherhood, and then move on, rarely disturbing her for more than a quick hello. It was difficult to feign interest in which brand of baby food was best, or how a dinner recipe had turned out.

Lately, she was more interested in moving on to experimenting with a much more difficult endeavor...Ben. She'd been attempting to read him more and more often. Before all of this vampire drama had begun, Ben had been her best friend. Even after Mattie had become a vampire, Allie had spent years being Ben's closest platonic friend and confidant. To have him so thoroughly cut her out of his life, believing that she was no longer the Allie he knew, but just some vampire demon residing in her body, really hurt.

She suspected that he no longer fully believed she wasn't herself, but was unsure how to react to her as she was now. In the past, his frightened anger over the situation made him defensive enough that she couldn't read his thoughts. He was blocking her out, even if he didn't realize it, but she kept trying.

When she had snuck into his wedding reception to see Felicity, his guard had been down. He'd had no idea that she was there, and she had been able to read him then. It had felt so wonderful to reconnect with her old friend, even if he was unaware. She had done her best to remember that feeling, the key to opening his thoughts to her, to try to keep the tenuous connection strong in her mind.

Now, when she tried to search through thoughts and feelings to pick Ben out of the human crowd, she was usually rewarded, able to find and read his surface thoughts, however briefly. Those little snippets of contact had encouraged her. She kept trying, hoping that at some point she'd be able to break through to deeper perceptions. She had to be very careful though. She knew that if he ever suspected that she was reading his thoughts, he would jump to the conclusion that she was somehow trying to manipulate him, and he would never trust her again, ever. Their friendship would be over before it was even given a slight chance for rekindling.

She found Ben now, skipping a perfunctory check in with Felicity in favor of the more challenging endeavor; except, it wasn't very challenging at all. Not only did she find Ben easily, his thoughts seemed more open to her than ever. He was drunk. Not completely wasted, but drunk enough to let down his natural guard and give her a chance to delve deeper into his mind than ever before.

Something was wrong. Even after all of their years of not talking, she knew Ben well enough to know that this was not something as simple as a night out with the guys. He was alone, and it just wasn't like Ben to go out and get hammered anyway. She quickly discerned that he was upset with Felicity. More shocking was the reason why. It was Alyson. He was thinking about her...he knew. He knew that Allie and Felicity had been talking and seeing each other over the years, and that Felicity had kept it a secret from him.

Felicity had also known that Ben's father, Bernard, had a penchant for vampire killing; something they had both hidden from Ben. As it turned out, Ben had already known. Allie could lightly skim through the culmination of memories of Ben's dad, sneaking around, practicing with weapons, and having secret meetings, on the phone or in person, in which the killing of vampires was discussed. Ben had put it all together and known for a long time. He was mad that Felicity hadn't told him, but mostly blamed his father for bullying her into keeping the secret.

He was most hurt that Felicity had been having contact with vampires behind his back. It wasn't so much for the lie, although that pissed him off too; it was more that he was frightened. He was frightened that he would eventually lose her; that Felicity would some night decide that she was tired of being human and playing family with him, when money was tight or times were hard, and then she would just disappear into the night, to become one of the undead.

It made perfect sense, and yet, Alyson knew that it would never happen. She knew Felicity too well. Of course, the idea of becoming a vampire had crossed Felicity's mind, more than once, but Allie knew how important family was to the woman, and how much she loved Ben. She would not consider becoming a vampire unless some major betrayal decimated her family and took the decision from her hands. As long as she had Ben and Christian, she would never leave them. Ben and that little baby had some mighty fierce protectors, just between Alyson and Bernard, so it wasn't a true worry that Felicity would ever lose them.

Alyson was heartened to find that beneath the fear and anger over Felicity's secret friendship with Allie, Ben was also feeling...hope. If Felicity was still fast friends with Alyson, and had fought so vehemently to convince Ben that she was still the Allie they knew, then maybe she really was. Maybe all of the things he'd overheard from his father were untrue.

Vampires losing their humanity to become soulless demons who masqueraded as their host, without a trace of the true person left inside...could that be false? He kept thinking about Cain. As much as he had always seen Cain as a rival, and someone he did not particularly like, Ben had gotten to know him pretty well over the summer and fall he had spent serving the vampire coffee at the Downtime Café.

At first Ben had liked Cain a lot, considering him a friendly acquaintance, bordering on being a real friend, back when Ben had thought him human. Once that disguise was shattered and Ben learned he was a vampire, he had observed the man in an almost constant state of suspicion, waiting to see evidence of the demon his father had spoken of.

Cain may have done some things Ben didn't like, but he'd never shown a glimpse of anything to make Ben believe the man was truly evil. Like it or not, Ben had to admit that Cain was consistent in his ways, level headed and civil; consistent enough that Ben had begun to doubt it was an act. Ben tried to despise him, but Cain was a decent guy, someone Ben sometimes forgot that he shouldn't trust, and during those moments of letting his guard down, Cain had never betrayed him. It seemed that, vampire or not,

Cain was just a person – not wholly good or evil, just someone trying their best to find a balance and do the right thing when they could.

But Ben had seen Cain touch a cross…and his flesh had burned. Part of Ben wanted to use that evidence to support the argument that Cain was a creature shunned by God, and therefore, as a good and honest God-fearing man, Ben should shun him too. But is everything always truly that black-and-white? Are there not shades of grey and room for atonement and forgiveness?

As a lawyer, Ben wanted the evidence to neatly line up and support the argument to produce an obvious conclusion. However, having a little real-life and courtroom experience under his belt, he also knew that the obvious answer was not always correct. Sometimes, you had to trust your gut to sort through the smoke and mirrors and find the truth. A vampire being burned by a cross looked pretty impressive, a flashy display to easily prove guilt or innocence, but it was almost too easy; too obvious.

Are there gradations of sin and evil? If the man Ben knew as Cain, was really just a man whose body had been changed into that of a vampire, did that automatically make the man evil? Even if he had done bad things, did that mean he was beyond redemption? Could he never be forgiven or become a good man after an evil act? How many sins did it take to tip the scale, to move a person beyond salvation? Human criminals did their time and then were released into society, considered rehabilitated. Could such a theory hold for a vampire, who had spent years seeking atonement for past sins?

What about a vampire who did not sin? Alyson was a good person; he knew her, he loved her. Did becoming a vampire make her evil? He had worried that it did, but only because he had been afraid that it wasn't really Allie anymore. But what if it was…?

What if Ben's dad had been wrong and some vampires retained their human consciousness? If that were the case, and Allie was still herself, with the new powers of a vampire, that didn't have to mean she was evil. Allie would never kill someone… At least, he didn't think so.

Alyson broke the connection. She disengaged herself from Ben's thoughts, shaken by his desire to have faith in her, partially misplaced. She had killed. Not on purpose, but did that matter? She suddenly felt the desperate urge to check on Cain again and try to figure out whether or not Zach had been successfully brought back as a vampire, to ease her guilt over killing him, but she stopped herself. It didn't matter if Zach was a vampire. She had killed him, taken his human life away, and she had to live with that. It couldn't be fixed. It was done.

She wasn't evil though. People make mistakes, sometimes horrible ones, but that doesn't mean they should be beyond forgiveness, does it? The fact that Ben was finally allowing himself to question his prior judgment of her was such a relief. There was hope that they could be friends again one day! She had always known it in her heart, but damn the man was stubborn!

She needed to contact Felicity right away. Poor Felicity, having to confess her secret friendship with Allie, and knowing Bernard's secret all at once. That must have been some blow-out. It seemed to have happened a few nights ago. Allie felt terrible that she hadn't realized sooner. It had presumably happened while her attention was fully distracted with something else…like drinking.

She'd contact Felicity right away, to make sure she was alright. She was confident that Ben and Felicity would get through it, kiss and make-up. It would just take a little time. Once things had blown over a little, maybe she could see about setting up a reunion with Ben! She needed to take small steps, and take things slowly, but it felt so good to know that Ben was opening up to it, and soon the healing process could truly begin to mend their friendship. Maybe she could even convince Mattie to come…

Chapter 4 - Fireworks

Ben

Ben and Felicity's house
Sagaponack, Long Island, New York
An evening in late June

"Mattie too?" Ben asked, pleading for reconsideration.

Felicity sighed over his reluctance to fully commit to the reunion plan she and Allie had devised. "Yes. Ben, you have to stop thinking of them as two vampires, and start thinking of them as people who used to be your friends. And while you're at it, stop thinking of me as being on their side. I am on the side of peace and rekindled friendship. I'm here to support you, and they should have each other for support. We've all been through some very emotionally difficult times. They are not our enemies, just some old friends; a couple, like us."

Ben frowned. "Right...or maybe they're just a couple of vampires out for a meal, and we're the main course."

"Cut it out. You know you don't really believe that, so stop being so difficult. If they were out for blood, there would be much easier ways to get it, and if they didn't want to be friends, then dealing with us would just be a big pain in the ass, wouldn't it? Why would they bother? Come on, we can do this however you want to, but we are doing this. We can choose a crowded public place like a restaurant; wherever you feel safe, but please don't say no."

It had taken a few days of discord, a few lonely nights at the bar trying to drink through his distress, some silent treatment and some arguing, but Ben and Felicity were finally back on solid ground as far as their marriage went. Now she was pushing the limits...typical.

In some ways, his wife could be terribly stubborn and unrelenting...just like him. She was far more subtle though. She didn't mind losing an argument, although she would fight vehemently for what she believed in. She knew how to lose with grace, and then come back with subtle feminine manipulation and manage to get just what she wanted anyway. Ben had to admit, no matter how savvy he was in a dispute, in some ways, he had met his match in Felicity.

It was not long ago that he had come to the horrifying realization that not one, but two vampires had been invited into their house. Felicity had been in touch with her ex-lover, the vampire Cain, and Alyson, Ben's dear friend of the past who had allowed herself to be turned into a vamp by his other lost friend, Mattie.

The idea of Cain being in his house, with his wife and child, unbeknownst to him, was upsetting...to say the least. He believed Liss when she told him that it was an accidental meeting, at least in her eyes. He couldn't completely trust Cain's motives, but he believed that Felicity wasn't trying to carry on a secret relationship with the man. She loved Ben and the life they had together. He just wished she wouldn't be so naïve as to always trust that everyone else in the world wanted to see their marriage succeed as much as she and Ben did.

Alyson; knowing that Felicity had been continuing an active friendship with his long lost friend for all of this time, behind his back…that still hurt. It wasn't so much the betrayal that hurt, but his own fear. He had spent years believing Alyson had been lost to the world when she had been changed into a vampire. A new creature with some of Alyson's characteristics had been created, but the Allie he knew was no more. Was that true? Now he wasn't so certain. Felicity had never wavered in her beliefs though. She trusted Allie thoroughly.

It had been traumatizing for him all those years ago, when his best friend Mattie had been killed and turned into a vampire. Then to have Alyson, his other close childhood friend, make the decision to become a vampire as well, in order to join Mattie, had been devastating. Things overheard from his father, Bernard Everheart – Vampire Hunter, had led him to believe that his friends were no longer in existence within their bodies. They were said to be demons only mimicking the humans they had once been.

To learn this was untrue; that his friends were mostly unchanged, and that he had been wrong, would be a wonderful relief, but also a terrible burden of guilt. It would mean that Ben had shunned his friends for no good reason, abandoning them in their time of need. That was not the man he wanted to be.

Leave it to his father to mislead him and mess up his life…again. Ben's vampire hunting father, Bernard, had entrusted Felicity with the knowledge of his mysterious double life; a secret that he had never seen fit to reveal to his son. Felicity had kept Bernard's supernatural admission from Ben, knowing he would be hurt that Bernard had confided in her while continuing to keep the secret from him, and hoping to persuade Bernard to tell Ben about it himself.

Unfortunately, Bernard never did disclose the secret to Ben. When Felicity learned her husband had already figured it out on his own, and that she knew about it as well, she felt terrible, knowing that Ben felt betrayed by her. He couldn't blame her too much for those lies however; he rested that blame on his father's shoulders.

Ben wanted nothing more than to live a normal, human life with his wife and their baby boy. These supernatural secrets were like landmines of broken trust scattered throughout their marriage, threatening to blow their relationship to bits. How had he let this happen? He had been so blindly stubborn that he had refused to acknowledge the situations that should have been openly discussed. He had made his own wife feel that he was unapproachable on the subjects, forcing her to keep secrets from him to try to spare them the stress on their marriage.

After some soul-searching, Ben had come home, firm in the decision that being angry and carrying grudges accomplished nothing. Those kinds of burdens had weighed on him for too long. He needed to decide what he wanted from life and do what was necessary to achieve it, without letting his own obstinacy get in his way. That didn't mean Felicity shouldn't be held accountable for her actions though.

She'd been relieved to see him come straight home, rather than go sit at the bar again to avoid seeing her before bed. She wanted to rush into his arms, but he hadn't let her. "Is Christian asleep?"

"Yes," she'd answered quietly.

"We need to talk."

"There's nothing more to say," she'd tried to assure him. "I'm glad it's all out in the open, and now we can move on."

He'd just stared at her for a second. "Actually, *I* have a lot to say. I'm not just going to let you dump all of this crap on me, and then have to carry on and pretend it's fine…no matter how much I love you."

"What more can I do? I told you, I am one hundred percent committed to our marriage, our family. I love you too," she'd insisted. "I didn't like having to hide things from you. I allowed myself to feel like I was forced to because of other people, and that was wrong. I knew it was, and I should have stood up to it and told you. I shouldn't have let it go on."

Ben had sighed. At least they were both on the same page. "I'm not really mad about my dad," he'd told her. "Well, I'm not mad at *you* for it. He was delusional and secretive long before you came along."

"Do you really think so?" Felicity had asked. "That he's delusional, I mean. 'Cause as imposing and lethal as he tries to portray himself…well, he seems to pull it off pretty accurately."

Ben remembered raising an eyebrow at that. He'd only heard the pompous talk behind closed doors. He'd never seen his father in action. "You think so?"

"It's true, a lot of the time he comes off like someone I'd imagine being in one of your dark comics; so taken with his own impression of himself that it's almost funny, but other times, he kind of scares the shit out of me," she'd admitted. "It's a good thing he's on our side, because I've seen him behead first and ask questions never; gives the concept of first impressions a whole new importance."

Ben had shaken his head with a slight snarl of a chuckle playing about his lips. "I know he's good, but you should hear the way he talks to people. Nobody is as good as he boasts."

"What people?"

"On the phone. I'm kind of surprised to hear you say that he's so quick to action, because if he *was* a super-villain out of the comics, I get the feeling he'd be the guy who goes into a whole self-important monologue tirade that allows his nemesis plenty of time to escape."

"I thought he was one of the good guys? And who could he possibly be talking to on the phone about this kind of thing?" Felicity had asked.

"I have no idea. Moving on… About Allie…you're right. You've tried to tell me and I never let you. It's hard to accept that you let it get this far, but I can't hold it against you; not if it's really her." He'd swallowed the lump in his throat and forced himself to ask, although his voice came out quieter and more unsure than he had heard from himself in a long time. "Is it really the same old Allie? Is she really still my lil big sis?"

Felicity's eyes had melted with compassion at the plea in his voice. He hoped to God she wouldn't lie just to comfort him. If he'd wanted that, he could have believed it from that first night. "She is the same old Allie, Ben…only times ten. Think of Allie, and then think about what she would be like if she suddenly had super powers and almost no fear of consequence."

"Are you trying to scare me?" he'd asked, half-jokingly.

"She's not out of control, and she hasn't changed any more than you'd expect. She's not exactly the same, but she's still Allie."

Ben couldn't help but laugh. "God help us all. I'm still not ready to see her. It'll take a little more getting used to…knowing she's been in our lives all this time, even if only on the fringe…if it's even really *her*. She's not why I'm mad."

Felicity had taken a deep breath in preparation for the final confrontation, before voicing his concern. "Cain."

"Do you love him?"

"Do you love Allie?"

"It's not the same."

"No," Felicity had admitted, "but it's not all that different. My time with Cain was so long ago, Ben. It's in the past, and now I am totally in love with you. I promised myself to you because I love what we have, and never want it to end.

I've moved on from Cain, but even though he's not in my life, I still care about him as a friend. Don't ask me to turn my back on that. I don't plan to see him again, and he's promised to keep his distance, but please don't expect me to shun him. I've already made my choice.

I want you to have faith in me, and to know that when I saw him the other night, there was nothing exchanged between Cain and I that would have been any different even if you'd been there. It was an unexpected meeting, and we both dealt with it as gracefully as possible. He is just a friend now, and he wishes us the best, he really does. Can you handle that?"

He'd felt her eyes pleading for him to love her again, fully, without mistrust or reservation. She was his partner, his lover, the mother of his child, his everything, his Liss. "I want to," Ben had explained. "I don't want to be the jealous guy, who's so insecure he can't be level headed about a situation, but it really pissed me off that he was here. You have to understand, babe. Knowing that you kept secrets from me, knowing that Cain was here, longing for you…"

"He wasn't…*longing*. We are just friends."

"Yeah, I know, but don't try to tell me that he wasn't wishing you were his, because even you know that would be a lie. I'm a jealous man, Liss. I can't help it, and I'm done apologizing for it, because no one could ever be my partner the way that you are; and the way you melt my heart and set my body on fire is something I am not willing to risk losing, *ever*. I love you and I need you to be *mine*. No doubts, no straddling the line. It's in or out, and God knows, I want in," he'd told her, as he'd forcefully pulled her into his arms and slid his hands to cup her ass.

Just pulling her close and feeling her body against him after spending the last few nights distant, had been enough to send heated desire racing through his fingertips to build throughout his body and culminate in a quickly swelling ache in his groin. He needed to possess her again, driven by the fierce pounding need to pleasure her past petty arguments or doubting fears, and remind her of his claim upon her, his undying devotion. Thick, hot, and human, a love inexorably intertwined with their shared understanding of each other, of life, of hopes and dreams realized and made possible *by* the human condition, not in spite of it.

"Part of me wishes I had some kind of venom of my own," he'd admitted, "so I could mark you like some alpha male animal and show the world you're unequivocally mine." He found her left hand and raised it to his lips for a kiss. "Somehow, a little ring made of diamonds and gold doesn't seem to cut it."

As he'd dropped her hand, she'd tilted her head to bare her throat in an odd gesture, as though he were a vampire. "Would you like to cover me in hickies?" she'd asked him teasingly. "Maybe I should get a few 'Property of Ben' tattoos…"

He'd sighed, knowing her heart. They were a team, unquestionably loyal, loving and willing to fight through anything for each other. The fact that one look from those heavy lidded, passion-filled green eyes of hers, while she moistened her lips with her tongue, could make his muscles tense and tremble, while his cock strained and wept for freedom from within his pants, certainly didn't hurt.

She wouldn't let him talk until he laughed, and even then, she had forced his mouth to concentrate on things other than conversation. Chemistry they had in spades. If only everything else were as easy as making love…

Tension broken, wounds mended, faith restored, things were good again…for a while. Then she'd started in with the reunion idea. She wanted him to agree to a sort of double date with the vampire couple, Allie and Mattie. The groundwork had been laid. He was no longer so vehemently against seeing them, so now she wanted to make it happen, quickly and painfully, before he could back out; like ripping off a Band-Aid.

"I'll have to think about the location," he said, stalling his answer.

"But you'll go?"

Ben sighed. He wouldn't be surprised if she had already arranged the whole thing, and his acceptance of the invitation was a mere formality. "When are we supposed to do this?"

"Whenever you want, but soon," she warned him. She wouldn't tolerate an open-ended acceptance. She wanted him committed. "I'll have to talk to Allie about details but I know she can't wait to see you."

"Alright," Ben acceded. "Call her."

"Um, it doesn't really work like that. She hasn't got a phone."

"Then how are you supposed to get in touch with her?"

"She's telepathic now," Felicity explained gingerly.

Ben let that sink in, realization and memory melding together as he briefly relived his only experience of seeing Allie again after her change. The intrusion in his mind, her reading his thoughts and responding before he'd even had a chance to voice the words, the way he had been terrified that the demon pretending to be Allie was somehow in his head, reading cues from his memories to perfect her charade... "She is telepathic, isn't she? Can all vampires do that?" he asked in trepidation. This was new ground for him, and he didn't like the implications.

"No," Felicity was quick to assure him, "but she can. I'll have to wait until she contacts me, since it certainly isn't something I can initiate on my own."

"She reads your mind...like, regularly?"

"Not really. We just chat sometimes without having to be together, or talk out loud."

"She reads your mind," he repeated.

Felicity rolled her eyes, trying to make him feel as though he was making more out of it than it was, but he wasn't going to let it be glanced over so easily. "Okay, yeah. She reads my mind, but not all the time. It's not like she's reading *all* of my thoughts, just what's relevant to the conversation. She doesn't poke around private stuff."

"How do you know?"

"Because Allie wouldn't do that. She tries to be very respectful."

Ben let out a little bark of a laugh. "Allie? Respectful? Now I know she's changed." Felicity made a face to show that she wasn't amused by the comment. "Well, you have to admit, if you're trying to convince me that she's the same old Allie, *respectful* is a strange way to go." Ben didn't know how Felicity managed not to crack a smile. Getting this point across must be very important to her.

"It is Allie, and Mattie too. Do you think you're the only one who's grown up a little over the past eight years? Becoming a vampire has forced a little more responsibility on Allie than you may realize. We've been through a lot, and we've all grown and changed over the years." She reached up to run her fingers through his hair at his temple on one side with a sultry grin. "Don't you think they'll notice your new silver sparkle?"

He rolled his eyes, stifling a groan. Recently his temples had become increasingly sprinkled with some silver-grey hairs throughout. It was only a slight handful on each side, but having such dark hair made the silver show pretty obviously. His father had quite a bit of grey in the same places, and apparently, Ben was going to be blessed just the same, and early too.

He'd thought he might at least be spared until he was thirty, but here it was, a few weeks before his twenty-eighth birthday and the silver was sprouting. Felicity swore it was sexy. He wasn't so sure, but so far, he hadn't loved the idea of trying to dye it, so there it had stayed. "That's it. I'm dying it."

Felicity laughed. "You'd better not. I love it. Can I set up the meeting?"

This time Ben didn't stifle his groan, but let it voice his discontent with extra grumbly emphasis. Felicity ignored it, forcing him to answer. "Fine. When Allie shows up in your head to chat, you can tell her I'm in. But I'm bringing stakes and crosses. I don't care if you think it's rude."

She smiled, just happy to get her way, no matter how it was accomplished. "You can bring 'em, but you won't need 'em. Trust me, it'll be a wonderful reunion, and perfectly safe. Now when should we do it? They should come for the fourth of July!" she suggested with hopeful excitement. "We've got an amazing view of the fireworks over the Sound."

He looked at her as though the idea was absurd, which, of course it was. "Sure we do, which is why your mom and dad, your brothers, their girlfriends, and almost everybody we know plans to be here for a kickin' party. We're not inviting vampires to that! Not unless you want to see some *real* fireworks!"

"You're right. Sorry, dumb idea."

"Tell you what, why don't we ask your parents if they'll take Christian home with them after? Think they're up to it?" Felicity's father, Jim, had undergone emergency surgery a few weeks ago for a burst appendix, giving them all a terrible scare. He'd been touch and go from the infection for a few days and Felicity had been so distraught that Ben had insisted on taking off work so they could drop everything for a trip back home. Luckily, he was making a full recovery, but babysitting might be a bit much to ask.

"They'd love it! Dad's been doing much better. The doctor gave him the okay to make the trip, and it's not like Christian's running around or anything yet, so I'm sure it's fine."

"If they can take the baby, and we have the house to ourselves, we can meet Allie and Mattie the next night. We can have them come here."

"*Here?* I thought you were all bent out of shape over the idea of vampires at our house."

Melanie Nowak   Destined for Divinity - Part 1 - Home of the Bloodthirsty   Chapter 4

"Forgive me for over-reacting," he said sarcastically, "but we'd only lived here for a week, and you'd already secretly invited almost every vampire we know..." She pursed her lips, refusing to admit that he was right. He continued. "They don't have to actually go *in* the house. We'll have the yard set up from the party and we'll meet them out on the deck. I'd rather be home than in public, anyway. The house is still a safe place to go if we need to get ourselves someplace that they're uninvited fast; and they *will* be uninvited, agreed?"

"Fine. Completely unnecessary, but yeah, maybe it would be nice to have them here. Good plan. I'll set it up," she told him with a smile.

~~~~~~~~~~~~~~~~~~~~~~~~~~~~~~~~~

That's it, he was committed; not that it wasn't something that he wanted. The idea of seeing Allie and Mattie again filled him with a hundred misgivings circling in his head, but it was also something he had always felt was inevitable.

He couldn't avoid facing them forever, and with them, his own tendency to evade possibilities that were emotionally difficult to deal with. There were instances in which he was still unsure of the truth, but he needed to investigate them for himself once and for all, and stop dismissing them to spare himself the anguish.

If Matt and Alyson really were still the same people that had been his friends before being turned into vampires, then he owed them a huge apology, and a chance to speak to him of all the things he'd never let them explain. Most of it wouldn't be easy to hear, but they had been his best friends at one time, and if those people were still within them, then he had been wrong to turn his back on them.

If they could not convince him that they had a trace of their former selves still within them, then at least he would finally know for sure...and he would have to handle it as he saw fit.

Felicity was so relieved that he had agreed to the visit. She had decorated the yard in a spectacular fashion for the Independence Day family barbecue, but he knew that she had taken it even further, knowing that she was decorating for Alyson and Mattie the next night as well.

Ben was getting in his sword training, out in the sideyard. They still had some time before family and friends should be arriving, and Felicity insisted that she didn't mind if he worked out while she took care of the finishing touches. She always made it sound as though she was very

99

compromising about his work-outs, but he knew that secretly she just liked to watch.

He wore only his loose sweats, barefoot on the grass, as he ran through a series of lunges with the new katana his father had given him for his birthday. Trading in his fencing foil for the Samauri sword had been an adjustment, but the thin sword was almost as elegant as a rapier, and much more practical if he ever actually needed to use it. It had been a few months now, and he was finally comfortable with the new heft and balance of the blade, but he hadn't named it yet, despite his father's persistent urging.

A thin sheen of sweat covered him as he swung the sword in the hot July sun. He fought to keep his focus, as he heard Felicity's friend Deidre arrive early and come in the yard gate with her son Jerry. She froze for a moment, gripping the toddler by the hand as they were both surprised by the sight of Ben posed before them; sword outstretched in front of him. "Hi," he uttered, barely glancing at them.

"Sorry..." Deidre stammered, shaking off her shock with a smirk. "I knocked at the door, but I guess no one heard me."

"I'm up here, Dee," Felicity called from the deck.

Deidre's eyes were still glued to Ben as she gave Felicity a wave. The toddler at her side tugged on her arm. "Mommy, he's like a warrior!"

"He certainly is," she agreed with a smile. "Lookin' good, Ben."

Ben sighed and lowered his sword, waiting for them to pass before he could continue. "Thanks."

Deidre went up the steps to the deck with her son in tow, as Ben got back into opening stance to begin again. The girls closed the stair gate to keep little Jerry from wandering down into Ben's way as they sat and talked. Out of his peripheral vision, Ben saw Deidre immediately cup her hands over Jerry's ears as she addressed her friend. "Holy shit, Felicity. If that man was mine, we'd have ten kids by now. I've always thought Ben was hot, but when did he become so freakin' body-licious?"

Felicity chuckled as Ben tried to ignore them. "He has been hitting the swordplay pretty hard lately, but it's nothing new. He always looks like that. You just saw him last week."

"Yeah...in a suit. I didn't see him half naked!"

"You should see the other half," Felicity confided with a grin.

Ben lowered his sword again and slumped his shoulders. "You ladies do realize I can hear you, right?"

Deidre gave him an unapologetic grin. "Well dude, you are seriously ripped. I mean, look at you! You look like you could be in one of those big superhero action movies...or *Magic Mike.*"

Felicity gave her friend a light reprimanding smack with a smile. "Deidre!"

"XXL," Dee finished tauntingly.

Ben avoided Deidre's stare as he retrieved the sheath for his sword off the grass and housed his blade. "Okay, on that note, I'm done. I'm gonna hit the shower...although it sounds like you need a cold one more than I do," he told Deidre with a raised eyebrow and a laugh.

~~~~~~~~~~~~~~~~~~~~~~~~~~~~~~~~~~

The Fourth of July celebration had been a great success, going off without a hitch. He had to admit, Felicity had become quite the homemaker since moving here. A few of the local ladies had begun inviting her for brunch, and she'd been picking up a lot of cooking and decorating tips. Ben kept teasing her about being a socialite in training; she turned out one heck of a party though.

Christian had gone home with Felicity's parents this morning, to give Ben and Liss a few days alone. Ben missed his boy already, but felt so much better to know that he was safe at his grandparent's house, far from here. Felicity's parents were great with him; he would be fine. Now Felicity was out shopping again, to pick up a few extra things for tonight's guests. Who ever heard of serving wine and cheese to a couple of vampires? Only *his* wife.

Before she had left, he had forced her to verbally un-invite Allie from the house, along with another vampire whom he refused to mention again thereafter. She swore to him that no other vampires had invitation, so if at any time they felt at all threatened, all they needed to do was step inside.

Ben slowed the car to wait for some kids to be finished lighting leftover fireworks in the road; it was just dark enough. Judging by the amount of screamers and bottle rockets they'd listened to the night before, he couldn't believe they had any left. Once the coast was clear, he continued past and then pulled into his driveway behind Liss's new minivan. Good, she was home.

When he'd called earlier on her cell, she had still been on the road. The local liquor store had been out of what she'd wanted, and she said she wanted to try somewhere else before getting home. He'd been worried that she would be late. The last thing he wanted was to have Alyson and Mattie showing up while he was alone and unprepared for them. This evening was going to be difficult enough for him. He needed Felicity to help him ease into things.

He parked the car, went up to the house, unlocked the door and went inside with the flowers that he'd picked up on the way home. Liss was so sweet, so badly just wanting to see him reunited with his old friends and to have them all get along in harmony and happiness. He wasn't sure things would work out that way, but bless her sweet, trusting heart for wanting it. "Liss, I'm home."

The house remained quiet. It was so strange to hear complete silence, especially lately. Christian was six months old, and he had just learned how to scream. He'd nearly given both of his parents a heart attack the first time he'd done it. Now that he knew he could make the noise, he thought it was great fun. When he was home, a blood-curdling scream could erupt from his room at any given moment, even during the dead of night.

The pediatrician assured them it was only a phase, and hopefully it would be short lived, as he eventually discovered something new and moved on. In the meantime, for this weekend, grandma and grandpa could have the joy of listening to it. They'd been warned.

Liss must be out back setting up the table. He walked through the house and out the French doors to the yard. A breeze was picking up, making the ocean loud and choppy. Not great for night sailing, but it looked beautiful. The white froth of the waves stood out against the dark of the water, almost glowing in the light of the newly risen moon.

"Liss?" She wasn't there. Had he missed her in the house? Maybe she was in the bedroom getting changed. "Liss?" He put the flowers down on the kitchen counter as he went inside for a more thorough search. The house wasn't that big, she should hear him. Where else would she be?

He looked out the front window, reassuring himself that her car was there. Where could she go with no car? He tried to stay calm through his rising alarm. She was probably next door talking to a neighbor or something. He picked up the phone to call her cell as he walked back out the front door to look around.

Ringing…ringing…she wasn't picking up…and it was still ringing. His heart stopped as he realized that he heard music. The musical tone of Liss's cell phone was coming from somewhere nearby. He walked toward the sound, near the car, but it stopped. It had gone to voicemail.

A cold chill went through him as he stood there behind the car trying to squelch down his rising alarm. There were still groceries in the back… He looked down at the cement at his feet, half-expecting to find her slumped there on the driveway, drained of blood…exactly as he'd found his mom about a dozen years ago. She wasn't there though. Had she even gotten out of the car? He raced to the driver's side and ripped open the door.

"Liss?!" he called desperately. The car was empty. There was nothing on the front seats; he didn't even see her phone. It wasn't in the holder she usually kept it in while driving. She had taken it and gotten out of the car.

He backed up and stood for a moment, looking around in distraught confusion. Then he dropped himself to the cement of the driveway next to the car and looked underneath.

Felicity's purse; it lay on the ground just under the car, along with her keys. She'd never even gone in the house. He sat there cursing himself for not noticing that he'd had to unlock the door. He picked up the keys and pulled out her purse. Sure enough, her cell phone was in its little pocket on the side.

He held back the sobbing gasp that came to his throat, shaking him with tremors. Where was she? Panic threatened to take him, but he held it back and tried to think logically. What had happened? Someone must have taken her, but why?

Flashbacks of his mom still pummeled his thoughts. He had been sixteen when his mom had last beeped the horn for him to come out and help with groceries. He'd paused to put on his shoes, and when he'd come out, there she was, dead on the driveway at the back of the car. How many times had he gone over it in his head? How long had it taken him to find and put on his shoes? Two minutes? Three? It had happened so quickly.

What had happened to Felicity? He tried to feel grateful that he hadn't found her, because at least she wasn't dead, but it was hard to be relieved for that. Who had taken her, and why?

Vampires…this very night they were agreed to meet with two vampires, and Felicity disappears? Quite a coincidence. There was no blood; he checked the white cement of the driveway all around but couldn't find a drop. That didn't mean she hadn't been bitten, but it was a good sign. Maybe it wasn't a vampire, but some random human psycho…

He quickly searched his immediate surroundings once more. Nothing…the mulch and flowers lining the driveway remained undisturbed. Even the sand that always seemed to be dusting the driveway and sidewalk was clear of any footprints, except his own. He thought there could be some scuffling disturbance right next to the car door, from where Felicity must have exited the vehicle, but they seemed un-approached from any other direction, and they led nowhere. Where had the attacker come from, and where had they been able to take her without signs of a struggle? It was as though someone had appeared out of thin air; she had simply been taken hold of and disappeared…

He picked up the home phone off the ground. He was about to dial the police, but something made him enter his dad's number first. "Dad, Felicity's missing. I think someone's taken her, by force…from our driveway." As the statement remained unanswered for a second, he knew his father was reliving his own personal horrors. "I found her phone and her purse under the car, but she's gone. It can't have been more than twenty minutes ago. I'm calling the police, but…I need you to look for her. Okay?"

After another second of silence, his father answered, steady and calm…his business voice. "I'll be right there." Without answering, Ben hung up the phone and dialed 911.

Chapter 5 - Play the game

Sindy

Kana Susamiş Icin Ev
Montauk, Long Island, New York
A few weeks earlier…in mid-June

"Fly? You can't be serious."

Zach was still having a hard time processing everything that he could be capable of, but Sindy knew there wasn't time to break him in easy on the idea. "I'm telling you, you can do it. Allie does it all the time, easy. I talked to Arif again last night, and he is never going to let us out of this place until he has Allie under his control. He wants her bad, and he's worried we'll spook her. If we want out, we're going to have to make a break for it, and this is the only way I see us standing any kind of a chance. My back is against a wall here."

"Doesn't look that way to me. I don't want to give you any ideas, but I'm sure you've already considered all the angles, and I don't get your thinking. If Arif wanted you to bring him a white-eyed vampire, why haven't you just handed *me* over to him? Rat me out and you could be living in one of them big mansions with an entourage of your very own. So what's stopping you? Obviously you don't like me very much."

"Zach, that hurts…" He raised a questioning eyebrow. "Okay, I may have considered it," she admitted.

"You just couldn't do that to me?" he asked with a smirk of a smile.

Sindy let out a small huff of a laugh. "You don't know me very well. You'd be surprised what I could do…but I made you."

"So?"

"So, don't you think that Arif knows that? He had spies on me! I know for a fact that Kieran knows it was me who made you, not Allie."

"Kieran…the guy whose house we're in?"

"That's him. An impish blonde elf of a vampire who is a pain in my ass and…actually, all of this is kind of his fault! What do you think would happen if Arif found out that I gave you white eyes? Earning V.I.P. status would be one thing, but I am not looking forward to spending an eternity of nights chained up in Arif's basement, turning every human he shoves at me into a United One.

Creating a vampire is not only exhausting, but every vampire I make has an intimate and unbreakable bond with me until they're dust. If you go through excruciating pain, I'll feel it too. I made you as a favor for Allie, but pumping out an army for Arif is not my idea of a life of luxury.

There is nothing good for either one of us here, long term. We have to get out of here. We'll go for a walk through the gardens. When I think we're in a good spot and the coast is clear, I'll embrace you. That'll be your cue to take us up; straight up and the hell out of this place."

Zach and Sindy both jumped as someone entered the room. They had become so used to the comfortable illusion of privacy and superiority that came along with residency at Kieran's estate, it hadn't even occurred to Sindy that they might be so rudely interrupted without warning.

It was a woman in her mid-thirties, beautiful and impeccably styled, but severe in expression. She wore just enough make-up to look exotic and lovely without being over-done, the spare shadows of silver and blue over her eyes contrasting with her mocha skin. She wore a sarong-style dress of purple and blue, her dark hair parted in the middle and then pulled tight into a clip, that allowed the length of her dark curls to fall down to the small of her back.

A large male vampire stood behind her, silent and imposing. His mark revealed him to be no older than Sindy herself. He was a cadet of little rank. His stare was unnerving, but undeniably it was the woman who was in charge of this situation, human though she was. Her gaze swept the room, and then came back to settle on Sindy. "The Master summons you to his chambers."

Sindy and Zach had done a thorough search of the bedroom and ruled out being eavesdropped on through hidden microphones, but they hadn't expected outsiders to be admitted to the house and allowed upstairs unannounced. Sindy let out a huff of breath at the interruption, hoping that she sounded more annoyed than alarmed, and that nothing incriminating had been overheard. "I just met with him in his office last night. Unless he's ready to let me head back out and finish my mission, I have nothing more to say to him."

The woman scowled at her for a moment, in disapproving confusion, and then shared a glance with her guard, who was smiling at Sindy's misinterpretation. "His *bed* chambers," he clarified with a smirk.

Zach laughed at the woman in disbelief, as though it was some sort of joke. Sindy froze, knowing Arif wasn't one for humor...it was a serious command. It was too soon for initiation into the coven. Her mark from Cain was still in full effect. That meant this directive had to be purely for Arif's entertainment. That creep was ordering her to his bed? How dare he! However, one look at the guard and a moment to consider her position, and she realized that it was in her best interest to play along, especially if she wanted to keep protecting Zach.

She needed to keep Arif from getting suspicious that she had anything to hide, until she and Zach could fly the coop. That didn't mean she was going to service the man like a concubine, but she'd save her negotiations and arguments for the Master himself.

She squinted at the servant to show her disapproval over the woman's glee, and then turned to Zach for some quick last instructions. "Don't leave the house, and don't get too fangy with anyone."

Zach gazed at her in absolute astonishment. "Seriously? Dude summons you to his bed? Are you okay with that?"

She gave him a brief but level stare. "I don't have much of a choice. I've done worse things for less. I can handle it. Just stay here. I'll deal with him and come back as quickly as I can, so we can spend some time alone together, maybe we can go for a romantic walk in the gardens...okay?" She was definitely going to be in the mood for a walk when this was over with, a walk right into the sky.

Sindy let the woman and her guard lead her over into Arif's mansion, upstairs and through the hallways, but became confused when they didn't head towards the suite that she knew to be Arif's rooms. "Where are we going?"

The woman kept walking, but looked back over her shoulder with a smile of amusement. "I can't bring you to him looking like that," she said, her voice dripping with delighted disdain, as though Sindy was incredibly naïve.

They reached a large room that may have once been a bedroom, but no longer held a bed. Now, it was a dressing room that would make almost any woman's jaw hit the floor. The focal point of the room was a very large, three-way mirror, in front of a little platform. The remainder of the room was filled with racks and racks of clothing. It was all arranged by size, as indicated by small tabs on the poles, and the sheer assortment of gorgeous fabrics and colors was almost overwhelming.

The walls of the room were covered with racks of scarves and hooks that dripped bracelets and necklaces, with the exception of one section filled with shelves of stunning pairs of high heeled shoes, sandals and dainty slippers. In the corner stood a cabinet of tiny drawers that surely held beautiful assortments of earrings, hairclips and various treasures. To the side, was a counter-top covered in lipsticks, brushes and little cases of eye shadows and powders. It was backed by another large mirror and had three chairs before it, for applying make-up.

As Sindy stood in the doorway, taking in the contents of the room, the woman entered and turned to face her. The guard vampire took up a station in the hallway just outside, and then gave Sindy a nudge so he could close the door. The woman eyed Sindy discerningly, and then headed for the clothing racks. Under normal circumstances, this could be a lot of fun, but this was one session of dress-up Sindy was not looking forward to. The woman waved her hand towards Sindy, seemingly indicating her dress, as she began picking out clothing. "Strip that off so we can get to work. The Master doesn't like to be kept waiting."

By the time they were finished, Sindy was dressed in something that seemed a cross between lingerie and belly-dance attire. The beaded bra-top was very revealing, and well-padded to boot, making Sindy glad she had slimmed her figure the last time she had phased. She had decided that it would be smarter not to try to attract any extra attention around the compound if she could help it…not that it had done her much good. Still, she was glad she didn't have too much excess to spill out over the top she'd been given. The skirt was bad enough.

The woman had ordered Sindy to don a copper colored G-string panty, which in itself, wasn't objectionable, until Sindy realized that the skirt she was given was not actually going to cover it. The skirt was basically a low slung waist band, with beautifully colored, shimmering scarves attached to it. The thin scarves were spaced so that skin could be seen between each, and unless she took the daintiest of steps, the G-string was clearly visible…along with all that it did not cover.

Sindy's protests against the outfit were ignored. The woman's only response to the insults Sindy muttered was "My name is Saruca. If you continue to address me by anything less appropriate, I can happily find you something less flattering to wear; something not quite so…modest." At that, Sindy bit her tongue and endured the rest of the woman's fussing, until Saruca tried to show her how each scarf could be individually removed from the skirt. Sindy shooed her away with thinly veiled disgust over the idea. At this point, she wasn't planning to give Arif anything more than a piece of her mind if she could at all help it. She certainly wasn't going to be doing a strip tease.

Next came hair and make-up. The woman was clearly well practiced, and pinned Sindy's hair up in an intricate design of jeweled clips and loose tendrils, with what felt like admirable artistry. She needed to constantly tell Sindy to stop fidgeting and sit still, but it was terribly hard to be patient, when Sindy could not see the woman's progress. The mirror was empty of all but Saruca.

Once satisfied with her hair, Saruca chose the supplies she would use to paint Sindy's face. The woman smiled, and remarked how she loved to work on vampires, as their skin was preternaturally flawless, pale and smooth as porcelain. Sindy sighed and tried to watch, to see if she could guess what was being done to her, but Saruca was usually in the way. Not that Sindy could actually see what she looked like, but each stroke of blush and line of eye make-up had the curious tendency to show briefly in the mirror, as though painted onto the air, before its continued contact with her skin made it fade to invisibility.

Although elaborate, the application didn't take long, due to the woman's obvious skill. Saruca put down her last brush and exclaimed over Sindy's beauty, telling the vampiress that she should wipe the petulant expression off her face and be grateful that she had been given such opportunity to impress the Master. Even with the vast selection of ladies available to him, he should find Sindy irresistible.

Sindy stood, not trusting herself to respond, but instead trying to formulate what she might say to Arif once she arrived. Even knowing him, and his egotistical tendencies, she was having trouble swallowing that he had the audacity to expect her to behave like one of his human concubines.

Saruca selected an assortment of bangle bracelets and a large pair of hoop earrings for her to wear. Then she brought a large piece of iridescent, sheer material that changed its autumn inspired colors from russet red and gold, to olive green with every movement. It was to be wrapped around Sindy as a shawl, while she was transported to her final destination. Saruca admired her handiwork while artfully draping the material as though she was wrapping a present, explaining that Sindy's full loveliness was only to be revealed to the Master himself. Sindy tried not to gag over the woman's subservient adoration for the creep.

Sindy ignored the jealous glares she received from other women they passed in the hall, and the covetous appraisals she seemed to be the subject of from every vampire guarding the checkpoints they passed through. When they finally reached Arif's chambers, Saruca paused outside the door, most likely receiving telepathic instruction. She then opened the door, punching a series of numbers into a keypad before it unlocked for her with a beeping noise and an audible click.

With Sindy in tow, Saruca made her way through an opulently appointed sitting chamber, with lush carpet and a roaring fireplace. Then they went through an open set of lovely French doors, to a large music room, floored with beautiful Italian marble, in the center of which stood a gleaming and lovely black baby grand piano, complimented by an exotically lovely harp in the corner.

Finally, they reached what could only be the actual bedroom. It was through an archway cordoned off with sheer curtains of an iridescence and color palate similar to the cloak Sindy wore. Saruca swept the curtain aside, and gave Sindy a nudge to enter. She deposited the vampiress in the room, and left with a swift curtsy, letting the curtain swing closed behind her. Sindy stood watching her leave, the space silent, until Saruca had retreated from the parlor and Sindy heard the front door close and lock behind the woman with a digital beep.

Arif's bedchamber was large and sumptuous, as Sindy might have expected. The room was decorated in red and gold, dominated by a huge four posted, canopy bed, draped in tied-back sheer curtains like the one in the doorway. She turned to find Arif himself reclined on the bed, dressed only in a black robe and propped up on one elbow, eyeing her with amused delight. His long, black hair was loose and flowing down behind him. His slight facial hair had been trimmed to just a neat mustache and goatee to balance the thick eyelashes and thin brows that gave him a look that was polished, dark and sultry, and yet masculine and mesmerizing.

His handsome features paired with his obvious power and preternatural vampire allure made him quite a provocative sight, but Sindy was unswayed. She had found his position attractive at one time, and he *was* physically appealing, but his sheer arrogance and his belief that he could bully her into submission disgusted her to the core. The way he'd ordered her to be primped, preened and dragged here at his whim grated down her nerves until her original acceptance of just sleeping with him, to keep him mollified and ease his suspicions, was out of the question. At this point, he'd be lucky if she left his manhood intact!

"Sindy, my dear, you look simply ravishing," he purred from the bed.

She narrowed her eyes as she placed her hands on her hips, refusing to appear docile in any way. "Don't get your fangs all aquiver just yet. I'm only here to talk. What do you want from me?"

He smiled, sitting up further on the bed, to better take in the full vision of her. "Isn't it obvious? I expect a display of your desire to be accepted into my coven," he explained with a grin.

Sindy pulled her sarong-cloak tightly closed and crossed her arms over her chest. "Years ago, I came to you, newly turned and alone. I did a strip tease in your office, and offered you free reign over my body," she recalled with thinly veiled self-loathing over the act. "I said I would do *anything* that you asked of me, if you would grant me residence here.*"*

Arif's grin broadened. "I remember."

"You turned me down," she added resentfully.

"I did," he conceded with a slight nod.

She uncrossed her arms to replace her hands back onto her hips in agitation. "Well, that offer is off the table now," she informed him.

"Is it? Then why are you so charmingly dressed?"

"Out of respect. I didn't want to humiliate you in front of your lackeys by refusing you outright, but this is as far as it goes."

"How considerate of you." He seemed more amused than grateful for her cooperation. She tried to cool her temper and play it smart.

She took a step towards the bed, which undoubtedly pleased him. "You're making a big mistake keeping me here," she told him gently, trying to appeal to his intellect. "You need to let me return to Cain's estate, so that I can finish what I started with Allie. You've given up on me too soon; I was so close. Every night that I'm away, her trust in me will fade. You'll ruin all that we've worked for, and miss your best opportunity to get her here willingly."

Arif stood from the bed and approached her, his demeanor now more menacing then seductive. Sindy forced herself to stand still, not backing down from him or allowing herself to appear intimidated as he moved in close. He cupped the side of her face and drew closer, as though preparing to kiss her cheek. "I think you greatly misinterpret your position here," he whispered. "All that *we* have worked for?" he asked, repeating her words with an arched brow. "You speak as though you believe us to be aligned, when the fact is, you are nothing but a hired whore."

"I'm not…" she stammered indignantly, as she backed out of his grasp.

He interrupted her harshly. "I hired you to seduce someone into trusting you, manipulate them into taking you into their private confidence, and then lure them into my compound. Whether or not the means were sexual, is irrelevant. I may not have given you a deadline, but you will have to agree that I have been most patient, and at this point, I am uninterested in giving you more time. When a whore brings climax within reach, but does not deliver it, she does not get paid."

Sindy opened her mouth, trying to think what she could say to improve her position. Finally, she decided that her best course of action was to tell him the truth of what she wanted. "Fine. You want to consider me unsuccessful? Then I guess there is no place for me here. I'll go on my way, and you can figure out how to get Allie here yourself." He laughed. Not a good sign.

"As I thought I had made clear, leaving this compound, that you once so desperately desired entrance to, is no longer an option. I cannot risk you interfering with my plans for the United One. You may not have proved very useful to me in the field, but here I can have you serve a purpose. You are not my guest, you are a prisoner," he said, pursuing her once more, as she slowly backed away.

She froze, as she reached the wall and felt the cold surface against the skin of her back through the thin cloak. Was the situation was dire enough for drastic measures, or was she still best off trying to reason with him? He reached up to gently touch the side of her face, and then let his hand trail down to brush the side of her breast as well. "And as such," he continued, "nothing is *off the table.*"

She glanced down at his hand on her body and then looked back up into his eyes, fighting to keep her composure. With every cell in her body, she was just itching to phase into mist…and perhaps reform as a wolf to rip his throat out, even if it would only be a temporary discomfort to him, but she knew such defiance would only add to her problems. "You have dozens of women," she quietly reminded him imploringly, "who would be happy to do anything that your twisted little heart desires."

He smiled, taking the edge of the thin cloak that covered her, and slowly pulling it away to leave her exposed in the skimpy costume she wore as he spoke. "And now, you are one of them."

She briefly wondered if Arif was able to feel her emotions through empathy, the way that Allie could, making her show of bravery count for nothing. She sincerely hoped that skill wasn't in his arsenal. She took a deep breath, allowing the indignity she felt to overcome her rising panic. Anger always served her better than fear. "I obeyed your request to see me, and I even let your minions dress me up in this ridiculous outfit as a show of goodwill. I came to negotiate with you, because I've always admired your intelligence, and I thought you'd see what a mistake you're making in keeping me here, and you would send me back out to do my job. If that's not the case, then we are done here." She slid sideways against the wall and away from him, very relieved that he did nothing to stop her.

She felt bolder as she reached the curtained doorway. Maybe Arif respected her bravado. "I'm going back to Kieran's," she informed him. "Do you want me to count to ten or something, so your guards don't take you for a minute man?" He said nothing, but simply fixed her with a level stare. Maybe that last remark was going a bit too far... "No? Then I'll let myself out."

She swept the curtain aside and walked out into the music room towards the parlor, heading for the door to the hall. Arif's voice followed her. "You will not be leaving my quarters until I order you out," he told her.

She didn't bother to stop or answer. She had reached the door. She panicked for a moment, when she realized that the combination lock might not allow her to open it from the inside, but before she could even try it, the door opened of its own accord, and two very large vampire guards stood blocking her exit. They stepped forward, closing the door behind them. One of them glanced over her shoulder towards Arif, and then looked back down at her. "I think he wants you to stay."

Sindy also spared Arif a quick glance over her shoulder before laughing at him and the guards in relief over the realization that she was not without recourse. "You can't hold me here against my will," she informed them, turning towards Arif, and knowing it was true. Her faith in her vampire skills transformed her fear into relieved defiance. "And you absolutely can't have any of *this*, without my say so," she said, brushing her hand over her breast and down the length of her body, as he had done to her earlier. "And I *don't* say so." She looked up at the guards in annoyance. "So get the fuck out of my face."

The guard directly before her leered, grabbing her throat with one hand in a swift strike. He dug in his fingers, forcing her chin upwards, but as he squeezed to hold her tighter, she let her throat thin until there was nothing but mist in his grip. He seemed very confused, but his partner was unshaken, and hooked one arm around her waist and the other got a tight hold of her arm. It didn't matter; she just finished her phasing and turned completely to smoke. Her costume of scarves fluttered in the air where she had been, while her beaded bra and jewelry fell to the floor with a clattering of metal on metal that was quickly swallowed in the carpet.

Unfortunately, the door was closed and the thick pile of the rug before it made her doubt her ability to pass through underneath. She couldn't remain as mist for long, and wasn't very skilled at maneuvering as smoke.

There was nowhere else for her to go; she was going to have to reform. She settled herself into the middle of the parlor, as Arif came through the music room to stand in the doorway and watch. She stood, now nude, in the center of the room between Arif and his guards. She held her head high. "I told you, you can't hold me against my will."

Arif met her eyes with a smirk. "I've disrobed you."

She rolled her eyes. "Hmmmph. Nice work. Take a good look, because this is all you're getting, asshole. *You can't touch me.* I think I've been pretty reasonable, and I was even trying to save you a little face, but now, I'm done with these games. Let me out, before I find a way to really humiliate you."

Arif chuckled and folded his arms, as though settling himself to watch what she might do. "My men care nothing for what you might tell them, and they will not open the door without my order." As he finished speaking, the men moved towards her, goaded by a mental command from their master. Both men came at her, once again trying to grab hold.

One look at Arif's smug expression and Sindy lost it. Forget trying to be civilized. She turned and leapt into the air, letting herself explode free of her human body, and shift into mist that floated weightless for a second, during which, time seemed to stand still, as the occupants of the room froze in shock.

She pulled herself together, shifting into her wolf form and letting her suddenly solid weight carry her forward with great force. She lunged at the vampire closest to her, raking him with her claws and sending him sprawling. As he hit the floor, she turned while atop his stomach, dug in her claws and tensed her muscles to leap, eliciting a loud groan from the man.

She jumped for the second vampire, her front paws meeting his shoulders and pushing him down in front of her. She vaulted over him, past Arif and through the music room in a giant bound. As she landed in the archway to the bedroom, she tore down one of the curtains as it tangled around her front paws, but she was untroubled and leapt again to land on the bed.

She skid and turned, making a mess of the coverlets, and then shifted back into human form for a moment, to be free of the curtain and assess Arif's reaction. "See what you've made me do? Now you're going to have dog hair all over your bed. Open the fucking door."

"As you wish," Arif answered, as his men regained their feet and gingerly assessed the damage her claws had done. The door opened, as promised, and four more male vampires came through, closing it behind them. "Seize her," Arif ordered. His arrogance was un-nerving, because despite her wolf display, he sounded bored.

Sindy shifted back into wolf form. She may have a hard time actually killing vampires this way, but if she gutted them all, they would be out of commission for a while. As satisfying as it would be to threaten Arif himself, she knew she couldn't kill him unless she took his head off. The guards wouldn't give her time to do such damage, and it would undoubtedly just piss him off and make him feel the need to teach her a lesson. By taking out the guards, maybe she would gain some respect in his eyes, and convince Arif that it was in his best interest to leave her alone.

She made a run for the door, snarling as viciously as she could manage. It was immensely satisfying to note that most of the guards looked like they were scared shitless, but when she managed to attack one of them, and locked her jaws around his throat, the stabbing pain that shot through her head immediately dropped her to the floor.

The momentary agony was so severe, that she lost her form. Her transformation to mist seemed to dull the pain, but she couldn't focus on reforming the wolf, and found herself lying naked and human-looking on the cold tile when it subsided. The vampire she had bitten was bleeding from the throat, but not too badly. He held a hand to the wound on his neck as he backed away from her.

"You cannot bite them," Arif explained in amusement. "They are marked."

She looked up at him, as she sat up and shook off her shock. "Lucky them, or I'd have ripped most of their throats out by now." Arif gave her a slight nod and a grin, as she stood and looked at the men, daring them to come at her again. "I can't bite them, they can't hurt me. I guess we're at a stalemate then." Actually, she could still do a good amount of damage with her claws, but the instant migraine had really thrown her for a loop, and she was beginning to think it would be nice if she didn't have to give any more displays of strength just now. She fixed her stare on Arif once again. "You've had a good show and we both know where we stand now. Enough of this shit. Let me out."

Arif just looked off into the distance, his eyes unfocused as though he was listening to something that only he could hear. He became suddenly pleased and met Sindy's gaze with a gleeful expression. "But the real fun is only just beginning," he said, as the door opened behind her.

Another vampire entered the room, an unimposing Asian man, who was casually dressed in black jeans and a tee shirt that said "Baby Metal - Gimme Chocolate!" on the front. He looked to have been in his early twenties when turned. He stood in the open doorway and crossed his arms, assessing the room's occupants and then fixing his attention on Sindy.

Sindy made her way towards the man, refusing to wait and see what Arif thought was going to be such fun. If all of the vampires behind her couldn't hold her, what was this jerk going to be able to do? "Get out of my way," she told him as she made to push past him out the door.

She actually did make it into the hallway, before he grabbed hold of her arm and kept her from getting any further. She tried to yank back out of his grasp, de-materializing her arm in the process, but the man held tight. She felt the molecules of her arm loosen and separate, preparing to turn into smoke, but the man's hold somehow prevented her from fully accomplishing it. After a second, her arm solidified. She couldn't shift. He dragged her back into the room, as she gasped in unready surprise. "What the hell?"

Two of the other vampires stepped forward and closed the door, as Sindy was shoved back into the middle of the parlor. Arif approached, pleased with the development. "I don't believe you have been introduced to the newest member of my Senior Guard. This is Jin. He will be keeping you in your human form for the remainder of the evening. While I find your wolf incarnation to be beautiful in its inherent brutality, you can see where it is an impractical allowance. I'm afraid we'll need to strip you of it for now."

She stood mute trying to process his claim, as remembered snippets of information came back to her. She should have known about this possibility, expected it. Alyson had told her that Arif had a vampire that could negate the powers of others. Alyson herself had the skill and had practiced it on Sindy once or twice, to her great discomfort. How could Sindy have forgotten? Wow, she had really played this wrong. She had thought she'd had a measure of protection in her power, and in reality…she had nothing but whatever her snide comments had earned her from Arif.

"Fasten her to the bed," Arif ordered. Four men came forward and scooped her off her feet, taking hold of her extremities. Without her ability to shift, one man would have been plenty. She was powerless against them, but they were taking no chances. She struggled anyway, sheerly on principle.

"You may want to calm yourself. It would be a pity if you forced me punish you and risk disfiguring such exquisite beauty."

The men held her tighter, trying to force stillness, and her struggles diminished a bit at the threat, but she answered him mentally with a flare of rage. *You can't disfigure me...I'm a shape shifter, you moron.*

Arif smiled as his men brought her closer. *Is that a challenge?*

She would have spit at him if she'd had the chance, but the men threw her onto the bed. They quickly regained their hold on her arms and legs, as the other vampires brought out chains attached to manacles that would fasten her wrists and ankles to each of the bed's posts.

They were putting her in *cuffs,* really? This was getting way out of hand. "Why?" she screamed. "Why are you doing this? Those women out there worship you. Why do you want *me?*"

Jin stood by and watched, enjoying the view of her, nude and flailing, on the bed in the grip of her captors. Her pathetic attempts to struggle were nothing but annoyances to the strong men that secured her, and barely gave them pause. Arif approached the bed, as the men finished their work. One of them stooped to retrieve and untangle the doorway curtains to be hung again as Arif spoke.

"Why do I want you? Do you think this is about desire?" Arif asked with a chuckle. "Are you conceited enough to believe that you are so attractive that I cannot bear to be denied the opportunity to avail myself of your charms? Silly girl, this isn't about *want,* it is about power. I have it...you don't respect it."

"You're powerful, I get it." Lying naked, chained to the bed, stripped of her own power and dignity, completely helpless and surrounded by strong vampires, even she knew that her concession sounded like far too little, too late.

"I don't think that you do. You seem to think that my orders hold no weight or consequence for being ignored. How long did you think you would dally with Cain, rather than further my plans, with only feeble excuses to deliver? I was very patient with you, but it only served to make you bolder."

"That's not true!" she insisted. "I was doing what you wanted. I told you it would take time and finesse. If you wanted me to do it right, I needed more time."

"Perhaps...but I still feel that a lesson in carrying out my requests expediently is in order here. Now you have been ordered to my bed for my enjoyment, and you will learn that my orders are to be obeyed." He straightened from where he had leaned over her, and addressed the guards. "Leave us."

The men began to file out of the room, but Jin remained leaning against the wall, observing Sindy with a wicked sneer. He lost the expression when Arif directed him to leave as well. "Wait in the parlor," Arif told him. "I trust that is still within your range."

"Yes, sir," Jin answered, as he left through the curtained doorway.

"And close the doors," Arif called to Jin, who had just passed the piano, and reached the set of doors that separated the music room from the parlor.

Jin turned, a hand on each door, as he made ready to close them behind him. "You just want me to sit out here in the parlor?" he asked. "All night?"

Arif turned to look at him through the curtain in annoyance. "And all day if I wish. And keep your focus on dampening the girl. No distractions."

Sindy could no longer see Jin from where she lay. She could see nothing but Arif looming before her. She could imagine that Jin wasn't thrilled with the prospect of spending the next twenty-four hours focused on disarming a woman he couldn't even watch, but unfortunately for Sindy, he didn't seem willing to argue about it. She heard him close the double doors with an ominous click that left her alone with the Master.

Arif removed his robe. He wore nothing beneath it. His skin shown with an almost golden cast, accented by the dark curls that began thinly on his chest and then thickened as they reached his navel and devolved into dense curls below. His member emerged from the soft down, erect and ready for whatever heinous deeds he had in mind.

"Tell me," he said, speaking casually, as he folded his robe and laid it across a chair neatly, as though taking comfort in his complete control of his surroundings, "when you were leader of your own coven, how did you enforce the obedience of your underlings?"

Sindy stared at him mutely, as the taut chains dug into her ankles while she tried in vain not to hold her legs so open before him. Her coven? Was he really going to raise examples from her past to try to justify his own actions? She swallowed and found her voice, hoping it didn't sound as feeble to him as it did in her own ears. "Venom."

"Ah, yes, venom. Something you have ensured I cannot use on you at the moment. Venom drew them back to you and influenced them, surely, but what was it that really kept them in line? What encouragement had they to do your bidding?"

Sindy shook her head, trying to deny the parallel he was obviously trying to draw. "They weren't like us. They were pretty stupid. It didn't take much to get them to follow instructions…if they could even understand the instructions."

Arif was unwilling to accept so simple an explanation. "I will tell you how you kept your power…fear; carefully cultivated fears, and a system of rewards. You made certain they were frightened to try to exist without you, or to displease you, and when they were obedient, you gave them reward. Like doling out treats to good doggies, you granted sexual favors and took them into your bed." He slid his hand along the pillowcase next to her head, as though admiring the soft fabric, and then let his hand stray to her shoulder, his fingertips just brushing the side of her throat. "Sex and fear…we are not so different, you and I."

She shrugged her shoulder, her arm pulling against the chains in an attempt to cause him to remove his hand. He took it back slowly, with a smile, as though submitting to her request through great generosity.

"Is this supposed to be the reward or the fear? Just so I'm clear," she asked him, with a snarky sass that she could display through her fright only due to years of projecting such an image at all costs.

"I haven't decided yet. Let's see how the evening progresses, shall we?"

She squinted at him through slitted eyes, unamused. Her voice was a low growl that doubtless reminded him of her wolf. "I never forced any of my vamps to do anything they didn't want to."

Arif's gentle hand turned hard as he used it to grip her throat. "Like dying? Did they ask you for death? Young men, just entering the prime of their lives, plucked from humanity to do your bidding. Don't try to take the moral high ground with me, young lady. I know you too well. We do what we must to better things for ourselves. You used what worked, as do I."

As he finished speaking his eyes suddenly changed color in the space of a blink. They unexpectedly became a beautifully smoldering violet purple, hypnotizing and provocative. Sindy found herself unwilling to look away from his spellbinding gaze, although she tried to remind herself that without biting her, he had no true control of thrall over her. She was not one of his minions…yet.

"Your mark protects you from the full effects of my skill," he confirmed, loosening his hold on her throat, "and yet, still you feel the compulsion, don't you? My powers of alluring enthrallment are un-matched. Even through your disdain, you find me seductively compelling…true?"

"Yes," she admitted with a whisper. It was no use lying.

"And yet a truly strong vampire of independent will, such as yourself, is aware of the spell. A human retains memory of my mastery over them only if I allow it, but a vampire is aware of their actions, and understands they are forced to do my bidding, even when they are powerless to prevent my control.

I could grant you the pleasure of ignorant bliss if you submitted to it. Were you to grant me control, I could compel your actions and yet you would have no memory of it at all."

She grimaced as he leaned back a bit, giving her a moment to break from his gaze and assert herself. "No! Are you crazy? I would never! If you're going to make me do things, I at least want to know damn well what happened!"

"Really?" he asked, studying her with mild curiosity. "It would not change your actions; only spare you the humiliation of remembering them."

"No thanks."

"Interesting. Your spirit intrigues me. I thought self-preservation of pride would make you want to shield yourself. Especially considering your troubled past. I wouldn't want to call up painful memories for you."

His tone was meant to be full of consideration, but she knew he wasn't actually concerned for her emotional distress, he was sending her a message. It struck a chord in her that filled her with wrath she could barely conceal. He knew…about the sexual and physical abuse she had suffered as a child and teenager. The bastard knew, and had no problem promising to recreate it for her.

She bit her tongue until she tasted blood. He watched her, waiting for a response. When it was finally clear that she planned to keep her mouth shut and her emotions in check, he went on. "Well, you've plenty of time to reconsider your stance on the matter. I cannot truly compel you until your mark fades.

Perhaps by the time it does, you will have earned my trust and esteem. I am a fair and honorable leader. Those who show proper respect are treated respectfully in turn. I do not make a habit of compelling my coven. They do my bidding for favor, not out of force or fear."

"I thought you didn't even want me in your coven? You turned me away last time because you said I was too much of an independent thinker; stubborn and hard to control."

"That is true."

"I haven't changed much," she informed him with a smirk.

"No, but back then your temerity came from a place of rebellious adolescence, which I find annoying, and not at all attractive. Now, you have found maturity, inner strength and confidence to fuel you. Unleashed it can be a nuisance, but harnessed it is a quality I can admire. Back when we first met, I had not been aware that you had such a rare and beautiful eye color. My court is lacking a red-eyed vampire at the moment, so I have decided that you will stay. A tamed wolf still has bite. It is just as dangerous as a wolf in the wild…only it is better fed."

"I doubt I'll ever be that hungry."

"We'll see if you still feel that way a few nights from now… You are an amazing creature. If you prove yourself a lady of sophistication and strength, who deserves to be treated with dignity, perhaps I will grant dignity. But displays such as the one here tonight," he warned with a gesture towards the parlor, referring to her wolf rebellion, "will earn you only torturous degradation. Understood?"

"Yes," she said through gritted teeth.

"Vampires of my coven call me Master…or at the very least, sir," he informed her. "It is a sign of recognition for my authority over them."

"I'm not a member of your coven yet," she reminded him quietly.

He smiled. Luckily, he seemed amused rather than annoyed by her small show of defiance. "True, you are not. Perhaps you never will be…we'll see what I think of you once your mark fades. But, whether I feel you have earned the honor of initiation or not, I will earn that 'sir' from you…quickly, I am sure."

He moved back a bit from the bed, swiping his hair back to fall behind him in soft ebony waves, and then smiled, as though posing for her. "You have not remarked upon my body, graciously revealed for you. To have been granted immortality in such a form, I have been truly blessed, wouldn't you agree?"

She took a moment to glance him over. His body wasn't particularly impressive, but nice enough. He did have a certain masculine beauty about him that drew the eye. No one could ever claim to find him revolting in appearance, but she was finally learning to appreciate the old adage, 'beauty is skin deep'.

He waited for her response. She wouldn't be stupid enough to blatantly insult him. If his powers of telepathy and empathy were anything like Allie's, she couldn't tell him so simple a lie anyway, and he *was* a handsome man. "Not bad," she remarked, indifferently.

"Indeed," he replied dryly. "I notice that you now sport your original, true form." He moved to sit next to her on the bed again, leaning over her intimately and lightly running his hands over her body with a familiarity that made her want to squirm and turn away. Being pawed by jerks was nothing new, but it felt very different when she wasn't the one making the decision to let it happen.

She forced herself to lie still and ignore his touch. If he took things much further, she'd find herself automatically resorting to retreating to the far corners of consciousness, where she could be numb, just like she used to. Arif had offered to spellbind her thoughts, sparing her knowledge of what he would do to her, but enthrallment was un-necessary. She was a master at blocking out defilement. It had begun with her father, but it was an art form at this point. How else could she give her body to so many men, to gain what she needed to survive all of these years? Some of them were fun to bed, when things were on her terms, but when she had no choice…she could do what she needed to. They couldn't truly touch her anymore. She should've just let Arif have her to begin with, sparing herself the trouble displaying self-worth had bought her.

She forced her eyes to focus, and her ears to hear his words. She would not go bury herself in her subconscious…not yet, she needed to stay and listen. Perhaps he could still be reasoned with. His body did not touch her, only his fingertips trailed along her skin. The way he took his time, stroking her and talking, was very different from violators of the past. Unlike others, he was in no desperate rush. She got the impression that he did respect her mind at least, that he considered her a worthy entity to speak to, unlike the human women he simply ordered about. Could he be…lonely? Perhaps she might use that to her slight advantage somehow.

He continued with his observations of her body. "It's quite appealing, this slender body, although I can see why you have become fond of experimenting with adding plumpness to further encourage men's desires," he added, giving her firm little breast a squeeze. "Either form would please me. I enjoy variety."

"Thanks for the tip," she spat out sarcastically, letting him know she was not emotionally defeated. She had a feeling he somewhat appreciated her sharp tongue at times, as a novelty. Perhaps it got boring being around only subservient slaves. He might be more lenient with her if he admired her, however grudgingly.

She dropped her mental guard for a moment. If Arif's powers of telepathy were anything like Allie's, then he could read her surface thoughts as long as she wasn't trying to hide them. She wouldn't be so defiant as to voice all of her thoughts out loud, but she wasn't above letting him read a few.

I'm not a frightened little girl anymore. I am a powerful creature of the night, who has learned to wield her strength and own it. I won't allow anyone to try to turn me into

that scared little girl ever again. I know who I am. "Did you bring me here for conversation? Because I'm a better listener, when I'm not fighting chains. If you're planning on doing more than chatting, then just do it already. I'm getting bored."

He considered her for a moment. He'd read her thoughts, she was fairly sure. Hopefully, he found her unbroken resolve impressive, rather than taking it as a challenge. Finally, he smiled. "But isn't the anticipation exhilarating? As vampires with heightened senses and awareness, we become accustomed to knowing what to expect from people. You will find that expectant anticipation and mystery can revive the interest we often find fading from our nightly existences."

So, his interest needed reviving, did it? Not a job she wanted, but at least if he found her interesting to have around, he wouldn't have her killed. She wasn't sure if that was an improvement for her. If release was denied, did she really want to spend her time like this? "So, clearly I should expect the *anticipation* to be the biggest thrill of the evening then?" she said with a pointed look at his crotch. "It's kind of a relief that you already know that, because I'm not so good at faking it."

He laughed, more amused than offended. "Make no mistake; I could thrill you if that was my wish. Just as I have read the horrors and fears of your youth, I can also pluck the longings and fantasies from your mind, and have you begging me to fulfill them. Women worship at the foot of my bed, in awe of the experiences I can provide…should I choose.

You are here so that I may prove my power, not my prowess. Mark the difference. Shall I claim you? Would that teach you respect, earn your loyalty? For you are bared here before me, mine to claim."

She met his eyes with a serious and level stare. "I came to you for a title and rank among vampires, not for a degrading fuck, but like you said, we do what we must to get what we want. I won't say that I haven't had some respect for you, because I always did, to a point. Good job obliterating that by the way, but I'm not afraid of you, and I never will be. You know what I want, and you're in a position to do whatever *you* want. So what are you going to do?"

He weighed her words, with no expression to betray his thoughts. After an interminable moment, he stood from the bed and affected to be suddenly tired of her. "I'm going to take a bath."

She was still watching him in confusion, when three human women entered the room, apparently at his mental summons. She tried to ignore them, although her keen senses picked up their delicious scents and tracked their heartbeats, tempting her thirst. The girls immediately stripped off their clothing and bowed their heads as they moved to stand before him. They snuck adoring glances at Arif and seemed as though they could barely wait to please him.

"My attendants," Arif explained to her, "here to bath me."

Sindy couldn't help but let out a huff of sarcastic disapproval. Was he trying to show her that he didn't need her body? *Good...have fun with your bathing beauty Barbies and leave me out of it!*

"You scoff at their obedience. Do you even comprehend the depth of their devotion? They would lick me clean like cats with their tongues if I required it of them." He turned to address them. "Go on and run the bath for me, ladies."

They disappeared into the bathroom as Arif kept his gaze trained on Sindy. "Simple, broken women I have. Intelligent women who do not know their place can be quite annoying; but women of spirit, intelligence, and charm, who *also* know when to display complete obedience, are quite rare. There are only two such women currently under my rule. One is unflinchingly loyal, but too odd and unstable to be considered a serious companion. The other, well...she has displeased me of late. Perhaps you should keep that in mind, when considering your opportunities for placement here, and the level of title and rank that you truly aspire to attain.

Intrigue me. Earn my true interest, and there could be a place of power for you here, the likes of which you never dreamed. It is not your spirit I wish to break, only the bonds that restrain your aspirations. Do not let your pride keep you from the path to loftier goals. Submit your trust and obedience to me, and you may receive more than you ever imagined in return.

But play your cards cleverly. I have no patience or tolerance for your petty insults. They show not true courage, only an ignorant lack of foresight. Your expressed view of me will directly determine how I view you, my dear. I suggest you choose your words and actions wisely."

He turned his attention to the door as it opened and another servant entered. Sindy recognized Saruca, the woman who had prepared her for this 'visit' with Arif. She carried a tray that held a plate of sugared donuts and pastries.

Arif gestured for the tray to be placed on a table, and Saruca did so with a bow of her head, and then retreated. As she left, Arif called into the bathroom, which had begun to resonate with the sound of water running. "Rebecca, come here a moment. I have something for you."

One of the girls came out to answer the summons; a lovely young thing, with dark wavy hair and a full, luscious figure. Arif smiled in approval of her swift obedience, and gestured to the plate. "For you, dear."

Oddly, she seemed less than pleased by the offering. She answered with timid reluctance. "But I've already eaten, master."

"Then you will eat again. I enjoy how its flavor infuses your sweet blood." Without further protest, she nodded and took the plate. She picked a piece of sugary crust off one of the pastries and popped it into her mouth, to show her compliance, and then took the plate into the bathroom.

"She is diabetic," Arif explained to Sindy. "An interesting variation of flavor, when levels are precariously balanced; delicate to maintain, but worth the effort. As I said earlier, I enjoy variety."

Before Sindy could process and respond to the explanation, Arif departed for his bath. She was left lying spread eagle on her back, naked on the bed, chained to its posts, and subjected to listening to nearly two hours of water splashing amidst feminine laughter and Arif's occasional remarks and moans of delight.

Saruca returned, and stood in the entryway to the bedroom. Arif must have called her telepathically, and now she waited for him to emerge with instructions. She stood for a moment, still and businesslike, but soon couldn't help but notice Sindy's discarded clothing and jewelry still on the floor. She collected it, and then turned her eyes to Sindy. Upon closer inspection of Sindy's appearance, she became very annoyed. Finally, she inched closer to speak to Sindy in a harsh whisper. "What have you done? Your hair…your face…all of my work, ruined!"

Between the shape shifting, struggling, and her treatment as she was restrained, Sindy was sure that the artistry Saruca had made her up with was indeed all but erased.

"Saruca," Arif said with slight reprimand for speaking to Sindy, as he entered the room. "Rebecca is in need of her insulin."

Saruca bowed her head and showed him a case held in her hands. "Yes Master, I have it here." Before leaving for the bathroom, she couldn't seem to help but wave a hand towards Sindy. "I trust this one was prepared to your liking? I took particular care with her for you."

"Yes, your work was skillful as always, but then, little skill is needed for such a lovely canvas." Saruca dropped her eyes, as though it was overstepping to take such pride in her work. "Saruca, you may want to hurry with the insulin. She was beginning to taste a bit acidic, never a good sign. She's passed out, I'm afraid," Arif informed her matter-of-factly with a nod towards the bathroom.

Saruca rushed to the bathroom in distress as Sindy shook her chains for Arif's attention. "You put that poor girl into a sugar coma, just so you could have a tasty treat?" she asked in outrage.

Arif simply smirked at her disapproval, and then snapped his fingers. "Kira," He called, as a different girl emerged from the bathroom. This was a nude blonde, dreamy eyed and stumbling, although whether she was high on venom, or some other intoxicant was impossible to tell. She carried something, and after a moment, Arif snatched it from her before it spilled. He brought it to Sindy. It was a shot glass of blood. "I saved you some."

Sindy turned away from it as best she could. "I don't want that."

He tipped it to her lips anyway. She couldn't truly avoid it without having him spill it on her. It smelled wonderful. Resisting it wouldn't make much of a statement or difference, as it had already been drawn from its victim. She was so thirsty... Who knew when Arif was going to plan on giving her anything else while she was restrained here? Finally, she drank it. It was actually very good, but she refused to comment.

Arif smiled, calmly addressing the human behind him. "Kira, will she live?"

The girl looked up at him in adoration. "Who?"

"Rebecca," he supplied patiently.

Kira nodded. "She's okay." Arif must already know her status through his telepathic link. He was asking for affirmation for Sindy's benefit. "She can't play anymore though," the girl said with slurred disappointment. She noticed Sindy on the bed and moved closer, as though discovering a treasure. "Maybe *she* could join us. She's real pretty." She looked up at Arif in askance. "I've never played with her before. Is she allowed, or has she been naughty?"

Arif glanced at Sindy with a sly smile. "She's been naughty, I'm afraid."

Saruca came back out of the bathroom, the third girl helping her to carry Rebecca, who was conscious, but only barely. Arif spoke as he watched them leave. "Send me Fatima as replacement. I'd like her to dance." He then turned, taking Kira by the arm and leading her through to recline on a chaise lounge in the music room.

Sindy shook her head in disdain. Did he have any idea what an ass he was? And what was the point of keeping her here to be ignored? He'd made his point. She was sore, aching and thoroughly humiliated. Why didn't he just release her back to her rooms already? "Arif," she called.

He completely ignored her, giving all of his attention to Kira. She tried twice more, but although he must have heard her, he did not bother to respond. Sindy pulled uselessly against her chains, but it served only to make her wrists and ankles hurt worse. She swallowed her pride and called out once more. "Sir?"

As she had expected, the title of respect caught his attention. She hated to give it to him so easily, but maybe it would goad him to release her. As Kira lay across the chair, he turned back to hear Sindy speak. "Are you just going to leave me strapped to your bed all night?" she asked.

He came back towards her a few steps. "Oh, I'm sorry. Did you want to join us? I was under the impression that you were uninclined."

She couldn't help but roll her eyes. "No, I don't want to join you, but I believe you've proved your point." He raised his eyebrows, questioning her. She continued, grudgingly. "I better understand your position of power here now, so…you can let me up now, sir."

"I've proved my point, have I? My point was that my orders are to be obeyed. You were ordered to my bed for my enjoyment."

"Yes, and I can see that having me in such a humiliating and uncomfortable position, for so many hours, has been very enjoyable for you," she pointed out.

"Indeed. As you can see, my physical needs are currently being well satisfied by others far more fully than you could accomplish. However, I *have* found your discomfort rather enjoyable. Enough so that I would like to continue it, until some other form of entertainment comes to mind."

Yet again, the door opened and another young woman entered. She was scantily dressed in a belly dance costume similar to the outfit Sindy had worn. "Ah, Fatima, you look ravishing. You're to dance for me," he told the girl, as he moved into the music room and swung closed its curtains without so much as a glance back in Sindy's direction.

Music soon began to play, and once again, Sindy was left alone to listen to the sounds of Arif's entertainment from the other room. It hurt her neck to crane and try to watch the vague shadows of fluid movement from the dancer through the curtains, and she soon gave up trying. Her arms and legs ached from being spread wide on the bed, but at least that was her only true discomfort. Things could be a lot worse. Perhaps in another hour or so, they would be, but for now, she could only close her eyes and try to sleep.

~~~~~~~~~~~~~~~~~~~~~~~~~~~~~

Sindy awoke to find Arif standing over her. He leaned casually against the bedpost, once again dressed in his robe of black velvet, staring at her. She looked up at a noise, and saw that the curtains to the music room had been left open.

Saruca and one of Arif's male vampires were there, helping Fatima and Kira to leave. Both women looked inebriated to the point that they could use all the help they could get. They were drunk…in every sense of the word…being inebriated with alcohol and Arif having drunk from them as well, making them high on his strong venom. Eventually, the guard vampire needed to scoop Kira up into his arms and carry her so that they could make it out the door. They left, passing Jin in the parlor, and closing its double doors behind them.

Once they were alone, Sindy looked back to Arif, who had never taken his eyes from her. "I never tire of gazing at the beauty that is the female form," he told her. "Of course, this is a less than flattering pose for you," he added with a grin, "but what it lacks in elegance, is made up for in its inherent helpless supplicance. Vulnerability can be quite appealing on you, my dear. Still, your sour expression does mar the vision."

"So, let me up already. I can guarantee it would improve the look on my pretty face."

Arif chuckled. "Perhaps it is your face I am tired of gazing at."

She sighed. "It's nearly dawn, Arif. Let me go. You are in charge and you always get what you want. I know that now. I'm not arguing…I get it."

He said nothing, but the male vampires returned to the room and flanked the bed. They began to unlock her chains.

"Thank you," she said with quiet relief. It felt so good to bend her arms and legs again. Unfortunately, she could only flex them for a moment before the guards took hold of her again.

"Turn her over," Arif ordered. The men forced her to flip over onto her stomach and began to chain her again. "I think that will be a nice change of view, don't you agree?"

Sindy tried to struggle, but could not accomplish anything. "You've got to be kidding me!" she yelled at him in disbelief, although much of the sound was lost within the pillows.

Arif smiled to one of his guards, who was obviously enjoying the view. "Her pert bottom is quite a pleasant sight. I'm finding it more enjoyable already; and the position also muffles her mouth, how convenient."

The guard gleefully agreed. "That ass looks ripe for plunging, if you ask me."

Arif gave him a sidelong glance. "I didn't." The vampire took the cue to gather the other guards and leave, now that she was once again fully restrained. "Comfortable?" Arif asked, once they were alone.

"Seriously?"

He sat on the bed next to her and took the opportunity to squeeze the cheeks of her buttocks and give her a light smack, enjoying the way it rippled over her flesh. "You'll stay the day, and the night again if I so desire." He punctuated his words with a sharper slap on her ass. Then he stood and moved to enter the large dressing room next to the bath. She heard the sounds of closets and drawers opening, before he returned, fully dressed.

"I have some business to attend to before first bell, but never fear, I'll be returning shortly to keep you company."

Sindy spent the next hour testing Jin's focus in the hopes that he had gotten bored and forgotten to continue dampening her shifting skills, but it was no use. It was as though she'd never had the ability. Her powers were useless while Jin carried out Arif's orders.

As the first bell rang to mark dawn's approach, a new human woman entered Arif's suite. As all of them were, she was beautiful. She had very fair skin in stark contrast with her hair that was almost black, and her large eyes were ringed with thick lashes and dark eyeliner. She entered with an attitude docile and obedient, until she looked around and spied Sindy on the bed. She came into the room further and spoke with snippy resentment. "This is my day. Who are you?"

After spending the entire night restrained prone on Arif's bed, Sindy was in no mood for a condescending attitude from some snotty human bitch. She allowed her eyes to glaze over red and bared her fangs with a hiss of breath that made the girl jump back a step in surprise. "I'm a vampire. I believe that means you are supposed to mind your own damn business and not speak unless spoken to. Who the hell are you?"

The girl was chastened as she dared to timidly look up in answering. "Forgive me, miss. I hadn't realized. I'm called Ambrosia. I'm scheduled to attend my Master here in his chambers for the day. I'm always to arrive by first bell in order to prepare myself for him."

"Great," Sindy spat out sarcastically as she let her fangs retract. "So stop staring at my ass and go prepare yourself then."

The girl bowed her head subserviently. "Yes, miss."

As she moved into the room, Sindy noticed Arif in the doorway behind her, wearing a broad grin. "Even in such dire seeming circumstances, you seek to assert your authority. I do like you," he remarked to Sindy. "Ambrosia, return to the harem quarters. I will summon you later if I have need of you. Right now, I have unfinished business with my special guest."

Ambrosia was resentful to be denied her time alone with the master, but left without another word. Arif came to sit next to Sindy on the bed, gently stroking the side of her body. Sindy sighed, getting very tired of this endless game.

He affected not to notice or care that she didn't want his attention. "Tell me, how old were you when you left home?" he asked.

"Sixteen."

"Sixteen? And your whole life, your father had taken liberties with your body, isn't that so?" She looked up at him with hatred in her eyes. How did he know so much? He couldn't truly read her deeper thoughts. She wasn't under venom control and she knew she was too strong for him to read her otherwise.

"Don't be so surprised. I know much about you. When I found you, upon disposing of Amos, your maker, you asked for my mark for protection from others, remember? I granted you my bite and read everything I cared to know the night we met. Unfortunately, I did *not* know the color of your eyes at the time, because you didn't even know yourself. Amos had convinced you that you were a lesser vampire of no consequence, and that is what you believed. That is why I did not take you with me, or accept you into my coven when you later approached me. I already believed you were unworthy of my time; just a young damaged girl who would be more trouble than use to me, but my, how you have grown.

It took you sixteen years to rebel against your father; sixteen years to work up the courage, the strength, and the belief that you deserved to be treated with respect. It was that boy who drove you over the edge, wasn't it? Benjamin, the boy you wanted me to help you claim. He was your trigger. Did you come to realize that as long as you were under your father's hold, you could never truly be with him? Is that what pushed you to act?"

Sindy lie there, her face buried in the pillows of his bed. There didn't seem a point to keeping things from him. Ben's love hadn't driven her to rebel against her father, it was the fact that she thought Ben had loved her, but when she'd balked at consummating their relationship, he'd discarded her. To be fair, she had totally freaked out on him, PTSD style, but he'd been so hurt and insulted that he hadn't let her explain. "He rejected me," she admitted quietly.

"Ah...denial, I thought it was merely your vampire nature that he resented. To have faced rejection from him while human... No wonder you were so passionate to master him. I believe that you deserve him, by the way. Love him or hate him, you had the right to turn him, regardless of Cain's feelings over the matter. But that was none of my affair. You've moved on, haven't you?

You have been forged in fire, my dear, and the malleable hot mess that you once were has cooled into a hard, cold and calculating wit, sharp enough to cut away unnecessary emotion to get what you desire...most of the time. You're going to have to work on controlling that temper, though," he told her with a grin.

He raised his legs to rest his ankles crossed on the bed as he relaxed next to her, comfortable and content with her company. "Out in the world, beyond my immediate coven, my influence reaches quite far. I lead an amassed army of weaklings and fools, following me out of fear. But far more important to me, are the more powerful underlings I hold much more closely. As you know, I lead a core coven of vampires who are strong and independent. They follow me not because they fear me, although many of them do fear me," he confided with a smirk, "but because they are smart enough to know what I can do for them. They have great respect for my power."

He patted her on the thigh and then rose to undress for bed. "Do you know what I have learned about respect and loyalty? It is more firmly given when someone believes I respect them in return." He finished undressing and returned to her side, once again nude. He looked down at her with lazy longing.

"I could easily defile you, and don't think that I wouldn't enjoy it. I could also mine your thoughts to gain further hold over you, through your fears, but I think I would rather earn your devotion through what I do *not* do, than force your frightened subservience."

Sindy said nothing. She couldn't help but think that it was simply more convenient for him to grant her some respite, because he had to wait for her mark from Cain to fade anyway, before he could truly control her. He could rape her, but he couldn't win her true obedience. Maybe he was going to leave her alone for now. Somehow, she didn't exactly find herself filled with gratitude.

"I'm currently weary of my concubine's affections. I think I'd rather a day of quiet rest." Arif rose from the bed and looked down on her. "I am going to spare you further humiliation," he announced, "and allow you to rest comfortably here with me, without restraint. Can I trust you to behave yourself?"

He produced a key to hold in front of her. She silently nodded her head. She'd rather be allowed to leave, but if he wouldn't let her leave, at least it would be nice to lose the chains. It was a very large bed. She had trouble believing that he might actually leave her alone to get some sleep for the day, but anything was better than handcuffs.

He unlocked her wrists and ankles, massaging them a bit. It took a decent amount of willpower to keep from yanking them out of his light grasp, but she allowed his touch. "There," he cooed, "I'm sure this will be much nicer, won't it?"

She didn't answer as he shut the dim light next to the bed and lay down on his back. After some thought as to what might be the most advantageous move on her part, she lay down next to him and snuggled close enough to put her head on his chest. With some amused surprise, he lifted his arm to put around her, pleased by the act. She closed her eyes, forcing her body to relax and melt into his. What else could she do, race for the door to be met by Jin in the parlor?

As she had surmised, he was quite tickled by the show of supplicance on her part, allowing him to feel she was giving herself over to him…without actually having to give herself to him. She was relieved when he seemed satisfied with that. She hoped that he didn't awake during the day and decide that he'd like to sample her body further after all…but even if he did, she'd endured worse.

"Remember my generosity," he whispered to her in the quiet. "When I allow you freedom of the compound once more, if you do not display proper indebtedness, I can return you to the chains, or worse, and force loyalty through less pleasant methods. Do think upon the sort of position you might like to attain, should you remain with us, once other matters have been dealt with."

Brief thoughts flitted through her head of how she might take advantage of her immediate freedom. Jin suppressed her shifting powers, but she might still manage to injure Arif somehow as he slept; it didn't take long to realize that her chances were slim though. Everything in the bedroom seemed made of shining lacquer and rich soft materials, not a piece of accessible wood in plain sight, unless she planned to try and discreetly hack up his furniture. He had little to fear from her, and he knew it. That's why he had freed her. Even if Jin fell asleep, she was locked in without much in the way of options. She was better off playing the game.

She peeked up at him through her lashes, suitably subservient and tamed, for now. "Well," she answered with a sly smile, "I'm not making any promises, but *if* I decide to stay, you know I'd want the highest position I can get. I like to be on top." Arif was pleased by her answer. He didn't seem concerned with her addition of the word 'if', even though it was definitely a big 'if'.

He seemed certain she would come around; self-assured bastard that he was. "I think a little stay here will do wonders for your point of view, my dear. Give it time. Have a good rest, and think of all we have discussed," he told her smugly.

Emotionally drained by the night's events, somehow Sindy managed to sleep. Her nervous anticipation of Arif's reaction to her in his bed was quickly lost to exhaustion. The next thing she knew, she awoke to feel him caressing her side. It was sunset. "Time to wake, my darling shiftress."

She pulled up the thin sheet to cover her exposed skin and rolled away from his touch. He ignored the gesture. "I've been thinking of your wolf form. I found it to be quite beautiful...even if it did get dog hair on my bed," he added with a smile, as though sharing a private joke. "Do you enjoy changing form?"

"Sure." She answered flatly, without emotion, adding mentally, *We're not chums...you can skip the chit-chat.* The thoughts probably weren't strong enough for him to catch, or if they were, he chose to ignore them.

"What does it feel like, to shift?" he asked.

"It feels just like you would think it should feel," she replied, a bit harshly, "freeing...powerful."

He ignored the bite in her voice and caressed her thigh through the thin bed sheet. "I would think it would be quite a novel experience to have a vampire of such talents...for a lover."

She shook her head with a frown. "It doesn't make a difference. It's not like I use it in bed."

"Perhaps you should," he suggested with a smile.

She glowered at him in disgust. "Not a chance in hell. You are a sick twisted fuck."

He smiled with a breath of a laugh. "Do not be offended, you should be flattered. The ability sets you apart as uniquely appealing. The opportunity for variation intrigues me."

She roughly sat up in the bed, holding the sheet close around her and trying to keep herself from saying something that would land her back in chains...

Nope, she couldn't bite her tongue *that* hard. "You want variety? How about the next time I shift into a wolf, I bite off that pecker you're so inexplicably proud of, and rake my claws down below your belly until they rip open your scrotum...just for fun? Would that spice things up enough for you?"

He gave her a tight-lipped grin and stood from the bed. "There's that pesky temper again... You're not like other women I've kept."

"You don't say?" she spat back sarcastically.

"Your sharp tongue is growing on me, though. When I initiate you into my coven, do you think I will be able to control the actions of your wolf, as I will your human body?"

Her eyes widened at the implication, but she said nothing. He smiled. "We'll put the idea aside for now. I have business that must be attended to early this evening. But I have thoroughly enjoyed your company, chaste as it may have been. It would serve you well to think of the opportunities presented to you here. I have a position of power and a multitude of luxuries to bestow upon you, for such small concessions in return," he informed her as he went to get dressed.

Jin and Saruca entered the room; he must have called to them telepathically. Arif returned, fully clothed and gestured towards Sindy. Saruca had brought her a simple black sari to wear, and helped her on with it as Arif spoke. "I'm releasing her from my quarters," Arif told them formally. "Escort Miss Sindy to our seamstress," he told Saruca, "so that she might have garments made for her more befitting a vampire seeking acceptance to my inner circle. Take her to the salon as well. Then you may return her to residence at Kieran's estate, so that she might enjoy her stay there until permanent accommodations can be made.

Jin, I believe you can release hold of her powers now. Treat her with dignity, and I am sure that she will prove herself worthy of it."

With that, she was handed off to two of Arif's vampire guards, and escorted out of the mansion, with Saruca following behind. She was brought to the seamstress, as promised, who had a little shop near the common house. Sindy was given permission to choose a dress, shoes and undergarments off the rack for herself. Then she spent the next hour or so being measured and picking out materials and designs that she liked for a few more outfits to be made to her specifications.

After the dressmaker's, she was brought next door, to the salon, where she was treated to having her hair and make-up done once again, along with a mani-pedi. By the time she was finished, half the night was gone, but she was looking and feeling much better, especially after they provided her with a few cups of previously collected human blood for refreshment. She understood the game now. Arif would show her that he was insurmountable as an opponent, useless for her to fight against. Then he would shower her with luxury and kindness, so that she would be happy to be kept as an underling.

Did he actually think that she was shallow and stupid enough to let herself be so easily swayed or bullied? Even with her shifting ability back in swing, she knew she would need to do some planning if she hoped to escape the compound. The entire place was fenced and patrolled by guards and dogs. Her wolf could cause quite a commotion, but would likely be captured or killed before actually getting out. She never did learn to get the hang of her bat form, so flying was definitely out…unless she had Zach to do the flying for her. She would just have to bide her time and wait for her chance to have him fly them both out together. She hated to wait; it was pretty nice to be pampered though…

When she was finally dropped off alone, back at Kieran's estate, there were two handsome human men standing waiting in the front hall. The vampire cadet in charge of the door offered no comment and ignored them in favor of a phone conversation he was having at the entry desk. The humans bowed their heads upon her entrance, and then each dropped to kneel on one knee. After she observed them in stunned silence for a minute, one of them spoke.

"Miss Sindy, I presume? My name is Lindsey Valentine, but everyone calls me Val, and this is Brett. We have been assigned to assist your every need, miss. A gift from the coven master Arif."

She looked them over in shock. They were both impressive male specimens, in wonderful shape and very good looking. They were dressed in the standard loose white cotton drawstring pants she had seen many of the human men wearing around the compound, and open white button down shirts to match. Val had fairly long, shaggy layers to his light brown hair and was clean-shaven, with baby blue eyes. Brett had shorter dark hair, with the scruff of a few days beard and sultry brown eyes. The predator within her found their scents to be alluringly divine. "A gift, huh? Clothes, shoes, and men…he certainly knows what to get the girl who has nothing."

"Nothing? If I may say so, miss, I can see that you have charms that far exceed our expectations." He glanced at Brett with a smile, as though he couldn't believe their luck to have Sindy for a mistress. "We are honored and eager to be of service."

"Is that right?" Did they have any idea that they were offering themselves to a bloodthirsty vampire? These guys couldn't know how ridiculously lucky they were that she had been practicing superior self-control lately, because they smelled damn delicious, and even after the few cups of blood served at the salon, she was parched. She closed her eyes for a moment, trying not to inhale their enticing masculine scents too strongly.

After a moment, she opened her eyes to find them both staring at her in anticipation of her reaction to them. "Stand up," she told them. "Let me have a good look at you." She walked around them as they rose, inspecting them as she took in the possibilities. They were both unmarked. "Where did you guys come from? I mean, did he have you kidnapped from some modeling agency or something? Do you have any idea what you're setting yourselves up for here?"

Val chuckled. "Yes, ma'am. We're well aware that you will require some of our blood at times, and no, we weren't kidnapped. I'm not a model. I'm…well, I was an Ad Exec., but I've been spending long weekends and vacations here for a little while now. Those little visits have already earned me more than a year's pay at my day job, so I figured I'd sign up for a formal tenure. Who needs a nine to five daily grind when you can have an all-expense paid, easy and interesting term, and come out set for the next twenty years?"

Brett looked over at him a bit skeptically but then answered Sindy's question. "I've only been here twice before, for a week each time, but there's no work or anything going on at home, so I let them recruit me. I've got to say, I was pretty nervous. The last time I was here, they assigned me to some crazy woman."

Val looked at him as though *he* was crazy and shook his head as he mumbled, "What is wrong with you? *Never* speak like that about a vampire! You want to get thrown into the reform cellar?"

Brett was quickly sobered by the reprimand, and tried to explain himself without incurring Sindy's ire. "She didn't treat me harsh or nothing. She wasn't all bad; she just acted kind of whacked." Val shook his head again, in disbelief at the man's lack of personal censorship. "I just meant…well, you're much prettier than she was, miss. I'll bet you're nicer too."

Sindy couldn't help but be amused by the exchange. Val gave Brett a fierce glare to shut up now, and brought the introduction to more acceptable closure. "Please forgive him. Your lovely appearance and personal preferences are not for us to comment on. Whatever your wishes, we are here to serve you, Miss Sindy."

She gave him a sly grin for his docile obedience. "So, you guys are getting paid for this?"

Brett seemed hesitant to open his mouth again and possibly get into trouble. He let Val do the talking. "Yes, miss."

"How much?" she asked, curiously. What was the price of indentured servitude these days?

"I've signed up for a ten year term, miss. We are provided with food, clothing, health care and accommodations for the duration of our stay, and if we serve the term honorably, we receive one million dollars upon departure."

"A million dollars?" she repeated in disbelief.

"Yes, miss...at least. I get $100,000 for each year of duty, plus bonuses for outstanding service." *If you survive*...Sindy added mentally.

At this point Brett spoke up. "I'm only here for three. I get $250,000 when I'm done. Ten years is a long time."

Val scoffed at him. "You're only twenty-one. You'll be signing up again when you're done, trust me. Don't you want to be a millionaire before you're thirty-five?"

Brett eyed Sindy again, seeming to think that Val might be right, but still not entirely convinced. "We'll see how it goes."

Val also looked Sindy over again with a grin. "For the right assignment, I'd do this for free. And I do believe I just won the lottery."

Sindy smiled. She could get used to some service from this guy. Hell, they were both pretty hot. "How old are you?" she asked Val.

"Twenty-six."

Old enough to have some smarts and not get on her nerves, yet young enough to show her a very good time. "Nice. And you've been here before. You know your way around this place pretty well, huh?"

"Yes, miss."

That could come in handy... "Good to know. So, who have you been assigned to in the past?"

"All different vampires, miss. Lorelei, Tomas, Nico, Cat, and Peter."

"Really?" Sindy questioned him with a smile and an arched brow. She noticed Brett was giving him a very odd look. "Women *and* men?"

Val smiled, unfazed. "I'm straight...very," he assured her, as he dared to let his eyes travel her body. "But I do what I'm told. Most male vamps are usually just looking for a harem guard and gopher boy that they can take blood from when they need it. But even if they want more, as I said, I'm here to follow my vampire's orders implicitly. I'm fine with that. My personal tastes aren't your concern."

Sindy gave him a broad smile. This guy was going to do well here, regardless of whom he was assigned to. "No wonder they pay you the big bucks. Too bad I may not be here long enough to make full use of you." They'd probably like to question her over that remark, but she didn't offer explanation, and they wouldn't be so bold as to ask. "Let's go boys, upstairs."

As they reached the top landing, Sindy spotted Kym exiting one of the bedrooms. The woman stopped before her with a respectful bow of her head. "Good evening, miss. I see you've found your presents. They're very impressive, if I may say so," she added with a wink.

"Yeah, happy birthday to me," Sindy replied. "Where's Zach?"

"I'm not sure, Miss. He's been sort of bouncing from bedroom to bedroom."

Sindy let out a huff of a chuckle as she shook her head. "Of course he has. This place is like a freakin' bordello. Well, the next time he bounces out here, let him know I'm back, and tell him I'd like to see him."

"Yes, miss."

Sindy led her new companions to Kieran's master suite and closed the door. "Here we are. This is home, for now. Make yourselves comfortable."

Val went to sit in a lounge chair, but Brett began stripping off his clothing. Sindy gave him an odd look as he pulled off his shirt. "I didn't say you had to get *that* comfortable. Eager to get things started, are you?" Brett froze and began to put his shirt back on, sheepishly. "It's okay. Do whatever you want." She glanced around the room, taking stock of things, and noticed a small rolling bar in the corner. Zach must have had it brought in. "Either of you guys want a drink?"

Val answered her with a question of his own. "Do you?" he asked in a deep, quiet voice that was very seductive to her inner vampire. He knew just what he was asking and it was making him damn irresistible. Arif hadn't given her more than a shot glass to drink all night and day. She'd had two small cups of blood at the salon, but that had just been enough to keep her civil…the hunky proximity of these guys was quickly reminding her that she was starving.

She did her best to hide her blood thirst and keep herself in check, so she didn't end up lunging at these guys like a monster. Did he know just what he was flirting with, in tempting her like that? "All in good time," she replied with a smirk. "Let's see if we've got any decent alcohol stashed in here." She opened the lid and found a full bottle of Southern Comfort. "This'll do just fine." She held up the bottle for the guys to see. "A little Comfort for you?"

Val broke into a broad smile. "Yes ma'am."

Sindy found two shot glasses under the bar and poured them each a drink. "Brett, come do a shot." She held up the bottle in toast to them, after giving each of the men theirs, and then swigged a hefty amount straight from the bottle herself. She saw Brett watching her. "Don't worry kid; I'll be sure to save you some."

At that remark, he eyed her even more curiously. "How old are you?"

"Brett!" Val interjected in reprimand.

"She called me *kid!*"

Sindy just smiled. She sometimes forgot that to the rest of the world she still looked like a teenager, rather sexy and mature for her age, even when she'd been human, but still...she was often treated as a barely legal young lady, sometimes it could be very annoying. However, unlike most people she dealt with, these guys knew that a vampire's age couldn't be determined by looks. For all they knew, she could be older than their grandmothers.

"I'm older than either of you," she informed them sternly, teasing them for their temerity. She let that sink in for a moment as they wondered just how old she might be. "I'm twenty-seven," she finally admitted with a grin. She only had Val beat by a year. "Did you guys just get here today?" she asked, after taking another swig from the bottle.

"Day before yesterday," Val answered as she passed him the bottle for a refill. He passed it to Brett after filling his glass.

"So, where've you been sleeping?"

"Quarantine," Brett informed her with some resentment.

Val explained. "They gave us all kinds of inoculations and checked us for every disease you can think of. We're clean."

"It's not like I'm worried I'll catch something," she said with a laugh.

"They can't risk us infecting the populace."

"Oh, right. Speaking of infecting the populace..." She reached over to hit the intercom buzzer on the wall. "Anybody heard from Zach yet?"

"No, Miss," was the reply.

"Well, don't forget to tell him I want to see him. He can come right to my room, even after daylight. Thanks." She briefly scanned the house for his mark, but of course, Zach was keeping it shielded. She thought she should be able to feel his proximity though; he was marked by her. Even if he was here, he shouldn't be out of range, but there was always the possibility he was out at the bar. She'd wait just a little longer. She didn't want to call attention with an all-out search.

She found the men watching her. She didn't need to explain herself, but felt odd just to ignore them. "Zach's another vampire. I made him."

"Oh, is he your boyfriend?" Brett asked, as though that were the reason she hadn't asked them to take off their clothes.

"He wishes! No, he's not my boyfriend, but I need to talk to him. I'm not going to be able to relax until I do."

Val put down his glass and spoke to her, comfortingly. "Well, I'm sure he'll turn up. It sounds like he's just out having a good time."

"Probably."

"Maybe you should try to chill out and have a good time too." He gave her back the bottle of alcohol.

"Maybe," she agreed uncertainly as she chugged some more from the bottle. "Maybe I should," she said more assertively. "You two are mine, right; a gift from the coven master, Arif?" she added facetiously. They nodded their heads. "Well, in my experience, Arif can be pretty damn fickle. Maybe I ought to hurry up and mark you both, before he decides to try and take you back."

Brett seemed uncertain of the meaning, but Val knew exactly what that would entail, and seemed totally game. "Sounds like a plan to me."

~~~~~~~~~~~~~~~~~~~~~~~~~~~~~~

A few hours past sunrise and some very satisfying drinks later, Sindy was roused from bed by the sound of the intercom buzzing. She gestured to it and Val stumbled over to hit the button for her. "Yes?" she asked.

"Forgive the interruption, miss." It was Kym. "I thought you would want to know, I've completed a thorough search of the house. Zach is not in residence, and he hasn't signed anyone out to accompany him anywhere. He visited the bedrooms of two of my girls on the night you departed for your meeting with the coven master, but he left them well before dawn yesterday. No one has reported seeing him since. I've called over to the Common House, but he hasn't been seen. I don't know where else he might go to retire for the day."

"How can that be? Nobody's seen him, in over twenty-four hours?"

"No, miss. He's gone."

Part 2

Enemies and Allies

Chapter 6 - Restraint is sexy

Allie

Mattie & Allie's trailer
Somewhere, Upstate New York
Independence Day evening

"We're not going," Mattie insisted firmly.

Allie's mouth fell open in shock. Once she recognized the set determination on his face, she almost felt like throwing a temper-tantrum worthy of a three year old…but she refrained. She was trying to give Mattie a chance to be a stronger partner in their relationship, respecting his opinions and wishes, but it was getting to be a real pain in the ass! He was always so freakin' responsible and it always seemed to squash her fun. In hindsight, most of the time he was actually being reasonable…and right, but it was still annoying.

"We *can't* go, Allie. You know we can't. A night at Felicity and Ben's house, really? Why would you even set that up?"

"Do you have any idea how long I have been trying to get Ben to agree to see us; how delicate this is and how badly I want it?" she pleaded.

"If you wanted it that badly, you should have set it up a few years ago, before things got so tense."

"I was kind of busy. Besides, Ben wasn't ready then."

"Well, I'm not ready now, so he'll just have to wait." Surely, he could hear the thoughts she was projecting, that he'd better get ready damn fast, because she wasn't going to let him screw this up, but he wasn't swayed. "Allie, we are supposed to be in hiding! What could possibly make you think it's a good idea to have drinks with the son of a vampire hunter, and the ex-girlfriend of a guy we're hiding from?"

"We're not hiding from Cain!"

"I think Sindy is working for Arif. Sindy is with Cain, so yes, we are hiding from Cain, for now."

"That's stupid. It's not like Cain will be there. It's just Ben and Felicity."

"We're not going, and so help me, if you try to mess with my head or compel me with those eyes, I will never speak to you again, Alyson, never."

Allie stared out the window, trying to decide how hard she wanted to fight him on this. He was probably right, but damn it, why did vampire stuff have to keep interfering with what she wanted to do? Hiding the fact that she was the United One, and trying to avoid Arif and his goons was becoming a real fun-suck. "Stop making it so windy, you'll screw up everyone's fireworks," she observed.

Mattie rolled his eyes, but curbed the weather. "We can still go to the lake tonight and watch the fireworks, but tomorrow night we are staying home."

"I'll bet they have way better fireworks in the Hamptons, and we could get there before they're over if we hurry."

"I don't care. Everyone who is a problem for us is out there and we're not stupid enough to go and visit them."

Allie groaned, defeated. "Fine, I'll tell her we're not coming."

"No! Don't even speak to her at all! Radio silence, remember?"

"That was just from Cain," she corrected him.

"It is from everybody. Jesus Allie, how can I hide you if you keep telling everybody what you're doing? Are you tweeting it too?"

"No, wise-ass, I closed all my accounts after you had that conniption over my last facebook status. Totally unwarranted by the way, since I was using an alias. Now, I am socially cut-off. I hope you're happy."

"Forgive me for worrying that someone might crack the code to your secret identity, *Vampire Tinkerbell*."

She narrowed her eyes and stuck her tongue out at him, before getting back to the question at hand. "What about Felicity and Ben? We can't just not show up!"

"Of course we can. In fact, that is a great idea. That way, if it is a trap, they'll all be waiting for us, far the hell away from here."

"It's not a trap," she muttered grumpily.

"Fine, I'll tell you what. Give her a quick check in to tell her we aren't coming, but that's it. No details, no chit chat. Just that we'll have to reschedule because you're busy, okay?"

She gave him a grudging smile. "Thank you sweetie."

"And we're staying home." He pulled her closer, into his arms, trying to coax her out of her hostility. "Just you and me...that's not so bad, is it? I'll try my best to make it an evening to remember."

144

~~~~~~~~~~~~~~~~~~~~~~~~~~~~~~~~

Allie found herself moaning, panting and gasping for air, not because she needed to breathe, but because it was the only suitable way she could audibly express the maelstrom of rapture she was experiencing.

Mattie let his tongue trail a possessive lick of ownership up the side of her tender throat, and then hushed her by placing his lips over her own. He shuddered with the final release of his satisfaction, and then let his tongue convey to her his own grateful contentment.

Mattie ended the kiss and then rolled aside, to leave Allie smiling at the ceiling in a bewildered state of afterglow. Mattie had been displaying quite the sexual appetite lately. She suspected it was to keep her too distracted to complain about being cut off from her friends. A few nights ago, on the 5th, they'd had some super-hot sex after the hunt she'd taken Mattie on to keep her mind off of their missed rendezvous with Felicity and Ben; and he'd been very attentive last night and the night before as well, but somehow, this unexpected quickie was just as satisfying; fast, hot and totally titillating. Less than fifteen minutes before, she had been slowly awakening from her daily slumber, when her lover had immediately made known his erotic desires. What a way to wake up!

She turned her smile on him. "Well, someone woke up with a mission on his mind," she teased in blissful giddiness.

He rolled to his side, to face her, and gave her a guilty grin as he ran his fingers across her cheek. "Actually, I was very patient," he informed her defensively. "I've been up for almost an hour. You were calling me…"

She looked at him for an explanation. "I guess you were having a dream or something; apparently a really hot dream. You were sort of projecting the feelings to me…it was such a turn on. Been a while since we played it straight missionary, and I just couldn't stop thinking about it, so…yeah, I guess I was on a mission."

She couldn't remember what she was dreaming about, but it couldn't have been any better than the real thing. "Consider it mission accomplished. I'm still humming like a tuning fork!" She was too. God, but the man could make her feel good. "You know I totally worship you, right?"

Mattie laughed as he rose from the bed. "Worship?"

Allie stretched and ran her hand down her body, from her ribcage to the top of her thigh, just barely inching her splayed fingers to caress the tender skin on the inside of her leg. Her body felt wrung out and fulfilled from her recent climax, and yet even her own touch threatened to stoke her desires back to a quivering quest for more. "Like a God," she assured him. "The things you do to me? Damn, you even make vanilla taste exotic!"

He laughed, pleased by her claims of his prowess, but not quite comprehending how strongly she meant it. She sat up slightly and met his eyes with a smoldering gaze. "I'm gonna want me some more of that later…slow speed next time. Make me beg."

Now she had his full attention. He moved to rejoin her on the bed. "Why wait for later?"

Allie kept his gaze, trying to convey the seriousness of her next words. "Because right now, you might not survive it. Right now, I need blood; lots, and lots of blood…" Along with the throws of passion, Mattie had awakened her body to its most basic carnal need. Her lust had been satiated for now, but her thirst was thriving, and it was urging her to drain him dry. If she didn't drink something pronto, she might not be able to keep herself from staving off the drive to attack.

Mattie often denied himself sustenance, but he knew better than to mess with *her* thirst. He quickly rose from the bed to go get her something from the kitchen. "Lots and lots, coming up."

Allie tried to wait patiently, distracting herself by examining the trembling thrill she still felt from their exploits. It had faded a bit, but she still felt unexplainably revved and ready. "My God Mattie," she said as he re-entered the room, mug in hand. "My senses are still strummin'."

He grinned as he gave her the warm mug of blood. "Glad to be of service."

She gave up the thought for a moment, as she chugged down the contents of her cup. Mmm, it was pretty fresh. Of course, drinking blood that had been gathered from livestock wasn't nearly as delicious as drinking from live game…especially if the game you hunted was human…but this would do. She needed more. Luckily, Mattie had known she would. He left as she heard the beep of the microwave. The second cup he had already put in for her was ready. He went to retrieve it as she chased the last drops with her tongue.

He brought the second mug, and waited patiently for her to gulp it down and refocus on him. She could feel the blood working in her, recharging her and giving her new energy and clarity of thought. The sensations she had mistaken as aftershocks from Mattie's affections were still there, and they weren't from Mattie.

"Do you feel that?" It sort of felt like the warm physical current she shared through her blood bond with Mattie, except that it wasn't him. She felt him…and then something else, separate. "I don't think it's you."

Mattie frowned, disheartened, having been suddenly stripped of the mantle of God-like lover, capable of having such an effect on her. "Gee, thanks."

"No, I'm serious. What is that? Can you feel it?"

"Feel what? Tell me what I'm feeling for."

She put down her mug and tried to examine and describe the feeling. "It makes me feel all tingly. It's like...a mark, it kind of feels like a mark."

"But it's not me?" he asked warily. She shook her head. "Maybe it's Cain."

She considered it for a moment. Could she be feeling her mark with Cain, come to find them? She shook her head lightly. "I don't think so. It's similar, but it doesn't really feel like *him*. Besides, you'd feel him too. I don't even know if it is a mark. I just don't know how else to describe it. Here, feel this," she said, as she projected the sensation to him through her empathetic telepathy.

Mattie seemed surprised and less than pleased by the perception. "Does Cain really make you feel like that?"

Allie sighed. "Not *just* like that. It's not him, but Cain and I do share a mark, Mattie. You know what that feels like. You have one with him too. I don't ask you how good that feels," she remarked teasingly. Mattie rolled his eyes as Allie got out of bed and began to get dressed. "Easy, baby; you know you rock me like no one else." She paused to give him a swift kiss, and continued pulling on her jeans. "It's not Cain."

"One of your meals then," Mattie conjectured with distaste.

She sat next to him and shook her head. It wasn't impossible, but they were nowhere near the sight of her last hunt, and this mark didn't feel like anyone she could place. If it was a human she'd recently drunk from, she was pretty sure she would recognize who it was. Besides, if they were close enough to feel, she'd see her mark on them.

Mattie tried again. "What about the shade you marked? Arif's guy, Kieran?"

She thought about it, but it just didn't match. "No."

"Did he look familiar to you? I feel like I've seen him before."

"Sure. We met him in Atlantic City," Allie supplied. "Remember?"

"No, I mean before that. Did he go to school with us or something?"

Allie chuckled. "He is way older than us, he just looks young. I never met him until the meeting with Arif. Anyway, this feeling...definitely not him. I remember what he felt like."

"Oh, really? I guess he felt as good as Cain does, huh?"

Allie didn't even bother to comment. As far as she knew, Mattie had never marked anyone but she and Cain. To him, marking was a very intimate thing. But by this time, Allie had marked dozens of strangers, and felt the enjoyable sensations of connection that went with the marks. Mattie seemed willing to dismiss marked human meals, but the idea of marking other vampires did not sit well with him. She was better off just steering away from the topic. "I don't know who or what it is, but I'm going to find out," she told him, getting up to finish putting on her clothes.

"What? What are you doing?" Mattie got up and began to dress as well, not to be left behind.

"I want to go and see what that is. Don't you?"

Mattie paused to look at her steadily. "You're feeling something intimate like a mark, possibly from some stranger. No, I can't say that makes me want to rush you out the door to investigate."

She ignored his plea for caution and left the bedroom. He followed her out and rushed to tie his sneakers as she slid on her flip-flops. She grabbed her hoodie from where it hung on one of the coat hooks on the wall by the door and hurried outside. She put up her hood for some anonymity as she left the trailer. There was nothing he could do, but follow and complain. "Slow down, what are you planning to do, just walk around trying to feel the source of this?"

She turned to look at him with the sparkle of unrequited curiosity in her eyes. "Why not? You got something better to do? Let's go!" She started off towards the road, heartened to feel that the sensation was getting stronger. If it was a mark, it was on someone who was moving towards her just as quickly as she was coming to meet them. She knew she should be more cautious, but it felt friendly and familiar somehow, like someone she knew, although she couldn't place it.

Mattie was having a hard time keeping up, but she couldn't help but move more quickly towards it. Who was making her feel this? Mattie pleaded from somewhere behind her. "Don't you dare lose me. What if it's a trap?"

"It's not a trap," she insisted, boosting the words with telepathy as Mattie fell behind. "It's just one person." She could make out a figure ahead. "It's…"

"Sweet Cheeks!" It was Zach, the guitarist she had drunk from and killed. He looked as good as ever, tall, dark, slim and sexy. He even had his guitar slung over his back. The last time she had seen him, he was dead as a doornail, and now…he looked good as new, better even.

He approached with a roguish grin and a glint in his eye that showed her he had come through his change with every bit of the incorrigible spunk he'd had before he'd died. He spread his hands and tilted his head in appreciation of her as he came closer. "Damn mama, I was looking for you, but I didn't think you were gonna be this easy to find, or nearly this much fun... Ooh baby, you feel good!"

She knew just what he meant. The sensations she was feeling were definitely coming from him, and obviously went both ways, but why? She was having a hard time digesting the fact that he was here, and erasing the image she had of his dead, lifeless body staring glazed at the ceiling when last they'd been together. "Zach, you're alive," she stammered in shock.

He shook his head in mock disappointment. "That's not what they tell me."

Her mouth hung open for a moment in guilty chastisement. "Oh...yeah, I am really sorry about that."

He smiled as he stopped to stand before her, his arms still spread and giving his hands a little wiggle to show how he was enjoying the sensations her closeness was providing. "Don't sweat it. I ain't never felt nothing *this* good alive."

She gave him a little secretive grin over the feeling and put a hand up a few inches from him, to see how it intensified with his proximity. "What is that?" She finally couldn't resist resting her hand on his chest. As she'd anticipated, a thrilling charge ran through her hand as she touched him.

He looked down at her with a smirk. "I don't know, but why don't you move that hand a little lower?"

At his words, she removed her hand with a guilty start and backed up a step...right into someone. She quickly turned to see Mattie had come up behind her. She'd been too distracted to notice. "Oh, Mattie...this is Zach," she explained.

Mattie didn't even bother to look at her. He had already locked eyes with the man before him. "So I gathered."

Zach gave him a lazy smile. "You a vampire too?" he asked.

"Yes," Mattie answered steadily. "But I'm not going to make you feel nearly as good. I'm her husband."

Zach never lost his grin. "Is that a fact?" he asked with unapologetic humor.

Allie was too busy contemplating the feelings they were sharing to pay much attention to any rivalry brewing. "What is this?" she asked, turning to Mattie as she gestured between her and Zach. "You really can't feel it?"

Mattie didn't bother to answer. He just stared at her with a grim expression before voicing his own suspicions. "I thought you said Sindy made him?"

"She did," Allie answered. "My mark on him disappeared when he died. We shouldn't have any connection at all!"

Zach gave a low rumbling chuckle that demanded their attention. "Maybe your body just couldn't bear to give me up," he suggested with a seductive leer.

Allie arched an eyebrow at him. "I don't think so."

Mattie took a step forward, and spoke with a voice full of quiet foreboding. "Hey pal, maybe you didn't hear me the first time. This is my wife."

Zach took on an expression that immediately told Allie this was not going to end well. "Maybe *you* didn't realize that the last time I saw *your wife*, she was snuggled in my lap, nibbling on my neck," he shot back, smugly.

Zach didn't notice the sudden severe gust of wind kicking up around them, or the clouds silently closing in overhead, and the sudden drop in temperature, but Allie was very keenly aware of these changes, and what they preceded.

I was just out for blood baby, it was all talk, I swear. She told Mattie silently as she quickly put a hand behind her to grab and squeeze Mattie's thigh in reassurance. She spoke to Zach with determined severity. "Zach, I only wanted a drink. I was just playing the part," she explained.

Zach ignored the fact that she was trying to diffuse the situation, and grinned at her suggestively. "You play nice."

Thunder cracked loudly overhead, making both Allie and Zach jump as lightning arced across the sky behind them to be lost among the clouds. "Play time's over," Mattie informed Zach ominously.

Allie just stared Zach down, daring him to say a word as she spoke quietly to her husband. "Reel it in, Mattie." She hoped to God that he knew how to keep it under control. She had a feeling that his restraint was thinner than could be considered safe at the moment. "Sorry, Zach, but I'm *not* one of your groupies. I was the one puttin' on a show."

"Whatever you say, sugar," Zach said amicably, but then he leaned forward for a last conspiratorial whisper. "But I know you were into it. I was there."

She must have been right in her assumptions that Mattie was barely restraining himself, because as Mattie focused all of his control on the weather to prevent an unfortunate lightning strike, he let go of his psychic shields and his mark flared into view.

Zach noticed and commented on it. "Well, ain't that purdy? Is that supposed to intimidate me? 'Cause I've got me one of those."

As Zach dropped his psychic guard and let his mark show, both Mattie and Alyson were taken aback. It was bright and strong…fully as strong as Alyson's. "Whoa…" Allie muttered.

Zach smirked at Mattie's speechless reaction. "Now, I think that there is what you call a mark. Am I right?" Zach asked, with a grin.

It hadn't even occurred to Mattie and Alyson that Zach was shielding his mark up until then, a pretty impressive practice for a new vampire, but now that they realized it, and saw the nature of his mark…it was all too reminiscent of Allie's.

Mattie didn't even bother to address Zach, but questioned Allie again with uncertainty. "Are you *sure* you didn't make him?"

"It was Sindy, I swear!" Allie repeated desperately.

Mattie shook his head in wonder. "I thought you said she wasn't very good at it?"

"Looks like she's improving," Allie admitted quietly.

Now Zach addressed Allie in wounded accusation. "You left me in the hands of a hack? Now darlin', that's just cold."

Allie ignored the allegation. "Where is Sindy?"

"She um, fell in with a less than desirable crowd. Bunch of vampires bent on serving some Master guy. I thought I'd do better to come and find you. Cults ain't really my scene. She pointed me in the general direction, and as soon as I felt your vibe, I knew I'd made the right choice. Something like the mojo we're sharin' just can't be denied, can it?" he asked, daring Mattie to object.

Allie narrowed her eyes at Zach, and then gave Mattie a glance to observe his reaction. He had shielded his mark again and the thunder and lightning seemed to have moved on, but the wind was still terribly strong. "Please, let me handle him," she asked quietly, imploring Mattie to stay civil. She needed to figure out what was going on before he goaded Mattie into toasting him or beating him to a pulp.

Zach answered with his own whisper. "Please…handle me."

Allie let out a huff of annoyance. Was this idiot *trying* to get himself killed? Luckily, Mattie seemed to have gotten his emotions under control, in turn calming the weather as well. He could see that Allie was unimpressed by the guy's behavior. He'd do better to let Zach tick her off and push her away on his own. "Relax," Mattie assured her in a voice of dead calm. "I won't fry him…yet."

Zach was stupid enough to take Mattie's patient demeanor for granted. He gestured to Allie again, indicating their shared connection. "No offense bro. I didn't set this up, but it does feel like we're meant to be together."

Mattie spoke to Allie under his breath. "Maybe I'll just give him a ride in a tornado…let him get tossed out a few miles from here, huh?"

Allie chuckled appreciatively before whispering back, "Restraint is sexy, remember?"

"On you," Mattie clarified. "Restraint is sexy on you. I'm feeling more like the bull."

"Look," Allie said louder for Zach, although he must have heard her prior whispered exchange with Mattie. "I don't know what this weird vibe between us is, but it's not an invitation. I'm taken, so cool your engine. And you shouldn't be flashing that mark around out here, especially if it means what I think it does." She paused before asking the dreaded question. "What color are your eyes?"

Zach shrugged with a little smirk. "Last time I looked, they were brown. Got a mirror?"

Allie could tell he knew exactly what she was asking and was just being a smart-alec, trying her patience. She may have been attracted to his talent and his look, not that she'd ever admit that to Mattie, but she was really getting tired of his attitude. "I think you know damn well what I'm talking about. Look, I'm sorry about what happened to you, I really am, and I realize that you don't really know me, but I happen to be the most powerful badass bitch you are ever gonna meet. So do yourself a favor; don't jerk me around. And you'll stop trying to bait my man, if you know what's good for you, because if he wasn't such a secure and respectful guy, he would have turned you into a little pile of dust by now."

"Is that so?"

"Damn straight," Allie responded. She let her eyes flash into their white brilliance as she spoke, commanding him to recognize her dominance as a vampire. "So you'd better stop getting on my nerves," she warned him, "because I have no problem killing you…again."

Zach put up his hands in surrender. "Hey, hey, I didn't mean to bring out your inner dominatrix, though I gotta tell you, power is sexy as hell on you, kitten."

Thunder rumbled in the distance as Mattie took his attention. "While we're laying ground rules here…her name is Alyson. Not Mama, Baby, Sugar, Darlin' or Kitten, and definitely not *Sweet Cheeks*. Got that?"

"Loud and clear," Zach assured him, although he still had a lilt in his voice that sounded more amused than respectful.

Allie was still staring at him through her vampire vision, and not only was she disheartened to notice that he didn't seem as mesmerizingly affected by her vampire eyes as other vampires usually were, but she had noticed something else disturbing as well. She could see Zach's eyes shining with a beckoning brilliance, even though he had not shifted.

To humans, his eyes were indeed brown, as he'd said, and not at all inhuman. However, to Allie, and any other vampire that looked upon him with their heat seeking vampire vision, Zach's eyes held the allure of a United One. If that was what *her* eyes looked like too, it was no wonder Mattie got all bent out of shape when she didn't wear her tinted glasses. His eyes were white – they must be. How had this happened? Did Sindy know? She must...

"I can't believe Sindy just let you take off on your own. She was supposed to stay with you for a while, teach you some stuff. At the very least, I would have thought she'd bring you to Cain, considering the circumstances. How long have you been out on your own? Have you been drinking?"

He just smiled through her deluge of questions and speculations before finally answering. "Sindy says I've got your eyes," he remarked, as he let himself shift to reveal that it was true. Damn, those eyes looked powerful and seductive as hell rimmed with his thick, dark lashes and paired with his sinisterly sexy face.

Mattie instinctively looked away, having had plenty of experience dealing with Allie in such a state, but Alyson just couldn't stop staring at him. It wasn't as though he had any inordinate power over her, she was definitely his superior strictly due to her age, and she didn't feel as though he was putting her in thrall, it's just that his eyes were so...beautiful.

Allie shifted back, turning her own eyes blue once again. Once Zach followed suit, she continued to question him. "What else did she say?"

"She gave me the basics. I'm a vampire. I've seen *True Blood,* what else is there to know? Since we're not out to the public, they don't actually sell it in bottles at the bar, as far as I know, so I've been drinking from the tap. I've managed on my own for a few nights now."

"Tap? Like...people?" Allie asked in shock. "You've been drinking from people?"

Mattie answered before Zach could. "What else did you expect Sindy to teach him? I guess Cain didn't catch up to them before they split; pity."

Allie just gave him a level stare. Cain had been hoping to meet Zach as soon as he awakened, and assess his temperament as a vampire. Mattie had mentioned to her that if Zach seemed incapable or uncontrollable, Cain would probably feel obligated to dust him, which, while upsetting in Allie's eyes, hadn't been anything Mattie was going to lose sleep over. Now that he'd met Zach, his feelings over the issue hadn't changed much. Not that Allie could blame him.

"Look, we need to talk about a few things," Allie told Zach. "You can't just go around killing people!"

"No?" Zach asked facetiously. "It's pretty easy."

"No! You need to come with us for a little, while we straighten some stuff out. Our trailer isn't far from here. You can sleep on the pull-out."

Zach didn't seem to object to the idea, but Mattie interjected with a protest. "This guy isn't coming home with us!"

"He has to Mattie. He's my responsibility. We can't just let him leave."

"I agree." *Who said he was leaving?* Mattie asked her silently, as some distant thunder punctuating his intent.

Mattie, you can't, she telepathically replied.

Sure I can. I can stoke up the storm in a heartbeat. I don't know what you're feeling, but I'm getting some bad vibes off this guy. Cain should've never let him wake up.

"Mattie, give him a chance," she said aloud, for Zach to hear as well. *That's not what I meant. I know you* could *kill him, but it's not right.*

Why, because you think he feels like some kind of kindred spirit?

No! Because that's not you.

I've killed before, Mattie reminded her.

In self-defense. Zach isn't trying to kill us, Allie insisted.

No, Mattie agreed. *He's trying to drive us apart.*

Then you killing him wouldn't be self-defense, it would just be selfish. Let him say what he wants. I'm not going anywhere.

Zach watched them warily during their silent exchange. Now he spoke with a bit of a grin. "Seems your secure and respectful man is feeling a little threatened."

Mattie, I know what I felt when I killed him, how I hated myself for it, and I have to live with that. I don't want you to have to carry the same burden. You've never killed without good reason and you don't have to now, even if he is being a jerk.

Zach continued, "I don't need to cause trouble between you two lovebirds. Plenty of groupies in the sea. I can just be on my way."

"Zach." Allie reached out to touch his arm and keep him from leaving. The dynamic connection between them sent a surprising current through her at the touch, and caught her off guard for a second. She didn't remove her hand, but the feeling did seem to die down after a moment, still feeling pleasurable, but able to be ignored while she spoke. "Don't go."

She wasn't sure if Mattie had noticed any reaction from her at the touch, but he stood staring at them both as he sent her his thoughts. *What do you want to do? I can tell you right now, if you plan on training and mentoring the guy yourself, you can do it alone.*

Allie shook her head a little. Zach looked down at her, as though the gesture was meant for him. "Well, if you want me to stay that badly," he said, looking up at Mattie, "I guess we can work something out."

We'll take him to Cain, she told Mattie telepathically. *What else can we do? We have to figure out why he's like me, and he needs to have some kind of training. We can't just turn him lose on the world, and I'm not letting you kill him. Cain will know what to do.*

Mattie shook his head, still unsure. *I don't know...we left Cain's because we didn't want Arif or anyone else to be able to find us. Going back there makes us vulnerable again, don't you think? Besides, Cain's place is like a six hour ride from here. Maybe we can have him meet us someplace.*

Okay, but until then, Zach will have to stay with us, so we can keep him out of trouble.

"Great," Mattie muttered.

Allie took her hand back, still wondering at the amazing sensations Zach caused in her. It must be because he was a United One, the only other of her kind. "There are things going on that you don't understand," Allie explained to him.

He laughed. "People keep telling me that."

"I'd like you to stay with us for a little while, and let us take you to meet someone who can help us understand things a little better."

Zach nodded, seeming interested and reasonable about her course of action. "Well, you did make me what I am," Allie began to protest but he held up a hand to shush her. "I know Sindy did the deed, but it was only because of you, so if I should be listening to anyone, I guess it would be you. I'm happy to stay, as long as your man don't mind," he added with a glance at Mattie. "You go ahead and do whatever you think you need to."

Alyson looked to Mattie as well. He was just standing there, arms crossed, annoyed, but resigned. "Fine," Mattie finally agreed.

"No more radio silence then? I can call Cain?" she asked.

"Please. Call him right now so we can drop this guy off and get on with our lives already."

"So we're looking to get to a phone then?" Zach asked.

"She's telepathic," Mattie corrected him.

By the look Zach was giving them, he didn't seem to understand. "Tele-what-now?"

155

Mattie sighed with impatience. "It means we can start heading out to his place tonight," Mattie encouraged Allie with a pat on her shoulder as he began walking back to the RV.

Zach watched Alyson for a moment as she concentrated on other things, then he followed behind Mattie. "Is it far to this guy's place?"

"Buffalo," Mattie answered shortly.

"Well, damn. That's way the hell up north, ain't it? I was planning to head down to the island myself. What do you say? Shame to waste beach season in fuckin' Buffalo," Zach commented.

"What do you care? When we're done with Cain, if you want to go spend a day lying out at the beach, please, be my guest." Zach smiled at the jibe as Mattie continued. "Anyway, we may not have to go all the way there. Allie will try to contact him first and see if he can meet us halfway."

"This it?" Zach asked, as they reached the trailer.

Mattie just looked at him irritably for a minute. "Do you see any other trailers around here?"

"Guys, be quiet, will you?" Allie shushed them. She stopped in front of the door. "I can't hear him."

"Who?" Zach asked.

"Shut up." Mattie stepped between him and Allie. "What do you mean? You can always hear Cain if you want to. This guy's yammering shouldn't matter," he said, jerking a thumb towards Zach.

"I'm not getting a damn thing," she insisted.

Zach watched her for a second and then shrugged. "Maybe you're in a bad reception spot. It's like that in the mountains."

Mattie shook his head in disgust at the guy's naiveté. "She's using telepathy, not cell service, idiot."

Finally, Allie unfroze and yanked open the door. "I don't get it. I know it's been almost a month, but our marks are usually strong enough to last at least another week or two. Maybe he's sleeping or something. I'll try again later. Let's just get moving." She held out an arm for Zach to enter the bus. "Welcome to *our* tour bus," she said, cracking a slight smile.

Zach slowly climbed the steps to enter. "I hope this one's more fun than the last one I was in."

Mattie entered behind him as Allie answered. "I doubt you'll find it much fun," she admitted, with a pointed glance at Mattie, "but I can almost guarantee that you won't die this time...I hope."

Chapter 7 - It's complicated

Cain

Cain's estate
Near Buffalo, New York
A few nights earlier...

"This house is beautiful!" Dawn exclaimed, as they entered the front hall, "...and big. How many vampires live here?"

Cain smiled, looking around the large, empty space. Although Sindy, Mattie and Alyson hadn't been terribly loud or intrusive, the house did feel significantly silent without them around. "There were a small few vampires staying here with me until recently. At the moment, it's just me."

"Wow. Just you, in this huge place? Doesn't it get lonely?"

He never used to get very lonely, until he'd been reminded of what he was missing. Cain shrugged. "I read."

She became animated in finding a common ground. "Me too! Well, obviously," she admitted, feeling sheepish over her quick excitement. She'd been reading when he'd found her.

"I have some...neighbors...I can visit with now and then. I don't actually spend all that much time here alone anyway. I'd rather be out finding and helping others like you. Let me give you the tour," he offered, leading her out of the front hall.

By the time he had shown her most of the house and headed upstairs to the bedrooms, it was nearly sunrise. "That's my room, down at the end of the hall."

She peeked down the way to his open door, through which she could see his bookcase, filled with favorites read too often to keep down in the library. "You really do like to read, don't you? One look at that library downstairs and I felt like Belle from *Beauty and the Beast*...except you're already a Prince Charming so...big improvement over her situation."

He simply raised an eyebrow with a smile as she went on. "I've never met a guy who loved books as much as I do. Are you sure you're not available? These days the guys I meet don't survive long enough for more than opening conversation, if you know what I mean."

He laughed, shaking his head. "Sorry. But there are plenty of guest rooms. Let's get you settled into one."

"This one's nice," she said hopefully, gesturing toward the room right next to his.

It was a large room, nicely kept with a feminine appeal to it. It was Sindy's room. She had taken to spending her days in his bed while she'd been in residence, but the room was still filled with her things. "Perhaps we can find you another," he said, falteringly. Dawn looked apologetic, noticing his reaction. "The room was occupied until recently," he explained. "I'm not sure if they might be back."

"Sure, no problem. Sorry," she was quick to apologize. "Just tell me where you want me."

"Any of the others is fine," he assured her, leading her down to see the rooms at the other end of the hallway. She chose one and sat on the bed with a quiet 'thanks'. He shook his head with some regret. "It's a pity you couldn't get back into your apartment to pack a bag. There are some toiletries and things here that you can use though," he said, leading her to follow him back out towards the bathroom, "and…" he ducked in to look for something in the linen closet. "Yes, I've got something here you can change into for the day." It was a set of the loose black clothing he kept for the Crimson Coven. Sindy called them 'Ninja Scrubs'. He had left a few up here for his last guests over the past holiday.

Dawn took the clothing gratefully. "I can't wait to get out of this sweat-suit! I didn't have anything with me when I left, not even my purse. I haven't had a change of clothes since the police staked out my place."

"We can go out tomorrow night and pick up a few things for you," Cain offered. "In the meantime, make yourself at home and rest easy. You're safe here. And if you have nightmares worse than you can handle, I'm just down the hall. Don't be worried to wake me."

"Thank you," she said, with a warm smile. "Thank you so much."

~~~~~~~~~~~~~~~~~~~~~~~~~~~~~

The next evening, Cain was happy to be back at home in his kitchen, moving about in his nightly routine, making coffee and such. He actually found himself humming a snippet of song in a content and even chipper mood. The sorrow of lost love and anxiety for the future always lay just beneath the surface of his exterior, but he had woken in such good spirits, that he refused to think on deeper things and spoil the mood.

He felt fulfilled, helping others again, and serving a satisfying purpose. He was still worried about Alyson and Mattie, but was trusting them to be responsibly independent, and was allowing himself a break from worrying.

As the coffee perked, Cain prepared two mugs of blood, in preparation to share a meal with Dawn when she awoke. She would be thirsty, and it would be easier to have a mug to immediately put into her hand, than to argue over hunting.

He was right. She downed two full cups before even asking him where he'd obtained the liquid. "I've never tasted blood like this," she finally exclaimed happily. "It's not as good as from a person, but way better than that other stuff you were trying to push on me."

He laughed. "It's from deer I have on the grounds. Blood always tastes better when it's from something a bit wild and free. I hate to admit it, but their somewhat nervous natures tend to add a bit of flavor that is reminiscent of the pheromones you can taste in a human victim brought out with fear. Not a flavor I would encourage one to seek out, but for a vampire, it does have natural appeal."

She had finished her beverage and stood to put the cup in the sink. Cain stood as well, and she turned to him with a question. "Do you have a laundry room? That sweat-suit of mine could use a good washing."

"Of course, but as I said, I'll be happy to take you shopping for something else to wear."

"Thank you. That is really generous, and don't think I won't take you up on it, but I feel kind of funny going out in public in this," she explained, looking down at the black hospital-type scrubs she was wearing.

Cain grinned. "Understood. Perhaps we can rectify that."

He took her to Sindy's room. She seemed hesitant at first, knowing he had been reluctant to give her the room, but he assured her that she could enter. Sindy had amassed quite a wardrobe at his expense. Surely, Dawn could find something suitable to borrow from it.

At his encouragement, Dawn began going through the closet, while Cain sat on the bed. "I hope you'll stay for a while," he told her. "Young as you are, your body has been taught to prefer the blood of the hunt. It's going to take a little while to distance yourself from that and learn to control your addiction. Our craving for fresh human blood is an addiction, and to treat it as such will give you more of an understanding and strength to master it. I think staying here for a bit, where plenty of animal blood and moral support are available, with limited human interaction, would make it easier for you."

She let out a little chuckle. "Great, my whole life I never smoked, drank, did drugs, or any of that, and somehow I end up an addict in rehab. Maybe I should've had more fun when I had the chance."

Cain shook his head at her regret. "There's no shame in having lived a responsible life."

"Responsible? I couldn't afford drugs if I wanted to. Every spare penny I had went to pre-order books for all my series. Reading was always my addiction. I should've worked in a bookstore."

Cain couldn't help but utter a wistful sigh. "I knew a girl who worked in a bookstore once."

"Wow…you've got it bad, don't you?"

"Got what? What have I got?"

Dawn laughed at his cluelessness. "The love bug! When you told me that you weren't interested in romance, I thought maybe you were just being polite because you didn't find me attractive, but you really are already smitten with somebody else, aren't you? Makes sense. Why else would you have all of these women's clothes? So, what's her name?"

He couldn't help but lose his smile and become withdrawn. "It's complicated."

"That's a funny name," she teased. "Just wondering who's the lucky lady whose clothes I'll be wearing. It wasn't supposed to be a trick question."

Cain shook his head and looked away. "Tis tricky nonetheless."

Dawn stared at him until it was obvious he wasn't going to elaborate. "I still can't believe you're real. You show up out of nowhere, totally going out of your way to set things right for me, handsome and helpful, with this mansion and that accent, using words like *'tis* and *nonetheless.*"

Cain had to crack a small smile. Mattie and Alyson were always reprimanding him for using such words. "Forgive me if I sound a bit archaic. I don't actually speak to people all that often. I'm not entirely *down* with all the new slang…or hip…or jiggy with it, or whatever."

Dawn had to reign in her laughter before commenting. "Clearly, but you came to talk to me. You're helping me so much." She held up one of Sindy's sexy dresses from the closet. "Won't she be jealous?"

Cain shook his head in dismissal. "No. This is what I do…or, what I did, before other priorities took precedence. I help others. Since my other priorities have taken themselves elsewhere for the time being, I am trying to stop moping about and carry on with my own ambitions."

"Why were you moping? Your girlfriend left?"

Cain sighed again, lying back on the bed. "Which one, the woman I love, or the woman I am supposed to love?"

"Oh…*that* kind of complicated. Well, whose clothes are these?"

"Sindy, the woman I am currently involved with…or was. We've spent a fair amount of years in and out of each other's lives. She was staying with me here until recently, often sharing my room. She left on a personal errand and never returned, so perhaps she doesn't care for me as deeply as I'd thought."

Dawn's eyes widened. "She just disappeared? Maybe something happened to her. I mean, I can't imagine she left *you* voluntarily," she said with a smirk.

"No, I don't think there's cause for alarm. It wouldn't be the first time she's disappeared on me. I went after her, and found that she went to be with a man she's had dealings with in the past, so it seems her choice is clear."

"That's the woman who used to wear this dress?" she asked, pulling out another very short dress with a plunging neckline. It was definitely made for someone with a great deal of pride in their body, and a great desire to show it off.

"Yes," he answered with a sheepish grin, "although I never thought such daring garments were necessary. She could command a man's attention wearing a sack, and have them begging her to drink their blood."

"Sounds like she was pretty…pretty stupid. What would she need with other men? She had *you,* and she left."

Cain sat back up on the bed and shrugged, unwilling to put any stock in that argument. "She's not stupid, she just has goals and ambitions I wouldn't agree with. It seems the tender heart she keeps hidden inside is at war with her thirst for power. I was hoping that she'd sorted things out. Maybe she has. Maybe she wanted more than my heart had to give. Try as I might to embrace the present, she knows my heart lives in the past. She is a smart woman. It was her drive and intelligence that drew me to her."

Dawn found yet another ridiculously sexy dress from the closet and held it up for emphasis. "Her *intelligence* attracted you? Really?"

"Yes," he asserted, after a brief chuckle.

Dawn looked at the garment, holding it in front of herself and seeming to decide that she couldn't pull it off. "Something tells me this isn't the dress of a woman who worked in a bookstore," she remarked as she replaced it in the closet.

"No," he admitted with a sigh.

"So, bookstore girl, she's your true love then?" He gave a shy, reluctant nod. "So, maybe it's good that Sindy left. It wasn't meant to be. Now you can go and be with your true love."

"It's not that simple. I'm afraid that ship has sailed."

"Don't be silly. There's always room for a happy ending." Dawn gave up on Sindy's closet full of revealing dresses, abandoning it for the dresser in the corner. She looked to Cain for his nod of approval and then went through the drawers. "If she's your true love, you can't give up that easy!"

If only it were that simple. "I admire your optimistic attitude and appreciate your eagerness to help, but trust that some things should be left alone. She is out of my reach, by my own design, and better for it."

After a short search, Dawn was rewarded with some more simple clothes she could be comfortable to wear, and picked out something she thought would fit. "Your true love, she's not dead is she?" she asked. He lightly shook his head. "Then she isn't completely out of reach."

Cain met her gaze with a level stare before disputing the statement. "She is a happily married human woman with a child."

"Oh…yeah, that's a tough one."

Cain stood from the bed, seeing that Dawn had found what she needed, and led her from the room. "My path is to be walked alone for now, and there are others I should be focusing my attentions on; others who need my help…like you."

Dawn gave him a sympathetic smile. "Focus away."

~~~~~~~~~~~~~~~~~~~~~~~~~~~~~~

Routine is a comforting contrivance. Less than a week later Cain had settled back into his old familiar ways. Long before he had ever met Felicity, Sindy, Alyson, or even Mattie, he would spend his time wandering the countryside, seeking out young vampires in need of his guidance. He often worked to help them in their own territories, but sometimes he brought one home to stay with him until they felt capable to be independent, such as he had done with Mattie, and Dawn.

Forget romantic attachments and entanglements. This was his mission, to make a difference in the lives of those who needed help, and to make the world a better place. Acting as mentor to The United One was an honor and responsibility he would always pledge his devotion to, worthy to take precedence over his other concerns, but if the United One needed time and experience on her own, to mature into the leader he knew she would one night become, then he should focus on his prior goals. Sinking into constant contemplation and pursuit of personal emotional endeavors was not an option.

He'd given Dawn leave to wander the grounds. He hadn't mentioned the Crimson Coven to her, but he rarely told anyone of them. They were usually the epitome of discretion and would not be seen by her unless he had cleared her with them first. She would simply have a peaceful walk around the property, never knowing that she was watched and protected by the coven.

She returned, carrying a bundle of papers in her hand. "I brought up your mail for you," she told him, coming to join him in the parlor.

He hadn't collected the mail in some time, so there was a nice sized stack. "Thanks, but I'm sure it can all go right in the rubbish bin. The bills are all set up to be paid automatically out of my accounts. They're probably just advertisements. No one writes to me."

She rifled through the mail, pulling something out to prove him wrong. "Well, someone did. Look. This isn't garbage, it's a letter."

He took the large envelope from her, hesitant but curious. He turned it over and observed the return address. There was a sticker with a scrolling foil design around the edges. Above the address, the name read 'Everheart'. He took a very deep breath and let it out slowly while staring at the label. Finally, he opened it and read the letter.

Dear Cain,

I hope you don't think it's inappropriate for me to be writing to you, but we had photographs taken of Christian, and I thought you might like to have one.

I want you to know that although it was unexpected, I am very glad that we had our accidental visit the other night. You have always been so supportive, truly wanting the best for me, even though I know it must be difficult for you at times. I am so grateful for your continued friendship.

I know that I am very blessed to have my family. I am truly happy with my life, and I appreciate that much of it is due to your influence and encouragement. Although we cannot be present in each other's lives, I hope you know that I always consider you a dear friend in my heart, and you are missed.

I wish you happiness and the best of luck in your endeavors. I know that the world is a better place for your efforts.

With love,

Felicity

He stared at the letter for a long time, before finally fishing for the photograph in the envelope. The baby was happy and smiling, with chubby little cheeks and a sparkle in his beautiful gray eyes. Perhaps those eyes might change to match the lovely hazel green hue of Felicity's one day.

Dawn was respectfully quiet, but doubtless she was curious. He handed her the picture. "Her son," he said softly. He knew she would realize who the 'her' must be.

"Aw, he's so cute." After a moment of chewing her lip in thought, she commented further. "Wow, she still keeps in touch, huh?"

"Not really. It's been over seven years since we parted, and I've only seen her twice. She's never written before." Although, he had written hundreds of letters to her…unsent.

"It's nice, that she sent you a picture of the baby…right? I mean, I'm sure she sent it with good intentions." She became unsure, worried that his feelings might be hurt. "She's not trying to rub your face in it or anything, is she?"

"No, of course not," he assured her. Felicity had surely agonized over whether to mail it, but she knew he would accept the letter with the gracious fondness with which it had been sent. Baby Christian, named for him, her first love. "Does it hurt to wonder if she loves her husband more than she would love me if I let her? Of course, but I hope she does, because I believe that having a family makes her happy, and is her destiny, not mine. It hurts, but I can bear it."

In the letter, she had mentioned their meeting as though it had just happened. The letter must have been sitting in his mailbox for weeks, uncollected.

He planned to go put the envelope in the box where his letters to her were locked away, but Dawn stopped him. She'd been sorting through the rest of the mail, when she came across something she thought deserved his attention. "Look, a postcard." She handed it over to him, although he was certain it was just more junk mail.

The picture was a lighthouse on a rocky shoreline under a bright blue sky. Print on the bottom identified it as Montauk Point, Long Island. This couldn't also be from Felicity, could it?

He turned it over and was startlingly disappointed to find that it was definitely not *from* Felicity, but was quite possibly *about* her.

> *Cain,*
>
> *I am disappointed that Alyson has not yet come to join me. She would find my compound a place most befitting of her presence.*
>
> *I have a mutual friend to you both staying here presently. Unfortunately, she is not finding my hospitality at all to her liking. Perhaps you can persuade Alyson to come and take her place.*
>
> *Have Alyson visit the lighthouse. My emissaries are ever present there and will escort her to my facility for a trade. Do have her come soon, as your lady-friend is most unhappy and wearing on my patience as a gracious host.*
>
> *Arif*

Cain read the postcard. Stared at it, and then read it again in mute shock. Finally, Dawn could not stand to wait in polite silence anymore. "What is it? Who's it from?" He handed it over for her to read, as he tried to decipher the message. "Who's Alyson?" Dawn asked.

"She is another young vampire I have been mentoring."

"Like me," Dawn said with a smile.

"Yes...but Alyson is a bit special. She is more powerful than any other. I've spent the last few years helping her to discover what she is capable of, and how to keep it under control."

"So where is she now?"

"I don't know."

Dawn waved the card for emphasis. "This guy seems to think you do."

"He knows she was staying here with me, but she left."

"Another ex-girlfriend," Dawn asked with an arched brow.

Cain shook his head with a smirk. "No. She left with her husband, who was also staying here with me. They are good friends of mine."

Dawn shrugged. "So call her."

"I can't..." he admitted. He had no way of getting in touch with Alyson or Mattie. Perhaps that was a good thing. "And I shouldn't. I don't know why Arif is so eager to have Alyson under his control, but it must be for his own personal ends. Whatever those ends are, I doubt they are anything that would be very good for Alyson...or the world. She is better off staying as far away from him as possible. It worries me not to have her under my protection, but perhaps she was smart to leave." He looked at the envelope from Felicity that he still held. "But who is the hostage?"

Dawn's eyes widened. "Hostage? What hostage?" She looked back down at the postcard, to read it again. "Oh, I get it. Well, who are you both friends with?"

Cain was staring at Felicity's envelope. It couldn't be. Arif should have no reason to bother with Felicity. His spies must know that Cain hadn't been keeping in touch with her. They had no reason to believe he was still fond of her after all of this time, did they? She had only come here once, and it was a few years ago, although he had unwittingly visited her more recently... Had he been followed?

Alyson had a much closer relationship with Felicity, but their correspondence was telepathic. Arif could not know about that. Alyson had only been to visit Felicity once or twice that he knew of. With her powers of speed and flight, who could possibly follow her?

Just as horrific certainty began to creep into his mind, he thought of something to allay his fears. Felicity was now married to Ben, who was son of Bernard Everheart, the feared vampire hunter. If Arif's spies had managed to observe Alyson's contact with Felicity, they must know this. To abduct the daughter-in-law of the Vampire Hunter would be an absurd amount of risk to the coven. To incite Alyson, Cain, *and* Ben and Bernard Everheart to attack his coven...Arif wouldn't dare.

"Sindy," he said with disappointment.

"Sexy dress girl?"

Cain nodded. "She has been sneaking around and telling lies since she arrived here. I suspected that she might have been working with Arif, but hoped to have been wrong."

"I don't get it. Working with him how?"

"I've told you that we had been in and out of each other's lives. Well, a little over two years ago she showed up here injured and in need of assistance. I healed her and took care of her, and offered to let her stay, as she assumed I would. She became close with me again, and with Alyson and her husband Mattie as well. She and Alyson became friends, and Sindy led her down a path of temptation and trouble, hoping to then lure her to Arif, on the premise that he could better mentor her than I."

"But that didn't work," Dawn confirmed.

Cain gave a snort of derision. "The temptation and trouble leading worked like a charm. Fortunately, Alyson knows that while *I* have her best interest at heart, Arif's motives are unclear, if not downright sinister. She wouldn't go to him."

"Except now he's saying that he kidnapped someone that he won't give back unless you trade him Alyson...and you think it's Sindy?"

"It makes sense. He ensconced her here to forge a friendship with Alyson and find her way into my heart as extra leverage, knowing that Alyson values my opinion. She couldn't lure Alyson away with her, so now she's gone back to Arif, to pretend she is a hostage.

Arif thinks that I would compromise Alyson over Sindy, feeling more dedication to a romantic relationship than a platonic one. He doesn't realize that while I may have been fool enough to fall for Sindy emotionally, I've still harbored doubts about her loyalty. I suspected that she was working for him all along. I'm not going to run over there with Alyson in tow in exchange for Sindy, especially since I know she's been in league with him the entire time."

He turned the postcard over again, looking for a postmark, but there was none to let him know when it had been delivered. Arif must have had one of his lackey's put it into his mailbox directly. "I think I have a contact number for Arif somewhere. Perhaps I'll set up a meeting with him to further clarify details of his proposal. He doesn't need to know that I haven't got access to Alyson at the moment. I'd like to know exactly what he is planning, even if I refuse to play a part in it. As for Sindy, if she wants to be a part of his coven so badly, he can have her."

Chapter 8
My apologies for the abduction

Felicity

Somewhere just beyond consciousness
Evening of July the 5th

Something smelled sickly sweet. Felicity's head was pounding, but not nearly as quickly as her heart, once she remembered her last few moments of consciousness.

She had been preparing for Alyson and Mattie to visit. Anxious, excited, and nervous as to how things would go, she had been out picking up a few bottles of wine and some snacks, as a distraction if nothing else, in case the evening became awkward. Ben would surely receive their company better with a few glasses of wine in him.

It was *Allie* though; how could this not be a wonderful reunion for all of them? Ben and Matt had been best friends long ago, and Allie was like a sister to him. Felicity was confident that after the initial hesitation and distrust faded away, Ben would be thrilled to spend time with his old friends again. With the baby staying at her parent's house, they had all evening to visit.

It was a bit nerve wracking that she hadn't heard a peep from Allie telepathically since they made their initial plan, but Allie was known for being a bit flighty and unreliable for little things. She may not be in touch, but she wouldn't dare forget this evening's plan. Allie was really excited for it, and had promised she and Mattie would be there. She was probably busy with her own stuff, convincing Mattie to come and be forgiving. Men could be so stubborn…she knew that well!

Felicity had worried all the way home that she'd get a speeding ticket. She'd been running late and racing as fast as she'd dared. Then, just before arriving home, she'd heard from Allie, a sudden and unexpected voice in her head. *We aren't coming*, her friend had announced, sounding filled with disappointment. Allie hadn't elaborated, but promised Felicity she would be in touch when she could and was terribly sorry. Felicity couldn't do much but assure her that they'd figure out a plan to postpone, and that she understood. She'd call Ben as soon as she got home, if he wasn't there already. As disappointed as Felicity was, he would probably be relieved.

She had pulled into the driveway, noting that she had still managed to beat Ben home. She had thrown her cell phone into her purse and whipped open the car door, eager to go around and grab her packages out of the back.

The moment she had truly been out of the car and closed the door, someone had grabbed her from behind. She couldn't see them, but felt a very large, strong form behind her as someone had hugged their arms around her body and immobilized her. She'd barely even let out a breath of surprise before she had felt a cloth pressed to her face, smelling of something strong and sickly sweet.

Her muscles had tensed as she'd sought to try to turn away and run, but she was grabbed and squeezed until she could barely move, let alone fight back. Fear had raced through her and she had held her breath for as long as she could, but struggling wasn't even an option. She was crushed in the grip of a large man's muscular arms, as tightly as though she were wound in the grip of a boa constrictor. His body felt huge, looming behind and above her.

She was forced to take a small breath or suffocate, but had then bent and brought up her leg to give a good kick behind her, hopefully into her attacker's groin. The kick couldn't connect well, because besides the fact that her extremities were beginning to feel tingly and go numb, and her vision was fading fast, the ground also seemed suddenly to tilt crazily to confuse and disorient her. Then…the ground was gone.

Felicity had felt a rush of wind, and an odd sinking feeling in her stomach, as though she was in an elevator. She was going up…and passing out. She couldn't even try to understand what was happening, because her mind felt so hazy, and the world was going black. No matter how she'd tried to fight it, consciousness had fled beyond her.

Now she slowly awoke, although the cloth was gone, she was still unable to get that odd and disturbing scent out of her nose. The ground was back. She was lying on her side, on the soft coverlets of a bed. No one seemed to be touching her, but that wasn't very comforting, because her wrists were firmly bound in front of her with duct tape, and her ankles were secured together as well. There was another piece of duct tape covering her mouth. At least she could breathe through her nose, even if she couldn't quite shake that strong smell from whatever had been used to knock her out.

The room was dark. Details were difficult to discern, but it seemed she was in an unfamiliar bedroom. The moment she began to stir, a deep masculine voice spoke from somewhere out of sight. "Good evening. My apologies for the abduction, but I was obligated to bring you here, and I felt the chloroform was the quickest, most dignified way to accomplish that without harming you."

Felicity froze in fear. Dignified? What about her current situation could this man possibly consider dignified? Where was she? Far from anyplace Ben would be able to find her easily. What was going to happen to her? Panic began to set in… She began struggling to rip her hands from the tape, but it was impossible. The best she could do was get herself into a sitting position.

The man spoke again, sounding annoyed. "I'd appreciate it if you'd remain calm and quiet please. You're in no immediate danger. When you're ready to listen, I'll explain why you're here."

Felicity could not seem to think of anything but trying to free herself, unreasonable and impossible as it was. The man's words were just a deep, scary rumbling voice in the background of her panic.

He moved into her view and barked her name, loud and imposing. "Felicity!" Her attention was jerked from her bonds and she looked up to see her captor. A huge, bald man of color stood before her. He was much taller than her husband, who was just over six feet, and he had a width and muscle mass to him that stole her breath. Although his sheer size was frightening, he didn't look sinister or malicious, as she would have expected. He was handsome, well dressed and watching her with an almost patient expression.

As she took in the impressive size of the man, she remembered how it had felt to be held and forced into submission by his brute strength. Holding her still to breathe the chloroform had been nothing to him. It would be just as simple for him now to subdue her again if necessary. Once again, she thought of his statement that he had tried to abduct her in a dignified manner…and then she thought of all the other things he might do to her, if he had a mind to be less dignified. That thought froze her more surely then any order from him.

He seemed pleased that she had stopped her squirming. He spoke, his deep voice inducing a hint of menace in her ears, simply for its unfamiliar baritone, even though he seemed to be trying to comfort her. "I understand that you're frightened, but please try to remain calm. Right now, I am the only thing standing between you and a true nightmare. I plan to treat you respectfully, but I do not like chaotic commotion in my house. Don't irritate me."

His house? Where the hell was she, and why? The fact that he planned to be respectful to her was slightly reassuring, but she couldn't imagine how that could mesh with the fact that she was currently tied up on his bed. And he thought he was shielding her from the true nightmare?

"I'd like to remove the tape," he informed her. Apparently he wanted to warn her before he moved closer, allaying her fears of his intentions. She nodded, allowing him closer while holding back her panic. He took a knife from his pocket, and she was very glad that he had told her it was for the tape *before* she had seen it. He moved to cut the binding from her wrists, but paused. "Don't make me sorry that I'm allowing you such freedom."

She nodded, timidly, and he cut her wrists and ankles free, speaking as he did. "It was just for the flight really. If you came to, I couldn't have you flailing about while we were a hundred and fifty feet in the air. I wouldn't want to drop you," he added with a smile. She could only stare at him in mute bewilderment. They had been flying, hadn't they? She remembered being carried into the air.

Sudden realization came upon her; this man was not human. He had to be a vampire, one who could fly, as Allie did. As if he weren't already scary enough.

He continued speaking as he moved to take the tape from her mouth. "But I trust that you'll behave yourself now that we can talk. There is nowhere you can go, and nothing you can do to over-power me." He grinned again at that statement, as though daring her to disagree. "I am not going to hurt you."

With that last reassurance, he removed the tape from her mouth so she could speak. Before saying anything, she took the opportunity to take some deep breaths through her mouth. The smell from the chloroform was just about gone, but it felt good to allow herself deep breaths again.

"Who are you?" she asked quietly, once she regained her composure. "What is this?"

"My name is Elric. I work for the coven master Arif."

Memories of Arif flashed through her mind. Whenever she thought of him, she pictured the first night they had met. He had been standing in the road, negotiating with Cain, and then moved to assess her where she'd sat on the back of Cain's motorcycle. Cain had called her *My Lady*, and Arif had begun eyeing her as though appraising her value, and the fact that she was unmarked. *I do see the lady*, he had said, *and I must remark, that she is not…yours.* The words sent cold chills down her back every time she thought of them.

"You're in a private community, under his command."

"Why? Why is he doing this? What does he want with me?"

The man seemed distracted, as though he wasn't even listening to her. His attention was drawn to the bedroom door. He seemed about to get up, when the door was opened by someone outside. A lovely black woman entered casually, seeming at ease and unconcerned. She was older than Felicity, but in wonderful shape, as her dance leotard clearly showed.

She was speaking as she opened the door, before noting the occupants of the room. "Elric I'm leaving for class…oh." She noticed Felicity on the bed and seemed at first shocked, and then somehow hurt. She quickly wiped all expression from her face and lowered her eyes. "My apologies, Master. I didn't know you were indisposed."

Elric settled back into his seat and dipped his head in a nod, forgiving her trespass. "It's all right, Latisha."

"Who is this?" the woman asked. Felicity took a breath to speak, trying to decide if this woman could help her, but Elric gave her a fierce stare for silence. Latisha ventured a guess on her own. "A new addition to our harem, sir? …My replacement?" She said it with quiet and dignified certainty, although the slight edge of resentment in her voice couldn't be denied.

Elric looked up in alarm at her distress. "No. She's not mine. I won't be marking her. She is…part of the mission I was sent on."

The woman clasped her hands before her and pursed her lips. It looked to Felicity as though she didn't believe him. "I see. You don't usually bring your work home with you. Why is she here?"

"Because I have deemed this an appropriate place for her to be," Elric informed her with authority. "Any other questions?"

The woman was un-intimidated. If anything, she looked like she was irked by his show of dominance. "No, sir." Her tone wasn't truly factitious, but it was obvious the woman wasn't going to let it go…they'd be speaking of it later.

"Then leave us." She bowed her head and began to swing the door closed. Elric stood, unhappy with the exchange. "Latisha. This woman is your salvation."

Latisha stopped, turning to look at Felicity again. Felicity was still peeling bits of tape stickiness from her hands and mouth, as she watched the scene play out before her. The woman observed her for a moment, as seeming comprehension of the true situation dawned. Elric spoke again, quietly. "I do what I must."

She nodded her head respectfully. "Of course, Master. You always do. But I wonder if the price will ever be too high."

He met her eyes. "Never."

She evaluated what she saw in his gaze and then lightly shook her head. "Perhaps it should be."

As the door swung closed, Elric let out a disgruntled sigh. Felicity wasn't sure how she fit into things, but somehow, after seeing the woman dare to challenge Elric and affect him emotionally, he seemed a bit less scary...for a gigantic vampire. He may have kidnapped her, but from what she could tell, he wasn't a crazy monster. He did seem to have a heart and a conscience, even if it hadn't stopped him from abducting her.

"Please, I need to go home," she begged him quietly.

He looked at her as though she was ridiculously stupid to think that her plea would affect him, after the trouble he'd gone through to subdue and transport her. Okay, maybe he didn't have *that* soft a heart.

"Look, you're a hostage. Understand what that means; you aren't in any immediate danger. You're to be kept here until certain demands are met, and then I'll return you to your home, safe and sound. All you have to do is keep from pissing anyone off while you're here, and you'll be fine."

"A hostage for what?"

"I'm not at liberty to say. But just so we're clear, you aren't in danger, as long as you cooperate. If you get it into your head to try to run, or hurt someone, all bets are off. I could have easily tied you up in a more public holding cell, where others would have access to you, others who haven't got much in the way of manners. I chose instead to bring you into my home where I can keep a better eye on you, but if you try to pull something and it puts a member of my harem in danger, I will not be very forgiving."

"Harem?" Her voice held a note of slightly shocked disbelief at the word, as though he must be joking, but the look he gave her in return showed he was not in the mood for humor. She remembered things Cain had told her long ago, of vampires who kept humans as pets...an unsettling thought. Should she expect any less from a vampire who worked for Arif?

"I am a large vampire with a thirst to match," Elric reminded her firmly. "I have nine humans in my care, and still I need to drink from strangers and animals, because their blood is not enough to quench my body's demands."

"Of course. They feed you. I should have realized. It just threw me for a sec, because the word 'harem' makes it sound like something sexual. Sorry."

Elric fixed her with a stare before speaking again. "Cain marked you," he confirmed, "in the past." She shyly nodded her head. "The two of you were close. I'm sure he drank from you regularly. You understand what that experience can be." There was no use denying it, although she wasn't comfortable sharing such intimate knowledge with this stranger, and she wasn't sure what it would mean for her current situation. "The humans in my care will be here for years," he continued.

"Years?"

He nodded. "I am responsible for their well-being, physical and emotional. I drink a moderate amount from each of them weekly, and while they're permitted to have relations with others within the community, for some, their weekly evening with me is their only physical contact with another. How unsatisfied would they be if the desires I awakened in them with my bite remained unfulfilled? How unhappy would it make them to believe I found them beneath my attentions? I'm not a cruel man. They provide me with their blood and I do for them as they desire.

I have no need to explain my living arrangements to you. *Harem* is the accepted term, being both accurate, and kinder to my ear than *herd* or *stable* as some other vampires choose to consider their wards.

It doesn't really concern you. I'm simply providing explanation as a courtesy. You are here in my home, because I have a great respect for the vampire Cain. I know that he favors you, and for him, I will keep you as safe and comfortable as I can. I am not interested in your judgment."

She nodded, timidly. "I'm sorry. Thank you. I appreciate your kindness," she assured him. "So, what happens now?"

"Well, you might have a few days to settle in here, before I need to bring you before Arif."

"A few days? I can't be here for *days!* I have a baby at home. I only pumped enough milk for him until tomorrow. I can't stay here. What about my husband, he must be going crazy with worry! What do you need me for anyway? I'm not special to anybody important. I make terrible leverage. If this is about Cain, you might as well just let me go now, because he left me, you know. We're ancient history."

He cocked an eyebrow at her. "Please don't dissolve into hysterics. I have no patience for hysterical women," he informed her with a sigh. "And don't insult my intelligence by pretending you mean nothing to Cain. While your feelings for him may be arguable, it is clear that *his* depth of emotion for you has never wavered. The master has read as much from those around him consistently in the past, and any who know him can easily believe it is true, regardless of your present involvements. And honestly, trying to convince the vampires here that you are unimportant would be rather stupid on your part. Unimportant equals disposable…drinkable. You're better off just keeping your mouth shut.

The sort of leverage you provide for the master is none of your concern, and it will take as long as it takes. You'd better hope that you are important to somebody, because if you aren't, you'll find yourself a permanent resident."

She opened her mouth in outrage, but could not even think how to answer. Finally, she let out a small huff of disgust. "So if Cain doesn't come for me, you expect me to join your *harem,* where you'll do me the considerate service of taking me into your bed once a week after you force me to let you drink my blood? You have got to be kidding me."

He smirked at her disdain. "I haven't got room in my harem for you," he informed her. "Which means you'll be put up for auction and given to the vampire of highest rank who fancies you, considerate or not. Judging by your current demeanor, I'd say it will take a great deal of taming before they can get a decent meal out of you without a fight, so you wouldn't go to a vampire of high rank…or morals." He fixed her with a steady stare and a smile, which surely stood out in stark contrast with the look of horror that must have stolen over her face. "As I said, you should hope you're important to *someone* who has something the master wants to trade for you."

~~~~~~~~~~~~~~~~~~~~~~~~~~~~~~~~~

Felicity was brought to a very nicely appointed bedroom down the hall. It was fairly large and sported a queen-sized bed, but Felicity was made to wait in a chair in the corner as Elric had a cot brought in and set up for her.

"This is Latisha's room," he explained. "She is the only woman in residence without a roommate, an honor she well deserves, but I believe this is the best place for you to stay for now. Your security here serves not only my best interest, but hers as well. Once she fully understands your significance, she will be more at ease knowing she can keep an eye on you. A word of advice, she is a strong, smart, and very practical woman. Mind her, and don't test her patience.

I'm setting a guard outside the room. Settle yourself and I'll have something brought in for you to eat. Latisha will be returning shortly."

True to his word, Elric soon had two women enter the room with a small folding table. One put it in front of the armchair in the corner and set it with a glass and two pitchers, as the other waited to set down a tray of hot food. Felicity was surprised to see that it looked like a very nice meal. "What is that?" she asked quietly, as the women were about to leave.

One of them turned to answer as the other held the door for her. "Chicken Marsala with fresh green beans in a brown sugar glaze. Chef's specialty, it's delicious," she answered with a confidential grin. She gestured towards the two small pitchers that had been placed near an empty glass. "Apple cider is in the larger one. The other is water. Is that alright?"

Felicity was a bit dumbfounded for a moment by the woman's sincere question; asked as though Felicity might demand she run out and find something more suitable. "It's great, thanks."

"Enjoy."

She wasn't very hungry, and worried a little that the food might be drugged, but it smelled wonderful. What reason would they have to drug her again? She was already completely under their power, and she was doing her best not to seem unruly. She hesitated, but had just been about to succumb to tasting the food when the door opened.

Elric entered the room, closing the door behind him. He observed the untouched plate. "I hear it's quite good." He noticed her hesitation. "I'd taste it for you, to show you it's safe to eat, but that wouldn't prove much, would it?" he offered with a smile.

Besides the fact that he was a vampire, immune to anything that would hurt her, it would take a ridiculous portion to have any effect on a man of his size anyway. She shrugged sheepishly and gave in to tasting the food. It was delicious.

He came closer and lifted the pitcher of cider for her approval. She gave a small nod and he poured some into her glass. "Latisha should be on her way." He checked his watch. "Her last class should be over by now, and I have a few things to take care of before sunrise." He paused, closing his eyes as a small smile spread over his face. "Excuse me for a moment," he said, as he turned and opened the door.

Felicity could see Latisha approaching from down the hall. Elric stepped out to meet her, leaving the door open a crack. It took Felicity a second to understand how he had known she was coming. Obviously, the woman was marked by him. The memory of that intimate connection came back to her...how it had felt to be marked by Cain, her body so in tune with his and knowing when he was near. It had been a long time since she had truly thought about details and nuances of vampire existence, never expecting to be immersed in the vampire world again.

The door was still slightly ajar, and she realized that she could hear her captors' conversation if she listened intently. Latisha was speaking. "For how long?"

"I don't know," was Elric's answer.

"Am I putting her on the schedule?"

"For me?" Elric asked in disbelief.

Through the crack in the door, Felicity could see her give the man a shove, not that it moved him an inch. "No, wise ass. Not the blood schedule, the community calendar; classes, work shifts?"

He rewarded her defensiveness with a grin. "No, hopefully she won't be here long enough to bother. I'd like her to tag along with you. I need her watched."

"That's a duty for a vampire. You have a cadet in your service. Let him guard her."

"I've already assigned two cadets to the task, but there is no one I trust more than you. I'd like to have you with her, as an extra set of eyes and ears to keep them on their toes. I worry that if another fails me, you'll suffer for their indiscretions."

"Two guards is plenty. She's not going anywhere. I'm busy, Elric. Tomorrow night I'm teaching two aerobics classes, one ballet, and two belly-dance sessions."

"Latisha, I wish I could watch her personally, but I can't, and you are the only person I trust as though I were watching her myself. I don't just want her kept secure, I want her kept in decent spirits as well. Maybe she'll enjoy joining you in class, you're an inspiring teacher."

"How am I supposed to concentrate on teaching a class while worrying about a hostage?"

"I could chain her to a dance bar for you." Felicity hoped he was joking. Elric continued. "What if I excuse Jordan from his shifts and have him accompany you both?"

"Jordan is gone tomorrow, remember?"

"Damn."

"The trade is at sundown. The new guy, Craig, will be quartered in quarantine for the next two weeks, he'll be moving in after." Latisha watched him quietly for a moment. "It worries me that you let Jordan go to that woman. You should make some time for a proper goodbye," she suggested.

Elric laughed. "I already have. And don't worry about him. I've given him all the warnings and he says he can handle it. He wants to be in her house to be closer to George. He's in love. Let him go. I believe Craig will be an asset in time. Leaves me short on trustworthy muscle until he settles in though."

"You've met him before?"

"Briefly, in the reform cellar. I know he'll be grateful I've taken him out of Cat's care, I can tell you that."

"Oh…" Her tone was a bit somber, but then she smiled with a new thought. "It's been a while since you had another proper rooster in the henhouse. You know, girls like a shiny new toy. Are you planning to keep him on a tight leash?" she asked teasingly.

He smiled. "No, he can interact with you all as he pleases. I'm not worried. It's good to re-arrange things now and then. The ability to deal with change will serve you all well."

"Because we won't be here much longer?" she asked in quiet hope.

There was a long silence. Felicity strained to hear, wondering if they were truly silent, or if they were whispering and she had missed something.

After a moment, Felicity saw Elric nod his head towards the door. "We don't have to leave. That woman bought you permanent residency."

Felicity pretended to be eating, as she saw them both turn to peek at her through the door crack. "But you said she was only a hostage. What if things don't work out to the master's liking?"

"It doesn't matter," Elric assured her. "My mission was to collect her, and I have. Her abduction was the price of your permanent status, no matter the final results of the situation."

"And how many more atrocities will you be forced to commit in his name? You do these things for my sake? I should be ashamed. When will it ever be enough?"

"What I do is my own burden, and this will be the last. As long as she is secure while in my care, I have fulfilled my end of the bargain."

"I'd like to say I'm relieved, but his bargains are always subject to change."

"He wouldn't dare, not this time. He knows he has pushed me far enough. You will be allowed to stay for the duration of your natural life."

"Fair enough. I've told you I'd accept that, but is that going to be sufficient for you?"

He sighed. "No, but it's a start. I'll work on it. I know we haven't got much time."

Latisha put her hands on her hips, "What's the rush? Am I getting too old for you?" she asked dangerously.

He laughed. "I'll wait until you're ninety if that's your wish."

"I liked the other options better."

Elric moved closer and lowered his voice even more. "We've gone over this. There are no other options right now."

Latisha seemed to disagree, but Felicity couldn't make out what she was saying, because she was whispering so quietly. There was a chair next to the door. Felicity quietly stood from her table. The two in the hall didn't notice; they were too engrossed in their conversation. After a moment of indecision, Felicity crept to the chair by the door and settled herself there. It would be obvious that she had been eaves dropping, but these people had kidnapped her, so she wasn't going to worry much about being polite. As long as she wasn't causing a problem, hopefully she wouldn't be punished for it.

"He has global influence," Elric was saying. "Trust me, I know the connections he has and they are no joke. If I left without his blessing, he would be insulted and he would have no qualm about calling in favors to make an example of us for it."

"What if we go the other route? You've gained a lot of influence. There are those who would back you up."

"Not now. It's too risky. I don't have enough vampires of age and power on my side. Arif's maker is here, with an escort even older. We couldn't possibly prevail against that sort of authority. Even rebels respect elders of that status. I'd lose half of my supporters."

Latisha's suggestion was barely a breath of a whisper. "What about Cain? The enemy of your enemy is an ally. You've said you liked him."

"I believe he is a solid man, but even he may not be enough. Besides, it's not his problem. I can't ask him to get involved in this."

"He's already involved. Your situations are separate, but the solution is the same."

"He'll have no love for me. I'm holding someone he cares for as prisoner." Elric gestured towards the crack in the door, pushing it further ajar. He gestured towards Felicity's table, but of course, she wasn't there. There was a slight moment of worry from Latisha and Elric as they quickly pushed the door open completely, but they relaxed as they saw Felicity in the chair near the door. Elric gave her a stern look of reprimand for changing her seat.

Elric finished glaring at Felicity and looked back to Latisha. "She is here with you until further notice. I'm putting a guard at the door. I'll come to collect her at sundown so you can teach your classes tomorrow night, but I'll be bringing her back when you're done. I have business to attend to and I can't have her trailing after me everywhere I go. I'm sorry, but you'll have to arrange a replacement teacher for the rest of the week so you can stay with her." After that command, he left without another word.

Left alone with Latisha, Felicity was uncomfortable with what to say, if anything, about the overheard bits of conversation. After a brief silence, Latisha finally sighed and spoke.

"Welcome to *Kana Susamış Için Ev.* I doubt you'll take offense when I say that I hope your stay with us is a short one."

Felicity only had time to offer a smile before Latisha was busy bustling around the room, getting extra pillows and a blanket for the cot. "Things are pretty much nocturnal around here," she explained. "I'm going to need to get some sleep today, I've got a full schedule tomorrow night. You can watch television, or read if you want." She put down the pillow she was holding and looked at Felicity in all earnestness. "This house was built to be secure. Everything is connected to a state of the art security system. You can't open a window, a door, or even mess with an air duct without bringing armed guards. I don't need to have you restrained while you're in here, do I?"

Felicity shook her head, as Latisha continued. "I know you wouldn't try to hurt me, because no matter who you might be important to, or why, Elric would drink you dead if you even thought about hurting me, damn the consequences. Do you believe that?" Felicity nodded yes, and she meant it. "Good. Smart girl. I'll go see if I can find you a change of clothing for the day. I think Caroline is about your size. I'll be right back."

Latisha returned with light cotton pajamas that fit Felicity comfortably. When Felicity emerged from the bathroom, and thanked the woman, she simply smiled and nodded. The remainder of the evening, Latisha kept to herself. She showed Felicity how to work the remote for the television, and then spent the night sitting at a desk in the corner of the room doing paperwork while referencing some sort of sign-in logs. Before she was done, a bell sounded from out in the hall. Latisha barely looked up from her forms. "Dawn," she explained to Felicity, and then kept working. It was two bells and nearly three more hours before she closed the books and announced she was going to bed.

She gave no comfortable opening to talk, noticeably by design. Felicity could tell the woman was uncomfortable with the arrangement, but she wanted to bring up Cain somehow. "Latisha," Felicity called as her hostess exited the bathroom, ready for bed. "Can I ask you…?"

"No," Latisha cut her off before she finished the question. "I'm not in the mood to talk. You can keep watching television, but I'm going to sleep. I suggest you try to do the same, because I doubt you'll get much sleep during the night."

~~~~~~~~~~~~~~~~~~~~~~~~~~~~~~~~

After a long, restless day, her nerves frazzled from worry and nervous waiting, Felicity had finally managed to fall asleep…and then an alarm went off. Felicity blinked groggy eyes as Latisha woke, rose, and began to get ready for the evening. Felicity sat up and rubbed the sleep from her eyes. From what she could tell through the curtains, it was still light out.

Latisha brought the folded pile of clothing Felicity had been wearing when she was taken, and lay them on the foot of the bed. "Get dressed. Time for evening check-in."

"It's not even evening yet."

"I'm the coordinator, I have to be there early. Let's go."

Once dressed, Felicity followed the woman out of the room. As they passed the guards Elric had stationed at the door, Latisha offered them a brisk "*good* evening", and the two vampires turned to follow them downstairs. Latisha put down the stack of papers she had been working on during the day, on a desk near the front door, and the guards moved Felicity to sit on a sofa in a large parlor near the entrance of the house.

As Felicity watched Latisha come and go, getting things ready, other women of the harem slowly began to gather and lounge on the sofa and chairs. When one of them tried to speak to Felicity, the guards quickly shushed her. Felicity was not to speak without leave from Latisha, so after a few curious looks, the women only spoke to each other. There were five women so far. All seemed fairly happy and comfortable with each other, voicing the normal friendly conversation and casual complaints you would expect from any other small group.

As two more women came downstairs, Latisha checked her watch with an annoyed sigh. After a moment, one last woman came rushing down the stairs, and Latisha was obviously satisfied by her arrival. She stood from the desk and clapped her hands, causing the conversation to stop and the others to form a line facing her at the door. There were now eight women in line, all lovely, although of many different ethnicities, and body types, ranging in age from twenty-something, to women into their forties.

Latisha greeted them with a smile. "Good evening, ladies. As you know, Elric is back in residence. We'll pick up the cycle from where we left off, making tonight night six; that's Natalie."

She consulted her papers and then took a small disposable cup from the table. "Okay, Beverly." The woman at the end of line stepped forward. She was likely in her mid-thirties, tall, lovely, and olive skinned with long dark hair. She took the cup from Latisha, who then turned to pour her some water from a pitcher on the desk into a second cup.

As Beverly accepted these things, Felicity realized that there were pills in the first cup. Felicity furrowed her brow. "You're drugging them?" she asked in indignant astonishment. Everyone looked at her as though she were ridiculously insane, as one of the guards gave her a nudge to remind her that she was not permitted to speak.

After a moment and a swallow, Beverly gave her a piteous smile. "They're vitamin supplements," she explained.

Latisha gave Felicity a look of annoyance for the disruption and then consulted her papers before speaking to Beverly again. "They're going to need you for some extra hours with the seamstress this week. A bunch of special clothing is being made for a visiting lady vamp, so you're double shifting and being excused from your classes."

Beverly nodded, threw her cups in the garbage and stepped back into line as Latisha called another name. "Tia." This was a fair, thin, young blonde woman. Latisha consulted her notes. "Medical says you're skewing towards anemic again, so you're on extra iron supplements," she said, nodded towards the cup of pills she had just given the woman.

Tia was annoyed. "Great. I can barely take a dump as it is," she grumbled.

Some of the women giggled as Latisha replied. "I'll tell Elric to take it easy on you and give your count a chance to go back up, but you still have to take the iron, at least until your next check-up." Tia rolled her eyes and took the pills as Latisha continued. "You're in the kitchen this week. Early shift." Tia's mood was much improved upon hearing her assignment, and she turned to give a black woman further down the line a big smile at the news.

"Carmendy," Latisha called, giving more cups to a pale, curvy brunette of about twenty-five or so. "Custodial, early shift."

"Again? I was just on custodial duty a few weeks ago," she complained.

"Yes, again, and it was a month ago. If you don't want to get stuck with the community service jobs, then finish earning your skill credits for something else. Until then, quit complaining. Someone has to clean the bathrooms. Report to the maintenance building for assignment."

"Yeah, I know the drill."

"Natalie," Latisha called, giving a set of cups to a very dark skinned woman with shortly shaved hair. She stepped forward and took them with a nod and a smile. "You're with Elric tonight. He's got a lot going on, so make sure you report to his room early so he can give you instructions before he's off and running." Natalie nodded and took her pills as Latisha asked, "How are things in the kitchen?"

"You tell me," she responded with a grin.

"Delicious as always. You're the best."

"It helps when they give me staff that knows how to prep," she added, giving Tia a wink.

Latisha carried on with the list. "Delilah."

A white woman with large, dark and sultry eyes stepped forward. She was about Felicity's age. Her long brown hair was up in a sporty pony-tail, and she had an athletic figure to match. Latisha handed her a cup. "I think they're changing up the schedule for the tennis courts for next week. Give Chris a call before lessons start so you guys can make sure you're on the same page, okay?"

The woman took her pills with a nod. "Gotcha."

"Emily." A smartly dressed woman in her forties was called up. She was a blonde, with a good figure and a no-nonsense demeanor. "I assume all is well over in the coven master's offices?" She accepted her pills with a smile and a nod, and resumed her place in line.

Latisha readied the cups and checked her papers for the last woman in line. "Caroline, you're serving in the bar over at common house this week, early shift." Felicity recognized the name as the woman who's pajamas she had been lent for the day. The woman was a bit shorter than Felicity, and a bit heavier as well, but very pretty with shoulder length strawberry blonde hair and large blue eyes.

When she stepped forward to take her cups, Latisha didn't give them over easily, instead staring at the woman for full attention first. "According to medical, you're up another pound."

Caroline shrugged and took the pills. "It's just one pound. Elric doesn't mind," she added with a sly grin.

"You still have to abide by community standards. You were given a range when you got here, and if you go under or over it, medical is going to intervene, no matter what Elric thinks; coven rules. I put you in my late shift aerobics class."

"Oh, come on, I hate aerobics." Latisha raised an eyebrow. "No offense, Tish, but all that jumping around just seems pointless to me, and it makes me nauseous."

"Medical put a note in the records. If I don't show an effort to do something, I'll get cited for negligence, and they'll just cut your meals."

"What about tennis? Schedule me on the court with Delilah and I'll play hard, I promise."

Delilah gave her a wicked sort of grin. "Oh, I'll whip her into shape," she promised Latisha. "But a word of caution," she warned Caroline, "I don't tolerate whining." Caroline just made a face at her in response.

"Fine." Latisha made a note in her papers, and then put them down on the desk with a sigh. "I'm sure you're all curious about our visitor," Latisha began, with a nod toward the sofa. "This is Felicity. She's not joining us; she's only here temporarily. She will be accompanied by Elric or myself at all times, and is to be treated cordially as a guest. Any questions or comments?"

Delilah spoke up to the others. "I told you she wasn't the replacement."

Carmendy replied with a pout. "I miss Jordan."

Latisha rolled her eyes. "I meant comments *for* our visitor, not about her," she clarified.

Carmendy leaned forward to see Felicity better. "Hi Felicity, welcome to the house." Now she turned back to Latisha. "I still miss Jordan."

"He'll be out of quarantine and moved in with his new harem next week. You can see him in the dining hall. Felicity is not his replacement," she confirmed.

Now Caroline spoke up, "No, I hear his replacement is a man," she said with excitement.

The other girls began to comment all at once, but before Latisha could quiet them, a bell rang loudly from somewhere outside. The women all became quiet immediately and looked to Latisha for dismissal. She paused and then quickly commented on their speculations. "Yes, his name is Craig, and he'll be moving in next week. We'll have plenty of time to discuss him later. Have a good night!" With that, the women all scattered to their separate assignments.

Felicity anticipated getting up from the sofa and being led somewhere new as well, but she was ignored. Latisha seemed about to sit at the desk when one of the vampire guards took the seat instead. She gave him a stern look, but he only sat back and made himself comfortable. Latisha barely bit back a grumble of annoyance, and took the phone from in front of the guard, moving it to the other end of the desk and making a call. The second guard remained standing at attention next to Felicity.

Latisha spent over an hour making phone calls, most of which began professionally, but quickly dissolved into friendly conversations. Suddenly, the two guards came to stiff attention. Felicity looked to see Elric casually coming downstairs with Natalie on his arm. Latisha wrapped up her phone call and came to stand before the desk to greet him.

Elric said something quietly to Natalie that made her smile, and then gave her a kiss on the cheek when they reached the bottom of the stairs. "Take care of that for me and I'll see you back here around four," he said to her. She nodded and left through the front door.

Now Elric approached Latisha, sparing a glance for Felicity. "Good evening ladies. I trust you had an uneventful day?"

Latisha gave him a smile and a kiss. "Yes, and now you can have her for an uneventful evening. I've got to run."

Elric spent a moment admiring Latisha as she walked away, before turning his attention to Felicity with a sigh. "How are you holding up?"

"I'm okay," she answered quietly. "Thank you for asking," she added after some reflection. "This place is a lot different than I pictured it."

"How's that?" Elric asked with some amusement.

"Well…" she began, trying to decide how she could voice her thoughts without being insulting, "for one thing, everyone is so busy. The word 'harem' evokes this image of a bunch of woman lying around in lingerie with nothing to do but compare Kama Sutra notes or something."

One of the vampire guards at the desk behind her laughed. Elric raised an eyebrow. "I'm sure those discussions take place at some point…but I guess it depends on the harem," he told her with a smirk. "As for the lingerie…that depends on the harem too. I feel there is a time and place for all things, and that is how I run my household.

Kana Susamiş Icin Ev is a fully functioning, almost completely independent community. We bring in some food and supplies from the outside world to supplement the gardens, but the vampires and humans who reside here are all expected to do their parts to keep things running smoothly.

Vampires receive their assignments according to their rank in the coven," he explained with a glance at the guards. "Humans alternate community service assignments for twenty hours each week, or if they have a skill, they can contribute to a specialty service. For example, Natalie is an excellent chef, so rather than work menial labor positions, she is assigned to lead the kitchen staff."

"Just twenty hours a week?"

"Doesn't sound so bad, does it? Humans are also accountable to attend twenty hours of activities and conditioning classes each week as well; classes that teach them everything from graceful movement, to poetry reading and even the lost art of polite and witty conversation."

"Conditioning classes? Sounds like brain washing sessions, to me."

"The classes are what you make of them. I encourage those in my care to view the classes as an opportunity offered to expose them to arts and culture they may not otherwise encounter. They should absorb what pleases them and take the rest with a grain of salt. Classes in social grace, manners and polite speaking are not *so* unnecessary. You'd be surprised how many humans have lost the ability to feel comfortable in a social situation. It's almost sad. There is no hiding behind texting here, and true conversation consists of more than one witty sentence you can express in a tweet, or whatever other new social media is popular these days.

When spending an evening accompanying their vampire, humans may find themselves at a formal gathering, and be expected to interact with others showing grace and ease. My ladies often join me when meeting others for the theater or a fancy party. I expect them to be suitably charming good company."

"Oh, now I get it, you're teaching them to be blood donor Stepford wives."

He chuckled. "I believe our system is modeled on a combination of ancient Arabic practices and those of the Japanese Geisha, infused with modern practicality. Human donors are expected to balance lessons of culture and entertainment with physical activities in order to keep them mentally and physically in good health, and to enhance their appeal to the vampires of the compound."

"Stepford wives," she repeated, stonily.

"While I do have social relationships with other vampires, I share my residence with these humans. When I'm not busy elsewhere, I am spending my free time with them. There's more to my nights than blood and bedroom, you know. If all of my humans were little more than vacuous dolls, I would find them terribly boring and they would grate on my nerves rather quickly."

"Wouldn't bother me," one of the vampire guards chimed in.

Elric gave him a withering glance. "Well, let's hope the four humans in your care are simple enough not to mind being treated like toys. I do hope you're kind to them, at least."

The guy gave a broad smile. "Oh yeah. I treat them real nice. They got it good, being mine."

"Lucky ladies, all," Elric added, facetiously. "Now, if your curiosity is quelled for the moment, I have a few things to take care of this evening, so we should get moving."

The vampire guards rose to follow, when Elric suddenly stopped and turned back to Felicity once more. "Have you been fed?"

Felicity was so hungry, she didn't even resent him for phrasing the question to make her sound like a pet. "Not since last night."

He shook his head. "My apologies. Latisha forgets to even feed herself half the time. She's always in such a rush, she relies on yogurts and things she keeps stashed in her studio. Come, let's get you a meal."

She followed him to the kitchen, guards in tow. There was an eclectic spread set out on the counter: sandwiches, fruit salad, pastries and breakfast things. It seemed odd, considering it was actually about 10 p.m., but it looked marvelous, and considering she had just woken up and was starving, it wasn't unwelcome.

"Choose something you can eat while walking," Elric advised.

Felicity quickly grabbed a bagel already spread with cream cheese. Elric selected a small container of orange juice for her, from the refrigerator, and they were out the door.

Felicity tagged along, flanked by her vampire guards, as Elric visited several buildings, checking in with various vampires, giving orders and collecting reports. He was given a great deal of respect from everyone they met, and seemed to be generally liked, although he kept things professional and not overly friendly. The tour of the compound that Felicity received in the process was a strange experience, if only because it was all so terribly…normal.

It seemed like a nice, peaceful gated community, someplace she would want to live, if she didn't know its' true purpose. There was a large dining hall, through the windows of which many people could been seen eating, laughing and seeming to have very friendly, social meals. They passed a small theater, a beauty salon and some shops, and a sports complex with a pool, tennis courts and a large building for indoor facilities. It was not at all what she had envisioned.

There were humans out on their own, but most of them were going from one place to another, without dawdling. They were a bit quiet and subdued, but no one seemed to be terribly upset or depressed, and although manner of dress varied greatly, no one wore the shackles and chains that she had somehow expected…even if it did seem silly in retrospect. No human was leaving this place unauthorized. That was quite evident after they made a stop at the front gate guard building and kennels. No collars were needed for these human pets.

After a few hours, it seemed their rounds were through and Elric brought them back to his house, with promises of another meal for her within. When they entered, Latisha was sitting on a couch in the parlor, along with three of the other women. "You're back! Come join us," one of the ladies invited with a bright smile. It was a lovely young brunette. After a moment of thought, Felicity was able to produce her name, Carmendy. The others were Tia and Natalie, if memory served.

Elric turned to one of the vampire guards that had been following Felicity around all evening. "Go and fetch Felicity some lunch from the kitchen. She can take her meal in here with the ladies." The guard obliged, while the other took up a place at the desk by the door. Elric entered the front parlor, and Felicity timidly joined him, and sat in an empty armchair, as all of the ladies gave her their attention. Carmendy patted the space next to her on the couch for Elric, but he instead crossed to take hold of Natalie's hand and give it a kiss. "You wouldn't expect me to slight Natalie, would you?" he asked Carmendy with a smile.

Carmendy gave him a playful pout. "Sorry, I'll try to be patient," she promised, mouthing him a kiss. "Elric, we have a favor to ask."

Elric shot her an amused grin, understanding better why she had been trying to cozy up to him. "Am I not going to like this favor?" he asked, with a glance towards Felicity.

"Oh, it has nothing to do with *her*," Carmendy assured him. "We want a beach day, Elric. It's been so long, we're almost as pale as the dead." Both Carmendy and Tia folded their hands before them, as if to beg.

Elric shook his head. "I don't know. I've got a lot going on right now." The girls gave Felicity pointed looks of resentment, but Elric corrected them for it. "It's not her fault, but I've got a lot of responsibility at the moment."

Carmendy tried again. "Well, it's not like you're going to come. You don't need to worry about us. We did it lots of times last summer, but this year you've been so distracted that we haven't been allowed to do anything fun."

Elric laughed. "What a lie! I took you all out clubbing two weekends past."

Tia nodded with a smile. "That's true. That was a lot of fun. Remember that guy that kept buying me drinks? *He* was fun."

Carmendy accepted the rebuke, grudgingly. "Alright, true. But that was two weeks ago, and we need some daytime fun. We're like wilting flowers, Elric. We need some sunshine. Please?"

Elric took in the hopeful faces of Carmendy and Tia, and then looked to see Natalie also raise her eyebrows in hopeful anticipation of his answer. When he gave a consulting glance to Latisha, she just shrugged with a grin.

The vampire guard that Elric had sent to the kitchen came back with a wrapped club sandwich that he handed to Felicity, and a bottle of water that he set on the coffee table. Elric weighed the request in his mind for a moment, until the vampire went to settle himself in quiet conversation with the other guard at the front desk. "Well," Elric began, "I do love the scent of my sun-kissed beauties after a day at the beach…all sea-salt and coconut oil…"

Carmendy rose and came to him, practically sitting in his lap as she leaned to give him a kiss on the cheek. "I promise we won't get sun-burned."

Elric paused to breathe in her scent before urging her to rise and return to her own seat. "Alright, I'll check the schedule. I can probably excuse you from duties and arrange escort for you early next week."

Tia clapped her hands in childish glee as Carmendy blew him another kiss. "Thank you!" She turned to Felicity in excitement. "You can hang out with us for the day, if you want. It'll be nice to have someone new. Beach days are so fun!"

Elric shook his head sternly. "She can't go. Don't give me sad eyes, Coven Masters' rules. She has to stay here."

Latisha nodded. "I can stay and look after her," she offered.

"Wouldn't you like a day at the beach?" Elric asked.

"Not if you need me for something more important."

"With any luck, Felicity won't even be with us anymore by then. You should go. You deserve some fun with your sisters."

Felicity had been taking in the entire exchange silently, but now couldn't help but to ask Elric, "You're letting them all go to the beach…in the daytime? Any escort you send would have to be human, right?"

"Yes…so?"

"Aren't you worried they'll leave?"

"Leave and go where?"

Felicity raised her eyebrows in surprise at his lack of concern. "Anywhere! They could run away down the beach, or swim to a passing boat or something!"

Elric laughed, and the girls looked equally amused. "Carmendy, you're not going to swim out to an island to escape me, are you?"

"Escape you?" she asked with a superior smile. "You can't get rid of me. I've put in some serious time here. I'm waiting for Latisha to retire so I can finally be your favorite! No offense, Tish."

Elric replied to Felicity, "It is a private beach with limited access, and trust me, the coven has well paid human security, so losing harem members is not a concern, but I wouldn't even bother with the escort if it wasn't coven protocol. They aren't going anywhere. Ask them yourself, I don't mind. Fulfill your curiosity. Ask them anything you want. I know their hearts."

Felicity waited a few seconds and then gave in to questioning the girls. "Don't you want to be free?"

"Free to go where, to do what?" Carmendy asked. "Look at where I live. Look at what I do all day. My clothes, my food, my friends…and I have the undying adoration of this magnificent sexy beast. Why would I leave?"

Felicity couldn't help but blush at Carmendy's obvious affection for Elric. It was very apparent that Latisha was also well satisfied to stay, but what about the others? They couldn't all be so happy, could they? She looked to see what Tia and Natalie thought of her question. They didn't say anything, seeming to think Carmendy's answer was sufficient. "I know you're addicted to his venom…" Felicity admitted quietly, suddenly realizing what an influential factor that could be.

Natalie laughed. "Fuck the venom. Not that I'd give it up, but it's not the addiction, it's everything. I signed up for this job. Best paid ten years of my life and enjoyable too. I've got three left and I wouldn't change a thing. I know some of the girls were involuntary recruits, but I think they're all pretty satisfied to stay."

Tia giggled and then covered her mouth shyly. "Sorry, but I was just thinking of evening check-in. I can't believe you thought they were drugging us!" she told Felicity. "I know you're new and you don't really get how things work here yet, but we're fine. We don't need you to worry for us, We're big girls and we know what we want."

Carmendy nodded. "Right now, I'm thinking I want to express my gratitude," she said with a wink at Elric.

Natalie leaned forward to give her a playful swat of reprimand. "Be grateful on your own night. She's right though. You don't have to worry about us. We're happy here."

Elric elaborated for Felicity's sake. "I'm sure you think they're just saying that because I'm here, but I do believe it's true. I have no heart or patience to keep someone in my home who does not wish to be here. I won't lie to you, there *are* vampires here who treat their humans like property they delight in keeping against their will, and have the right to abuse, but I am not one of them.

I carefully select members of my harem, because I plan to have a long relationship with them and I want them to be happy."

"What about the other humans," Felicity asked, "the ones kept by vampires who aren't like you?"

Elric sighed. "Arif is the coven master here, and he has final say over how the place is run. He makes the rules, but part of holding a high rank in this coven means that I have input on those procedures and rules. I regulate things as best I can…and then I mind my own business."

"Are there other high-ranking vampires here who think like you do?"

"Byron," Carmendy answered, but she received a stern look for it.

"A few," Elric supplied.

Felicity glanced towards the cadet vampires at the desk, but they weren't paying attention. "Then why do you stand for it?" she asked quietly. "Why do you put up with the others who abuse people?"

Elric stared at her long enough that she began to wish she hadn't asked, but then he answered. "I am the trusted captain of the senior guard in this coven…a rank I have worked very hard and long to attain, under the strict guidance of the coven master. I do my best to regulate things as I can."

Felicity lowered her voice to the softest whisper, knowing that Elric would be able to hear her. "Overthrow him. You could run this place the way you run your home, having consensual mutual relationships, instead of treating humans like slaves. You and the others should get rid of Arif and change things. I know Cain would help if you asked, and he knows others…."

Elric gave her a disapproving glare. She couldn't tell if it was for show, or if he really was abhorrent to the idea, but after the conversation she had overheard between he and Latisha, she felt she had to take a chance and throw it out there. Finally, he answered her gravely, although whether the answer was truthful, she hadn't a clue. "Madam, I would never entertain such a mutinous notion."

He rose from the couch, and held out his arm for Natalie to join him. "If you'll excuse us, ladies. I'm afraid this lively discussion has made me rather thirsty."

~~~~~~~~~~~~~~~~~~~~~~~~~~~~

Felicity spent the remainder of the evening with the rest of the girls of the house, watching television, and talking about nothing but pleasantries. Latisha kept near but seemed distant, refusing to do more than offer brief comment in the conversations. Felicity looked forward to the prospect of getting her alone before bed so they could really talk, but Latisha never gave her the chance. Once sequestered in the bedroom towards the dawn, she readied Felicity's bed and then went to the door. "I have to be down the hall for a bit. The guards will be at the door if you need anything. Get some sleep."

Was Latisha going to speak to Elric about trying to get Cain's help? Felicity wasn't sure what Cain could do, or whether she should have been so bold as to offer, but she knew Cain's heart. If he could help, he would. She would just have to wait and see what unfolded.

She finally fell asleep, and was awakened by Latisha's alarm just before sunset again. Latisha came and gave Felicity a nudge, as she walked by to get herself dressed and ready for the evening. "Come on," she urged Felicity. "We have to find you something to wear."

"What?" she asked groggily. "I can just wear my own clothes for another day. Maybe I can go home soon."

Latisha took Felicity's clothes off the chair and dumped them in a hamper in the corner. "First of all, they could use washing. Secondly, you have an audience with the coven master tonight. Into the shower, while I find you some clothes. If you aren't dressed well, it'll just tick him off."

Felicity sat up, rubbing her eyes with a frown of indignation. "I'm sorry, was I supposed to have planned to wear a formal gown for my impromptu kidnapping?" she asked, sarcastically.

"Don't sass me," Latisha replied with a sigh. "Come on. Once you're washed up we'll go try some stuff on you. There is a gorgeous selection of clothing that will fit you in Caroline's wardrobe."

Once Felicity had showered, wrapped herself in a robe and towel dried her hair, Latisha took her by the hand and led her down the hall, past the guards, to Caroline and Beverly's room. Eventually they found a simple but pretty sheath dress of green that the girls insisted contrasted beautifully with her hair color.

Felicity couldn't help but feel disheartened that she didn't look slimmer in it. It had been a while since she had worn anything other than loose sweats or yoga pants, and the extra baby weight was still stubbornly apparent. Luckily, the cut of the dress was as flattering as she could hope for, drawing attention up to her neckline, away from her tummy and hips. The flat shoes she had been wearing would work with the outfit, so that was one less concern. She hadn't bothered with heels in a while either, and didn't love the idea of trying to walk in them now.

"Why am I being taken to Arif…it's some kind of meeting?" she asked in excited trepidation. "Do you think I'm being sent home? Has someone come for me? Do you know what he wants from them in exchange?"

Latisha rolled her eyes. "Elric left a message that said bring Felicity to *Susuzluktan Saray* by 10 p.m. That's all I know."

Guards ever in tow, they walked next door to the beautiful mansion. Felicity paused before the grand house, taking in its splendor. Turrets and decorative finial-topped towers gave the sprawling estate the impression of being a royal castle. There was a circular driveway before the entrance, with a large fountain centered behind it, and the lawn was bordered by meticulously trimmed hedges and night-blooming flowers.

"*Susuzluktan Saray*. It means *Palace of Thirst,*" One of the guards told her with a grin, after observing that Felicity had stopped to take it all in.

Latisha checked her watch and then took Felicity's arm. "Come on."

They were checked in at the door and escorted to a large boardroom in the back of the house. Felicity needed to be nudged along several times, because she couldn't help but be distracted to stare at the opulent beauty and grandeur of the house. They were brought inside the meeting room, surprised to see that it was fairly full…of vampires.

A large table was in the center of the room, but hardly anyone was sitting at it. There were a dozen or so vampires standing around talking, until their entrance. Felicity and Latisha were the only visible humans in the room, and every vampire there seemed to sense it immediately. They all turned to look and assess the new arrivals. Felicity didn't recognize any of them, but she could swear a few of them tilted their heads a bit, as though catching her scent. Felicity was suddenly, painfully aware that she was unmarked, and to these vampires, that meant she could quite possibly be construed as the 'refreshments'.

Her vampire guards brought her to a clear space against the wall, where she and Latisha were apparently expected to stand and wait, for what she didn't know. Once they were settled, the guards promptly ignored the ladies and began to socialize. Felicity froze, in terrified silence, praying for the rest of the vampires to stop staring at her and go back to their previous conversations.

"Are you okay?" Latisha whispered.

As the concealing hum of conversation finally picked back up in the room, Felicity gave her a frightened glance. "We are in a sealed room with over a dozen bloodthirsty vampires," she responded quietly. "I realize that for you, this is just *Tuesday,* but for me, this is a good reason not to be okay. I'm freaking out!"

"No one is going to hurt you."

"You don't know that," Felicity whispered, harshly. "I know you live here, so maybe you're just desensitized or something, but these are vampires…blood drinking vampires. You get that, right? They may not have immediate plans to hurt me, but if I'm not useful to them, they also don't particularly care whether I live or die. When they look at us they don't see people, they see food."

"They aren't all like that, and you damn well know it. You've been a consort to a vampire before. It may have been a long time ago, but don't pretend you don't know better. Pull it together," she ordered, with a glance around the room. None of the vampires seemed to be observing them any longer, having moved on to other interests.

"Consort…? Oh. Cain is different," Felicity asserted. "He doesn't survive off of human blood. Vampires that drink from humans have a totally different vibe. Maybe you can't tell the difference, but I can. Cain only drank from me for marking…and for emotional reasons. I was never food. The vampires here would drain us dry in a second if they felt like it, because that's what we're for. We're like cattle to them."

Latisha raised her eyebrows and her voice in shocked insult. "Are you trying to tell me that you think my man sees me as food?"

Felicity was immediately chastened and quick to apologize. "I'm sorry. Elric seems to be above that."

"Damn right he is."

Felicity cracked a smile. "*Your man?* There are quite a few other ladies in that house who might see it differently. I thought he was your *master?*"

Latisha looked around to see that no one was observing them any longer. She moved closer to Felicity, to whisper. "Do I strike you as a woman who would have a master?"

"Not really, no."

"Hell no."

"That's why I don't understand why you're here…any of you. Especially knowing some of you actually signed up for it! Believe me, I get the attraction," she whispered grudgingly, trying to suppress the memories of being in Cain's bed that tried to surface. The way his touch had felt on her skin, how he'd savored her scent and kissed her throat… "But being kept *here* seems so stifling…and if you did love a vampire, why on earth would you want to share him?"

"I don't expect you to understand, but we're happy. We're a family. The others want security and being here gives them that. They have food, shelter and someone to take care of them while they're here, and financial security when they leave. As for me…" She lowered her voice to the barest whisper at Felicity's ear. "Elric and I have something that goes deeper than you'll ever know. He needs the others to feed him. They nourish his body and he satisfies theirs. I'm fine with that; I know his heart and that's what matters. This compound is where we live. It provides us both with safety, comfort, and luxuries under protection we wouldn't have elsewhere. In order to stay here, we play the parts. The word *master* is just a word. It means nothing to either of us, between each other, or used among vampires. Relax. Follow the rules, and you'll be just fine."

Latisha backed away, giving her a little pat on the back as she did. Felicity took a deep shuddering breath. "Easy for you to say. You're under marked protection. They all look at me like I'm on the menu." Latisha just shook her head dismissively and looked around the room. Felicity questioned her quietly. "Do you know all these vampires?"

"Not all of them, but most; some better than others. They're mostly Senior Guard, under Elric's direct supervision." She nodded discreetly towards a man who appeared to be in his mid-thirties. He had light brown hair and a haze of stubble across his face. He stood at the window, seeming uninterested in socializing with the others. "That's Byron, one of Elric's most trusted comrades."

Latisha discreetly pointed out a small group standing towards the center of the room; a woman with two men. The men were each fairly handsome, middle aged and large enough that another would think twice before crossing them, but the woman stole all attention. She was just as tall as the men, and had a strikingly strong sort of unconventional beauty. Her long, straight, golden blonde hair swung behind her when she turned to observe those around the room. "Those are Tomas, Richard and Lorelei. Lorelei was head of the guard before the position was given to Elric. It was her screw up that demoted her, but she's always resented him over it. She's the haughtiest bitch you'll ever meet," she added in a whisper.

Just then, the door opened and a woman walked through, commanding a silent pause in the room, for although her entrance was quiet, she had an air of importance about her…and she was gorgeous. A delicately featured beauty, she wasn't very tall, but held her head high. Her bright red copper curls were piled up and fastened with a headband that gave the distinct impression of a crown. Jewels dripped from her neck, drawing attention to her ample bosom, offset by her tiny waist. A man entered behind her, also arresting and darkly handsome, but he was overshadowed by his companion's radiant beauty. She spoke with a crisp British accent that made her sound somehow royal to Felicity, and a bit of a snob.

"Forgive our delay," the woman announced to the room, not sounding a wit apologetic. "You may take your seats to begin now." A vampire guarding the door leaned to politely inform the woman that they were indeed still awaiting the arrival of the coven master. She looked a bit annoyed that despite being fashionably late, she had not been late enough to have been awaited. After a moment of purse-lipped composure, she responded, "Well, if I am going to be made to wait, someone ought to bring me a drink while I'm kept idle, don't you think?"

Latisha leaned closer to Felicity to whisper, "Maybe I was hasty with the haughty bitch warning...looks like Lorelei may have some competition."

"Who's that?" Felicity asked in wonder.

"I have no idea... There aren't many woman in vampire society. The ones who can survive the brutality of such an existence, aren't usually the kind of women who tolerate each other well."

Someone brought the woman a wine goblet filled with blood, and she and her companion moved into the room to join Lorelei's group.

"Elric," Latisha said quietly at Felicity's shoulder.

Felicity looked, grateful for the promise of familiarity, but did not see him. "Where?"

Latisha had her eyes closed. "He's getting closer. He'll be here in a minute."

"Oh." She must feel the arrival of his mark.

As predicted, a moment later Elric entered, holding the door and stepping aside for Arif. As the coven master paused in the doorway, all vampires in the room fell silent, bowed their heads and then quickly took their seats at the conference table, making Felicity feel very exposed to attention, she and Latisha being the only ones left standing, besides Arif and Elric with the guards at the door.

While the head of the table was reserved for Arif, the foot of the table was where the redhead's companion moved to sit. He first pulled out a chair next to his for the woman, before taking his seat of honor. Elric briskly walked into the room, passing Latisha and Felicity with barely a pause, and going to the head of the table to pull out the chair for Arif. As

Arif neared them to pass, Felicity tried to flatten herself to the wall, wishing she were invisible.

Arif stopped before her, giving her a slight bow that seemed mocking rather than respectful. "The lovely Felicity, so glad you could join us. I do hope you've been kept in good health and spirits during your stay thus far."

"You..." Before she could think of a reply suitable to sum up her outrage and disgust over his absurd attempt at charm, after having her kidnapped and held prisoner, he captured her will with his gaze. His eyes were a hypnotizing mix of lavender and violet, the color filling each entire orb, swimmingly sparkling and beautiful. The color turned to deep purple as it converged upon the black slit of an upright pupil that drew her into its center.

Without thought or control, she found herself raising her hand to be taken into his for a kiss. Without breaking their gaze, he gently brought her fingers to his lips. Words tripped over her tongue of their own accord. "You are too kind, my lord, to have invited me into your coven's inner sanctum. I am truly honored."

Arif lowered her hand and smiled. "I'm sure you are."

He blinked his eyes, with a slight nod of his head, and once again he had the dark brown iris' and rounded pupils of a human man. He kept her attention for a moment more with a smirk, before moving on.

When he finally released her hand, she had to resist the urge to wipe it clean on the skirt of her dress. As an involuntary chill shivered down her back, her heartbeat began to quicken, thumping in her chest so hard and fast she worried that the vampires must hear it. She took a shuddering breath, and was for a moment startled by a touch at her hand once more. It was only Latisha. She slipped her soft, warm fingers into Felicity's and gave them a squeeze; a more human gesture, helping to calm and comfort her.

Arif had controlled her... He had controlled not only her actions, but her words as well. She had still felt like herself, thank God, being aware and of her own mind, but she'd had no control whatsoever over her behavior. What power! How could such a vampire be opposed? If he could so perfectly turn her hatred into apparent polite goodwill with such ease... What other devious acts could he coerce, without allowing even a voice to protest, but instead forcing spoken invitation? The thought was more chilling than the idea of any of these other vampires attempting to drink her blood. Let them drink if they would...but keep her actions her own...

Arif was taking his place at the table, standing next to Elric, who was holding his chair. "Thank you Elric," he said with a slight nod towards

Felicity, "I applaud you on yet another job well done. I can always count on you."

Before sitting, Arif seemed to remember something, turning back to the human ladies. "Latisha, congratulations to you as well. It is my pleasure to inform you that your status here has now become permanent. For your years of loyal service, I grant you unlimited invitation. Above and despite the regulation limits governing our other resident donors, for as long as you wish to remain, let *Kana Susamış İçin Ev* be considered your home." He looked around the room after his pronouncement, that all vampires should take note and acknowledge the allowance.

Latisha's soft voice quietly cut through the room in answer. "I humbly thank you, Master of my Master." Latisha stepped forward and performed an unexpectedly elegant but simple gesture of dance that culminated in a falling, sweeping bow of respect towards Arif. The motion ended with Latisha's head bowed down upon her arms, which were stretched forward to touch the floor.

Arif was quite pleased by the display. "You are indeed an asset to our community," he told her. "Take your leave of us now."

Latisha rose, with an uncertain glance at Elric. Both Latisha and Elric's eyes darted to Felicity. Latisha took Felicity by the arm to lead her from the room, but Arif reprimanded the action. "The woman stays,"

Latisha could do nothing but drop her arm and bow her head. "Yes, my Lord. Thank you." She gave him a quick curtsey and left the room.

"Lorelei," Arif called out as he finally took his seat. "While I am yet unfinished with Miss Felicity, perhaps it is best she not be present during vampire business. Take her out into the hall until I have need of her."

Lorelei looked annoyed to have been charged with a task she felt beneath her, and thereby excluded from the room, but then she rose with a gracious smile and a voice of saccharine obedience. "I'd be happy to."

Felicity watched, wide-eyed with dread, as the vampiress walked the length of the room to approach her. The woman almost looked as though she'd prefer to drain Felicity outside the door just to be rid of her, and return to the room. When she stopped before Felicity, true reason for dread unveiled itself. Lorelei's eyes transformed into purple portals of captivation, just as Arif's had. "Come with me."

Lorelei turned, and Felicity could do nothing but follow her out into the hall. The door to the room closed behind them with a loud and echoing sound. Before Felicity could even wonder where they might go, Lorelei gave her further instruction that could not be ignored. "You will wait here with your mouth shut, and your mind blank," she ordered.

The next thing Felicity knew, she was being led back into the room by Lorelei. She suffered a moment of disorientation, as she felt to have suddenly awoken from sleep while walking. Had anything else happened while she was out in the hall? She didn't think so, but she couldn't really remember. How much time had passed? It was very unsettling, not to know.

Some amount of time had apparently gone by, because most of the vampires within seemed to have left the room, although she couldn't recall noticing anyone having walked past her in the hall. The only vampires still present were Arif, Elric, the beautiful red-headed woman and her male companion.

The man remained seated at the far end of the table, long opposite the Coven Master. He was very handsome, with pale skin and dark hair and eyes, but although his appearance was attractive, something about him seemed very cold. Even Arif, wretch though he was, had an appealing allure that made the unsuspecting want to be drawn closer to him, while the other man made Felicity want to run away.

The man handed the woman next to him a briefcase he had just been given by Elric. "You don't mind, do you dear?" he asked, his European accent making his words sound very precisely enunciated. He barely gave her his attention, and did not seem to even entertain the idea that she might answer him to decline. The woman opened her mouth, but then closed it again, as though she'd thought better of arguing with him. She set the case on the table, opened it, and perused a few papers, forms of some sort. She seemed to decide that the details on the forms were in order, and began counting the apparently large sum of money that was also within the case.

Felicity was brought by Lorelei to stand at the corner of the table between Elric and Arif. Arif addressed them when they arrived, with a nod towards Lorelei, who then took a seat at the table on the other side of Arif. "Cain's *lady* of nights long past…we meet again. You're looking…human."

The words felt like a many barbed insult; Arif's way of acknowledging that for whatever reason, he thought Cain felt she hadn't been fit to turn, and as a result she was older, wearier, ever as vulnerable…human. She found herself unable to answer, which was just as well, considering the responses that sprang to mind.

"I hope I have not made a miscalculation estimating your worth. So far, you are not proving nearly as valuable as I had hoped. It seems Cain is no longer so eager to rush to your rescue." He looked her up and down, condescendingly. "I suppose I should have guessed."

Felicity tried to swallow over the lump in her throat. He was lying, he had to be. Human and married though she was, she knew Cain. He loved her, and even if he had never planned to see her again, he would not desert her while she was in need. He would rather die than leave her here in the hands of this creep. He would come for her...he had to.

Arif smirked at her, as though aware of her thoughts and amused. "Fortunately, I have other avenues through which you might be wielded to produce the result I desire. I'm sure *someone* would like to see you returned home, and will do as I ask to make it happen. I understand you married someone who knew the vampire Alyson before she was changed. I've sent an emissary to see if your husband might be of some use to us in gaining what I desire for your safe return. Tell me, does he keep in touch with his old friend? Does he have knowledge of *your* supernaturally murderous friends and sordid past?"

Felicity was shocked by the question... Did Arif really not know to whom she was wed? Before the thought could even fully form, Arif was distracted by the red-head at the other end of the table.

She looked up at him as she closed the case before her. "If you want something from Cain, you simply should have asked, darling. Under the right circumstances, the man is butter in my hands."

"How so?" Arif asked.

The woman's companion did not look pleased by the exchange. "Maribeth, I have asked you to remain uninvolved." The beginning of her name was pronounced as one would say the word 'marigold', with a short *i* sound, and the man's accent made it eerily familiar to her ears. "This is none of your affair."

Felicity suddenly stared at the woman with the fresh shock of recognition upon hearing her name... Maribeth.

It was like randomly encountering a celebrity you knew only from motion pictures or television, that you never thought of as a person you might actually someday meet. She had heard stories of this woman in intimate detail.

Maribeth was Cain's maker. Once the human wife of Cain's brother, she had tempted him from his own human wife, centuries ago, leading him down the road of sin and shame that had ultimately destroyed his life, and then she had drunk every last drop of his blood as the wreckage had barely settled.

She'd been abducted and turned into a vampire, and then returned to draw him into an unending sojourn upon the earth as one of the undead with her. To make matters worse, she had also drawn him into decades of decadent and deadly existence, killing, stealing, and ignoring any ethics of conscience and faith. It was only when he'd found the strength to break away from this woman, that he had been able to become the repentant guardian of human life that Felicity had fallen in love with so long ago.

Cain had even admitted to her that this woman had an unexplainable effect on him, that had not only seduced him against his better judgment, but now kept him from reducing her to dust. Her wiles had too often been his weakness, and although he professed to have outgrown her, he could not seem to harden his heart sufficiently to remove her from the world; deadly merciless as she might be.

Awe, fright, disgust, terror… Felicity stood and stared, her mouth agape. This was the woman who had so easily and completely captivated Cain with her irresistible charms, that Felicity had sought to emulate and then erase her from Cain's memory, the first time they had made love. Seeing her now, regal, haughty, contemptible, and yet undeniably an enchanting vision of beauty and grace, Felicity somehow felt a fool to have ever hoped to have outshined the woman, in terms of romantic appeal and temptation.

However, she was comforted by the woman's manner, to know that her own gentle, honest soul must have attracted Cain's kind heart more truly than Maribeth's, dead or alive. Cain had loved Felicity more than any other before her, he had said so himself. No matter Maribeth's mesmerizing allure; Felicity had won Cain's heart.

A moment of guilty reproach fluttered through her mind. She should not care who was greater in Cain's affections. She had a human husband of her own now, and Cain was free to cherish whomever he pleased.

Still, the past knowledge might serve her well. She thought back on Cain's brief and grudgingly vague accounts of his time with Maribeth after their change. He had described her as spoiled, fickle, maddening, and sometimes cruel, alternately dispensing loving adoration or despicable deeds of wickedness, depending on her quickly shifting moods.

Somehow, her ways seemed more chilling because she hid her intentions behind the polite and flowery façade of a 17th century noblewoman, a role she had always aspired to, but only very briefly attained and then lost while human. Her seductive smiles and poetic phrases of polite lies could have equal chance of being amusement to her, or veiling murderous intent. This was not a woman Felicity had ever wanted to come face to face with, even disregarding awkward aspects of their having a shared ex-lover.

Arif turned to gaze at Felicity, as though she had spoken her shock aloud. "Cain's maker?" he asked in astonishment, catching the knowledge from her mind, and then looking back to the pair at the other end of the table. "Drake, is this true?"

The man looked insulted, and answered, after giving Maribeth a disapproving glare. "You will address me as Master in mixed company," he told Arif, imposingly.

"Forgive me, Master. But is it true?"

"It is. This is she."

"Then why have you kept this valuable asset from me? You know influence with Cain could greatly assist my endeavors."

Drake narrowed his gaze. "Your endeavors are not my concern, and my consort is not an asset for you to wield. I only wished to be kept abreast of your progress. I have no intention of becoming involved in the messy aspects of it. We are done here for tonight. Come Maribeth."

He stood from the table and put out his arm for Maribeth to accompany him from the room. She looked up at him before rising. "But Drake dear, perhaps we should hear him out. I'm curious." His eyes flashed purple and he gave her a look of dark foreboding that made her quickly stand. She took the case in one hand and Drake's arm in the other. Both Arif and Elric stood in polite deference to her impending exit, although Lorelei remained seated. Maribeth turned to smile politely at the men. "Best of luck then," was all she managed to say before Drake briskly escorted her from the room.

The moment the door closed behind them, Lorelei took Arif's attention. "Master, I have news." She looked distant for a moment, receiving some psychic communication from elsewhere. Elric took the opportunity to meet Felicity's eyes with a small smile of reassurance. Then Arif became agitated. Lorelei must have relayed the news to him telepathically.

"Are you sure?" Arif asked aloud, with a dangerous edge. Lorelei only nodded. Arif stood from the table. "Well, it seems our meeting is cut short. I have arrangements to make concerning others."

"Perhaps Cat could be of assistance," Lorelei suggested with a grin.

Arif considered her proposal and grinned. "Indeed. Elric, thank you again for your service. That is all."

Elric stood and moved towards Felicity, but Lorelei stopped him. "The girl is coming with me," she announced with some sinister glee. "She'll remain safe here within the walls of *Susuzluktan Saray*, until the master arranges for an exchange."

202

Felicity's heart sank and she gave Elric a desperate glance, but there was nothing he could do. He gave her a look of piteous apology, before he bowed his head to Lorelei, and followed Arif out the door.

Chapter 9 - Insurance

Sindy

Kana Susamiş Icin Ev
Montauk, Long Island, New York
Earlier that evening

Sindy awoke with the nightfall, unsettled to find that while she could feel the warmth of Val's comfortable form through her nightclothes, still spooning her from behind, the bed in front of her was cold and empty. "Where's Brett?"

Val's voice answered her, groggy with sleep. "He had a class."

"What class?" she asked in confused alarm.

Val cracked an eye open as he rolled to face him. "I don't know." When it was obvious she wasn't going to accept that as an answer, Val was forced to actually wake up a bit and think on it to give her a true response, however grudgingly. "Social grace and etiquette or some shit."

"I don't remember him telling me he had that tonight."

Val sighed and rubbed his eyes. "It's a required class. It's on the schedule."

"Do you have any classes tonight?"

She could tell that he was a bit grumpy to have his sleep disturbed. Apparently, he wasn't a 'morning person'…even at nine o'clock at night. "No. We've been with you for like two weeks. Don't you know the routine by now?"

"Nine nights," she corrected him.

"We alternate. Stop worrying. I'm here with you all night to attend your every need. I have my classes and duties tomorrow night. Then Brett can stay here to answer all of your questions and tell you to stop being paranoid."

She sat up and looked down at him with an offended stare. It was true that Sindy had been terribly on edge since Zach's disappearance, making her much less fun of a mistress than she might have normally been for these guys, but it wasn't Val's place to show his disappointment over her short patience. He was usually subservient and respectful, but maybe the novelty was wearing off a bit for him. "You're not trying very hard for that bonus lately, huh?"

He became immediately repentant and gave her a small smile. "Please forgive the tone," he said, while finding her hand to bring to his lips for a kiss. "But the comment was justified. You need to relax. Lay down and snuggle with me." He still held her hand, and pulled it to wrap her arm around him.

"I don't feel like snuggling."

He rolled back over to look up at her with a sigh. "You're so tense. Why don't I give you a nice massage?"

"Oh sure, now you want to suck up to me," she shot back with a smirk.

"Miss Sindy, I will suck anything you desire. That's what I'm here for."

"No thanks. I'll be the one doing the sucking, but first, let's have a chat. Has anyone been asking you questions?"

"Just you, mistress."

He sounded dangerously close to being snide, but she ignored it. "Have you met with the coven master, Arif?"

Val sat up a bit, nodding. "I've met him. All the humans have to spend an initiation period under his supervision before we're allowed to serve vampires of the coven. He approved my placement here with you."

Sindy tried not to show her impatient annoyance with his answer. "I know, but have you met with him more recently?"

"No. Is something wrong?" She shook her head, but he was unconvinced. "It's that Zach guy, isn't it? Ever since you found out that he left, you've been acting all jumpy. Are you worried about him?"

"No. I'm sure he's fine. It's not a big deal at all." She sat in silence for a moment, knowing she was walking a fine line as to how much she should say. Without Zach's flying ability, she didn't know how she was going to manage to get out of here on her own. The fact that Zach had obviously flown the coop without her was making her feel very disheartened about her own chances of escape. She couldn't fly! She might shift into her bat and see if that was enough just to get her through the fence, but she hadn't worked up the nerve to try it.

It might prove easier to play along for a while and see if some better opportunity offered. However, not knowing Arif's stance on things was keeping her on edge and really paranoid. "I just don't understand why Arif hasn't spoken to me about Zach's disappearance."

Val shrugged. "Maybe he doesn't know."

She fixed him with a discriminating stare. "With all of his underlings, lackeys and spies…you don't think he knows *everything* that goes on in this place?"

"No, I don't. That's like assuming that the company boss knows what glitches and screw-ups the secretaries whisper about around the water-cooler. I think that *he thinks* he knows everything he needs to know, but when you have that many people working in an organization, you can't assume everyone always reports what they should. I'm sure he thinks everything is always under control here in his own backyard, whether it's true or not. Either he doesn't know, or he knows and doesn't care because it's not a concern."

"You're right. Zach was just a nobody vamp that I dragged here with me. Why should Arif care if he left? One less mouth to feed."

"So why are you so worried about it?"

"I'm not. Forget it."

"Look, if this is some kind of problem for you, then let me help. What are we dealing with here? What can I do? Do you think he might still be in the compound? Because, I know this place really well. I can help you find him. I could show you secret tunnels and places that no one else would even know to look."

She stared at him for a moment, suspiciously, and then adopted an expression of distressed surprise. "Val, I'm surprised at you, suggesting I go sneaking around where I don't belong. I would never violate the hospitality of the coven master that way."

He was momentarily confused and a bit chastened, but then he began to grin. "You think I'm setting you up. I'm not though. I'm sorry if that was out of line, but I just want to help. You can trust me, really. Can't you tell that? When you bite me, it's so…it's pretty amazing. I know it's even more than that to you. It's like you possess me, totally, so intimately… Can't you like, read my mind and stuff? I wouldn't dare lie to you."

She smiled at him, content to leave him guessing about her abilities. Before coming here, it had been a long time since she'd interacted with a human who knew what she was. Drinking from Val and Brett had solidified their amorous addiction to her, but other than that, she had interacted with them more as equals than as a vampire should. In this unfamiliar territory, with her worry and uneasiness, she hadn't truly been enjoying the benefits of mastering them, and had let them become a bit too comfortable with her. She should remember to use awe and curiosity to her advantage, along with a tiny, but ever present, dose of fear, of course.

She shifted into her vampire state, just to add a mesmerizing and intimidating edge to her words. "I know you wouldn't try to lie to me, Val. That would be incredibly stupid on your part," she agreed with a sinister, fang tipped grin. "You're not stupid, are you Val?"

He shook his head, staring in wonder at her paranormal appearance. She gave him a more sincere smile. "Neither am I. I know you crave my approval and attention, which I am very happy to give you, but I also know who pays the bills.

You're not just here for the truly amazing experiences I can provide; you're here for the money. I can approve all the bonuses you want, but I'm not the one paying it out in the end. So no matter how loyal you may be, when the coven master decides to take you back and pick your brain, anything I wouldn't want him to know, had better not be in there, for your sake and mine.

You're nothing to him. He could have you for a snack and feed your body to his dogs." She let the truth of that statement sink in for second before she continued. "I am a vampire of great power," she assured him, "but I am also a grateful member of his court, who follows the rules, and trusts her loyal humans to feed her, and keep her warm in bed, nothing more. Got that?"

"Yes miss."

His heartbeat had quickened with her words, betraying his nervous excitement over her inhuman authority. She needed to remember her place here, and theirs. As much as it had been nice to feel she could have a confidant in this unfamiliar and possibly hostile territory, this man was supposed to be nothing more to her than a warm body; a sex slave, servant and food. No matter what her larger problems here may be, she was on her own.

Val remained silent and motionless, gazing at her crimson eyes in awe. Her vampire sight showed the hot blood within him, beckoning her to drink. She licked her lips and leaned closer, to whisper to him softly. "Now…let the sucking begin."

~~~~~~~~~~~~~~~~~~~~~~~~~~~~~~

Sindy crossed the road and made her way from the little row of shops and services, back towards Kieran's estate that she had become very quickly accustomed to thinking of as her own, being the only ranking vampire in residence.

The dresses she had been fitted for were finished, and she had spent a lovely evening at the coven seamstress' shop, trying them all on and choosing more shoes and bags to match. All of this, after another spa treatment at the salon. She was definitely getting used to life here at *Kana Susamiş İçin Ev.*

As she neared the house, she noticed Elric had just emerged from Arif's mansion, *"The Palace of Thirst"*, or *Susuzluktan Saray,* as the coven master liked to call it. Elric's path would be converging with Sindy's as she passed his home to get to her destination.

She felt a warm current of relief upon seeing him, although there was truly no good reason for it. She didn't know him well, but he was the only vampire here that she had known prior to her current situation, and who had shown her a hint of kindness. She met him with a smile, pausing in his path after hoisting her shopping bags a bit higher to keep them from the ground. "Elric, you're back."

He seemed preoccupied, and she was disheartened to observe that he didn't look particularly happy to see her. She knew she didn't mean much of anything to him, but he'd usually seemed at least appreciative of her appearance and cordially charming in the past. Now he just looked very aggravated and annoyed to be delayed by her for pleasantries.

Elric was always well dressed, and there was something very alluring about seeing this huge man wearing perfectly fitted dress shirts, cardigans and slacks. He never looked flashy or smug, but he was definitely a man who took pride in his appearance, even without a mirror. His large, muscular form had always struck her as incredibly sexy, and he had a handsome face as well, but at the moment, his dark mood suddenly made him seem more intimidating than comforting, familiar or not.

Seeing that he didn't seem inclined to stop, Sindy began walking so that he would hopefully be happier to speak with her without worry for delay. "How'd it go?" she asked.

He didn't seem to know what she was asking. She tried again, giving him a conspiratorial grin. "Weren't you supposed to be out kidnapping someone? Whiney human woman, red-head, just pretty enough to turn a man's head, but too insipidly sweet and stupid to use it to her advantage...you know who I'm talking about."

Elric stopped and stared at her for a moment, in the way that any normal, innocent person might look if she had randomly asked them how a kidnapping had gone. But Elric was not a normal or innocent person, he was an elder vampire, whom Sindy was certain had been involved in much darker activities than kidnapping in the past. So, why did he seem to find her questioning so unsavory?

"The woman Cain favors…Felicity," he provided grudgingly.

Sindy's eyes narrowed to a slit at his description. Felicity was the one woman who had managed to keep Cain's attention, despite time and distance, while Sindy had to fight to keep him focused on her, even while she was in his very bed. *The woman Cain favors…* "That's her," Sindy confirmed. "How'd it go?" She glanced Elric over again, and tried to envision how he might look to Felicity. She had to smile. Undoubtedly, the woman had found him terrifying.

"How am I supposed to answer that?" He had a distant look in his eyes, almost speaking more for himself than for her. "There are very few things I have been a part of here that I can honestly say 'went well'. As a matter of fact, I think the entire mission was a fucking disaster."

Sindy squinted at him curiously. "I wouldn't think snatching an unsuspecting human woman half your size should have been very difficult for you."

He stared at her for a second before answering. "That's part of the disaster," he replied. "Excuse me, but I've got some plans to make," he said shortly, leaving Sindy behind.

What the hell did that mean? Did he manage to kidnap the bitch, or not?

It wasn't that Sindy wasted much time thinking about Felicity lately, or wanted anything truly bad to happen to her; she didn't really care *that* much. However, Sindy had been chasing Cain since before he had even met Felicity. After all of Sindy's efforts, the way that little Miss Priss had casually captivated the man was almost insulting. If Arif had plans to abduct her and disrupt her perfect little human life for a bit, Sindy felt zero guilt over enjoying the idea. Arif wouldn't actually kill her; he wasn't stupid enough to turn Cain that drastically against him. After the indignities Sindy had suffered, knowing Felicity had a good scare and some discomfort coming her way was kind of satisfying.

Elric had rushed off to his home, so Sindy was just going to have to forget about Felicity for now. If the mission had failed through some screw-up on Elric's part, Arif would find some other way to get what he wanted; he always did.

Sindy was just happy that Arif seemed focused on things other than her right now. She would head back to Kieran's, and keep herself out of trouble and otherwise occupied until she could learn what was going on in the big picture.

Sindy stood on the porch, shifting her bags so she could try to open the front door before her. Telepathy sure would come in handy right now. She needed to call Val or Brett to come and help her with all of her new clothes and things.

She wondered who was scheduled to attend her tonight. Although the guys alternated being at her beck and call, they often hung around the house even when they weren't scheduled, unless they had other duties, so she sometimes lost track.

She finally got the door open and approached the vampire cadet at the desk before her. "Don't just sit there, help me." He cocked an eyebrow at her, rather than rush to help, which was really annoying. She let out a huff of disgust. "Fine. Page Val and Brett to come down and take my bags."

"Sorry, I can't do that." She looked up at him with a harsh scowl for his disobedience, but he was quick to explain. "They just left."

"Both of them? I didn't authorize that."

"I know," the cadet answered with a smirk. "He did." The vampire pointed to the sitting room off to the side. Arif was there, standing with his hands clasped before him and with a large attendant on either side of him.

He seemed to enjoy her astonishment at seeing him so unexpectedly. "Sindy, my dear, you look lovely as always. I see you have been enjoying the benefits you have been granted."

She dropped the bags at her feet, in as dignified a manner as she could manage. "Arif, what a pleasant surprise," she said with a false smile to hide her shock. "I was beginning to think you'd forgotten about me," she scolded him teasingly as she came forward to take his hands and give him a kiss on the cheek.

He was taken aback by the reception, and she worried it was too much, but a little smile stole over his face to let her know that she had pleased him. "I'm a busy man. I'm afraid business has kept me from paying you a visit sooner, though I've missed your signature blend of seductive wiles and snide wit."

She gave him a sly smile. "Well, you have this whole coven to run. Of course, you're busy. Your compound is amazing. I don't know how you do it."

He observed her for a moment, and then gestured to the open door. "Take a walk with me."

She tried not to show hesitation as she walked out the door, leaving her bags behind. Was he taking her back to his quarters again, to be either threatened and beaten, or ravaged and adored? She had no clue. Her mark from Cain had weakened, but was still in force.

Did Arif know about Zach's disappearance? He had to know. For all she knew, he might have had Zach taken into custody the moment he was out of her sight, and have him locked in a cellar somewhere. Maybe she should tell him, express concern and keep him unsuspicious of her.

Arif walked silently beside her, making her feel uncomfortable, as though he expected her to speak first. "I've been hoping to have time to talk to you," she began cautiously. "I didn't want to bother you with trivial stuff though. I know you have a lot to oversee."

"My time is precious, but I'm here now. Tell me your concerns. Have the humans I provided not been to your liking?"

"Oh, they're great. Thank you for them. Did you send them somewhere?"

"Not to worry, they're accounted for. I see you have been enjoying the amenities at your disposal, so what's troubling you?"

"Well, I haven't seen Zach in a while. Did you have him moved to other quarters?" Better to let him think she assumed he knew what was going on better than she did.

He squinted, assessing her for a moment. "That is just what I have come to speak to you about. It has come to my attention that your protégé, is currently unaccounted for. I thought you might tell me where he was."

She widened her eyes. "I don't know. I assumed he was in some lucky lady's bed somewhere. I didn't realize he was unsupervised. I'm sure he'll turn up."

"Yes. However, given your attachment to him, as his maker, I'm sure you could have determined his whereabouts the moment you thought to look for him."

"I didn't though. I haven't got a clue where he is, I swear. I don't feel him at all. This place is pretty spread out though. I guess he could be over at the performance studio with his guitar, or maybe he's shooting hoops down at the basketball court."

Arif gave her a look of disbelieving reprimand. "I'm sure your perceptions reach further than that." As they walked, Sindy noticed they were approaching the common house. Arif led them up the pathway and then paused at the entrance to the building. His guards waited attentively to open the door for him when he was ready to enter. "Have you felt his presence since you returned from your stay in my chambers?" Arif asked her.

She paused, trying not to seem disgruntled by the memory, or alarmed by his questioning. "Um…I don't think so, but I can't say I really noticed. I haven't drunk from him since the night we got here, so our bond isn't all that strong. Anyway, I've been pretty preoccupied with the generous gifts you left for me."

"Indeed." Arif gestured for the door to be opened, and led them inside. "That is all you have to say? You have nothing more to offer on the subject?"

"I'm sorry, but I can't say we were all that close. I just made him for Allie. I don't know him very well and I don't know where he'd go," she insisted as they entered and crossed the common room, past the sitting area and bar, towards a desk that guarded a door in the back. Other vampires and humans watched their progress curiously, but Arif acted as though they did not exist. Sindy continued as she followed him, flanked by his guards. "I was curious if you'd moved him, because I would hate for him to be getting into trouble and disrupting your community, but since I hadn't heard anything, I wasn't really worried about it...until now, I guess. Why would he leave someplace that was giving him fresh blood and babes? That doesn't make sense. He's got to be here somewhere."

Rather than answer, Arif led her to the door and opened it for her, revealing stairs to a lower level. She didn't really know what was down there, never having been through the door, but considering snippets of conversation she had heard in the past, and the way the humans always avoided the area of checkpoint before the door at all costs, she had a feeling it wasn't good. She glanced at the door, and then back at him. "Where are we going?"

Arif ignored her immediate question, instead giving her a more encompassing explanation. "A thorough search has proved that Zach is no longer within the community, and I cannot risk that you may somehow follow his departure. I still have need of you here."

"How could anyone just leave? There are guards everywhere." Arif didn't offer comment, but he didn't look happy about the fact that his formidable security had somehow been breached.

Sindy looked back at the stairs in alarm, the term 'reform cellar' coming back to her from an overheard conversation. "It doesn't matter anyway. I'm not going anywhere. There is so much opportunity for me here, why would I leave? Especially after our last conversation about possible positions you might offer me," she reminded him, with a hint of sexual innuendo. She'd been uncompromising while in his bed, but she understood that he almost enjoyed it as being all part of the hunt; the chase and struggle before the kill, as it were. He could have raped her easily, but he'd rather play mind games and feel he had tamed her. "I've thought a lot about what I could have here, and I think I'd like to stick around."

"Wonderful, and I will be sure of that. I regret to inform you that the dignified freedom you had been granted must be so short lived, but I cannot be constantly worried for your whereabouts."

"So you're going to lock me up?" Sindy asked in outrage.

"No, of course not. I save such extremes for those who have greatly disappointed me in some way. I can see that you have done nothing but try to make yourself pleasing to me, since the time we spent together in my chambers," he assured her, with a very appreciative glance over her appearance. She was wearing one of her new dresses, a short, tight, red number that hugged her curves beautifully. Her long black hair and new leopard print heels and bag really made it pop. She knew she looked stunning.

He continued with a grin. "I have been contemplating how I might ensure your continued residence with us until initiation, without compromising either your freedom and enjoyment of my home, or my coven's security. I have come up with a compromise I believe to be fair and comforting. Come with me."

He descended the stairs, and she had no choice but to follow, his goons closing in and descending behind her. They came down the stairs to a small landing entryway into a nicely finished basement. It was a warm and inviting oak paneled room, but there was an odd sort of table standing tilted upright in the back. The table had straps secured to the sides of it, evidently to be used as restraints. Standing next to the table, awaiting their arrival, was Jin, the vampire who had so effectively cancelled out her shifting abilities during her last visit with Arif.

"What is this place?" Sindy asked in alarm.

"I thought it best if we could handle things in more controlled, private surroundings." In emphasis of the statement, one of the guards closed the door, making the space suddenly silent and cut off from the comfortable sounds of light music and conversation upstairs.

"There's nothing to handle," she insisted. "I'm telling you the truth. I have no idea where Zach is. You imprison people down here. I haven't done anything to deserve that!"

"No, of course not. I want you to continue to enjoy your stay in my community with the freedom to move about the grounds as you please. However, until I am able to put my mark upon you, I cannot be certain of your complete dedication. As a shape-shifter, you have the unique ability to evade the community guards…as you so deftly demonstrated for me in my bed chambers."

She lowered her eyes in regret over the display. She should have better controlled her temper, knowing it wouldn't really get her anywhere but into trouble.

Arif continued his explanation. "That jeopardizes the security of my home and makes my coven very uncomfortable. You can understand that, can't you? The idea that you might take it upon yourself to leave us is a bit troubling. I cannot allow that possibility at this critical time.

So, regrettably, I must deny you your shifting ability for the time being. I am sure you will agree that is a fair compromise. With that small concession, you can still enjoy complete freedom here without causing concern."

"Some freedom. I have to have Jin follow me everywhere I go? Is he going to sit in the corner and watch me sleep, too? And when I'm in the shower?"

Jin made a derogatory face at the suggestion. "Trust me, that wouldn't be my dream assignment, princess. I've got better things to do than babysit and gawk at you."

Arif chuckled at the remark. "Dear me, no. Jin is far too valuable a resource as a member of my senior guard for such a mundane task. His talents are in demand elsewhere, and you are a lady deserving of your privacy. Now that you are behaving with the dignity I expect of you, I would not think to compromise you in such a manner."

"And just how *are* you willing to compromise me?" she asked him warily. "How do you plan to keep me from shifting?"

"Another of my senior guards has developed a rather ingenious procedure for such a predicament."

"Procedure?" she repeated flatly. "Can't say I like the sound of that."

Arif smiled as though she had praised his resources. "One of Cat's contributions. I don't think you've yet had the pleasure of making her acquaintance. She is a woman of some unique, although odd, genius. A bit daft in her ways…but smart as a whip."

Sindy wore a tight-lipped grin. "She sounds darling, but you know, Jin isn't actually all that bad. Maybe he *should* just keep me company for a while. I'm sure he'd be much more reliable than some crazy procedure."

Arif gave her a grin meant to reassure her. "Sindy, my dear, there is no need for alarm. I can assure you that the effects are only temporary and completely reversible. There will be no permanent damage."

"Damage?" she confirmed in alarm. "You plan to damage me?"

"Relax. It's been fully tested and is perfectly safe. Jin has other assignments, and I'm sure you'd rather continue the indulgence of the accommodations and freedom you have been granted, than spend your time here chained to my bedposts. Let me put my mind at ease, and we can all go back to enjoying our evening."

It sounded too reasonable to argue, but she was still slightly terrified to learn what he had in mind. He took her hand to move her closer to the table, admiring the shift of her tight skirt as she walked. "That is a lovely dress, by the way. Is it of your own design? Isn't our seamstress a wonder? So talented. Stunning garment. It suits you. Take it off, please."

"Excuse me?"

"Your dress. I wouldn't want it to be ruined. Remove it please."

"How's it going to get ruined?"

"It isn't, because you're going to take it off now." He placed his hands on her shoulders and gently spun her around to unzip the dress for her. "Don't worry, you can have it back as soon as we're through."

Sindy allowed him to remove the dress and hand it to one of his guards, who carefully draped it over a chair in the corner. She stood in bra and panties as the men played their eyes over her. They seemed very appreciative of what they saw. Too bad she couldn't enjoy it. She felt as though she was waiting for execution. "How is this procedure done, exactly? Does it hurt?"

Arif gestured toward the table, and the guards moved forward to help Sindy over to it. After a moment of frightened hesitation, she allowed them to strap her to it. It wasn't as though she had much of a choice. Arif smiled at her cooperation, and answered her prior question. "I'm afraid it will be a bit uncomfortable, but I'm not concerned. You're a strong girl."

Before Sindy had time to worry any more, the door to the stairway swung open and an accented soprano voice cut through the room, demanding attention. It was high pitched and breathy like a poor imitation of an oriental Marilyn Monroe. "I'm here kiddies. Are we ready?"

The woman dropped her bag at the door and waltzed into the room as though walking a red carpet, head held high, shoulders back, chest out, pausing within the room to pose, as though for a photo. If the paparazzi *were* here, they'd be having a field day...so would the Fashion Police.

Cat was tiny and fair, and had probably once looked like a beautiful little china doll, but now she looked more like something out of Cirque Du Soleil. Fluorescent yellow hair was teased into a cloud around her head, with streaks of bubble gum pink and a blinding orange that hurt your eyes.

Her false eyelashes were so long and adorned with orange glitter, that it was a wonder the woman could see.

She wore a short, cute little pink and orange jacket over a revealing yellow bustier, with a printed mini-skirt that practically defied gravity with its stiff flare, over yellow leggings and tall pink boots. The heels on her boots were of an odd design, being terribly high, but with no true heel. All of the lift was gathered under the ball of the foot, and they were so high, Sindy couldn't imagine how the woman was actually walking in them. It must take superior balance and control, but the woman made it seem effortless.

Her outfit had very clean, bold, futuristic lines to it, but was so overwhelmed with minute details of pins and appliqués, that it was difficult to take in and decipher, although everything was impeccably matched and obviously chosen with great care. The color scheme matched her hair, and the theme seemed to be stars and planets. The overall effect looked like someone had taken a glue gun to Judy Jetson, and crafted her within an inch of her life using spot-on accessories.

Sindy took in the appearance of the woman in disbelieving awe. "I'm being tortured by Effie Trinket???" she quipped with a raised eyebrow.

Arif swept forward to take Cat's hands into his own and cover them with kisses. "Cat, you twisted temptress. You look arresting, as always. We are ready for you, my sweet."

Sindy tried not to gag at the display. Jin saw her reaction and moved closer to whisper, "That's Cat. She's Harajuku."

"Hara…what?"

"It's a district in Tokyo; kind of a fashion mecca."

Cat strode towards them, giving Jin a superior smirk and refusing to ignore his whispered explanation. "Harajuku isn't just a location, it's a way of life. I transcend fashion. I am an ever evolving work of artistic mastery in personal expression through fashion." After posing with her hands in the air for them to take in her full vision, she moved closer to Sindy, strapped on the table, which was tilted vertically so it was almost standing upright.

Sindy couldn't help but stare at the headband the woman wore, which allowed a tiny, sparkly star and moon to dangle above her head at a jaunty angle. Cat grasped Sindy's hand within its restraint, checking her nails. They were bright red, each tipped with a swath of leopard spot design from her recent trip to the salon. Cat seemed to approve. "You've got a bit of style to you."

Then, catching Sindy off guard, she let go of her nails to pinch and squeeze Sindy's cheeks. "Pretty face. Can I start there?" she asked, turning to Arif.

Arif spoke to intervene. "Now, Cat, I cannot allow you to pollute such natural beauty. Besides, I have promised to leave her with a measure of dignity. Keep it subtle and coverable please, as long as it's effective."

Cat practically ignored him, turning Sindy's face this way and that to look at her. "Cheek piercings are in," she insisted. She dropped Sindy's face to better assess the rest of her body. "Besides, she's so scrawny. I need some meat to work with. That means I'll need to use what I can, undignified or not," she added with a very impolite tweaking of Sindy's right breast through her thin, lace bra.

Arif sighed. "Very well, but discreet please."

Sindy caught his gaze over Cat's shoulder with an angry stare. "Very well? No, it's not well. Not at all. What's she going to do to me?"

"What's she going to do to me?" Cat repeated, mockingly. "*Shizumaru.* You just relax yourself. I am going to keep you from wearing these chains for the next month, that's what."

"How?"

"With a brilliant invention of mine," Cat answered smugly. She snapped her fingers and one of the guards moved to bring her bag from where she'd left it. Once in her possession, she pulled from it a power tool about a foot in length. She brandished it proudly, and after a moment of observation Sindy was able to conjecture what it was, having had a father who had worked construction jobs...until she'd killed him.

Her eyes went wide at the realization. "You invented a nail gun?"

"It's a modified nail gun, smart ass. Now it shoots these." She pulled a small box out of the bag and held it up for Sindy to see.

"Toothpicks...seriously? What the hell is that going to do?"

Cat scowled at her in annoyance. "If I put one through your heart it will shut you up damn fast."

Sindy narrowed her eyes in derision as Arif intervened. "Now Cat, I think Miss Sindy deserves an explanation. After all, she is being very cooperative."

"Cooperative my ass," Sindy interjected, impatiently. "What's it for?"

Cat backed off, put the power-nailer down on a table off to the side, and pursed her lips as she eyed Sindy. She seemed to be deciding just how thorough of an explanation Sindy was capable of comprehending. She picked up the box of cocktail toothpicks and moved closer once again, rattling the sticks inside with rhythmic shakes of the box.

"Our blood cannot abide contact with wood, you must know this." She opened the box and pulled out a large toothpick, adorned with little loops of transparent yellow cellophane at the tip. She brought it closer to Sindy, pinched between her fingers like a dart about to be thrown. "That is why when it pierces the heart," she said, just touching the tip of the toothpick to the bared skin above Sindy's bra, with a sharp prick, "the epicenter of a vampire, the vampire explodes into dust. It's like a severe and instantly fatal allergic reaction."

She continued, while dotting little pricking touches of the point to Sindy's skin in various places. Sindy tried not to give the woman the satisfaction of seeing her squirm as Cat continued her explanation. "That is because the main seat of control for vampire blood in a human body is the heart. Think of your body as a hive for lots of little vampire-blood bees, and sitting in your heart is the queen," she said, with a last sharp little jab at Sindy's breast. It didn't draw blood, but it made Sindy let out a small gasp that brought a smile to Cat's face.

Satisfied, Cat gave up teasing Sindy with the toothpick and instead began to play with her long dark hair. "The secondary control center, seat of the king perhaps, is in the hub of the central nervous system, the brain stem, which is why beheading is also fatal. These two leaders, the king and queen, they need each other. Without one or the other, the body is lost, and the blood self-destructs." Cat dropped the strands of Sindy's hair she had been admiring, and suddenly addressed her directly with a demanding tone. "What happens if you are staked elsewhere?"

Sindy swallowed the lump in her throat, remembering various times she had been stabbed with a piece of wood, and managed to survive. "Nothing. It hurts, but we heal."

Cat smiled and patted her on the head as though she was a good doggie. "The blood can retreat to other parts of the body before more than a few cells turn to ash. Once the stake is removed, the vampire blood can safely return to the area and repair the damage." Cat held up the toothpick again to admire its point. "But what if the wood is not removed?"

As she asked the question, she turned with blinding speed and threw the toothpick like a tiny dart, with inhuman precision and force, to embed itself into the side of Jin's neck. The action was so fast that it took a moment for the occupants in the room to even realize what had happened when Jin let out a grunt of pain.

Jin gingerly felt around the spot for a moment. The toothpick was buried in his throat almost to the cellophane. Cat smiled and blew him a kiss before turning back to Sindy. "What if the wood remained buried in his flesh?"

Sindy wanted to enjoy Jin's discomfort, but was too busy pondering Cat's question. She thought back to the time Allie had tried to pierce her ears. The earrings weren't wooden, but they had been forced by their backings to stay in place. The concept was similar. "It wouldn't heal."

Jin plucked the thing from his neck and threw it back at Cat, but without her unmatched speed and agility, he couldn't hope to do any damage with it. It barely touched her shoulder before it hit the floor. She gazed at him in disapproval, her eyes now a bright pink color, nearly bright enough to match the shades of neon bubblegum in her hair.

She turned back to Sindy with a broad grin. It was very disturbing. "That's right. If the wood is not removed, healing is slowed to an almost human rate, because the vampire blood won't risk contact with the substance. It hides away in other parts of the body until the threat is gone."

Sindy still didn't understand how this fit together with her impending procedure. "What good are non-fatal stake wounds going to do?"

"When a portion of your body does not contain significant amounts of vampire blood, not only is it unable to heal, it also cannot change shape. It is the vampire blood that takes apart each portion of your body to be reassembled into something new. If the vampire blood cannot reach a part of your body, that part will remain locked in form. Now do you see where this is going?"

"So, you're going to shoot me up with toothpicks, to keep me looking human?" Sindy asked in mild horror.

Cat nodded. "Basically, yes. Pretty cocktail toothpicks."

"Why? What's the cellophane do?"

Cat looked up from admiring another toothpick she had pulled from the box. "Nothing. The first model I constructed used golf tees. They worked alright, but they were so big that they left awful lumps and welts. Toothpicks are sleeker."

"Okay...but why use the kind with cellophane?" Sindy repeated, grudgingly thankful that toothpicks were indeed much thinner and sharper than a golf tee.

Cat grinned. "I just think it's funny...and fashionable. You'll look like you have multi-colored measles when they start to come back out," she conjectured with a giggle. "Let's get this party started," she said, holding up the toothpick towards Arif for his approval. He stood in the back of the room, observing silently with arms crossed, and gave Cat a small nod.

Cat retrieved her air-gun and turned back to Sindy, showing her the toothpick before inserting it. "Oh look, a pretty red one to match your eyes."

Sindy searched out Arif on a wave of panic and met his gaze. "Arif, are you really going to let her do this to me? I'm not going anywhere, I swear."

Arif gave her a loving little look and then shook his head with supposed regret. "A little insurance never hurt anyone," he told her.

"Actually," Cat interjected, "it's going to hurt a lot."

~~~~~~~~~~~~~~~~~~~~~~~~~~~~~~

Twenty-four toothpicks. Twenty-four, two-inch long, cellophane topped cocktail toothpicks had been driven deep into her flesh, sunk below the surface until the only evidence of them was what looked like the worst case of chicken pox ever. Bleeding, oozing holes…two in each calf, three in each thigh, one in each buttock, two in her stomach, one in each breast, two in each forearm and two in each bicep.

She was supposed to be grateful they hadn't bothered to put any in her face, despite Cat's insistence that cheek piercings would be an exotic nod to a fashionable trend. When Arif told Cat that none should go into Sindy's face or neck so she wouldn't be *too uncomfortable,* Sindy almost bit her tongue clean through to keep from uttering an acid response. She hoped Arif managed to read it from her though. She wouldn't dare speak it, but he couldn't blame her for thinking it.

He simply remarked that he was glad they didn't need to mar her beauty, and he was satisfied with the wooden hoop earrings Cat had fitted her with. She was forbidden to remove them, but truthfully, as long as her *body* was anchored in form, she wasn't going anywhere.

After assuring Sindy that the holes in her body would close over and the pain would eventually lessen, they had dressed her and sent her back to Kieran's house; two of Arif's guards practically carrying her.

As soon as they arrived, Kym took one look at her and pointed up the stairs, insisting that the men continue carrying her and put her into bed, because it was obvious she wouldn't be able to make it up there on her own.

They dumped her on the bed, without much care for being gentle, dropped her purse and high-heeled shoes in the corner, and left. After the shock of pain faded, from being dropped at an angle that caused a few of her toothpicks to shift and make her feel like she was laying on a bed of nails, she was able to roll onto her back and lay still without much pain…other than the throbbing aftershocks that resonated in every hole…

At least there were none in her back, and those in her butt had been driven in downwards from the top curving swell of her cheeks to be almost vertical when she was standing. That meant that when she was lying down, they were perpendicular to the bed, rather than jabbing into her worse. She could lie here without exasperating the pain. Great.

This was Arif's brilliant compromise to allow her the indulgence of freedom throughout the compound. She couldn't even imagine trying to get back up off the bed. They must believe she would feel better eventually though, and be capable of activity, because she had a standing appointment with the medical center each evening. Although the vampire blood within her was loathe to touch the wood invading its space, it would eventually find a way to begin expelling the toothpicks by moving the muscle and skin around them. If they began to pop back through, Arif wanted to make sure that the medical center would 'diagnose' and keep track of her 'multi-colored measles', to push them back in expediently.

She lay on the bed, trying to decide if the pain was fading. Nope, not a bit. After a token knock, the door opened and Kym came in with a pitcher and glass for her. "I've brought you something warm, Miss." She put the tray down on the bedside table and began to pour. "Can I bring you anything else?"

Warm sounded good. "Val. Bring me Val. Brett too. I want them both."

Kym hesitated, noticeably stalling her words as she finished pouring and set down the pitcher. "Let me help you sit up better so you can drink," she offered.

Sindy stared at her, and then finally allowed the woman to help her up. It was painful, but manageable. Under Sindy's unrelenting gaze, she finally answered. "I'm afraid Val and Brett are unavailable, Miss. I have strict instructions that you are to be served animal blood only."

"What? Why?"

"I was only told that human blood would be detrimental to the procedure you've endured. They said you would be incapacitated for a short time, and that my ladies and I should care for you, but you are not to be served human blood, even after you're feeling better. My apologies, Miss."

Human blood would speed the healing process. Arif didn't want her drinking to undo Cat's work. Kym retrieved something from the tray and handed it over for her to see. It was a credit card of some sort. "This is yours, Miss. To be presented whenever you are served animal blood from the reserves, here or at the commissary. It keeps track for you, of your daily rations."

"Rations?" Sindy asked in disbelief.

"There is only so much blood to go around. All of the lesser ranking vampires receive a card. But never fear. It has been made very clear that you haven't been given a lower station. You are to be treated as a vampire on level with the Senior Guard, but your portions are being controlled…for health reasons."

Sindy let out a huff of disgust. They *really* wanted to keep her healing rate to a minimum. She should have known. "Can't Val and Brett come in anyway, just to keep me company?" She felt sore, humiliated and her wounds were still stinging. All she wanted to do was snuggle under the covers with her warm boy-toys to comfort her and go to sleep until this nightmare dissolved away into something better.

"I'm sorry, Miss, but they've been sent back to quarantine until their marks from you fade. Perhaps when the coven master has remarked them, he will consider sending them back on loan for a while. Until then, my ladies and I are at your full disposal for anything you might need. If you'd like, I can see if perhaps another male can be borrowed for a time."

"Forget it." She didn't want sex, she wanted someone she knew and felt comfortable with, who could hold her and make her feel better. Stupid of her, to get attached. The coven master giveth, and the coven master taketh away.

She spent the rest of the evening and the next day in bed. She wouldn't have gotten up the next evening either, but shortly after sunset the intercom buzzer went off. She ignored it, but soon Kym was knocking on the door and then trying to get her up and dressed. Escorts were waiting to take her to the medical center for her nightly check-up.

Sindy was surprised to find that her wounds were all visibly healing over nicely. They still hurt, but you couldn't really see them anymore, especially once she was washed up and clothed.

The nurse was human. She was a very stern woman in her forties, who could look lovely if she tried, but was all business and no sympathy. Sindy asked if the pain was ever going to go away, but got no answer.

After inspecting each entry site with poking, prodding fingers, the nurse told Sindy to toughen up and stop wincing. "You're a creature designed to endure for centuries, and you're going to whine about a few splinters?" She rolled her eyes and let out a sigh of disgust. "I'd chop off my pinky to be in your shoes. If you're going to complain, don't do it in my office."

With that, the woman left Sindy to get dressed and get out. Her escorts were waiting for her outside the center. They were a couple of vampire cadets. She came out to find them lounging against the building casually. One of them was smoking a cigarette, but he tossed it the moment Sindy was spotted. Both guys stood at attention for her. Apparently, her rank was still considered above theirs.

"Everything okay, miss?" one of them asked hesitantly.

Sindy suddenly realized that the other vampires and humans of the compound did not know what had been done to her. Other than those who had been present, and the nurse, her indignities were private, and she was still outwardly seen as a vampire of status here. Even Kym didn't seem to know specifics, only that she was going to need extra care last night.

If Sindy had free reign of the place, and was going to be given special treatment, she might as well try to enjoy it. They didn't know she felt humiliated, or that she was in pain. Perception was everything. She held her head high, and allowed herself to exude the confidence of the powerful seductress she often portrayed herself as to the world. "Everything's fine. You boys don't need to head back right away, do you? Let's go find something fun to do."

Chapter 10-Whatever it takes

Ben

Ben and Felicity's house
Sagaponack, Long Island, New York
48 hours since Felicity's disappearance…

Ben handed baby Christian back to his mother-in-law as he shook his head, unable to accept her offer.

"Benjamin, please. You need the support of family right now. Look at you… you shouldn't be alone."

He knew he was a wreck. Who wouldn't be? He hadn't slept, eaten or even showered since Felicity's disappearance. Between his relentless questioning of the police and being questioned by them in return, alternately searching blindly and then racing back to the house, afraid not to be there in case of news… He was in no shape to care for his son and in no mood to be taken care of.

"I have my dad," he reminded her weakly. She knew just as well as he did, that his father may have good intentions, but was severely lacking in the emotional support department.

She furrowed her brow at him and hoisted Christian to sit on her hip. Ben pleaded with his eyes for her to understand. He wanted Christian far away from here, safe at his grandparent's house. It may seem more practical for his mother-in-law to stay here with him, but Ben needed privacy and leeway to talk to his dad. He was almost certain that supernatural circumstances were to blame, and maybe his dad could accomplish what police couldn't… But first, Ben needed a chance to confront him about it…about everything.

"Grace…" She gave him a look of reprimand for using her name. "Mom, I can't tell you how grateful I am to have you to take care of Christian for me right now. I know you want to be here, but you should be home with Jim. With the police coming and going and all the commotion, I really think it's better for Christian at your house anyway." She knew that was not really the case. The police were not spending their time here anymore. Without a lead or a ransom request, there was nothing here for them. "You know I'll call you as soon as I know anything. Please, I need some space to figure this out. If the police can't discover what happened, maybe I can. I have to. I have to find her."

The police had informed him this morning that while they were continuing the investigation and doing everything they could, after forty-eight hours, the chances of finding Felicity alive, or at all, were growing slimmer. They had nothing to go on, no suspects, no true sign of foul play even, other than finding her dropped purse in the driveway. She could have run off willingly somewhere or been abducted, but either way, they did not even know where to search or who else to question, other than him.

His mother-in-law put a hand on his shoulder and gave it a squeeze. She didn't know why he was so adamant, but she knew how much he loved her daughter, and if there was a way Ben could get her home safely, he would. She'd let him be. "I've got enough baby clothes and things for at least a week," she assured him, with a nod at the diaper bag and suitcase. "Don't worry about the formula, he'll take it. I put the food I made you in the fridge. There's directions on everything. I hope the cold doesn't make the sticky notes fall off. Make sure you eat. You're all muscle and no meat."

He tried to laugh, but it came out as an oddly choked sounding breath of air. "I'll be okay."

"I know you will. She's okay too. I can feel it. If something awful had happened to her, I would know. Give the police a chance. They'll bring her home, you'll see."

Ben nodded dutifully, hoping to God that she was right. He leaned forward to give Christian a kiss on the head goodbye. That smell…*Baby Magic* lotion and powder. It almost made him want to take the baby back, rather than give him up for any longer. "Are you sure you can handle him? I know you've had your hands full with Jim as it is…" Felicity's father was still recovering from recent surgery. He'd come through everything fine and was up and around, but making him follow doctor's orders and take it easy was a chore. Surely, the last thing Grace needed was a baby in the house.

"Oh hush. If there is one thing I know how to do, it's take care of boys…no matter how old and stubborn they are," she said, giving him a loving pat on the cheek. "Felicity's got three brothers, don't forget. They say girls are harder…but Felicity was always the one I could count on not to get into a lick of trouble."

Ben offered her a true smile. If she only knew… "I'm going to find her and bring her home, Grace…whatever it takes."

Grace nodded, blinked back tears and then adjusted the baby again. "I'll call you when we get home."

Ben helped her get everything into the car, strapped Christian into his car seat and waved goodbye as she pulled out of the driveway. Another car stopped in the street, waiting for her to leave so it could pull in. Perfect, it was his dad.

Ben tried to decide how to begin the true conversation, while making them both coffee, as his dad sat at the kitchen table. His father had asked a few questions and made a few comments, but nothing to hint that he may have further information to share.

"And they still haven't come up with any leads?" Bernard was asking, as Ben handed him his cup and took a seat.

Ben rested his head in his hands for a moment. "No dad, they haven't got a clue. You haven't found anything?"

Bernard looked almost puzzled. "No. You know I've been looking, but if the police couldn't come up with anything to follow, what could I find?"

Ben squinted at him, his anger building over the charade his father insisted on hiding behind. Now that things had settled down enough for privacy, he could finally bring everything out into the open. "The police don't even know what they're dealing with, so I don't really expect them to find her. They haven't got the resources of a vampire hunter."

Bernard must have been shocked by the accusing revelation, but managed to keep his poker face. He stared at Ben for a long time, and finally let out a snort of breath with a hint of a smile before taking a sip of his coffee. "How long have you known?"

"How long has it been going on?" he asked in rhetorical retort. "I know everything…everything I care to know, anyway." He clenched his jaw and his fists as he recalled the bare minimum of his memories to sum up his disgust. "I know how you've always snuck out at night for it, leaving mom and I alone, even when I was little. And I know how you used to meet that blonde whore right in our fucking driveway, like you had no shame."

Now Bernard's composure became defensive anger. "Watch your mouth."

"She killed mom, you know that, right? I saw her there."

His father's eyes grew wide with shock before glazing with unshed tears. "I loved your mother. I've made mistakes…wrongs I can never right. But I try."

Ben refused to be moved by admissions of regret and acts of redemption. "She's a vampire, isn't she…the blonde?"

Bernard swallowed over the lump in his throat and gave a slight nod. "Her name is Lorelei."

"Is?" He echoed, with a lilt of surprise. "So you haven't dusted her yet?"

Bernard fixed him with a steely stare. "It's on my to-do list."

"Good." Ben acknowledged the vendetta and put it aside for now. This could not devolve into emotional accusations over the past. Felicity needed him. "I have to find my wife. I think vampires took her. I need you to tell me where to look."

Bernard shook his head in confusion. "She's not your mother. That was different. Lorelei has no reason to harm Felicity. Not everything is about vampires."

"This is, trust me," he insisted forcefully. "Felicity and I had friends…who were turned." Bernard's mouth fell open in shock. "They were supposed to meet us at the house the night Felicity disappeared. I never saw them."

"These *friends,* you think they betrayed you?"

"I honestly don't know."

"You know they're different after they change, don't you? They enter into symbiosis with a demon. No one could be the same after that. Who were they?"

Ben hesitated. He was still unsure who to blame or what to think, and giving his friend's names to a vampire hunter was pretty major. He wanted to find out what had happened and then deal with Allie and Mattie himself, but he couldn't very well expect his father to help if he didn't know who he was trying to find. If Mattie and Alyson were responsible for hurting Felicity, they were already as good as dust in his mind anyway.

"Mattie." Ben watched the name register. Ben had been a teenager when Mattie had gone missing and their other friend Davy had been killed. His father nodded, as if he'd suspected as much. He had to have known that David's death was the work of vampires. When the cops had found him, his throat had been mutilated and his body drained of blood. Mattie had eventually been declared dead, but his body was never found.

Ben closed his eyes and continued in a whisper. "And Alyson."

Bernard went pale. "I'm sorry," he said quietly when he found his voice. His father knew how close they used to be, how much Allie had meant to him.

He wanted to say more, but Ben stopped him. Further explanations could come later, right now, he just wanted to be done with discussions and feel like he was doing something useful to help Liss. "You're the vampire hunter. I need you to track them."

"I can't. I can see marks…auras, but only if they're nearby. It's not like they leave glow-in-dark footprints. I can't follow them any better than the police could."

"You can see marks?" Ben asked in surprised wonder.

"Yes. It's a signature sort of glow…"

"I know what a mark is," Ben cut him off, impatiently. "I know more than I ever wanted to know about vampires."

Bernard looked his son over with discerning curiosity. "Really?"

"Marks, venom, stakes and crosses, I probably know more about them than I do about you; self-taught, of course. I'm smart, strong, I'm even good with a fucking sword, but not good enough for you, I guess. You never thought I could handle it, so you spent your life lying to me and trying to hide it."

"I was trying to keep you safe!"

"Well, you suck at it."

"You're still alive, aren't you? I know you can take care of yourself. I've made sure of that. You're good. It's not about skill. I wanted you to have a normal life; to have a family you didn't have to sneak away from at night; to have the opportunity to be the father and husband that I never was."

That hit home. It was the truth…he could see it, feel it as he'd never understood it before. All these years he had resented his father for excluding him. He'd always known that in Bernard's own mind it was 'for his own good', but that seemed a lame excuse. He'd always thought his father was unimpressed with his skills and deemed him unworthy of the secret. Now it finally dawned on him; belief in Ben's skills was irrelevant. Bernard wasn't trying to protect him from vampires…he was trying to protect his son from becoming a man like himself.

"It consumed me at first," Bernard admitted quietly. "It seduced me…"

"She," Ben corrected him. "*She* seduced you, and you let her."

"It wasn't just her, it was her kind; her abilities, her immortality, everything… I let it suck me in, until I lost hold of my life. By the time I realized the demons vampires really were, it was too late to go back. I was in it all too deep. I tried to pull away. I uprooted everything to move away and hide us, to start new. It didn't work though. We'd shared blood, she and I. Lorelei was in my head. I would have to have travelled to the other side of the world, hidden for months until her hold on me wore away, and even then, I don't know if she might have found me.

I should have tried harder, I guess, but we had a sort of truce, she and I. She didn't reveal my location to her coven, and I kept the area clear of lesser vampires, taking out the bold and disobedient before the coven would have cause to investigate. She let me go, and I was a fool to believe that she still cared about me enough to let me have my life. For a long time, it seemed that way. I rekindled things with your mom and we were happy, the three of us. You know we were. We had a good life."

"Did mom know?"

"No. None of it."

Ben wanted to curse him; to blame his dad for not warning her, somehow arming her against the creatures that had ultimately taken her life…but a part of him was very glad she hadn't known. They *had* been happy. Whether his mother had been truly oblivious to Bernard's secret outings in the wee hours of the morning, or not, she had always seemed happy. Ben had been a teenager when she'd died. If she were constantly troubled and worrying, Ben was pretty sure he would have noticed.

The truth of it was, when he was younger, before his mom's death, Ben had thought his dad was some sort of superhero, a secret agent that snuck out at night to meet with his supernatural sidekick to fight crime and champion justice. He'd always known Lorelei was supernatural somehow, before he had ever even heard of vampires. She moved with a grace he had never seen, and the way the moonlight shone on her perfect alabaster skin, with her hair so long that it almost brushed the ground behind her as she walked, she had seemed otherworldly to him as a child.

He would never forget the time that he had been peeking out his window, watching her talk with his father, and she had looked in his direction. It seemed too distant for their eyes to meet, but she had seen him, he knew. He'd always wondered if he'd been mistaken, because it should have been too far for him to see, but her eyes had looked purple, glittering and hypnotizing as she'd caught his gaze and smiled. An alien, an angel, an Amazon warrior; he didn't know what she was, but he was entranced. He'd thought she was good, and special, and he'd envied his dad for knowing her… He knew better now.

"I don't think Lorelei killed your mother. Our affair was over and she didn't want anything more to do with me. Lorelei was supposed to have killed me years before, when we ended it, but she'd disobeyed her coven master's wishes. He went mad with jealousy when he learned I was alive. She came to warn me, but by then I had been secretly killing random vampires for quite some time, and was certain I could defend myself against any he would send. The coven knew of my offices in the city, but I only travelled by day, so they couldn't follow me home. Lorelei knew where we lived, but your mother refused to move again, so I had to trust that Lorelei wouldn't betray us."

"I remember...you wanted us to move and mom wouldn't go."

Bernard needed to stop for a sip of coffee and a deep breath of composure. "I should have put my foot down, but your mother was so happy there, entrenched in her job and with her friends. I couldn't force the issue without explaining everything, so I let it be. I was the target, not her. I killed every vampire the coven sent to find me, easily. Arif had no idea that I could see their marks coming from a mile away."

"Arif? I know that name..."

Bernard shook his head. "You couldn't possibly."

Ben sat silently as he recalled a conversation that felt like it had taken place a million years ago. Something Felicity had told him, when he had found out that Cain had bitten her. *He was afraid that Arif would hurt me. Hell, I'm afraid of Arif too! You should have seen the way that he looked at me,* she had said with a shudder. *If I'd understood about this whole marking business, I might have asked Cain to do it, right then and there.*

Cain had marked her as his personal property all those years ago, so that a vampire coven leader named Arif could not claim her. Ben had thought it a disgusting excuse for Cain to drink her blood...but after he had experienced being marked firsthand, by Sindy, he realized that along with its awful bond and effects, it did also offer a measure of protection from other vampires.

At this point, Arif should have long forgotten about Felicity. Ben could not imagine why Arif would bother to come looking for her now, but if he had found her, this time, she wasn't marked.

"Maybe this isn't about Mattie and Allie..." Ben admitted, now uncertain.

"If they knew where to find you and were planning to come, then it seems obvious that they arrived early so that they could steal Felicity without your interference."

Ben shook his head, still unconvinced. "But Felicity's met with Alyson before. I didn't know, but they've been friends. If Allie was going to hurt her, she would have done it already."

"What about the other one?"

"Mattie? I... I don't know. When she was human, Alyson was sure that he was the same, or she wouldn't have chosen to go with him..."

"She was a fool, and now she's tricked Felicity as well."

"I can't believe that."

"Your vast knowledge of vampires tells you otherwise?" Bernard asked in condescension.

Ben took a deep breath. "I can't believe that, because if it's true, then they've already killed or turned Felicity and there's nothing I can do. I will not give up until I see my wife for myself, and if she's been turned, *I'll* deal with it...and I'll deal with Alyson and Mattie too. This is not your fight. I need you to find them for me because I can't do it alone, and I think you at least owe me that much, but I'm calling the shots."

"Do you really think Arif may be involved? Considering the size of his coven, I suppose it's not unlikely that your friends may have been inducted."

"If Arif is at the bottom of this, he's yours, but not until I say. If he knows where Felicity is, then you can't be seen until I get her back, or you'll blow the whole thing. Okay?"

"Whatever it takes."

Chapter 11

The enemy of your enemy...

Felicity

Kana Susamiş Icin Ev
Montauk, Long Island, New York
The same evening

Arif entered the dressing room and put up a hand for silence from the human woman Saruca. "I'll handle it. Leave us." He looked very annoyed to have been called away from his own business in order to interfere with such trivial concerns as the care of a mere human. Well, Felicity was annoyed too.

"I am told that you have been refusing to change your dress, and resort to rude insult or utter hysterics whenever given an order. I am not going to need to have Lorelei following you about and directing your actions for your entire visit, am I? What is wrong with you, girl?"

"Oh, I'm sorry," she spat out sarcastically. "Is holding me prisoner an inconvenience for you?"

Arif just rolled his eyes and handed her the outfit Saruca had been trying to push on her for the better part of the last hour. "You've been away from home for a few nights now. I thought you would welcome a wardrobe change."

She scowled at him. How dare he try to pretend he was being considerate! "This isn't mine," she informed him, smoothing her hands down over the front of the modest dress she wore. "I was given it to wear from Elric's harem." She snatched the offensive outfit out of Arif's hands and held it up in disgust. It was an indecipherable pile of sheer scarves and beaded pieces, that Felicity had no desire to try to figure out how to put on. "I didn't have to wear this kind of stuff at Elric's house. His harem lent me regular clothes to wear, like sweat pants and tee-shirts."

"Elric allows his women to dress like slobs in his home. I don't. You will wear what you have been given."

Felicity fished the strap of the sequined bra out of the tangle with her finger, and held it up further for emphasis. "You expect me to dress like some Arabian slut?"

Arif's smile made her anger smolder hotter as he only met her protests with patient, soft-spoken explanations. "It is standard home attire for my courtesans. They wear what will be pleasing to my eye, for my favor is their greatest desire. There is a saying: *Yemeği yemeden önce gözlerinle yemelisin.* It means that you should want to eat the food with your eyes, before you taste it with your mouth."

Was he kidding? "Well, I hate to break it to you, but I'm not auditioning to be one of your meals in heels."

"That is clearly evident. You should be honored that I am allowing you access to the very extensive and expensive wardrobe of my harem." He looked her up and down, to add with a smirk, "You should also be grateful there may be a few items within that might be altered to fit you…with luck and an expert seamstress."

Felicity threw the garments to the floor in outrage. "You condescending, spiteful, narcissistic little man! You may think you own these poor women," she yelled with a gesture meant to encompass the house, "but you most certainly do not own me, and I refuse to let you disrespect me like this."

Arif raised an eyebrow in amusement. "Did you just call me *little?*" Apparently 'condescending, spiteful, and narcissistic' weren't points he was going to bother to argue. "I can assure you that my concubines all find me to be quite adequately proportioned in all respects," he told her, smugly.

Felicity made a gagging noise at his egotism. "That's because they've never met my husband, who resembles a Greek God compared to you, you nauseating, metro-sexual priss."

Now he seemed truly insulted, but his gaze bore into her and then he smiled. "Your husband *is* quite finely made, as I can clearly see from the stunning visual your memory provides."

Unsettled by the fact that he could so easily read her mind, Felicity faltered in her anger, giving him opening to continue. "But no mere man could hold a candle next to the flames of passion that I could easily consume you with, should I choose to initiate you into my harem. Your husband could never know you as I would know you. He could never read your every secret desire and stroke your fantasies to fulfillment as I could.

Your husband is but a mortal man of flesh and faults. I am the God of the pair, the true embodiment of ecstasy."

"You wouldn't dare touch me," she growled at him. "No matter what else happens, you know that if you touch me you will die for it."

Arif took a step closer and then gave her true cause for alarm. His eyes became purple. She stood frozen, unable to flinch away, and then, to her horror, she found herself raising her own hand to lovingly cup the side of his face. Her fingers caressed his cheek, pausing to trace the soft lines of his facial hair and rub her thumb over the curve of his lip. His words whispered upon it, giving her chills. "My dear girl, I would never stoop so low as to lay a single hand upon you."

As she dropped her hand from him, she felt in control of herself once more, frightened and trying not to tremble. She met his brown eyes and steeled herself not to appear terrified, even if he could read the truth from her mind.

"I think I'm going to be sick," she muttered in disgust over his attentions.

"Good, maybe it will help you fit into your new clothing," Arif answered, without missing a beat.

Felicity blinked at him, and then tried to assert herself once more. "I am not wearing that."

"Then you may spend your time here nude, it's your choice. If you would like to continue your show of protest, I can simply control you myself to disrobe, thus sparing you from having to give in voluntarily, but I thought you might prefer to change in private."

After a second, she stooped and picked up the clothing from the floor. He smiled. "I'll have someone come to collect the dress for return to Elric's harem. I would advise you not to continue with further displays of outburst during your stay. Poor Saruca really deserves better treatment. Your comfort and well-being are not nearly as integral to my plans as you might assume. Your continued health would be convenient to my cause, but not entirely necessary, so I suggest you cooperate. You would be a fool to anger me. I am the most powerful vampire on the continent."

He turned to leave her, but she couldn't help but dispute his claim. "No you aren't. The most powerful vampire on the continent is about ten times stronger than you in every respect, and she just happens to be a really good friend of mine."

Arif turned back to her and smiled. "I'm counting on it."

Realization stole across her. "Oh my God…that's what this is really all about, isn't it? You don't want Cain. It's Allie you're after".

"Indeed. Cain is simply a tool to be used to my end, and removed when his usefulness has passed. He will convince your good friend Alyson to submit herself to my demands to ensure your safety. When she agrees to trade her cooperation for your release, you can have her bring you whatever clothing you desire. Until then, you will wear what you are given. My harem's wardrobe has been graciously opened to you, and that is a stunning selection Saruca has chosen from it for you. The color will bring out the green in your eyes."

Felicity refused to let him walk away. "What do you want Allie for anyway? No matter how jealous you are of her powers, or what kind of threats you make, she can't give them to you. It just doesn't work that way."

Arif chuckled. "You think to tell me more of vampire physiology than I know? I do not bend to the whims of anything so petty as jealousy. My intentions do not concern you, but you can rest assured that Alyson need not be harmed if she sees fit to cooperate with me to my ends.

You, on the other hand, are not the only means of persuasion I can produce. It is clear that you are dearer to Cain than to Alyson, and if she is not convinced to come to terms for an exchange, or should you prove too difficult to keep, other tactics will be enacted, and you can become a fully initiated member of my stable, or a fine feast for my men. Your fate is up to you.

Now, if you'll excuse me, I have more important matters to attend to than your wardrobe fitting. Good day, dear."

~~~~~~~~~~~~~~~~~~~~~~~~~~~~~~

Felicity tried to better wrap the sheer scarf around her hips to try to disguise the fact that her pants were sheer as well. Wasn't the long slit down the side of each leg enough? She had never worn so many pieces of detailed accessory clothing in order to feel so naked!

She changed her mind, wrapping the scarf over her shoulders instead, deciding that the pants would have to be good enough on their own. There was no way she was going to walk around in front of other people wearing nothing on her upper body but a glorified bra. It was a gorgeous piece of artistic beadwork, and thankfully, it had silk scarves flowing down from the band under her bust, to hide her midriff. However, being a slightly overweight, nursing mother had given her bosom a plumpness that left her bursting with cleavage to indecent proportions.

Saruca told her to stop fussing, and pulled her along the hall until they reached a door with a guard stationed to the side. He nodded permission for her to open the door, and the women entered.

The room was a beautifully furnished sitting room, decorated with all dark polished wood and leather. An assorted collection of lovely antique lamps gave the room a cozy, warm glow. There were several large, comfortable looking chairs arranged around a coffee table in the center, but Arif stood against the far wall by the window, looking outside, down upon the grounds. The only occupant in the room, he didn't bother to look up at their arrival. Saruca and Felicity were forced to stand at silent attention for a few moments, until he chose to acknowledge them.

He finally turned and looked Felicity over with an approving eye. "You are such a foolish woman," he told Felicity. "You fought so hard to stay so plain, when a bit of proper packaging has you looking absolutely delectable. Thank you, Saruca. Lovely work, as always."

Saruca bowed her head, and then departed the room. Felicity was left standing there hating the fact that she looked gorgeous. After finally having to relent to Saruca dressing her in the revealing harem outfit she had been given, Saruca had also insisted upon doing her hair and make-up.

With her hair curled and pinned to the side, and her eyes done expertly with smoky shades to match her outfit, Felicity had to admit, it had been a long time since she remembered looking this good. Arif had been right, the dusky brown and plum colors in her clothing and eye shadow did make the green of her eyes pop. She looked arrestingly exquisite. Knowing it had been done for *him,* made her wish she could crawl under a blanket and hide.

Arif approached her and she stood still as a statue, wondering if there was any way that she could possibly oppose him, if he tried to control her actions again.

"No, not really," he responded to the thought with a smile. "Humans are powerless against me. It takes a bit more effort to handle those whom I have not bitten, but I've had plenty of practice. Even other vampires cannot fight against my control, if they are foolish enough to allow my venom within them."

She said nothing. What could she say? Even her private thoughts were open to him. She simply stood, waited, and prayed for her time here to be over.

"I too hope that my terms are quickly met, so that you might be returned to your home…although, with a little effort, you are even lovelier to look at than I remembered. I don't suppose I'll mind having you around for a while." He gave her a lecherous grin and then moved towards the corner of the room furthest from the door. "Come here, girl." She squinted at him, insulted by the way he addressed her, but then obeyed. She would rather obey his directives, than have him take over her body to force the action.

Once she arrived, he pointed at the floor. "Sit." She looked back at the six cushy chairs arranged in the center of the room, but he snapped for her attention. "On the floor, now."

"Are you kidding me?" He didn't bother to reply, as the stern look he was giving her was more than enough of an answer. She sat on the floor, folding her legs beneath her and trying to arrange her scarf for modesty.

He smiled. "Good girl." He then walked to seat himself in the nearest armchair. "You are not to speak a word unless I address you myself," he ordered. She nodded her understanding as the door opened.

To her chagrin, it was the vampires Maribeth and Drake who entered. The domineering man gave her the creeps, and Maribeth made her feel like an illicit spy, for knowing so many intimate details of the woman's past without her knowledge. She tried not to meet their eyes as they entered, hoping not to attract their attention. Arif rose in response to their arrival, greeted them both, and crossed to kiss the lady's hand before leading her in, with Drake behind. After they were sufficiently within the room, one of Arif's servant girls followed, pushing a cart that held a warming carafe and several glasses. She poured and served each of the vampires a glass of blood, and then bowed and exited the room, leaving the cart behind.

Once settled, Arif waved a hand towards Felicity. "Pay no mind to my new pet. I thought I'd keep her here to look at, rather than tempt my men. Things will go more smoothly if she remains unmarked. She does look delicious though, doesn't she?"

Drake gave Felicity an appreciative stare that made her feel sullied, but Maribeth didn't even spare her a glance. After a pause, Arif took back their attention. "Now that the larger coven business has been settled, I thought it would be nice if we could speak in a more intimate setting. I am so glad to have you joining me here once again. I know you've been traveling quite a bit."

Although Arif's comments were directed at Drake, it was Maribeth who answered. "Honestly, I'm bored with Europe presently. I find myself with the urge to visit home now and then, but it's never the same as I'd like it to be. Even Canterbury with all of its old estates isn't quite the same. I visit places I used to call home and now they're tourist attractions, homogenized and repackaged to represent old splendor, but they're completely different to me. I find no solace there. It's depressing. Coming here to the states is much more interesting right now. Everyone who is anyone is here at the moment."

Arif gave Maribeth a gracious smile. "Indeed."

She took his reply as encouragement to continue. "Besides, I've been thinking about this lovely little retreat of yours since our last visit. I did have a wonderful time. Perhaps you can arrange for Lorelei and I to have another evening to ourselves? She and I had such fun."

Drake spoke before Arif could answer. "Maribeth, do stop your incessant, inane prattling about Lorelei using her thrall as a parlor trick for you. It's all I've had to listen to for weeks."

Maribeth knitted her brows in a pouting expression of disapproval that somehow looked adorably sexy on her delicate features. "You can't blame a lady for enjoying some proper subservience, can you? I'm practically nobility and I haven't ever had nearly the treatment I deserve."

Drake was apparently unaffected by her sultry sulking. "Over three hundred years ago, you were married to a Baron who renounced his claim and title almost immediately upon receiving it. You are hardly royalty, dear."

Maribeth now seemed truly displeased by the remark, rather than just putting on a pout for show. "At least Lorelei knows how to have fun. I do love a new toy, and I can never get you to give me any."

"That's because you can't manage not to kill them all almost immediately. It's a nuisance to have to keep replacing them," he told Arif with a scowl.

Felicity couldn't help but let out a breath of disbelieving shock over the statement. She was horrified when it was clearly audible, and caused all eyes to turn to her. Drake dismissed it and Arif only gave her a look of warning, but Maribeth commented on it. "What's wrong with your human? She looks as though she's seen a ghost or something."

Drake sighed. "Maribeth, a woman of the breeding and station you claim should know when to hold her tongue. Stop boring us with your pleas and questions. I'm here to discuss business matters."

Maribeth opened her mouth in insult, but kept quiet as Drake turned his attention back to their host. "Arif, I have found the perfect location for your vessels. I've purchased the property and have the surrounding area sufficiently secured. You can have them moved in at your ready."

Once again, Maribeth interjected. "Oh, is that what you purchased the boarding school for? I wondered. I couldn't understand what you'd want with it otherwise. Arif, you aren't moving your coven, are you? Because this is definitely a much nicer spot."

Drake spoke in a voice of quiet foreboding. "Maribeth, please. It is none of your affair."

Arif chose to pretend that she hadn't spoken at all. "Wonderful, sire. I do thank you for your interest and assistance in my endeavor. My ladies have already been preparing for the move. The west wing suites will be cleared by the end of the week, and I'll have escorts transfer them over. The timing couldn't be better. We're almost ready for the change."

The words seemed to spark interest and brighten Drake's mood a bit. "I must admit, although I didn't originally want to be involved, this could be history in the making. I always knew you had a spark of ingenuity in you. I'd like to discuss your proposed methods of change."

"Of course." Arif paused to glance at Felicity, who was sitting quietly in the corner. "Let me have someone come and tend to the girl for me, so that we might have some privacy."

Drake raised a hand to stop him before he called in an escort. "No need to summon anyone. Maribeth can take her."

Maribeth seemed just as disturbed by the suggestion as Felicity was. "Excuse me?" the vampiress asked.

Arif also responded dubiously. "The human's life is currently of some value to the situation. Her safety assures that all of our plans for the upcoming event will be successful."

Drake was unconcerned and seemed pleased with the idea of getting rid of his consort for a while. "Yes, I understand her significance. Maribeth can be trusted, can't you darling?"

"Trusted to do what?" Maribeth asked hesitantly as she observed Felicity.

"Just take the girl and keep an eye on her. Don't let her out of your sight while Arif and I have a private meeting. You can take her to the dining-room for some food or something, she looks a bit pale," Drake told her.

Felicity knew she shouldn't speak, but had to say something to keep from being sent away with this woman. "You don't need to bother her, I can just stay. ...Of course, I will do as you please," she found herself adding...but the words were Arif's, not her own; a reminder that she had absolutely no say in the matter.

Maribeth was still trying to argue with Drake over it, however. "Do I look like a nanny?" she asked in insult.

Arif put his hand on her arm for soothing attention. "You needn't leave the house or look after her for long. She can be delivered to Saruca in the harem quarters if you'd be so kind as to provide her trusted escort. Any of the guards can tell you the way. Then I will see if perhaps Lorelei can arrange for some time to spend, so you two might share some entertainment later on," he promised.

Drake did not bother to try to persuade her as nicely. "Need I impose the order directly?" Drake asked with a dangerous edge, his eyes shifting to their purple brilliance. "Your age is impressive, but do remember the authority of breed and power present. Take the woman and leave us. Please me now, and I shall remind you later of the benefits of being on the other side of subservience."

Maribeth's eyes flashed orange with outrage at the suggestion, but she rose from her seat without a word. She shot Felicity an icy look, and then turned for the door. Felicity immediately rose and followed her out of the room. As the door closed behind them, Maribeth walked a few paces, past the guards and around the corner of the hall, before stopping with a hushed outburst of indignation. "Benefits of subservience? The nerve of that tyrant! Thinks he's got the power to order me about, does he? I ought to pluck those purple eyes from his head. He doesn't know who he's dealing with."

Felicity had followed discreetly behind, and now couldn't help but widen her eyes and shake her head. "No, I'm sure he doesn't."

Maribeth paused to shoot her a very discerning look, that this mere human had had the nerve to answer the rhetorical question. "Who are you again?"

Felicity contemplated how she might answer to gain Maribeth's interest as more than an insolent meal. Rather than try to remain unnoticed, she might fare better to try using the woman's ire to her advantage. She didn't plan to spend the next couple of weeks sitting around waiting to be rescued while worrying that Ben or Cain would get themselves killed trying to help her. She needed to see if there was anything she could do for herself. At least Felicity *did* know who she was dealing with, better than anyone here might guess. Perhaps Maribeth could be convinced to help her in some subtle way, if she didn't anger the woman into drinking her. "I'm someone who knows exactly who she's dealing with," she answered with a bit of reverence.

"Do you, now?" Maribeth replied, sarcastically.

"With all due respect."

Maribeth stared at her for a minute, lips pursed and a look of contempt upon her face. "Well, jolly good for you. Cor… I'm twelve times your age, and have traveled the world over. This is indubitably your first time outside of your town, and your safe little life…and you think you *know* me."

"I'm sorry. I didn't mean to insult you. I'm incredibly in awe of you, actually. I've lived some, but I know it's nothing compared to the things you've experienced, the trials you've endured."

Maribeth squinted at her for a moment, seeming to remember her associations and realizing that perhaps Felicity did know something of her. "That's right…you're here for Cain, aren't you?" She came nearer, causing Felicity to suddenly freeze and feel that perhaps her approach and the familiarity with which she'd been addressing the woman had been a big mistake. Maribeth lightly ran her fingers through Felicity's dark red hair. "Still chasing after shadows of me, is he? And he's spoken of me too, how terribly sentimental of him." She laughed and let the strands of Felicity's hair flow from between her fingers. "Arif may not have been so misguided after all. Christian never could resist rushing to the aid of a damsel in distress. I ought to know. You may be the latest…but I was the first."

Felicity cautiously nodded. "You made quite an impression on him."

"Of course, I did. The question is, have you?"

Felicity lowered her gaze. "Maybe not. So far, Arif says he isn't coming."

Maribeth expelled a small breath of a laugh. "Yes. Well, I certainly haven't heard anything from him, but Arif has been known to lie."

"They want Cain to convince his friend Alyson to do something for them. Do you know what they want her to do?"

"Something only fit for a vampire's ears, I'm sure," Maribeth replied, dismissing her. She tilted her head, considering something, and then suddenly turned and began to walk briskly down the hall. After a moment, she looked back to Felicity, and then continued down the hall. "Chivvy along, girl."

After a brief glance about and a stern look from a nearby guard, Felicity followed after. They made their way down the hall and then turned down an unfamiliar passage. After following her a bit further, Felicity worked up the nerve to ask, "Aren't we supposed to go that way?" She pointed back down the hall.

"What's down there?"

"The harem quarters."

"No, you're accompanying me elsewhere at the moment."

That sounded like it had the potential to be either a welcome opening for plans of escape…or something much more troubling. "Why? Where are we going?"

"To satisfy my curiosity." Maribeth paused in her brisk pace at a junction in the corridors. She looked down each passage, seeming to have become disoriented within the large mansion. She turned to Felicity. "Where would the west wing be?"

Felicity tried to get her bearings. She had no idea of the location Maribeth wanted to visit, but… "The staircase is that way, right?" Maribeth didn't follow her thought process, but nodded. "Meaning the front entrance is down that way too." Felicity closed her eyes, picturing herself standing before the house. "Then sunset should be over there," she said, pointing to the passage on their left.

She opened her eyes to see Maribeth smiling at her. "Making that the west…and the west wing will be in that direction as well. Clever." She began walking the way Felicity had indicated. "Come on girl, keep up."

"My name is Felicity."

"I didn't ask."

Felicity followed, trying to remember anything she might have heard regarding the west wing, but nothing came to mind, other than what Arif had just said about relocating its residents.

Maribeth spoke as she walked, seeming to have warmed up to the idea of Felicity being an actual person, rather than just an encumbrance. "I'm not supposed to be off poking around," she confided, "but as long as I've got you tagging along, I look like an escort on an errand. Paired with the age of my mark, no one will dare question me. I'm even older than their master."

"The vampire Drake must be pretty ancient, huh?"

Maribeth looked back at her, curiously. "What makes you say that?"

"Well," she began timidly, "I know Cain is an elder, which earns him a lot of respect among vampires, but you're Cain's *maker*." She was sure to infuse the statement with as much awe as she could muster. "I figure anyone who thinks they have the right to order *you* around would *have* to be ancient. Who else could assume that kind of authority?"

"Who indeed?" Maribeth was thoughtfully quiet for a moment. "He's unequivocally powerful, but I'm not convinced he's actually older than I am," she admitted.

"Really? The way he spoke to you…"

"I shouldn't take that from him, I know. He's got such a commanding presence…it can be quite attractive at times, but I'm not sure how I let myself become so far under his spell. It's not really like me at all."

"I can tell you're a very strong woman."

She narrowed her eyes, giving Felicity a look of warning that the words spoken had better be believed, and not just to stroke ego. "The strongest. I like a strong man, as well. I do," she asserted after a pause.

"There's a difference between strength and cruelty," Felicity offered quietly.

"Both attributes have their uses. I may have been drawn to kind-hearted gentlemen in my youth, but soft-spoken tolerance never propelled anyone to greatness."

"Well, I'm sure Drake is very respected among vampires," Felicity commented carefully.

"Yes." Maribeth responded, in quiet thought. "Although, I am beginning to think I might be missing gentle charms. I certainly wouldn't mind having complete control of myself once more. Have you ever been handled by them; those with purple eyes?" Felicity nodded, with a shudder. "The novelty wears rather quickly, I can assure you…at least when one is on the receiving end."

She became thoughtful, speaking more for herself then Felicity. "Perhaps it is time I started planning my exit strategy." She looked up from introspection to address Felicity directly. "It's a delicate matter, leaving a man of power."

Felicity nodded. "I can imagine. Ending a relationship is always hard, but with a vampire like Drake… You'd definitely want some support."

"Support? From whom…you?" Maribeth peered at her with a smirk.

"Well, I know you wouldn't want to seem vulnerable in front of other vampires here. If you ever need someone to talk to…"

"I realize this isn't a discussion that I ought to be having in your presence, but one would assume that you would know your place better than to take part in it. Could you be daring to think that I need someone like you to hold my hand? As though we're going to be girlfriends, braid each other's hair while we call men pigs and have a good cry or something?"

"No! Obviously not. I just meant, it would be hard to leave Drake because you wouldn't want to make enemies…unless you had reliable allies."

"What sort of allies?"

"Other vampires, of course. Vampires who don't approve of the kind of manipulation Drake and Arif wield. The enemy of your enemy, maybe?" she added, thinking of Latisha's remark to Elric.

Maribeth smiled. "I see. You think to align me with Cain and the others to further your own ends. I'm not a fool, and who said Drake was an enemy?" she asked with a snicker. "Simply a lover's spat, nothing more. It's not your concern."

A guard entered the hallway and began walking towards them. Maribeth turned on her heel and continued down the hall to the west, away from the guard. Felicity glanced back at him, and then hurried to follow Maribeth.

They came to a broad corridor with a guard at each corner of the entrance. Maribeth barely paused, and then took Felicity roughly by the elbow and sauntered towards them. She had actually already walked right through, when one of them turned to question her. "Excuse me, miss? Can I help you with something?"

Maribeth turned and paused to give him an expression of surprise and a smile. "No, not at all, but thank you so much for asking. Such manners are a rare treat these days…and I do love a man in uniform." She looked both men up and down with obvious appreciation. "Pity I'm busy, but perhaps if I hurry you'll still be here when I get back?" The vampire nodded after sharing a glance with his partner. Maribeth continued before they could say anything. "This is the west wing, isn't it? We're expected. I'll be sure to make it quick," she added with a wink.

Before the guards could even decide whether or not to protest, she was off down the hall with Felicity in tow, and through the set of double doors at the end. Once inside the closed corridor, all seemed very quiet, cut off from the rest of the house. They were in a short hallway that opened into a large parlor that had several closed doors leading elsewhere. Maribeth took stock of their surroundings and seemed unsure where to go from here.

Felicity took the opportunity to try to rekindle informative conversation. "Do you know for sure if Cain even knows I'm here?"

Maribeth shushed her and paused, cocking her head as though listening to something. She looked very surprised and puzzled. After a few minutes of interminable silence, Felicity dared to ask, "What is it? What do you hear?"

Maribeth knitted her brows with a small frown. "Something I haven't heard in a very long time." She walked decisively to a door in the back of the room, and Felicity had no choice but to follow. Once there, Maribeth very quietly cracked it open to peek inside. She then opened it and went through.

Another hallway. As they slowly advanced, Felicity began to hear what Maribeth must have been listening to. It was the sound of a baby crying. Just recognizing the sound made Felicity's milk laden breasts ache. She froze, suddenly terrified that somehow they had abducted Christian and secreted him away here…but no, it wasn't him. She wasn't sure how she could tell, but she just knew. This was someone else's child.

They found their way to the door from which the sound was emanating. Maribeth inched it open just in time to see a woman enter from a door on the other side. She didn't notice the cracked open door, but instead went to soothe the baby. She wasn't harsh with him, but wasn't particularly loving either. It was doubtful this woman was the baby's mother. The child was lifted from one of three cribs. The other two held older toddlers, sitting and playing with toys as they watched the woman calm the baby. When one of the little boys looked in the direction of the door they were spying through, Maribeth immediately clicked it shut.

She and Felicity shared a confused glance, and then Maribeth went further down the hall to investigate another room. It was fairly quiet, but the slight sounds of older children playing could be heard from within. She didn't even bother to open the door, just stood listening for a moment, and then turned to retreat.

Felicity followed, quietly horrified. "Why are there children here? They aren't drinking from children, are they? That doesn't even make much sense. I would think they'd be harder to care for, and they don't have as much blood as an adult. Who would do that to a child?"

"They're only slightly marked," Maribeth informed her, and then continued on back the way they had come.

"Slightly? What the hell does that mean?" Felicity asked in disgust.

Maribeth answered her in a harsh whisper. "It means they were likely marked for the sake of being marked, and aren't being regularly drunk from. They aren't food…at least not yet. It's a control thing."

The next time Felicity tried to speak, she was quickly and fiercely shushed. A door further down the hall was opening. Three children came out, all boys, between the ages of perhaps eight and ten, followed by an older boy who looked to be thirteen or so. The children all stopped to look up at the women in surprise, until the older boy hurried them along. He barely glanced at Felicity, but observed Maribeth almost as though he was in shock, and then gave her a very respectful nod of his head that was almost a bow, before ushering the children into another room.

"Who was that?" Felicity asked, once the door had closed behind the boys.

Maribeth looked puzzled. "I've never met him. He was human, but...by his reaction, I would swear he could see my mark..."

"How...?" The double doors at the entrance opened, cutting off Felicity's question. It was the guard Maribeth had flirted with on the way in.

"Did you find what you needed?" he asked.

Maribeth quickly turned on her considerable charm and gave him a winning smile. "Yes, thank you. All done." She shot Felicity a look as though she resented the woman's presence. "I've got to go and drop her off at the harem quarters...unless you think you could ask your friend to do it for me, so I could stay here with you for a bit?"

The man dropped his stern countenance and considered it for a moment. "I can't," he told her regretfully. "He's not allowed to leave his post."

She batted her eyes at him. "What a pity. Well, perhaps I can come by later. I do like to keep things new and interesting...if you think you might dare for a tryst."

"I'll be waiting," he replied with a smile.

She blew him a kiss as she took Felicity by the arm to leave. "I'll be off then." She hurried down the hall, pulling Felicity with her, until they were back at the sitting room where they had left Arif and Drake. Maribeth entered, ignoring the guards' protests. Both men looked furious to be barged in on and interrupted, but when they saw who it was, Arif simply sighed, nodded his acceptance to the guard and the door was closed behind them.

Drake still looked angry. "Why've you still got her in tow?" he asked with an annoyed glance at Felicity.

Arif spoke in a tone calm and understanding, trying to diffuse Drake's ire. "Please accept my apology. Were you unable to find Saruca to take her?"

Maribeth gave Arif a token smile, but spoke with an acidic tone. "It's fine. We've been enjoying some girl time. I'm curious though...what are the babies for?"

Arif looked shocked. Drake questioned her with quiet outrage. "Can you never simply do as you're told?"

"Children, small toddlers and babies; rooms full of them!" Maribeth insisted in shocked disgust.

"It's none of your concern, dear," Drake hushed her.

"But what's he want with babies?"

"Some vampires consider children a delicacy. Don't tell me you've suddenly become sensitive, darling. Mind your business and leave it be."

"You know I don't like children, to eat or to play with. They're bothersome," she assured him. "But babies…" He gave her a look of annoyance, but she was clearly horrified and could not let it go. "They are so difficult to bring into the world as it is. Do you have any idea how many things have to go exactly right just to birth one, and be assured of its survival? It's a damn near miracle the human race sustains itself. For a mother to overcome such odds and nurture life within her until birthing a baby…and then to have someone steal that baby away…it's just not right, Drake. We're not monsters."

"Actually, that is exactly what we are, Maribeth."

"No…not really. Grown people, they take their chances. They have their shot at life. If they are so careless as to give us a chance to steal their blood and cut their life short, so be it. But a baby hasn't even had a chance to see what they are to become. A baby needs to be with its mother."

Drake raised his eyebrows and then gave her an amused smile. "Your protest is duly noted, darling. I'll see that Arif keeps them off the dinner menu then. Now run along and deliver the human properly."

Arif spoke up with smooth assurance. "My dear lady, you may trust that the children being kept here are cared for most lovingly. Rest easy, that they are not meant to be meals. I attend them personally to ensure that their development and education is a top priority. They are truly blessed to have been chosen for the futures they have in store.

Now, if you please, have faith that all is well, and allow one of my men to take Miss Felicity to the harem quarters for you, so that you might go and find Lorelei. I've arranged for you ladies to have a delightful evening together. She is awaiting you in the common house lounge."

Maribeth smiled, graciously. "See Drake. Arif understands the chivalry of soothing a woman's concerns, rather than shushing her to be silent." The door opened and a vampire came in to retrieve Felicity for proper escort as Maribeth continued. "Thank you, Arif. I'll be off to find Lorelei then. Forgive the interruption."

Maribeth didn't even bother to spare Felicity a glance as they left the room to go their separate ways. Felicity had no idea what the woman actually thought of her and her suggestion to become Cain's ally, or whether it would make a difference to her position. She knew only she was being taken to the harem quarters, to be locked up for yet another interminable term of waiting…and was afraid to even wonder what she was waiting for.

~~~~~~~~~~~~~~~~~~~~~~~~~~~~~~~~~~~~~

Saruca led her back to the area of the house where the harem bedrooms were gathered. They passed the large dressing room filled with clothing, mirrors and make-up, where Felicity had been prepared for her meeting with Arif. Further down the hall, Saruca seemed to pause before a few different doors before deciding which they should enter. She finally reached a room that had enchanting music coming from within, opened the door and led Felicity through.

The music stopped as they opened the door. It was a large beautiful bedroom, with two full sized beds. There was a gorgeous, thin, young, dark haired woman seated on the bed furthest from the door. She had been playing a flute, and looked less than pleased by their interruption.

"This is Felicity," Saruca announced. "She is most important to the master, and will be staying here temporarily. Guards will be posted outside."

Without even bothering to tell Felicity who her new roommate was, Saruca then turned and left, closing the door behind her.

After a few moments of awkward silence, during which the woman looked her over with what Felicity could only interpret as resentment, the woman began to play her flute again. Felicity took a step further into the room. "You play beautifully. What's your name?"

The woman only briefly paused. "Ambrosia."

"Really? That's pretty. Is that your real name, or did *he* give that to you?" The woman looked at her as though the question was incredibly rude... Maybe it was. Flustered, Felicity sought to explain herself. "You just don't often hear of women being named after desserts...anyway, hi. I'm Felicity. Have you been here long?" The woman resumed playing before Felicity finished the question, which went unanswered. Trying not to let it ruffle her, Felicity sat down on the empty bed.

Ambrosia lowered her flute. "You can't sit there. That's Kira's bed."

Felicity opened her mouth in protest. "Where am I supposed to sleep?"

Ambrosia shrugged. "The floor?"

She was clearly planning to resume playing, when Felicity interrupted her again. "Well, Kira can ask me to move when she gets here."

Ambrosia squinted at her for a moment and then shrugged. "Whatever. Can I get some practice in now? The master wants me to come and play for him in less than an hour, and I have to learn this piece. I need to impress him tonight. I got gypped out of my last session with him, and if he isn't pleased with me tonight it will probably be a whole week before I get a fix."

"A fix?" Felicity asked, blankly.

Ambrosia scowled at Felicity's naivety. "Venom."

"Oh."

"I take it you haven't been initiated yet?"

"No, and I never will be. I'm only here temporarily."

Ambrosia raised her eyebrows. "Good. More for me."

"Doesn't it bother you? He treats you all like pets and he's totally using you. I know the venom is kind of addictive, but still, I'd think you'd be *happy* if he didn't call you to his bedroom so he could treat you like a sippy sex doll."

Ambrosia arched an eyebrow at her with a smirk. "Sippy sex doll? I like that. If he ever gets tired of Ambrosia, I'll have to suggest that one." Felicity was off-put to find that she couldn't even tell whether the woman was being sarcastic. "Have you ever had sex with a vampire?"

Felicity uncomfortably averted her eyes before answering. "Yes."

Ambrosia shook her head. "Well, either it was a long time ago or your vampire didn't know how to *work* it. Trust me, none of us would ever give up our turn voluntarily. Even if he's not in the mood, we do our best to coax it out of him, any way we can get it. It's in *all* of his fluids you know, and if he's having a group night, we all fight over it, believe me."

Rude or not, Felicity could not even try to pretend she wasn't disgusted. "Excuse me, I think I just threw up in my mouth a little."

Ambrosia didn't seem to be insulted, but rather seemed to think that Felicity was just too inexperienced to understand. "The more venom you can get, the better, believe me. If you aren't slated for initiation, it's your loss. You're a little on the chubby side for his tastes anyway. Now, if you don't mind, I need to practice. Why don't you go do some sit-ups or something?"

Felicity opened her mouth in shock over such treatment, but couldn't quite muster up a response. Ambrosia immediately began to play again, and wouldn't have heard her anyway. Felicity turned away, sitting on the bed and wishing that such insult brought out fierce anger in her, rather than humiliation and hurt, but she just didn't have much fight left in her at this point. She knew this nasty woman wasn't worth getting upset over anyway...but she still found herself blinking back tears.

After some more practice, Ambrosia left to prepare herself for her appointment with Arif. Felicity was glad to be rid of her, but unfortunately, it didn't do much to ease the tension. Felicity was left worrying and wondering when the girl's roommate, Kira, would show up and what animosity she might bring.

After an hour or so alone, Felicity tried to sleep in Kira's bed, fitfully anxious that any moment the girl would show up and kick her out of it. She tossed and turned, trying to calm her mind so she could get some much needed rest. At least if she could sleep, time would go by that much faster, and hopefully get her that much closer to returning home.

She tried to relax, and picture Ben lying next to her, strong and warm, cuddling close. Just the thought of him made her long for his comforting presence even more, making her unsure if it was any better than just lying in the bed with a mind full of worry.

She imagined the way he'd press himself close against her from behind, spooning her, and wrapping his arm around her shoulder to pull her into him. So vividly could her mind reproduce the feeling, it almost seemed he was there. It was amazing how clearly she could envision the sensation of his firm, well muscled body holding her, penetrating her, causing her to ache for him...desperate for satisfaction. Her mind calmed, anxiousness replaced by a flood of longing for her husband's touch, the caress of her own hand between her thighs a poor substitute.

Eyes closed, she imagined she could feel him nuzzling her neck from behind. He graced the side of her throat with gentle kisses that felt so real they made her sigh. Tension built and grew, pulling her further and further into the fantasy and towards the brink of ecstasy, until she was finally rewarded with passionate release. Again, she felt her throat covered in whispering kisses...*absolutely delectable.*

Her breath caught as she became aware of her surroundings once more. She was slightly shaken by the realism of her fantasy; it wasn't like her at all. She couldn't recall Ben ever saying those words to her, and they didn't seem like something he would actually say. Where had she gotten that from?

A noise at the door startled her. She barely had time to compose herself before it was opened by vampire guards. They were escorting a blonde human woman. Kira was being returned to her room. Felicity wondered if she would be ordered from the bed, but Kira didn't seem to be in a state of mind to care that Felicity was in her space.

The woman was too intoxicated to walk without assistance, and after the guards made a brief observation of the room and Felicity's whereabouts, Kira was unceremoniously dumped onto Ambrosia's bed. Rather than protest over being in the wrong bed, the drunk girl merely mumbled something incoherent, and then passed out, proceeding to snore quite loudly.

Felicity sat up, as a guard addressed her gruffly. "You'll remain for the rest of the day. Someone will be coming to collect you after sunset to be dressed and readied for another audience with the master." With that, the door was slammed shut. Kira barely stirred. All Felicity could do was to lie back down and try to get some sleep, until it was time to see Arif.

~~~~~~~~~~~~~~~~~~~~~~~~~~~~~~~

Felicity sat in Arif's formal office, on a large pillow on the floor in the corner. The arrangement made her feel uncomfortably like a pet, but she was grateful for the cushion after spending the night before being made to sit on the hard floor without one.

After a broken day's sleep, she spent the early hours of the evening in the harem quarters being bossed around and made to feel as though she were an insulting inconvenience to everyone in residence. Then she was roughly made to wash, dress in another costume much like the one she had worn the night before, and have her hair and make-up done once again. She finally received a sparse meal, and then was deposited in Arif's office to await his arrival.

Arif finally entered, looking very handsome in a long, fitted kaftan jacket of midnight blue, the edges gorgeously embroidered in swirls of gold. It was open, revealing the collar and sleeves of his deep blue silk shirt, its top buttons open just enough to show the gold chains that lay against his chest.

Arif's naturally curly hair had been brushed out until it was straightened into waves, soft as ebony cotton, and his cologne was a subtle but alluring musk. His beard and mustache were meticulously trimmed and detailed, and his eyes darkly rimmed in naturally thick lashes; he looked particularly seductive this evening. It wasn't hard to understand why the women of his harem seemed to find him entrancing. However, one look from him, filled with smug arrogance and delight over her distress at being his captive, immediately filled Felicity with disdain.

After a moment of enjoying how uncomfortable it made her to have him staring at her in her skimpy attire, he gave her a final appraisal with a smirk, and then remarked, "I trust you had a restful sleep, filled with pleasant dreams?"

She was almost frightened to even think of her brief fantasies of Ben before she slept, lest Arif read them from her mind...but was it possible he had read them already? Felicity's eyes widened as a knot of disturbed disgust began to clench her stomach. Or perhaps, Arif had *put them there...?*

Nausea rolled over her at the thought, which was quickly becoming a sickening certainty as she observed the sight of his smarmy smile. He winked at her and then turned away, as though she was of no further interest to him. "I've a busy evening ahead," he informed her, after which, he promptly ignored her.

Thoroughly revolted, she was just as happy to be spared his attention. She was made to sit there silently for hours, as he took phone calls and had various meetings with several different vampires. At first Felicity tried to listen in, and figure out what was going on, but nothing seemed to be of true interest to her. It was a lot of discussion over who was or wasn't performing their routine duties, the shifting of schedules, payment calculations, and things she couldn't hope to understand or care about. After a while, she just tuned out the conversations and prayed silently for Alyson to become aware of her telepathically, or for Cain or someone to figure out how to extract her from this place.

Arif finished reprimanding and insulting a young male vampire who apparently was too stupid to retain his rank, and the berated vampire left with his proverbial tail between his legs. Arif swiveled his chair so he could stare out the window pensively as he mentally consulted with someone about the next meeting on his schedule. A smile stole over his face, and he turned to share his glee with Felicity. "This should be fun. Straighten up and show some pride of appearance," he told her, while tugging down the cuffs of his own silk shirt and opening a button near the top to expose more of the gold chain that lay against his chest beneath. "I can't show you off properly if you're slumped in the corner like a rag doll."

Felicity managed to hold her tongue, but didn't make much of an effort to sit any straighter.

"I have a bit of news you'll be happy for," Arif informed her.

That perked her up quickly enough. "Is someone coming for me?"

"Yes, although not one I had hoped. Since Cain and Alyson haven't come rushing to make a trade for you, I've had an emissary make contact with someone who might actually want you back." Felicity was too busy trying to figure out what he was implying, to be insulted by his tone.

"Your husband," Arif provided. "My informant Kieran tells me that the man you married was quite close with Alyson while she was human. Very convenient for me. Perhaps that can be used to our advantage. Coupled with the fact that he is vested in your well-being more than any other at the moment, I think he will make the perfect intermediary for us."

"Ben...?" she sputtered in disbelief. "You had a *vampire* contact him?" She kept herself from adding, *Did he kill it?*... No sense letting Arif know that her husband was capable and dangerously hostile when necessary, if he didn't already know. "Does he know where I am?"

"He has been assured that you are being kept in good health and will be returned safely if demands are met. Kieran has given him the time and place for a meeting with me tomorrow. I have graciously agreed to allow you to join us, so that he can rest assured that you are unharmed."

"I'm going to see him tomorrow?" she repeated in excitement. Although thrilled over the prospect of seeing him, part of her was filled with absolute dread over the thought of Ben having to negotiate with this awful man, especially after spending the afternoon listening to how complicated and manipulative Arif could be when dealing with others. But if anyone could handle it, Ben could, and thank God he would know where she was and hopefully how to arrange for her to go home. She had never even dared to dream that Ben would be at all involved to help her, if only because he had no way of knowing what had happened to her or who to deal with to get her back.

"The man you married...Kieran suggests that he is the same man that the vampiress Sindy had requested aid in securing all those years ago. If so, then apparently she was unsuccessful." Felicity gave a little non-committal shrug, but Arif smiled. "Interesting. I'll have to keep that in mind." He turned his attention to the door as someone gave a light knock. "Enter."

The door opened to admit a vampire for his next appointment. Unlike the others thus far tonight, it was a woman, tall with long dark hair. The shock of recognition was almost as disturbing as when Felicity had first seen Maribeth...but this was someone she was much more disappointed to see.

It was Sindy herself, looking more posh and polished than Felicity had ever remembered. Stunning high heels added to her height, and with her short dress, made her legs look a mile long. She wore dark stockings, which marred the effect a bit...sheer would have looked better, but she was gorgeous regardless. Her dress hugged her body as though made specifically to show off each sexy curve, offset by long flowing sleeves. Her hair had pieces pinned up in a twisted design to the side, but was mostly loose down her back and shone with a sleek, dark brilliance.

Her make-up was sparingly, but expertly done, darkening her luscious lashes outlining her eyes, accentuating high cheekbones and giving blush to her full lips. Felicity suspected Saruca must have had a session with her. Sindy was always a beautiful woman, but other than the dark eye-shadows

Chris had smothered her beauty with in the past, most of the time she was without benefit of make-up. After being primped and preened by an expert, she looked like a movie-star.

The one thing that made Felicity feel a bit better about her old rival's appearance, was the fact that as she first entered the room, Sindy had an expression upon her face that crossed somewhere between repugnance and fright when met with Arif. She didn't even bother to look at Felicity; just another of Arif's human slaves sitting on the floor. Sindy entered the room and looked down at the floor as she did a slight nodding bow of respect. "You wanted to see me?" she asked.

"I always enjoy seeing you, divinely dark and seductive vision that you are," Arif purred as he took in the details of her.

Felicity watched the woman transform at the words, as though visibly putting on a persona to play the part. She peeked up at him through thick lashes and seemed visibly moved by his attractive appearance. The corner of her mouth slid upward into a smirk of a smile and she rested a hand upon her hip. She now presented the perfectly balanced image of confident sexuality and aloof boredom.

"Well, if you want to keep me around to look at, you're going to have to start feeding me a little better," she informed him.

"Now, now…you know your restricted diet is only temporary, and for good reason. You'll be back on human blood soon enough."

Sindy let out a dissatisfied breath of disgust. "I don't need carte blanche, but a glass now and then wouldn't make much of a difference, would it?" As she begged the question, she glanced in Felicity's direction, as though Arif should pull out a knife and slit her wrist for Sindy to sample. "Come on, sugar daddy, share the flow."

Felicity could read the exact moment when recognition set in on the vampiress' face. She did a visible double-take and her eyes got very wide when she realized who it was that sat listening in on their discussion. "Holy shit…you actually nabbed the bitch," she gasped, turning to Arif in shock. "Painted her up real nice too. Your staff even managed to make plain Jane look hot to trot." Felicity refused to meet her eyes or even speak. She simply held her head high and looked out the window as though uninterested in the woman's reaction or opinion. Sindy turned back to Arif, almost accusingly. "I thought Elric said it didn't work out."

Arif chuckled. "In a century of service I can count on one hand the number of times that Elric has ever disappointed me. I thought it might be good for you to observe that when I give an order to an officer of my coven it is carried out thoroughly and promptly. Elric was asked to deliver me this woman, and so here she is. I can only hope that you will learn to produce such satisfying results as well."

Sindy opened her mouth in outrage, not only insulted by Arif's attitude, but by the fact that he meant to belittle her in front of Felicity. "Are you comparing Elric's mission to grab a clueless, unarmed human woman, to my job of luring in a powerful, highly dangerous and guarded vampire?" she demanded in disbelief.

"I was simply pointing out the level of competence I expect in my ranks, although I must say, your own performance *was* severely disappointing. Do you think you might strive to do better in the future, or have you decided perhaps that holding a rank in my coven is no longer your desire?"

Sindy stared at him for a moment with frightened calculation playing upon her face. "Of course I still want rank here...the highest. Don't you think I'm worthy of it?" she asked, puffing out her chest a bit and looking down at Arif in haughty challenge.

Arif smiled, looking her over in approving appreciation. "My dear, I believe you are worthy of all sorts of positions. I consider them often."

Felicity grimaced as Sindy gave the creep a satisfied wink in response. "The oddest thing though," Arif continued. "Medical has informed me that a few of your inhibitors have gone missing."

Sindy quickly lost her smile. "I don't know what you mean. They just checked me a few hours ago. They didn't say anything."

"That's because they don't report *to you.*" Arif crossed to her and roughly tugged up her sleeve to reveal her inner forearm, which was bruised and had scabbed over cuts in two small spots; one on her wrist and another up near the crook of her elbow, as though there were actual holes dug into her skin. "Two from your left arm."

Sindy shrugged, lightly pulling her arm from his grasp. "I guess they fell out. You said they would."

Arif squinted at her in doubtful suspicion. "Indeed. There's quite a bit of damage on your arm, for you not to have noticed their *accidental* displacement."

Sindy sighed. "They were itchy. I think I was scratching at them in my sleep, but I thought they were still in there. I didn't know they'd fallen out, really."

"Well, since they have come out so much sooner than expected, we'll have to have them replaced...just for peace of mind."

"You don't have to do that. It's just my arm!" She sounded almost desperate. Felicity wondered what exactly he wanted to put into her, and why. It had to be something pretty bad if it caused scabs and bruising on a vampire, considering how quickly they healed.

"It's merely until your initiation. Then I will help you remove them myself, so we might explore *everything* we are capable of together." Sindy seemed to blanch at the suggestion, but Arif ignored her reaction. "Reveal your mark, if you please."

After a moment of hesitation, Sindy must have complied, because Arif smiled. "Very good. See? You have only but another week to endure such indignities."

"I think it's more like two," Sindy corrected him.

"Nonsense. We don't need to wait for all trace of him to dissipate, only for his mark on you to become weak enough for me to cross. Sufficiently faded, I can overcome it to accomplish the task. A week.

That will do just fine, because there is a vampire of my senior guard whom I have just demoted this evening. That will leave a vacancy in one of our larger residences. It shall be gifted to you upon your initiation. I've already set aside some unmarked humans for you. I think seven will do. Would you like to regain Val and Brett in the group, or would you prefer an entirely fresh new stable?"

His promises gave Sindy pause to reconsider her feelings on the matter. "Oh…um, sure. I'll take back Brett and Val. That'd be fine. Seven?"

"Yes, standard allotment for a member of my senior guard. Of course, Elric governs nine, as the head of command, but considering that you are being inducted past the cadets and lower guard, to directly hold such a high rank, I think seven is very generous."

"Definitely, more than fair," she agreed.

"I'm glad you think so. To have been passed eyes of such a color, you have been truly gifted, my dear. You are going to be quite pampered here, and I ask comparatively little in return. Obedience will buy you the decadence and security you deserve, remember that. I'll escort you to the common house, so Cat can give your arm its supplemental treatment. Let me just summon the guards to bring Saruca, so that she might take our Miss Felicity back into her custody."

Sindy sighed. "You don't have to come. It's only my arm, I can handle it."

"Nonsense. Of course I'll accompany you." It was unclear whether he did not trust Sindy to go and take care of whatever the treatment was on her own, or if he would simply enjoy being there to watch. Maybe a little of both. He raised his finger in the air for her to wait. "Just a moment." He wandered over to the window, clearly in conference psychically with someone else.

A few very uncomfortable minutes passed. Felicity tried not to fidget as Sindy stared down at her in disdain. She looked as though she'd like to say something, but Arif was too close for her to dare. Good, Felicity had no desire for conversation. Felicity found herself admiring Sindy's shoes, rather than make eye contact, but after a moment, her eyes wandered to the woman's legs. A dark spot had drawn her eye. Upon closer inspection, she realized that Sindy's legs also seemed to be covered in scabbed bruises, like the ones on her arm. The dark stockings hid the injuries, but from Felicity's close vantage point, she could make out the marks through the hosiery. What had been done to her?

Arif finished his silent exchange and let out an exasperated sigh. "Excuse me a moment. I'm afraid I have to go and take care of something first."

"That's okay, I know you're busy. You don't need to come," Sindy tried again to assure him.

He fixed her with an authoritative stare. "You will remain in this room until I return for you." He glanced at Felicity as an afterthought. "Keep an eye on her for me, will you? She is to be kept unmarked. Saruca is awaiting a guard escort so she can come and collect Felicity for transport." He gave Felicity a pointed look. "Can't have you wandering off where you don't belong again, now can we?" As though her foray to the west wing with Maribeth had been her fault. "Not to worry, there are guards posted outside the door if she gives you any trouble," he assured Sindy with a smirk, as though they were there for the vampiress' protection rather than to guard her from leaving as well.

"Oh, good…thanks," Sindy grumbled, as he turned and left the room.

The moment the door was shut, Sindy let out a huff of disgust, but then composed herself and turned to Felicity with an evil grin. "Well, look at you, all gussied up and degraded into playing vampire's pet…again."

Felicity stared at her in disdain. It just figured Sindy would have a position of power in this place, even if it was under Arif's strict authority. She may not be free to do whatever she wanted, but she was in a better position than Felicity. After a moment of biting her tongue, Felicity answered with quiet tenacity. "I was never anyone's pet."

Sindy shook her head with a smile. "That's not how Cain tells it."

"Cain would *never* call me a pet, *ever*…you lying skank." She couldn't help but mutter the added insult. She didn't want to let Sindy get the better of her, but the bitch always knew how to push just the right buttons.

"Ooh, sounds like I struck a nerve. I didn't say you weren't spoiled and pampered like a beloved little poodle, but you were still a pet, whoring out your body for venom. At least now you look the part."

"You're one to talk. I'm here against my will. You're the one sleeping your way to the top of the trash heap. Talk about degrading. Looks like you'll take all sorts of abuse just to keep from feeling worthless, huh?"

"You'd better watch your mouth, missy, or I'll have you punished like a bad doggie."

"You may have some pull around here, but I'm a valuable hostage, you can't do anything to me. Anyway, it sounds more like you're the one about to be punished. What are you letting him do to you?"

"None of your fucking business." To punctuate the statement, Sindy leaned forward and gave her a sharp shove on the shoulder. The unexpected force knocked Felicity's head back against the wall. "And I can do what I want, as long as I don't leave any permanent injuries. That gives me plenty of room to play."

The shock and resentment of the act hurt worse than the pounding in her head, but Felicity knew that Sindy was probably right...to an extent. She sat back up and narrowed her eyes as she rubbed the back of her head. "Hey, what do you think Arif would say, if I told him that along with your arm, it looks like both legs need some more *treatments* too?"

Sindy lost her smug expression. "Don't you dare."

"But I'm really concerned about you," she said, with sarcastic sympathy. "He's obviously forcing something awful on you, and if I'm worried and thinking about it, Arif is bound to pick it up in my thoughts. I can't help it," she said with a false smile.

"It's not your concern, so you'd better not think about me at all and just worry about yourself. What a surprise, Strawberry Shortcake is once again poking her nose in my business and trying to ruin my life."

"You think *I'm* ruining *your* life? You were already dead when I met you! Then you tried to kill me, you slept with my boyfriend and tortured my friends!"

Sindy let out an amused chuckle. "Actually, I tortured your friends first, then I slept with Cain, repeatedly, for years. He's a *really* good lover." Felicity turned away rather than give Sindy the satisfaction of watching the hurt and disgust on her face. The thought of Sindy sleeping with Cain tarnished her treasured memories and made her feel ill. Sindy chuckled.

After a moment, Felicity collected herself and turned back to her. "Go ahead and try to rub it in all you want. So, you were with Cain. You forget that I'm not frozen in time, like you. I don't live in the past. I've moved on.

My husband and I love each other very much. We're really happy together, and you can't touch that.

If Cain really was with you, then that just makes me feel bad for him, because I know he was just clinging to you so he didn't have to feel alone. He'll never feel for you the way he did for me. How could he, when you're such a pathetic bully? You brag about torturing my friends like it's some kind of joke? Cain could never love someone like you. I wouldn't get too comfortable, because once Cain really gets to know you, I doubt it's going to last. If it was anything real, then you wouldn't be *here*, would you?"

The vampiress stared at her with a cold hard glare. "You don't know me."

Sindy's voice was a low grumble, infused with some unexpected hurt emotion that really caught Felicity by surprise, making her feel like the bully she had just accused Sindy of being. Sindy's eyes were becoming glassy with unshed tears of humiliation and hurt. Felicity averted her eyes, ashamed to have stooped to such insult. "You're right, I don't. I'm sorry, that was really mean."

"And technically, Ben and Allie were *my* friends first."

Felicity was prepared to ignore further digs over Cain, but couldn't help but be dumbfounded with outrage by the last statement. "*What?* Ben and Allie hated you when I met them…with a passion. It had nothing to do with me."

"They were coming around, until you showed up."

"Oh my God, you are so delusional."

"I'm delusional? Cain dumped you. So what do you do? You latch onto Allie in some sad attempt to get him to give a shit about you again. So pathetic!"

Felicity took a deep breath and let it out slowly. "I can't believe I just apologized to you. You are a fucking psychopath."

"Yeah, well, I was abused, tortured, killed and then tortured again, in that order, so who could blame me for losing a few screws? What's your excuse?"

Felicity stared at her, open-mouthed, never doubting for a moment that the description of Sindy's life was completely accurate. She almost felt bad for her. "You know, it doesn't have to be like this. I don't know what I ever did to make you hate me so much, but I bet if we worked together, we could both find a way to get out of this place," she suggested in a whisper.

"Who says I want out? Maybe this is exactly where I want to be." Sindy raised her hands, gesturing to indicate the expensively furnished room they were in, to accentuate her statement. It caused the flair of her sleeves to fold down, exposing her forearms, and their scabbed over bruises.

"You're looking pretty beat up for someone who is exactly where they want to be."

Sindy hastily pulled her sleeves back down with a grimace. "Shut up. What do you know? So I've got some sob stories of my own. If I've learned anything in my life, it's that you have to take care of yourself, because nobody else gives a shit. I get backed into a corner, and who's coming to my rescue?"

"Maybe if you weren't such a bitch, people would want to help you."

"I don't need your help, or anybody else's."

"Fine, then get away from me. I don't have to talk to you."

"Actually, I could make a really good case for forcing you to do whatever I want. You're on my turf now, and bruises or not, I'm pretty hot shit around here."

"Yeah, as long as Arif gets to use you for his twisted entertainment; and whatever that is, I don't want to know. Luckily, I don't plan to be here for long."

"I wouldn't put much stock in those plans, honey. I hope you don't think Cain is coming to save you, because he doesn't really care about you anymore at this point. He's mine now. I'm the one he's sitting at home missing, hoping I'll come back for a visit. And Alyson…she is way over her head into some deep shit you can't even imagine. She's not going to risk her neck for *you*. Face it, it's looking pretty likely that your only way out of here will be in a body bag. Until then, be a good girl and at least you might get to have a little fun for a while first. I wonder what Arif plans to do with you after everyone gets bored of this. Maybe I'll pick you up at the next auction. I could use a housemaid for the new diggs."

"I'm not staying, and I don't need Cain or Allie to save me," Felicity informed her, fighting for fortitude. "We're going for negotiations tomorrow, and once my husband finds out where I am, he and his dad will get me out of here. You'll see."

Sindy actually laughed at her. "You think your human husband is going to storm a fortress full of powerful vampires…with his *dad?* What kind of dipshit did you marry?"

"I didn't marry a dipshit," Felicity told her with a true smile, full of quiet confidence. "I married an Everheart; Benjamin Everheart. His dad's name is Bernard. Maybe you've heard of him?"

The shock on Sindy's face was absolutely priceless. It took the vampiress a moment of recovery to find her voice. "You married my Ben?"

Now it was Felicity's turn to laugh. "He was never *your* Ben, and yes, I did."

"His father is the vampire hunter," Sindy confirmed in quiet awe.

"I know," she answered with a broad grin.

"Does Arif know that?"

"If he doesn't yet, he will tomorrow, and I for one, am looking forward to seeing him quake in his stylish silk shirt."

Sindy shook her head as though Felicity was still screwed. "Okay, so you've got plenty of heroes planning to rescue you at any moment, but hopefully they aren't stupid enough to try and storm in here, because that will just make everything a big fucking mess. Arif will be totally pissed off and just kill you and Ben both. There is no way Ben's going to be able to get you out of here without giving up whatever Arif wants, even with his dad's help...and then Arif still might decide to keep you, just for spite against Cain. You've got to know that."

Felicity had no idea whether Sindy was right or not, and she wanted to have faith that Ben and Bernard would be able to figure things out better than Sindy could predict, but suddenly it all just became too much. While trying to keep a brave front in the face of Sindy's onslaught, she had desperately clung to the hope that somehow Ben and Bernard would be able to save her. To have Sindy dismiss the idea so easily, crumbled the last of her confidence, whether Sindy was right or not.

Felicity looked down, to try to gather her strength and hide her watery eyes, but that only made her notice the embarrassing harem costume she was in, and the fact that her middle was far too chubby to look very appealing in it unless she was standing up and sucking in her breath for all she was worth. It was the last straw, breaking the strength that had been holding back her tears.

Of course, Sindy noticed almost immediately. "Are you crying? Oh my God, what a pussy you are. Nobody's even done anything to you."

Felicity looked up in outrage and swiped her arm across her face. "I was abducted! I have a little baby at home, who is probably crying inconsolably because he doesn't know where I am or what's going on. I've never been away from him for more than one night. He's too little for anyone to explain to him that it'll be okay and that I'll come home soon...and I don't even know if that's true.

I'm breastfeeding, and they must have run out of my milk by now. He's never had formula. He probably won't even drink it. And do you have any idea how much pain I'm in?"

Sindy looked insulted over the remark. "*You're* in pain?"

Felicity lightly cupped her breasts, which were overflowing the sequined bra she was in. "My boobs feel like water balloons about to explode! I have to express milk in the shower just to get some relief, and it's just washing down the drain while my baby is home crying." The last words were spoken as she once again deteriorated into tears.

"Alright, let's not get dramatic. Someone will give the kid a bottle. He'll survive. Get a grip and relax. I'm the one doing the toughest balancing act of my existence here. You have no idea how difficult a position I'm in. You're just taking a forced vacation; big deal."

"At least you're here because of choices *you* made and you have some free will. I didn't ask for this! You have no idea how hard this is for me. You think I'm on vacation? It's awful enough that I have to be away from my husband and baby and spend each night wondering if my captors are going to get bored and thirsty enough to kill me, but I'm surrounded by bitchy Barbie dolls to boot.

You can't even imagine what that's like. Every woman here is young, thin and gorgeous. I don't exactly blend right in." She wiped her eyes again and tried to compose herself with a sniffle. "I am not old, and I know I'll eventually lose the baby weight…I hope, but you all make me feel so damn tired and undesirable, everywhere I turn. It's humiliating. I've got bags under my eyes and stretch marks on my thighs, and every other woman here has a figure that defies gravity. It may be the least of my problems, but it still sucks."

Sindy smirked at her, making Felicity regret opening up and showing any sort of weakness to the woman, but a part of her just could not believe that another woman couldn't understand and sympathize with her position, even Sindy.

Sindy let out a huff of breath and shook her head. "And people think I'm the shallow one? Those stretch marks are a badge of honor that I will never have the opportunity to earn, whether I'd want them or not. You created a whole 'nother human being. You may not be much, but you are a mom, and most people automatically sympathize with you and respect that."

Felicity lowered her eyes and wondered if Sindy really might be jealous of her humanity in that way. Before she could think of something to say, Sindy continued. "I have to fight and claw my way to earning any inkling of respect or power I've got. Do you remember what it was like to be sixteen? No one takes you seriously. I am a twenty-seven year old woman, and I still get treated like an incapable teenager."

"That might be a result of your behavior more than your appearance," Felicity responded, sourly. "Are you seriously trying to make me feel bad for you because you will forever have the body of a beautiful sixteen year old? Because if you are, I may just have to smack you, vampire or not."

Sindy answered with a derisive snort. "I love what I am, but everything has its drawbacks. I don't know all your business, but between Cain and Allie, I'm sure you've been given the choice to be turned at some point. You chose to be human, even though you had the oldest, strongest, hottest vampire I have ever met, agonizing and panting after you like a puppy. Then, you move on, and somehow manage to marry the strongest, sexiest *human* man I've ever known."

Sindy swallowed, looking as though she was choking on the words. She continued in a voice deep and filled with resentment. "You lucky bitch. I'll bet you have a real nice house, don't you? Clearly you're getting three square meals a day," she added with a smirk and gesture towards Felicity's figure. "And on top of it all, you have a little legacy waiting for you at home; a baby who thinks you are his whole world right now. So he's spending a few days crying at grandma's house, big deal. When this is over, he'll never even remember that you were gone.

You're in strange place full of scary vampires, I get it, but nobody is going to let anything truly bad happen to you, because they don't want Cain, Ben and Bernard on the eternal vengeance train. You get to go home to your cozy little life when this is over. So forgive me if I'm not filled with sympathy that you aren't feeling like the sexy center of the universe here. Boo fucking hoo."

Felicity sat up straighter, trying to put things into perspective. She couldn't help but eye Sindy's beautiful young body and wonder what it would really be like to never age. Appealing as it seemed, one thought of the baby she would never have had a chance to have with Ben, and she knew she had made the right choice. It was worth it. "Do you really think they're going to let me go home?"

"Not without a lot of hoopla so Arif can wring what he wants out of Cain or Ben first, but yeah."

"I think he wants something from Allie."

"Well then, who better to convince her to give it to him then Ben and Cain, right? She sure as hell wouldn't listen to me."

"You?"

"Long story, but in the end, I'm sort of glad it didn't work out. In fact, I kind of hope Allie manages to stay the hell out of all of this, even if it does complicate things for you. Ben is a pretty smart guy. Who knows?

Maybe he'll figure out a way to get you back without going through Allie, although I can't imagine how, not without help from the inside…"

Felicity processed the suggestion and then eyed Sindy, quizzically. "The inside… Are you saying you might want to help me?"

Sindy shrugged. "I wouldn't say *help*. I don't know what I could do anyway. If you haven't noticed, I've got my own problems to deal with. But if the opportunity arose to get you out…I might. Think of it more as me wanting to get you out of my face. Besides, the sooner I can give you back to Ben, the better. Whether you deserve it or not, ensconced in your perfect little human life is just where I want you. Married, mortal and leaving a big empty space in Cain's bed." Sindy couldn't resist giving Felicity a sly smile as she rubbed her hand down the side of her body suggestively. "I've been having a wonderful time making him forget you ever existed," she confided, gleefully, "and the last thing I need, is for him to feel guilty and worried that you're here rotting away in Arif's cellar.

If Ben wants you back, I'd be happy to throw you over the fence to him. But don't get your hopes up. I have a feeling I'm going to be kind of busy for the next few nights," she warned, reaching lower and rubbing one of the scabbed over bruised spots on her leg.

Both women were startled by the door opening as Arif himself re-entered the room. They both jumped a bit guiltily, but Arif didn't even notice. He wasn't even looking into the room, but having a discussion with Saruca who stood in the doorway with him, backed by two vampire guards. "Ladies, time to go."

~~~~~~~~~~~~~~~~~~~~~~~~~~~~~

Midnight, the appointed time to finally meet with Ben. After an interminable day spent wondering how she and Sindy might possibly be able to help each other, and whether the vampiress knew Maribeth, who also might be persuaded to assist them somehow, Felicity finally gave up, worried that Arif would read the thoughts from her head. After being changed into more appropriate clothing for the outside world, Felicity was ushered into a car with Arif and a few other vampires. They arrived at the designated meeting place, a diner, and sat in the car for what seemed like forever as Arif's guards positioned themselves in various spots around the location.

Cat, who had been sitting with her eyes closed, still and silent as stone for the entire ride, now shifted impatiently. She was a lovely, petite, oriental vampire, but oddly enough, seemed to be dressed like Cat Woman this evening. She wore a sleek black outfit consisting of a sexy bustier, and very long gloves that covered her arms and tipped each finger with a sharp long nail of shining silver. She had a belt slung over the hips of her spandex pants that sported a thin tail in the back, and she wore ridiculously high heeled thigh-high black boots. Her short dark hair was cut in a cute bob, with straight bangs across the front, and the outfit was completed by a headband with small triangular ears on top.

She was a bit strange, but other than being a vampire, hadn't given Felicity any reason to dislike her. Arif, on the other hand, seemed to handle the woman as though she was a child. He coddled and fussed over her one moment, but then gave her stern clear directions the next, as though she couldn't be trusted to use common sense. As Cat began to wiggle some more, Arif now shot her an annoyed glance for her fidgeting.

"I'm done meditating," she explained in a sharp yet breathy whisper. "You know I don't like confined spaces. I need out."

Arif hushed her. "Just a moment, darling."

After a brief pause, the driver exited the vehicle and went around to open Cat's door. She sprang out of her seat and was little more than an inhuman blur of motion, before coming to rest under the lights of the restaurant entrance. "Better," she purred with a smile.

Arif nodded his approval. "Go on inside and see that all is in order. I'll be keeping a full mental link. We'll follow shortly."

The driver closed the door and Arif leaned back and closed his eyes. Felicity waited quietly until she couldn't stand it any longer. "Is he in there?"

Arif didn't even crack open an eye. "He is."

"Then what are we waiting for?"

"Patience. I want to be sure all is to my liking."

Felicity smoothed her hands down her skirt in nervousness. Thankfully, she had been given back the green dress she had borrowed from Elric's coven to wear. She would have died of humiliation and shame if Arif had paraded her out in public to meet Ben in the harem get-up. Besides, seeing such indignities would doubtless cause Ben to lose his temper; something they could not afford at the moment. "Is he alone?" she asked.

"So it would seem."

"Then what more do you want? You have vampire guards everywhere, and with your powers, you don't even need them." A smile stole upon his face and he opened his eyes to meet hers as she continued. "He is my human husband. He's not a threat to you," Felicity insisted, pleading for him to let them go in. "He just wants to find out what you want from him to get me back. He doesn't care about your vampire politics."

Arif weighed her words and then gave a slight nod of agreement. "Very well." Arif's door was opened for him by the driver. Before getting out, Arif closed his eyes and spoke, seemingly boosted telepathically to the guards he had positioned inside. "I don't think I like the table. Have him moved to a booth in the back."

When Arif finally allowed them to enter the diner, they were met in the vestibule by Cat, who took hold of Felicity's arm in a grip hard enough to leave a bruise. It was surprising to feel such strength from the petite and dainty seeming woman. Felicity shifted in her grip. "You want to take it easy? I'm not going anywhere."

As Arif went into the dining area, surrounded by three of his men, Cat flashed startlingly pink eyes at Felicity and bared her fangs in a smile. Felicity was suitably frightened into stillness. No matter how much time she spent with these vampires, a display like that was always chilling. Cat kept her eerie gaze trained on Felicity as she spoke. "Sorry, sometimes I forget how fragile humans are. You'll notice that Arif has put more guards protecting himself than he has put on you. That's because he knows that I need no help to keep you in my possession. You might want to behave yourself."

The woman spoke truly. Arif did not seem to be concerned about Felicity's security in the least. Felicity couldn't help but spend the next few minutes wondering just what range of formidable powers a vampire with pink eyes might possess, to make him so assured that Cat would have no problems.

Cat held her back while Arif went further inside. Felicity strained to see past him, and finally spotted her husband in the back of the room. Her heart leapt at the sight of him, even though he looked as though he hadn't slept in a week. He was nicely dressed and handsome as always, but the dark circles under his eyes and unshaven stubble of beard across his cheeks and chin betrayed his worry. He wore a grim expression and seemed very anxious indeed when Arif approached him and Felicity was nowhere to be seen.

Felicity lost sight of them, as guards surrounded the pair. They spoke for a few minutes before Cat gave her arm a small squeeze. "Show time." Felicity was escorted to the back of the diner, and the guards parted, leaving clear space between her and Cat, and where Arif stood with Ben.

The moment Ben saw her, looking healthy, lovely, and unharmed, enormous relief showed on his face. "Felicity!" Ben obviously meant to rush to her, but would need to pass Arif and his guards to do it. He stopped himself to judge Arif's demeanor.

"By all means, hug her, kiss her, assure yourself she is well and unbitten. Did you expect that I was not going to keep my word?"

Ben didn't bother to respond and needed no further urging. He hurried forward to take Felicity into his arms. Being enfolded in her husband's embrace had never felt more comforting. True to his word, Arif gave them a few moments, and his guards did nothing to restrain their reunion.

"Liss," he whispered. "Oh God, Liss, I thought I'd lost you." Ben hugged her tightly to him, as though he did not want to have to let go. "Are you alright? Tell me he hasn't hurt you and you're alright."

She nodded against his shoulder. "Where's Christian? Is he okay?"

"He's fine. He's with your mom."

She nodded again, hugging him tightly, unable to find any more words that she could trust not to come out as choking sobs of relief. She was not home yet, and relief would have to wait.

Arif spoke, reminding them of their audience, and gestured for Ben to get into the booth. "Please, sit. You can keep her next to you, on the end."

As per Arif's instruction, Ben entered the booth first, and Felicity got in next to him. Felicity realized that by blocking him in with her, Arif was keeping full control. He had spent the last few nights learning to manipulate Felicity flawlessly with his powers, and she would be unable to move a muscle if it was not Arif's wish to allow it. Ben did not understand this though, and still seemed confused by Arif's willingness to allow Felicity to be close with him in the booth.

"Let me assure you, I have no trepidation over your actions," Arif explained as he took a seat opposite them in the booth. "We are quite heavily guarded at the moment, and I have power you have never even dreamed of. If you attempt to remove her from my presence, or endanger me in any way, your wife will be left with deep emotional scars and mental incapacities that will make you wish I had simply killed her. Are we clear?" Arif's eyes shifted to reveal their purple vampiric brilliance, and after showing them to Ben with a smile, he trained them on Felicity. Ben affected suitable surprise and awe over the display, but worse than that, Felicity trembled as she could feel the power in that gaze, and knew that she was his to command.

Arif ignored the glare that Ben had now trained on him in insult over the threat as the vampire continued. "I have spent some enjoyable time learning the workings of your wife's thoughts and actions these past nights.

She is quite a susceptible conduit for telepathic influence. I can promise that there will not be a thought in her pretty little head that I am not privy to. So feel free to fondle her and whisper any secrets you'd like."

A waitress approached, eyeing Cat and the guards that were still standing around the booth. "We have a larger table over here," she said, trying to get them all to move and sit.

Arif turned his violet eyed attention to her. "We want only to be left alone," he told her in a firm but gentle voice.

The waitress stiffened for a moment at the sight of his purple gaze, but then nodded, her eyes glazed over and an accommodating smile on her face. "Take all the time you need. I'll make sure nobody bothers you," she assured him with a little crinkle of her nose.

Once she was gone, the guards moved to take up stations around them as Cat took a seat next to Arif. She leaned closer to Felicity with a grin. "He's handsome," she said with a glance at Ben, confiding her approval.

Ben observed the woman for a moment, questioning Arif. "Who's this?"

The woman smirked and answered for herself. "They call me Cat."

"Like the animal." Ben nodded, eyeing the fuzzy, black cat-eared headband she wore.

She squinted at him, as though he was being terribly naive. "No...like the street. Evidently you've never been to the north side of Omotesando, Tokyo."

"...Evidently." Ben squinted at her in confused bewilderment for a moment, before turning his attention back to Arif. "Why are you doing this? What do you want with Felicity?"

"I don't want anything from Felicity, charming as she may be," he said with a smarmy smile at her. "I require the cooperation of another vampire in order to accomplish a task I have been long working on. My hope was that you or Felicity might have sufficient influence over this vampire to find and persuade them to lend me their assistance."

Ben adopted a shocked expression. "A vampire? I'm just a guy who wants his wife back. When the blonde kid came and told me who...and *what* had taken her, I could barely even believe half of what he said. I'm still trying to process it. What makes you think I could possibly be capable of doing anything you couldn't do yourself?"

Arif sighed. "Don't waste my time with games. Do you think I am a fool? You needn't bother affecting surprise over my nature or request. I know exactly who you are, Mr. Everheart, just as you know me. I will admit, I was uninformed initially, but it wasn't difficult to put together.

Your wife did an admirable job of keeping your identity and connections from me at first, but it wasn't long before I learned to navigate the configuration of her thoughts, once I gave her my full attention." He turned another grin on Felicity that made her turn away uncomfortably until Arif continued speaking to Ben.

"I found your identity inconvenient and a bit troubling at first, but I have come to realize that it could prove very beneficial indeed. Your past associations with Alyson and any information and abilities that you have inherited from your infamous father make you quite uniquely capable of successfully performing the task at hand."

Ben bitterly narrowed his gaze. "My father and I aren't very close, and I'm pretty sure that all I've inherited from him are these premature grays and a predisposition to alcoholism, so just leave him out of it and tell me what it'll take to get my wife back. Better yet, maybe you'll realize that you don't want to make this any worse than it is, and let me take her home now. I don't think I can do anything for you, and while I may not like my father much, he has a pretty self-inflated ego and a dramatic propensity for avenging injustice, whether I'd want him to or not, so I doubt you want him involved. Surely, you can handle your problems without us."

Arif smirked in amusement. "Your wife also doubts your abilities...how emasculating for you. She does not seem to think that you are capable of the task I require." Felicity gave Arif a dirty look for voicing such betrayal. She hadn't truly been doubting Ben's capability, but that wouldn't even matter. Now that Arif had said it aloud, Ben would always wonder if he'd read it from her mind.

Arif smiled at her and went on. "That is a pity, because if you cannot accomplish my request, I will simply keep Felicity for myself and find some other means to get what I desire. She looks delicious." He leaned forward over the table, as though weighing Felicity's favorable characteristics, and then raised his eyebrows as though just considering a new idea. "She might even make a good vampire...even if Cain didn't seem to think so.

If you're incapable of helping me, perhaps the vampire Cain would be better suited to carrying out my favor. If I were to turn the lady, I am sure he would be interested in doing whatever I'd like in order to acquire her for himself when I am through."

Whether he had read it from Felicity, Ben, or divined it on his own, Arif knew just how to push Ben's buttons. Ben immediately spoke against the idea. "I can do it. What do you need?"

Arif was pleased by his quick response. "I need someone turned into a vampire...by your dear friend Alyson."

"Why don't you just do it yourself?"

"If only I could... I need it done with *her* blood. It must be hers, no one else's. Since she has shown unwillingness to turn others, and it is a complicated task, best done voluntarily, a nice sampling of her blood will have to do. If she will not do it for me, then I need a good deal of Alyson's blood, so that I may use it to change whom I desire."

Ben looked as horrified as Felicity, and he didn't even know that Alyson was The United One. "How am I supposed to do that? Alyson isn't going to give me her blood, and I hear she's a strong vampire. I don't know how you think I could possibly take it from her. If you know as much about me as you say you do, then you know that Alyson and I are not *dear friends* anymore. I haven't even spoken to her in years!"

"Relax. The task is not as difficult as it would seem, I need only to know that you are not averse to accomplishing it. If it were simple, would you do it?"

Ben glanced at Felicity, who was staring at him wide-eyed. She certainly didn't want to remain in Arif's power, but she couldn't ask Ben to betray Alyson. Besides, Alyson was The United One. Felicity wasn't even totally certain what that meant, but she knew it was something that made it unacceptable for Arif to have control of her blood. "Ben, you can't. We'll find another way."

Arif was quick to speak against her. "There is no other way...unless you would *like* for me to turn you. Once you are a vampire, I am sure that Cain would bring me every last drop of Alyson's blood if I requested it, in order to mentor you himself and keep you from my continued possession."

"You're not turning her," Ben asserted. "What do I do?"

"It's very simple. You need only to tell Alyson that you want to see her. Convince her that she must come alone to meet with you, in the interest of re-kindling your friendship."

"I don't even know where she is."

"With the skills of the famed vampire hunter at your disposal, I'm sure that won't be a problem for you. Should your father be willing to assist us in this, I would be willing to take the price off of his head."

"I don't think my father has been very troubled by any bounty you've put on him. You've been unsuccessfully hunting him for how long now?" Ben pointed out snidely. "He seems perfectly comfortable with things as they are."

Arif was unamused and fixed Ben with a level stare. "Don't let his cavalier attitude fool you. My coven members have taken great sport in hunting your father all these years, and although he has managed to avoid capture thus far, I am sure the hunt is wearing on him.

If you are not close, as you say, he must recognize this as an opportunity to make amends with you by helping to retrieve your wife. Let him hunt Alyson for you...just don't let him kill her. Have him find her, and once she has been located, lure her to a place of my choosing so I may subdue her myself. I will then release your wife, in return for you letting me keep Alyson for my own ends."

"Even if my father finds her, how am I supposed to lure her anywhere?"

"She was once fond of you, surely you can convince her to let you talk to her. You can even tell her that you want her help in regaining Felicity from me. That would not be a lie. She is good at sensing lies...but you are naturally defensive and difficult to read. If you stick with twisted truths rather than outright lies, you will fool her.

Once you have brought her to me, I will have the means to dampen her powers. Even if I cannot coerce her to create a vampire for me, she will still be defenseless. She will be restrained so I can take the blood from her and make the change myself. She must be well controlled, for it will take some time for such a great deal of her blood to be drawn, but as long as she is alone, my trusted team can accomplish the deed."

Cat shifted and purred at the thought. "Oh yes. We know what to do."

Ben ignored her to question Arif. "Will it kill her?"

"The drawing of blood will not, but when we are through, if she is uncooperative, her death may prove to be a necessary measure. Is that a problem for you?"

Both men took a moment to glance at Felicity, knowing her life was at stake. Ben shook his head. "The Alyson I know is already dead. This vampire may have confiscated her body, but her soul is gone. If she won't do what you want, and is perfectly content to leave Felicity here to rot, then I don't have a problem doing whatever it takes to buy Felicity's freedom."

"Ben..." Felicity tried to protest, but Arif cut her off.

"She has a protector, her lover and maker. It may be difficult to separate them. If she refuses to come alone, you may need to...distract him for me."

Ben took a deep breath and let it out again. "Her lover, Mattie. Yeah, I know him. If he really loved her, he wouldn't have turned her. He's never been a match for me. Vampire or not, I can take him."

Arif smiled. "Wonderful."

"Ben, you can't," Felicity insisted, tearfully. "You can't agree to this, it's horrible! You can't betray them, and it might get you killed."

"What do you want me to do, Liss? Leave you with this guy?"

Felicity opened her mouth, at a loss what to say. She made the terrible mistake of glancing over at Arif, and suddenly felt the disorienting loss of control over herself. Arif locked her in his mesmerizing vampiric gaze, and took over.

"Yes," she heard herself telling her husband. "If it means betraying Allie and Mattie, then I'd rather you left me here. I won't let you do that to them and get yourself killed in the process." Ben looked as upset by the words as she felt.

"You know he won't truly kill me," she continued, her gaze locked to Arif's, "because he'll want to see if he can use me to manipulate Cain. So, let him turn me. There are worse fates. Let Cain be the one to do his dirty work. I'm sure he'll do it. He'd do anything for me. Maybe not while I'm human, but if I was a vampire? Without a doubt. At that point, maybe he could even talk Allie into cooperating so no one else has to get hurt. Allie loves Cain like he's family. She'll listen to him. At this point, without me there, I don't know if she'd even agree to meet with *you.*"

As the last words left her lips, her will was released with a mental command to be silent. The pain on Ben's face was devastating. She wasn't sure which hurt him worse, that Cain seemed to have usurped Ben's place in Allie's heart, that Felicity sounded as though being turned into a vampire was a perfectly acceptable solution, something Ben had always secretly feared she wanted anyway, or her casual determination that Cain was more willing and capable of helping her then Ben was.

Ben looked as though he'd been punched in the gut. It was awful to see the despair on his face. After a moment, his expression turned grim and determined. Cat stifled a giggle, and Ben refused to even glance in Felicity's direction. He addressed only Arif, with a voice deep and fierce. "Give me a time and place. Alyson will be there. I'll take care of Mattie."

Arif smiled. "A wise decision. And Mr. Everheart, I hope you won't be having second thoughts once our meeting here is through. If you or your father seek to oppose me in this, if the famed vampire hunter persuades you to help against me rather than using his skills to my ends, I'll simply change your wife immediately, rather than waste more time. In fact, if you decide to renege on our agreement, not only will I take your wife, I think I would be well justified in acquiring you as well.

I believe my new mistress would fancy you as a plaything. You remember the vampiress Sindy, don't you?" Felicity could clearly see the remembrance of Sindy drinking from him flash across Ben's face. When he was younger, he had spent many a night fighting to keep from becoming one of Sindy's mindless love slaves. Arif smiled at his reaction. "Yes, you would make a fine gift of a pet for her, should you prove yourself untrustworthy."

The threat obviously flustered him, but Ben tried to keep his face neutral and calm. "I'll do what you want, but Felicity had better be kept comfortable and healthy until then, and if you touch her…"

"Mr. Everheart, I would not jeopardize our agreement by defiling your wife," he assured them with a wicked smile at Felicity. "I haven't touched you, have I dear?"

"No." How else could she answer? It was true, even if he had invaded her mind and perhaps been psychically involved in suggesting her sexual fantasy, being an unwelcome voyeur. He had mentally forced her to caress his face once or twice, as a display of control, but *he* had never inappropriately touched her. A short answer of agreement was the easier option. There was nothing Ben could do about it anyway.

She refused to meet Arif's eyes and let him control her again. He may be able to read her mind, but she was fairly sure he couldn't force her actions without keeping eye contact, as long as he hadn't drunk from her. Arif smiled with a nod and continued. "I want this plan to succeed. It would be much easier for me then having to turn your wife and bother dealing with the vampire Cain. I have plenty of women of my own. It is Alyson that I need. Your wife will be held safe and unharmed until the exchange."

Ben nodded, and then finally allowed himself to look at Felicity again. She had tears in her eyes. She blinked them away and silently begged him for forgiveness for Arif's words. Ben turned back to Arif. "You know, if you were to give her to me now, I would still help you. Let me take her home, and then I'll do whatever you want. I might be difficult to read, but I'm sure I'm not completely immune to powers as strong as yours. You can feel my true intentions, can't you?"

Ben leaned closer, imploring the vampire. "I've been so wounded by Alyson. Can't you feel it? Mattie too. Sneaking around, carrying on a friendship with my wife behind my back, without thought to how much danger they put her in…

Allie chose to abandon our friendship so that she could be with vampires. So take her. What do I care? Let me take Liss home and I'll help you hunt her down, I swear. If Allie has any residual feelings left at all, then she should feel so guilty for ditching me, that I would make fine bait for your trap. You don't even need Felicity anymore. I'm in."

Arif grinned, amused by his entreaty. "I do feel the truth of your betrayal by your friends. The anger in you towards them is undeniable." Ben nodded, holding his breath. "It is very reassuring, but I will keep your wife with me all the same. I am certain you will perform that much better with such strong incentive. I wouldn't want you to forget your focus."

Ben let the air out of his lungs in disappointment. "I won't betray you. Please."

"Be sure that you don't." Arif snapped his fingers and Cat produced a business card from somewhere to hand Ben over the table. "Felicity's life is in your hands," he warned with a smile. "My spies will be watching."

Part 3

Vicious Survival

Chapter 12

Sales, swords, and weather-stripping

Cain

Cain's estate
In a little town somewhere near Buffalo, New York
The evening before

The woman sitting next to him smelled so good…human, healthy, delicious…and she had no idea that her very life was in his hands. Cain tried to ignore her scent as she leaned closer to point something out to him on the papers before them. "See, it's in this clause here."

"Yes, whatever, it's fine. Where do I sign?" he asked impatiently.

She glanced at him in amusement. Regardless of the fact that she looked to be more than a good decade or two older than Cain's appearance, this lady had been flirting with him all evening. She wasn't unattractive, and the vampire in him found her even more tempting than the man, but Cain had not called her here for her company or her blood, and was trying very hard not to allow her human nature to distract him. Even so, she of course assumed he was being flustered by her advances rather than the beckoning lure of her pulse.

She smiled, still leaning closer to him than strictly necessary, and finally handed him the pen. "Here," she said, pointing to a line, "then again on the last page." He flipped through the paperwork as she watched him with a grin. "I still don't understand though. You realize you're offering them almost twice what the land is worth, and that's not even accounting for the farm from a business standpoint. The equipment's not included in the sale. I understand they're behind on the payments and most of their machines are likely to be repossessed…unless of course they have a large profit from the land sale to pay off their debts."

"Fine, this will help them out then. They can pay their bills, sell the equipment and keep the profits. I won't be continuing with the farm. They can harvest what's there before they go. I just want the property. I'll pay their worker's for the season if needed. They'll have to look for positions elsewhere. No one is to trespass on the land after closing."

"Alright, if that's what you want, but that's a lot of money to throw around. Are you sure you won't be needing to take a mortgage?"

"No, I can manage it. It will be quicker and easier without bank involvement. I don't mind paying extra. Consider me a sympathetic neighbor. That farm has been in their family for generations. I know it must be very hard for them to let it go. The least I can do is compensate the widow fairly. Her kids have been working hard but they don't want to be farmers, they want to go to college, and she can't run that place on her own. She hasn't got a choice but to sell."

The woman sighed and began staring at him with that annoying doe-eyed look again. "You're so sweet. Most buyers would take advantage of this kind of opportunity. You don't see much in the way of compassion these days."

He gave her a vague nod as he signed the paper. She pointed out another line further down in need of his signature as he spoke. "I've been waiting a long time for that property to become available. Considering the sad circumstances in which it occurred, paying well for it is the least I can do. Is that it?"

She held his gaze for a moment, not answering his question. "Is there a Mrs. Herald we'll need to consult with?" she asked.

"No. I'm a widower myself."

Now she was all sympathy and consoling mews of pity. "You poor thing."

"It was a long time ago." She furrowed her brow a bit at that, and then became even more compassionate. He didn't look old enough to have outlived a wife by many years, meaning his spouse must have met a premature death.

A slight sound from the back hall drew his attention. The real estate agent didn't notice, but he knew it was Dawn, sneaking around where she shouldn't be. "Is there anything else you need from me to close this deal?"

The woman's eyebrows lifted in a surprised smirk for a moment. "The purchase?" she asked with a lilt of humor... as though there was another deal in the works in her mind.

"Yes. The purchase, are we done?"

"Yes, I think that's all I need for now. Your offer is so generous, I can't imagine she'll bother to counter it. I'm betting you can now consider yourself the proud owner of 600 acres of farmland adjacent to your own. What do you have here, if you don't mind my asking?"

Cain glanced in Dawn's direction, hoping she'd remain out of sight. "112," he answered shortly. He stood from his chair, a cue for the woman's departure.

"Well, aren't you the land baron with a heart of gold?" she teased. "Do you have plans for it, or are you just securing it as an investment?"

"I like my privacy." As she rose from her chair, he took her elbow to guide her to the door.

She seemed tickled by his chivalry and flashed him another big smile as she spoke. "If I need anything else, I've got your number. You've got mine too, don't you? Don't be afraid to use it. I'll let you know when the closing date is set. It shouldn't take more than a few days for you to hear from me, since there aren't banks involved. Then it'll just be a matter of how long the family needs to shut things down and move out."

"Wonderful," Cain said with a smile as he showed her to the door. "I look forward to hearing from you."

The woman beamed at him for the remark. "Well, I look forward to calling you." Suddenly the smile dropped from her face in exchange for a look of unwelcome surprise. Cain turned to see what she was looking at. Dawn had come up behind them, silently. To the real estate lady, she looked like nothing more than a barefoot girl in a sundress, but to Cain she looked like a predator stalking its prey. Thank God her eyes were still brown, at least. "And who is this pretty young thing?" the woman asked with thinly veiled jealousy.

Cain shot Dawn a look of disapproval. "My niece. She's visiting for a bit."

The woman smiled, as though she didn't believe him. "Oh, your niece. How nice."

Dawn gave the woman a broad smile. "Good evening ma'am. Were you leaving? You could stay for a drink..."

The woman spared Cain a glance, but couldn't help but see his blatant disapproval of the invitation. "Thanks, but I think your uncle is eager for me to make some phone calls and work my magic." Cain nodded in agreement. "Well, I'll just have to take a rain-check then and let you owe me a drink next time, hmmm?" She pretended not to notice Cain's stark lack of enthusiasm over the idea. "You two have a nice visit."

Cain shooed her out the door onto the porch. "Thanks for coming out."

"Not a problem. Call me anytime, really."

Cain practically closed the door on the woman before she was finished speaking. He spun to face Dawn, who stood behind him in the entryway. She didn't even appear apologetic as he reprimanded her. "I told you to stay upstairs this evening until I came for you."

"You took too long. Buying some property?" She didn't even seem to care what he thought of her eavesdropping.

"The farm next door. The Crimson Coven has been ranging over there to hunt as it is. I'll be happy not to worry about them being seen by anyone." He'd divulged knowledge to her of the vampires that inhabited his property, in preparation for meeting with Arif. He wouldn't allow her to come with him and she had balked at being left alone. "I'll have the property fenced like my own, so I don't have to worry about humans wandering onto it."

"You've been waiting for them to sell it for a while, huh?"

"I've had my eye on it. It is adjoining my own, and it's the largest undivided parcel in the area."

"Did you kill him?"

Cain opened his mouth in shock. "The farmer? No, of course not! I've known the family forever. If that was the way I did business, I would have owned the land generations ago. What a question."

Dawn shrugged. "Most vampires would have."

"You don't even know any other vampires."

"Am I wrong?"

He laughed. "No, but I am not like most vampires. In fact, it has been my life's work to be a positive influence on *most* vampires, so I'd like to think the scale is slowly shifting. At some point, the ruthless and cruel shall be the minority, and we can consider ourselves civilized, regardless of our beginnings."

"I was pretty civilized just now. Did you notice? Not even a slip…and she smelled good."

He shook his head a bit with a smile. "I know. She kept leaning into me with her throat so exposed…" He took a deep breath and sighed. "The urge is always there, you know, even for me. You did well though. I was worried to have you close to a human so soon. That's why I asked you to stay upstairs."

"I know. Sorry, but I wanted to see if I could do it. Heck, even when I was hunting, I had enough control to wait for the right target, at least. You know how many people I had to smell go by that park bench without lunging for them? It's not easy, but I know I can do it."

Cain nodded. "I knew it too, I just worry. If I didn't think you were made well enough to have some control, you wouldn't be here. Speaking of control, we've some work to get back to before I leave."

Dawn sighed, frustrated with Cain's insistence upon her constant practicing to shield her mark. He was going to meet with Arif soon, and he would leave Dawn here, rather than have her tagging along after him and possibly becoming a liability.

"Do we have to?" she whined. "I'm safe here on your property. You said that Khalon guy was patrolling the place with his guards, right?"

Cain chuckled, as her description brought to mind the very inaccurate idea that he had some sort of vampiric military army guarding the grounds. "Khalon is a coven leader, and he and his vampires live here on my property, but they aren't really guards, per se. I introduced you to him so that he could recognize your mark and keep an eye on you. His coven will investigate any intrusions on the grounds, but they'll also be busy expanding into their new territory."

"Right, I guess they'll be exploring the farm, huh?"

Cain smiled. "I'm sure they already know it quite well. They've been secretly visiting it for years. They will be happy to have the farmers out of there though. Once we're given the go-ahead, they'll be out taking down the netting and small fences used to keep the varmints out of the crops. The local wildlife is going to have a field day feasting on whatever's left behind."

"And the vampires are going to be feasting on them; seems kind of cruel."

"It's the circle of life. Besides, they don't usually kill the larger game if they can help it. They do hunt plenty of small game, but when it comes to the deer, they drink some, and then leave the animal to heal so it can be fed off of again in the future. Otherwise, they would have depleted this entire region long ago. As it is, I am very happy to have been able to give them the much needed extra land to hunt."

Dawn grimaced. "You're not supposed to hunt deer out of season."

Cain shook his head with a smirk. "Our hunting may not be strictly legal, but neither is being a vampire. You're going to have to resolve this resistance you have to drinking from animals. It's still better than endangering humans, and besides, catch and release isn't actually hunting. Now stop changing the subject. We need to work on your mark studies."

"So what if I'm not so good at mark stuff? I'll practice while you're gone."

"The Crimson Coven will use your mark to find you in an emergency and they may ask you to cover it if they are concerned that a strange vampire is present. There are certain coven members designated as 'beacons', their marks remaining uncovered at all times. You need to be able to recognize and distinguish them from a stranger, so that you would know who to go to for help. I know it seems unlikely, but I have had strange vampires with ill intentions lurking about here in the past, and I'll feel better once you've gotten the hang of this." She rolled her eyes at his over-cautiousness. "Alright, I'll tell you what. Why don't we put the reading practice aside for now and play a game?" he asked with a smile.

She seemed dubious that this was some sort of trick. In a way, it was. "What kind of game?"

"Hide and seek," he proposed playfully.

"Aren't we a little old for that one?" she asked with a smirk.

"Not the way I plan to play it," Cain told her with a grin.

Now he had her attention. She raised her eyebrows and tried to guess what he could be planning. "Is this going to involve stripping at some point?"

He let out a surprised chuckle. "No."

"Can it?"

"No! No offense, but mentoring you is supposed to be helping me to get my mind *off* of romance. Letting my heart and mind wander from the mission I've set for myself to help others has brought me nothing but pain. In case you haven't noticed, you are part of a desperate attempt on my part to escape that pain, so please, play along; be a nice, boring student in need of my full platonic attention and guidance, will you?" he reprimanded teasingly. "You'll go and hide, and if you can manage to keep your mark hidden as well, I'll have much less chance of finding you. I'll keep my mark visible. See if you can manage to see me coming and avoid me without being caught. We'll begin out in the yard, and if you can make it back to the house without getting caught, you win."

"What do I get if I win?"

"I don't know. What do you want?"

"No stripping, huh?" He gave her a stern look and she giggled. "I'm kidding. Boring and platonic, got it. I'd settle for skipping lessons for the night."

"Fair enough. I'll even give you a healthy head start, but if I catch you, you'll practice until I decide we're finished."

"You got it. I plan to get good at this really fast."

"Good…"

~~~~~~~~~~~~~~~~~~~~~~~~~~~~~~~

She *was* getting pretty good at it, but not good enough. Despite an almost ridiculous head start and some mediocre effort on Cain's part, he still managed to catch her before she made it safely back to the house. So, more lessons for the evening were in order.

After a few hours of mark discussion and practice, even Cain was getting impatient and found his mind wandering. *Was* it Sindy that Arif was trying to dangle before him as a hostage? Would she really flip her loyalties like that and try to put him in such an awful position? Many would say that it was nothing less than they would expect from Sindy, but he couldn't fully believe it. She'd changed…they had a real connection now, didn't they? Cain wanted to know exactly what was going on so that he could figure out how to negotiate and keep Alyson out of trouble. It seemed that many nights had already been wasted while the postcard sat in his mailbox. A meeting with Arif couldn't come soon enough now for his anxieties.

"I still don't understand how you can figure out age that way." Dawn's remark was met with only silence. "Hello, Cain?" Dawn waved a hand in front of Cain's face across the table until she had his attention once again.

Cain finally met her gaze with apology. "What? Sorry, I became lost in my thoughts for a moment. What were we discussing? Mark duration, was it?"

Dawn offered a sympathetic grin. "Um, about ten minutes and three topics ago. Welcome back. Are you okay?"

"I'm fine. Forgive me."

She assessed his expression with a frown. "You don't look fine. I guess the fun wore off. Worried about that postcard?" she conjectured.

"I don't know why it's bothering me so much. I knew Sindy was in league with Arif, deep down I think I always knew it, so why does it sting so badly that he's trying to use her against me?"

"Heartbreak hurts, even when you see it coming. Love stinks, ask anyone. They even wrote a song about it. You were still vulnerable and trying to get over that woman with the baby…what was her name?" she asked, apologetically.

"Felicity," Cain answered with a sigh.

"You were still heartbroken over Felicity, so being hurt by Sindy just compounded everything, like pouring salt in the wound."

"I suppose, but I waited years before allowing myself to kindle something with Sindy."

"Time doesn't matter. If Felicity was your true love, she always will be."

Cain shook his head with a small chuckle. "Good heavens, you're even more of a hopeless romantic than I am," he accused her teasingly. "But I think I know why Sindy's betrayal is eating at me, even if I did see it coming.

I gave Felicity up by choice, because I knew that in her heart, what she really wanted was a human life with a family, and I believed it was best for her. But Sindy has an entirely different future ahead of her, one we *could* share, yet she chose to abandon me for someone else. I don't know if she was the perfect woman for me, but I loved her the best I could, and she still left me. The hardest part is that she didn't even have the respect to tell me to my face. She just left."

"Maybe it wasn't a question of respect, maybe she just didn't have the courage to face you."

"Sindy may be afraid of her own feelings at times, but she's not afraid of speaking her mind, believe me. Many times I've written off her actions as products of fear, but perhaps it really is all just selfish disrespect as everyone claims.

Whatever the case, I think I deserve an explanation at least. I don't often think of myself as deserving much, but I deserve that. So, I will go to Arif as I planned, and listen to his ridiculous demands, with which I will *not* cooperate regardless. However, before I agree to discuss terms, I will demand to see Sindy alone. If she wants to pretend she hasn't been secretly dealing with Arif all along, and play out some charade of an innocent prisoner being held against her will, let her lie to my face. I'm not giving over Alyson for her."

"But what if he really did kidnap her and she begs for your help?"

"Surely that is exactly what Arif will coach her to say, but I cannot doubt myself any longer. I know what I've seen, the sneaking away for secret rendezvous, the lies… I think I know her better than Arif assumes and I have to believe that I'll be able to read the truth in her eyes. I'll either do what else I can to help her, or tell her how disappointed I am in her choice, and then I will leave the two of them to their designs, free to move on, knowing I've done all I can.

But none of this is your worry. Back to work. If I'm going to leave you on your own while I go and sort out whatever's been hinted at in that dreadful postcard, then I very well want to be sure that you know how to read and decipher marks. As I've said, the Crimson Coven will act as a guard and protect you, but they communicate over distance using marks, and you must be able to recognize them. Let's begin again. It will help if you close your eyes."

Cain demonstrated by closing his own, but Dawn's were focused over Cain's shoulder, glued to the glass doors of the parlor, and widening by the second with increasing alarm. "Cain…" He was busy revealing his mark and beginning to make explanations, forcing her to make another bid for his attention. "Sir…"

The formal deferment to his authority caused him to recognize her alarm and open his eyes. He followed her gaze, turning to see the glass doors of the parlor and what lay beyond. A large cloud of dark mist had gathered before the door and was now suddenly dropping low to siphon itself down below, through the crack between door and flooring.

Dawn stood and backed up in anxious worry. Cain also backed up his chair, but was not quite as alarmed. "Looks like I could use some new weather-stripping," he quipped as he stood from his chair.

The mist entered the room, rising until it was about the height of Cain, though still a few feet away. Once it was fully within the room, it began to solidify into the shape of a man. As they watched it take shape, Cain reached down to pull a stake from his boot and tossed it to Dawn. "A vampire," he told her. "I don't believe it to be a dangerous one, but neither is it a friend. Be wary."

Dawn backed away until she was off in the corner near the doorway, out of the thing's immediate scope of view. The smoke took shape into the form of a young blonde man with green eyes and a mischievous smile.

"You, you're the shade," Cain remarked in recognition, shaking his head. Kieran gave him a slight bow. Cain had spent many a night speculating with Alyson and Mattie over the possible suspects who might be capable of such transformation, and what color their vampire eyes would be. "Green, I should have guessed. What do you want?"

Kieran furrowed his brow, seeming momentarily forlorn. "What I want has never been consequential. I've been sent to speak with the lovely lady Alyson."

Cain narrowed his gaze. "What makes you think that you can enter my home uninvited, and demand audience with The United One?"

"All who come in peace are welcome within," Kieran responded with a clever grin, spreading his hands and quoting the plaque that Cain had once again hung outside, above his door.

Cain had to return the smile. "If she were here, the sign would not stand. If you've business with me, then speak your mind."

"Speak my mind?" Kieran asked with a smirk. "Never in all of my nights have I been given such leave. But then, *my* mind might be better kept silent. But forgive my lack of manners for not introducing myself to your guest," he said, suddenly turning to pierce Dawn with his gaze. She had been staring at him slack jawed and was abashed to have been caught looking. Kieran stood, unapologetically naked after shifting, and winked at her. "I'm Kieran…and you are?"

"Leaving," Cain answered for her, "to fetch Kieran a pair of pants, if you'd be so kind." Dawn nodded and left on the errand. "Thank you," Cain called after her. "She's none of your concern," he told Kieran sternly. "Why are you here?"

"On behalf of the Coven Master Arif, of course. I was on my way back from other errands when he asked that I stop in for a quick visit here. He wishes to ascertain that you are in receipt of his recent correspondence."

"The postcard?" Cain confirmed with some distain.

"What did you make of it?"

"Your Master is a bully and a fool if he thinks Alyson will succumb to his wishes through such manipulation, or that I would ever encourage her to do so. I don't know what it is precisely he wants with her, but threats will not accomplish what he desires. For the good of not only her own existence but for the greater good of vampire and humankind alike, The United One will remain independent."

"I see. I am supposed to ask Alyson herself if she feels the same."

"She isn't here, as you must know, considering your continued illicit surveillance of my property."

"Quite true. Alyson has not been in residence for some time now."

"If you already know that, then why do you ask for her?"

"I do as I am told. My orders were to report here and ask for The United One, to determine her stance over the matter, as well as yours."

Cain furrowed his brow as he gazed at Kieran thoughtfully. "And yet you did not see fit to apprise Arif of the fact that Alyson left some time ago?"

The corners of Kieran's mouth turned upward in a crafty grin. "He didn't ask. As I said, I do as I am told. I have quite a hierarchy of those I do service for, some out of enforced authority, some out of respect, some for friendship, and many overlapping gradations in between. Each order and request must be weighed and balanced against my personal indebtedness and opinion. My loom of loyalty spins a more intricate weave than I ever wished for, believe me."

"And the order from Arif to report Alyson's whereabouts did not carry the same authority as someone who would like for you to keep the information to yourself?" Kieran just shrugged and smiled. "You are a more complicated young man than I first took you for."

"And you are one of the few people I'll allow to address me as *young man* without feeling my usual frustrated insult over it."

Cain smiled, acknowledging the fact that Kieran was older than most gave him credit for, but was still a few centuries Cain's junior. Dawn returned with a pair of scrub-pants. She entered the room and timidly tossed them in Kieran's direction while trying not to look directly at him. It was a terrible throw, but Kieran just chuckled as he went to retrieve and put them on without comment. Once he had donned the pants, she came a bit closer. "I brought a shirt too," she told him, showing him what she still held.

"Keep it; I don't plan to be here long," he said, making himself at home on a kitchen chair.

"Thank you Dawn," Cain said. He barely glanced at her, but she understood that the words were clearly a dismissal, and made herself scarce. Cain had the distinct feeling she was eavesdropping from just out of sight, but he let her be and took the chair opposite Kieran.

Kieran smiled, leaning back and lifting an ankle to rest on his other knee. "I have a feeling you haven't grasped the full implication of things yet."

"What makes you say that?"

"The fact that you're still here and not out to separate Arif's head from his body was my first clue."

Cain's gaze bore into him as he leaned forward in his seat. "Then tell me what's really going on here."

"You're not going to like it."

"If you're going to tell me that Sindy has betrayed my trust and gone to Arif, only to be used against me as leverage in persuading Alyson...then I already know, and you're right, I don't like it, but it's not going to work."

"Don't you care for Sindy any longer?"

"There's only so many times a man can allow himself to be lied to before turning away. I may be tolerant, but I'm not a fool."

"So, you're letting Sindy go then?"

"To follow the path she chooses. It's not my responsibility to ascertain it is a wise one. I've given her what help and advice I could over the years, now her choices must be her own. It's disappointing to know that her choice has been to leave me, but I have survived worse heartbreak."

"Yes… I know you have."

Cain locked eyes with him for a moment. "*Is* Sindy with Arif?" he asked.

"As far as I know. She's not *with* him," Kieran said, using his fingers to make air quotes, "but she's there," he confirmed.

"Is she alright?" Cain asked. When Kieran didn't answer immediately, he continued, a quiet plea for honesty, beyond their separate loyalties. "Look, no matter your answer, I'm not going to put Alyson into Arif's hands. You must know that. Alyson isn't here and quite frankly, even if she was, I know in my heart that no one person's safety is worth allowing Arif access to such a powerful vampire. I'm not *that* sentimental of a fool. I have to be practical. The safety of the world outweighs that of any single soul. So please, just tell me if she is alright."

"I haven't spoken to her, and I haven't been back since she got there, but I don't believe she's in true danger at the moment," Kieran assured him. "A lot depends on how she handles things. She can be sort of…unpredictable."

Cain gave a quiet chuckle. "To say the least."

"She's not the hostage referred to on the postcard though."

Cain's smile deserted him as he looked up in shock. "What?"

Kieran uncrossed his legs, sitting up straight and raising his hands in surrender. "Don't dust the messenger."

Cain froze, feeling as though time had suddenly stopped, all sounds of the night drowned out by the ringing that began in his ears, dreadful worry clenching his heart and tightening his throat. "Of course it's Sindy," he insisted weakly. Kieran didn't answer. Cain stood. "Who?"

"He has Felicity."

Three simple words, that turned all else in the world meaningless. Cain's jaw was clenched tightly, as well as his fists, as he stood for a moment, frozen, and then turned decisively to leave the room.

"Where are you going?" Kieran asked, having expected more questioning.

"To separate Arif's head from his body."

~~~~~~~~~~~~~~~~~~~~~~~~~~~~~

It took both Dawn and Kieran to subdue Cain and drag him back to sit for some discussion before rushing off on a vendetta, and even then, it was clear that he was only restrained because he allowed it for fear of hurting either of them. They had him sitting again, but it still seemed likely that he might tear away from them to race to Felicity rather than listen to reason. "Is he insane?" Cain was demanding of Kieran. "Does he *want* me to kill him? He must. In fact, I think I'll use his own sword to do it. I've got Ash-bringer stashed away here somewhere."

Cain stood, shedding their hold on his arms and disregarding their protests to stomp off into the next room. Kieran and Dawn watched as Cain felt for something up along the tops of the china cabinets in the dining room. "Aha." Cain pulled down the sheathed sword from its hiding spot and held up his prize.

"That's not actually *his* sword, you know," Kieran informed him.

Dawn raised an eyebrow. "You're going to kill a vampire with a sword?"

Kieran turned to her with a smirk. "Not a bad method actually. If you're strong enough, you can take their head off in one clean swing."

"Oh...I guess. So why do people in books and movies always use stakes? Would it be better to use a stake?"

Cain unsheathed the sword, Ash-bringer, from its housing, holding it up for them to see. The sword was made of wood; a dark and beautifully lustrous red in color, and undoubtedly strong. It had a thin, keen inset edge of metal blade running along each side. The weapon was like a giant stake with a hilt and a sword's cutting edge. Kieran smiled and Dawn's eyes widened. "Oh."

Cain looked over the blade and then re-sheathed it. "Who's sword is it then?" he asked, while adjusting the strap that was attached to the scabbard, and putting it over his head to rest across one shoulder and down his back.

Kieran took a thoughtful moment before answering. "Someone who could give you some much needed help right about now."

"I don't need any help, and I don't care what Arif's plans are. The moment he touched Felicity, all rules of civil arrangement went out the window."

Dawn sighed in romantic admiration, but Kieran rolled his eyes. "Look man, I get it, really I do, but don't be an idiot. Don't you think Arif knows you'd do anything to keep her safe? That's the whole point, and he's made damn sure that there is no way for you to safely retrieve her unless you play by his rules. If you don't arrange for a trade, then he'll be expecting you to fly over there in a rage, and he'll make sure she's dead before you get anywhere near her. Think it through."

Cain eyed him for a moment and then sighed. "Alright, so who's the true owner of this sword and why should they help?"

"I said they could. I didn't say they *should*."

"Got a name for me?"

Kieran laughed. "You'll get a better answer out of the sword than you will out of me. That's pushing the restraints of my loyalty a bit far, don't you think?"

"Frankly, I haven't got a clue to whom you are actually loyal lately."

"Me," Kieran answered with a sly grin.

Cain acceded with a grin of his own. "Alright, so if someone didn't want you to tell Arif of Alyson's departure from my protection, then who else is it that wants to keep Alyson safe?"

Kieran shrugged without answering. After a moment of silence, it was Dawn who offered an answer. "Alyson, I'd imagine. And her husband, of course."

"Of course," Cain agreed, giving her a nod of thanks before continuing to question Kieran. "And have you seen them?"

"I've got to go. Should I tell Arif to expect you?" he asked teasingly.

"I'd rather you didn't."

"Right…but have I any reason to be loyal to you?" He left the question hanging with a secretive smile. "I'll let Arif know that you are unhappy with his methods of persuasion, but will consider meeting with him to discuss it directly. I'll tell him you'll meet with him at midnight, three nights from now; give you a chance to figure out what you're doing. See you then."

With that, he allowed himself to dissipate back into a cloud of fog, the borrowed pants dropping to the floor below him. His eyes and smile were the last to fade, reminding Cain eerily of the Cheshire Cat of Wonderland…

Cain opened the back door for him. "Next time, I'd prefer you knocked," he called after, as Kieran's cloud of mist blew out the door like smoke on the wind.

Once Kieran was well gone, Cain turned his attention back to Dawn. "Lessons are over, and I do hope you're ready to be left on your own, because I've no time to lose."

"Dashing off to her rescue is totally romantic, and don't let me stop you, but what are you going to do, exactly? That guy is probably right. They know you're coming and they wouldn't tell you where they had her if they didn't expect they could defend against you. You're going to have to make some kind of deal. Maybe you should go find Alyson first."

"Alyson... Even if I knew how to find her, I can't do that. She is better off remaining hidden, even from me. What I said earlier, still remains true. I cannot sacrifice the safety of all for the safety of one...no matter who that one is. Alyson is too powerful to give into Arif's hands. I need to find another way."

"What about the guy who owns that sword?"

"I don't know who that is. It could be anyone." Cain thought about what Kieran had said: *You'll get a better answer out of the sword than you will out of me.* Cain drew the sword from its scabbard and inspected it. It was beautifully made, but didn't seem to bear any identifying marks to give a clue to whom it might rightfully belong. Cain was just giving up and re-sheathing it, when something caught his eye. On the very end-tip of the hilt was a small symbol. Cain pulled the sword out and held it up, straight in front of him at eye level and then laughed. "Well, look at that."

There was a small, sideways figure eight with a heart below it. Dawn came closer to question him. "Do you see something?"

He showed her his discovery. "Do you know what that is?"

She squinted at it for a moment. "Obviously that's a heart. Above it, isn't that the symbol for infinity?"

"Yes, it means forever... Everheart."

Chapter 13 - I Spy

Sindy

Kieran's house, *Kana Susamiş Icin Ev*
Montauk, Long Island, New York
Later that evening

Sindy lay alone, hidden under the covers in the large king-sized bed, trying to ignore the renewed pulsing ache in her left arm from the new toothpicks she'd been shot up with. The ones she'd already had throbbed and hurt all the time, but she'd almost forgotten that they'd hurt this much more when first going in. She'd only just dug them out last night, and had been hoping that her arm would have healed over sufficiently to escape the notice of the nurse during her evening medical check. When the staff did not mention it her, she thought she'd gotten away with it. In fact, it had made her bold enough to spend another two hours digging three more of them out of her legs as soon as she'd had some time alone.

Unfortunately, the nurse must have reported the transgression to Arif without saying anything to her. That meant that if she had any chance at all of ridding herself of the wood and shifting to escape, she was going to have to get out every single toothpick in the 24 hour period she had between medical checks. That meant getting out a toothpick an hour. It sounded possible, but she had found that it wasn't nearly as easy as it seemed. Not only did it hurt horribly to try and dig holes in her skin and fish around for the little buggers, how was she going to be able to see what she was doing to reach the ones in her butt, and the backs of her thighs?

Arif's promises of power, a lovely home and a harem of humans at her beck and call had almost seemed a worthy trade for suffering these indignities, but seeing the look on Arif's face as she had been once again injected with these cruelly sharp pieces of wood, snapped her back to her desire for escape. He'd kept asking her about Zach, as though he assumed she knew more about his escape than she was telling, and her disloyalty was a thorn in his side. Not only would the toothpicks keep her from escaping as well, but he seemed to enjoy watching her suffer.

How much more would he enjoy having her under his complete control once he was able to mark her? No amount of blood or money could be worth living in fear again of what someone might want to do to her. Plus, once he could read her mind, he might discover that she had given Zach white eyes. What might he force her to do for him then? She'd rather take her chances on the run.

She knew one thing though, it wasn't going to happen today. It had taken her about two hours to dig two toothpicks out of her left calf and one out of her right, but by the time she had finished, she was in awful pain and felt sick to her stomach. Then she'd been summoned to see Arif.

Luckily, she had put aside a pair of dark stockings for just such an occasion, so her handiwork wasn't visible, but she was stressed to the max. She attributed the fact that Arif hadn't bothered to check the rest of her body, leaving her leg wounds unnoticed, to dumb luck and the fact that he had seemed very busy and distracted with other things, but surely it would be seen tomorrow at her check-up.

The time with Arif had eaten up the rest of her evening and there were only about two hours until sunrise. She would have privacy for the day, but that only gave her fifteen hours to get out her remaining twenty-one toothpicks. It was theoretically possible, but she was exhausted and nauseated just thinking about it. Right now, all she could do was lay still and wait for the agony to recede.

Pain pounded through her arm like a sick parody of the pulse of a beating heart. Her body wanted the wood out, out, out. The flesh around her new wounds was freshly angry and sharply protesting, but her existing embedded toothpicks fought to painfully remind her of their presence as well. She had to get them out. How could Arif expect her to exist like this for any amount of time? She could walk and talk and try to make herself forget the pieces of wood invading her flesh, but they were always there, pushing into her and making her blood rue their trespass.

Fuck this. She had to get them out today or the progress she had made by taking the three out of her legs would be lost. The fact that she was missing more toothpicks would be discovered, and rather than a light reprimand and a few more shots, who knew what they would do to her? This could be her only chance.

She tried to summon the will to get up, take out the little knife she'd found squirreled away in one of the dresser drawers, and start digging into her body again. She lay with eyes closed, alone in the bedroom. All was quiet, so when a man's voice broke the silence, she couldn't help but jump and let out a gasping scream.

"What a nice welcome home surprise." Kieran stood right next to her, arms crossed and a superior smirk on his face for finding her in his bed. Her jumping scramble away from him angered her injuries. She tried to hide her wincing reaction and instead spoke to him in irritation. "How did you get in here?"

Kieran cocked an eyebrow at her. "I live here. This is my bed."

"I know... I mean... I didn't even hear the door."

"I'm a spy," Kieran reminded her. "Sneaking into places unobserved is my specialty."

Sindy sat up better and threw back the covers, glad she had not bothered to undress before lying down. At least Kieran was fully dressed as well, but taking in that fact made Sindy even angrier at herself for not being more observant and hearing him come in. If he was dressed, he hadn't turned to mist. He'd snuck in the old-fashioned way. "Sorry, Arif told me I could stay here, since you wouldn't be back for a while."

Kieran still wore that annoying smirk of a smile. "Is that what he told you?"

Sindy carefully swung her feet off the side, trying not to awaken new pain while preparing to leave the bed. "I'll ask him to put me up somewhere else."

Kieran walked around and stepped in front of her, blocking her from getting up. "You'll do no such thing. Arif put you here because he thought I'd want you here. He knows I've had an eye for you."

"Is that so? And here I thought he was saving me all for himself."

"No offense, but it's your talent he's interested in, not you. Until you're marked, he hasn't got much use for you. I, on the other hand, am someone he wants to do his very best to keep happy right now. As the go-between, a lot is riding on me, and he wants to keep me satisfied. Since you're currently...incapacitated, he thought you'd make a nice present wrapped in my bed-sheets."

Sindy stared at him in shock for a moment. "Don't get any ideas. I'm not as incapacitated as you may think."

Kieran chuckled. "I know better than to underestimate you, but I also know that you are in no shape to be calling the shots. Trust me, I know exactly how debilitating your treatment was."

So he knew about the toothpicks then. "Really?" she asked him, sourly. "Was that your brilliant idea?"

He backed up, giving her some space. "No." He sounded offended, but she couldn't read his eyes, as he immediately turned to press the button on the intercom next to the bed. "Send Daphne in please, and have her bring an empty glass." When he turned to face her again, he seemed surprised and hurt by her accusation. "You think I would do that to you?" he asked quietly, gesturing towards her body. "Cat came up with the prophylactic toothpicks, I just got to be the guinea pig."

Her eyes widened as shocked realization came over her that he had endured just what she had. She didn't know what to say, and he continued before she could speak. "We were fresh out of shape-shifting vampires 'til you came along. As a shade, I'm the next best thing, so I got to be the lucky lackey they tested it on. Hurts like hell, I know, and I'm betting they more than double-dosed you compared to what I got, so you can expect your fair share of sympathy from me."

He paused, giving her a slightly hurt and level gaze for her assumption that he had played a part in her ordeal. "I don't plan to take advantage of you. I wouldn't anyway. That's just not how I play."

"I appreciate that," she told him sincerely, but then added with a teasing smirk, "but are you trying to tell me that you've got ethics? You're a spy! Besides, something tells me that you don't keep a high rank in this coven with pesky morals holding you back."

"My rank came with my eye color. Yours will too, if you want it. Rare breeds get special treatment. As long as I don't piss off Arif, I'm sitting pretty stable. I don't have aspirations for higher accolades, just keeping the status quo. I don't play to win, I just enjoy the game."

"Exactly what game are you playing?"

"The one where I know just enough about what's going on, to stay the hell out of the way. Ride the highs, skirt the lows, and reap only enough reward to keep my Jiminy Cricket quiet. No harm, no foul. You on the other hand, don't seem to know how to keep yourself out of trouble."

"Yeah well, flying under the radar was never my style."

"Clearly, but lying to the coven master?" He clucked his tongue at her in disapproval. "Not your best move."

"I wasn't lying. I didn't help Zach escape," she insisted.

"I never believed that's what you were lying about." Before she could dare wonder what he was talking about, there was a soft knock on the door. "Come in."

It was one of his pretty young human women in a pale lavender satin slip dress. "Yes Master Kieran?"

Kieran smiled at her respectful inquiry. "I believe our guest could use a drink." He crossed to the top dresser drawer where Sindy had found the knife she'd used to dig out her toothpicks. He pulled out the knife and then paused. Could he tell that Sindy had used it recently? He looked at it, and then slowly passed it under his nose, smelling the blade. He gave Sindy a sly smile, and then continued speaking. "I'm sure Daphne's sanguine sweetness is better than anything you've had in a while. Tonight you can have my share. I know they've been keeping you on strict rations of animal blood only, to slow the healing process, but I won't tell if you won't," he stage-whispered with a wink. He looked to Daphne for approval. "You don't mind, do you?"

The girl shrugged and shook her head. "My blood is yours to use as you wish, Master." Kieran moved closer to her and took her hand into his for a kiss. Then he turned her hand to face palm up and sucked gently on her wrist, wetting the spot and numbing it with his venomous saliva, before using the knife to slice and bleed her into the glass she held.

After letting a small wincing sigh escape at being cut, the girl continued to speak to Kieran. "My body's yours too. I hope you'll still request my company this morning. I've missed you."

Kieran gave her a little nod of acknowledgment, and then released her arm. "Thank you Daphne. You can leave us. Don't leave the house though, I might call you later."

Sindy smirked at the comment as the girl closed the door behind her. "Just like a man. Take what you want and leave her waiting by the phone."

Kieran grinned and handed Sindy the glass of blood. It smelled so good, she could barely mumble a "Thanks," before taking a drink. She tried to sip it slowly, rather than chug it down as she really wanted to.

"Pretty, isn't she?" Kieran asked. "I lucked out. I acquired her sight unseen just for the name. Leftover childhood cartoon crush... So, where is Zach?"

Sindy licked her lips and lowered the glass. "I don't know. I'm his maker, not his keeper. Jerk took off on me and left me to face the torture for it. I have no idea where he went. All I can tell you is that he isn't here and he isn't dust."

Kieran shook his head as though disappointed in her. "I can't believe you turned him."

"Well I couldn't let Allie do it."

"No, you couldn't," he said, thoughtfully. "I love it when people surprise me."

Sindy shrugged it off and took another drink. "I should've just let her. Sure would have saved me a lot of trouble."

"And it wouldn't have made any difference at all, would it? Not that anyone else realizes that." He reached forward and took her empty glass as she tried not to look too freaked out. He seemed to be hinting that he knew about Zach's white eyes. "I know why he felt he had to leave..." Kieran told her, "what I don't understand, is why he left *you.*"

"You know kids these days, no respect for their parents. He doesn't give a shit about me, he was just worried about saving his own ass."

Kieran was unconvinced. "Still, he was in no immediate danger. As long as he was careful, he had some time left before he had to worry. I've got a pretty nice place here. I know if *I* was sharing this suite with you, I wouldn't be in a big rush to leave. Did you two have a spat or something?" When she didn't answer, he began to look at her with a smile of surprised realization. "You weren't sleeping with him, were you? You don't have to answer, the humans will tell me. They always know everything. That's why he wasn't attached to you. You wouldn't give him any," he conjectured with a laugh.

"Your bimbos were willing company enough, he didn't need my attention. He had plenty of playmates to keep him occupied, and if you know me as well as you claim to, you know that sex has nothing to do with how attached I feel to someone."

"Maybe...or maybe things have changed. Normally, I would say you'd have no qualms about sleeping with him if it would help you out...even though the guy is kind of a douche."

"He's not a bad guy," Sindy said, defensively.

"For a douche. But I think you're off your game. Even though you sleeping with him would have made him feel somewhat indebted to helping you out of here, you couldn't do it. You were feeling guilty."

"What do I have to feel guilty about? I use sex to lure in meals all the time."

Kieran shook his head with a smile. "Those are humans. Besides, that's the old tune...the song has changed. You forget that I've been keeping track. I know it's been a long time since you bothered to get into it, especially since Cain finally let you in. Now you just lure them with promises and foreplay. You're trying to be faithful, aren't you?" He said it like he found the idea terribly cute.

How stupid. She didn't even bother to answer him, so he went on. "Do you think you love him? Maybe you do, in a way. But it's not real love, is it? It's not the breath catching, pulse pounding, shivers of excitement kind of love."

She glowered at him in resentment for asking so candidly before she finally answered. "No…it's not; because I'm dead, wise-ass. I don't breathe. My heart doesn't beat. I haven't got a pulse to pound and I don't shiver. Spy on me all you want. It doesn't mean you know how I feel."

"You might think you love him, but it's not him, you know. You don't really love *him*, you love what he gave you."

"Clothes and shit?" she asked, indignantly. "Thanks for thinking I'm shallow as a shower."

"Not the clothes. What he gave you every day you slept under his roof."

"What did he give me?" She paused and rolled her eyes after hearing how that sounded. "Are you trying to be crass or something?"

"A home." She stared at him with a blank sort of fear in her eyes. She knew it was Kieran's job to be observant, but she hadn't thought he was the type to see so far beneath the surface. "Before you went to him, how long had it been since you'd slept safe and sound? Dorm rooms, dumpy motels, barns and abandoned houses; always wondering how long you can get away with it before you're forced to move on. How long had it been since you didn't have to worry about where your next meal was coming from, and how hard you were gonna have to work for it? How long since you felt surrounded by friends and family…since you truly felt *taken care of?* Had you ever felt it, even when you were human? I don't think you ever did. Cain gave you that.

It's a big world out there. It's nice to feel you have someplace to come home to. Believe me, I know. Why do you think I put up with Arif? I understand what Cain gave you, better than anyone. I understand why you think you love him."

Sindy glared at him to drop it. "I didn't sleep with Zach, because Zach is a douche."

Kieran laughed. "Must be weird, having a connection like that with someone you barely know."

She shrugged. "Nothing new for me. I'm not really known for being discriminating, even in that."

"How many have you changed?"

"Eleven." Eleven souls, lost to the world; lives cut short, just so she could have a meal and a protector, or a lover, or both.

"Wow, that's quite a record for someone so young."

"I'm not exactly proud of it. It's a testament to my incompetence more than anything. The early ones were basically mistakes. I thought I could keep a stable, like you do, but I over-drank them all. The others...I tried to use them as a lesser guard, but I didn't really make them very well. Out of all the guys I changed in the past, only two of them came through it decently. Then one of them betrayed me and the other one got dusted, so...yeah, spreading the wealth hasn't worked out all that well for me."

"Zach came through just fine. And to be fair, Marcus was already pretty much brain-dead when you found him in that hospital, so he doesn't really count."

She squinted at him, wondering just how much he actually knew about her past. "How about you? Got the process down to a science?"

"Nope. I've never made another."

"Never?"

"Not on my own, anyway." He sat down on the bed next to her. "It was a condition of my creation. The guy who turned me made the master and I vow that I'd never make another. I did get assigned to a group turn once though; kind of an experiment. Sketchy ethics where the vow was concerned, but I guess Arif figured it was worth the risk. I consider that one on his head, not mine.

Can't say I enjoyed it. Then again, I never enjoy any activity that Lorelei and Cat are involved in. You think you're dark? Those girls have some seriously twisted tastes, let me tell you. I have no desire to make more vampires. If you ask me, there are too many in the world as it is."

"Well, you aren't missing much. Besides, what more could you want? You've already got the whole harem thing going on."

"Right? This is a great gig."

She was going to have to start believing it was great, because obviously she wouldn't be digging out the rest of her toothpicks under Kieran's watchful eye, and she doubted she'd be getting another chance. It was looking like *Kana Susamiş İçin Ev* was going to be home sweet home for a while. "It is...isn't it?"

"Sure. I'll have you know that women fight over positions in my harem. I am the most sought after assignment in the whole community."

"Is that a fact?" she asked, with a smirk over his arrogance.

"Absolutely true."

"Cause you're such a stud?"

"Cause I'm never here. They get to live in my house, use the community amenities, and rather than play harem girl and get sucked on all the time, they just report to the medical center once a week to donate blood for use at the bar. I come home every four to six weeks to renew their marks and stay for a weekend. Other than that, they mostly get left alone, and I'm sure they like it that way."

Sindy watched him for a moment and realized that he was speaking the absolute truth as he saw it. "Don't sell yourself short. They talk about you like you're God's gift. You saw the way Daphne was fawning over you just now."

"Of course they treat me like that; they're not stupid. Neither am I. I may look young, but I'm not naïve enough to think they're all smitten by my boyish charm. They fight for spots in my bed because they want to make sure I like them each enough not to trade them for reassignment. They don't want to give up their sweet spots here to get stuck with some vamp who'll monitor their every move and expect them to deliver their blood and bodies on a regular basis. They kiss up to me once a month and then I leave them alone. Everybody's happy…I guess. I was a penniless virgin when I got here, so I guess I can't complain."

Sindy snorted with surprise at the remark. "How old were you?"

"You first."

"Sixteen."

"Damn. I knew you were a teen, but I thought at least you could vote."

"I was mature for my age."

"In a very good way," he agreed with a smile.

"You?"

"I was *almost* sixteen."

She looked him over in surprise. He was tall and seemed older to her, but that must be some of his true age showing through. "Jeez, that's young."

"You probably only had me beat by a few months. I'm way older than you now anyway."

"When were you turned?"

"Summer of '69, just like the Bryan Adams song."

She did a quick mental calculation. "So, you're like…sixty? I never would have guessed. You don't act it."

"Why should I?" he asked with a laugh. "I've never really had the responsibility of being an adult, and quite frankly, it sounds really boring. I've found that experience serves better than maturity in most situations. Peter Pan had a pretty sweet gig. I'm not complaining."

She had to smile. Peter Pan was actually a perfect description. "So, what happened to you?"

"Woodstock. A lot of vampires like to claim to have been there, but I really was. That's where I died. My parents had forbidden me to go," he informed her with a smile. "They thought I was a dumb kid, sneaking out and melting my brain doing 'shrooms and listening to psychedelic shit. I should've known better than to idolize a bunch of hippies. I was supposed to be like my brother Liam and always do the right thing. He was fighting over in Vietnam...never did come back.

I wasn't as bad as my parents thought; I was just a kid, but I wanted to go and I wasn't going to let them stop me. I hitched from Sweet Valley Pennsylvania over to Bethel, and had the greatest, and last, weekend of my human life."

"At least you had a kick-ass goodbye party," she said with a chuckle. "Woodstock...pretty wild. So where's the guy who turned you? What's his deal?"

"My maker's an elder named Krasimir. He took off after he made me; Bulgaria I think. I'd like to meet him again someday though. He was some kind of spiritual disciple for this society called "The White Brotherhood"; all about harmony and love. Not exactly your typical vampire."

"Peace and love...yup, sounds like Woodstock to me."

"Bulgarian style. This guy wasn't just some hippie, he was the real deal. I think Arif met him on one of his trips back to Turkey and brought him here, trying to get him to join the coven. Vampire shades are very rare, and Arif is big on breed diversity. He wants every talent at his disposal. Krasimir wouldn't stay, but he made me as a sort of parting gift. No hard feelings, you know?"

Every talent at his disposal... That summarized Arif's obsession with the United One in a nutshell. Kieran was watching her quietly, seeming to sense her conclusions. She shrugged it off, bringing him back to his story. "So, why you?"

He smiled. "Just lucky, I guess. They were looking for someone old enough to take direction, but young enough to be inconspicuous. Kids make great spies. No one takes us seriously or pays any attention to us, really. Also...I think they kind of liked my eyes," he added with a grin.

Kieran's human eyes were a beautiful shade of green. Sindy couldn't help but feel drawn to lean a little closer, gazing into them. "You do have amazing eyes."

He smiled and briefly changed them to reveal his vampire eyes, also green, although brighter and flecked with a very inhuman looking lime color. Kieran let her look for a moment, and then changed them back to his human visage. "Thanks. Anyway, Krasimir changed me, presented me to the master, and the rest is history. So, how about you? What's your story?"

"I ran away too. My dad was abusing me, so I left," she said, shortly.

"That sucks. He was knocking you around?"

"Only when I wouldn't spread my legs."

"Oh."

Sindy sighed. "I ran off to the city and started walking the streets. I figured if I was going to be sexually abused, I might as well get paid for it."

Kieran gave her a sympathetic smile. "How'd that work out for you?"

She let out a mirthless chuckle. "You remember the girl in *Pretty Woman* who *didn't* get to sleep with Richard Gere? Her life was cake compared to mine. I was so stupid. I thought I was such hot shit that guys would pay top dollar for me."

"I'd pay top dollar to be with you," he told her matter-of-factly.

She ignored the comment, trying to hide her smirk of a smile, and went on. "I made enough to rent a dumpy room and keep from starving to death. I figured I was just biding my time until I was old enough to dance in the clubs, where the real money was. Then I met Amos."

"Your maker."

"The one and only. He paid me double the usual, but he was pretty homely, so I didn't think much of it. He bit me on the first night. I even kind of knew it. I remember being like, 'Dude, what the fuck?' Then the venom kicked in. It made me feel so good, I figured he must have slipped me something, but I lived. I couldn't afford my own drugs, so anything that made me forget my troubles and sink into bliss wasn't something I was going to question too closely. God, I was an idiot.

He came back a few nights later. I could feel him coming. It was so weird. He bit me again and I knew it was fucked up, but he left me the money and I woke up okay. Whenever he came around I didn't turn him down. After a few more times, there was a night he didn't pay me and I put up a stink. He threw a ten at me and told me that the next time I'd be begging him to do me for free. He was right.

He stayed away for over a week, and it drove me insane. Not only didn't I realize I was addicted to his venom, but he stayed just within range, so I could almost feel him, but never see him. It was sick. I couldn't sleep, I couldn't think. He would call me with my mark, but he wouldn't let me find him. I finally ended up wandering the streets in the middle of the night. I could feel that he was so damn close. I laid down right on the concrete and begged him to come and take me.

He did, and after that, he told me that I was his, and I couldn't deny it. He came back regularly and I would drop everything to feed him. I could be in the middle of making a deal…it didn't matter. Amos couldn't be ignored or disobeyed, which sucked because he wasn't paying me and it was really cutting into business.

It got so I could hardly afford to eat. I was panicked and jittery all the time, waiting to feel him coming. Even on nights he left me alone, John's stayed away 'cause I looked like a junky. I was getting real thin, like those starving kids they show on TV guilt commercials. I was anemic too, so I could barely drag myself off the mattress to hit the streets in the hope I'd see him.

He was totally over-drinking me. I was a goner. It was just a matter of time. Then one night, a feeding was more than I could survive. I died, and for some reason, he chose to turn me.

You know, after he turned me, he just left me there in the dump where I'd been staying? I didn't know what the hell was happening to me. I was confused, and frantic, and thirsty as hell. I was going out of my mind and he didn't come back for me until two nights later. He told me he'd made me into his minion, and that I would always belong to him now. He said only he could stop the desperation and pain, and that if I ever left him, I would die. Then he fed me, and it was so amazing, I had to believe it was true.

He took me back to his place and never let me out of his sight, unless he was leaving me locked up to go out by himself. I was only with him for a month or so. I'd like to think that if it had gone on much longer, I would have eventually managed to get away from him, but during those first few weeks, he had me too terrified to risk it.

He used to bring humans home for me to practice using venom on. He was actually a pretty good teacher. He liked to show me his venom skill because he liked how it impressed me, but mostly, he treated me like shit. I was his personal slave. He'd say 'Come here', and I never knew if he was going to show me something useful, smack me in the face, or bend me over. I might as well have stayed at home.

I was starting to wonder if that was all my life would ever be…endless nights of being treated like dirt, starved until he let me drink a little from whatever victims he brought home before he finished them off. It was awful."

Kieran looked thoroughly disgusted on her behalf. "I remember."

Sindy paused to look up at him. "What do you mean?"

"You had such potential, and he squashed it completely, making you exist in filth and fear. He didn't deserve you in the least."

She continued to stare at him. "No...what do you mean, *you* remember?"

"That's where I found you, in his apartment," he told her, matter-of-factly. "What a surprise you were; a beautiful gem he had kept hidden for himself. You were a dark, dusky jewel trapped and buried beneath his gross gluttony. I wanted to set you free, dust you off and see you shine." After a moment of reminiscence, he met her eyes and then looked away, sheepishly. "Sorry, sometimes I get poetic."

"What are you talking about?"

"When I saw you at Amos' apartment... Amos had a squabble with a coven member. I was ordered to find him and issue a warning; demand that he swear fealty to the coven. I followed him home and I saw you there."

"I never saw you."

Kieran smiled. "I'm a shade. Amos never saw me either. I never did give him the warning, you know."

"You didn't?"

"Nope. I watched him for a few nights, the way he treated you, and when I couldn't stomach anymore, I went back to the coven. I told Arif that Amos said he wasn't afraid of our coven and spat in my face."

"Even Amos wouldn't have been that stupid," Sindy remarked, wide-eyed.

Kieran shrugged. "I knew that, but Arif didn't, so Amos was dust."

She was shocked with disbelief that someone she didn't even know would do something like that for her. "Why? Why would you lie?"

"He didn't deserve any better; you did." She stared at him blankly, trying to digest that. "I knew that Arif wouldn't want you, but at least you'd have a chance to be out on your own, off of Amos' leash. You know, I tried to check back in on you, to see if you needed any pointers, but after Arif turned you away, you disappeared. Most new vamps don't last long on their own. You had me really worried."

"I went back home. I had some debts to settle." She shifted, eyeing him in a new light. "So, wait...for all of these years, you've been stalking me?"

He shrugged, unapologetic. "Sort of."

"I can't decide if that's creepy, or kind of sweet."

He laughed. "Well, in my defense against creepiness, I *am* a spy. I was just doing my job. And out of everyone I have ever been asked to observe, you're the only one I've ever been interested in enough to keep tabs on beyond orders."

"Flattering…in a twisted sort of way."

"Hey, in the time I've been stalking you, I've seen *you* stalk more than your fair share of guys. Ben, Luke, Chris, Paulie… Shall I go on?"

"They were human. I'm a vampire. I'm supposed to stalk humans. That's what we do."

"Yeah, but you've turned playing with your food into an art form."

She gave him a satisfied smile. "Why, thank you."

"So, I think we can both agree that stalking is not an unpardonable offense in this situation."

"Fair enough."

"After Arif wouldn't let you join the coven, it took me forever to finally find you again. That's how I bumped into Cain. We'd heard of him, but he'd always managed to stay out of our way. I knew Arif would be interested in him, and it was a good excuse to get the coven to travel up that way so I could keep tabs on you and make sure you were alright. It looked like Cain was giving you a rough time, so I convinced Arif he owed you a favor or two, having dusted your maker and all."

"That was all because of you? Why'd you do all of that for me?"

He shrugged. "Seemed like the right thing to do."

"But you must see lots of bad stuff. I'm sure you don't help everyone, like some do-good vampire superhero."

"You like that type lately, don't you? But you've already got one of those."

"Role model?" she asked with a smirk.

"Na, leave it to Cain. I'm a little too ADHD for the whole life quest bit. I wanted to help you. Call it a random act of kindness."

"So after the whole deal that went down with Ben and Cain, I went off on my own. Why didn't you approach me then? I never even knew you existed until I went looking for Arif years later."

Kieran shrugged. "I was busy. You'd cut loose all your underlings and it looked like you were just discovering your shifting abilities. You seemed to be enjoying the time alone, feeling pretty empowered and independent, so I let you be. I do have other interests besides following you around, you know. It's not like I'm obsessed with you or something… Jeez, curb the ego."

She laughed as the sound of the morning bell rang throughout the house, and outside too. Dawn was approaching. "Bedtime," Kieran noted.

Sindy glanced down at the bed. "Is *that* why Arif put me here? He figures I owe you."

Kieran just gave a non-committal little shrug. "What do you figure?"

She thought about it for a minute. "I figure it's all your fault that I let Allie kill Zach, which led me to being here and getting nailed...literally."

Kieran smiled in acceptance. "Then I guess you get the bed, and I'm in a guest room." He stood and made his way to the door. "Want me to send in a human to keep you company? They're all women, but I'm sure they'd be happy to oblige."

"No thanks. Let them all fight over you."

He nodded. "Have a nice day," he said with a smirk as he left the room, closing the door behind him.

~~~~~~~~~~~~~~~~~~~~~~~~~~~~~~~~

As night fell and the bell informed all vampires within the compound that it was safe to emerge from their daytime lairs, Sindy stood in the bathroom, one foot resting on the toilet seat, so she could inspect her leg. The wounds from where she had dug out her inhibiting toothpicks were healed and gone, showing nothing but unbroken skin and a slight discoloration. She could hardly believe her luck.

Although she'd had the daylight hours to herself, she had been afraid to continue her handiwork with Kieran in residence. She'd thought for sure medical was going to nail her this evening for having dug out three toothpicks yesterday, but it seemed they would never even know. It must have been the human blood. Kieran hadn't allowed her much, but it had been enough to accelerate her healing. The medical team would never know about her transgression.

That meant that if she was left alone after her check-up, and could trust that Kieran was busy elsewhere, she should have enough time to dig out the rest of the toothpicks, shift forms and sneak out of this place! The wolf was too conspicuous...she'd have to use the bat form, which was not something she was looking forward to trying, but even if she couldn't fly, she'd be small enough to squeeze through the fence unnoticed. If it could get her out of here, it'd be worth it.

The intercom buzzed, out in the bedroom. "Miss Sindy? Time for your physical." It was Kym, at the front door desk. Sindy had just enough time to finish dressing before there was a knock at the bedroom door. Her escorts had arrived.

She opened the door, expecting the young cadets who had been assigned to take her to the medical center each evening. Instead, it was Kieran who stood at the door, fully clothed. "Where's my escort?" she asked him in surprise.

"I'm it. Arif needed the cadets for something, so he asked me to take you."

"And you thoughtfully obliged," she said, batting her eyes and giving him a false smile for his lame attempt to spend more time with her.

"Why wouldn't I? I'm a trusted coven member. He tells me to jump, I ask how high," he replied with a smirk. "This isn't going to take all night, is it?"

"I sure hope not," she answered with a laugh. "Let's go."

"After you," he said with a chivalrous sweep of his arm.

She spoke as she lead him out into the hallway and towards the stairs. "About last night, I'm sorry for laying all my baggage on you. You didn't want to hear about that stuff."

Kieran chuckled. "Have you never met another vampire? That's what we do. We swap creation stories. It's traumatizing for all of us. It's not baggage, it's how we understand each other."

"So we each know just what *kind* of crazy monster we're dealing with?"

"Exactly."

"Wasn't so traumatizing for you, though. You got high for a few days, heard some great tunes, and now you're immortal."

"True, I had it pretty easy, but don't let that fool you, it doesn't make me any less crazy."

She smiled. "I'll keep that in mind."

"I'm sorry about what happened to you. I'm glad that it made you who you are, but I'm sorry you had to go through that."

She felt exactly the same way. No one had ever expressed such a lucid understanding of sympathy for her position before. "Thank you."

"If it weren't for the venom, you totally could have handled Amos, vampire or not, you know that, right? If he didn't have you all strung out, he would have been putty in your hands."

She turned to him, curiously. "You think so?"

"Totally. Manipulating guys is what you do best. But you don't have to keep collecting conquests just to prove you're strong. Trust me, on behalf of men everywhere...we know."

She had to laugh, but then gave him a light smack on the arm as he held open the front door for her. "That's not what I do."

"That's exactly what you do. You're always trying to prove to yourself that you aren't a victim anymore, and handling men is easy for you now."

"It is, isn't it?"

"Except for Cain. He made you work for it."

She paused in the front walkway, insulted. "I got him though, didn't I?"

"Yep. You always get your man." He moved forward and took her arm, to escort her to the street. "So, who's next?"

"Who says I'm done with Cain? Besides, I'm a little busy trying not to be someone else's conquest at the moment."

"You're not talking about me, are you? Because I'm not trying…"

"Yes you are, but no."

He laughed. "Arif," he concluded, with a gesture towards the coven master's mansion next door. "I suppose he pitched you the whole glitz and glamour power package? He's in the market for a new favorite, you know."

"I thought you were his favorite," she responded with a false smile.

"I have a feeling I'll soon be falling from grace."

"Is that so?"

He shrugged. "Nothing lasts forever."

"Have you been a naughty boy?" she asked him with quiet suspicion.

"All my life," he replied with a grin. "I am his best spy, but Lorelei has always been his best girl…until now."

"Can I tell you a secret? I don't really want the job."

"I thought positioning yourself to be here was all part of the master plan."

"Turns out, my plan sucked."

He offered a smile. "That happens sometimes. So…you don't want to be his best girl, or you don't want to be here at all?"

"That depends," she told him carefully. "Which answer sends you running back to Arif to tell him I need more toothpicks?"

"Whose bed you want to be in is your business," he assured her. "For now, you're in mine. I plan to thank Arif and tell him we had a day to remember."

"We didn't do anything. That's kind of misleading information. I thought you were his best spy?" she reminded him facetiously.

"A good spy knows what's worth reporting, and when to just smile and nod. Let him think you made me happy. What's the difference?"

"Well, it might just tick him off. When he ordered me into *his* bed, I wasn't very cooperative. He threw a big hissy fit over it."

"Really?"

"Actually, he stood by calmly while having a bunch of guards throw the hissy fit for him, but he was still a big baby about the whole thing. He decided I needed to be taught a lesson about obeying orders."

"I'll bet he was just lovin' an excuse to flex his coven-master-muscle," he conjectured with a smirk.

She nodded with a chuckle. "Oh, he flexed, alright. I never gave in though."

"Is that a fact?" Kieran asked with a surprised smile. "See, I knew you were trying to be faithful to Cain."

"No I wasn't," she insisted, giving him another smack on the arm for the accusation. "Believe it or not, and I never thought I'd hear myself say this, but I'm kind of getting tired of using sex to get my way all the time. Letting guys grope me night after night, it's just not that much fun anymore."

"There's no challenge in it. It's too easy for you," he said with an appreciative glance at her.

"Thanks," she answered wryly.

"But I could see where it'd be more fun when it's just for fun."

"Yeah. I didn't think I needed to bother with Zach, and by not letting him screw me, maybe I kind of screwed myself, but that was just bad judgment. I can be practical about it. I had actually planned on sleeping with Arif just to make things easier, but then he really pissed me off and it brought out my stubborn streak."

Kieran laughed. "Serves him right. His loss. I'm sure he was disappointed."

She shrugged. "I doubt he really cared; he gets plenty of booty. It hurt his pride more than anything. Even the self-proclaimed slut wouldn't sleep with him. You might not want to bring it up. I'm guessing it's kind of a sore spot for his ego."

"Even sluts have standards. But for the record, I don't think you're a slut. I think you're skilled in the art of deceptive drinking and creative negotiation. Sluts give it away for free. And I am *definitely* going to tell Arif that we had a wonderful time yesterday...if you don't mind," Kieran added with an evil grin.

She thought about Kieran's position and how it would feel for him to casually mention her acceptance of him, and had to laugh. "Go for it."

As they crossed to the medical center, a black limousine pulled through the driveway in front of *Susuzluktan Saray*. Sindy saw her usual cadet escorts come down the front steps of the building on either side of a woman; it was Felicity. They held her by the arms in a firm grip, and brought her down to the limo. After she was within, they closed the door and stood guard next to the car, waiting for Arif.

Sindy paused. "That's right. Arif's taking *red* for negotiations tonight, isn't he; to try and convince someone to help him get a hold of Allie?"

"That's the plan," Kieran answered, observing the car.

Sindy shook her head. "You really think that'll work? Allie's not going to come for her. They were barely friends like a million years ago."

Kieran cocked an eyebrow at her. "Actually, the woman and the United One are very close. You spent how long supposedly gaining Alyson's trust, and you didn't know that? You're a shitty spy."

"I'll leave the spying to you," Sindy huffed. "It's not like Allie ever hung out with Felicity, or talked about her." Kieran shrugged. "Even if they're BFF's, Alyson is a powerful immortal super-being, why would she sacrifice herself for some stupid human? I know Felicity's meant as leverage to sway Cain too, but what's Cain gonna do, besides flip a nut? Cain's strong, but Allie's stronger. He might dramatically brood until Allie's sick of him, but he's not going to get her to give herself up."

"He's talked you into a thing or two in your time. The question is whether Felicity is sufficient motive for him to *want* Allie to give in. Anyway, they aren't meeting with Cain tonight, although that'll happen too at some point. They're going to see Felicity's husband. Supposedly he has influence over Allie too. Arif is leaving no avenue untried. He wants Alyson convinced that she needs to comply, no matter who does the convincing. It's not a sacrifice he's after. He just wants a nice sampling of blood from the United One, then they're both free to go."

"That's it? Maybe it *will* work then. I don't know if she'll listen to Ben, but if it won't kill her and Cain's pushing for it, I doubt even Mattie could keep it from happening. Cain'll probably have her here to donate within a week. So, what's Arif going to do with her blood?"

"Does it matter?"

"I'm sure Cain could think of a few unsavory things to argue against it, but if Felicity is in jeopardy he'll give up in a flash. He'd do anything for *her*."

Kieran wore that annoying smirk of his again. "You sound a little bitter."

"I'm just sick of her and her charmed little life."

Kieran glanced at the guarded car again. "I don't think she's feeling very charmed at the moment."

"Good."

Kieran watched her, warily. "You two have a bit of history, don't you? Am I going to have to put extra guards on the girl?"

Sindy chuckled. "What do you think I'm going to do, kill her?"

"Maybe...or free her."

Sindy felt a frantic wave of panic wash over her, that her conversation with Felicity may have been overheard, but she straightened and recovered her confidence. If they had been overheard, Arif would have known last night that she'd pulled some toothpicks out of her legs, and he would have replaced them while shooting up her arm. Chances were slim she could do anything to help Felicity anyway...and she wasn't even sure if she wanted to. "Why would I do that? Let little Miss Sunshine see what it's like not to have everything her way for a change."

"You know, she's married now, with a baby. She's been extremely upset."

"So? Did you *want* me to help her? Come on, Arif can threaten all he wants, but it's not like he'll ever really kill her, not unless he wants Cain to have a holy conniption. So the bitch gets to spend a week reading by the pool away from her husband and cranky baby. Boo-hoo. Look what they did to me! She's lucky I don't make things worse for her while she's here. Oh, but everybody feels bad for poor Felicity; so typical."

Kieran smiled at her passionate disgust over the issue. "Extra guards it is."

~~~~~~~~~~~~~~~~~~~~~~~~~~~~~~

Sindy's medical check went more smoothly than she could have hoped for. The human blood she had drunk had managed to heal the wounds where she had dug the toothpicks out of her legs so that the nurse never gave it a second glance. At first Sindy worried that perhaps the staff was just playing it cool and waiting to report directly to Arif like last time, but they really didn't even look her over well enough to have seen anything.

It didn't hurt that Kieran had come in with her, and spent the entire time being incredibly charming and distracting to all of the nurses. Apparently, they all knew him well and were flattered that he'd stopped in for a visit. He seemed to have a lot of power in the coven community, being known for pulling strings and fulfilling requests. The staff was so busy asking favors and promising favors in return that they barely even glanced at Sindy.

Before she knew it, Kieran had dropped her back off at home, and was headed out on errands of his own. He told her he'd be back before dawn, but she could keep the bedroom. Apparently, he was looking forward to arrangements he'd made to sleep elsewhere.

Sindy sent for some animal blood, a few bottles of alcohol, and then told the staff that she wanted privacy from them for the rest of the evening. She was finally alone, ensconced in the bedroom, with the entire night and day ahead of her. There should be plenty of time for her to surgically remove the rest of the toothpicks and get the hell out of this place once and for all.

If she were to stay, she might manage to stomach suffering through Arif's desirous requests until he finally bored of using her body, and then she could live the lifestyle she had always dreamed of, but was it worth it? What if he found out she could create a white eyed vampire...then what? No matter how appealing Arif's promises of power and luxury, she knew in the end, her freedom was worth more.

She took a good long swig from the whiskey bottle she held as she stood in her bra and panties, locked in the bathroom, trying to inspect her body. Not having a reflection in the mirror sucked. She could feel the toothpicks that had been jabbed into her butt cheeks and the backs of her upper thighs...oh, could she feel them, but she couldn't see what she was doing to dig them out properly. Those would have to be last. Maybe if she managed to get all the others out, she could turn most of her body to mist and somehow get the rest out that way.

Her arms and legs seemed the least daunting. She would start there and hope that the encouragement of seeing progress and the consumption of a lot of alcohol would be enough to get her through the tougher areas later on.

After another shot of whiskey, she swapped the bottle for the knife, and got to work. The knife was sharp, at least. Sitting in the bottom of the bathtub, she was able to make a nice, clean and precise cut into her calf, next to where she could feel the toothpick. She couldn't see it, but it was close to the surface.

Under her vampire blood's direction, her body had been slowly squeezing and contracting the muscles around the wood to try to make it work its way out. Another good slice, bisecting the first, and she felt the blade touch wood. Now all she had to do was dig around a bit with the tip of the knife until she could maneuver it into a position where she could pull it out with the tweezers she'd found in the medicine cabinet. A little blood pooled at the site, obscuring her view, but there wasn't as much as she had expected. She hadn't been fed well enough to have much extra.

Jeez, it hurt. At one point, she wondered if the prolonged poking, digging and prodding with the knife was almost worse than some quick clean amputation would be. It wasn't a serious consideration, even if it might work, but she wasn't sure how she was going to get through this. Eventually, she had to stuff a washcloth into her mouth, to give herself something to bite down on and muffle the cries she couldn't manage to stifle on her own. Her stomach turned with every gentle jab of the blade, no matter how delicately she tried to handle it. She could deal with pain and discomfort; she had plenty of experience trying to numb herself to whatever was being done to her body on various occasions, but that was more easily done when she didn't have to focus on anything else. It was difficult to pay attention to what she was doing *and* have to feel it. She kept having to stop, look away and give the pain a chance to subside so she could clear her focus.

It took almost a half an hour, but she got the damn thing out. Not bad, time-wise, but this was just the first one, and was in what was irrefutably the easiest location. One down...twenty more to go. This was going to be a long, miserable night, but knowing Arif was busy elsewhere gave her incentive to carry on.

Around 4 a.m. she ran out of alcohol. She'd tried to pace herself, but its effect was so dampened by her vampire nature, that she'd needed to drink it fast and steady to help dull the pain. Despite some valiant efforts to get shit-faced drunk, her mind was only slightly foggy, but that was a good thing, because she could work through it. She'd gotten out nine toothpicks from her arms and legs, but there were still twelve left, and their positioning was going to prove challenging.

She needed another break. There was only so long she could endure this tension and torture before her hands began to shake so badly as to be useless. She allowed herself to slump back against the side of the tub and close her eyes for a moment.

She must have passed out. When she opened her eyes she immediately knew that more time had passed than she would have liked. She had no idea what had woken her, or what the hour was, but her body could tell that the sun had already risen well up into the sky. The bathroom door was still locked and all seemed quiet in the suite. She sat up and tried to take stock of things.

Her limbs looked positively gruesome, with numerous spots having been sliced and gouged, and despite the fact that she'd been on such light rations, she'd still made quite a bloody mess with her handiwork. She had soaked through two towels, and made a smeared, drippy mess wherever she touched. Although most of it was thankfully contained in the tub, the bathroom still looked like a crime scene.

She tried to stand, but suffered a terrible wave of dizziness that made her think better of the idea. Maybe she ought to just sit here for another minute and recuperate. The haze of the buzz she'd been under had lifted, and the thought of trying to continue her self-mutilation was absolutely nauseating, but she was not nearly finished.

Something caught her attention near the door, a dark haze, near the space at the floor. Sindy blinked, wondering if her vision was clouding...but she knew she wasn't really drunk any longer. By the time panicked alarm flooded through her at the realization of what was actually happening, there was nothing she could do. It was too late.

Kieran had siphoned himself under the door as mist, and was now taking shape before her. He stood over the tub, looking down at her mutilated body. Sindy just lay there in her underwear, feeling a painful bloody mess. What could she possibly do or say? Her activities and intentions were beyond obvious.

Kieran folded his arms and shook his head. "It's a good thing there aren't any other vampires in the house. I could smell you from out in the hall."

She glanced down at her legs, covered in blood, and realized that it must be true. "You gonna turn me in?" she asked. He didn't answer. After a moment of silence, she couldn't look him in the eyes any more. She was having a hard time reading him and the tension was too much. He'd always been friendly and flirtatious with her, but she had seen him drop his smile to become seriously ruthless in an instant when needed, and he had always appeared unflinchingly loyal to Arif.

She lowered her gaze. Kieran was naked from shifting. She uncomfortably tried not to stare at his body, turning away to look at the bloody mess she'd made of the tub instead. He unfolded his arms and his demeanor softened.

"I'm not turning you in..." he told her with a smirk of a smile, "I'm turning you out. You don't belong here, and digging those things out is your only chance for freedom. I'm no surgeon, but I'll do it for you, if you want."

She looked back up to meet his eyes, hardly believing her ears. "Why would you? If I escape, you could get in big trouble and you know I'll have to do a serious disappearing act. You'll never see me again."

"I can handle trouble. So disappear...you'll manage. You think I'm *that* hung up on you?" he asked her teasingly. After a second, he nodded with a shrug. "Okay, so maybe I am, but you know what they say, if you love someone, set them free."

"You don't *love* me," she assured him. "Anyway, if they leave, they were never truly yours."

"Yeah, but if they come back, we could have one hell of a good time together."

She chuckled and cocked an eyebrow at his tenacious pursuit of her affections. "I can't come back. Arif would have me dusted on sight."

"True, but vampires live a long time...things change. I think I'll take my chances that I'll see you again somewhere along the way, and considering this will be my second time majorly helping you out, I think this time you'll owe me," he pronounced with a grin. He came forward to take her hand and try to help her stand and step out of the tub. It took her a few minutes, but she was finally able to feel steady as he held her and unlocked the door.

He turned back towards her, and on a whim, she leaned forward and gave him a small kiss. It was just a brief, soft touch of the lips. It was so unexpected, he didn't even really have time to try to kiss her back before she leaned back from him just enough to break contact. He accepted her departure from his lips gracefully, eyeing her with a bit of surprise. "Are you drunk?" he asked.

She realized she reeked of whiskey. "Not nearly as drunk as I should be," she admitted.

"We can fix that. Let's get you on the bed and I'll call up some more liquor for you before we get started."

He helped her out into the bedroom. She wrapped her arms tightly around his neck, trying to ease her descent and lessen the pain as he lowered her onto the bed. Once settled, she whispered, "Thanks," and let go.

He grinned as he straightened up from her. "Don't thank me yet. This is going to hurt like a bitch."

"Don't I know it?"

He used the intercom to call up some supplies. While they waited, he went to the bathroom to clean up a little and retrieve the knife and tweezers she'd been using. He brought in a few clean towels too. Shortly after, there was a knock at the door; a girl had arrived with his request. Rather than let her in, Kieran went out to the hall to retrieve the items.

Sindy found it strange and amusing that Kieran had still not bothered to put any clothes on. The human girl didn't mention his nakedness, that Sindy could hear. Kieran must walk around in the nude all the time at home, so that he could easily shift at will. He was pretty nice to look at, so she certainly didn't mind, but it was odd to get used to. She wondered what the humans thought of it.

Kieran returned with a few bottles of Jack Daniels and a large, dark pitcher. "This is for now," he said, handing her a bottle of alcohol, "and these are for later." He put the rest on the bedside table. "Blood," he explained. "It's getting cold, but it's human."

"Score," she said, pushing aside the J.D. and reaching out for the blood.

"Not yet. Save it for when we're done. You'll need it to help heal you if you want to have any energy left to shift."

She pouted, but accepted the liquor bottle instead, knowing that he was right. "You sure you want to help me?" she asked him. "This could really screw things up for you."

He waved a hand as though he wasn't concerned. "To be honest, I've been planning an exit of my own. After forty-five years of loyal service, I consider my debt paid. I used to think I'd wait for fifty, but the timing seems right now. Arif is getting on my nerves...and I'm not the only one. I have a feeling the coven is heading for major upheaval, and I think I'd rather avoid the ruckus.

Besides, Allie is the real deal, The United One. She's like, a sign or something, don't you think? I know to you she's just been...Allie, but you have to feel her power, right? It's...divine."

"Divine?" she asked in disbelief. "As in, God-like?"

Kieran seemed dead serious. "Yeah, totally."

"She's not God, she's just a vampire."

He chuckled. "No, she's not God, but she is a Goddess among vampires. You know it's true. Her blood is special, and like it or not that girl is destined for divinity. I don't know about you, but I'd rather follow *her* wishes then obey some self-righteous coven master."

Sindy narrowed her gaze and shook her head. "How spiritual and un-materialistic of you. You're willing to trade in your sweet spot here because you want to go follow after Allie?" she asked with a smirk.

He gently took the bottle from her so he could take a swig of his own. "I didn't say I planned to follow her, but I certainly don't want her for an enemy. I may not have been around for centuries, but in all my life I have never seen anyone who deserved the respect that she does. You said it yourself once, you told her that she was a Queen. I heard you."

"That was just to get her to stop worrying about obeying Mattie and Cain all the time."

"It was true, and you knew it when you said it. Believe whatever you want, but that's how I feel." He gave her back the bottle. "So...once we're through here, what's your plan?"

She shrugged. "Put on a robe, head outside and find a fence, I guess. I don't have time to make complicated plans."

He furrowed his brow as he cleaned off the knife with an edge of one of the towels. "Those fences are tight, too tight for a wolf. Gonna try and mist your way through?"

That would be a nice simple solution, but she doubted she could manage it. Unlike Kieran, she could only remain dispersed as mist for a very short time, and she was not experienced enough to navigate while in that state. With her luck, she would wind up reverting back into human form with the fence jammed through her middle. "No, I'm too limited for that to work. The bat will fit."

Kieran raised his eyebrows. He must know that she had refused to partake in bat-shifting sessions with Tempest and Allie because she was afraid of using the form. She was terrible at it. She could not maneuver well in her bat form, and flight was out of the question. "I just need to squeeze through. Once I'm on the other side I can use my wolf. Then they'll never catch me."

"It's a double fence, you know, with about a ten foot gap. They let the dogs run the space in between. Trust me, you do not want to be caught. They are fast, and catching you would be great fun for them."

Sindy was briefly tormented by flashbacks of the first time she had tried to use her bat form, and she had been caught by a fox. It was frightening, painful, and not something she'd like to repeat. She shuddered. "Then I'd better make sure they don't see me."

"Keep it quiet and quick. They're more than just *dogs,* you know."

"What do you mean, more?"

"Well, Arif feeds them blood."

"Blood?" she asked, in surprise.

"*Vampire* blood; his very own."

She made a face of disgust. "What the hell for?"

"One of Arif's pet projects. He raises them from pups and feeds them his blood. He's very proud of them. It gives them a bond. Plus, if he gives them enough of it, sometimes traces of his powers carry over too."

Sindy blanched at the bad taste that suddenly invaded her mouth at the thought. "How creative of him. He's got a thing for dogs, doesn't he?"

Kieran shrugged. "He's still trying to perfect the process to get the levels just right. Ever heard of the Montauk Monster?"

"The what...? No."

Kieran shook his head with a blanch of disgust. "A couple of years back, he gave one of the Dobermans too much. It started to turn..."

"Into a vampire?" she asked, incredulously.

"Sort of. It was incomplete. It was still alive; couldn't take the sun though. We hoped things would level out eventually, but it never stabilized. It went crazy and took off before we could put it down. Ended up down the beach. All its hair burned off but it didn't turn to dust. Partial transformations are tricky, and I'm betting that wasn't the first time it's happened. Poor thing probably died a slow and painful death."

Sindy shuddered. "Probably?"

"We lost track of it and some beach-goers found it before we could reclaim the body. They thought it was some kind of demon. Spawned some local legends for a while. They dubbed it 'The Montauk Monster'. Google it, it was in all the papers."

She recalled observing the group of Dobermans with Zach from the car during their arrival; demon dogs indeed. "Fabulous. So what else can these dogs do, besides go insane and inspire urban legends?"

Kieran chuckled. "Arif's been more careful lately. He hates losing them, they're very close."

"I'll bet," she muttered in disgust.

"The best he's been able to do is lengthen their lifespan and boost their thought ranges to be more receptive to him. But there are a few who have become truly telepathic."

"Great," she mumbled, sarcastically.

"That means catch the attention of the wrong one, they'll all be there." Sindy was rethinking her plans in shocked dismay as Kieran tried to reassure her. "You can do this, though. Just be quick and stay focused. Arif has no reason to be suspicious of you or have them on high alert. You should get through. Then what?"

"From there, I don't know what I'll do. Arif's going to want my head, so I should just go 'lone wolf' for awhile, out in the woods somewhere, under the radar."

"Sounds lonely."

She shrugged. It wouldn't be the first time she'd gone off alone that way, but she wasn't looking forward to it. "Without some formidable protection, I don't really have a choice, do I? Although, I guess I could always head over to Cain's and see if your *Goddess* Allie would help me out. She definitely owes me a favor."

He chuckled. "Yeah, she does, but she's not there. She and Mattie took off when you left...which is supposed to be a big secret, by the way," he added, thoughtfully, "but I doubt you plan to tell Arif, and I thought you should know."

"Thanks."

"Glad I could save you a trip. It seems my bonds are loosening..."

"What?"

"Nothing." He became thoughtful again for a moment. "Do you *want* to go back to Cain's?"

"I think what you're asking is whether I want to go back to *Cain*...minus the *s."* He opened another bottle of whiskey without answering her, and took a swig. "I don't know," she told him truthfully. "The Crimson Coven is there. They might take me in. If I was accepted as a full member of the coven, I could hide out under their protection for a while."

"Sounds like you've got a plan." It was hard to tell what he thought of the idea. He'd probably rather she stayed alone, so he could try to join back up with her at some point, but joining a large coven would be the safer way to go.

He put down his liquor bottle and picked back up the knife. "Let's get this going. Where are we at?" he asked, with a gesture over her body.

She sighed. "I have twelve left."

"Twelve?" he repeated in disbelief.

"Well, I started with twenty-four."

"Wow, Arif must really be feeling paranoid."

"You think?"

"Okay, don't worry. The sun's not down yet. We still have a couple of hours before they'll be looking for you at the medical center. I think we can do it...if you can handle some quick and dirty surgery." He raised the knife, questioningly.

"If you've got the balls, I've got the bottle," she replied, lifting the Jack Daniels in salute to him.

After a pointed glance down at his exposed crotch, he said with a smirk, "I think we're set." She chuckled appreciatively and took another draw from the bottle. "How do you want to do this? Should I give you a magic marker to make little X's for me, in case you pass out?"

"I won't pass out," she assured him. "I already did most of the easy ones, though. I've still got one in each upper bicep, two in the back of each upper thigh, one more in each butt cheek, and then two in my stomach, and one in each breast," she explained, as she took off her bra. She didn't bother to take off her thong panty; it wouldn't be in the way.

"Is that all? No problem," he quipped with a grin, eying her bared breasts.

"And stop smiling," she ordered him, as she lightly cupped and covered her breasts, protectively. Even just that light gesture made the toothpicks within painfully pierce deeper into her flesh. "This is not going to be fun."

"It's not going to be much fun for me either, you know. When I pictured you naked in my bed, this wasn't what I had in mind. But I can do it. It won't be pretty, but I can get them out, and you'll heal."

"I know."

"Alright, why don't you lay on your stomach? We'll start at the bottom, and work our way up."

Kieran turned out to be fairly skilled with the knife, and by the time he had gotten the third toothpick out, he'd found a technique that seemed to work pretty well. Sindy was twisting the bed sheets up in her clenched fists and smothering herself in the pillows to keep quiet, but they were making good progress, and the gulping swigs of Jack Daniels she took between each new round definitely helped. Horrible as it was, it was a huge relief to be able to focus on dealing with the pain and let Kieran do the work.

They were in the home stretch. The evening bell rang to announce that the sun had just set, but Sindy wouldn't be expected for her check-up for at least another hour. They only had two toothpicks left to go.

"Found it. Tweezers," he said, holding out his hand as he held the knife steady, buried in her arm just below the shoulder.

Sindy lay on her stomach again, her face turned away from the wound as she passed him the tweezers. He was about to take them, when he suddenly jerked the knife sideways and grabbed for the bridge of his nose with his free hand. "Ow!"

She cried out in pain of her own from the unexpected motion. She looked over her shoulder at him, curiously. "Hello? I'm the one having holes dug into my flesh. What's your problem?"

"I don't know. I just had this sharp pain all of a sudden, like somebody smashed me in the face. Ahhh." He dropped the knife and almost fell off the edge of the bed.

"What the hell is wrong with you?"

"I don't know. My back. It feels like my back is broken."

Sindy eyed him speculatively. "How's your chest…and your throat?"

"Fine. Did you not hear me say my face and my back? Isn't that enough? What the fuck is going on?"

"I think I know…liar."

"What? Why am I a liar? I mean, besides the fact that I often lie…but not to you. Not recently, anyway."

"You said you've never made another vampire."

"I haven't."

"You sure about that? Because this looks like a classic case of transferred pain; the gift of parenthood. If your neck and chest don't hurt, then at least your offspring hasn't been staked or decapitated. You're still in pain, so they can't be dust yet, but it sounds like somebody is getting their ass kicked. Who did you make?"

"Nobody…"

"Well, if it's not you, then you're feeling somebody else." While Kieran thought about that, Sindy used the tweezers to pull the exposed toothpick out of her arm herself. Once finished, she looked up with a weak smile. "How you doing? One left. Are you up for it?"

Kieran thought about it for a moment and then took the knife and tweezers from her. "Yeah. I think I'm okay now, but that was seriously weird. Let's hurry up and finish this."

She pinpointed the exact spot on the upper bicep of her left arm where she could feel the last toothpick buried. Kieran made an incision, and was using the tip of the knife to gently catch the edge of the wood, when his hand flew to the back of his head and he closed his eyes, obviously in great pain. "Holy shit," he mumbled through gritted teeth. He dropped the knife and backed away from her to fall to his knees on the floor. After the shock of unexpected pain began to wear off, he tried to whisper explanation. "My head, it feels like someone just took an ice-pick to it. What the hell?"

"That's got to be really bad for junior. You wouldn't feel it unless it was life threatening. If you concentrate, you can probably tell where he is too, if you felt like lending a helping hand."

"Concentrate, you mean while trying to keep my head from exploding? Who could live through pain like this?"

"A vampire, that's who. Ain't we a lucky bunch?"

Kieran took a few moments to recover while trying to decipher the situation. "I don't understand, I've never…"

"Never say never." Suddenly, Sindy felt her words cut off as her throat constricted with a sharp, squeezing pain of her own. "Oh, fuck."

"Not you too?"

"It's Zach. Maybe he's with your guy." She winced again. "Whoever they are fighting, they are definitely losing."

Kieran stared at her thoughtfully for a moment. "This isn't teamwork. I have a feeling our kids aren't getting along."

"So you *are* somebody's daddy?"

He barely nodded, "I've got to go."

"What are you going to do?"

"Teach them to play nice together, I guess."

"We wouldn't even be feeling it, if this pain wasn't super serious. One of them will be dust before you even get there. Did you figure out who Zach's up against?"

"Yeah, I think so...and it's someone I really don't want to see lose." Without giving her a better answer, Kieran leaned down to surprise her with a quick kiss. "You've got this, right?" he asked, indicating the wound in her arm. "I have to go and stop the fight...now. I can't afford to wait...if he's dusted...it would just be awful. I have to stop it."

Sindy sighed. She didn't really want to let him run out on her, but she had been damn lucky to have his help in the first place. "Okay, go. But who is it?"

He shook his head, not ready to explain. "I'll tell you later. And I'll tell Kym that I'm taking you to medical so you won't need an escort, that should buy you some time. Be careful. I'll see you on the outside." With that, he suddenly dispersed into a cloud of smoke and flew out the door.

"Sure, go ahead. Don't worry about me," Sindy called after him. "I'll just lay here and do surgery on myself."

Chapter 14 - Vicious

Mattie

Mattie & Alyson's trailer
Somewhere upstate, New York
A few nights before…

Zach made himself at home on Mattie and Alyson's couch, lounging and putting his feet up on the cushion next to him. "This place is pretty sweet."

Allie took note of Mattie's reaction to Zach's shoes on the clean couch cushion, and immediately went over and shooed Zach's feet down so she could sit there instead. "Thanks." She gave Mattie a small smile. *I can't believe he survived the change! He was dead for a few minutes, so I wasn't sure he would.*

Forgive me if I'm not overjoyed, was Mattie's response.

"I can't believe we just bumped into you like this," she said aloud to Zach.

Zach grinned and spread his hands, "Crazy, right?"

Mattie eyed him suspiciously. "It is quite a coincidence."

Allie noticed his distrust. *I don't know why we can feel each other, but it makes sense that if he happened to cross my path it would be easy for him to just keep following the feeling,* she told him privately.

Mattie nodded. *I guess. I know when I feel you, it always makes me want to get closer.* He mouthed her a kiss.

Zach leaned back into the couch with his hands behind his head. "Tell me again why we're headed up to Buffalo?"

"Hopefully, we aren't. We have a friend there," Allie explained, "who's experienced in mentoring new vampires, but I don't even know if he's home. He's been known to travel, so I'm going to try to get in touch with him before we go anywhere. Maybe he's nearby and we can get him to come to us. He can help you learn what you can do, and how to control it."

Zach raised an eyebrow. "I don't need a mentor. I can figure it out myself."

"Normally, maybe, but you're kind of a special case."

"Because I have white eyes, like you," he concluded with a smile.

"Exactly."

"Did this guy teach *you* stuff?" Zach asked.

"Yes, he's helped me immensely. He's wonderful."

Zach acknowledged Allie's obvious fondness for Cain with a glance at Mattie and a smirk. "Oh *really?* Is he cute too?" he asked condescendingly.

"Not like that," Allie reprimanded, giving Zach a light smack for the remark. Both she and Zach were immediately surprised to attention by the thrill that ran through them as Allie touched him. Apparently, there was some kind of odd, marked sort of connection between them, for their shared white eyes.

Alyson quickly scooched further from him on the couch, and snuck a quick peek at Mattie to see if he'd noticed. He had, but only shook his head a little and tried to ignore it.

It was bad enough Allie didn't seem to realize that her open and familiar attitude often came off as flirtatious, now this guy was going to get treated to electric thrills from her touch to go with it? He had better not be staying long.

Alyson re-settled herself in the opposite corner of the couch and answered Zach's remark. "Yes he's cute, but he's like a brother to us, closer even. We're coven mates."

"Coven-mates, huh? Then why aren't you still there?"

Alyson glanced at Mattie before answering. "We were just taking some time to ourselves, but it'll be good to see him again. I know he can be a big help to you."

Zach crossed his arms and then swung his legs to rest ankles crossed on Allie's knees. He was trying to touch her again in any way possible without seeming overt about it, but Allie wasn't stupid enough to allow it, at least not in front of Mattie. The moment he touched her, Allie stood, dumping him off. Zach gave her a mischievous grin as she went to sit on the kitchen bench instead, speaking to Mattie telepathically as she went. *Thank you, for keeping things in check outside.*

You don't have to thank me. I'm not a monster. I do have some self-restraint.

She grinned. *And it turns out that you were right, restraint is sexy.*

I'm glad that's your stance, because obviously this guy's got next to none.

She gave Zach a reprimanding glance and answered Mattie in her head. *He's just feeling full of himself right now, from all the power. I know you had a rough time being turned, but when it isn't so traumatizing, being a new vamp is quite a trip.*

Oh, he's full of something, alright.

Seemingly unaware of the silent exchange, Zach continued with the prior conversation. "I don't need any help from this guy, Cain. I sure as hell wasn't planning to go all the way up to Buffalo. Pure Chaos has a gig in Brooklyn this weekend. They need me."

"Who's Chaos?" Mattie asked, as he went to stand next to Alyson. He put his arm around her, reminding her of the voltage in their own personal shared mark, and hoping Zach got the implied message,

Allie responded for him. "His band…and *no.* Are you crazy? You can't play a gig. You can't see them anymore. I'm sorry, Zach, but that is a non-negotiable rule of becoming undead. You can't go back."

Zach sat up, spreading his arms as though innocent of any impure intentions. "I'm not gonna bite 'em or nothing. I just wanna play. We're good, you know. You've heard us. We were going somewhere. I can't let them down. How are they gonna play without me?"

Mattie could tell Alyson felt devastated to have been responsible for ripping this guy away from his life. Mattie almost felt a little badly for him as well, knowing how he had felt to lose his own human life, but he wasn't going to dwell on it. It was done and couldn't be changed; the price of Allie's mistake. She knew it too. "I'm sorry, Zach, but that's just the way it is. They'll have to find a new guitarist."

"They can try, but I'm irreplaceable."

"I didn't say they'd find someone as good," she clarified with a warm smile, "just someone else."

Zach slumped back into the couch again. "This sucks. You never saw your family to say goodbye?"

Mattie shook his head. "They think I'm dead. It was hard, but necessary."

"I wasn't speaking to anyone much in my family anyway," Allie told him, "so I don't even know if they've noticed, but I never plan to see them again."

Zach eyed them both suspiciously before asking Allie, "Who turned you?"

"Mattie did," she said, putting her arm up to caress him lovingly.

"How'd you meet him?"

"Gosh, I've known Mattie forever. He was best friends with my neighbor, so we kind of grew up together. He was my boyfriend before he died."

"So he came back for you?" Zach clarified with a superior smirk. "What makes you think your relationships are any stronger than mine? That band is my life. We're brothers, just as close as you guys were. Why can't I go back for them like he went back for you?"

"It's not the same," Mattie asserted. "Allie already knew about vampires before I changed. Trust me, it's different. Besides, your white eyes put an even sharper spin on things. You cannot go back," he repeated, sternly.

Allie took a softer tone, "Not now anyway. Meet Cain, then we can talk about it more after he's had a chance to weigh in."

Zach snorted in derision. "Why should I care what he thinks?"

"Cain is an elder," Mattie told him, offended by the disrespect. "He's been around long enough to know a thing or two about these kinds of situations, and he deserves respect."

Zach dismissed Mattie's reprimand, becoming excited by a new thought of his own. "An elder? That's right. Vampires can't die, can we? Awesome."

Mattie narrowed his eyes in refute. "You can die. Trust me. You just won't die of old age."

"So, how old is this guy? Like a thousand?"

"No. There aren't any vampires around that are that old," Mattie explained, "at least not that I've ever heard of. Supposedly, they all wiped each other out back in the 1600's over some kind of 'breed war', and almost went extinct. Now they're repopulating, and Cain is one of the oldest you'll meet. I think he's 350."

Allie leaned forward to appeal to him quietly. "Zach, we really need you to meet with him, okay? Please?"

Zach locked eyes with her for a moment, and then acceded. "Fine."

"Thank you," Allie said with a sigh of relief. "I couldn't seem to get in touch with him before, but I'll try again later." She smiled and searched for something to reward him with for the cooperation. "Hey, why don't you play something for us?" she asked, waving her hand towards his guitar case, where it leaned against the couch.

Mattie rolled his eyes, and even Zach seemed dubious. "What…now? I don't have an amp."

"That's okay," Mattie assured him. "You don't have to play."

Alyson would not take no for an answer. "He's really good Mattie. Wait 'til you hear him. I can jack it into our stereo system, I think."

"Really?" Zach asked, warming up to the idea. Alyson's obvious excitement over the thought was hard for him to resist.

"Sure, I used to work the sound board at a bar and our equipment sucked. It was always crapping out, so I learned to be creative. I'll have to play with the levels and it won't sound as good as an amp, but I can get it to work. Let's jam!"

"Don't," Mattie pleaded, "you'll blow out my speakers."

"No we won't, I promise," she said, standing to give him a swift kiss. "Besides, you've got to hear this guy play. You won't believe how talented he is!"

Mattie groaned a bit. "With his new supernatural speed and dexterity, I'm sure he's a guitar prodigy. I think I'd rather get us going," he told her, as he made his way towards the driver's seat.

"Holy crap, his vamp abilities will affect his playing, won't they? He'll be unparalleled; he could be a legit rock star!" Allie exclaimed towards Zach, with glee.

Mattie turned to her with a snort. "Oh yeah, what could possibly go wrong with that plan? Haven't you ever read Anne Rice's *Queen of the Damned?*"

Allie scoffed at him. "Baby, I *am* the Queen of the Damned."

Mattie sighed and answered drolly. "Why don't you try and choose a role model who *didn't* want to murder half the population of the world?"

Zach looked to Allie in confusion. "What is he talking about?"

"It's a book." Allie answered with a smirk.

"Oh. I don't read."

Mattie chuckled. "Big surprise."

~~~~~~~~~~~~~~~~~~~~~~~~~~~~~~

The guy was good on the guitar, Mattie had to give him that. After hearing him play, at least Mattie could better understand Allie's enthusiasm for the musician, even though the guy's presence in their home still pissed him off. As the night wore on, Allie claimed that she still could not seem to reach Cain telepathically. She swore she had tried several times throughout the evening, but she'd been so caught up in Zach's music, that Mattie had a feeling she hadn't been trying very hard.

Around 4:30 a.m., Allie finally admitted she had to give in and retire to the bedroom for the day.

"Already? I've still got plenty left in me," Zach exclaimed, hefting his guitar higher in a bid to persuade her to stay up.

"Sorry, I just can't..." Allie told him as she disappeared into the bedroom.

"She's pretty sensitive to the sunrise," Mattie explained. Dawn was still almost an hour away, but he knew Allie's body demanded she seek shelter in the darkened bedroom long before light threatened the sky. Mattie set up the pull-out couch for Zach to sleep on during the day, and joined Allie in the bedroom. He made sure to lock the door before getting into bed. Zach should be tired and do nothing more than sleep during the day, but he wasn't taking any chances.

When Mattie woke the next evening, Zach was still passed out on the pull-out couch, as expected. He woke up as Mattie was preparing a mug of blood for himself in the microwave.

As Mattie retrieved the warm beverage, he decided to go and hand it over to Zach, rather than drink it himself. Something told him that keeping the guy well fed would help diffuse any friction.

"What's this?" Zach asked, dubiously, as he took the mug.

"Breakfast."

Zach sniffed the mug's contents suspiciously, but then downed it without further comment. Mattie heated up some more for himself and then took Zach's empty mug for a refill.

It was about an hour of awkward small talk before Allie finally emerged from the bedroom. She was all smiles, but refused to talk much or try to contact Cain telepathically until she had well satisfied her thirst with several helpings of blood. Once she finally attempted to reach him, she insisted that she still couldn't pick up any trace of him.

"That's really weird..." Mattie observed.

"Yeah, but I wouldn't worry. He might just be shutting me out."

"He can do that?" Mattie asked.

"He doesn't do it often, but he's gotten better at it, and if Sindy's there, they could be kind of busy..."

"That's okay," Zach chimed in. "Give me a chance to jam the rest of my playlist for you."

Mattie wasn't sure he could stomach another concert from this guy, no matter how good he was. "I think I'm going to get us rolling," he told them.

"Shouldn't we wait until I can talk to Cain?" Allie asked. "What's the rush? I'll get through to him. We can relax for a little while first."

Mattie began straightening up and stowing things for the ride. "We're a long way from Cain's. It couldn't hurt to get moving and meet him halfway." He got in the driver's seat and waved towards Zach, hoping to assuage Allie's disappointment. "He can play while I drive. Just keep it down," he said, shaking his head. "My poor speakers will never be the same."

Allie blew Mattie a kiss as he turned his driver's chair around. "We won't hurt your stereo," she promised.

"You'd better not," Mattie called over his shoulder, as he started the ignition. "And try not to make my ears bleed."

Maybe his weather prediction somehow tied him into forecasting the future... After half an hour of being constantly accosted by high-pitched guitar shrieks and wails, Mattie wouldn't have been surprised to actually find blood dripping from his eardrums. He yelled into the back...again. "Turn it down!"

It's rock and roll. It's supposed to be loud, was Allie's response in his head.

Mattie didn't bother to answer, he just slammed the partition closed behind him, and kept driving. If he'd had any idea that they'd be heading back to Cain's so soon, he wouldn't have allowed them to wander so darn far south. Without being able to drive past dawn, it was going to take them two nights to get there.

A few hours later, Zach finally got tired of playing, and the guitar was replaced by the radio, but it wasn't as much of an improvement sound-wise as Mattie had hoped. He focused on pulling up properly next to the gas pump, rather than be distracted by the raucous noise Zach and Allie were making in the back. It sounded like they were having an awfully good time...too good.

Putting the trailer into park, he tried not to jump to irate conclusions as he shut the engine and climbed from the driver's seat. He turned to open the partition that separated the cab from the living quarters, as Allie let out another little scream of excitement. "What the hell is going on back there?" he asked, wincing over the fact that he sounded just like his dad...*don't you kids make me pull over...*

Mattie took stock of the situation, almost afraid of what he was going to find, but Zach wasn't even anywhere near her. Allie was perched on the sofa, while Zach sat on the edge of the kitchen bench. As Mattie entered, Zach stood and went over to Allie to give her a high-five. He was clearly ignoring Mattie's ire.

Allie hesitated, but still smacked his hand before giving Mattie her full attention. Given a legitimate excuse, she just couldn't resist the temptation to touch the guy again... "Hey babe. Check it out, we're playing *Extreme Quarters!*"

Mattie walked over and turned off the radio for some blessed silence. "You're doing what?"

"It's a game," she explained brightly.

Zach gave him a sly grin. "What did you think I was doing to make her squeal like that?"

Allie took back Mattie's attention before he could spit back a reply. "Watch," she told him, holding up a quarter for him to see.

Mattie glanced around for the shot glass she'd be aiming for. It was placed against the wall in the little hallway that led to the bathroom. It was straight ahead from Mattie's point of view, but from where Allie was sitting, it was practically around a corner. She could barely see it from where she was, let alone toss a coin into it. "That's an impossible shot, the glass is way over there."

"I know!" she replied with a lilt of excitement. "Prepare to be amazed," she promised, as she tossed the quarter into the air. She threw it underhand, arching upwards and towards the hallway, but as it got there, it seemed to slow down in speed, until it was practically hovering in the air. After a brief, wobbly second, the coin made a decisive right turn, and then plinked down into the shot glass. Zach let out a little whoop of congratulations as Allie turned to Mattie, all smiles. "Isn't that wild? Did you know I could do that?"

Mattie paused thoughtfully, and then sighed. "I did, actually. Moving things with your mind, it's called telekinesis. Remember when you unlocked the door for us that time, right before dawn? I told you about that."

"Oh yeah... Jeez, I've got too much going on to keep up with. It's amazing!"

"Lucky you," Mattie mumbled, not even bothering to hide the edge of resentment in his tone.

Zach clapped his hands together and then held one out to Allie, palm up. "My turn. Coin me." Allie fished another quarter out of a cup she had on the table and handed it to Zach. "Look," Zach said to Mattie. "I can do it too."

"Of course, you can." Mattie didn't even bother to watch Zach make his shot. He tore Allie's attention away with a question. "Can I speak to you for a minute please?"

Allie gave Zach a thumbs up as his quarter went into the shot glass, before answering Mattie mentally. *Sure, what's up?*

"In the bedroom?" Mattie clarified aloud.

What for? He can't hear us like this.

Mattie gave in with a sigh. *This is not a good idea.*

Playing quarters? Allie asked, incredulously.

We are supposed to be on a serious mission here.

Allie let out a little huff of a laugh. *Mission? Somebody's been playing too much Black Ops. It's not a mission, it's a road trip. Road trips are supposed to be fun. Look it up,* she reprimanded. *What's with you, anyway? Why do you hate him?*

I can't believe you're asking me that.

Nothing happened, Allie assured him, irately. *I didn't sleep with him, I killed him.*

I know, Mattie assured her. *But if you were going to have an affair, it'd be with someone like him. He's just your type.*

He is not! You are my type, stupid.

Oh, you like stupid guys? Mattie asked, sarcastically. *Then he's perfect for you.*

Zach went to dump their quarters out of the shot glass, giving Mattie a pointed glare for disrupting their game, as he got back in position to shoot again. Mattie ignored him and continued his telepathic conversation with Allie. *It's obvious the whole dark musician thing turns you on. Sometimes I wonder why you're even with me.*

For your information, it's not musicians who turn me on, it's freedom of expression. The whole creative vibe is something I really admire. It's part of what I see in you. You're an artist too, you know. Your photography, your poetry...

Nice try, but no one ever threw their panties at a guy wielding a camera. And I wrote those poems like a million years ago, and they suck.

They do not! They'd make great lyrics.

They aren't songs, they're bad poetry.

Most songs are, she told him with a smile.

I'm not a dark and mysterious artist, Allie. I'm safe, and you are not one to play it safe. So, if I'm wasting my time, tell me now, and you two can go make beautiful music together.

Alyson looked far more hurt than he'd expected. He was distracted for a second by the sound of another of Zach's quarters plinking into the shot glass, but Alyson never even glanced his way. She stared at Mattie until he met her eyes again. *The only time wasted, is time spent not believing in us. This guy is nobody special to me, and you know it. So I like his music...I am still more passionate about you, than all of my other interests combined. Making love with you is the only music that touches my heart. And for the record, sometimes a girl needs to feel safe.*

She raised herself to put her arms around him and give him a deeply passionate kiss to prove her point, until Zach cleared his throat. "Do you guys want me to leave?" he asked snarkily.

Yes, Mattie thought fiercely.

"No," she assured him with a smile. Zach chuckled and went back to throwing quarters.

Mattie took back her attention. *I don't think it's a smart idea to start showing this guy what he can do.*

Why not? Cain's going to do that anyway, isn't he?

Wait until we are at Cain's in controlled circumstances, please. What if you give this guy all kinds of information about his power, and then he goes off half-cocked and unstoppable on a killing spree?

Allie raised her eyebrows at him in disbelief. "Doubtful," she said with a snort, forgetting to keep silent, for Zach's sake. Zach flashed her a grin, and she continued the thought to Mattie secretly. *But you're right. Sorry. I didn't mean to. I didn't even remember that I could do it. We were just playing quarters and it came out. The trailer was bouncing through pot holes and it was really hard to make honest shots. I was so intent on trying to control my throw, all of a sudden, it began to levitate. It was so cool! I wasn't trying to play teacher, we were just passing the time, honest.* "You should join us in a game," she invited aloud. "Lighten up and have some fun."

As though playing quarters with two opponents who could levitate their coins at will could possibly be fun for him. "No thanks."

Why don't I ride up front with you for a while?

"We're at the gas station. I've got to go fuel us up."

"Oh, okay. Well, we'll come with you, stretch our legs," Allie offered.

Mattie almost waved her back to their game, but decided that making Zach pump gas would definitely be preferable to leaving him in here to have fun with Allie while Mattie did it. He let them follow him out of the trailer.

"Want me to try working my mojo on the pump? Bet I could get it to fill us up for free," Allie offered.

"No, I've got some money. Hey Zach, make yourself useful," he said, with a wave towards the gas cap, as he went inside to pay. He paused and turned to yell back to Allie before going inside. "Should I add on some extra for the Charger?" he asked. Allie's car, the classic '69 dark orange Charger was being towed on a hitch behind the trailer.

"Na, don't bother," Allie answered after a pause for thought. "It's got at least half a tank."

When Mattie returned, Allie was chatting as Zach pumped the gas, "Nothing fancy under the hood, but it runs like a champ."

"She's a beauty," Zach said, admiring the Charger. "Were those the keys I saw hanging on the peg board inside? I could drive it for you, if you want; give the hitch a rest." When no one answered him, he smiled. "I'm sure Mattie wouldn't mind letting me take it for a spin, would you Matt? It'd get me out of the trailer for a while. I'd follow real close and treat it like gold."

"I don't think so," Mattie answered.

"We'll be there soon anyway," Allie told him.

Mattie checked his watch. "Soon, but not soon enough. We'll never make it before sunrise. We'll have to stop for the day and get there tomorrow night. Zach, why don't you take shot-gun for the rest of the way?"

"Afraid I'm getting too cozy with your girl?" Zach asked, winking at Allie.

Allie answered for him. "No, I told him I was getting sick of you. Mattie, we can drive with the partition open if you want. I know we were being distracting, but we don't have to play Quarters anymore."

"Aha," Zach said. "The truth comes out. You're afraid to keep playing me because I'm getting better than you."

"Kiss my ass," was Allie's reply.

"Gladly," Zach answered, punctuating his reply with an air kiss and then a brief but obscene tongue wiggle.

Wind kicked up, blowing back Zach's hair as Mattie's anger flared over the gesture. "Dude, are you fucking kidding me?" Mattie asked. "Are you seriously going to stand there and make obscene gestures to her right in front of me?"

Allie shook her head in disapproval. "Not cool, Zach."

Mattie took a deep breath and blew it out, trying to keep calm. Just one more day, then they could dump this dick off at Cain's and be done with him. He took Zach by the arm and turned him towards the trailer. "Get in the cab, sicko."

Zach had the nerve to make a face to Allie as though Mattie was being totally unreasonable. "Why is that sick? She's a vampire. She probably hasn't taken a shit in years. I'd be honored to tongue that puckered little hole of hers."

The next thing Zach new, Mattie had him by the throat, pressed up against the side of the motor home. The wind was whippin', and a sudden downpour of freezing rain began.

Zach smiled down on Mattie, trying his best to appear unaffected by the choking hold, and then called to Allie over his shoulder. "Hey Sweet Cheeks…you'd love it," he promised with a grin. Thunder rumbled and Mattie couldn't stop himself from tightening his grip on Zach's throat. *That's it. This asshole is toast.*

"Sure you want to do this, sport?" Zach asked, his voice coming through as barely a choked whisper, but punctuated clearly with some aid from telepathy invading Mattie's mind. "Cause if you want to go at it, I'm more than ready."

Zach nonchalantly raised his hand to grab Mattie's wrist, but rather than try to break Mattie's hold on his throat, Zach simply began to squeeze.

"Guys, stop," Allie insisted from behind him.

As Zach squeezed harder, Mattie could feel the superhuman strength within him. To crush the bones in Mattie's arm would be nothing to this creep. He was a United One. Mattie had sparred with Allie plenty of times, and knew her strength… It was more than he had ever wanted to really mess with, and she had never *wanted* to hurt him.

Hail began to pelt down; stinging, almost marble-sized balls of ice that made noisy pinging sounds as they battered the cars. Mattie let go of Zach's throat, and as he did, Zach released his forearm, although Mattie couldn't help but notice the discolored indent left there. Zach shook his head a bit, trying not to be fazed by the hail that didn't seem to be troubling Mattie any.

Mattie nodded towards the trailer door. "Get in," he growled.

Zach finally broke eye contact, using a hand to shield his face from the hail, and was quick to duck his head and go inside. "Yeah," he acceded, "nobody wants to stand outside in this shit."

Mattie just stood there, holding the door as Allie approached and hugged close to him. She looked up at the sky for a moment in wonder. Although there was rain and hail pelting down all around them, she and Mattie were mostly unaffected. He was barely even wet. It was as though there was a small space of clear weather, only directly over Mattie's head. Mattie looked at Allie and gave her a small smile, trying to seem un-rattled by the whole exchange. He held out his hand, palm up for a moment and then inspected the little lump of hail that landed there. "Doesn't bother me."

Allie gave him a kiss before going inside. *What a jerk. I am so sorry. Just one more day Mattie, and then Cain can decide what to do with him.*

Mattie eyed her thoughtfully for a moment. *You can negate his powers, you know. You can shut him off, the way that other vampire did to you that time.*

Her eyes went wide. *Holy shit, you're right.*

Do me a favor, Mattie asked her mentally with a little grin, *keep that in mind.* Not that he wanted to have to ask his wife to rescue him, but if things came to that, he wasn't above having Allie help.

I will definitely keep that in mind. Until then, I'll keep my distance and he'll back off. You're right, this trip is a serious mission. No more games.

Rather than ride up front as Mattie had suggested, Zach had made his way back into the living area, and stretched out on the couch, making himself comfortable. Allie stepped inside, took note of his smug smile and immediately made a beeline for the back bedroom. Before closing the door and keeping to herself, she gave Zach a parting mental word of advice. *Stop being such a prick.*

She let Mattie in on the directive, and also let him be privy to the fact that Zach tried to contact her once or twice during the rest of the ride, with telepathic conversation of his own, but she shut him out. Apparently, he wasn't as unaware of that ability as he had seemed...or he was a fast learner.

Allie spent the ride locked in the bedroom alone; she wanted to work on practicing some of her shape shifting abilities anyway. Mattie didn't say a word to anyone. He just got back in the driver's seat and floored it towards Cain's. The sooner they got there, the better. He had been right in his earlier assumption though, there was no way they were going to make it there before dawn.

He finally gave in at 5 a.m., around twenty minutes before sunrise. He had been about to pass a strip mall, when he saw that it included a butcher shop. He pulled into the parking lot. It was as good a place as any to wait out the daylight. The shop hadn't opened yet for the day, but according to the sign on the door, they'd remain open until 9:00 p.m. tonight. Although it was cutting it close, he should have about a fifteen minute window after sunset, just enough time to try and buy some blood from the place when he awoke.

Once Mattie had the trailer locked up tight with all of the shades drawn, he went and grabbed a blanket from the closet. He didn't even bother to pull out the bed for Zach. He didn't say a word, he just threw the blanket towards the guy where he was laying on the couch watching television, and then went to join Allie in the bedroom. He slid the door closed loudly...about the closest equivalent to a slam you could achieve with a pocket door, and locked it.

Allie was already in bed and seemed to be sleeping. It was pretty close to dawn, and although Zach didn't yet seem to be quite as affected by the daylight, Alyson couldn't stay awake if she tried.

Mattie couldn't sleep. He spent most of the day tossing and turning until he finally dozed off a few hours before sunset. He was awakened by a noise outside. It sounded like someone had slammed a car door. Mattie sat up in bed. The sun was still setting. It wouldn't be fully dark for a while yet, but it was close enough that Mattie could head outside soon without much of a problem. The sun would be slipping below the horizon by the time he was up and ready to go out.

He climbed from the bed and dressed quietly, although he couldn't have woken Allie up even if he'd tried. She would be comatose for at least another hour, if not longer. He left her sleeping peacefully, closing the door behind him. Surprisingly, Zach was already up. He was in the kitchen, inspecting the last of the blood in the sole remaining container in the fridge. "This all you've got?"

"For the moment."

Zach swirled the blood around in the bottom of the container a little, and then turned to Mattie in all seriousness. "Hey man, sorry about last night. I was just messing with you. I didn't mean for it to go that far."

Mattie just stood mute for a minute. Clearly, this was where Matt was supposed to tell him it was okay…except it wasn't. He finally nodded his head, but then looked Zach in the eyes with a steady stare. "Allie is with me. Don't disrespect that again, or we're going to have a big problem."

Zach smiled, seeming amused that Mattie would stand up to him. "Understood. Maybe thirst was clouding my judgment," he speculated with a teasing grin. "I know one thing, if you expect me to keep my fangs in check, we're gonna need a lot more than this for breakfast, and soon."

"I know," Mattie told him. "I'm on it. There's a butcher shop right here. Why don't you take a walk over there with me, and we'll see what we can get?"

Zach grimaced, and moved the shade aside from the window a bit to peek outside. "Right now, are you crazy? I'm not going out there. It's not even dark yet."

Mattie checked his watch. He didn't have time to wait. If the butcher shop decided to close a few minutes early, they were screwed. "Scared of a little sunshine?"

"Ever been out in it? I'm not scared, but I'm not stupid."

Mattie put on his mirrored sunglasses and pulled the hood up on his sweatshirt. Alyson was always antsy, bordering on panic-stricken, when faced with daylight. Even knowing that the sun couldn't hurt her if she kept her skin from being exposed, she was extra sensitive to it; it must be a United One thing. "Fine. Wait here, you big baby. I'll be right back."

Mattie left the trailer, shoved his hands into his pockets and hurried across the parking lot. He reached the butcher shop door just as the lighted 'open' sign went dark. In a panicked rush, he tried the handle. It was locked, but a young woman came to open it. "We're closing," she said, not backing up to let him in.

"Couldn't you take one more customer? ...Please?" Mattie asked, taking off his sunglasses and pulling down his hood. He could see that the young lady was affected by his plea. Between his bright blue eyes, light smattering of freckles, reddish gold hair and winning smile, he had a trustworthy, country boy sort of charm that he had learned women often found disarming.

The woman shifted her weight and sighed. "I've already started breaking down the slicers," she told him by way of apology.

Mattie's grin broadened. "No problem. I don't need anything cut. It'll be a quick and easy order, I swear."

She thought about it a moment, but let him inside. "Alright, come on in. What do you need?" she asked as he followed her back towards the counter.

"I don't suppose you sell blood?"

She turned around to stare at him for a moment. "Blood?"

"My grandma's got this old recipe..." It was an often used explanation that was usually met with a head nod and a smile...*how sweet, he's helping his grandma....*

The woman just kept staring at him as though he was very odd. "A recipe for what?"

"Black pudding. She's from Ireland and used to make it with her mum." That was actually true, but Mattie had never seen or tasted it, only heard about it. When he had been human, he'd thought it was incredibly disgusting that his grandmother wanted to make and eat such things. Now, if she only knew...

The young woman seemed dubious. "I don't know..." She turned around to yell into the back. "Dad, do we sell *blood?*"

An older gentleman came out in response. "Blood? Sure. We get some beef blood in now and then, but I don't know if I've got anything fresh. I'll take a look."

The girl turned back to Mattie, as surprised as he was relieved. "Apparently we do."

The man returned after a few minutes. "I've only got a quart of fresh, mixed with vinegar." Mattie blanched. This was a common practice that some places did to keep the blood from clotting...but it tasted awful. The man noticed Mattie's reaction. "I've got two gallons pure, but it's frozen."

"I'll take 'em. Give me the fresh too, I guess." The vinegar mix could be Zach's meal.

The girl chatted as she rang up his order. "So, have you ever tasted the black pudding? Is it gross?"

"It's...kind of grown on me."

"Well, maybe you could invite me over to try it sometime," she suggested, looking at him hopefully.

Mattie paid, giving her an apologetic smile. "I think my girlfriend might object, but thanks for helping me out," he said, raising the bag in tribute to her as he turned to leave.

By the time he left the shop, it was almost fully dark outside. Hopefully, he could defrost some blood, fix himself a mug and get them moving on the road towards Cain's before Allie even woke.

The trailer was very quiet when he entered. He'd expected to see Zach lounging on the couch, but the space was empty. Mattie put his bag down on the counter, and looked around, warily. He hadn't expected Allie to be up yet, but where was Zach?

A sudden stab of fear went through him...he shouldn't have left Allie alone with the guy, even if it was only for a few minutes. But Zach wouldn't want to hurt her, would he?

Mattie crept silently down the hall towards the bedroom. A quick glance showed him, with disappointment, that the bathroom was empty. The bedroom door was partially open. Not good.

There was movement inside. That was a relief, because if the room had been empty, Mattie didn't know what he would have done. Rather than charge in, as his tensed muscles were just itching to let him do, Mattie paused, trying to see through into the room, without being seen.

Zach was in there, alright. It took Mattie a second to process what he was seeing. The covers of the bed had been thrown back, but all that lay on the bed was Allie's rumpled nightgown. Alyson herself was being held by Zach. She was still unconscious, draped across his arms, nude. As Mattie took in the knowledge that Zach must have undressed her while she was sleeping, Zach began to whisper quietly to the woman in his arms.

"Alright, come on baby. Just a short walk to the car. I'm not going to hurt you." He began to turn towards the door, and would have seen Mattie any moment, but something odd happened. Allie began to dematerialize into smoke. As she did, Zach became very annoyed, although, oddly enough, he seemed to have expected it. "No, no. Come on, damn it."

The cloud of mist that once was Alyson hovered over to the bed, and then reformed her body, still peacefully sleeping. Now Mattie realized why Allie was nude. Zach must have tried to lift her once before, and been met with the same results. Alyson still seemed completely unaware, but apparently, the vampire entity within her was at least minimally alert, and refused to let her be manipulated without her knowledge. Well, Allie was always blaming random acts of self-defense on the blood. Mattie was very happy to see she hadn't just been making up excuses.

Zach grunted in frustration and then grabbed the edge of the blanket. Obviously, he was thinking that if he wrapped Allie up, he might have better luck. That might work, but Mattie sure wasn't going to give him time to try.

"Get your hands off her."

Zach froze with a guilty start, but then turned around slowly with a condescending grin. "Mattie. I had hoped we could avoid an ugly scene. Face it buddy, you had a good run, but she belongs with me now. We're soul mates...she can feel it and you can't deny it."

"You don't even have a soul, dirtbag. You don't deserve to look at her, let alone touch her. Back off."

"Why's that? Because she let you tell people you're her husband, just to spare your sensitive little feelings? You may have made her, but you don't own her. You're not enough for her. You never were and you never will be. You know it. You haven't got any real claim over her."

Mattie tried not to let the words rattle him, even if he sometimes suspected they held a grain of truth. He kept talking, although he'd really just love to end this guy and be done with it. He needed to stall for time. As much as it killed him to acknowledge it, Zach was too powerful for him to take on his own. It would be much easier if Allie could wake up and strip the guy's powers first. That's all he needed her to do, make it a fair fight. Then Mattie would be more than happy to pound the guy into dust personally, United One or not.

"Her mark says different," Mattie reminded him. "She's with me by choice. What did you think you were going to do, kidnap her, and she'd be okay with that? Like she would suddenly think you were awesome and she'd be yours? She'll never be with you, no matter what kind of magic tinglies you think you can make her feel. She sees right through you, pal, and no one, no matter how powerful, can ever claim to *own* her, not even you. She's The United One."

Zach allowed his eyes to shift into their pure white vampiric brilliance as he spoke with a sinister smile. "*She's* The United One? I'm just as powerful, or have you forgotten? No, you didn't forget. That's why you haven't made your move. You walk in on me laying my hands on your naked woman and you want to stand here and have a chat? You're waiting for her to wake up, because you know you don't stand a chance without her. The United One…she may have been the *first*…but who do you think you're talking to?"

Mattie's eyes narrowed to mere slits as he stood in the doorway and murmured, "The last…the last mistake she'll ever make."

Zach rushed him and Mattie backed out into the hall. He'd like to get the guy outside where at least he had a chance to try and use his own powers of weather manipulation to help him. Zach grabbed for him, but missed as Mattie ducked under, having had some slight experience in evading Allie's speed and skill. He managed to get in a nice right cross to Zach's jaw before slipping out of reach again, but he knew that avoidance would be short lived.

Once Zach got out of the cramped hallway, his speed and strength would be unmatched and Mattie was in big trouble. The punch he had landed had to have hurt, but Zach was more amused by it than injured. He was certain this would be a quick and simple fight for him, and Mattie was afraid he was right.

"You know," Zach said as he pursued Mattie down the length of the trailer, "from what I remember, vampire blood has a real nice kick to it. I'm thinking I could use a good meal right about now."

Zach came for him, eyes white and fangs bared. Rather than stand and fight, Mattie turned and raced for the door. The trailer was already shaking in the hurricane force winds that were now swirling outside. He needed to get Zach to follow him out the door.

Mattie ripped open the door, but it was pulled from his grasp and slammed shut again. Mattie froze for a second in confusion. When he tried to reach for the door again, it unexpectedly swung open forcefully and slammed him in the face. Fucking telekinesis…

Mattie reeled back from the blow, and before he could gather his wits to try again to get out, Zach grabbed him from behind. As he pulled Mattie backwards, thunder crackled and lightning arched and struck the front steps at the open doorway with a sizzling strike that left scorch marks.

Zach jumped back, dragging Mattie with him, and stared at the doorway in awe. "Is that *you* stirring up that shit outside?" he asked in realization. "Well then, we'll just have to make sure we stay in here, safe and sound." The trailer door slammed shut again at Zach's mental command, the lock clicking in place for good measure. "Now, where were we? Oh yeah, I was about to have some breakfast."

Zach pulled Mattie in close to bite his throat, but was painfully startled when he discovered that Alyson's mark protected Matt from his bite. While he was momentarily stunned, Mattie took the opportunity to elbow him in the face. "She's with me," Mattie reminded him. "I told you disrespecting that would make problems for you."

Zach's nose was bleeding, and his head must have been pounding from trying to cross Allie's mark, but he clutched Mattie by the shoulders, unwilling to let him go, no matter how Mattie struggled. "I forgot about the fucking migraine thing. Well, I guess I'll just have to settle for kicking your freckled ass."

True to his word, Zach tossed Mattie down onto the floor like a rag doll and gave him a few good kicks. Mattie almost vomited after a couple of shots to the kidneys. Then Zach rolled him over for more, and he felt and heard the crunching of bone as ribs cracked with each kick. The power behind this guy was definitely something to be feared. Mattie tried to crawl out of range, but Zach picked him up and threw Mattie against the kitchen counter. He pinned him there and followed up by pummeling him with his fists, blackening Mattie's eyes and breaking his nose, despite Matt's valiant efforts to defend himself.

All of a sudden, with a loud, explosive crash, all of the windows on their side of the trailer blew in, showering shards of glass into Zach's face. The wind raged like a tornado outside and Zach was forced to let go of Mattie to pull a long, sharp piece of embedded glass from his cheek. Mattie hoped it hurt like hell, but the cut began to heal the moment Zach pulled it out.

Mattie felt like a jumble of broken bones covered by one giant bruise, and he could barely see, but began to make his way towards the door again with desperate determination. Some distant part of the back of his mind couldn't help but be amazed and annoyed that Alyson could be asleep through all of this, although he knew it wasn't anything she could control.

He reached the doorknob, turning the latch to unlock it and trying to pull it open. As Zach tried to grab him to pull him back, Mattie was able to transfer a mild shock of static electricity from the doorknob through himself like a conductor. It wasn't enough to hurt someone, but it achieved a frightened delay as Zach felt the shock and backed off, trying to figure out what Mattie had done to him.

Mattie pulled the door open and tried to stoke up some lightning again. The storm was raging, but lightning was a tall order, taking a lot of power and control. A small bolt of lightning struck the antenna on top of the trailer, but caused no real harm, as the trailer was grounded and no one was touching its exposed metal. Mattie cursed the clumsy effort, and crawled out the open door and halfway down the steps. If Zach followed, maybe Matt could call down another strike and hit him. There was a good chance that Mattie would be hit as well, but at this point, he didn't care. Maybe his powers would help insulate him from it.

Zach did follow him, but only so far as to grab Mattie's legs and drag him back inside. The last thing Mattie saw outside was lightning striking the ground at the foot of the trailer. Zach pulled him back and telekinetically slammed the door in front of his face. So close…

Zach lifted him high and smashed him down, breaking Mattie's back over the top backing of the kitchen bench, and then swung him around and threw Mattie against the wall by the door. As Mattie hit the wall, it felt like fireplace poker suddenly pierced the back of his skull. Bone cracked, and pain like he had never known lanced through his head, upwards from the base of his skull.

He wasn't falling…he just seemed to stay there, halfway up the wall where he had hit, until Zach came and ripped him away…off the coat hook that had pierced the back of his head. The world went black…

As feeling was restored, excruciating pain made Mattie want to shrink away and hide back in the dark depths of unconsciousness, but he couldn't seem to close his eyes, and vision was slowly returning. He was being moved, jostled roughly about, with no regard for the agony each shift caused. He was dropped to the floor. He was in the doorway to the bathroom, he realized. Zach tried to close the sliding pocket door, but it bumped Matt's arm and wouldn't close all the way. Zach kicked and shoved Mattie further into the bathroom, not even looking, as his attention was drawn down the hall. He slid the door better closed, although it was still open a slight crack, and left to go meet Allie, where she was awakening in the bedroom.

Mattie couldn't see much, just the linoleum of the bathroom floor, and a small slice of blur from the bedroom through the crack in the door, his vision unfocused. He couldn't move at all, but that was a blessing, because he also seemed to have lost feeling in his body again, sparing him the pain of his breaks and bruises. The pain at the base of his skull was more than enough to deal with, so terrible he almost wanted to die. But he couldn't die...and he couldn't leave Allie. He tried to clear his mind enough to listen to what was happening in the bedroom.

Allie was moaning, louder by the second and clearly audible now that the wind had suddenly ceased. She must be feeling his pain as she awoke. She let out a scream and Zach called out in response, "Allie!" and rushed to her aide.

"Mattie? Mattie where are you? Mattie? Mattie!" Alyson was sounding more hysterical with each plea. Zach was trying to console her wild shrieks to no avail.

Through the crack in the door, Mattie could see Zach move towards her with something. It seemed he was wrapping her in a blanket, covering her and trying to calm her. "What happened? Where is he?" Allie demanded, her voice sounding more clear and confident now, trying to take control of herself.

"They took him," Zach said firmly.

"What? Who?"

"I don't know...these guys. They just showed up and broke in. I think they were after you, but Mattie wouldn't let them near you. They must have fought, but they dragged him out the door and took off before I even knew what was going on. I woke up to howling wind and glass breaking and Mattie was already out the door. I tried to follow, but they could *fly* and they carried him away. It was insane!"

"What?!?"

"Come on, get dressed. We need to get you someplace safe before they come back."

Allie was looking around, very confused. She stood, with the blanket wrapped around her. "Wait, he's *gone?* Why would anyone take Mattie?"

Mattie hoped the lilt of skepticism in her voice meant that she didn't believe him. Other vampires wouldn't have been able to enter the trailer without an invitation, and surely that was just one of the many holes in Zach's story. He hoped Allie could see that.

Zach didn't seem worried in the least. "I don't know. Maybe they want to use him as a hostage or something. Here," he shoved some clothing at her. It must have been what she'd been wearing last night, thrown over the chair. Zach turned around, but didn't leave the room. "Don't worry. It'll be okay. I'm here to help. I won't let them get you."

Allie began to sound hysterical again as she got dressed. "I can't hear him," she told Zach in a panic. "I can always hear Mattie. Why can't I hear his thoughts? I can't hear anything. I can't even read you!"

"Calm down, you're probably just too upset to focus. Come on, we can take your car. I've already grabbed the keys." He took her by the arm and hurried her out of the bedroom...and quickly past the bathroom.

"Oh my God." Allie wasn't given a moment to pause as Zach ushered her down the hall, and her attention was immediately taken by the sight before her. She was startled to see the mess of the living room and all the broken glass from the windows. As Zach rushed her through towards the door, Allie resisted and continued to question him. "You said they took him somewhere?"

"Yes, up into the sky. They must have been really powerful to take him like that, and I couldn't follow," he moved closer to her, taking her into his arms for comfort. "But don't be scared. Don't worry, I'm here. I'll help you."

Mattie couldn't really see them anymore, but all was suddenly silent. He couldn't tell if Allie was accepting the embrace, or had pushed Zach away...but if she had rejected him, why was it so quiet?

Finally, Allie spoke, but it was soft, without nearly the amount of disgusted inflection Mattie would like to hear. "Seems more like you're helping yourself."

Zach chuckled. "Just trying to be comforting, that's all. Wow, I keep forgetting what it feels like to touch you. You've never felt that with anyone else have you? 'Cause I've *never* felt that before. It's like we were made for each other."

The comment was met with silence. Mattie's heart broke when she didn't say anything to deny it. Was this hell? He must be in hell, because he could not move or speak, he was being forced to listen to this and Allie couldn't seem to hear his thoughts, or even know he was there. Couldn't she feel him?

Mattie's distress was suddenly quelled at the thought. She could feel him...she had to feel him. They were marked. Zach had told her that Mattie had been taken far from here, but Alyson had to know he was lying, even if she couldn't read his mind, because she could feel that Mattie was hardly more than a dozen feet away. Zach was inexperienced enough not to realize all the implications of the mark Allie shared with Mattie, but Alyson was no fool. She must be playing along, trying to buy some time to figure out what was going on.

Zach spoke with a quiet reverence, as though she amazed him. "You know there's something incredible between us, even though you're trying real hard not to admit it. Don't fight it."

"Why would I fight you?" she asked him quietly.

Suddenly, Zach let out a small exclamation of surprise, and maybe pain? Mattie strained to hear, trying to figure out what was going on, when he realized what Alyson would have done.

She'd either bitten him, or stabbed him with her hypodermic fingernails. Most likely, she had stabbed him, if she'd had a chance to alter her hands. It was an easy and sneaky way for her to subdue someone. Zach still wore the fading remains of a mark from Sindy, but Alyson must be strong enough to over-ride it. *How do you like that hug now, Zach?* Mattie thought with evil satisfaction.

"What the...?" Zach's voice trailed off as Alyson's talon-like fingernails sank their full length into his back, up under his shoulder blades from behind. Mattie was flooded with relief as Zach's system was flooded with Allie's venom. Zach tried to question her again in alarm to no avail. He couldn't think straight, and couldn't easily overcome such an onslaught of her strong venom.

He'd probably begun to slump against her, because Mattie heard some shuffling that might have been Alyson pushing him upright as she withdrew her hypodermic claws. "Stand up and be still," she told him authoritatively. "Why would I need to fight you?" she asked him again, teasingly. "I own you."

That's my girl, Mattie thought weakly, as he allowed himself to stop struggling so uselessly hard against his paralysis. He was helpless to move and apparently unable to communicate effectively with Alyson in thought, but she was smart enough to smell Zach's treachery on her own. She would be okay.

"If you thought I was going to believe that line of bullshit you were trying to feed me, then you're even stupider than I thought. Tell me what's really going on here. The truth this time," she asked Zach sternly, her venom ensuring that he was forced to confess.

"I was trying to bring you to Arif's coven. Bounty's a nice mansion full of babes and all the blood I can drink, so why wouldn't I? But even though you were unconscious, I couldn't get you into the car before you came to. Now that you're awake, I thought I'd try being your seductive savior instead. You're already hot for me, so why wouldn't you buy it?"

"Because I'm not an idiot." Alyson blurted out in shocked confusion. She was quiet for a moment, probably trying to recall some hint of the events of the day, during her slumber, but could not produce the memory; she'd been out cold. "Why couldn't I read your mind...or Mattie's?"

"I blocked you. Sindy said that I could keep other vampires from using their telepathy if I tried. It kept Arif from poking around in my head, so I figured it'd work on you too."

"That's why I couldn't reach Cain," Allie surmised in annoyed realization. "Where is Mattie, *really?* He hasn't gone far, I can feel him. He was hurt."

Zach answered with defeated acceptance of the inevitable. He knew that he could not hide his deed, as her venom forced him to admit the truth. "He kept getting in the way, so I took him out. He's in the bathroom."

Mattie could hear Alyson gasp in fear. She spun to look behind her, and met Mattie's eyes, staring blankly through the small crack in the doorway from where he lay on the floor within.

Alyson flew to the bathroom, slid open the door and knelt to take Mattie into her arms, dragging him out into the hall and trying to assess what was wrong with him. His eyes stared ahead, surely seeming blind and dull, like that of a corpse. His body must look horribly bruised and battered from the brawl, but it was the sickeningly odd tilted angle of his head that concerned her most...until she cradled his head in her hands. Her fingers met the unexpectedly cracked and squishy point of impact, becoming covered in blood leaking from the back of his skull...

The numbness that had settled over him fled, replaced by stabs of blinding pain as she shifted his head. She felt it too, choking back a sob at the onslaught. When her hand came away red, she quickly moved to better see his injury, and he heard her stifle a choked gasp at the sight. There must be a terribly messy puncture in back of his head from the coat hook, not only from his initial impact and impalement, but from being ripped off of it again by Zach. By some miracle, his eyesight and hearing were not completely obliterated, but he couldn't focus his eyes, his thoughts were muddy, and the many shard-like pieces of splintered skull jabbing into his brain felt fused into one large throbbing mess of pain.

"What did you do?" Allie asked Zach quietly, her voice trembling in shock. "Oh my God, what did you do to him?" She was cradling him in useless protectiveness, almost shaking in dismay and disbelief. She tried to take some small comfort in the fact that she could feel his pain. Although unresponsive, he was still in there. He wasn't dust. If he wasn't dust, he could be fixed. Mattie knew that crazy, impossible seeming fact must be true, and after fighting through a few moments frozen with fear, Allie knew it too. Safe in that knowledge, her frightened panic transformed into volcanic rage.

Her whisper to Mattie was a wrathful rasp in his ear. "Don't worry honey, he's going to pay," she promised.

She gently lowered Mattie back to the floor and turned to find Zach with a gaze that could melt glass. He was still frozen at the other end of the RV, where she had left him standing, waiting for her to release him from her last directive. "I trusted you," she told him in disgust.

As she looked down to Mattie again, lying broken and limp on the floor, her voice became quiet and regretful. "He didn't want me to, but I trusted you...and *this* is how you repay me; by betraying me and hurting someone I love?" She asked Zach in disbelief. She looked down and held Mattie's gaze for a moment, in a plea for forgiveness, and then, as he watched, her eyes drained of sorrow, and transformed into their white brilliance with a promise of revenge.

In a blinding blur of super speed she flew across the room to stop dead still with her hand crushing Zach's throat. She held him against the wall, forcing his chin upwards as she muttered to him with a rumbling growl of barely contained fury. "When I killed you the first time, I felt guilty; haunted with remorse, and regret."

Zach was still held in place by her venom enforced directive just as much as by her grip, but his eyes went wide at the phrase *the first time.* "Now...you're going to wish I'd left you dead." She squeezed her grip harder.

Zach's eyes were beginning to bug out. They rolled up to stare blindly at the ceiling, but then he managed to close them for a moment, and when next his eyes were opened, they too were the glowing white orbs of a United One.

To Mattie's great dismay, his lacrosse trophy that he had proudly displayed on the shelf over the television flew across the room to smash Alyson in the back of the head, and she never saw it coming. Allie's venomous hold on Zach had forced him to be still, but he was fully capable of harming her through telekinesis without lifting a finger.

The heavy trophy hit Alyson full force, making her let go of Zach in her surprise, and knocking her to the floor. Her paranormally hearty constitution and sheer fury kept her from staying down, but disposing of Zach was not going to be nearly as easy as it had first seemed.

"Let's not take it to that level," Zach said, levitating the trophy up off the floor again, and then mentally tossing it away from her, across the room. "You're mad," he told her, having the nerve to try and sound understanding, "I get that. You cared about the guy, but we both know that there was no future there. He's dead. Let him go."

Alyson rose from the floor, dazed and confused by Zach's attitude as much as the blow to the head. Zach must not have ever seen a vampire turn to dust before. He thought Mattie was dead, and that Allie should just move on and forget him...*as if.* He didn't have the experience to know the miracles of healing that could be performed, and he greatly underestimated the strength of true love.

Zach continued. "I didn't want it to play out this way, kitten, but the guy just didn't know when to give up. He was holding you back. Now you're free...free to explore some true potential."

Zach took a slow, uncertain step towards Allie. Her hold on him was fading fast. Her venom was an incredibly powerful toxin, but Zach was also a United One. He was young and inexperienced, but in all likelihood, he'd recently fed on human blood, and his body was fighting her venom like no other vampire could. "You don't want to go and give that Arif guy the reigns? That's fine, I understand. I didn't take the gig myself. Sindy told me that I couldn't be held, and she was right. Didn't take much practice before I flew up and out of there. You like your independence, like me, so forget about him. Maybe we should be thinking bigger."

"We?" she asked him in amazement.

"Think about the pair we could be. Sweet Cheeks, one touch and you can just feel that our bodies are meant to be together. I'm still new to all of this, but I know people are scared of the power you've got. I've got that kind of power too...together we could rule the fucking world, baby!"

Allie stared at him, her mouth agape in disbelief. "We could...or...I could crush you into a bloody pulp. Yeah...let's go with that."

Zach chuckled, tilting his head, as though she was being completely unrealistic. "Oh, come on. You're not gonna make me *fight* you? You don't want to end up like your boyfriend. Don't make me do that to you, sugar," he pleaded.

"You're the one that made this happen. It didn't have to be this way." Alyson's eyes welled up as she glanced back towards Mattie, lying broken and bloody on the floor. "We were trying to help you. Why did you do that to him?"

"Because as long as he was around, you were never gonna be with me."

"I will *still* never be with you."

Zach shrugged. "Your loss. Then we go with the other plan. I deliver you to that guy Arif, get nicely rewarded, and find some other groupie chic to vamp, who'll be grateful for the opportunity."

"Try it…see what happens." She looked at Mattie again, the burning ember of anger in the pit of her stomach once again fanning to flame. He was still in dreadful pain, and counting on her to heal him. She needed to get rid of Zach so she could help Mattie. She kept her voice steady, but ominous. Zach may be overly cocky, but he was still a formidable vampire. Rage would not serve her at the moment. She needed to keep her wits about her. "The betrayal hurt…but what you did to Mattie? Big mistake. You're not taking me anywhere."

He was actually fool enough to laugh at her. "I've got just as much power as you do, buttercup. I don't see you stopping me."

Allie smiled, keeping her cool. "Actually, you haven't got any power at all."

Zach looked over to the trophy again, and then spent a minute glancing around the room, evidently trying to levitate something…anything. He finally looked back at Allie in wonder. "You're blocking my powers?"

"This ain't my first rodeo."

After a second of assimilation, he spread his arms and waved her towards him. "Bring it on. I'll still crush you."

"How do you figure?" Allie couldn't help but ask.

"Have you looked in the mirror lately? Oh," Zach corrected himself with a laugh, "I guess you haven't, being a vampire and all. In case you've forgotten, you're just a tiny little thing. That body was made for loving, not fighting. Why don't you just give this up and let me love you like you deserve?"

Alyson was obviously disgusted by the very idea. "You're gonna make me puke before I kill you? That's your plan?" She moved closer, her eyes brilliant white and her own arms spread, palms up to display her talon-like nails, not that she planned to allow him the privilege of more venom to dull his pain. "You know, I'm starting to think there's a reason I'm called The United One. One is enough."

Zach held up his hands in surrender as she came towards him. "Just calm down and take a minute. You've told me off and done your duty. I know I was wrong to kill your man. You feel that connection between us though, don't you?"

Allie paused, as she could indeed feel the strangely intimate connection the two seemed to share. Zach was encouraged by her hesitation. "These feelings can't be denied, baby. There is something special, supernatural even, going on here. Don't be so hasty to just throw it away when we were obviously meant for more."

Alyson eyed him warily, seeming to weigh his words and giving him time to relax and let down his guard. "Let's start new," he cajoled her, taking a brave step closer. "I'll even let you lead. You strike me as a babe who likes to be on top."

Was this guy really that conceited and stupid, to think that she would just forgive him and decide to be his babe? She didn't bother to answer. Her well of witty repartee had run dry and distasteful. She just wanted it over. She needed Zach dead so she could go and help Mattie.

He inched closer, seeing that she was hesitating rather than attacking him. "Think about it, babe. You think touching each other feels good now? What do you think it'll feel like when things really get hot and slick? You've got to be curious."

She smiled at his comment, and he let out a sigh of relief and smiled broadly in return, beckoning her into his arms. Before Zach could realize she wasn't planning on submitting to his embrace, she reached forward and grabbed him. With one hand gripping his bicep and the other jammed under his armpit, she twisted and stretched her leg out in front of him. As she dropped to one knee, Zach was spun and thrown to the ground before her, landing on his back. She climbed to kneel on top of him and hold him down.

Zach was dazed, and struggled a bit, but somehow still seemed to think she might be playing with him. She mouthed him a kiss to keep him guessing. "I hope you don't mind...I can be a little rough," she teased. "And you're right," Allie told him with a sinister grin. "I do like to be on top."

Leaning down, she brought her face close to his and placed her hands on either side of his head, in a deceivingly loving gesture. Without further thought or delay, she let her fury take over. He leaned up a bit, as though to kiss her, but instead she twisted his head sharply to the right, snapping his neck.

He shuddered and thrashed before going limp, but she didn't stop there. Fingers wound into his hair, and clutching his ears, she began to twist and pull. Zach screamed, still conscious despite his paralysis, but Allie wouldn't stop until rewarded with a sickening tearing and popping sound. Her supernatural strength served her well as she grunted and pulled, unsatisfied until Zach's head was ripped from his body. As it came free, she felt him soften and finally crumble to dust beneath her. She dropped his head as it disintegrated in her hands and collapsed as a pile of ash on the floor.

Alyson stood, barely taking the time to brush the ash from her hands before racing back to Mattie, where she'd left him on the floor. "It's alright honey, he's gone. I'm here. I'm going to fix you. You'll be okay."

He was completely unresponsive, his eyes open, staring blankly before her, but he found that their psychic connection seemed unblocked and back in force. Seeing the way he looked through her eyes…nose broken and swollen, cheeks bruised, eyes blackened…he could understand her dismay. He couldn't seem to speak or move. Allie was un-nerved but barely paused an instant before ripping into her own wrist so that her blood would flow for him.

She tore her skin and let the blood drip onto his lips. He couldn't even seem to feel or taste it. After a few moments of this, she pressed the wound more firmly to his mouth, hoping that he would be able to suck and take the blood on his own, but he still could not move a muscle. He was trapped in an unresponsive state hovering just out of death's grasp.

She removed her wrist from his mouth and tilted his head a bit to better see his wound again. He could feel her tender fingers gingerly parting his hair amidst wincing apologies to him. Each touch was agony, but although she could feel his perceptions through her empathy, he couldn't seem to actually communicate with her. He could feel her now, within his mind, trying to read his thoughts. Now that Zach wasn't blocking her, she was as connected with him as always, but he was too far gone; his thoughts were too jumbled to make any sense, so they couldn't really talk. It was just as well. What could he do but assure her that he trusted her to do whatever was needed?

She ripped her skin again to pour some blood directly into the wound. Although she made a large gash in her arm, and was bleeding onto him quite a bit, it wasn't long before her arm healed itself closed and this time she paused before opening it again. It was going to take a hell of a lot more blood to start his healing and get him into better shape. Allie realized this. He could almost catch the flitting snippets of memories she recalled of other acts of vampire healing she had been witness to for reference.

"I can fix you good as new…" she assured him, "but I'm gonna need to fuel up first to do it. I need blood; human, and lots of it."

Mattie couldn't even manage to work up a protest over the prospect of Alyson going out and attacking someone for him. The excruciating pain was robbing him of coherent thought so that he could barely follow what she was saying to him as it was. He must be really bad off. He had to trust her to make the call. Let her do what she would.

"Honey, are you with me? I think you should try to stay conscious if you can. You've got a…a brain injury and I think I'm supposed to keep you awake. Or maybe that's what you do for a concussion… Is it the same?

I don't know if it even matters. Either way, I have to go hunt, but I'll try to stay connected with you, okay? I have to leave you alone, but I'll be as quick as I can. I'll stay linked with you the whole time, I promise. Don't be scared honey. I can take care of you. Don't worry. You just try to stay focused on me, okay?"

She leaned down to give him a kiss and then she was gone, out the door in a burst of speed so fast, he might have thought she'd teleported if she could. He could feel her telepathic presence in his mind. He tried to latch onto it, to see through her eyes and let her thoughts keep him shielded from the pain. It didn't work as well as he'd like, but it was better than nothing. He tried to meld with her as completely as he could. For fleeting moments, he was almost able to believe he was the one racing down the street, rather than lying here broken and battered.

Allie was soon in one of the seedier parts of town, making her way through alleys, desperately searching for someone, anyone she could bring herself to drain. "Come on," she muttered, her face turned towards the sky in a desperate plea to a deity greater than herself…praying for something she had no right to ask for.

Her gaze swept the street, briefly surveying each person that hurried by. "Come on, there must be someone…someone who doesn't deserve to be here as much as Mattie does. I can't let him suffer for my poor judgment. He doesn't deserve this…please."

After rushing about, frantically searching to no avail, she finally stopped herself and took a few deep breaths. "Looking like I'm on a desperate hunt is not going to get me anywhere," she reminded herself. After a moment of calm, she chose a dark empty street, where a couple of men were visible far down at the other end, and began walking down it. She stopped about halfway and checked her wrist, hoping her sleeves would hide the fact that she wasn't actually wearing a watch. It just seemed an appropriate gesture to convey that she was forced to wait for someone in a place she didn't care to be. It worked like a charm.

Before long, one of the men began to walk towards her, although the others had disappeared. He walked slowly, not to alarm her, but eventually reached her, greeting her with a sleazy sort of smile. "Hey there. I don't think I've ever seen you around here before. You lost or something?"

Allie gave him a polite smile and a look of uncertainty, as she invaded his mind and assessed his demeanor. Knowledge of the dark deeds in his past made her smile with relief. He was perfect. She could exact vengeance for his victims while taking him as a victim of her own. "No, I'm not lost. I'm waiting for someone," she explained. As she spoke, she could sense someone else approaching her from the other direction. Apparently, one of the guy's buddies had gone around the block to cut her off. She pretended not to notice, as the first man spoke again.

"Someone left you standing out here all by your lonesome in this neighborhood? Shame on them. Who are you waiting for?"

She turned around to face the second man with vampiric white eyes and a smile as he closed in on her. "You." Before he could react to her sudden inhuman attention, she reached out and put her hands to his shoulders. "Take a nap," she told him, as she pulled him towards her and head butted him hard enough to knock him unconscious, then turned to deal with his friend before the guy she'd knocked out even hit the ground. She didn't bother to try to subdue the next one. She just lunged for his throat and sank her fangs into his flesh.

Without thought, restraint, or the slightest hesitation, she savagely tore his skin and began sucking and swallowing down his blood as fast as it would come. The guy let out a strangled yell and tried to throw her off of him, but she gripped him with the power of a vice. He might as well have been fighting a stone statue. To end his struggle, she plunged her needle-like fingernails into his shoulders and injected him with venom while she drank.

She drank and drank, as never before, reveling in her indiscretion, using his blood to re-energize herself. Sudden thoughts of Mattie raced through her mind, his well-being the incentive for this trespass. Was he still linked with her telepathically? Was he disgusted by her heartless display of violent, remorseless feeding?

Mattie read her every thought as though each notion was his own, but could not seem to convey his acceptance and forgiveness to her. It didn't matter. She had already taken too much, the guy's heart was struggling to pump through nearly empty chambers. With or without Mattie's approval, the man she held was dying. As his heart beat its last, she sucked the rest of the blood that would flow from the corpse in her arms and then dropped him to the street.

She returned to the other guy, where he still lay motionless behind her on the ground. After checking to find that he still had a pulse, she hefted him up into her arms. Not only had she knocked him out, but her order beforehand for him to sleep should keep him out even if he wasn't truly unconscious. This one she would bring home for Mattie, whether he wanted the blood or not. If her blood was going to heal him, it would help if his body had some raw material to work with.

She glanced around, suddenly wary of being seen as she realized that she was now in fact a murderer; no question about it. She couldn't leave the one she had drunk just lying on the street to be found. Uncertain what to do, she stooped down and grabbed his arm, taking him as well. It was awkward, but she was strong enough to manage it.

She took straight up into the air, levitating high enough to avoid being seen, and then quickly flew back to the motor home. Mattie's consciousness wavered, flickering in and out as he tried to track her progress. He had sunken into oblivion for a moment, when he was revived by sounds of Allie outside, attempting to open the door while carrying both men. After a second, there was silence. Then the door burst open of its own accord, Allie remembering and using her telekinetic ability to open it for her, as she struggled to bring the bodies of the two men inside.

She dumped them both on the floor while telekinetically closing the door behind her, and then she rushed to Mattie's side to check on him. She was greatly worried by the fact that she could not seem to communicate with him telepathically. He could hear her thoughts but he still couldn't seem to send her any of his own. It almost seemed that her thoughts were his own, as his brain didn't seem up to having any independent ideas at the moment.

"I'm back honey. Are you still with me? Time to get down to business." She hefted him up into her arms and brought him to the bed, lying him down and rolling him onto his stomach, so she had better access to the injury on the back of his head. Being moved made everything hurt worse, the heavy ache that had settled over his head and body turning back into glaring jabs of pain with every shift. Allie felt it too, trying to settle him as gently as possible.

Agony took over and his vision flared to an intolerable brightness of white, but only for a moment. Then the brightness faded back into normal vision and Mattie felt a tingling warmth on the back of his head, the first sensation besides pain that he had felt since she had found him. The room smelled of her blood, she must be flooding his head injury with it, so that he could heal.

He found that he could finally close his eyes, some small bit of control and semblance of life coming back into his body. He closed his eyes and allowed himself to let go of consciousness, secure in the knowledge that Allie was taking care of him now. He'd be okay.

At some point, he woke to find that he was cradled in her arms and being given her blood to drink. She'd somehow slashed her own throat, and was hugging him to her. His lips locked onto the wound and he sank into a comforting haze of suckling sustenance until he lost consciousness once more.

The next thing he knew, he was lying on his back again. Allie had him propped up and was trying to get him to drink. The blood at his lips was human, and it wasn't in a mug. He could smell it, fresh, warm and beckoning, a man's bleeding arm held right under his nose. It was almost touching his lips, but he hadn't parted them yet, although the change overcame him automatically the moment the offering was presented to him. Despite Alyson's attentions, he still needed more blood, badly.

"Mattie drink. I cut him with a knife, so he isn't marked." Mattie's eyes were closed, and when he still made no move to bite the man, Allie sighed. "I refuse to let you feel bad about this, Mattie. These guys were rapists and thieves. There is no way in hell that they deserve to live more than you do, and at this point, I'm gonna kill the poor bastard either way, so you might as well take the blood."

Mattie opened his eyes to try to focus on her face, although she remained maddeningly blurry to him. She was visibly relieved to see him respond, even in that small way. "There you are," she whispered. "Thank God."

"You're vicious when you're panicked," he remarked, groggily.

"I'm not panicking. You're going to be fine. And from now on, I'm going to be vicious when I need to be, so get used to it. There was no excuse for this happening to you, Mattie, none. I am so sorry. I shouldn't have trusted him. He could have killed you," she exclaimed, fear rising in her voice through her tears, as she realized the absolute truth of the statement. "He thought he did. The only thing that saved you was the fact that he was inexperienced and stupid…dumb luck. You're always protecting me. I should have been there to protect you."

"It's not your fault."

"I am too strong to have allowed something like this to happen to you. I let my guard down. Never again."

"Never again sounds good," he whispered with an attempt at a smile. "Don't be so hard on yourself. I'll be okay," he hoped… He could manage to think and speak again; he wasn't dust, but at the moment, the pain made death almost sound like it would be a nice peaceful respite.

The look on Allie's face suggested that she may have caught the thought. "Damn right you'll be okay, because you are going to drain this guy, now," she ordered with a pointed look at the human in front of him. "You need the blood."

Mattie slid his gaze towards the face of the unconscious man that was practically laying in his lap. He looked blurry, washed out in color and unreal. Alyson followed the gaze and then reached for the man's head. Before Mattie had even realized what she meant to do, she took hold of the guy's chin, placing another hand at the back of his skull, and gave his head a malicious twist. The man's neck gave an audible snap. She let go and he slumped limply next to Mattie on the bed as Alyson rose. "Drink, while it's still warm," she ordered. "It's on me."

Mattie lay there in shock for a few minutes, closing his eyes and taking in the small details of the man who lay before him, dying. No more slight sounds of breathing, no more heartbeat…but the warmth of the body seeped through the sheets, tantalizing Mattie's cold skin. What could he do? He drank. As his fangs sank into the flesh of the man's arm, something in him rebelled against drinking from a body without a beating heart, but as soon as the blood touched his tongue, still warm and in good supply, all hesitation was immediately forgotten. Good God… Human blood, thick, rich and still fresh; just what his body needed. He sank back into a hazy state of semi-consciousness, focusing only on sucking and swallowing.

Alyson sighed in relief, satisfied that she had done all that was needed for now, to send him on a speedy path to recovery. Mattie suddenly felt her attention drawn to the door, through the connection they still shared. Someone was approaching the trailer, and now knocked at the door. He could feel Alyson's alarm grow, as she balanced the sound of the knock with the fact that there was a dead man draped over Mattie's lap on the bed, and another lying on their kitchen floor.

She quickly left the bedroom. She dragged the corpse of the first man she had killed through the kitchen, and shoved him into the shower stall in the bathroom. She then gave Mattie a last glance as he fed, before closing the bedroom door and making her way to see who their visitor could be.

Mattie hadn't the strength to do more than continue drinking, eyes closed and all energy focused on the blood, better, purer than anything he had ever drunk other than from Allie herself. Human blood, straight from the source; his body rejoiced at finally being directly given what it was made to consume.

With the bedroom door closed, Mattie could barely hear Alyson as she answered the front door. He let his mind latch onto her telepathically once again, as she had left their connection intact, and he could see and hear through her senses almost as though they were his own.

"Kieran," Allie exclaimed in wary surprise as she opened the door.

It was indeed Kieran, standing at the door, naked and looking very distressed. "Is he okay?" he asked.

Kieran began to fidget impatiently as Alyson refused to answer, staring at him suspiciously. "What are you doing here? How did you find us? I thought I told you *not* to find us," she realized with slight alarm.

Kieran closed his eyes, looking as though he had a migraine and was not in the mood to answer questions. "Is Mattie alright?" Kieran asked again.

"You aren't under my mark anymore, are you?" Alyson asked, again ignoring his question and trying to observe if he still had any of her venom left in his system. His mark was hidden from view.

Kieran distinctly wanted to dispense with the explanations and barge past her into the trailer, but after a moment, he took a deep breath, holding his hands to his head and letting the air out slowly, trying to calm himself. Finally, he looked up at Alyson, clasping his hands before him and trying to appear respectful. "Your Majesty, forgive my haste. I've just…been under great stress."

She raised an eyebrow at the title, trying to determine if he was always going to address her with such formal flourish since her display of power over him, was being sarcastic, or if he was just trying to kiss her ass, but he continued. "No, your mark no longer governs my actions…at least I don't think so." He seemed momentarily distracted and uncertain over the prospect.

Mattie could feel Alyson's own uncertainty. "Why should I trust you?" she asked. "You do work for Arif, and I'm starting to think I shouldn't trust anyone…"

"You shouldn't," Kieran agreed. "But I'm not here on behalf of anyone but myself, and you can do whatever you have to, to assure yourself that I'm not here to betray you. I'll tell you again what I expressed during our last rendezvous, when you so charmingly tricked and drugged me into submission, and this time, I'm not under the forced influence of your venom, I'm just telling you the truth.

You are The United One, a vampire clearly superior to any other, and the only one to whom this pure blood of mine from the old country has ever reacted with such deference. I'm just a hippie kid from Pennsylvania, but my maker was a foreign elder of great power, and his blood in me knows that you are the true leader of our kind. You're young, and maybe a little naïve, but you are the chosen one, a goddess among vampires, and as such, I swear my fealty to you."

"I'm not naïve," Alyson told him, insulted.

Kieran laughed. "Look back on this moment and tell me that again in fifty years. I may work for Arif, but I'd rather place my full loyalty in a young, naïve deity than an elder experienced in maliciousness any night. You *can* trust me. What more do you want, the still beating heart of a virgin lamb?"

Alyson blinked, opened her mouth, and then closed it again. "I'm not a deity. I'm just a really powerful vampire," she muttered. She reached out for him and Kieran didn't shy away. She clasped the bare skin of his shoulder, as he stood unclothed from shifting. There was no current left between them, her mark had truly faded away, but through her empathy Allie could tell that he was telling her the truth as he believed it, and that he was also deeply worried and in some pain.

"Are you okay?" she asked.

"I'm fine. Can I come in?"

Allie sighed, and backed away, opening the door. "Sure. I invite you in."

"Thank you." Kieran barely glanced around at the disaster that was their kitchen and living area as he entered, but instead made his way directly back towards the bedroom. Before opening the door, he paused turning back to Alyson. "May I?"

Allie folded her arms, curiously amused by his confidence. "How do you know where he is?"

Kieran glanced around the tiny motor home. "Where else would he be?"

Allie smiled to accede his point, but then shook her head. "No, I mean…how do you know he's anywhere?"

"Everybody's got to be somewhere." Without waiting for further consent, Kieran reached out and slid open the door.

Mattie lay on the bed, propped up with the dead man lying draped across him. Mattie's face was mostly hidden. He had pulled the man up closer and had now been drinking from the crook of his neck, although it was difficult for their guest to tell if he was still drinking or had passed out again. All was quiet and still.

Kieran gave Allie a last token glance for invitation. She rolled her eyes and nodded. It wasn't as though she was going to kick him out *now*. "Go on in."

Kieran entered, as Allie ducked into the bathroom and grabbed a towel. She shoved it at him to wrap around his waist; not that it mattered much to *her* if he wanted to walk around naked. Being a shifter herself, she understood the annoyance of clothing at times, but Mattie would surely be more comfortable if Kieran didn't walk in with her while naked. Kieran wrapped the towel around himself without comment over it. "What happened?" he asked.

"I trusted someone I shouldn't have," Alyson admitted remorsefully.

"Zach, I know. But what happened? Where is he?"

Allie narrowed her gaze at him again, wondering how he knew it was Zach. "He's a mess on my rug, soon to be resting comfortably in the bag of my vacuum cleaner," she replied, waving back towards the living room, and what was left of Zach's ashes on the floor.

Kieran winced as he realized what the consequences of that might be. "Wow, I hope Sindy's okay."

Allie ignored the comment. "How did you know Mattie was hurt? Can you feel him somehow? You can, can't you? Why? How is that even possible?" Kieran didn't answer. He was angling his head to try to get a better look at Mattie's injury without disturbing him. Mattie just lay there, healing, tasting the blood on his tongue, eyes closed, listening. Presumably, he looked to have passed out.

"Don't make me drug you again," Allie threatened.

Kieran greeted the threat with a smile. He'd probably enjoy it. "They say we can feel the pain of severe injury in a vampire of our making, no matter the distance. The agony of excruciating physical trauma, and even death, is felt as though it were that of the maker." He looked up with a small grin. "I never really believed it though. I was certainly never in a position to know…until now."

"You?" Allie asked in outrage. "You did this to him?"

"I helped turn him into a vampire, I didn't bash his head in. You act like it was a curse. He may believe that, but you don't. It wasn't my idea. I was barely even involved. I was just a donor following orders, one of seven. But yes," he confirmed, looking down at Mattie. "Luke, I am your father, as the saying goes; one of them, anyway."

Mattie's eyes flicked open, taking the sight of Kieran in with his own eyes and then looking to Allie. "See, I told you he looked familiar," he mumbled.

Allie rushed to sit next to him on the bed, moving the corpse aside and brushing the hair back from Mattie's face. "Mattie. How are you feeling?"

Mattie squinted up at Kieran again. "Kind of pissed."

"Wait a minute," Allie said, turning back to Kieran. "Following orders? You mean *Arif* did this to him? Why? Why would Arif order seven vampires to go out and turn some random guy?"

"To create a vampire like you. He was trying to make The United One."

"*Trying* to make a vampire like me?" she repeated in astonishment.

Kieran nodded. "It didn't work, as you know. And it wasn't random, they just got the wrong guy."

"Who were they trying to get?"

Kieran took a deep breath, and then sighed, shaking his head, deciding against opening that can of worms. "It's complicated, and if you really want to know, we can get into it later. Right now, I would really like to make a long awaited apology to Mattie. I was forbidden to identify myself to you," Kieran explained. "But I'm just breaking rules all over the place now, so what the hell?

Look, I've always wanted to apologize for everything you went through that night. I wasn't there for most of it. The shade always gets to be the look out, so I just got called over to feed you and then sent back out to keep watch, but I know Lorelei and Cat. They're each bad enough on their own, being held captive by the two of them together must have been a nightmare. I heard you were pretty traumatized, and for that, I am deeply sorry."

Mattie didn't say anything. He just wiped his mouth shakily with the back of his hand and tried to sit up better. Pain shot through his back and legs. Apparently, the blood was being kept too occupied healing his brain and keeping him conscious to worry about getting to the rest of his body yet. "Get this thing off of me," he muttered to Allie, shoving at the dead man on the bed. She pulled the corpse away from him and laid it in the corner. "You're sorry?" Mattie asked.

"Yeah. There was nothing I could do."

"You could have stopped them."

"No I couldn't. We were under Coven Master's orders to turn you, and Lorelei was head of the Senior Guard. If she wanted to mess around with you first, what was I supposed to do about it? You don't understand, you've never been part of a coven. Not the little group you played house with at Cain's, I'm talking about a real coven. It's all rules and protocol and politics. You follow orders or you're dust, and you don't want to piss off your superiors, trust me. My hands were tied."

As Mattie thought things over, Allie spoke quietly in the silence. "It wasn't his fault, Mattie."

Mattie looked up at her with understanding, but gently shook his head. He opened his mouth to speak, but pain stole the words. Allie felt it and cut him off. "That's enough for now. You still need rest, lots of it." She looked to Kieran and then began to shoo him out the door. "Leave him be, let him heal."

Kieran tried to resist her shoving him out the door. "Okay, but we need to talk. I want to help."

"You want to help? How about some advice on how to dispose of bodies?" she asked, indicating the dead man in the corner.

Kieran seemed to think it was nothing to worry over. "Don't give it a second thought. I'll take care of it."

Allie glanced over to see that Mattie had closed his eyes again to try to recuperate. She continued in a whisper. "I don't expect you to. It's my mess. I'll clean it up. I just don't have much experience with this sort of thing. What do you do, dump them in the river?"

"What good is being a supreme being, if you don't have others to do your dirty work for you?" Kieran quipped.

"I'm not looking for that."

"I know, but I've got this... as long as you'll let me return when I'm done. We *need* to talk."

Allie sighed with indecision. "If you've got something to say, just spill it. I was thinking I should get us on the road. I don't like staying in one place too long...especially now that I've got dust on my hands."

"Dust? Oh, Sindy isn't going to come looking for Zach."

"You know where Sindy is?"

"I'll come back and tell you everything I know, but...you can't stay here."

"That's what I said."

Kieran suddenly became uneasy on the verge of panic. "No, I mean I just realized...you really need to get on the move, *now*. If I felt Mattie's pain, you can bet that his other makers did too. It's a no-brainer that you two would be together, and now they know where to look."

"Oh my God." Allie looked around the trailer in panicked worry, assessing how quickly she could get them on the road. "We've got six other vampires coming after us behind you? Maybe you should have opened with that!"

"I only just thought of it. There are only two though. Cat and Lorelei are the only others still with the coven at this point. Lorelei wouldn't be able to track him far enough before the pain ended to actually find you. I only felt the very worst of it while it was happening. If I couldn't fly, I never would have found you before losing the direction. But Cat...Cat is fast, as fast as you."

Allie's eyes widened. That was a very scary thought. Kieran gave her a look of slight reassurance. "I don't know where she is or what she's doing. She isn't here yet, so she may not even have the presence of mind to realize the pain would lead her to you. She's brilliant, but crazy, and kind of short on common sense."

"Wonderful," Allie muttered. "A super fast, crazy, evil genius vampire may be on our trail? This just keeps getting better. Take the bodies and go. I have to get us out of here!"

"Let me meet you somewhere."

"No way! Even you have to realize what kind of risk that would be."

"I'm the one giving you the warning to leave, I wouldn't betray you! My allegiance is yours, first and foremost. I swear it. Can't you feel it? Read it from me, it's the truth."

There was an uncomfortable silence as Allie weighed everything in her mind, feeling rushed and unsure, before finally conceding. "Fine. Get rid of the bodies for me, and I'll think of a place we can meet up when you're done."

"Bodies...plural?"

"There's another one in the bathroom," she confirmed, sheepishly.

"Consider it done."

"Okay, but if you make me regret trusting you, you are going to wish I let you die quickly. That's a promise."

"Yes, ma'am."

She returned to the bedside and leaned down to give Mattie a kiss on the cheek. "I'll be right back," she promised.

Mattie was almost embarrassed by the wave of panic that washed over him at the thought of her leaving again, now that he was aware enough to worry about her. She reassured him with a mental nudge. *I'm not going anywhere, I'm just going to help him outside. I'll stay in contact, just like before.*

Mattie's tension eased as his thoughts groped for and found the line of communication that would allow him to see through Allie's eyes and know things were okay. She helped Kieran get the bodies out the door, glancing around nervously, but then paused, as it was obvious he wouldn't be able to carry both of them far. *Let him take the car,* Mattie suggested. She ducked back into the trailer to grab the keys to the Charger, but they weren't on their hook. After an annoyed search she paused and remembered, Zach had said he'd taken the keys. Sure enough, she found them on the floor after an uncomfortable moment of sifting through his ashes, and brought them outside.

"Here," she said, tossing them to Kieran. "You can take my car. Just don't get blood in it or the smell will drive me crazy."

Kieran smiled and made a token inspection of the bodies before dragging them over to the car. "Not a problem, I don't think you left any."

With one body in the trunk, and the other stowed in the backseat, Allie quickly gave Kieran a rendezvous point that she hoped was sufficiently far away and a bit off the beaten path. She watched him drive away before returning to Mattie's side. "I've got to get us on the road," she told him, as she made sure he was tucked in and stable. "Try to get some rest."

One look at the destroyed remains of the trailer's kitchen windows and the disaster that used to be the living area, and Allie knew there was little she could do as far as the preparations they normally went through before driving. The R.V. was a wreck on wheels and she just needed to leave it be and get them on the road. Allie got them moving with a frantic sense of dread that Cat was going to catch them before they were able to get some distance. It took quite a few miles before she was able to relax a little. She had no doubt that she would be able to handle a lone vampire, no matter what their talents were, but she needed more time to tend to Mattie. Besides, if Cat did catch up to them, she would be in psychic connection with Arif; something which held all kinds of bad implications.

Allie finally reached the place she had told Kieran to meet them, pulling the trailer into the lot behind an old building and putting it in park. She went back to Mattie, relieved to be able to hug him close and offer him her throat. He sank his fangs into her vein, gratefully. Comforted by her embrace and the healing ambrosia of her blood, Mattie suckled her throat until he was able to allow himself to sink back into the deep, dark oblivion of healing sleep.

Mattie woke at Kieran's return, and observed that the shade was fully clothed this time. After a second of odd recognition, Mattie realized that he had stolen the clothes off one of the dead men he'd just gotten rid of. Kieran was alone. Apparently, he was staying true to them and they had succeeded in keeping themselves hidden from Arif's coven.

Mattie addressed him, the resentment of the memory of his turning giving him energy and clarity to speak. "You..." he began as Allie escorted him into the bedroom and closed the door behind her. "You helped them turn me into this."

Kieran crossed his arms and cocked an eyebrow. "If I hadn't, you would have been rotting in the ground for the past decade, so I don't know what you're angry at me for. Anyway, it wasn't my decision. I told you, I was just following orders. It wasn't my fault."

"It's the fault of anyone who contributes to allowing covens like that to rule the vampire world," Mattie insisted, sitting up to better express his ire. "Cain described a coven as a group of vampires existing together as a family, to help and support each other, and that is what a coven *should* be. Not some twisted hierarchy in which everyone allows evil and treachery to reign because they're too afraid to stand up and stop it."

Kieran looked insulted that Mattie was accusing him of following out of fear, but rather than answer, he just shoved some laundry off the chair in the corner and sat, crossing his feet up on the edge of the bed.

Mattie gave his legs a shove, and when Kieran removed them from the bed, Mattie continued. "Torturing and turning me was just one small injustice. I'm just one guy. Think of the incredible amount of small injustices this coven has perpetrated. Then add them to the depths of larger evil doubtlessly going on behind closed doors. He was trying to create a United One? Are you fucking kidding me? If that's true, then who knows what other little experiments this guy has going on? He's probably doing things that half the vampires there wouldn't even want to stomach, but they're afraid to speak out, so they turn a blind eye. That's how men like Hitler rose to power. Inaction might be the greatest transgression of all."

Kieran took it in, neither denying nor defending himself against Mattie's accusations. Once the last of Mattie's words died away, he asked, "What can I do?"

"We can try to change things," Mattie suggested quietly.

After some thought, Kieran tried to hide a smile, as he added authoritatively, "Do, or do not. There is no try." He smiled, explaining himself after a short pause of silence. "Sorry, after the Vader thing before, it had to be said."

Allie returned the grin and asked, "Who do you think we are, the rebel alliance? I've got to tell you, no matter how strong the *force* may be in me, I can't say I feel like rushing over there and fighting a hundred vampires just for the chance to kick Arif's ass and start a vampire revolution."

Kieran chuckled. "Well, why don't you let me tell you guys what's really going on over there. I have a feeling it may foster some of that fighting rebel spirit."

A look of trepidation flashed over Allie's face to match the sinking feeling Mattie had in the pit of his stomach. "Why, what's..." Alyson began the question but suddenly faded off with a faraway look in her eyes. Mattie knew that look. She was in telepathic communication, but with who?

"What is it?" Mattie asked.

"Fear..." Allie answered uncertainly.

So, it was empathetic then. "*Who* is it?"

"Felicity." Alyson spoke the name with such dread that Mattie felt a chill travel down his spine...or maybe it was just phantom sensation from his injuries. "Oh my God! When...?" Alyson's question trailed off like the others as she stopped speaking aloud and replied only in thought.

"Are you talking *to* her, or about her?" Mattie asked. Alyson was only known to have long distance communication with Felicity, or with Cain. At least if she was talking to Felicity directly, she knew her friend was still alive.

Allie was shaking her head, looking very upset. She gave Mattie back her attention briefly. "I'm talking to her now. She's been abducted...by Arif. He took her prisoner last week! I can't believe I didn't know! I could have stopped him!"

"You've been kind of distracted, between sharing tinglies with Zach and what with me getting pulverized and you going on a killing spree," Mattie reminded her weakly. "Even before that, you were trying to show me how you hunt *without* killing. I'm sure control like that takes a lot of focus. I was showing you some of my new moves too," he added with a smile, remembering how he had teased her in bed with his control of electrical current. "We've been a little busy..."

Allie still seemed mad at herself for being so unobservant. "Right...those weird vibes I was feeling from Zach were definitely a distraction when he first came on my radar." Mattie dropped his smile. Allie gave him a sympathetic nudge, that she hadn't meant to downplay their lovemaking. "It's been a very distracting time all around. Plus, I think Zach knew more than he was letting on about telepathy. As soon as we met up, I think he may have been blocking all my outside communication." She glanced at Kieran and then made for the door. "Excuse me for a minute. I need to go process this, and make sure she's okay."

Mattie lay back again on the bed, a bout of nauseating dizziness passing over him. As Allie left the room, Kieran pulled his chair closer to the bed. "You knew about this?" Mattie asked.

Kieran nodded. "I was going to tell you. Don't worry, she's alright...for now. How are you? That must have been some brawl between you and Zach."

Mattie closed his eyes as a wave of pain washed from the base of his skull and up over his head to settle into a dull pounding. "Yeah," he whispered.

"You must have some serious fight in you, going up against a United One and surviving to tell the tale."

"Yeah, you can measure how formidable I am by all the broken bones and the big hole in my head."

Kieran chuckled. "You got lucky. I know it doesn't feel that way, but you did. Even the fact that you held him off as long as you did is impressive." He glanced towards the door, but Alyson was still occupied in the other room. "Listen, you've obviously suffered some serious damage." Kieran seemed anxiously worried over Mattie's state, which was kind of unsettling. "It's amazing that you seem to be functioning so well. In fact, that was a pretty rousing speech from a guy with a big hole in his head."

"I think the hole is closed now," Mattie muttered, peering at him, wondering where he was going with this. "So?"

"So, I've seen vamps deal with some serious head injuries in my time. You'd better take it slow for a while, and...well, I wouldn't be surprised if you had some issues. Just take it easy and know that with trauma like that, you will still be healing for some time before things get back to normal."

The way he said *normal* made Mattie very nervous. "I feel normal now; kind of shaky and in a lot of pain...but normal. What kind of issues?"

"I don't know, depends on what part of your brain was damaged, I guess. You could have memory loss, stuff like that. Clearly your reasoning and speech are both fine, as evidenced by the whole 'Arif's coven is evil' lecture. How's your hearing, vision...?"

"I guess my eyesight has been a little...off. Things are blurry sometimes, washed out... They get too bright, and then dim..."

Kieran nodded. "Give the blood a chance to fix everything. It should come back fine."

"I think my memory is okay...but I guess if I was forgetting stuff, I wouldn't know, would I?" he asked with a nervous laugh. "I can't move my legs well though. I'm pretty sure I've got some broken ribs and my back is killing me."

Kieran gave him a sympathetic smile. "Believe me, I know. I didn't feel it all, just the worst of it, but some of those injuries nearly knocked me out of the sky while I was trying to get here."

Mattie laid quiet, taking stock of things. He didn't feel like he was having any problems with thought comprehension, but if he had brain damage, would he be cognizant of it? He felt the dull, fuzzy feeling of taking too much cough medicine, but nothing he couldn't function through. "In Allie's nightstand," he said, waving Kieran towards the drawer. "There's an anatomy book."

Kieran opened the drawer and began to oblige, but paused. "You sure her nightstand is something you want me digging through?" he asked with a smirk.

"Just get the book and don't look at anything else," Mattie directed irritably. As though his worries over brain injury shouldn't trump privacy concerns...even if Allie did have a few sex toys in there...

Kieran pulled out the textbook. "Convenient."

"Tempest gave it to her to help with shape changing. See if it has anything on brain physiology."

Kieran looked it over, but seemed very disheartened. "I'm working with a 9th grade reading level here...this shit is technical."

"Find a diagram. Everything's labeled."

"Yeah...in *Latin.*" Mattie just closed his eyes and waited for Kieran to stop complaining and find something useful for him. Eventually he must have, because after some more page turning he muttered, "Okay, here we go." Mattie opened his eyes to find Kieran studying him. "Base of the skull mostly, right? How high up is the injury?"

Mattie leaned forward a bit, trying to indicate where the puncture had been. He was almost afraid to touch it, but once he did, he was very happy to find that it did seem to have healed shut, tender as it was.

Kieran consulted his diagram. "I guess that would be the cerebellum, and maybe part of the oc...occipital lobe...?"

He looked to Mattie, as though questioning his pronunciation, but Mattie just shrugged. "What does that mean?"

"I have no idea. Hang on, there must be a glossary or something."

Kieran flipped more pages and finally seemed to have found something that was worth reading. He went over it silently until Mattie prompted him. "Well?"

"I'm sorry dude, there's a lot of stuff here to wade through. The very bottom seems to be motor function, equilibrium, steadiness, stuff like that. Up above it, in the occipital lobe, that's all about vision; color, clarity, field of view."

"Sounds accurate. Anything else?"

He shrugged. "That's where you got hit. All the thought process and memory stuff seems to be up front."

Mattie sighed in relief. Not that he wasn't in tremendous pain and worried about what he was dealing with, but physical stuff he could handle. It would heal...hopefully. To lose functions like reasoning and memory, those were things he wasn't certain he could ever get back. Of course, if he had been badly injured in those areas, he wouldn't be aware enough to be so worried about it, but it was still a relief to know. It may hold him back a little, but it wouldn't change him.

Allie re-entered the room, looking furious enough to spit nails. "He is so dead." She paused when she saw Kieran quickly close the large book in his hands. "What are you doing?"

"Nothing," Kieran assured her, shoving the book back into her drawer.

Mattie reassured her. "Just a little research on my injuries. Don't worry, I'm going to be fine."

"Good, because forget all that stuff I said earlier, about not rushing over to fight Arif. You're getting me in there," she told Kieran, "and then he is dead. A few minutes alone with him is all I need."

Mattie held up a hand for her to slow down. "I said I'm *going* to be fine, but it's gonna take a while. I'm not in any shape to keep you from getting yourself killed, so please don't go charging in before I'm well enough to stop you."

Allie raised an eyebrow. "Like you've ever been able to stop me? Besides, this is major. Felicity is trapped in the hands of that sleaze. She is freaked out, and I lost connection with her before she could even tell me anything useful. I don't know what happened. I was cut off, like someone disconnected the telepathic phone line."

"Jin," Kieran surmised. "Arif has him dampen out all paranormal activities periodically, including telepathy. He and Lorelei are the only known telepaths in the coven, but ever since she betrayed his trust a while back, he's been kind of paranoid, and with the idea that Alyson might be trying to snoop around in someone's head, I'm sure he's got Jin working overtime. Especially after his meeting with Ben."

"What?" Both Allie and Matt asked in shocked unison.

"Yeah. I'm supposed to be spying on him right now. In case Cain doesn't come running with The United One in tow, Arif is also enlisting Ben to use his dad to try to find and convince you...or capture you. Whatever gets him your blood. He's getting impatient."

Mattie was outraged. "He's sending the Everheart's after us now?"

Allie threw her hands up. "That's it. This is crazy. I'm not giving anyone my blood, and Ben and Cain aren't going to be able to convince me, or capture me, or do anything but get themselves killed. I'm going in there and I'm dusting him," Allie announced, daring them to dispute it.

Surprisingly, it was Kieran who spoke against it. "Bad idea."

"And where does your loyalty lie again?" she asked with a raised eyebrow.

He smiled. "Oh, I'm done with Arif and his ego trip. After the way he has dealt with your arrival into the world, I don't care if he's dusted. Good riddance."

"So, you don't think I could do it?" she asked him, dangerously.

"My Queen, you could surely accomplish whatever you set your pretty little mind to, but I think the results you desire are better accomplished from a different angle. Sneaking in on your own is not the best plan, even if you are all-powerful."

"Thank you," Mattie said, giving Allie a nod of agreement.

Allie thought about it for a second, and then nodded. "Okay, maybe you're right. I could probably use some back-up. We should get Cain."

Mattie was quick to refute that idea. "No!"

Kieran shook his head with a puzzled smile as he put a hand on her shoulder for attention. "Why do you always think you need to look to someone else to lead you? That's not what I meant."

She was still looking at Kieran in wonder, when Mattie finished his protest. "Like it or not, Cain is the last person we should contact."

"Why? We can use all the help we can get."

Mattie sighed. "Allie, you know I've trusted Cain with my life, but what would you do if Arif was holding *me* prisoner, threatening to kill me, and would only release me in exchange for a sample of your blood...which he would almost certainly use to create a master race of vampires under his control, who would wreak havoc on the world?"

Allie immediately knew the answer. "I'd give him my blood to get you back; figure out how to save the world later."

"Good answer, but it proves my point. Like it or not, we can't trust Cain on this one. Felicity means too much to him."

Allie wasn't convinced. "But Cain wouldn't betray me like that, Mattie. You don't know him like I do...the way he thinks. It's like he feels it's his duty to sacrifice everything for the greater good, a punishment for his sins. Like if he isn't suffering, then he must be doing something wrong."

"He's Christian, not Catholic," Mattie corrected her with a chuckle.

"He's Cain, and he would never willingly hand me over to Arif. He'll find another way to save Felicity."

Mattie nodded in understanding, but was still unconvinced. "Maybe, but all the same, you'd better keep the radio silence in effect for a while longer. No telepathy...at all. Anyway, Ben's the *vampire hunter*," Mattie added in disgust. "Let him be the hero."

Allie frowned over his bitterness. "That's not Ben, that's his dad."

"Like father, like son. I've seen both of them wield a sword, and they are no joke. You and I are keeping our heads safely attached to our necks and out of their way. Got it?"

Kieran stood, arms crossed. "Are you two finished yet? Because I've got an assignment I need to get back to, and I already know what you need to do. Leave Cain and the Everhearts to me. Screw the sneaking around. You need to go big..."

Obviously, he had some sort of plan in mind. It seemed as though Allie could read his intentions, but wasn't quite ready to give him the floor yet and spoke herself. "Kieran's right." Her focus trained on Mattie, serious and steady. "Some night, when something happens that I just can't stand by and watch, I'll have to stand up to it, reveal my powers over vampires everywhere, and use them to take my place as their leader and make things right," she quoted.

Mattie gave her a look that said she was being ridiculous and dramatic. "Says who?"

Allie laughed. "Says you. Your prediction, weatherman, remember?"

Kieran nodded. "She needs to make a statement; go over Arif's head and take control...of everyone."

Mattie could tell that as much as Allie wanted to be on board with the idea, she was still very unsure of herself. "I'm with you, but...I'm just supposed to swoop in and assume that everyone is going to listen to me, just because of the color of my eyes? What if I try to command them and they laugh at me...or try to kill me? If we're talking about Arif's coven, then I would assume these are some pretty loyal and ruthless guys."

"You can do it. Trust me, I know what I'm talking about. I'm not just some dumb kid, and I don't give my loyalty to just anyone. I've been around, and I've been a faithful member of Arif's coven for forty-five years. You think I'd throw that away on a whim? I believe in your power, and I know other vampires will believe in you too. You just need to show them who you are. Image is everything. They crave someone to guide them. We're lost...all of us."

Mattie smirked at him. "*Lost?* Like that vampire movie from the eighties?"

Kieran returned the smile. "Yeah, *The Lost Boys* is a pretty accurate way to describe us, and we are all just looking for a Peter Pan to lead the way."

Mattie gave Allie a teasing grin. "Would they settle for Tinkerbell?"

"She always ran the show anyway," Allie said, giving him a withering glance as she put her hands on her hips and rose herself a foot into the air to stand taller above them. "If I'm meant to be a ruler, then damn it, I'm gonna stand up and lay down some rules. Don't you make me *order* you to be at my side."

Mattie looked from her to Kieran, knowing full well that with Kieran backing her up, he couldn't talk her out of it. This had the potential to be a complete disaster...but it just might work. He finally relented with a little shake of his head. "I hope we're not going to regret this...*My Queen.*"

Chapter 15 - The "i" in team

Ben

Ben and Felicity's house
Montauk, Long Island, New York
The same evening

Ben met his father out on the back deck overlooking the ocean. He took a discreet look around as he handed Bernard the martini he'd requested. It seemed very private out here; nothing but empty beach and the crashing of the waves to muffle their conversation, but Ben never doubted for a moment that Arif somehow had spies watching him. He'd been warned, and he wasn't taking any chances.

His father took a sip of his drink and then nodded thanks for it. "I had an interesting meeting last night."

"So did I," Ben answered quietly as he sat.

This gained his father's surprised attention. "Really, who with?"

"You first."

Bernard eyed him curiously, but relented. "Well, apparently your friend Alyson has become kind of a big deal." Ben had filled his dad in on some of the encounters he'd had with vampires in the past, including what he knew of Alyson's decision to become one. "One of my sources knows a vampire who defected from Arif's coven after failing in a mission to capture her. The vampire must've thought she was pretty important to Arif if the punishment for failure was worse than having to spend the rest of his afterlife in hiding. So, why does Arif care about her, and why were the orders to capture, and not kill? What's so special about Alyson?"

"I don't know, but she is my key to getting Felicity back."

"It is likely that Alyson is responsible for Felicity's disappearance. It's classic vampire behavior, to hurt those they loved most in life. It's not difficult to believe that she would harm your wife to torture you, her dearest friend."

"No, Alyson didn't take Felicity."

"But you said she was the key..."

"Alyson isn't the kidnapper, she's the ransom."

His father stared at him as he deciphered the facts. "Arif," he grumbled.

"I need to get Alyson for him."

"Ridiculous! To defeat a serpent, you don't feed it, you cut off its head. I'll assassinate the miscreant once and for all, and retrieve Felicity myself."

"No! You can't. He knows you'd love the opportunity, but he has Felicity under his twisted powers of influence. His spies are watching us. If you make one false move, he will kill her, change her, or scar her psyche beyond repair. I want her back, whole and human, not as a vampire or a helpless vegetable. Please dad, for once in your life, respect me enough to trust my judgment. We need to find Alyson. We can trade her for Felicity and then leave the vampires to their own battles."

"You would do that, give Alyson over to him?"

"Wouldn't you?"

"In a heartbeat, but you're a bit more sentimental. She is no longer the friend you knew, but I know what Alyson meant to you."

Ben sighed. "I don't know if she is or not, but she made her choices. Now I have to make mine. I need you to help me find her. Any leads?"

"Nothing fresh."

"You said your guy's friend was supposed to capture her. Where was that?"

A strange grin spread across Bernard's face. Ben became impatient as his father paused before letting him in on the joke. "Your wedding."

"What?!"

"I take it she didn't come give you a hug and kiss while she was there."

"No...but it might explain why Felicity spent half the night in the ladies' room. What the hell was Alyson doing leading Arif's vampires to my wedding, and why didn't they manage to catch her?"

"Possibly because I beheaded one of them before they had a chance."

"You... You were decapitating vampires at my wedding?" Ben asked in outrage. "How does that happen without my knowing about it?"

"Well, I'm sure Felicity just didn't want to upset you."

"Felicity knew about it?!"

"I tried to be discreet, but you can't expect vampires to be civilized. I dealt with it as I saw fit. The guests weren't disturbed and I didn't even get any dust on her gown."

"It was right in front of her?" Just when he thought his angry disbelief had hit its peak... Ben took a deep breath and blew it out slowly. "I don't even know why I continuously allow myself to be surprised by the shit that gets pulled behind my back these days. I will hear more about this later, but it doesn't help us much now. That was two years ago. Alyson came for the event, that doesn't mean she's been hanging around. She could be anywhere. How are we going to find her?"

A voice called up from down below them on the sand. "You can't."

Both Ben and his father stood, in alarm, to look over the beach-side railing, although Ben already recognized the accent and knew who it must be.

Bernard reached for his sword, but Ben put up a hand to stay his draw. Cain stood at the foot of the steps leading up to the deck from the beach.

The vampire looked just the same as Ben remembered him. His light brown hair was just long enough to blow off his shoulders in the wind. He wore an unassuming dark tee shirt and faded jeans with his heavy boots, and stood on the sand with his thumbs hooked into his front pockets.

Although his appearance was almost identical to when they had last met, about seven years ago, Cain used to seem much older than Ben, for good reason. Of course, Ben knew that the man was, if he could be believed, *centuries* older than him, but they now looked to be the same age, in appearance anyway. In fact, the bits of grey in Ben's hair caused him to appear the older of the two.

Ben looked down on him in distain. "You."

"Me."

"Somehow this is all your fault, isn't it?" Ben muttered angrily.

"Not really, but whatever helps you sleep at night. I'm sure you'd love to make me the bad guy."

Bernard was alarmed by Cain's sudden appearance, but didn't seem overly hostile towards him, just on guard as he asked, "Who is that?"

The vampire wasn't quick to give his attention to Bernard, but rather looked up at Ben with a quiet sort of confidence that conveyed his maturity more strongly than his appearance. He was self-assured in a way that came off as patient rather than condescending. It made Ben self-conscious of his own quick temper that he worried may seem childish to someone of Cain's vast experience.

Cain ascended a few of the stairs as Ben held up a hand to stall his father's question a moment longer, but now Cain gave the man an acknowledging smile and answered him on his own. "Allow me to introduce myself."

Cain simply stood there, looking up at them, but Bernard suddenly drew his sword and gasped in shock. He paused only for a moment, and then it seemed he was poised to jump the rail and attempt to decapitate their visitor. Cain must have revealed his psychic vampire mark.

Ben was trying to decide if he should let them go at it for a minute or two before breaking things up, but Cain rolled his eyes and put a hand up in the air. "Stand down, hunter," he ordered.

"You know me?" Bernard asked warily. He didn't lower his sword or relax his stance, but at least he remained on the deck.

"I know of you. I've spent the last three decades avoiding you. Do you really think I'd walk up and introduce myself if I wanted to kill you?"

"Are you unafraid of me then?" Bernard asked, with a lilt of cocky insult.

Cain smiled. "You're quite infamous in these parts. In fact, I use stories of you to frighten young vampires into behaving themselves, as though you're the boogey man, but I'm not afraid of you, no."

Bernard squinted at the vampire and tightened his grip on Hikari, his sword. Cain noted the gesture. "Don't take it personally. That doesn't mean I don't respect your prowess. Frankly, I've just got more than my share of things to worry about, and self preservation isn't usually that high on the list. However, I do have things to do, so being dusted at the moment would be a bit inconvenient. Perhaps you might put that away so we can talk?"

Bernard studied him, seeming a bit awestruck. Ben had never really seen that expression on his father, and wasn't thrilled that it was Cain who had elicited it. "You know him?" Bernard asked his son, without taking his eyes off their visitor.

"Unfortunately," Ben muttered.

Bernard took a step closer to the rail. "You're the oldest I've seen...by far." Cain shrugged with a slight nod, as though the fact was uninteresting. "How is it that I haven't seen your mark before? Even if you masked your own, you still have to feed. Do you just kill them all?"

"You'll find that I'm a bit more civilized than that, thank you."

"If you don't kill, then why haven't I seen your mark on your victims?"

Now Cain seemed insulted. "Perhaps that's because I don't victimize people." He took a few more steps upwards to the deck before looking to Ben for permission, sounding a bit impatient after the insult. "May I?"

"Felicity's uninvited you," Ben announced with a certain smug satisfaction.

Cain looked up, surveying the deck with a raised eyebrow. "We're outside."

"Just thought you should know."

Cain let out a huff of a breath with a smirk. "Thanks."

"Come on up," Ben grumbled, leaving the railing to return to the table.

As Cain reached the top of the stairs, Bernard hesitated for a second, but then sheathed his sword and backed up, unlatching the gate to allow Cain entrance. Cain paused for an uneasy moment, and then passed him to join Ben at the table.

Bernard continued to stare at the vampire as he sat. Ben realized he must be studying Cain's mark. "Wait...I have seen your signature before...on Felicity!" He made the claim as though it was a pronouncement for Ben to attack the man.

It certainly evoked feelings that made Ben want to comply, but he settled for giving Cain a sour look while he explained to his father. "It was before we were together. They were *in love*," he added bitterly.

Bernard looked ill. "Felicity's smarter than that."

"You mean smarter than you?" Ben asked bitterly.

Bernard chose to ignore the dig. "You can't be serious."

Cain tore his gaze from the locked stare he'd been holding with Ben over the table. "Dead serious," Cain told Bernard. "I don't play with people's emotions. Despite what you may believe, a relationship between a human and vampire need not always be treated as a game."

Ben didn't know whether Cain knew anything about his father's past, but that was the wrong thing to say. Bernard put his hand back to the hilt of his sword as he stepped towards Cain, menacingly. "Was that barb aimed at me?"

For the first time it seemed Cain took Bernard a bit more seriously, becoming very still and holding the man's gaze, warily. "No," he answered quietly, but firmly. "I do not know you, sir, or the details of your personal affairs. I apologize if I've touched on a tender subject. I only meant to clarify my own feelings over the matter." He turned to give Ben a piercing look. "Your son has been inclined to believe that I take the devotion of Felicity's heart lightly, which is most certainly not the case."

"That's good to hear," Bernard answered, taking back his attention, "as long as you keep in mind that her heart is devoted to my son."

Cain answered with quiet sincerity. "As I am well aware. My name is Cain, by the way. Perhaps you've heard tell of me, as I've heard of you?"

Ben could see by his father's reaction that he had. He seemed impressed... *Great,* Ben thought in annoyance.

Cain continued with his introduction. "Love and loyalty are the strongest guiding forces of my existence, alongside my faith."

Ben rolled his eyes with a sigh. He was so tired of Cain's constant declarations of nobility…whether he believed them or not. Then again, maybe someone who gave the involuntary impression of being a blood-thirsty monster couldn't be blamed for putting forth a little extra effort to dispute the reputation.

Cain focused on Ben in strict earnest. "We haven't had opportunity to talk since I left. You should know that I ended my relationship with Felicity so that she might focus on humanity, and have the life that she desired and deserved." He glanced up to include Bernard in his explanation. "I believe that she has chosen a worthy man to share that life with, and I have stepped aside giving my blessing."

Bernard surprised him by speaking out. "I believe you." Ben was a bit shocked that his father did not seem nearly as skeptical as Ben would have expected.

Ben scraped his chair back from the table. "Am I supposed to be grateful, like you did me a big favor?" he asked Cain with as much angry sarcasm as he could muster. "Our marriage doesn't depend on your approval."

Cain seemed appropriately apologetic. "Of course not. I only want you to know that I never sought to interfere in your lives. I respect your marriage, Ben…your family. I hope you believe me when I tell you that I wish nothing but happiness for you."

After a moment of silence, Ben nodded, grudgingly, and Cain continued. "However, it has come to my attention that Felicity is in danger. If the danger were of human nature, it would be unfair for me to interfere."

Ben let out a derisive huff of a laugh. "But that wouldn't stop you, would it?" He could instantly read on Cain's face that he was right. The vampire wouldn't let anything bad happen to Felicity, whether it was his place to prevent it or not.

"I can't honestly say," Cain admitted, falteringly. "But the fact is, vampires threaten her now, and such jeopardy is a situation I am equipped to rectify. I plan to find and remove her from danger by whatever means necessary. As you are her husband, I thought I should do you the courtesy of consulting with you over it before doing so."

"Gee thanks," Ben quipped sarcastically. "What a guy." He shared a glance with his father and then turned back to Cain. "Look, I don't know how much you really know about the situation, but if you honestly want to help, you'll get me in touch with Alyson. She's the one who can help me fix this mess, and I'm betting you know where she is."

Cain raised an eyebrow at him. "I have no idea where she is, and she'll not solve your problems but only serve to make them worse, for everyone," he informed them, dismissively. "We don't need Alyson's involvement. I can handle this without her, and quite frankly, without you." Cain stood, as though prepared to leave. "Enough time has been wasted already. Shall I include you in my plans, or be on my way?"

Ben glanced around nervously. If Arif's spies were watching, he couldn't have them thinking that he and his father were going to team up with Cain against Arif, even if he could use the vampire's help.

If Arif suspected betrayal, he would destroy Felicity's mind. Ben worried already that being seen with Cain was incriminating enough. He needed to stick with the original plan. "Please, at least let me speak to Alyson. You know how close we were, and I think she was the last one to see Felicity. Just have Allie meet me somewhere so we can talk. You can get a message to her, can't you?"

Ben stood as Cain fixed him with a discriminating stare. "He's already gotten to you, hasn't he?" Cain asked. Ben could tell that he knew Arif had asked him to betray Allie, and it disgusted him. "I hope Alyson has left the continent."

Ben closed his eyes, taking a few deep breaths. He wasn't even sure if he *would* betray Alyson, but he had to do something, and he knew that he couldn't let Arif's spies hear any more. "Don't say anything else. If you aren't going to help me find Allie, then just go."

"Really? You'd rather let Felicity die, than accept *my* help to save her? Perhaps I misjudged you after all," Cain muttered in disgust as he turned to leave.

Bernard was quick to defend his son, no matter how impressed he may have been over Cain's age and civility. "He doesn't need help from the likes of you. My skill and sword are behind him."

Cain narrowed his eyes. "You don't even know what you're dealing with."

Ben held up a hand to lightly push his father to step back. "Please, dad, just let him go. We'll find her ourselves."

Cain opened the gate to descend the stairs to the beach, but all three men were startled when he was suddenly blocked by a dark, swirling mist that solidified into a young man standing in the way.

"You're not going anywhere," Kieran told him with a smirk. "I didn't work this hard to coordinate everyone just to have the three of you fuck it up in a pissing contest to see who's the better hero."

"But..." Ben stammered, trying to understand, "you work for Arif."

Bernard let out a huff. "Does he? Then why don't I just execute the spy, and we can do as we please?" Bernard suggested, once again drawing his sword.

"No!" Ben jumped to stay his hand, but Kieran was already dissipating into smoke and swirling out of reach to reform on the deck behind them.

Bernard was taken aback by Kieran's avoidance, and lowered his sword in aggravation. "Benjamin, if there is one thing I have learned, it's that you will never persevere while playing by their rules."

Kieran spoke in Ben's defense. "He's just trying to play it safe, for Felicity's sake. Talk to them, Ben. You don't have to keep playing double agent. The only spy Arif has watching you, is me, and I'm not going to say anything."

"Why not?"

"Because he's been in power long enough." He turned to Cain with a small smile of seeming apology. "I couldn't say anything to you until I knew for sure, but the plans are made and my restrictions are now lifted. The true master of all vampires has chosen to reveal herself, and she is not very happy about all of this."

All three men looked at him quizzically. Cain seemed amused, while Bernard was confused, and Ben was just trying to take it in and understand. The true master? Who was he talking about? *"She?"*

"Yes. She finds the whole thing very upsetting and she'll be rectifying it shortly, but we may need your help."

Cain chuckled. "Are you speaking of The United One?"

"Who else?"

Bernard and Ben still didn't know what the vampires were talking about. "The United One? Who's that?" Bernard asked.

Cain grinned. "Alyson."

"Alyson?" Ben repeated, in shock. "But she's..."

"Divine leader of us all," Kieran pronounced, cutting him off, "to whom I have pledged my undead devotion until such night as I am dust, for she is my rightful queen."

~~~~~~~~~~~~~~~~~~~~~~~~~~~~~~

Ben still couldn't quite wrap his head around the idea, even though the vampires had tried to explain it several times. He and his father had been exchanging information with Cain and Kieran for over an hour, and trying to formulate the best plan to extricate Felicity from the situation, but every time they spoke of Alyson as some all-powerful deity type creature, Ben couldn't help but falter. "Alyson?"

Cain patiently tried to make him understand. "It doesn't matter who she was in life, Ben... And she still is the Alyson you knew, by the way." He pointedly ignored a huff of disagreement from Bernard, and continued. "But the blood that has been introduced into her body has made her into a vampire unlike any other. All vampires can see it in her eyes. We know it inherently, and the blood within us responds to her authority. It cannot be denied. She is an evolved creature, born of the highest powers of every breed, above all vampires. She is The United One."

Ben processed and tried to accept the concept. "Arif wants to control her."

"Can't be done," Kieran interjected with firm certainty.

Ben laughed. "No, I wouldn't think so. Alyson was out of control even when she was human."

Kieran gave him a look of warning. "She's not out of control, she is beyond the control of others. Mark the difference." He waited for Ben to nod in agreement before he continued. "I have to get back to her. We have a lot to do and she needs my advisement. You can trust that the coven won't oppose you, Alyson and I will see to that. I'm hoping Elric will be swayed to our side. He'd never admit it, but I know he's been waiting for just such an opportunity. You'll only have to deal with Arif and those very few who are most closely loyal to him; Lorelei, Cat, Jin, and maybe one or two others."

Ben recognized Cat as the woman who'd accompanied Arif at their meeting. At the name Lorelei, both he and Bernard blanched, but Kieran either didn't notice, or decided to ignore the reaction and continued speaking. "Most of the coven will stand down, I'm sure of it. Oh...but I don't know if Drake and Maribeth will still be there."

Ben had never heard those names before, and they didn't seem to mean anything to his father either, but Cain looked as if he'd been struck a blow. "What?"

"Drake, he's Arif's sire," Kieran stated simply.

"I see." Cain paused for a moment, putting that together in his mind. "I should have recognized the connection by their shared condescending arrogance."

"I take it you've met," Kieran said with a laugh. "The woman is his consort."

"I know." Cain turned a steely stare on Bernard. "She's mine."

Bernard squinted at him strangely. "Your what? Lover, protégé?"

"No. Mine to deal with. Don't touch her." He turned to include Ben in the warning as well. "If she is threatening your life, then of course she is fair game, but I'm betting she's more of a background player. She shouldn't give you any trouble."

"Who is she?" Bernard asked.

"You'll spot her easily. She is a stunning woman, fairly petite with porcelain skin and flaming red hair. She was twenty-eight at death, but now she's older than all among us."

"Even you?"

Cain chuckled. "Yes, even me, but only by a year, if that. She's my maker."

"*Your* maker?" Bernard asked, stunned.

Ben wished he could see Cain's mark, as his father and other vampires could. Was it really impressive enough to cause such a fuss? So he was old. Big deal. "What's she doing with Arif?"

"Nothing too devilish, I hope; I doubt she's deeply involved in his plot. She's probably just found herself in the midst of things while there on Drake's arm. She's mischievous at times, and can be downright evil if she's a mind to, but she hasn't normally got the patience to carry out grand scheme plans. Thank goodness, because she *has* got creatively cruel manipulation down to a science."

Cain sounded bitter enough that Ben was sure the woman had somehow broken his heart. "Maybe Arif brought in your ex as a distraction for you, or as some sort of leverage to sway you somehow," Ben suggested.

Cain shook his head with a smirk. "I doubt it. She's long lost any hold she ever had upon me. She's not my favorite person, but neither is she truly an enemy. Felicity is meant to be the leverage against me, I can assure you."

Ben gave him a look of resentment, that the vampire's feelings for *his* wife should be so well known and exploited. Cain noted his expression and quickly carried on. "If anything, it may be a stroke of luck to have Maribeth with them. I doubt she's any strong loyalty towards Arif."

"But is she at all loyal to you?" Bernard asked.

"I couldn't say. We have our differences, but have managed this long not to kill each other. If things became dire, I think she might back me. She's honestly lucky that I haven't dusted her already for some of her past antics, and she knows it. You can't have a history as long as ours without having a certain understanding of one another. I think she has softened a bit as of late. She's likely just bored and tagging along after Drake for lack of anything better to do. Leave her to me. But speaking of exes..." Cain added, suddenly seeming to have remembered something. "I'm afraid

Maribeth and Felicity won't be the only exes I'll have to deal with." He paused before adding, "Sindy is with them as well."

Bernard looked to his son, defensively. "The one you told me about? The vampiress who bit you?"

A wave of resentment flowed through Ben over the name as he nodded. "Sindy is on your ex-list too now, huh?" he asked Cain, in disgust.

Cain took a moment to contemplate the answer. "Ex or current, I'm not quite clear actually. We *were* together, but she snuck out to meet with Arif and hasn't returned."

Ben chuckled at his answer. "Sorry, Romeo, Sindy is definitely with Arif. The guy even threatened to give me to her as a gift if I didn't follow his instructions. He called her his *Mistress*. Face it, you've been played."

"I think Arif is counting his mistress before she succumbs," Kieran interrupted. "She's *not* with him, actually."

"You told me she was..." Cain disputed.

"I told you she was there, but not *with* him. She was there, and she was in league with him, that's true, but she's since reconsidered her position."

"Oh, has she?" Cain asked facetiously.

"The last time I saw her, she was enacting her exit from his coven. I wish I could go check on her, but there's no time. I need to hurry up and iron out our plans here, so I can get back to The United One. You'll be seeing Sindy back at your estate if all went as planned. She had ideas of going to Khalon's coven for sanctuary."

Bernard let his hand graze the hilt of his sword, menacingly. "Well, if she dares to show up here, we'll be ready for her."

Both Cain and Kieran were insulted by the gesture, but Ben couldn't help but smile, that his father wanted to defend him from her...even if it was too little, too late. Cain gave him a stern look. "I'm sure that won't be necessary."

"She's already paid for her poor decisions," Kieran assured him. "She's looking for a place of retreat and recovery at this point. Don't go picking fights."

Bernard puffed out his chest a bit. "I don't pick fights, like some schoolyard bully. I defend humanity from those who feel they have the right to prey upon the unsuspecting populace. You may be vampires who have perfected your civil charade, but I never forget the company I am in and the horrors you inflict upon your victims. I stay my sword only for Felicity's sake."

Cain glowered at him over the indignity. "Rest assured, I'll be inflicting no horrors for you to avenge. Need I spend the evening looking over my shoulder? If that's the case, perhaps I should make an exception and dispose of you now, before you compromise our plans and your lack of self-control costs Felicity her life."

The corner of Bernard's mouth twisted upwards in a satisfied smirk. "I do worry you after all, do I? I've agreed to a temporary alliance, and my word will not be broken. I am savvy enough to accept what truces are offered to further my own ends, but that does not make me sympathetic to your plights, or that of your various ex-lovers. Your vampire girlfriends are your problem, and if they get in my way, they will be no more, whether they have reconsidered their treachery or not. It is easy to reconsider and beg forgiveness once forced into a corner of submission. That does not make one deserving of mercy."

Kieran laughed. "Sindy won't be begging anyone for mercy, I can guarantee. Back that vixen into a corner and you'll get that much more vicious of a fight. Just leave her alone. She's not involved any more, and as for her past pursuits and her biting you," he said to Ben, with a grin, "I'm sure you can find it in your heart to forgive her. After all, there are men who would beg to have been in your position. I know I would have."

The remark drew a curious look from Cain, but only served to make Ben furious. "You ignorant little shit. Having the soul sucked out of you really does screw your moral compass, doesn't it?" Kieran genuinely seemed surprised by his reaction. Ben turned to his father, his fury over past hurts suddenly renewed. "Maybe we *should* just dust her...and him too, while we're at it."

Kieran scoffed at the threat, as he momentarily turned himself to smoke, showing that anyone would be hard pressed to try and harm him.

Cain put a hand of understanding on Ben's shoulder, which he immediately shrugged off. "You won't even see her," Cain assured him. "If Kieran is correct, she's long gone already from Arif's control. Let's not stray from our focus."

Ben wouldn't be pacified, still railing against Kieran's comment. "You have no idea how fucked up that is. If a woman was beaten and raped, would you tell her she should forgive the guy, because other women would beg to be in her place?"

Ben glared at Kieran, who had lost his smirk and was now quick to apologize. "Sorry. Guess I hadn't thought about it like that."

Ben took a deep breath, acknowledged him and chose to move on to the matter at hand. "Fine. How do we do this?"

Kieran nodded, relieved that personal feelings aside, Ben was willing to defer to his knowledge of the situation. "Without letting Arif know it, we need to work as a team. That means knowing when to step back from things. No offense, but Cain is our key player here."

"Just love to be in charge, don't you?" Ben asked Cain in annoyance. "You know, there's no *I* in *team.*"

Cain observed the angry glare Ben was giving him and raised his hands in innocence. "I'm not the one making this plan."

"Neither am I," Kieran insisted. "Not alone anyway. It is the strategy I devised in concert with The United One. She believes the plan is sound, and in her I will put my trust. Cain is the focus. Obviously *you* have the most interest vested in Felicity's safe return," he assured Ben, "but Arif will believe that Cain wants to save her just as much, and Cain has more persuasive power over Alyson."

Ben wasn't so quick to accept that. "How do you figure? He may be able to find her quicker, but Allie and I go way back. Why should she listen to him any more than she would to me? So he's an old vampire. Does it really give him that much power? I've never seen him do anything special."

Surprisingly, Cain seemed to agree. "I'm afraid Ben's right."

"The boy is *not* right," Kieran asserted. "You underestimate yourself, while Arif knows full well what you're capable of."

"The boy?" Ben asked in angry disbelief. Just when he thought they were going to be able to work together without too much friction. "Did you really just call me a boy? *Seriously?*" Ben asked, gesturing for the others to recognize that Kieran looked the youngest of all of them.

Kieran cocked an eyebrow at him. "I'm older than your dad."

Ben furrowed his brow in confusion over the remark, but then shook it off, giving his disgruntled attention to Cain with a wave of his hand. "He may have pulled that shit years ago, but I'm a grown man now. Neither one of you'd better forget it. I don't care how long you've been dead."

"I'm sure he meant no disrespect," Cain assured him. "It's simply a manner of perspective and having more experience."

Ben squinted at him, irritably. "Experience as a vampire, existing on the fringe of society as an outsider, not as a man. I've got more human experience. I'm older than either one of you lived to be."

Cain cocked his head in thought. "Aren't you twenty-seven? That makes it a tie, actually. I guess I just wear it well. However, my experience and youthful good looks aside, Ben is right. No one could believe that I would have power over The United One."

Kieran was still quick to dispute the claim. "Actually, you do, which is one of the reasons she and Mattie have chosen not to contact you directly...not yet. Not that they don't trust you, but your emotional attachments and influence, coupled with your power, make you uniquely capable of manipulating her; and Felicity is sufficient motive that Arif would believe you'd do it, even unconsciously."

Cain looked just as disbelieving as Ben felt. "What power? I've no powers of coercion and I've mentored Alyson for years. She and I have sparred many a time and she's always bested me in the end, through sheer supernatural strength and skill. She is unmatched. You said so yourself."

Kieran smiled. "Not if you play sneaky. You're a greater threat than you realize. All you need is a few seconds of surprise on her, and she's yours; and the emotional bond you share would easily buy you those seconds if you played it right. That's why I'm glad to see your loyalty to her hasn't wavered, despite Arif's hostage. You keep that loyalty strong and I'll show you how to fool Arif and rescue Felicity. Just don't get any ideas of giving in to Arif's demands or I'll kill you myself. The United One will not be compromised."

"I have no intention of handing Alyson over to anyone, but I still don't understand what power you think I have over her."

"You and I can have a little chat about that later. Ben and Bernard, we'll need you two to stay under-cover behind the scenes, if this is all going to go down without putting Felicity at risk any more than she already is."

Ben's mouth fell open in outrage. "Are you kidding? I'm not just going to stand back and wait to see if he pulls this off."

Kieran was unfazed. "Cain has already agreed to meet with Arif tomorrow night. We are out of time for arguments, the plan is set. When Cain sees Arif, he is going to be desperate for Felicity's release, and agree to lure and trade Alyson to accomplish it," he advised Cain with a nod. "I'm sorry Ben, but it's much more believable that Cain could do it, no matter how much you might want to. You just haven't got his resources.

Once Arif believes the trap is set, he won't really need you, but you want to be sure Felicity is delivered to you and not Cain, so you've got motive to keep on him. Tell Arif you want to help as planned, regardless of Cain's involvement. You told Arif that once Alyson was delivered, you would assist him, and handle Mattie if necessary, and that is exactly what you need to let him think you're going to do.

You resent Mattie and Alyson, for her choice to turn her back on your friendship for him. We all know that's true, and Arif loves a good revenge story. He'll be quick to believe you're on his side, at least he'd better, because the minute he thinks you're not following his instructions, he'll get suspicious, worrying your father's persuaded you to pursue his own vendetta, and he knows better than to let his guard down in the presence of *that* Everheart."

The comment made Everheart Senior sport a smug grin, but Kieran barely gave him time to gloat before continuing instructions. "Bernard, you should remain low-key as Ben's back-up until things get ugly, at which point we could sure use your sword to take care of any loyal coven members who don't know when to jump off a sinking ship."

Bernard nodded in agreement. "But what about Arif himself? If I have a chance to take him out, I'm not going to pass it up. He and Lorelei will both pay for my wife's death."

Ben answered his father. "Let's take care of *my* wife first, please. You'd better hold back and stick to the plan," he warned. "You can avenge mom's death on your own time, you certainly haven't been in a big rush so far." That drew a glance full of anger and hurt, but Ben was unrelenting. There may be good reasons that his father had been unable to exact his revenge thus far, but it was still the truth and Ben didn't have time to argue about it. "You blow my chance to save Felicity and I'll never forgive you. Once she's safe, I'll be more than happy to help you make them pay for what they did to mom and Felicity both."

Bernard was plainly unhappy to be spoken to thusly, but he made no comment. Kieran took it as acceptance and turned the lower half of his body to smoke, floating up over the railing of the deck and beckoning Cain to approach the stairs to follow. "I need to get back to The United One, but I'll meet with you again tomorrow. I know the motel you're in. Be ready for me at sunset."

"I thought I was to meet him at midnight?" Cain asked.

"Yes, but we've got to have a more private conversation about some vampire business before we arrive," he reminded Cain, with a pointed look at their present human company.

Cain stood, surveying Ben and Bernard, who gave him disgruntled glances at that, but he ignored them. Cain nodded. "Alright, but honestly, the only vampire business I want to discuss is how I'm going to liberate Arif's head."

Kieran gave him a twisted grin. "I remember. Brought your weapon?"

"Oh yes, I almost forgot." Cain opened the gate and jogged down the steps.

The Everhearts leaned over the deck to watch, unsure if they should follow. Cain quickly returned from where he had disappeared around the side of the house, carrying a very large, sheathed sword. As he better returned to their view, he drew the weapon.

The sword struck an odd chord of recognition for Ben. It shined with a reddish glow in the moonlight, its blade edged with glistening metal, but the body of the sword being made of some kind of wood. It was the same sword Ben had seen Sindy use to behead Marcus, unexpectedly rescuing him from the brute vampire in the school gym years ago. He had thought the sword looked familiar back then, like something he had seen in his father's collection, but it seemed implausible and he'd never had opportunity to ask about it. Seeing it again now, Ben was shocked, and found that the odd blade definitely tugged at some buried, inner recognition. He had seen this blade in his father's hands, hadn't he? One look at his father's face, and he was certain. He knew this sword.

"Ash-bringer," his father breathed. Cain gave only the barest nod. "Made of bloodwood; beautiful isn't she? How did you come by her?"

"She was a gift," Cain told them with a perverse smile, "from Arif."

Bernard was visibly floored by the admission. "Really?"

"Yes. I hope you don't mind, but I'll be using it to kill him."

Now Bernard smiled as well. "That's what she was made for. Of course, I had hoped to wield her myself..."

Cain sighed. "I wouldn't lay hold on a man's weapon without his blessing," Cain said, preparing to climb the steps again.

"No. I have Hikiri now," he said, pulling on the hilt of his katana just enough to show it's shining blade. "It pains me to say it, but you'll catch him off guard far more than I could, and it does give a sense of satisfaction to know he so misplaced his trust. One of his men stole it from me years ago. I've never seen the thief again, but I've made quite a few vampires pay dearly for it since."

Kieran seemed a bit uneasy, eying the sword. He'd doubtless spent a good amount of time avoiding it himself. He turned back to the Everhearts, as Cain made his way back to where he'd left his bike. "Ben, I'm sure Arif will be having me contact you after he speaks to Cain. We'll talk more then. Be ready."

Chapter 16 - Gifts

Cain

Montauk Highway, in the middle of nowhere
Montauk, Long Island, New York
The next evening

Cain pulled off the road into the entry of the Hither Hills Beach Access as directed, and shut down the motorcycle's engine. "Here?" he asked, doubtfully.

Kieran had met Cain at sunset as promised, and they'd discussed Cain's previously undiscovered vampiric gift. As Kieran had claimed, it would give Cain power over Alyson; not that Cain planned to actually use it, but it explained why Arif had so much faith in him to bring her in. It was quite an enlightening conversation, and Cain wished they'd had more time to talk, but all too soon, Kieran had shushed his questions and hurried him to his motorcycle. "We're to meet the Master in less than an hour, and in case you've forgotten, you can't fly."

Cain surveyed their surroundings. Where they had stopped, there was nothing but woods and a sandy path of a road heading down to the beach. "We're in the middle of nowhere," he insisted, glancing around again. They had been driving mostly through woods, and passed a small red sign about a half mile back, proclaiming the boundary of Hither Hills State Park. The road seemed to stretch on forever with nothing of note in immediate sight.

Kieran didn't even bother to answer him, but instead focused on a pair of headlights approaching from the other direction. A large black Hummer slowed as they were spotted, and it pulled off to the side of the road to join them. Byron, Arif's driver emerged from the car and went to open the back passenger-side door.

Arif stepped down out of the vehicle, the ocean breeze tugging at his long dark hair. He came to meet Kieran and Cain with a sinister smile upon his face, as Byron closed the car door behind him. Kieran gestured towards

Cain with a slight bow, the vampire having been delivered as promised. "Thank you for escorting him, Kieran," Arif acknowledged. "You may wait with Byron at the car." Kieran moved off as directed while Arif greeted his guest. "Cain, I was beginning to wonder if I would see you. You haven't reacted with nearly the urgency that I had expected."

Cain crossed his arms with a scowl. "Your postcard wasn't exactly clear as to whom you were holding."

"Does it matter? I thought you were out to save everyone; the humans from the vampires, the vampires from themselves..."

"Release Felicity," Cain demanded, grimly.

"Bring me Alyson," Arif countered with a shrug.

"What makes you think I would trade one life for another?"

"Wouldn't you?" he asked with an arched brow. "But Alyson's life needn't be sacrificed. I merely seek her cooperation."

"I thought you believed she was evil; a descendant of darkness doomed to be consumed by her thirst for power and destruction?"

"Do you still doubt my predictions?"

"She's shown me nothing to confirm them."

Arif smirked at him. "Really? Nothing at all? A well-behaved and model student for you, is she?" When Cain refused to comment, he continued. "Suffice to say, she is a phenomena neither of us knows exactly what to expect from. I do not seek to harm her, only to study her. Yet, despite my numerous and generous invitations, she has not seen fit to comply."

"She's not an experiment, she's a person, and she is unwilling to be studied by you."

Arif chuckled. "Indeed. That is why I have chosen to supply some incentive in Felicity. If Alyson is not inclined to join my coven for a time of observation, then I offer this alternative. Bring me Alyson and have her turn a human of my choosing. Once I have a vampire with white eyes to observe in her place, she and Felicity will both be free to go."

"And if Alyson refuses to change someone for you?"

"Then she will be restrained, I will draw a sufficient amount of blood from her and use it to perform the act myself. If her well being is of great concern to you, I will return her unharmed once the deed is accomplished, but if you want me to release Felicity, you must bring me Alyson. That is the deal."

"Even if I were to find Alyson and convince her to accompany me to meet with you, Mattie will never allow it."

Arif chuckled. "You'll have no trouble with him. The young Mattie is in no condition to protest, I can assure you."

A terrible chill of foreboding shivered over him as he asked, "Why? Has something happened to him?"

"Nothing of my doing," Arif assured him. "Lorelei has informed me that he was greatly wounded through some dealings of his own. Unfortunately, he survived the encounter. It would have furthered my own pursuits if he had not, but the timing is still fortuitous. Alyson is undoubtedly shaken and wanting to put an end to all turmoil at this point. The opportunity to fulfill my request without bloodshed should appeal greatly to her, and with you urging her as well, she will comply."

Cain could hardly concentrate on Arif's proposal. All he could think about was what might have happened to Mattie. Whatever the altercation, it was a relief to know that he hadn't been dusted, but it sounded like he was not going to be up for a fight. Had Kieran known? He had said he was recently in contact with Allie, so he must know what happened. Since he hadn't mentioned it, maybe Mattie wasn't as badly injured as Arif thought. Cain could not allow himself to be further distracted. He needed to stick with the plan. Knowing Alyson, rather than feeling broken and defeated by Mattie's injury, it probably fueled her anger.

As Cain pondered his position, Arif assumed that he was still unhappy with the proposal. "And yet, still you hesitate? Your lack of action thus far has already forced me to turn to much less reliable methods. Felicity's human husband seeks her safe return as well. He jumped at my offer far more eagerly than you."

"Her husband?" Cain scoffed. "And what could a human possibly do to accomplish your will?"

"Nothing so certain as what I know you can do for me, but the human was quite enthusiastic once the proper persuasion was applied, I'll give him that."

"I don't want him involved."

"I'm sure you don't," Arif responded in amusement, "but he may prove useful to me."

"No. Turn him away...and I will do my best to ensure Alyson's cooperation in exchange for Felicity," Cain offered, hesitantly.

"You will bring Alyson to me?"

"I don't know where she is, but I'll try."

"You have lost track of your dear coven-mate? Surely, your entwined mark betrays a relationship much too intimate to keep you from contact with her. I am unready to dismiss the human's cooperation so lightly, but bring me Alyson and I will be sure that you are well compensated for your efforts. I will turn Felicity."

"Beg your pardon?"

"I will turn her myself, and then release her to your care."

"No! She is to remain unharmed, unmarked and untouched. How can you possibly consider turning her to be some sort of compensation to me?"

"Do not be so quick as to dismiss my generous offer. Think about it. You want this woman, but your nobility has kept you from her. Let *me* do the dark deed. Not only will she be granted my unique and desirable vampiric talents, you will have your own desires fulfilled without guilt.

She will not blame you for taking her life, for it will be *my* trespass. You will be her rescuer. Her husband will not care for her in such a state. She will need you more than ever to guide her, and she will cling to you, her first love and protector. You really could not ask for a better reward."

Cain recoiled from the ghastly cleverness of the offer. "It is not your decision. I want her to remain human and unharmed. It is non-negotiable."

After a moment of pause, staring into his eyes to discern that this truly was Cain's wish, and not a token protest, Arif shook his head while lightly clucking his tongue in disapproval. "You are so foolish, but far be it for me to judge you for passing up such a unique opportunity. I suppose it is just as well that you leave the woman to her husband. You have your own woman to worry about, don't you?

You've spent so much time pining over the human, that the splendid vampiress who shared your bed has felt sadly neglected. So much so, that she came begging to me for comfort and affection. Sindy has been eagerly helpful in her attempts to gain my favor, to make up for your own woeful lack of attention to her. She has been working for me for quite a while, you know."

Cain refused to show how her betrayal had wounded him. "Well I'm sure after any true amount of time in your company, she thoroughly regretted her decision. In fact, I wouldn't be surprised if she's left you already."

"You wouldn't? Well, as it turns out, that is not the case. Not at all. As a matter of fact, she clings to me with a needy desperation I would not have expected from her. I guess I do bring that out in women though."

Lies...they had to be. Cain knew Sindy better than that. However, Kieran may have been mistaken in thinking she was no longer in Arif's power. Her exit may not have gone as planned. He wondered just how badly it might have gone, but it seemed Arif wasn't going to tell him. The coven master wanted to pretend she was happy as could be in his company.

"I'll believe that when I see it," Cain muttered. "Where is Sindy? Can we arrange a meeting? I'd like to speak with her myself."

He paused, pondering something, and then reached a conclusion. "You can have her. To be honest, I'm tired of her. She can be quite annoying, and though I have thoroughly enjoyed the erotic enticements she has to offer, I've decided that the novelty of her affections just aren't worth having dog hair in my bed."

Cain felt a chill shiver through him at the implications, as Arif turned back to the car. "Sindy, come out here, dear," Arif called with a snap of his fingers.

Arif's man opened the car door and after a moment, Sindy emerged wearing Arif's mark and a beautifully embroidered long sleeved, belted tunic with a deep v-neck, over black leggings. Cain was a bit rattled to find that she was indeed here with him, and strongly marked by him as well.

She approached, took in the sight of Cain with apparent surprise, and then lowered her eyes and edged closer to Arif in a subservient action that Cain had never believed he would ever see from her, *ever*. "Yes Master?"

The words flowed from her lips as smoothly as though she'd been his meek and humble servant for years, but Cain could barely keep his mouth from falling open upon hearing them. Arif gave him a smug smile and addressed her. "I am turning you over to Cain, dear. Your welcome in my home has been withdrawn."

Sindy reacted with apparent dismay at the news. "What?" After her initial shock she spoke to him in an ineffective whisper. "I don't want to go with him. I'm yours, remember? You said I was your special pet. You can't turn me away now!"

As disgruntled as Cain was with Sindy after her betrayal, the words still made him nauseous. Was it an act? She must think he would be jealous...and perhaps he was a bit, but really it was just upsetting to see her behaving like a broken concubine.

Arif answered her firmly. "I can, and I have. It's been fun, but I'm bored with you now. I fear Cain may be a bit cross with you for your betrayal, but he always has been the forgiving type, far more than I." Sindy clearly wanted to protest the transaction further, but Arif held up a hand for silence, ignoring her to turn his attention to Cain. "Do with her as you will, but you may want to save your reprimands for another night. I require you to deliver The United One to me at the Montauk Point Lighthouse by midnight tomorrow, and time is ticking."

Cain tore his eyes from Sindy in disbelief. "Tomorrow? I can't possibly! I don't even know where Alyson is!"

"Then I guess you'd better start looking. If The United One does not meet with me at the lighthouse by midnight, Felicity will be turned, whether it pleases you or not. Assuming she survives the transformation, she will remain my prisoner, held as a vampire, starved every night thereafter, until I have the blood of a United One with which to turn the human of my choice." He didn't bother to entertain any more protests. "Sindy, it has truly been a pleasure, but our dealings are done."

Arif gave them no further attention. He opened the car door for himself and climbed inside. The last that Cain saw of them, was a brief flash of Kieran's horrified face from inside the car before the door was shut and they drove away. Clearly Kieran had not known that Sindy had still been in Arif's company and he found it just as upsetting as Cain did.

As the car disappeared from sight, Sindy stood frozen next to him, staring at the ground. Cain watched her for a second and then sighed. As he did, it seemed she suddenly became aware of him again and met his eyes. "I can explain," she began tentatively, but then seemed to give up. "Do you hate me?" she asked.

Cain, short on patience, mounted his motorcycle. "I don't even know and I can't say I care to think on it right now. You can come with me or go off on your own, but I haven't got time for drama and explanations. What'll it be?"

She silently got on the bike behind him as he started the engine. He wasted no time and took off back for the rendezvous point he had set with the Everhearts. Now that Kieran had clarified for him exactly what he was to do, he wanted to discuss a few more things with the humans before finding Alyson and putting it all into action. He hoped that he could indeed find her. Arif was right in his observation that he still wore Allie's mark and his strong desire and distress shouldn't go unnoticed by her through their empathetic connection...in theory. He hadn't heard from her yet, but Kieran had assured him that he would.

It wasn't too long a ride. They arrived, but no one was in sight. Cain cut the engine, dismounted, and turned to help Sindy off the back. She seemed to have an inexplicable amount of difficulty, leaning strongly on his arm. "Are you alright?"

"I'm fine," she assured him. He moved away from the bike a pace, looking around, and she followed, eager to regain his attention. "So, what are you planning to do now? Are you really going to give him Alyson?" she asked.

He was trying to decide how to answer, when suddenly Sindy was clubbed on the back of the head, collapsing into his arms. Bernard

Everheart had hit her with his sword, strongly whacking her with the flat of the blade to knock her out. Cain was understandably surprised and dismayed. "What the bloody hell?!?"

"You're lucky she's still got her head," Bernard assured him. "Why would you bring her here?"

Ben came rushing to them from his place of hidden observation, taking in the situation. "What did you do?"

"I preserved our secrecy. You know that she's a plant, right? Arif knew you wouldn't desert her, although she clearly wears his mark. They have a telepathic and empathetic connection. While conscious, she is his eyes and ears in your camp. Do I really need to tell you that?"

Cain shifted Sindy's dead weight in his arms. "Of course, you're right," he realized. "I wasn't going to tell her anything, but what can I do with her? I can't just desert her, and I'm not letting you harm her, despite whatever history you might have," he added pointedly to Ben, who was staring at her in odd wonder. It was probably the first time he'd seen her in almost a decade.

Bernard shook his head at Cain's inexperience with such things. "You've never seen a violet-eyed vampire in action, have you? If you had, you would be much more worried...and careful."

Ben looked to his father, trying to be sure he had things straight. "Violet-purple eyes, they read minds and emotions, right?"

Bernard nodded. "Yes, but also, so much more. It is the mental rape of memories, feelings and knowledge. They can learn to wield actual mind control, causing actions and words not of the subject. It can be truly diabolical."

Cain shifted Sindy's weight in his arms, observing her in a new light. "I didn't plan to trust her, but I should have put it together better. She wasn't herself. Not at all. She may have been acting under Arif's control entirely."

Ben also seemed to be digesting the information. "Could he do that to anyone? Make them do and say things?"

Bernard answered as best he could. "Basically, yes. I've had some unwanted experience. Although, I don't think vampires are as easily controlled."

Cain concurred. "He'd have to bite a vampire in order to control them."

"Which he clearly has," Bernard confirmed with a gesture at Sindy.

"What about a human?" Ben asked in thoughtful worry. "Could he control a human to do and say whatever he wanted, without biting them?"

"It's safe to assume that a vampire with his experience might."

Ben shook his head in disgust. "I should have known." The men looked at him questioningly. "Felicity," he answered without further explanation.

"You've seen her?" Cain asked anxiously.

Ben ignored him. "What about us, how can we be safe from his influence?"

Cain was quick to reassure him. "Even a vampire as old as Arif has limits to his power. To control an unbitten human he is unfamiliar with should take direct eye contact at the very least."

Ben was briefly relieved, but then squinted at Cain in distrust. "What about you?" he asked. "Alyson can do those things too, can't she? If she has all powers then she can use mind control too...and you should know that. And they say you wear Alyson's mark." He said the last as though he found it obscene to think that Allie may have bitten him and sucked his blood.

Cain sighed as Bernard began to accuse him as well. "True, your girl Alyson must wield the power as well."

"She's not *my girl,*" Cain corrected with a smirk.

"No, she isn't," Ben seconded.

Bernard rephrased the statement. "She is your student. Is that fair to say?" After a nod from Cain, he continued. "Then how can we be sure that she doesn't hold sway over your actions now? Kieran says she is to side with us against Arif, but how can we know her intentions for sure?"

Cain's expression must have shown that he found the idea ludicrous. "We share a mark of the coven as a sign of protection towards one another for other vampires to respect. However, I can assure you that I am not under her control. The powers you speak of are ones that Alyson and I have chosen not to pursue and develop at this time. We deemed them distasteful and dangerous. I've never truly seen them used to the extent of what you're describing."

Bernard seemed skeptical. "Perhaps, or perhaps not. She may have used them on you countless times. You wouldn't know, would you?"

"Oh, I would know."

Bernard shook his head. "Causing the ignorance of the subject is a part of the skill. Trust me, I've seen it."

That drew an odd look from Ben, but Cain answered with a smirk. "With others maybe, but not with me. I always know, believe me. She learned very early on not to go poking around in here," he told them with a tap to his temple. "I have seen her wield it though, mildly, upon her initial discovery of the talent. She's caused Mattie to do a thing or two, without full comprehension of the trespass."

"Like what?" Ben asked.

Cain smiled, unwilling to fulfill his curiosity. "Nothing you need be concerned with."

"If she's used it before, how do you know she hasn't used it on you?"

"Because it doesn't work on me, not very well, anyway. I didn't realize why at first, but Kieran has confirmed the phenomenon. It's an aspect of my gifts."

"Gifts?" Ben asked.

"Yes, unique talents; skills bestowed with the blood of my vampiric breed. All vampires have certain gifts."

Ben narrowed his gaze. "You consider having a talent for murder a *gift?*"

Always looking to bring around confrontation... "No," Cain answered quietly, "but resisting mind control is a talent I am unashamed of and rather happy to have. It is a protection unique to vampires of golden eyes."

Bernard seemed very interested to hear this. "Really? Golden, are they?" he asked, observing Cain's eyes, although they were pale blue at the moment.

Ben answered for him. "They're not *golden,* they're yellow. I've seen them."

Cain humored him, with a grin. "Well, I haven't," he admitted, "so I suppose I'll take your word for it."

Ben steadily held his gaze. "What else can you do?"

"I think I'll keep that to myself." Ben was disgruntled by his answer. "Benjamin, I've mentored countless vampires of numerous generations, and yet I do not even see fit to inform *them* of all the things they can do."

"You don't?"

"No, so don't take it personally, but I'm not about to unveil my every last secret to *you.*"

"If you don't tell vampires what they can do, then that makes you a pretty lousy teacher, doesn't it?"

"That depends on what it is you think I am trying to teach. Knowledge of powers they might display would merely be temptation for them to display them and become powerful! One must learn to control instinct and act responsibly before being introduced to deadly weapons, wouldn't you agree? I have a hard enough time trying to keep them from using their fangs. Why on Earth would I hand them the key to unlocking more dangerous forces? I am trying to inspire a race of ethical creatures who respect life, not a legion of killing machines."

Bernard was staring at him in wonder. "I had heard that about you, but never would have believed it could be true."

"Well, it is."

"Many vampires resent you for it."

Cain laughed. "I know."

Ben spoke as once again Cain shifted Sindy's dead weight in his arms, becoming impatient. "Control and responsibility...have you been trying to teach Alyson that? You said she was your student, right?" Cain nodded. "That must be a fun class..." Ben imagined with a smirk.

"You have no idea," Cain told him with a return smile. "Look, we can discuss my philosophies and practices later. Right now, I need to figure out what to do with Sindy. Not to mention, find Alyson and plan our coupe; all before getting to Montauk Lighthouse by midnight tomorrow, I might add." Cain nodded over the men's shock at the short time frame.

Ben moved a step closer, studying Sindy's face, peaceful in her unconsciousness. "Why don't you just dump her in a motel?"

"To awake confused and alone? If I'm not telling her anything, Arif might decide to send his men to finish her off."

Bernard cut in. "If she is at all nearby, she may be under Arif's control when she revives. She could rejoin him against us, if we let her."

"You really care about her?" Ben asked.

"I know her faults," Cain admitted with a sigh, "but yes, I care."

"She's killed people...lots of people."

Cain sighed. "So have I. Every night I wish I could take it back, change the past, but I can't. Those people are gone and I can't bring them back. No one can fix it. No one can say that such horrible deeds deserve forgiveness either. It's not your place or mine to forgive Sindy for what she's done, or to punish her for it. It won't undo what's done, and I'm not about serving up judgment; I leave that to the Lord. I just want to make it stop."

Bernard looked as though he might disagree as to whom had the right to serve punishment, but Ben was just contemplating Sindy, thoughtfully considering her position. Finally, he asked, "Do you really think you can get Felicity out of Arif's control, unharmed?"

Cain met Ben's eyes with steadfast certainty. "I do."

Ben took a deep breath and then turned to walk to his car. He opened the door and then gestured to Sindy in Cain's arms. "I'll take her."

Cain assessed his demeanor, surprised by the offer. "Take her where?"

"I don't know...back to my house, I guess. I'm still coming back for tomorrow night, so that's as far as I'm willing to go. Will it be enough?"

"She'll be safe from others who are uninvited, but I don't know about Arif's influence." Cain did a quick calculation in his head. "That's still a few miles from the lighthouse, right? I don't know Arif's range. Normally, I'd think that was fine, but for vampires who have repeatedly shared blood and know each other intimately, distance may not be a factor."

"That's crazy, there's got to be limits," Ben insisted. "How can you know?"

"Because I know that if she has a mind to, Alyson can reach me from across the globe."

That admission took Ben by surprise. "You and Alyson are *intimately* close?"

Cain shrugged. "She is my coven sister." After a brief pause, Ben accepted that and gestured for him to put Sindy in the car. "Ben, I know how you feel about Sindy..." Cain began with worried hesitation.

"You couldn't possibly," Ben assured him with huff and shake of his head.

"To entrust her to your care is showing quite a bit of faith on my part."

"Then it's a good thing you're a man of faith," Ben retorted with a small grin. "My father may be able to help you find Alyson, but there's really nothing I can do at this point. Focus on getting my wife back to me unharmed and I'll see that Sindy is kept safely out of the way, at least until midnight tomorrow."

"And then what?"

Bernard gestured to her with his sword as Cain brought her to the car. "Chain her in the basement," he suggested, although both men seemed to think he was joking. "Come daylight you can leave her to go to the hardware store without much concern of her escape. Buy whatever you feel is necessary and before you leave her tomorrow night, be sure she is firmly secured to await our return."

Ben looked doubtful, but Cain outright laughed. "Chains can't hold her. I know her talents, and without her cooperation there is no one who might restrain her...except for me, perhaps," he added thoughtfully. "Chains won't help."

"They couldn't hurt," Bernard insisted.

Ben shook his head. "I'm taking her back to the house and I'll watch her until I leave. I don't trust her, but I don't think she's entirely stupid either. Her best move now is to stay out of the way. If things work out as Kieran planned, it shouldn't matter."

Cain lay Sindy across the back seat in Ben's car and then shut the door. "He's right, and I haven't got time to argue." He studied Ben and then gave him some last minute instruction. "I appreciate this, especially knowing your past together. Please, don't let her goad you into hostility. You can't trust her, but you can still treat her civilly, even if she might not deserve it...for me, please? If she's being difficult, just ask her to wait for me, close her in a room and ignore her."

Ben chuckled. "*If* she's being difficult? I think you mean *when.*"

"Probably...but she might surprise you."

"Well, I promise I won't stake her, but I do have a few crosses in the house if necessary. Don't worry. I know how to handle her."

Cain met his eyes steadily for a moment. "Somehow that doesn't ease my worries much at all." Ben just smiled and got into the car.

Chapter 17 - Skylights

Sindy

Drifting unconsciousness
Montauk, Long Island, New York
A few nights prior

Venom; warm and pulsing, infiltrating every vein and nerve. Heat flowing beneath her cool skin, the painful sting of fangs leaving her throat. She was so dizzy, nauseous, clouded, her body fighting so hard against it, but after the recent beating she'd endured in response to her attempted escape, she hadn't much fight left. *Please just stop and let it carry me away already. Either that or let me turn to dust and be done.* Arif's hands caressed her body, whispers in her mind brought about actions from her flesh without her will. What was she doing? Maybe she didn't want to know. At least it was better than the harsh and painful punishments...or was it?

Let it feel good, better than the pain. I always was so stubborn though, didn't want to give in, but now... Good would be better. I don't care anymore. Make me feel good and let it carry me away from this struggle. Everything hurts and I'm so tired. She tried to pretend she wasn't aware and wouldn't remember what he was doing. Back when Arif had asked her if she would want to know, she had been so proud and adamant. Maybe she should have asked him to erase the memories after all...

Sharp points driven into her flesh, over and over again. Not fangs with dulling venom, but sharp and unforgiving little stakes of wood, each one accompanied by the loud hiss-squeal-bang of the nail gun. She lost count and just prayed they would hit her heart and end it. Struggling to survive wasn't worth it, now that she knew what it was to truly be under Arif's control.

He seemed frustrated and bored with her now though. He'd finally gotten what he'd wanted, Cain's mark having faded just enough for Arif to circumvent its protection, he'd infiltrated her with his venom and invaded her mind and body. After the endless hours of parading her wolf around like a prized pet, controlling and experiencing the animal through his new link with her, playing with the form and compromising her in whatever bazaar ways he desired, he was frustrated and dissatisfied. The form was not his, nor could it ever be, and influencing her hadn't been as much fun as he'd hoped. He was feeling bitter, and once again, with the aid of Cat's infernal toothpick-gun, the shifting ability was denied her.

Dumped in the reform cellar, available for all other vampires to reprimand and use as they saw fit, Sindy lay on a mattress on the floor. The cutting bite of chains around her wrists and ankles, and the cool, damp air chilling her naked body, these were her only distractions from the pain as she lay waiting for whatever horrors other vampires who came would commit against her. They visited, one after the other. She lay prone, beaten, kicked and spit upon...used for pleasure, given pain. The night seemed endless...the day was worse. No sustenance, no mercy or respite. She was there to serve as a reminder to all of what it meant to go against the master.

Even as the sun rose in the sky, still others came through tunnels beneath the ground to spend their sheltered hours playing with the coven's newest toy. They taunted and mocked her, and she tried at first to show brave refusal to accept their barbs, but there came a point when it was better to retreat within herself and attempt to ignore them...and what they did to her. She kept her eyes closed, but their marks still invaded the darkness.

"Sindy?"

The familiarity of the deep baritone voice dragged her back to consciousness and caused her to open her eyes. Elric had entered the room, closing the door behind him. He seemed to be assessing her condition as she lay there watching him, blinking through blurred vision for clarity. Naked and chained, she felt helpless and resentful that he had pulled her out of her haze to be aware of whatever lay ahead. He'd always seemed approving of her appearance in the past. Apparently, he wasn't going to pass up the opportunity to get a closer look, if not more. "Come to take your turn?" she muttered bitterly.

He simply stared at her for a moment, and then approached, stopping just shy of the mattress she lay on. He looked so large and intimidating, especially from her current vantage point. She tried not to flinch and shrink away when he bent down towards her. Rather than reach for her, he reached out to where the chains that restrained her arms were fastened to a clasp on the floor. The way that they were attached, they could not be opened and removed without a key, but he was able to unhook them to let out more slack and allow her freedom of movement, rather than keep her fastened tightly to the floor. "Sit up," he commanded.

She narrowed her eyes, wondering what he had in mind, but after a moment, she did her best to comply. After being tooth-picked again, repeatedly beaten and raped, even just sitting up was a painful endeavor. He grasped the lapel of his jacket and she thought he was going to take it off, but instead he pulled something out of an inside pocket. It was a flask. Bemused, she took it when he unscrewed the cap and handed the container to her.

She brought it to her nose to sniff, but before it even reached her face she could smell that it was blood. She brought it to her lips, eagerly. It wasn't very warm, but it was human. After a few swallows, she looked up at Elric with confused appreciation. She got the feeling he was doing this on his own. Arif hadn't bothered to see that she was given anything since she'd been chained here, and although a guard had come down to check on her periodically, he only seemed to be concerned that she hadn't been dusted by anyone; other than that, he hadn't cared what they had done to her. This flask was an unexpected and much appreciated kindness, however small. "Thank you."

He brought out a handkerchief and small a bottle of water from his other pocket. She paused in her drinking, and after dampening the cloth, he gently cleaned her face. She felt unsure how to react to his kind and simple gestures, which seemed so intimately sweet, and yet somehow she could just tell that they were things he would do for anyone in her position, not just her.

She looked up into his eyes with a grateful smile, and then broke the gaze, feeling ashamed by her attitude the last few times she had seen him. She had fallen so far from grace...and he was a true gentleman, not seeking to berate her for it, but only trying to do what he could to make it bearable for her, trusting she had learned enough from the experience without him bothering to make her talk about it. He reminded her of Cain.

Elric gave the material to her, so that she could try to wipe away some of the grime from the rest of her body, as he rose and walked back towards the door, where he then pulled over a folding chair from the corner and made himself comfortable. It seemed he was planning to leave her to tidy herself up without hovering over her further.

She looked up at him, hopefully, as she finished her task. "I don't suppose you could be a hero and get me out of this hole?"

He couldn't look her in the eye as he denied her. "No. I'm sorry."

"You know what they're doing to me down here, right?" she asked him harshly, trying to appeal to the gentlemanly side of him that was obviously uncomfortable with the arrangement.

He forced himself to meet her accusing gaze. "Arif's methods can be very harsh...cruel even."

"No shit."

"This is not necessarily the way that I would do things, but I will say that he is usually fair."

"Fair?" She practically spat the word in disbelief.

"There are rules. They may not be rules I would impose, but they are the rules that govern. Vampires can be vicious creatures, and without rules we would exist in vicious chaos. Breaking a rule has consequences, and if you expect anyone, especially vampires, to follow the rules, those consequences need to be dire. You're not in here for no reason."

"He shot my body full of toothpicks!"

"Sindy, this is all a game; a cruel and dramatic game of negotiations. Don't tell me that you didn't know that before you got here. If you let it get this far and you submitted to his demands, then you have to follow them through. If you don't, then you pay the price. If you don't like it, then you'll have to learn how to navigate the game and negotiate better for yourself next time. You took a known risk. It didn't pay out."

She squinted at him, knowing that in a sense he was right, but still refusing to accept her fate. "You could get me out of here if you wanted to."

"Perhaps I could. But to make that stand against him, and change my advantage in the over-all negotiation, for someone who knew the risk and broke the rules, is not a smart move. Giving up what leverage I have, is a play best saved for last." He glanced down at his watch. "I'm here to make it easier for you if I can, but that's all I can do. I've only got my allotted hour, so you may want to drink that down quickly and try to get some rest," he told her, after which he crossed his ankles and sank down in the chair as though planning to take a nap of his own.

Each vampire of the compound was only permitted to spend one hour with her in the reform cellar during a twenty-four hour period, and it was first come, first serve. Apparently, Elric had scheduled himself an hour and was using it to allow her some small respite. It went by quickly, but if she was stuck here, then she was at least grateful to have some time in which she didn't have to worry who was going to come through the door and what they would do to her next.

When the time was up, Elric came to wake her and retrieve his flask. "I've got to go," he told her, apologetically.

He didn't offer any words of hope, but she'd gotten herself into this mess. She'd known the risks, and now she was going to have to wait out the punishment and hope something better offered in the future. "Thanks," she mumbled again, taking advantage of her new chain-length by trying to curl up so that she didn't feel so exposed.

He stopped and stared down at her, waiting for her attention, as though realizing that he couldn't just leave without offering her some kind word to cling to. "This won't be forever," he assured her. "Hang in there. Byron will try to come by later, but he won't be free to come until after sunset." It took her a moment for her to place the name, but then she remembered him to be the driver who had escorted her and Zach to the compound and given them humans to drink from. "He'll bring more blood for you...and give you some more peace and quiet."

~~~~~~~~~~~~~~~~~~~~~~~~~~~~~~~~

Unfortunately, the next vampire to visit her was not Byron, and neither was the one after. Two hours later, as the sun set and the door opened, Sindy looked up, hopeful that Byron had come to keep others away for a while. She was sorely disappointed. In fact, a cold lump of foreboding dropped into the pit of her stomach, and she almost wished that if it wasn't Byron, that it was just another lecherous man entering the room, looking to play with her body for a while.

It was a raspy, feminine voice, filled with authority that accompanied the visitor, as she spoke to someone outside the room upon entering. "Oh, I won't need a full hour...but I doubt she'll be much fun for anyone else this evening; not once I'm through."

Lorelei closed the door behind her, and then took in the sight of Sindy with a malicious grin. Sindy's chains had been fastened taught once more, forcing her to lie almost flat on her back on the mattress.

Although Elric had helped to clean her up a bit, she'd had another visitor since then. Once again, her hair was messed and she was feeling dirty, damp and used. Her condition, when she thought about it, made her feel ill, but it seemed to give Lorelei a sense of evil satisfaction. "There she is...the bedraggled little batgirl. Not feeling so fierce now, are you?"

Lorelei walked closer, in a meandering sort of way, as though lost in her own vicious thoughts, a smile playing upon her face. When she reached

Sindy, she looked down and her smile fled. "Do you finally realize what an ungrateful moron you are?"

Sindy just squinted at her for a moment, unsure what she was even talking about. Lorelei continued, annoyed. "Even now, you're too stupid to have learned your lesson. Arif gave you the opportunity to have everything!" she insisted in exasperation. "Just because he was tickled by the idea of controlling your stupid wolf-bitch! Which he apparently found to be a bit of a letdown, or you wouldn't be down here.

What an imbecile you are! You could have made him love it...worked the angle you were given and had everything handed to you on a silver platter...everything! Aren't you the slut that everyone was so impressed with because she knew how to work a man's fantasies to keep him eating out of the palm of her hand? He would have favored you over everyone in the coven; given you whatever you wanted. That was my role once. Do you know how long I have struggled to try to get it back? You waltz in on nothing but the color of your eyes and he was ready to hand it to you! And, what...you suddenly decide that you're too good for him? That being second in command to the largest coven on the coast is beneath you, just because he wanted you to kiss his ass a little?"

Lorelei made a face of disgust and then spit onto Sindy's stomach before turning and walking away a pace. "He's so powerful," she continued, in a calmer tone as she paced the chamber. "He's smart too. Look at what he's made of himself. And handsome, you can't argue with that." She turned to look at Sindy again in disbelief. "He's such an amazing lover... You're a fool," she pronounced, shaking her head at Sindy's folly. "When I was human, he brought me to heights of ecstasy I never imagined existed! I thought I would die from the sheer onslaught of pleasure. I guess eventually, I did," she confided with a chuckle.

She made her way to a closet at the far end of the room, opened the door and perused its contents. Finally, she chose something from within; it was a large, wooden baseball bat. She walked back to Sindy, fondling the wood as she spoke. "He was so generous and gentle when he brought me over. I will be forever grateful to him for all that he's given me. And I *will* be closest at his side again, especially now that you've reminded him what selfish, ungrateful bitches other women are."

Sindy found her voice, a thick and gravelly whisper from lack of water or blood. "He's all yours."

"Damn right he is!" Lorelei yelled at her as she smacked the bat into her own hand, making Sindy flinch back. Lorelei smiled in reaction. "Wondering what this is for?" She turned the bat over in her hands as though considering her options. "Maybe I should shove it up your snatch...since you're so sure it was too good for Arif. Bet you'd be wishing you'd made other choices then, huh?"

Sindy refused to display any sort of reaction. Lorelei watched her for a moment, and then returned her attention to the bat. "But no, you decided to play batgirl and try to escape through the fence," she said, smacking the wooden bat against her hand again. "Like a scared little pussy bitch, you turned yourself into a disgusting winged rodent and tried to run away. Well, guess what? You're not going to be running anywhere...not for a long time."

With her last words, she raised the baseball bat up high over her head and brought it down with great force on Sindy's right shin, breaking her tibia bone with an audible snap. Blinding pain radiated from Sindy's leg like an explosion, making her cry out in agony. Her scream only spurred Lorelei on further. Again, and again, the bat came down upon her...

The woman's anger was spent after only a few more horrendous blows, but the damage was devastating. Sindy's legs were broken messes of lumps and bulges where none should be. The bruising wasn't what it should have been, for lack of blood, but the pain was severe and left Sindy sobbing, despite her best efforts to keep quite.

After regaining her composure, Lorelei surveyed her handiwork. "Just enough, I think. I'm sure Arif won't mind...since I spared your pretty face." She spit at Sindy again, and then hefted the bat, smiling as it made Sindy try to shrink away. "You're lucky it wasn't my sword," Lorelei informed her. She then turned to replace the bat in its closet, and left without another word.

~~~~~~~~~~~~~~~~~~~~~~~~~~~~~

The moon rose again, as Sindy lay there trying to stifle her sounds of suffering and block out the pain. She couldn't even muster the will to hope for Byron anymore. She closed her eyes and tried to let her consciousness hide away, shutting out the world. She was just grateful to finally be left alone in the quiet, until... Whispers of instructions in her ears...or was it only in her head? Her mind became muddled as she felt Arif mining her thoughts and she tried desperately to shut him out. *Get out of my head!*

Confused and frightened, she wasn't sure if he was dimming her senses or she was just going mad from trying to resist. She found it hard to focus and she stopped bothering to try. More marks came. Freed from her chains, she was being carried somewhere. Vague sensations of being handled, washed, dressed... Arif was still in her head, invading her thoughts and clouding her senses. Commanded to blind and docile obedience and foggy haziness, she wasn't nearly aware enough of what was happening to her, and his telepathic whispers assured her that it wasn't worth worrying over. Sure, *now* he was going to block out her awareness. *I could have used that a few hours ago...*

Riding in a car, the smell of salty ocean air invaded her nostrils. He hadn't bothered to try to heal her. The pain was dulled by little more than a directive in her head. *It doesn't hurt anymore, you're fine. Leave the car and come to me, obedient and submissive.* She found herself able to walk, although the stabbing shards of agony she was assailed with tried to warn her of how unwise the action was. Her legs throbbed and ached, but she was forced to walk anyway, and the sensation eventually dulled, forcibly pushed from her awareness by other thoughts; instructions to be followed, actions, words. Cain was there, but she couldn't go to him, or even speak to him as she'd like. Her voice belonged to her master... It was so odd to hear herself speaking words she hadn't thought to say. It seemed a dream.

Dreaming was better than awareness, at least it dulled the pain, but the fogginess was fading and the throbbing, stabbing sensations of harsh reality were beginning to invade once more. Thirst racked her body with aching cramps as the trace lights of other vampires moved about in her mind like fireflies, until... They're gone.

It was finally dark behind her eyes. No more marks. Good. *Bring me blood or leave me the fuck alone already.* The room had stopped spinning. The venom was fading now, wasn't it? Then why was it still so warm? Growing warmth spread over her throat and face, stinging her eyes, even closed. *Isn't it bad enough to have my throat burning with thirst on the inside? Please let it fade. I need to rest. I can't do this anymore. It's getting hotter and burning and I can't fight anymore. Just leave me alone and let me rest. Can't you feel the coming dawn?*

Sindy sat bolt upright with the realization that sunrise was long past. The uncomfortable burning sensation she was beginning to feel was no longer venom within, but the sun creeping ever higher in the sky, seeking...finding her. She opened her eyes to find herself in a room flooded with sunlight, sunbeams of pain piercing through from somewhere above. With a yelping scream she grabbed the blankets that had fallen to her waist and pulled them up over her head. She lay huddled on a bed, thinly shielded from the sun's deadly rays. She tried to ignore the aches that her movement had awakened and sought instead to make some sense of everything. Vague and unwelcome memories flooded her mind from the evening before, hazy recollections of deeds performed by her body, and yet not her own.

"Sindy, are you alright?" A man's voice; full of concern, but definitely not Elric, Kieran, or Cain…or Arif, thank God.

"Where am I?"

"My bed. My beach house. You're safe."

The only house on the beach in the compound was Arif's, and she couldn't imagine someone there telling her she was *safe*. She must not be in *Kana Susamiş Icin Ev* then. That had to be an improvement. The man sounded familiar. He was human. She could smell him; masculine sweat, the scent of prey teasing her body as it ached with thirst. It wasn't Val or Brett. He was tantalizingly familiar, but who? Friend or foe? She couldn't quite place the voice. "Who are you?"

"Sindy, it's me…Ben."

After a moment's contemplation, she slowly lifted a corner of the covers to see his face; a handsome man close to hitting his thirties, hovering over her after rushing to the bedside in alarm over her scream. He hadn't shaved in days apparently; his face was thick with stubble. His short, dark, curly hair was mussed from restless sleep, and sported thin sparkles of silver over his temples. Could it be?

Years had passed since she'd seen him, and Ben's tall young wiriness had coalesced into a thicker, more muscular maturity of form. He had such broad shoulders, and his body had an athletic build, giving the appearance of strength despite the worn worry in his expression. She ran her eyes over his face, taking in every new little line and crease. There weren't many, but still…

"Everheart? Wow, look at you all grown up. You're gettin' old." He rolled his eyes, giving her a look of exasperation. Yes, she'd seen that look from him many times before. This was still the Ben she knew. She looked him over again thoughtfully, gazing into his golden brown eyes. "It looks good on you."

Was that a smile? Maybe just a hint of one. He hadn't expected a compliment; she'd caught him off guard. Memories of leaving the compound were returning to her now, humiliating and awful, but at least she was out. She smiled back and peeked out further to try and see some of the room, and the source of her nemesis, the sun. After a quick glance at the ceiling she turned back to him fiercely. "You put me under a skylight?!? You jerk!"

Ben winced. "I know. I'm sorry. I closed all the curtains when I brought you in. It was dark, and I completely forgot it was there, honest."

As though she needed yet another injury atop her breaks and bruises. She scowled at him, but decided that he was telling the truth. "Am I burned?" she asked, gingerly touching her cheeks. Her face felt sore and raw. Come to think of it, she had a pretty bad headache and a sore spot on the back of her head too...although she couldn't remember why her head should hurt. With all of the injuries she was racking up, she was losing track.

He looked at her with renewed interest as she tugged the blanket from where it was neatly tucked under the mattress, and then lifted the covers so that he could see her better, without giving up her shelter. "Not really, just a little red. You look...fine..."

Sindy noticed that he couldn't seem to take his eyes from her face. She had hazy recollections of Arif's servants removing her from the reform cellar to bathe and dress her. She'd been cleaned and coiffed to look in decent shape before being paraded in front of Cain, so she knew she didn't look like the pathetic mess she had been a few hours before. She wasn't sure why Ben was staring...

She suddenly became very aware that regardless of the fact that she was now a twenty-eight year old woman, she still looked every bit the sixteen-year-old girl Ben had known and cared for...forever ago, the age at which she'd died. She wondered what Ben made of that. He looked slightly awestruck, but seemed to like what he saw. "It's been awhile," she said with a small grin.

He guiltily averted his eyes. Yes, he still thought she was attractive, always had. She knew it. He'd rather die than admit it though, *after* she'd died that is. *Before* he'd been rather plain about what he'd thought of her appearance, especially when they were alone in the woods out behind the school; fun times. He cleared his throat and tried to pretend he didn't really notice her smile. "You haven't changed."

She thought about that for a moment. "You'd be surprised. Have you?"

Now he did meet her eyes again. He looked like he was trying to read through them to her soul, if she still had one. Never was very clear about that. Very disquieting...not to know. "I guess. Maybe we both have." He sighed. "I am sorry about the skylight. Maybe I should have listened to my dad after all," he added with a chuckle. "He wanted me to chain you up in the basement."

"I never liked your dad," she informed him. "Considering I just came off some time chained in a basement, I can't say I don't appreciate the upgrade...even with the skylight," she added with a twinge of bitterness.

Ben eyed her, curiously. "Cain said chains couldn't hold you."

"Did he? What a sweetie. Normally, he'd be absolutely right. Unfortunately, I'm a little off my game right now."

"Because you've got Arif in your head?"

She let out a sarcastic huff of a laugh. "He's not in here at the moment," she assured him with a tap on her temple. "Having him in my head I could handle. It's my body I'd like him to stay the hell out of." Ben gave her a look of distressed disgust over the comment. "And not in the way you're probably thinking...although, that was pretty unpleasant too." Ben looked away, visibly uncomfortable, and he didn't even know the half of it. "Arif...put something into my body that inhibits my powers. Until I get it all out, chains work just fine."

"Good to know," Ben replied with a smirk.

She took in his expression, realizing the compromising position she was in. Pleasantly familiar as he was, there had been a time when Ben would have been happy to try to kill her, on more than one occasion...but then again, when wasn't she in a compromising position these days? After everything she'd just been through, she'd be damned if she was going to let herself be intimidated by Everheart, of all people. "What am I doing here...with you?"

He took a thoughtful moment to answer. "Do you remember anything?"

"Some, but nothing I care to dwell on...or share," she added in warning.

He didn't push, but instead spread his hands in surrender. "Just trying to figure out where you're at," he explained. He sat back down on the chaise lounge where he must have spent the night. "I brought you here as a favor to Cain."

He was cooperating with Cain? That was a bit unexpected, but she nodded, her memory returning. "I was with Cain," she said, dredging up the groggy recollection, "and Arif, but I never saw *you.*"

"What were you doing with him, anyway? Last I heard, you were skipping out on Arif."

"Unfortunately, Arif heard that too, and he wasn't happy about it."

"What happened to you?"

"What *hasn't* happened to me? I'll tell you what happened, a nasty guard dog and couple more bitches named Maribeth and Lorelei." She stretched a little, testing out the telltale sting of her toothpick wounds and the aches and pains not yet receded from her last beating. It was a good possibility that the broken bones in her legs hadn't nearly begun to mend.

The toothpicks inhibiting her blood flow and Arif making her walk on them certainly hadn't helped. She closed her eyes, trying to sort through foggy recollections of what had taken place. She let her memory travel back to the beginning of the end for her escape.

~~~~~~~~~~~~~~~~~~~~~~~~~~~~~~~~~~~

The moment Kieran left her in his bedroom, Sindy realized that she'd no time to spare. She un-gently yanked the last toothpick from her shoulder, biting back a cry from the pain, and then rose to make her exit.

She threw a blanket over the bed, hoping the bloody mess wouldn't get Kieran into too much trouble. Servants to a vampire shouldn't think much of it. They'd undoubtedly cleaned up worse. She pulled on a slip-dress, without bothering to don underclothes, slipped on some shoes and hurried out the bedroom door. The cadet at the front desk paid her little mind. As a vampire, she was free to come and go as she pleased. Kieran had dismissed her medical escort, saying that he would bring her there himself, so she had free rein of the compound without question.

She made her way outside, and after a brief glance around, began to follow the road towards the front end of the compound. Behind her were only the houses of the Senior Guard, and Suzluktan Saray. She knew nothing lay behind their fences except for a small bit of beach and the ocean. She headed for the thin strip of trees that separated the houses of the senior guard from the townhouses and apartments of the lower coven members, towards the direction most likely to lead her out.

With the perimeter fence in her sights, she ducked behind a tree. Assured no one was near, she pulled off her dress, kicked off her shoes and stowed them in a bush. Now came the moment of truth. She forced herself to stand still and try to relax for a moment. If this didn't work, all of her efforts had been for nothing.

She took a deep breath, and then allowed her body to break apart, melting in on itself and then dispersing into a million particles of dust and mist. It felt amazing, so satisfying to be free of form. It dulled the pain of her recently emptied toothpick wounds and gave her an unparalleled sense of relief. She felt beyond bodily bonds of physical structure and discomfort. If only she could float away, a simple cloud untroubled by earthly restraints...but that was not her talent.

Already she felt the pulling and tugging that would inevitably force her to combine her particles into a form. She longed to form the wolf, but knew that would be a mistake. A wolf could not get through the fence to escape. It would have to be the form she dreaded. She became the bat.

Smaller than her other forms, she condensed her body matter into the size of a housecat. Her face was vaguely reminiscent of her wolf, with its long snout and large, upright ears. The flying fox, this bat was sometimes called, and it did resemble a fox, as its large almond shaped eyes could narrow to give the impression of a fox's clever cunning. When shifting to glittering red, to use her vampiric spectrum of sight, they gave the beautiful creature a look that was almost demonic.

Her toes were long, curved and claw-tipped, and could almost be used as hands; her feet were made for gripping branches and things more than walking, but it was the new size and shape of her arms that was most strange to her. They stretched out quite far, almost similar to her arms as a human, giving her a wingspan of five and a half feet, just a bit less than her height as a human. Below her strong shoulders, she still had elbows, wrists and even fingers, although they ended in claws that were elongated far past their once human length, and could not be separated individually. Only her thumb stuck out, an independent claw that could be used for gripping things. As her other fingers splayed out wide, thin but incredibly strong folds of skin between them formed truly magnificent wings. They connected from the tips of her fingers all the way down the sides of her body to her ankles. She could close them around herself like a cape, or spread them wide for flight.

The problem was, she couldn't really fly. It was a technique comprised of dozens of intricate calculations, instincts and muscle movements she was not born to and had not even come close to mastering as of yet. It frightened her terribly, and this animal that could be so beautiful in the air was odd, awkward and difficult for her to manage on the ground. That's why she rarely used the form. To be awkward and floundering was to be vulnerable, and her flying fox had only needed to fall prey to a true fox one time before shying her away from practicing the form further.

She stretched herself out, assessing the form again, before suffering a sudden surge of panic over her lack of protection here on the ground. She crawled closer into the bushes, trying to conceal herself as she observed the fence not far from her. It was a tall, black, iron fence of smooth vertical bars spaced about a foot apart, topped with decorative, but vicious looking, spikes. All she needed to do was to get through, cross the ten foot gap, and then squeeze through the outer perimeter fence to freedom.

It was the ten foot gap that worried her. She knew that it was patrolled by Arif's guard dogs, Doberman Pinschers that had been raised from birth being given small amounts of vampire blood to secure their loyalty and boost telepathy with their master and those who handled them. Sindy was going to make quite a spectacle flapping and crawling her way across the gap to the outer fence. She could only hope that the guard dogs were busy elsewhere.

She was about to make for the fence, when she heard people approaching, more specifically, vampires. Their marks were bared, but even without seeing their auras, Sindy would have recognized the two women immediately. Maribeth and Lorelei strolled down the path in her direction.

Maribeth was walking casually, absently twirling the end of her long copper braid of hair draped over her shoulder, as she observed the manicured grounds around her. The lovely, landscaped, park-like setting of the compound was broken into sections by small strips of forest dividing the different housing units from one another. The women were just approaching the bit of woods where Sindy was hiding. "I haven't been down this far before. Where are we going?" Maribeth asked her companion.

Lorelei was intently studying the fence-line as they walked, making Sindy much more nervous from where she crouched hidden within a bush. "I thought we'd visit the kennels."

Maribeth's face became pinched in displeasure at the thought. "I don't like animals," she complained. "I was forced to exist on a farm for a time, you know. Dirty, smelly, needy things, animals are."

Lorelei laughed. "These aren't farm animals, they're dogs; big, strong, smart and dangerous dogs. I think you'll like them."

"I doubt it, but if you insist."

At this point, they had entered the patch of trees, and passed by Sindy's place of hiding. She breathed a sigh of relief for not being seen. Good, maybe the women would be keeping the dogs busy elsewhere, giving Sindy a better chance at avoiding them. She gave them some time to reach their destination before venturing out from hiding. All was quiet, not a mark anywhere near her.

Sindy approached the fence and reached forward, gripping it with the tiny thumb-claws protruding from the top arch of each wing. She pulled her body forward and then turned sideways, squeezing herself through between the bars. It was tight, but she fit without much problem. It felt comfortable to tighten her claws around the bars and she longed to climb up them to a height of safety, but the fence was made of smooth, tall, vertical bars that were difficult to grip and climb unpracticed without sliding back down.

Sindy carefully observed her surroundings. The space between the fences offered no shelter whatsoever. There was nothing but grass, which had been mostly trampled down the middle into a dirt track from the constant patrolling by the dogs.

She jumped a bit as she heard some sudden frantic barking from off in the distance. The dogs were barking, from down towards the kennel. It didn't sound like ominous barking though. It was more the noise of animals begging for attention and treats. Lorelei was presumably egging them on, trying to show them off to Maribeth. Good, keep them all nicely occupied!

Sindy focused on the fence across the path and began to make her way there. After a step or two of awkward crawling, instinct wanted her to spread her wings and fly. She did so, managing to loft her weight a foot or two off the ground. She wasn't very coordinated, but it was better than actual crawling. She fluttered and floundered her way across with hopping jumps of brief flight.

She was almost there when a new sound approached, making her momentarily freeze in fear. The loping, galloping sound of a dog, running at full speed. How could it be coming up on her so fast without warning? Shouldn't she have seen its mark? She realized, belatedly, that the dogs must not have been fed enough vampire blood to carry their own marks; they hadn't truly been turned. Drinking blood from a dish wouldn't inject them with venom for marking, and these were not the vampire wolves of Khalon's coven that she was used to running the woods with, they were just dogs...with a bit of a boost in intelligent telepathy.

She jumped into the air, hoping a last good burst of flight would carry her to the fence. She did reach the bars, but not before the dog was upon her. It was a large, black Doberman Pinscher, with classic rusty/tan colored markings and alert, cropped-upright ears; a female. The dog was fairly tall and impressive, not too massive in size, but from Sindy's point of view, more than large enough to command frightened respect; about 75 lbs. of lean and mean pure muscle. The animal came into view and then pulled up short to a sudden stop, seeming very surprised to see a bat in its territory. It hadn't known she was there or been running to catch her, it had been heading to the kennels so as not to miss whatever commotion was happening there.

Sindy used the dog's pause of surprise to her advantage. She reached forward with a wing, grabbing a bar with her claw and tried desperately to pull herself forward and through. She had her body wedged between the bars, but couldn't be lucky enough to squeeze through out of danger before the dog regained composure from its surprise. It snapped for her, and

Sindy let out a squeal of pain as the dog's teeth bit down on her trailing wing, piercing through the thin flesh and ripping it as she was dragged back through the bars. It tossed her to the ground and then pounced and gripped her more fully by the body before she had a chance to scramble away. The bitch lifted her from the ground to shake her wildly. It was terrifying and disorienting, but Sindy had experienced this sort of treatment before.

This time, she refused to let an animal get the better of her. She closed her eyes and concentrated on disassembling her body. As her form disintegrated into mist, she was able to float up and away from the dog's snout, amidst the dusty dirt being kicked up from the ground during the dog's actions. She floated in a direction that she desperately hoped was towards the fence, unused to navigating in this state, but was forced to reform before she reached it.

The dog snapped its jaws in confusion as to where its mouthful had disappeared to, before it found her again and began barking in confused alarm at her eminent escape, focusing on the large dark cloud separating from the settling dirt. This dog was smart enough to understand that the smoke was somehow related to its former prey, and it was not about to give up and back down. Sindy allowed herself to become human for a moment, hoping that her sudden size would induce some confusion and give her some slight authority over the dog.

Sindy found herself up against the fence as she regained human shape, leaning on the bars, naked and human. It certainly did confuse the dog for a moment, but it took only a quick assessment for them both to determine that Sindy's soft skin was going to be no match for the dog's sharp teeth and powerful jaws. Her forearm was already gashed and bleeding from the hole the dog's fangs had made through her wing as the bat, along with other scrapes and bruises. The dog did a sort of double-take, and then began to bare its teeth in a snarl accompanied by a low rumbling growl that sent shivers down Sindy's spine.

"Sit! Stay," Sindy told the dog with as much authority as she could muster, as she tried to inch away from the animal. Sindy almost thought she could hear the animal's amused response in her head. *I don't think so...*

The dog lunged for her, and she dispersed into mist just in time to avoid the snapping bite of its jaws. The animal was stunned, as its forceful jaws clacked together on thin air. Sindy floated herself up and away, as far as she could manage, before being forced to take form again. This time, she had the wolf in mind.

Sindy's large black wolf was slightly bigger than her adversary, especially when accounting for her raised hackles and fluffed fur as compared to the Doberman's sleek, short coat. The wolf stood in the center of the space between the fences, the dog now standing between her and freedom. Sindy bared her fangs at the dog and began to circle away from it, trying to get close to the outer fence again, head low, hackles high, and a growl of her own coming from deep within her throat.

The Doberman was thoroughly surprised to suddenly find itself facing another canine. She backed up a bit, nostrils flaring as she tried to catch the scent of the unexpected wolf that now stood before her. The wolf's front leg had a deep gash in it, the carried over wing injury that hadn't had time to heal, and was now beginning to bleed. Her blood betrayed her scent as being the same person throughout, despite her form.

Sindy gave off another snarling growl, warning the dog to back down. The Doberman responded likewise again, undeterred, and seemed reassured when answering barks began coming from another pair of dogs approaching from the kennel. Apparently, this telepathic guard dog was taking no chances; she had called for back-up.

Sindy was almost up against the fence again; not a smart position to get herself backed into if she were planning to fight, but at this point, fighting was not her plan. The Doberman took a menacing step towards her, recognizing that she was trapped. Although she had some experience in fighting other wolves, Sindy wasn't sure how she would measure up against this vicious guard dog, and she wanted no part of dealing with the bitch's approaching pack-mates; all she really wanted was a chance to escape. She lunged forward with a ferocious, rumbling snap, hoping to back the bitch up and give herself some room.

The dog did jump back a little, although not seeming nearly as intimidated as Sindy would have liked. Sindy took the moment of respite to transform one last time. She barely had enough energy left to accomplish it, and couldn't manage to steer her clouded self through the bars, but rose up out of reach and formed the bat once more.

In mid-air she took shape and immediately started flapping her wings. She may not be a talented or experienced flyer, but those large wings gave decent lift, even with a tear in her skin from the dog's prior bite. It was enough to get her up over the beast's head. She threw herself against the fence and clung to it, attempting an only partially backwards-sliding climb higher up the bars and hopefully out of range of snapping jaws. Just a little further and she would reach the horizontal bar than ran across the top, securing the vertical bars together, just below their nasty spikes. As she reached the bar, she pulled herself up and then getting her hind claws onto it, pushed off it, flapping her wings and giving herself a nice boosting lift up past the spiked top of the fence and into the sky. She did it! She was flying!

Something hard thwacked into her back, nearly knocking the wind from her and messing up her newly begun rhythm of flight. Someone had thrown a rock at her! She lost height but flapped frantically, trying valiantly to recover her lift.

Another rock whizzed past her head, breaking her concentration, and then a third struck her wing. She wobbled precariously with dread certainty that she was never going to recover her flight now. Dizzy and disoriented, Sindy found herself plummeting towards the ground. She was awkwardly flapping and struggling just to lessen the blow of her fall.

Someone grabbed at her legs. She lost what little height she still had and felt a glancing blow against her. A hand had reached up and swatted at her, smacking her down to the ground.

"I got it!" Someone reached towards her and all Sindy could think to do was snap at the hand while trying to decide if she should shift form, or attempt to launch herself into the air again. The dog had been joined by two of its pack mates, and all three were barking incessantly so that she couldn't even hear herself think.

"Katil, down," a voice commanded. It was Lorelei, ordering one of the dogs to silence, but her voice was behind Sindy, on the other side of the fence. "Don't let it get away!" Lorelei pleaded desperately.

Sindy tried to back up, crawling out of her opponent's immediate reach. It was Maribeth who stood above her, seeming hesitant to grab for her again. Instead, she brought down her shoe upon Sindy's body, holding her in place and restricting her movement. "What is it?" Sindy flapped her wings as best she could and hissed at the woman, hoping to frighten her into retreat.

Lorelei yelled through the fence. "It's a shifter. Hold on to it!"

"The beastly thing tried to bite me!"

Her chances for escape quickly slipping away, Sindy gathered her energy for one last effort and turned herself to mist once again. As she did, Maribeth lifted her foot in surprise and Sindy was able to siphon herself away from the woman. Now she could become the wolf and take off into the forest, without the others having any hope of catching her again!

Sindy's strong, dark wolf began to take its furry shape, when she suddenly felt herself restricted. *No! She was so close!* It felt as though all power was flowing out of her and she found herself lying on the ground, settling into shape as a human woman instead. Lorelei breathed a sigh of relief. "That's alright. Jin's got her now."

Jin...the vampire must have been called, and was just getting into her range, in time to strip her of her powers and any chance to disappear into the woods. Sindy was exhausted from her escape attempt. Shifting form took an incredible amount of energy, and she hadn't drunk nearly enough human blood to support all of this activity, but she sat up, wondering if she could manage to run from Maribeth even while locked in human form. She could not give up now; after all her work to be free, it couldn't end like this! Would the woman try to stop her?

Sindy shakily got to her feet, steadying herself and tensing her muscles to run. Maribeth observed her with a haughty and detached sort of curiosity that made Sindy think the woman wouldn't be inclined to give chase. Without another moment's hesitation, Sindy sprang into action, sprinting in the direction of the forest as fast as her shaky legs would carry her. She glanced over her shoulder to see that, as predicted, Maribeth didn't bother to follow, but before Sindy could feel elated over the observation, she smacked into something almost as solid as tree, although less rigid and far more interested in her escape attempt.

It was a very large, strong vampire, who immediately grabbed her by the shoulders. She recognized the man as one of those who had helped Arif chain her to the bed. Sindy went wild, pulling and screaming, to no avail. Another vampire came to help hold her and she didn't stand a chance. Jin came to lend a hand as she was dragged back towards the fence, kicking and yelling at them to let her go. Finally, she was dumped on the ground at Maribeth's feet, closely surrounded by the men.

Was nothing ever destined to go her way? Sindy blinked in disbelieving defeat and looked up to find Maribeth smiling down at her, as she gave Sindy a light little shove with the toe of her shoe. "Well, well. Look who it is. One of Cain's strays."

Lorelei came to lean against the fence behind them. "You know her?"

Maribeth looked as though she was surprised and amused by this turn of events. "I do. Isn't she the one usurping your place in Arif's bed?" she asked Lorelei. Her tone tried to make the question seem innocent, but even Sindy could decipher it to be a thinly veiled barb used to tweak Lorelei's ego. "If she wants to flee, I say let her. Good riddance to the tawdry little trollop."

Lorelei recovered her poise of authority as she noted the amusement of Jin and the guards over the exchange. "Let her go? That would be against direct orders. We'll bring her to Arif...but I suppose there's no rush.

Perhaps we should play with her for a bit first," she said with an evil grin, stroking the head of Katil, the dog who sat obediently next to her, eyeing Sindy through the fence and licking her chops.

Jin seemed to share her interest in the idea, but Maribeth scolded them both. "Nonsense. Don't sully yourself with this strumpet...it's beneath you. Take her to Arif then...immediately."

Jin nodded. "Yes Ma'am."

Lorelei questioned Jin, insulted. "Since when do you answer to her?"

Jin grabbed Sindy's wrist firmly for escort and replied to Lorelei with barely a pause. "Since you're no longer head of the guard and her age out-ranks you. I agree; she should be taken to the Master immediately."

Lorelei eyed Jin and Maribeth angrily, but seemed to decide she should back down before her ego became further bruised. "Fine, take her. Make sure you tell him that I was the one who pre-empted her escape." She squinted at Sindy with a wicked leer. "I'll be sure to come visit you later, batgirl."

Maribeth spoke to Jin as one of the guards took Sindy's other arm, rather roughly, and the men began to force Sindy towards an entry gate further down the fence. "Handle her with care," Maribeth ordered. "I'm sure your Master would like the honor of disciplining her personally."

Jin seemed a little surprised by the plea, but nodded. Sindy knew she was in for some severe trouble, but was surprised to hear Maribeth speak on her behalf. Maribeth noticed her confusion. "Cain can thank me for you later."

~~~~~~~~~~~~~~~~~~~~~~~~~~~~~~~~

Sindy decided not to relay the episode to Ben. She wasn't even sure if he knew she was a shifter, and he didn't need the details. "Maribeth and Lorelei are vampires who work for Arif," she clarified.

Ben expression was very cold and stern. "I know who they are."

"You do?" Sindy questioned him in surprise.

"Maribeth doesn't actually work for him...she's just there."

"I know. I was simplifying. I guess Cain's mentioned her to you?" Ben nodded. "And how do you know Lorelei?"

Ben continued to stare at her with a grim look of anger, fiercer than she'd ever remembered seeing from him...and he'd been mad at her a lot. "Besides my new hatred for Arif, Lorelei has the unique distinction of being the only vampire that I've ever hated more than you."

Sindy raised her eyebrows and chuckled in surprise. "What an honor."

Ben didn't seem inclined to elaborate. He went on without explaining his reasons. "So they prevented your escape, brought you to Arif, and he bit you," Ben surmised, "putting you under his control."

His words inadvertently brought the memory of the moment to her mind. Arif had been furiously fuming over her attempted escape, but she had still held the slight hope that he might somehow respect her for trying. *"Did you really want a consort that was subservient and weak? Someone your coven would never respect? I see the appeal of what you're offering me, and I would stand at your side, but the toothpick shit has got to stop. You can't keep trying to control me. Think of how impressed the coven would be if I obeyed and adored you* without *wearing your mark!"*

Arif hadn't even bothered to consider her words. He'd laughed at her and bared his fangs with a smile. *"I don't need to impress them further, and I don't want them to respect you. What I want, is for you to be marked as* mine.*"*

Sindy shuddered, pushing the memory of Arif overcoming Cain's mark and piercing her throat, out of her mind. She refocused on Ben, sitting before her. "Yeah, they caught me and he bit me. That's the gist of it."

"So, how do I know he isn't listening in, or controlling you now?"

"He's not."

"Really? Because this is the most civil you've been to me in years."

Sindy opened her mouth in insulted outrage before finding the words to speak. "You think the only way I could be tolerable, is if I'm being puppeteered by somebody else? That's a whole new level of insulting. He isn't controlling me and he isn't lurking in my head...at least I don't think so," she added, uncertainly.

"But you don't know. You can't tell, can you? That's not your *gift.*"

"No. Sorry, I don't have much experience being connected with a telepathic vampire. I mean, I could tell when Allie read my mind, but that was different."

"Allie?" Ben asked in disbelief. He seemed surprised to hear that they'd been in contact. Sindy had to smile.

"All the time." She wondered what he'd make of the fact that she and Allie had actually become pretty good friends. He'd probably consider it proof that Allie was evil now for sure.

"Why was that different?" he asked.

"Because Allie never drank my blood. Look, I'm sure at this point Arif has decided that I've been dumped out of the action and he's got better things to focus on, but if you're worried he's listening, then don't talk to me, okay? Just answer me one question. How did I get here? Last I remember, I was talking to Cain. Where'd you come from?"

"*Do* you remember? *Everything* I mean."

Sindy averted her eyes and sighed. "You mean when I was under Arif's mind control? Yeah, I remember. Can't say I'm happy about it, but I didn't have a choice. It's like that, you know?"

Ben seemed to cringe. "All too well."

Sindy looked at him in surprise. What did he know about vampiric mind control? As far as she knew, *she* was the only vampire to have ever bitten Ben, and true mind control wasn't one of her talents, unfortunately. Ben wore no mark now. "Have *you* ever been…?" she asked.

He quickly shook his head. "No. Felicity. Apparently, Arif can get into a human's mind without biting them. I saw her, when I met with Arif. We spoke. I think *he* wrote most of the script."

Sindy widened her eyes, remembering the meeting Arif had taken Felicity out for. "That must have been a fun conversation…for him. Pretty shitty for you I'd imagine."

Ben lightly nodded without giving the memory any more thought. "Yeah. Anyway, Cain showed up with you tonight and you, um…collapsed. Cain asked me to take care of you for him, so I brought you here."

Sindy rubbed the aching sore spot on the back of her head with a raised eyebrow. "Collapsed, huh?" Ben didn't bother to confirm or deny the account. After all she'd been through, did it really matter? "Why would you help Cain?"

"I'm just keeping you out of the way. He didn't want to leave you alone."

"So you took me in for him? Aren't you the boy scout? Wasn't he worried you'd dust me?"

"A little," Ben replied with a grin.

"Plan to?" she asked with a quiet lilt of curiosity. Ben shrugged, as though he hadn't yet made up his mind, although she was sure it was just for show. Ben wasn't the indecisive type. If he'd really wanted to get rid of her, he would have done it while she'd slept.

"When all of this is over with, I plan to hand you back over to him in exchange for my wife," Ben explained.

She had to wonder if he might be explaining his reasoning more for Arif than for her, but she really didn't think Arif was listening, at least she hoped not. "What if Cain doesn't want to trade Felicity for me?" She had asked the question just to irk Ben, but as she voiced it, she realized it could be a true concern.

Ben glared at her for suggesting the scenario. "Then I guess you're going to have a problem, because I sure as hell don't want you."

Anymore, she added mentally. "I guess times have changed." She looked him over, still adjusting to the age difference. "We haven't even seen each other since..."

"The gym," Ben supplied for her.

"Right...we fought those vamps in the school gym. I was on your side for that one, you'll remember."

"I remember. I still had your mark from when you bit me," he added bitterly.

"Still sore over that, huh?"

Ben's gaze bore into her uncomfortably. He seemed to be trying to gain some unknown information from her appearance. "Are you really the same Sindy?" he finally asked, quietly.

She squinted at him. "Who else would I be? I told you, Arif isn't controlling me right now."

"I mean, are you still the same Sindy *I knew*...the Sindy who was human; or is she dead? Are you something new, taking over her body, or is she still in there?"

Ah...the Sindy he used to want, before she'd become taboo... Sindy sighed. Jeez, was he really going to get into this? "The Sindy you knew?" she asked, sarcastically. "She was weak. She worried about what other people thought. She was too fragile, even under the act she tried to put on to keep people from prying. She allowed herself to be backed into situations and have things done to her that she never should have had to endure," Sindy spat out, harshly.

"I know..."

"No, you don't," she barked back at him. "But then she made it stop. She got bit, and then she got turned...and it took some work, but then she got strong. She became independent and in charge of her own life... Yes...she died, but she was reborn, and she was finally okay, better than okay." Sindy paused, shaken. What had she done with her new freedom and strength? "And then she got cocky, and greedy, and once again, she let herself be backed into situations and have things done to her that she never should have had to endure," she said in aggravated realization. "So...yeah, I guess I'm still *exactly* the same. Is that comforting? Why don't you just dust me now and put me out of my misery?"

He just stared at her for a few moments, seeming almost sympathetic. She closed her eyes, her mouth a thin line of a grimace. When she opened her eyes again he was still just sitting there, watching her. "What, no cross in your back pocket today? No stake within reach? I guess you really have changed. The old Ben wouldn't have passed up the opportunity."

"Don't be so sure. The old Ben had his chances too. I'm just smart enough to make sure I have all the information before I do something irreversible...then and now."

Sindy smiled in amusement at his affected superiority. "I don't know, a couple of times there, you seemed pretty bent on killing me."

"Well, you really know how to piss me off."

"I do, don't I?" she agreed proudly.

"You never used to be like that, so I have to wonder, are you the girl I knew, or are you someone else now?"

"Maybe you just never really knew me."

"Maybe...but you've got to admit, you did a pretty good job of perpetuating my belief that vampires lose their souls and are not the people they were in life anymore after the change."

She sighed. "Okay, I probably wasn't the best version of myself when I came back. I went through some stuff and was pretty bent on vengeance at the time; not against you...at first, but that was the mindset. Like it or not, it was me then and it's still me now. Can't blame it on the blood. Turns out, I'm just a hot mess all on my own. Happy?" She didn't really give him a chance to respond. She wasn't in the mood for dredging up old stuff. "So why are you leaving Cain to rescue your girl while you're stuck here with me?"

Ben was obviously irritated over the matter. "The vampires have a plan and I'm not much of a player in it; but as long as it keeps Felicity alive, I don't care what they do. Let them drag Alyson to Arif and figure out how to make the trade. I trust Cain to handle it...for now. If I try anything, I'll get her killed."

"A bit of advice, make sure you're playing *some* part in it, because letting Cain do all the heavy lifting is only gonna look bad on you. Felicity is in there playing the piteous slave-girl and the only thing holding her together right now, is the idea that her big strong husband and his vampire-hunting dad are going to storm in there to save her."

That perked up Ben's interest. "You saw her in there?"

"Yeah," Sindy told him with a shrug. "We had a little chat."

"Is she okay? What do you mean by slave-girl? What's he doing to her? He said he wouldn't hurt her."

"She's fine. A little humiliated by the provided wardrobe maybe, but I don't think he's touched her or actually made her *do* anything. Relax. She's just being made to sit on the floor in the corner and look subservient. It's much better treatment than I got, believe me." Ben looked appropriately disgusted, not only with Arif, but with Sindy by association. Sindy caught his gaze, trying to redeem herself a bit. "I offered to try and help her."

"You did?" Ben asked with obvious skepticism.

Sindy slumped her shoulders with a sigh over Ben's disbelief that she might have done something decent for Felicity. "Yes, I did," she told him, defensively. "I'm not gonna say I treated her like my best buddy or anything, but I did want to try and get her out of there for you." Ben still didn't seem to be buying it. "I figured gaining some brownie points with vamp-hunters couldn't be a bad thing, right? I tried. It didn't work out though. I wasn't aware that I was on Arif's schedule for torture-time and it sort of messed up my opportunity to plan anything for Felicity."

"Oh..." Ben replied quietly. "They tortured you? I thought you were on their side."

"So did they. Arif got kind of cranky when he realized that wasn't really the case." Ben seemed to want details, but she just shrugged. "I survived. That's what I do. People turn my life to shit and I claw my way back up out of it. They say what doesn't kill you makes you stronger. At this point I'm fuckin' bullet-proof. I hope that's also the case for Felicity, because that girl could use a little backbone. What do you see in her anyway?"

"She's plenty strong, she's just been through a lot. You think I'd marry someone who couldn't hold their own? She's sensitive and a very caring person, but she knows how to keep me in line, trust me," he said with a laugh.

"She's like your *wife* now, huh? Does she cook you dinner and massage your shoulders after a hard day at work? Do you share all your secrets and snuggle under the covers on Sunday mornings, like they do in the movies? Living the dream?"

"Something like that." Ben looked away.

"And you guys have a kid?"

Now Ben's smile was undeniable as he nodded and answered. "A boy. Christian, he's six months old."

"Wow. A little Ben. A little baby boy to carry a piece of you forward in time." Sindy tried to ignore the imaginary biological clock that was pounding within her. The batteries had died in her clock twelve years ago. A few more years and she'll have been vampire longer than human. How long before these damn human instincts finally fade? "You're lucky."

"I know." She had the distinct impression that Ben was just realizing how lucky. "I need her back."

"If anybody can help her, Cain's your man. Don't worry, he'll save her. Cain's been waiting to be Felicity's hero for almost a decade. Of course, he'll find a way. You'd just better hope he's willing to give her back when he's done."

Ben gave her a look of annoyance and nodded. "He will." He was being so trusting. Not really a trait she remembered in him. Must have come with maturity, and too many years of safe complacency. He met her eyes again. "I don't know why you were trying to help her. I know it wasn't for me, and I'll bet it went far more badly than you'd bargained for, but thanks. I owe you one."

She had just wanted to make sure he didn't feel inclined to dust her. She hadn't expected him to be grateful. Now she felt kind of guilty for exaggerating her effort to help. She'd been pretty mean to Felicity, really, and Ben was being pretty decent to her, considering. She looked at him oddly. "Ben, think back a moment. I had you kidnapped. When you rejected me, I made Marcus beat the shit out of you. I drank from you in a publicly humiliating display and then I tortured you with your mark for weeks. I don't think you owe me. Come to think of it, I can't even say I'd blame you if you put me under the skylight on purpose."

He chuckled. "I didn't."

"I know."

"You killed Marcus for me," he reminded her.

Marcus, now there was a monumental mistake. The guy had been a criminally insane murderer, in a medically induced coma, when she'd snuck into the hospital and turned him into a vampire. Not her smartest decision. She'd eventually beheaded him just as he had been about to attack Ben. "He needed killing."

Ben lowered his eyes from her, in contemplation over other past hurts and transgressions. He seemed to have decided that she really was the same girl that he had known all those years ago. She knew just what he was thinking. Was he really going to bring it all up now? *Don't go there Ben*, she silently begged. Finally, he met her eyes once again. "Before...before *everything*, I was pretty rotten to you."

She gave him a fierce and narrow stare for actually voicing it out loud. The sound of his friends laughing, the stab of ice through her human heart when she'd realized that he didn't want her anymore. It all came rushing back.

He had really liked her, she was sure of it. She'd even thought it was love... of the new, tentative, teenage exploration kind, anyway. She had always existed on the fringe of the kids at school, first as the shy and quiet girl who was afraid to speak to anyone, living in fear and shame over her secrets, then as the weird Goth girl who was trying to be someone new to escape her old life. Either way, she had never felt accepted, until...Ben.

He hadn't cared that she was unpopular. He'd taken the time to find out who she was and he'd made it plain that he wanted to get to know her even better. She'd opened up to him...a little. Not about the abuse she'd been suffering at home, she'd rather die than tell him that, but she had felt like he cared who she was inside.

Until that fateful day, when she had ruined everything. They'd been fooling around and she was into it, she really was. When Ben had touched her it had made her feel special and tingly inside, not dirty and shameful. Being with him felt right. He'd wanted to go all the way, his first time, and she hadn't planned to stop him. But after things had begun, he'd said something...a word, a phrase, something she hadn't wanted to hear or even remember now. He had suddenly reminded her of her dad. It had freaked her out, totally. A flashback had assaulted her and made her yelp and try to jerk away. When Ben had tried to comfort her and understand her distress, she hadn't even assured him that it wasn't his fault, she had just pushed her way out from under him and run...fast and far... She had taken off on him.

She couldn't face him. She'd waited out the weekend, figuring she would talk to him in school on Monday, but when she had gotten to school the damage had already been done. Ben must have said something to his friends, because everyone was staring at her and snickering as she'd gone by. Some jock called her a "tease." Another mumbled "crazy frigid bitch" as she'd walked past. Something was taped to her locker...it was a card from *Candy Land*, the children's board game. *Queen Frostine.*

And there was Ben, standing with a group of his friends, talking...laughing.

Ignoring the surge of old hurt and anger, she forced herself to meet his eyes without expression. "Yeah, you were a real dick."

He accepted it, but sought to explain. "I was hurt, but I didn't mean for it to get like that, not at all. I only told Davy, but I guess he told a few of the guys and it spiraled out of control. I shouldn't have let them be so mean to you. I should have stopped it. I shouldn't have told him at all."

"You think?"

He went on. "I guess it was wounded pride. You always seemed so into me, and to have you urge me on and then suddenly take off on me was pretty cold. Things had always been so intense between us, and then just as we're going all the way, you freak out on me? I felt like you'd strung me along on purpose."

Her mouth hung agape in silent outrage, before she let out a huff of breath and looked away. "Ben, this was ages ago. It's done. Who cares? Just drop it."

"Drop it? I never even got to talk to you about it. You took off, and the next time I saw you, you were dead. I lost my virginity to you, and you screamed and ran! I spent years thinking I'd done something wrong to you...hurt you or something. It really fucked with my head."

"Well, you can lay down the guilt. I was damaged goods long before *you* ever touched me. It was all me."

He could see that there was more to it...something she didn't want to explain. Tough shit. She'd been humiliated enough over the past few days to last a lifetime. She wasn't baring her soul any further to anyone...not for a long time.

Despite her lack of elaboration, he suddenly seemed to put some of it together on his own. "When you came back, you killed your dad, didn't you?"

She gave him an icy stare, but finally decided to answer. "Damn right, I did, nice and slow. He deserved every bit of pain and suffering I gave him. Doubt it?"

He was a bit shocked and repulsed by the admission, but she could see the sympathy in his eyes; horror over the realization of what really must have been going on. She hated that look. "No," he answered quietly. "When he was murdered, I suspected it was a vampire, but I never put it together. I wish you would have said something, before..."

"Save it. Would have, could have, should have... I wasn't strong enough to stand up to him until I came back. Then I did what I did." So now he knew. She wasn't planning to wallow in it. "You weren't supposed to know, but when I came to you, you *knew* I was a vampire and it freaked you out. I didn't even think you believed in the supernatural. I didn't think you would know...that you could tell. It totally threw me off and screwed up my plans. I never even had a chance to explain anything to you. You called me an evil demon!"

"You lived up to the name."

"How did you even know what vampires were?" she asked.

"A lot went down while you were away."

"No shit..."

"Mattie got turned."

"I know. I didn't know back then, but I've seen him since, with Allie."

"Did they tell you Davy was killed?"

"Your *good friend* Davy Bradshaw?" The one he'd confided in about her; the one who had spread the rumors...

"Yes, and he was a good friend. He didn't always use the best judgment, but he was a good friend."

"I'm sorry. What happened to him?"

"Vampires, what else? I used to think Mattie did it. It was right after he'd disappeared."

"*Mattie?* He would never!"

"Which fit in with my whole 'vampires aren't the same people anymore' theory..." he explained.

"Oh. I guess I could see you buying into that. It's even true sometimes."

"Yeah?"

"Not for me, though. I'm still me, just...a different version of me." It felt so good, natural, to be able to just sit here and have a conversation with Ben, someone who actually *knew* her. Even with the blanket held tented over her head, it was almost like old times, before he'd started treating her like a monster. "A better version," she proclaimed, trying to recapture some of her confidence.

Ben let out a small derisive laugh. "Better?"

"Yes. Well, maybe not always," she amended, "but I'm working on it,"

"Okay, well, here's a tip. Less homicidal would be a big improvement."

"I've figured that out. Though, I hear you're quite the killer yourself."

"Only vampires."

"Like father, like son?"

"No. Not at all."

"Good. Be yourself. I kind of liked the old Ben...before you crushed my heart. Just be a better version."

"I am." He met her eyes for a moment before he continued speaking. "You're right, all that stuff was a long time ago, but it shouldn't have ended up like that. I feel like I don't even know how we got here...to this, to you thinking I want to kill you, and me wondering if I do. Point is, I was a jerk, and I'm sorry."

She gave him a little half smile. Did he have any idea how good he used to make her feel? He'd been her refuge, proof that she wasn't worthless trash. Didn't he know how she'd felt about him? Why else would she have spent so much effort on him after she'd died? Stalker, psycho effort maybe, but still...

She gave a wounded little laugh. "Yeah. You were a jerk."

Ben didn't dispute it, but wouldn't quite let her give him all the blame. "I'm still not sure it warranted the way you stalked me and made my life hell for a while there," he asserted, "but I'm not going to stake you. I hurt you, you hurt me back. Now we're even."

Even? After everything she'd done to him, he considered them even? Not by a long shot! An aching cramp of thirst and pain flowed through her as she tried to shift position on the bed. Okay, the torture had been pretty bad, even if it hadn't really been for him. She could accept 'even'.

She gave him a mischievous little smile. "Yeah, we can be even. Unless you're feeling generous. I'd be awfully grateful for a drink." Ben sat back, seemingly in alarm, as his increasingly comfortable demeanor quickly vanished. She couldn't help but smile. He was still frightened of her, even if it was only on a subconscious level. Like she was in any position to do him harm!

She took her eyes off of him, trying to hide her smile and let him ease back into some small level of comfort. "Arif's coven really drained me," she confided in explanation. "I'm gonna take forever to heal from all of this, unless I get some fresh blood," she said with a glance down, meant to indicate her many injuries.

Ben's alarm faded into an expression of disturbed sympathy as he tried to discern what her injuries might be. He really couldn't see much while she kept the blanket tented over her head. "What did they do to you?"

She took a deep breath and exhaled it roughly as she mentally counted the trespasses against her. Besides the toothpicks…chained, repeatedly raped and beaten…mentally coerced into doing things she'd rather not recall, all of it beyond her control.

Maybe it was some sort of karmic payback. But she had never been quite so vicious to any of her victims or underlings, had she? She wouldn't try to justify the deaths on her hands, but she wasn't into maliciousness or pain. Her victims had died in a euphoric dream state and those she brought back she had given a chance at immortality. Didn't that count for something? She'd always liked to think they had enjoyed the things she'd done, even though she had been the one in control. It had seemed kind of fun, when she *hadn't* been the one on the receiving end.

"Let's just say they had a *lot* of fun," she muttered. Ben gave her a discerning stare that went totally unacknowledged by her. "Look, I don't really need to breathe, but I can't say I'm looking forward to spending the whole day stifled under this blanket. As much as I would normally enjoy spending the day in your bed, how about you show me to the couch?"

Ben smiled but then shook his head and rolled his eyes. "Skylights in the living room too."

Sindy squinted at him. "And you thought this would be a *good* place to take an unconscious vampire to recoup?"

"Sorry, I didn't have harboring injured vampires in mind when I bought it. As a matter of fact, I'll bet my therapist would say that I've subconsciously chosen a retreat filled with as much sunlight as architecturally possible."

Sindy smirked at him. "You have a *therapist?*"

Ben gave her a level stare. "Yeah. Thanks."

She grinned. Yeah, she could take credit for some of that. "Where the hell are we again?"

"My beach house."

"You have a *beach* house? So, in effect you own *two* houses?"

Ben nodded and shrugged. "The other's an apartment actually, in the city; Upper West Side, Manhattan Valley."

Sindy raised her eyebrows. "Must be doing pretty well for yourself."

"I do okay."

"Got any rooms that aren't dust-inducing death traps? Servant's quarters maybe?"

Ben laughed. "No servants. There's a guest room though; no skylight."

"A guest room? And yet your first instinct was to put me into *your* bed. Interesting."

He narrowed his gaze at her in reprimand. "This is the only room with a lock on the door," he explained.

"Still leaves me questioning your instincts, Benny," she teased. "You locked yourself in here *with* the vampire?"

"I promised Cain I'd protect you."

"I see. And who was gonna protect *you?*" she asked, shifting to smile at him, fangs bared. It shook him up a little. So cute. He reached behind him and produced a cross from the back pocket of his jeans. She laughed. "So, you do still carry one."

Looking through her vampiric vision, she couldn't help but notice the hot blood within him. She blinked and shifted back, licking her lips as her eyes turned from red to brown again. He moved his hand up on the cross revealing the bottom of it to her. He had chiseled the base into a stake.

"I'm prepared to protect myself just fine, even from you."

"Good to know," she said, echoing his words from before and then mouthing him a little kiss.

He shook his head. "How about we put you in that guest room now?"

"Lead the way." She sat up and tried to slide her legs over the edge of the bed while keeping the blanket over her head. Oh man, they still hurt…a lot. She let them dangle over the edge a moment. Ben must have removed her shoes last night, but she was still wearing the tunic dress and leggings Arif had put her in so her injuries didn't show. Still, it seemed amazing that her legs weren't swollen like balloons; they felt so heavy and aching as they hung down to the floor; dead weight. Then she realized…no blood. She had practically nothing in her, so they couldn't swell. Somehow, that wasn't very comforting.

She knew it was going to be useless, but she shifted her weight closer to the edge, tentatively touching her feet to the floor. She tried to bite back her small exclamation of pain. Without much blood to run on, she wasn't healing nearly as fast as she was used to. She gave Ben a look of apology. He was already standing at the door. "Maybe I'd better just stay here with the blanket, after all. I can't walk."

He took a step back to her, studying her legs where they dangled in the shadow of the bed. "I *saw* you walk, last night."

She gave him a look of annoyance. Like this was part of some stupid plan to stay in his bed? *He* had put her here! "What you *saw* was Arif *making* my body walk. It wasn't particularly pain free. My legs are toast. Trust me, there is no way."

He seemed to feel bad and came closer to inspect them. "Sorry. What's wrong with them? Is there something I can do?" He suddenly met her eyes with a little smile, as he surmised her answer before it was voiced. "*Besides* feed you."

He smelled so good. His scent brought the thick rich taste of his blood to her tongue as though she'd only just drunk from him. His blood was so good…that was one drink she would never forget. "Help me get them back on the bed."

He gingerly took both legs by the ankles and gently swung them back onto the foot of the bed for her. Luckily, most of it was still in shadow. Only the pillow was truly bathed in sunlight. She hid back under the covers and managed to wriggle and pull her leggings down around her ankles. She carefully moved her feet out from under the covers, trying to keep the pain at bay with slow, gentle movements. "Pull those off for me?"

"What are you doing?"

"Trying to assess the damage," she told him with another painful kick of her legs. He finally came and removed the leggings for her.

"Ow! Gentle," she reprimanded him. She scooched her dress back down past her thighs and pulled the blanket to hold tented over her head as she gazed at her poor battered legs. Although the toothpicks had left small scabbed marks up and down her limbs, and she still had some scratches, they weren't terribly bruised, but she knew that was the deceiving lack of blood within her.

Ben still seemed to think they looked awful, all the same. "Oh my God, what did they do to you?"

"Don't sweat the superficial stuff. That'll heal. It's the bones I'm worried about. Do they look straight to you?"

Ben was still staring at her face, his expression a mixture of disgust and sympathy. "He broke your legs? ...Because you tried to run away," he guessed.

"Actually, Arif specializes in breaking people's spirits. My legs were courtesy of Lorelei and a baseball bat." He just looked at her oddly, in disbelief, but soon realized she was dead serious. She nodded towards her legs as her arms continued to hold the blanket over her head. "Could you see if the bones feel straight? 'Cause if they're not, they'll heal all fucked up."

She wouldn't be able to shift shape until she dug all of the toothpicks out…again…a prospect that made her terribly nauseated just thinking about it. She couldn't go through that at the moment, even if Ben was willing to help her do it. She thought of how Ben might react to having to dig splinters of wood out of her ass, and was afraid to ask. "If my legs heal crooked, I'll have to break them again or be stuck that way for a while. I'd kinda like to get it right the first time."

Ben looked horrified by the idea. Yeah, she was too. He stooped to lightly run his hands over her left leg. At first, he seemed very hesitant to touch her. She wondered if she felt terribly cold to him; his hands felt *so* warm on her skin. After a moment of acclamation, he began to gently press his thumbs to the bone that ran down the top center of her lower leg as his fingers cradled either side of her calf. She tried very hard not to flinch away or gasp with the pressure. He was gentle, slowly moving his hands down her leg, from knee to ankle. He kept his eyes on her leg, but she couldn't keep her own from the intent expression on his face. He was all business surely, but it was so good to feel his hands on her again.

"I feel some bumps, but nothing really jagged out of place or anything." She just nodded and closed her eyes as he shifted his attention to her other leg. As his hands completed their explorations, she noticed that he rested them on her ankle, rather than remove them. "Seems okay. I'm no doctor, but they feel good."

She opened her eyes to meet his gaze with an amused smile. "Do they?" He immediately dropped his hands from her leg and gave her a warning glare. She gave him a more sincere smile. "Thanks."

"I'll carry you. You want me to make sure all the curtains are closed first?"

"No, that's okay. The blanket's good enough. I'll take it with me."

She wrapped the blanket about her head and shoulders as Ben slid his arm under her legs. She smiled and opened her shroud to let him slip his other arm around her back, underneath. He hesitated before leaning close to lift her. "We're not going to have a problem here, are we? Can you handle yourself, or am I going to regret this?" he asked, giving her a look of warning.

"Tempting...but I think I can manage to restrain myself, just this once."

"You'd better. Those fangs touch my throat, and I'll have to tell Cain you slipped and fell on my stake."

"I'm on my best behavior, I promise," she assured him with a laugh, as he lifted her strongly from the bed.

He seemed very surprised by her insubstantial weight. He looked at her oddly and shook his head in disbelief. "You're so light."

"It's this diet I'm on. I haven't had a decent meal in years," she quipped. He didn't seem to find it funny. She couldn't help but notice that he was trying not to hold her too closely. "Oh come on, Ben. I'm a vampire, deal with it. Acting like I've got cooties is a little insulting. If you're gonna hate me, it should be because of the shit I've done, not what I am."

Rather than answer, he hefted her more firmly in his arms and nodded his head towards the end of the blanket hanging down. "You'd better cover up; the living room gets pretty bright this time of day."

She reached over and pulled up the blanket to cover her face as he made his way out of the bedroom and into the hall. It felt so warm and secure, wrapped in his arms. She snuggled her face into his chest within the blanket. Wow, Benjamin Everheart, carrying her to safety; the knight in shining armor that she'd always hated him for not being. Never thought she'd see the day. Weird how things change. Trapped close within the blanket, his scent beckoned. Apparently, personal hygiene hadn't been a priority for the past few days; she couldn't consider it a turn off though. His sweat smelled of anxious worry...fear, and that always translated as prey. God, she was thirsty.

He put her down gently on the bed and went to draw the drapes. "There you go; all clear."

She poked her head out from under the blanket as he moved away from her. Not bad. Ben hurriedly cleared the end of the bed of the piles of folded clothes that had been on it, and had to clear a bunch of baby toys and things off the floor before he could find a place to put the stuff down. Evidently, the room wasn't used for much but storage. It was of a very nice size, well decorated. It looked like a room in a reputable hotel. "This is nice."

"The bathroom's right across the hall."

She smiled at her gracious host. "Thanks. I won't need it. What I need is a favor." He just stared at her quizzically. "Got a phone book?"

"I'm not sure. What do you need it for?"

"I'm drained, like dry, and I gotta tell ya, you're lookin' and smellin' *real* good. You have no idea the self-restraint I showed just now. Seriously, you should be impressed. So unless you *are* feeling generous, I need to get me some blood. *Now.*"

Ben had that amusing look of alarm again. So cute, really. "And you're thinking what…pizza delivery boy?" he asked with a sarcastic edge.

She laughed. "I wish. I need you to find me a butcher, stupid. Three quarts should do it. Be a good start anyway, I might be here for a while."

He seemed confused. "You can drink from… That'll be okay?"

"Unless you want to offer something better."

Ben had already pulled out his cell phone was looking up the number as he moved to the doorway with a little smile. "I won't be long."

~~~~~~~~~~~~~~~~~~~~~~~~~~~~~~~~~~~

Ben's deliciously masculine scent betrayed his return. He must have showered. His human scent was now masked with soap and deodorant, but she could still pick out the musky undertones that were uniquely Ben; wonderfully tempting to her. Sindy was lying on her back on the bed with her eyes closed, just enjoying the appetizing fragrance. It seemed a long time that she lay there with his presence inciting her thirst. He had arrived quietly and didn't speak, but her senses didn't lie; she'd been aware of his approach almost immediately.

She concentrated and could hear the very faint sound of his breathing…and his heartbeat. Although he wasn't marked, once she consulted her inner-vampiric sight, she could easily see the life-aura of his living presence standing next to the bed. What was he doing? She allowed her eyes to flick open, her sudden awareness making him jump with a guilty start. He seemed to have been staring at her chest. "Did you want something, or are you just enjoying the view?"

Ben became flustered and then sought to explain himself. "You don't breathe," he said with a vague gesture towards her chest.

She grinned. "Been observing pretty *intently* have you?"

He was flustered again. "No. I just...noticed." He raised the white paper bag that he held, for her attention. "I'm back from the butcher."

She sat up eagerly and then winced from the pain. Damn...still? Without any blood, her healing must have slowed to a human rate. Human blood was what she really needed to speed things up, but animal blood would be better than nothing. Ben put the bag down on the bed next to her. He looked pretty anxious to leave. "Wait a minute." He turned back to her hesitantly from the doorway. She glanced down at the bag. She could feel its coldness seeping through the blanket where it touched her leg. "I can't drink it like that."

He gave her a look meant to convey the depths of disgust that would come of her asking him to prepare it for her. She slumped her shoulders and tilted her head in defeat. He was going to make her beg? "Come on, Ben, please? I know I'm in no position to be picky, but I'm not *that* desperate. You've gotta warm it up for me." Ben gave her a hard stare. "If you want to bring the microwave in here, I would gladly do it myself. Otherwise, I need you to do it. Come on, it's no big deal."

"Yeah, for you," he replied in derision.

"Don't think of it as blood, it's like...gravy, without all the extra stuff. People put blood in gravy, why do you think they sell it?"

He closed his eyes and shook his head. "I really didn't want to know." He looked back to find her doing her best to achieve an expression worth his sympathy. After some eye rolling and a heavy sigh, he grabbed the bag.

She mouthed him a little kiss. "Thank you."

He wouldn't meet her eyes as he grumbled. "How long?"

"Not hot, just warm. If you put it in a mug, it should only take about a minute." He turned to leave the room. "Oh, unless they had it in the freezer. Then it might take more, and you might have to warm up the whole container first, so it'll pour easy. Even if it's not frozen, unless it's super fresh, sometimes it gets all congealed."

At the word 'congealed', Ben visibly flinched. He spoke in an angry grumble as he stormed out of the room. "*Now* you owe me!"

~~~~~~~~~~~~~~~~~~~~~~~~~~~~~~~~

"Knock, knock," Ben said, rapping on the open bedroom door.

Although lying in bed, Sindy was obviously awake. She smiled at his pronounced show of not quietly sneaking in or watching her this time. "Come in."

"How are you feeling?" he asked, coming closer to the bed. He was holding another mug of blood for her, she could smell it.

She lost her smile as she fidgeted to try to take the mug from him, and was reminded that her healing was going far too slowly for her taste. "Frustrated, pissed off, thirsty..." she answered, bitterly.

Ben froze, his hand stretched out hesitantly to offer her the blood as his brow furrowed in slight apprehension. "Not really what you want to hear from a vampire."

She couldn't watch him trying to hide his inherent uneasiness without being amused. It helped her forget the pain and bought back her grin. She took the mug, but made no move to drink from it. "Relax. I don't plan to take it out on you."

"Glad to hear it. I just thought I'd come and let you know that the sun's gone down," he informed her.

"I know." He threw a puzzled glance towards the windows he had meticulously covered for her. The curtains were heavy and did not give much clue as to the state of the sky. "I don't have to see it, I can just tell," she explained.

"Oh. Do you...get stronger at night?"

Sindy glanced down at her legs, still feeling battered and broken. "That'd be convenient, but no, not that I've ever noticed. I'm always strong," she told him, with a steady stare of conviction. "I just need to be runnin' on the right fuel. There's only so much that animal blood can do," she said, putting the mug down on the nightstand rather than drinking from it. "It helps, but human would be better."

Ben gave her a look of warning. "I am *not* feeding you."

"Okay," she told him with a lilt of surrender. "Just trying to get myself out of your hair. I don't like being stuck here on the side-lines, any more than you like having to play Florence Nightingale to me." Whoever would have thought Ben would be nursing her back to health? She had to chuckle at the thought.

"What's so funny?"

"You... You, Cain, Elric, Kieran...even Zach to an extent; well, it just occurred to me that I am the most lethally dangerous babe that you will ever meet, yet somehow I keep ending up injured, with doe-eyed do-gooders trying to take care of me. Am I putting out a vulnerable vibe or something? 'Cause I've really got to find a way to put an end to that."

"Or...stop doing stupid shit that gets you injured. Trust me, when I think of you, *vulnerable* is not the word that comes to mind," he assured her with a smirk.

"No, but you've had some other choice words for me over the years, haven't you? You know, people are always calling me a bitch, and I won't say it isn't usually well deserved, but let me tell you something. You'd be cranky too, if you had to go through even half the shit that I've had to endure! After a certain amount of hell, you just don't have the patience for being nice anymore. I do whatever it takes to look out for *me*, and I'm not going to coddle everyone around me while I do it."

"Looking out for yourself... is that how you managed to get both your legs broken?"

She squinted at him in disdain. "No. As a matter a fact, I'm ultimately paying for trying to do a good deed for your friend Allie. See? This is why I'm not nice to people."

"For Allie?" he asked in surprise.

"Nevermind."

"You were with Cain, right? I'm not a fan, but at least he isn't violently vindictive...or so I'm told. I don't understand why you would leave him to go side with someone who would allow this to happen to you," he said with a gesture towards her legs.

"Arif had something that I thought I wanted."

"Did you get it?"

"I decided it wasn't worth the price...and that was *before* he started letting people beat the shit out of me," she told him with a mirthless laugh. "You know, all my life has been about negotiation, voluntary or not. Men use my body, and it gets me things...safety, shelter, power, blood...

I'm just a puppet. Men slip inside and make me do what they want, and I always figured it was a fair exchange to get whatever I needed. But Arif..." she said with a shudder, "he's the Master Puppeteer. I thought I'd let him play with me and I'd get what I wanted. I could have... I could have just let him use me. I've done it so many times in the past, but *his* manipulation is so literal, so complete, I realized that nothing I wanted could be worth suffering it. Maybe all I really wanted was to cut the strings once and for all...you know, like Pinocchio; be my own real person.

I'm tired of negotiating trades. Even when I was the puppeteer, luring in men and forcing them to obey my commands, it wasn't real, it was just a puppet show. I was just going through the motions." Ben nodded, a look of disgust on his face as he remembered how she had led her coven of lackeys around and ordered them to do things for her...things like attacking him.

She tried to make him trust that she understood how distasteful it seemed. "You know, I don't do that shit anymore. I cut them all loose and left it behind. For a while there, I was tasting shame-free independence, and it was pretty sweet. It may not come with power-trips and pampering, but it felt good, all the same. Why didn't I value it more when I had it?" she asked rhetorically, kicking herself for her short-sightedness. "Arif came along and offered me that powerful puppet position, and I jumped at it, out of reflex more than anything, I think. I should never have taken the bait. I should have trusted myself not to need it anymore; not to need anyone."

"Don't be so hard on yourself. Everybody needs someone. There's no shame in not wanting to be alone."

"Maybe, but no more puppets and puppeteers. I'm done with the whole exchange."

"There's always an exchange...of trust, friendship, love, but it doesn't have to be a negotiation, it's a relationship. It's not easy to nurture one, because there's always give and take. A lot of times you have to put someone else's needs above your own, because it's based on love and respect, not selfish gain."

"Respect?" she repeated with a lilt of humor. "Yeah, that is probably the one thing that has been largely missing from my past relationships."

"It's not easily earned or given, but it can be worth it. Allow yourself to give and accept that; you deserve it; everyone does."

"Wait a minute, Benjamin Everheart thinks *I* deserve respect?" She wasn't used to seeing this understanding, tender side of him...trying to comfort her. It felt like the old days, when her only problems that he'd known about had been high school cliques and mean girls. "And we're not talking about a healthy respect for the fact that I could bite and kill you right now, before you could even react...right?" she asked, unable to resist letting her eyes flash red momentarily, reminding him that she wasn't the helpless girl she used to be when he'd last tried to comfort her. "You mean like real, mature, respect?"

He leaned back a little, causing her to grin. "Don't be too flattered. There are a lot of things that I despise about the way you've conducted yourself. You've killed people, innocent people. And there is still a part of me that will forever hate you for making me live in fucking terror for almost six months, while you stalked me, marked me and constantly threatened to turn me into a mindless zombie slave."

She broke eye contact. It sounded so awful when you put it like that... She didn't usually allow herself to try to think of things from his perspective. "I wasn't going for mindless zombie. I wanted you to be a strong vampire, like me."

He ignored her and continued. "But there are still some things, some small things, that I respect and admire about you."

"Really?" she asked with hopeful curiosity. "Like what?"

"Well, for one thing, you're stubborn, like me. You know what you want and you don't give up. I'd like that quality much better if it wasn't aimed at me half the time, but I've got to admire your tenacity. You are strong. I just hope you've learned to make sure that you're going after the right thing, before you lock your stubborn sites on something."

She laughed. "Yeah, lesson learned, and leave it to me to learn the hard way. I think I'm going to value my independence for a little while, and maybe look before I leap next time."

"Good plan. So, Miss Independence, how long until you don't need my guest room anymore, do you think? No offense, but I fully expect to be bringing my wife home tonight, and I'm not sure she'd be thrilled to have you here for the homecoming."

She stalled her answer, reclaiming the mug of pig's blood to take a sip, but finding it had already gone cold. She wrinkled her nose in distaste. "Well, this shit is better than nothing, but it sure isn't the healing elixir my body was hoping for, so I can't make any promises. Animal blood can only help so much. I might be here for a while."

"Again, I'm not feeding you."

"I know. That's fine. And if you want to kick me out, that's fine too. I know you were doing Cain a favor by giving me a safe haven for the day, but it's not like you're obligated to keep looking after me. I'll take what's left of the blood you bought me and find someplace else to hole up for a night or two until I'm healed enough to hunt for myself."

"Hunt?"

"Animals. Human blood works quicker, but I mostly make do with animals these days. It's much stronger when I can drink it live."

"What kind of animals? How do you... Nevermind, I don't really want to know. Is there someplace I can drop you off...someplace else you can go?"

"You don't have to act all concerned. I'm not your problem."

"You're injured. I can't send you out the door when you can barely even walk. Besides, I told Cain I'd take care of you, and I meant it. That doesn't mean getting by with the bare minimum. If you haven't got anyplace else to go and you need to stay here until Cain can come for you, so be it. I expect him to follow through on his promises to me.

He really cares about you, you know. He knew you were under Arif's control, but he wouldn't abandon you, and he had no idea what you went through, I'm sure. If he'd known, he would have taken care of you himself."

"I know he would have. It's not like he hasn't done that and more for me in the past." Sindy felt a slight chill as she remembered the time her stomach had been ripped open by a Crimson Coven wolf and Cain had healed her. He had drained himself of blood, pouring it into her wounds and feeding it to her until her injuries had disappeared. She had never felt so truly loved and cared for.

The memory made Sindy freeze as it caused a nagging idea begin to tug at her thoughts. Her eyes suddenly widened with realization. "Oh my God. I know how it happened."

"How what happened?"

"Zach! I wouldn't let Allie make Zach because we didn't want her to give him white eyes, but then when I made him, his eyes turned white anyway, and now I know why!"

"Who's Zach? I haven't even got the vaguest idea what the hell you're talking about," Ben told her with a grimace of confusion. "Want to fill me in?"

"You wouldn't get it. It doesn't matter to you anyway."

Sindy ignored Ben's questioning as she thought through her suspicions. Vampire blood is made up of not only the same substance as that of a human's blood, but also carries within it microscopic organisms capable of directing and controlling it's host to an extent; the 'beings' responsible for directing and initiating change when a person is turned into a vampire. These organisms take up residence within a body, remaining there indefinitely, until passed into another body while being drunk during a bite.

Cain had given Sindy his own vampire blood - lots and lots of it. But it wasn't only Cain's... Cain had been existing in a coven with Alyson and Mattie for years. The three of them drank each other's blood often. She knew that they did, because they shared a mark of the coven as proof. Cain's blood had been regularly mixing with Alyson and Mattie's for so long now, that he must have just as much blood of The United One in him as Allie did; and then he had given it to Sindy.

That special blood couldn't do much of anything in her. She was already a vampire, and once changed, her body could not be made to work differently than it did upon her initial awakening from human death. The powers she had when she was made were her only abilities for eternity. There was always the possibility she had not yet discovered all she was capable of, but if it wasn't built-in during her death, she couldn't gain a new talent now. So, the powerful blood of the United One could do nothing but exist within her...until she made a new vampire.

That's what it wanted, what it waited for. When she gave her blood to someone else, the vampire organisms within her surely jumped at the chance to inhabit a new body, and when that body was turned into a vampire, they were able to transform it into the same sort of powerful creature that Allie had become; a vampire of all breeds, United. That was why Zach had white eyes.

Suddenly Sindy had another leap of comprehension. Although she had passed blood of The United One into Zach while making him, it was almost certain that there was still powerful united blood in her now. She'd given Zach a lot, but she hadn't given him every last drop within her. United blood was still in her body, waiting for an opportunity to pass itself into another...and Arif had drunk from her.

"Arif doesn't even need Allie anymore!" she blurted out in dismay.

"He sounded like he needed her pretty badly to me. I'm not really clear why, but he sure thinks he does," Ben insisted.

"That's because he doesn't know. He never knew about Zach, but if he figures it out, he'll be unstoppable. He could make as many as he wanted, a whole army of them! That can't happen."

"Sindy, I'm still in the dark here. What's going to happen?"

"Oh shit. What if he reads it from my mind?" she asked in frantic distress. "It'll be all my fault! We have to go and stop it. This is way bigger than just trying to get Felicity back. He needs to be destroyed, dusted, or we're all dead! I have to tell Cain and Allie. You have to take me with you tonight, Ben. I have to warn them."

"Calm down," Ben pleaded. "If he was reading your mind, it's already too late." Like that was supposed to calm her down? "Chances are, that whatever it is, he doesn't know. You said yourself that he's got better things to worry about at this point. You're out of the action and he probably isn't wasting his time in your head. I can't take you with me though. Bringing you to his attention will only makes things worse, no matter what it is you're worried about. If you show up at the lighthouse, he'll get in your head and make use of you just because you're there and he can."

She knew he was right, but she couldn't shake the panicked feeling that she should be doing something. How could she have this information and not do something about it?

Ben took her shoulders in a firm gesture of concerned understanding. "Look, there is already a plan in place. I'm not going to get into details, but you can believe that once Felicity is safe from harm, Arif will be taken care of. After all the shit he's pulled, there are too many people who want to see him dusted, and I'm betting he won't have nearly the safeguards in place that he thinks he does. It's out of your hands. The best thing you can do, is go back to sleep so you aren't thinking about it if he does check in. If there is any chance to take him out, believe me, somebody's going to take it."

Part 4

Divining Destiny

Chapter 18 - Inevitable

Mattie

Mattie & Alyson's trailer
Parked about an hour's drive from the lighthouse
The night of the exchange

Allie was making her last preparations to leave, and put their plans into practice. Mattie was still reluctant to let her go without him, but unfortunately, he wasn't in any kind of shape to join her...or stop her. Kieran had set everything up with the others, and assured them that Cain and the Everhearts were on board with the plan for 'negotiation' with Arif. Now it was time for Allie to make sure the rest of the coven would not come to his aid when she went to retrieve Felicity.

"If I visit the coven first, won't that tip my hand to Arif?" she asked.

Kieran was quick to reassure her. "Arif already knows you don't want to give him your blood. He thinks Cain's pushing you to do it. He doesn't expect you to just meekly turn yourself in, but I doubt he thinks you're as confident as to do what we've got planned.

He has no reason to suspect anything is going on at the compound and he's going to be busy preparing for the trade. Besides, I'm his eyes and ears, and I'll be feeding him the all clear that it's quiet and business as usual. He hasn't drunk from me since long before you did, so he can't really read me, but we know each other well enough that he can get what I send him if he checks in, and I'll be sending him whatever he wants to hear.

Even if he reads about it from someone else's mind, he won't think it makes a difference. He's too cocky for that. I bet he'd find it amusing. The important thing is that the coven will be confused and uneasy. He won't be able to count on them for back-up, but he'll figure he brought enough muscle with him to handle you, and that Cain won't let you back out of the deal."

Kieran became thoughtful for a moment and then gave Alyson a hopeful smile. "That reminds me...you should mark me again before we go."

Mattie was quick to question the suggestion. "What for?"

"He's counting on me to be on his side. My wearing Allie's mark will be a potent display of loyalty when the charade is dropped. It might even make one or two of his guards reconsider backing him. Besides, I am happy to offer my blood to give her strength."

Allie answered him as she threw Mattie a quick glance to show that he shouldn't be concerned. "I'm strong enough, thanks."

Kieran wasn't giving up that easily. "You want us to be in sync, right?" He tried to appeal to Mattie's concern for her safety. "We'll have better communication if she can read me clearly," he reminded them.

"He's right," Allie told Mattie, apologetically. Kieran seemed very pleased and was quick to expose his throat, but Alyson flexed her hand to reveal her hypodermic needle-like nails. "But I don't need to drink from you to mark you."

Kieran was visibly disappointed, but still met her gaze with a grin. "I'll take what I can get."

Mattie shot him a look of warning. Kieran's utter-devotion bit was grating enough; being openly thrilled by the effects of physical contact with Allie was going too far for Mattie's patience. She didn't seem to mind though. She gave him a smirk of a smile and then sank her nails into his shoulder, dosing him with her venom.

It was a very brief injection. She removed her nails before Kieran was even visibly intoxicated. "That's it?" he asked in disappointment.

"That's enough. You've got work to do and you need a clear head." At least Alyson seemed to be taking the impending altercation seriously. Mattie was worried she would underestimate their opposition. She seemed to catch his thought. She mulled over her own concerns for a moment, and then questioned Kieran. "Do you think Elric will side with us?" she asked.

"Elric, he's the one who can fly, right?" Mattie confirmed with a hint of jealousy. He was still a tad bitter over the time that the strong handsome vampire had taken Allie by the hand and flown up into the sky with her, far from view, for a short, private demonstration of his power. She was definitely intrigued by the man.

Kieran nodded, rubbing the injection site on his shoulder, apparently trying to facilitate the spread of venom from the spot to better infiltrate his system. "That's him, and you'd be lucky to have him as an ally, but whether he sides with us or not, I know he won't act against us. Trust me. Elric has been waiting for an opportunity to break free of the coven, and this is it."

Allie nodded, ready. "Okay. Let's do this."

"Allie, wait." Mattie tried to get up, but his damn legs still wouldn't work for him. The moment he put weight on it, his right knee gave out, crumpling under him as spearing pains of sciatica shot from his back down his legs. "Damn it."

Allie sighed, giving him a look of reprimand for trying, as Kieran helped him back up with a rebuke of his own. "Dude, besides the hole in your head, you were slammed over a bench, kicked and stomped on by someone with super-strength. You are out of commission, deal with it."

Mattie groaned as he got himself back into a sitting position on the bed. "I can't accept that. Maybe if I drink from Allie one more time."

Allie moved closer to take his hand. She felt terribly guilty for leaving him, but Kieran wouldn't let her be swayed. "No. No more. She's given you more than she should spare already. She needs her strength, and if it hasn't helped by now, it isn't going to. It needs time to work; time and raw material to work with." Kieran stood by the door and took Allie's attention. "Are you sure you've got down the form you want to use? It's awfully ambitious."

Allie adopted a mischievous grin. She had come up with an idea for some bodily alterations designed to inspire intimidation, awe and respect. Once again, not exactly the way Mattie would prefer for the coven to see her, but she was adamant. "It's pretty wild, isn't it?" she asked with a grin. "Is it too much?"

"Yes."

"No," Mattie and Kieran answered, respectively. "It's important every vampire recognizes that you're capable of things they've never seen before. It's perfect," Kieran told her, "if you can actually pull it off."

"I can do it," Allie assured them. "You're right though, I'm going to need my strength. I'd better leave now if I want to stop for a quick hunt along the way. It might take me some time to construct the body I plan to use, and I don't want to be rushed. I'll see you at the compound in like an hour or so?"

Kieran nodded. "I'll be there, but they won't know we're together."

Allie leaned down to give Mattie a kiss. "Don't worry. I'll be careful, and I'll feel better knowing you're here, safe. I have to do this."

"I know." Mattie kissed her again, unwilling to let her go yet. "I love you."

She met his eyes with a smile. "I love you too."

"Don't leave me worrying. Check in with me whenever you can."

"I will." She turned and left before he could say any more.

Kieran watched her go and then turned back to him. "Do you need anything before I head out?"

"Yes...actually, I do."

Kieran could tell by his tone of voice that it would be more than just a small favor. "I don't have much time."

"I know, but...you said I need raw material, right? The vampire blood is trying to heal me, but it must need more to work with."

Kieran sighed, glancing to the kitchen. "Your fridge is stocked, but I'll bring someone in for you, if you want." Mattie cringed at the offer. "Human blood would work better," Kieran reminded him, although he knew Mattie wasn't normally willing to condone taking a victim, no matter Allie had done for him earlier.

Mattie shook his head. "Does it have to be fresh? There's a hospital down the road. Couldn't we just liberate a few donations from the blood bank?"

Kieran smiled. "I guess so, but what's with the 'we'? You're not in any shape to come with me."

"Sure I am. My knee just buckled before. It's not really that bad, and I'm getting better every minute. Just get me into the car. Once I've had some more human blood, I'm sure I'll be fine. Then I can meet you guys at the lighthouse."

"Are you crazy? If you show up there you will only be a distraction to her."

"There is going to be more going on there than even she can handle, and you know it. I won't get fully involved. I just want to be there, in case she needs me. Are you going to help me or not?"

"She'll pulverize me!"

"First of all, you know as well as I do that's she's probably listening to this conversation right now, and could chime in if she was really planning to fight me on it. Secondly, she'll pulverize you if you make me try to do this alone."

Kieran seemed unsure whether Allie was actually privy to the discussion and Mattie wasn't even sure himself, but he was determined. "I am not going to lie in bed all night while this goes down. You know I won't."

Kieran grabbed his hand and helped get him upright out of the bed, draping Mattie's arm around his shoulder so he could help him walk to the car. "Fine, we don't have all night to argue about it, but if she's mad, it's on you."

Mattie chuckled. "She'll blame me anyway, she's my wife."

~~~~~~~~~~~~~~~~~~~~~~~~~~~~~~~

Kieran and Mattie sat in the hospital parking lot, surveying the emergency entrance, and the ambulance parked in front. A patient on a stretcher was being unloaded from the back, as a few family members hovered around, worriedly. With efficiency amidst the hustle and bustle, the EMT's finally moved everyone inside, and the ambulance pulled away, leaving the hospital entrance doors unattended and quiet. The vampires watched through the glass doors, as everyone moved through the entryway vestibule and disappeared into the emergency room.

"This shouldn't take long," Kieran said, as he moved to exit the car.

Mattie spoke before he could get out. "How are you going to do this?"

Kieran shrugged. "Same way I always steal things. I'll duck into the restroom, strip, and stash my clothes. Then I'll mist my way to a refrigerator, and nab some blood."

"And then what? Walk back to the restroom naked with your arms full of blood bags? You can't carry them while you're mist, and even if you could, someone would notice them floating down the hall."

"I'll admit, it's dicey, but I'm usually a lucky guy."

"This is a little too important to depend solely on luck. If you get caught they'll lock you up somewhere. How are you going to help Allie then?"

Kieran laughed. "Nobody can lock me up anywhere, unless they've got an airtight box. But I will admit, it's going to be tricky. Got a better suggestion?"

"Yes. I'm going with you. Check it out," he said, pointing to a wheelchair that had been left unattended at the entrance. "I can walk if I have to, but it'd be easier if you just get me some wheels and bring me in. No one will look twice at us. There's a blanket in the backseat that we can throw on my lap. After you do your thing, you can hand off the blood to me to stash under the blanket, while you go back and get your clothes. Then you just wheel me out with the blood on my lap. Should be simple."

"Alright, wait here." Kieran went and got him the wheelchair. No one was around to question them or try to bring them in for admittance. The small hospital was fairly quiet, and the staff was being kept busy tending to the new arrival. Once Mattie was settled, Kieran wheeled him into the deserted vestibule. They watched and waited until the desk clerk was on the phone, and then Kieran pushed him through into the waiting area, past check-in, and into the elevator.

It took a bit of wandering for them to find the blood reserves, but once they had the area scoped out, Kieran parked him nearby in the hall, and then left for the restroom so he could go stash his clothes and do his thing.

Mattie sat in the wheelchair in front of the doors to the blood bank, keeping lookout down the hall and waiting for Kieran's smoky return. A few people walked by, but were busy with their own endeavors and didn't question him. Eventually, he spotted a dark fog near the ceiling. It rolled around the corner from the direction of the restroom. The cloud that had to be Kieran floated towards him.

At that moment, Mattie was alarmed to hear more people coming from the other direction. A male doctor and another man turned the corner to come towards him, pushing a patient in a wheelchair. The patient was an elderly woman, loudly complaining of how she was unhappy to be here. Mattie tried to avert his eyes from Kieran's progress and desperately hoped that no one would notice the odd dark mist floating along the ceiling and pull a fire alarm.

Kieran's smoky presence stood out starkly against his surroundings, considering the bright lighting and the fact that everything was painted 'hospital white', but luckily, the woman in the wheelchair was keeping her companion's full attention. "So what if I was going to take them? They're my pills and you have no right to confiscate them! I am a grown woman and I know what I want. I certainly don't want to be here."

The doctor answered her with a tone of coached professional compassion. "Of course, you have every right to determine the treatment you'd like to pursue Mrs. Aberwhite. I'm here to help you do that however I can, but you have to follow the proper channels."

"That stuff you gave me doesn't even work. The other ones are much better. It's all pain medication. What do you care if I switch one for the other?"

"You can't just go taking some strange medication mom," the man beside them interjected. "What's wrong with you?"

"What's wrong with me? Why don't you read my chart, smart mouth?"

"Mrs. Aberwhite, those pills are a controlled substance and were not prescribed to you. Would you please tell me where you got them?"

The woman looked away, rather than answer. Her eyes fell on Mattie and she flashed him a mischievous smile. "None of your beeswax," she replied to the doctor, giving Mattie a wink.

Mattie moved his wheelchair back a little, as though trying to stay out of their way, although the motion also pushed against the doors to the blood bank, causing one of them to push in and open a crack.

The woman's son gave him a look of embarrassed apology for the commotion as they passed by. Mattie gave them a sympathetic smile in return, just happy that none of them had bothered to look up over his head at the mist that was now siphoning itself into the blood bank through the opening in the door.

Once they were gone, Mattie allowed the door to close and began to hear some slight sounds of movement from within the room behind him. Finally, he heard Kieran's voice whisper through the door behind him. "Coast clear?"

Mattie surveyed the silent hallway once more and backed his chair closer to the door again. "Yes, hurry up."

Kieran opened the door and dumped six plastic bags marked 'whole blood' onto the blanket in Mattie's lap. Mattie quickly folded it over to cover them.

"Don't hang around here," Kieran told him through the crack. "I've got to go back for my clothes. You'd better get lost in case anyone notices there's blood missing before I'm back. I'll meet you downstairs in the waiting room. Can you handle the chair?"

"I got it. See you down there...and don't get caught!"

"Who me? Never," he heard Kieran answer with a laugh, as he began to disassemble into a puff of smoke. Mattie held the door for him again until he was through, and then wheeled away down the hall. Mattie forced himself to move at a sedate pace, although he couldn't help but feel a bit of guilty panic until he had turned the corner and gotten some distance from the scene of the crime.

He finally reached the elevators just as the door was closing on one going down. "Hold the elevator," he called to the lone occupant. A lovely blonde woman was inside, and she reached out to hold the door for him.

Mattie managed to wheel himself into the elevator, albeit, not very gracefully. Once inside, he tried to maneuver the wheelchair to turn himself around and face the door. The woman helped him, and he flashed her smile, just grateful that he hadn't hit her with the chair or spilled the blood from his lap. "Thanks."

"Sure," she told him pleasantly, although she barely glanced at him.

Mattie saw that the button for the lobby had already been pushed, and was rearranging his blanket to be sure the blood bags were covered, when the door began to close. Unfortunately, his chair wasn't quite far back enough, and the door bumped into his footrests.

"Oh my God, I'm sorry!" the woman exclaimed, as the door's safety made it bounce back open again. "I am so sorry," she repeated as she pulled his chair back further into the elevator. "Here I am, just standing here smiling like an idiot, and I wasn't even paying attention. Are you okay?"

"I'm fine," he assured her, as she fussed over making sure his chair was positioned so the door could close. She smelled so good as she leaned over him, trying to adjust his chair. He could feel the beckoning warmth of her body-heat in stark contrast to the cool air-conditioning of the hospital. It made the vampire in him immediately surge to attention, reminding him of his thirst.

"Really," he told her again, trying not to breathe her in and hoping she would lean back before his fangs insisted on distending. "I'm fine." She stepped back from him as the door closed, but this time she actually gave him a genuine smile and met his eyes as he spoke to her; he was very relieved they were still blue.

Mattie forced himself to blow out a slow breath and shake off the urges that were trying to overwhelm his senses. "You look like someone who got some good news," he said, remarking on whatever pleasant distraction had kept her preoccupied, and hoping to distract himself with small talk. Conversation would help him to see her as a person...not as prey.

"My sister is having a baby."

"Oh wow, that's great. Congratulations, Aunt..."

"Lorraine," she supplied with a grin.

"Aunt Lorraine," he repeated formally.

"Ugh, when you say it like that, it sounds like an old lady name!"

"No it doesn't," he insisted with a chuckle.

"Sure it does. Welcome to the world, baby. Meet your old spinster aunt, Lorraine."

"You hardly qualify as spinster material," he reprimanded with a laugh.

"Tell my parents that. My *little* sister is upstairs having her second baby, and I'm still single."

"Do you have any cats?" he asked, suppressing a smile.

"Not yet," she answered with a giggle.

"That's a good sign," Mattie answered as he gazed up at her with a grin. She was wearing sweats and a tee shirt, obviously thrown on in haste when she got the phone call to come to the hospital, and her shoulder length dirty-blonde hair was a bit mussed, but nicely cut. Even without artifice, she was a stunning beauty to his eye, and while she was just beyond the fresh blush of youth, she was by no means old. "If you're still single, then it's obviously because you've got high standards," he informed her. "As well you should; you're gorgeous."

She immediately blushed, taken by surprise at the compliment. "Thank you," she mumbled, quietly. After a moment, she recovered and gave him a stern little smile. "I may not be old, but I'm definitely too old for you."

Mattie couldn't help but let out a little huff of indignant surprise. "Don't be so sure," he said with a sly grin. Why was he flirting with this woman? It was so unlike him, but she smelled so good...

"I'm twenty-seven," she informed him with a smirk.

"Really? Me too!" He realized the absurdity of the statement, even as it left his mouth. He'd been about to turn eighteen when he'd died, and hadn't aged since. Half the time he couldn't even pass for twenty-one...twenty-seven was really pushing it. She seemed amused. "I have this condition," he explained with a humorous tone. "It keeps me from aging. But don't worry, I'm not contagious or anything."

"That's something I wouldn't mind catching," she said, playing along, as the elevator bell sounded to tell them they had reached their floor.

The doors opened and Lorraine took his chair by the handles to push him. "Thanks," he said over his shoulder.

"Are you here alone?" she asked, looking around the empty space as she wheeled him out.

"My friend is upstairs. I'm supposed to meet him in the waiting room."

"Oh, I'm headed that way too. The delivery room was kind of crowded, so I told them I'd wait down here for a while," she explained, continuing to push him in that direction.

Mattie noticed a Dunkin' Donuts walk-up counter, down the hall a bit from the waiting room. The hospital was pretty empty tonight, but there was a bored looking attendant there working the register. "It looks like Dunkin' Donuts is still open," Mattie remarked, but regretted making the observation as he realized that he hadn't brought any money with him. "I'd treat you to a coffee, but I haven't got anything on me," he explained, apologetically.

"Then I guess I'll have to treat you," she told him, with a lilt of amusement.

"I wasn't fishing for that," Mattie assured her.

"It's fine," she told him as she wheeled him over to the counter. "How do you like it?"

"Just a little milk and sugar."

"Two medium regular coffees, please."

As though that's what he was thirsty for... Dark ideas and desires flitted through his mind, and he sat there wondering just what he thought he was doing. She completed the transaction and handed him his cup. He took it with thanks, feeling guilty for accepting anything from this nice woman, while he harbored ulterior motives... He wasn't truly going to take things any further with her, was he? He had a lap full of all the blood he should need. He should just go wait for Kieran and leave this woman alone. But it would be terribly rude to just wheel himself away from her, now that she'd just bought him a coffee.

"What's your name?" she asked him, as she began walking him to the waiting area.

"Matt." He glanced towards the elevators, looking for Kieran, but there was no one in sight. They reached a bench and she sat, while he quietly sipped his coffee, trying to decide if he should just thank her and go wait for Kieran at the car.

"So, Matt, what brings you in here tonight? You're not sick, are you?"

"No. I just...hurt my leg. The doctor wants me to stay off it when I can, but I'm fine."

"Glad to hear it."

"Mattie?" The stage-whispered call came from the other side of the room, near the elevators. It was Kieran, and he hadn't seen them yet. It took Mattie a second to recognize him, because he was wearing a set of light blue hospital scrubs covered by a white doctor's coat. He finally noticed Mattie where he sat with Lorraine, and began coming towards them.

"Is that your friend?" his companion asked, skeptically.

"Um...yeah."

Kieran approached them. "Hi," he said, taking the handles of Mattie's chair with a smile. "Ready to go?"

Lorraine stood, looking over Kieran. "Aren't you a little young to be a doctor?" she asked the seeming teenager.

"Just call me Doogie," Kieran replied with a wink.

"What?" Mattie asked in confusion.

Lorraine answered with a laugh. "Doogie Howser, M.D. See, I'm old enough to get that," she told Mattie, still trying to assert that she was too old for him. She looked back to Kieran, curiously. "How are *you* old enough to get that?"

"Reruns...and I'm older than I look," he said, turning the wheelchair to face Mattie towards the door.

"You too, huh?" Lorraine commented with an arch look at Mattie.

Mattie looked up at Kieran over his shoulder. "Hey, could you give us a minute?"

Kieran gave him an odd look and then threw a glance back at Lorraine. "Sure...but we've really got to get going."

"I know. Here," Mattie said, gathering up the ends of the blanket with the blood bags wrapped in it, and handed it to Kieran to carry like a sack. I'll meet you out at the car."

Kieran took a deep breath, as though to protest, but after Mattie gave him a glare of warning, he just took the blanket and left as asked. As he walked away, Mattie couldn't help but notice that his friend was bare-foot. He turned back to Lorraine and saw that she had noticed too. "I have a feeling something very strange is going on here," she said, suspiciously.

Mattie shook his head, at a loss for even a plausible lie. "You have no idea."

She didn't question him, but did seem to think it odd that he hadn't left with his friend. Why hadn't he? Indecision pummeled him as she stood there, staring. "I should be getting back," she finally told him.

"Wait, I was wondering..."

"You know, I'm flattered," she interrupted him before he could even ask her anything, "but I'm not into the whole cougar thing," she warned him.

He gave her a strange look. "Of course not, you're only twenty-seven."

"How old are you, really? Are you even old enough to drink?"

If she only knew. "Oh...I can drink. I don't usually, but I can. Trust me." She raised her eyebrows, seeming to appraise his appearance again as he continued. "Look, you don't have to give me your number, it's okay. But...how about a kiss?"

"Excuse me?"

"Just one kiss," he pleaded with a smile. "Throw me a bone...something to fuel my fantasies." He could hardly believe he was even saying this to her. Even voiced with a sexy, quiet confidence, it sounded so desperate and pathetic. It was never going to fly. Probably just as well. Let her turn him down and walk away. He should be concentrating on trying to get strong and help Allie. Although...Lorraine's blood would surely make him stronger than anything Kieran had carried to the car. He gave it one more shot. "We can be like two ships that passed in the night."

She wanted to pretend that she wouldn't even consider such a bizarre request, but he could tell she was tempted. "I'm not in the habit of kissing random young men," she informed him.

"And I am not in the habit of having the courage to talk to a beautiful woman. Please don't shoot me down. Everyone should do something a little crazy once in a while. Don't you think? One kiss?"

"You are crazy," she agreed. "You're also really cute, you know that?" She looked around, suddenly self-conscious. After another moment of indecision, she looked into his eyes and licked her lips. Mattie was unsure whether he had an inkling of the latent power to put people in thrall; Cain had suggested that all vampires wielded hints of it in varying degrees, but if Mattie had any of it, he tried to apply it now. After staring into his eyes for a moment, she seemed won over. "What the hell. One kiss."

She began to lean towards him, but was distracted by a noise from across the room. It was nothing, but it caused her to get behind him and wheel him around the corner into the vestibule, out of sight-line from prying eyes. "Perfect," he told her with a smile.

She came around in front of him again and shook her head a little, looking into his eyes with a smile. "I can't believe I'm doing this."

"It's just a kiss," he answered with a whisper.

She leaned down to him. At first, he could tell that she was trying to decide whether she would just give him a peck on the lips to fulfill her obligation, or give him a real kiss, but he put his arms up around her and met her lips with a sweet and tender kiss that made her stay for more.

He grasped her shoulders loosely, but made sure to position himself so that he could hold her strongly if he had to. The moment she gave in to give him a true, deep kiss, he knew she wouldn't be any trouble. The venom in his saliva affected her, although very slightly compared to what an injection would do. She seemed to lower her inhibitions and then became a little off balance. Mattie took the opportunity to sort of dip and turn her, so that she ended up sitting in his lap.

She broke from his lips, surprised at herself and trying to stand, but he gently held her place. She allowed it, meeting his eyes with a gasp and giggle of embarrassment over her brazen deed. "That was some kiss," she whispered.

"Yeah," he whispered back, as he leaned in for another peck on the lips.

She was willing to kiss him back, but he turned instead to bury his face in her hair and nuzzle her neck, giving her a few wet kisses there instead. His venom tingled and numbed the spot a little, but she began to protest and sit up. "Okay, I think that's..."

He didn't allow her to stop him. Instead, he tightened his hold on her and sank his fangs into her throat. Now she did struggle, but he held her firmly and forced his venom to pump throughout her system. She had barely made a sound to object, when he felt her shudder; her muscles untensed and he heard a sigh escape from her lips.

Enveloped in her warm, enticing scent, with his lips pressed against her skin, his fangs injected her with venom. He was nearly overwhelmed by the desire for her blood, but forced himself to wait as long as he could. He wanted her fully inebriated, so she would have no clear recollection of the trespass once he was finished. She slumped further into his arms, now having no will to resist him, and a quiet moan of astonished ecstasy escaped her lips as he withdrew his fangs and took the first pulling draught of her blood.

Years...it had been years since he had drunk blood from a living breathing woman, warm, thick, rich and full of life. This was so much better than the man Allie had killed and given him. Mattie had been so injured, he'd only vaguely been aware of that drink. This was a conscious act, and the full perfection of it was like a sudden wave of nirvana and devastation rolled into one, for he knew that he was headed down a rabbit hole... This was too good for him to think he would never taste its' like again. Drinking blood from this woman, from any human, was bliss that he had denied his body for far too long. It was sweet temptation to tread a dark path, and all he wanted was more and more. He had finally succumbed, as Allie had always been certain he would, despite his protests. She was right, it had been inevitable.

Hot damn, are you drinking someone??? Allie's exclamation burst into his head, as though summoned by his barest thought of her, shaking his senses back to alertness.

Quiet, you, he answered in thought. He held tightly to the woman in his arms and forced himself to stop drinking and asses her condition. She was completely intoxicated by his insidious serum, but her heartbeat was strong and she was breathing fine. He hadn't taken all that much yet and his body barely let him pause; he needed more. *Don't distract me,* he reprimanded Allie. He wished she wasn't so attuned to him, privy to his actions, but he should have known the intense rapture he was suddenly experiencing wouldn't go un-noticed by her.

Not another word, she promised. *Go get her, tiger.*

Mattie did his best to ignore her, and after a brief hesitation, allowed himself to continue drinking from Lorraine. Allie seemed gone from his thoughts. She'd been trying to get him to hunt humans for so long, now that he had finally given in, he knew she didn't want to bother him and turn him off to it; as though anything she had to say about it would shame him into stopping. The exquisite satisfaction of sucking the blood from this woman's throat was better than anything he remembered or expected the experience to be.

Drinking from Alyson, when she had been human, had its own special fond attachments to it, of course. It had been a memory to savor always. But even back then, he knew that each time he had sampled her blood it had tasted better and been more overwhelming than expected. It was as though he kept trying to downplay the experiences in his memory, to squash his longings, and was then surprised to find just how amazing it really was, once he gave in.

Thoughts of his experiments of drinking from Allie brought lessons from Cain to mind. He forced himself to heed Cain's teachings and pay strict attention to the woman he drank from now, keeping her vital life-balance his priority. He had always been so careful when he'd drunk from Allie, terrified to harm her. He knew how to stop when it was time.

Lorraine was a larger woman than Allie's tiny frame, and could stand more blood loss, but he wasn't going to take any chances. He could already feel the blood he had taken from her working through his body. His muscles sang with the infusion, and his legs were surely healing more and more every second. He forced himself to make his next swallow be his last, and gave the puncture in her throat a final lick and kiss before turning away.

He was startled to find Kieran standing before him. He'd been so engaged with Lorraine, he hadn't even heard the electric swoosh of the automatic doors to the vestibule, or noticed the other vampire's approach.

"Dude, right here? Seriously?" Kieran asked him.

Mattie licked his lips and hugged the woman to him protectively as he glanced around. "No one saw me."

"Good thing. What do you plan to do with her?"

Mattie hefted her slightly higher and held her out towards Kieran. "Here, take her for a minute."

Kieran took the unconscious woman into his arms as Mattie slowly attempted to rise from the wheelchair. "She's still alive," Kieran observed, mildly.

"I should hope so! I didn't take too much. She should be fine. I gave her a lot of venom though. Put her in the chair," Mattie ordered, as he moved aside.

Kieran settled her slumped form into the wheelchair, and Mattie leaned forward to arrange her limbs more naturally, putting her hands into her lap and gently swiping the hair from her face. "We can wheel her in and put her on a couch in the waiting room. People will think she just fell asleep," he suggested.

"I'm not going back in there to set her up all cozy. We should be long gone! They found my clothes in the bathroom. Why do you think I had to swipe these? They noticed the missing blood right away too."

"Well, you took too much! Jeez, didn't you leave them any?"

"I left some, but if I was going to go through the trouble to steal it, I wanted to make sure there was enough for me too. They'll be down here looking for suspicious characters before long; and that's pretty much our description to a tee. I'm surprised they don't have the place on lockdown already. At least it got you into walking shape again, I see. It's time to go."

"Yes, it was worth it," Mattie said as he looked down at Lorraine with a sigh. "Alright, let's go."

"She'll be fine right here," Kieran assured him as he stepped forward to the doormat, causing the doors to open.

"Wait," Mattie said, as Kieran pulled at him to follow out into the parking lot. Mattie quickly unsheathed his fangs again and used the sharp point of his right tooth to puncture his finger. He carefully balanced the bead of blood that formed there, while using his other hand to move Lorraine's hair and expose the place where he had bitten her.

Kieran shifted, restlessly. "That really isn't necessary."

"She's at a hospital. If a nurse or someone finds her before she wakes up, they might check her out. We don't need them to see a bloody bite on her neck on the same night that a bunch of blood was stolen. Do you want 'Vampires attack hospital' to be tomorrow's headline?" He rubbed the vampire blood from his finger onto Lorraine's throat, allowing it to mend the broken skin and erase evidence of his transgression.

Kieran chuckled. "Even if it was in every paper, no one would actually believe it. Let's go."

Mattie couldn't help but caress the woman's cheek as she slept, before pulling himself away. Kieran became impatient and pulled him out to the car. "Come on! I have to get to the compound before Allie does or she'll wonder what happened to me."

"She knows," Mattie told him as they got into the car.

Kieran just stared at him for a second. "Oh...I guess she would, wouldn't she?" he said, thinking about the intimate connection Mattie and she shared. "You seemed awfully attached to that girl," he observed with a smirk, nodding his head back towards where they had left Lorraine.

Mattie gestured for Kieran to start the car, and then looked out the window. "She was my first," Mattie told him, quietly.

Kieran started the engine and put the car in drive, but paused before pulling out of the lot. "Allie was your first," he corrected.

"You know what I mean. That woman was the first drink that was...nothing but a drink."

"Then why were you trying so hard to make her more than a drink?"

"Shut up and drive."

"I'm just saying, you made it kind of...personal."

"I made it personal because she was a person," Mattie asserted. "She still is a person, because I was careful, and I always will be." Kieran just smiled with a slight nod, but Mattie knew what he was thinking... Rookie. "They're people, not prey. If we try to dehumanize them, we'll only end up dehumanizing ourselves."

Good point. Mattie could feel the comforting presence of Alyson's attention wash over him with a calming sense of approval. *I like that.*

Chapter 19 - United we stand

Allie

Somewhere outside of *Kana Susamiş Icin Ev*
Montauk, Long Island, New York

Alyson tore her attention from Mattie and Kieran in her mind's eye, to focus instead on the man standing before her. The human was just some guy she'd found, parked by the side of the road, texting on his cell phone. She'd lured him out and now he was completely entranced. She'd enchanted him with her vampiric gaze, stepped into the woods with him in tow, and given him mental commands to stand silent and obey her every directive. She wanted to shift shape, look at herself through his eyes and make a final check of her form before heading to the vampire compound, *Kana Susamiş Icin Ev*.

She and Kieran had decided that if she was going to command the respect of vampires older and more experienced than she, her white eyes might not be enough. She needed to capture their attention immediately, and show them she was unique not only in eye-color, but with abilities unlike any vampire they'd ever seen.

Before she had learned to use more caution, she had unwittingly allowed a few strange vampires to see her white eyes in the past, with mixed results. Some seemed frightened or confused and steered clear of her, others acted openly subordinate, telling her that they recognized her as superior, and that they wished to join her coven, as though she was already some great leader. With Cain's assistance she had finally managed to shoo them away, although, right about now she would have been grateful for their support.

When she revealed herself to the coven, her eyes and mark should definitely make them nervous to dismiss her, if not outright submissive. Her new form was the final touch. She planned to give them quite a show.

Her body was basically the same as always, although she had made a few internal modifications, such as fusing her ribs to make a breastplate better protecting her heart. She didn't expect to need such precautions, but it was something Tempest had once mentioned, and she'd thought it was worth practicing. She was using her previously created hypodermic nails, with their internal workings for injecting venom, but she had modified them to be longer and more claw-like for visual effect as well. The most difficult part of her creation, the part she was most proud of and hoped would be the most visually arresting, were her wings.

As a bat, her arms transformed into wings, and her body already had within it the blueprint for this transformation. To make wings on a scale befitting her human body, without benefit of using her existing arms, had been quite a challenge. She did not like the idea of losing use of her human arms, and it had taken a great deal of work and creativity to force her body to allow both arms and wings at the same time, but she had finally done it...and damn, she looked spectacular!

To the human standing before her, she looked like a demonic faerie; something out of a fantastically dark and deviant wet-dream. She stood nude and nubile, her skin almost glowing in its paleness under the moonlight. The pink ends of her bobbed, platinum blonde hair nicely complimented her rouged lips and the blushing pink areolas of her pert breasts. She'd whimsically pointed her ears, the tips peeking out through her hair, as an extra touch, just to look a bit more inhuman.

Her wings spread out tall and wide behind her, a tad darker than her skin, large and intimidating, completing the effect. Her finger nails were long and wicked, and echoing them, sectioning the thin membrane of her wings, the fine bones of each wing-finger could be seen, all ending in sharp, protruding claws as well.

She had managed to eliminate some unnecessary internal organs for raw material used in making her wings; the extra flesh had to come from somewhere. She'd also had to sacrifice some vertebrae, losing height to gain bone material to work with. She hadn't much to spare, but hoped shrinking from 5'2" to 4'6" wasn't going to make a big difference. Everyone else was always taller than her anyway.

Her white eyes shone like sparkling diamonds, gathering and reflecting the moonlight. She smiled, exposing the tips of her fangs against her pink lips. The man before her thought she looked incredibly sexy, being so unexpectedly unique, inhuman and intriguing; petite but clearly deadly.

She was sure Mattie wasn't thrilled over the prospect of her standing before the entire coven completely nude, but she couldn't wear normal clothing with her wings, and as much as the idea of fashioning some kind of cool body armor intrigued her, she didn't have time to piece something together. She was planning to shift shape a few times throughout the evening anyway, so clothing would only be a nuisance. Besides, if she wanted to sway the opinions of a large group comprised mostly of men, being naked couldn't hurt, right?

It was time to go and pay Arif's coven a visit. Her trepidation over the prospect was quickly beginning to fade as she took in her appearance one last time. This was going to be fun!

She indulged the human's fantasies by coming forward to take him into her arms for a drink. Her wings closed loosely around them to hide their embrace, as she rose up on tip-toe to sink her fangs into his throat. Just a taste...to top off her reserves and ready her for the evening ahead. She sucked his blood, feeling deliciously thrilled by the private enclosure her wings made for them, and delighting in the erotic fantasies floating through the mind of the man in her arms.

With a mental command for him to forget her presence, she opened her wings and let him slump to the ground. His breathing was slow and heavy in his venom induced slumber. They were only a few feet from his car; she wouldn't bother to move him, he'd see it when he woke. He'd be a bit confused, but she wasn't going to worry about it. It was time for business. She emerged from the trees, spread her wings and took off into the air.

She couldn't actually use her wings to fly. She hadn't nearly created the necessary muscle mass or proper structure to lift her body weight, even tiny as she was, but it didn't matter. She had enough muscle control to flap them for show and use her magic of levitation to lift herself through the air.

She wasn't far from the private vampire compound, *Kana Susamiş Icin Ev*. Following Kieran's instructions, after passing over the last development of homes on the south side of Lake Montauk, she left the highway to head southeast over the forest towards the coast, out near the tip of the south fork.

She could see the Montauk Lighthouse rising up in the distance, about five miles ahead of her. She'd been trying intermittently to contact Felicity telepathically, but Arif seemed to have found a way to block her communication in his vicinity. Maybe that would work to her advantage... If Arif wasn't letting any telepathy through, then the odds were that he might not even find out about her visit to the coven. He was either going to block communication or let it through, he couldn't have it both ways. *Hang in there Felicity,* she thought to herself. Onward to *Kana Susamiş Icin Ev*.

She found it easily from the air, although it was very isolated. She could see buildings nestled in the trees below her. She took one looping pass from high up, getting the lay of the land, before allowing herself to slow and drift down lower. She attracted the notice of the guard dogs, who began barking furiously as she passed overhead. She paid them no mind and kept flying over the development towards the beach, off to her right.

She navigated over the road that lead through the community until she found the building that Kieran had told her to look for. Arif's impressive mansion rose tall and intimidating at the far end of the compound, just before the coast. Its huge expanse of front lawn ended in a circular drive and a large fountain stood before its entrance. It might have made a nice landing spot, but that was not where she was going. Kieran had advised her to land on the broad, flat rooftop of the sprawling building before Arif's, the common house. He had assured her that it was the central meeting place for all within the community, and was where she would attract the most notice.

He was right. There weren't many people in the streets, but the few who were immediately saw her approach. After a moment of staring awestruck, each ran into the building to bring those within outside for her arrival. She hovered in the air, her giant wings spanning at least eight feet across as they flapped slowly and caused a downdraft of air that looked to be keeping her aloft.

A crowd was gathering, mostly comprised of vampires, but with a few frightened humans huddling in the street as well. They were all talking at once, staring, pointing and exclaiming to each other. Her eyes were blue at the moment, but even so, the vampires seemed to be in awe of her form; that was its purpose, so far, so good. She drifted towards the front of the building and allowed herself to lightly touch down on the edge of the roof, just one story above the ground.

"Get Elric!" she heard someone order with hushed sternness. A human immediately fled the crowd on the errand.

Allie allowed her wings to partially fold behind her, lowered but still open enough to make her seem larger than life, despite her small stature. The elbow joints of her wings rose pointed above her head, a single thumb-claw on each sticking out sharp and curved.

She looked around and spotted Elric, the very large black man easily recognizable from a distance. He was coming from another house a bit behind her but not far away, following the human. He hadn't seen her yet, but she knew instantly once he had. He stopped for a moment, shocked at the sight of her even from afar, standing on the roof of the building in all her glory.

He walked faster, but she didn't wait for him. She wanted to begin before anyone with authority thought to question her. She looked down at those before her, demanding their attention. As they hushed, she spoke with strong command, and broadcast her words telepathically as well, to echo in the minds of all present.

"Vampires of the coven master Arif, I have come to reveal myself to you, and to all vampires, the world over." She spread her wings a bit for emphasis. The crowd was silent, bereft of response in their wonder. "Behold, The United One."

There were whispers of reverent awe, and some of disbelief. A few had heard the title before, and those who hadn't were questioning those around them, but all were unsure what it should mean to them. Elric pushed his way to the front of the gathering before her, but said nothing. He recognized her and seemed as shocked as the others by her wings, but also a bit amused, as he took in her appearance. Luckily, the other vampires didn't notice his expression. They couldn't take their eyes off her.

Alyson did not let her gaze linger on him. She didn't want him to feel he had opportunity to address her yet. She could feel that some of the other vampires were becoming frightened. Elric dropped his smirk to become more serious, wondering just what she thought she was doing, and a few of the others were beginning to look to him for protection. That was not her goal.

She quickly continued. "Like you, I too am a vampire, born human," she assured them. "My body was infused with blood that was descended from darkness, but I am destined to rise above that darkness," she claimed, raising herself a good fifteen feet into the air above the roof for emphasis, flexing and flapping her wings slowly for effect, "and to become the divine leader of us all."

"Who is she?"

"Look at those wings!"

"I've never seen a vampire like her..."

There were whispers of wariness and distrust amongst the vampires below her. "What does she mean? We already have a leader..." They weren't thrilled with the master they had, but they weren't necessarily looking for a new one. They looked to Elric for guidance, Arif's senior guardsman and the man positioned to hold authority in his absence. He acknowledged those around him and then stepped forward for Alyson's attention.

Elric spoke with clear, stern command. "You dare to challenge the authority of the master of this coven?"

There were nods and whispers of approval at Elric's words of defiance. Alyson flapped her wings strongly for attention and then settled back down on the rooftop. "Arif has declared himself as your master, and you have accepted his leadership by choice, or in some cases by force, but I am being lifted to lead you not by my own will, but by the divine right of prophesied destiny." With her last words, she revealed the brilliance of her mark and her vampiric white eyes, letting her gaze survey all of the vampires before her.

Now the murmurs amongst the crowd were once again tinged with awe. A small few actually stepped back and lowered their heads, as though acknowledging that she was their superior, but most simply seemed uneasy. They were intimidated by her eyes, her mark, and the confidence she displayed, even as she stood over the crowd as a nude, petite young woman. Never had they seen a creature such as her. They knew she represented more than just what they saw... It struck them on a deeper, carnal level within their blood. They felt the power of her eyes and didn't quite know what to make of it. She lightly jumped from her perch, the crowd instantly parting and shifting to clear a space for her as she landed on the ground, wings spread and then folding behind her.

No one wanted to get within reach of her, but they also couldn't take their eyes from her, and were happy to get a closer look. She decided that she didn't like how they all towered above her in height. Her wings had served their purpose; she had their attention. Now she would appeal to their sense of unity in species.

She rose a few feet in the air, and suddenly seemed to disappear in a swirl of smoke. There were gasps from those before her, but just as they had begun to whisper and speculate, she returned. First, she reformed midair as a true bat, causing surprised exclamations as she circled quickly above them all, showing off her shifting abilities. Then she misted again, and formed as her normal, human-looking self. She was still nude, pretty and petite, but her eyes remained vampiric white.

It felt good to be her normal height of 5'2" again, but she was still tiny compared to those around her. She levitated, rising to hover just above their heads, to be seen by all. She estimated that there were a good thirty vampires present now, although all of the humans seemed to have fled or been ordered indoors.

"The color of my eyes is a sign, a signal for you to recognize the truth of what you can feel inside. I am born of the blood of all of you...every breed, every vampire, united, and so I am called The United One." Another murmur rolled through the crowd, hearing the title confirmed once more.

Some of the older vampires had heard stories. "I am a creature known before only in legend, and prophecy, a harbinger of great changes to come among vampire-kind."

The crowd separated to give wide birth and clear a space as she floated down to the ground again and walked forward to be among them. "I do not wish to lead through fear or violence, because we are not evil beings. An act of evil is a choice." She was aware of a few vampires closing in behind her who silently scoffed at her proclamation. She spun to face them, causing them to widen their eyes and almost bite their tongues like school children caught mocking the teacher. "But I *will not* be ignored or disrespected," she warned them, boosting the words further with a telepathic broadcast to them again, as her white eyes bore into their hearts and minds. "I am here to show us all the path to true greatness, and cannot allow the petty, selfish acts of other vampires to stand in the way of that."

Like a flash she spun again, the vampires behind her nearly falling over themselves to get out of her way as she neared them. She paused, and then from stillness she suddenly sprinted forward, circling the outside of the crowd in a blur of speed faster than even vampire vision could follow. She leapt and came to a stop, perched above them, balanced on top of one of the stone pillars that marked the entrance up the path to the door of the common house.

"For who would deny the power I possess?" she asked in a booming voice that carried even to the furthest vampire in the crowd. "I am The United One, sent among you as a sign of destiny, and through your acceptance of my power, I shall unite us all. I am the true leader of all vampires," she insisted, once again taking to the air, this time without benefit of wings. "I am above all masters of all covens."

The vampires were a bit shocked to hear such open challenge to the rule of their master, but wouldn't dare dispute her claim. They were not afraid to look to Elric to stand up to her, though. That was his job. "Again, you challenge the master," Elric said, speaking for the group, "but I notice you don't dare to face him directly. If you feel you are above his rule, then these words are for *him* to hear from you, not to be spoken behind his back, like a coward."

Alyson's eyes flashed with the fury she felt, and those closest took a step back from her in response. So that was how Elric wanted to play it? After a moment of trying to read his intent, she decided that he wasn't opposed to her personally, but was challenging her for the sake of the coven, so that she might be forced to prove herself to them. "Your coven master knows me," she informed them. "Arif, thought to deny me my power." Clouds rolled in across the clear sky and the warm summer air turned cold as a frigid breeze began to blow. "He hid his knowledge of me from you. He tried to lie and deceive me," she told them, "but of course I knew the treachery in his heart. He ignored the message of unity I embody. He thought to possess me, like an object to be coveted, so that he could steal my blood and use it to his own ends..."

She raised her hands into the air, further stoking up the wind and bringing a hesitant rumble of approaching thunder for her ire. "But who could ever hope to contain or possess *me*? He will pay for his blasphemy," she promised, as a bolt of lightning streaked across the sky, followed by a clap of thunder loud enough to make everyone jump.

She became aware of Kieran joining the group. She couldn't see him, but felt his presence through her mark on him. She tried not to let him distract her, as she tried to find her place to continue her speech. Her words sounded rehearsed and formal in her ears, but she was afraid to stray from the carefully crafted script she, Kieran and Mattie had come up with. "I have come to reveal myself to you, because you deserve to know the truth. He wants to keep me hidden from you, but I will be heard! And you have been warned. Do not seek to interfere on his behalf," she cautioned, "or you will share his suffering. He'll receive from me only what he deserves. So I issue a warning to all: Despite any orders he may try to enforce upon you, do not position yourselves against me."

Alyson hopped down from the pillar, causing those closest to her to step back in alarm. She allowed the stillness of summer humidity to return once more, and sent waves of warm kinship and soothing reassurance towards them all. "Do not be afraid," she continued in a softer tone. "I wish only to enlighten you, not to enslave you as coven masters have done. I am kin to each and every one of you, bound by breed and blood...I know you. I am your sister. Every secret you hold, every power you wield, I share with you. Like Arif, I see into your minds and I feel the truth in your hearts, but *I* do not use the skill to control you."

Unsure if she spoke truly, some of them seemed very nervous to think of what she might see within them. Without sharing blood, she couldn't delve deeply into their thoughts, but they were nervous, and some of them were more easily read than others. She chose a gruff looking man, whom she could sense had a particularly dark past, and approached him, lightly touching his shoulder with a smile. "Do not be without hope for change. We all have darkness in our pasts," she said, surveying the crowd.

"We should all be rightfully ashamed of the sins we've committed, even me. But I will rise above them," she told them, taking to the air once again, "and I offer you all the opportunity to do the same; a new beginning. We can't comfort ourselves any longer with the lie that what we are makes us exempt from sin for the things we've done. We can't change the past, but we can mold the future. I signal a new path of evolution for our kind, a path of power in choice."

Elric unfolded his arms and loosened his stance, coming closer to her, truly intrigued by her words. "Vampires kill...we do dark deeds. It's in our nature."

"You don't believe that," she insisted. "Each of us has the will to be what we choose. We can change."

"How do you think you can accomplish this change? Just by overthrowing one master of one coven?"

"The word *master* will no longer apply," she explained, "because we are each master of our own destiny." She could feel her words reverberating through the crowd, striking a receptive chord in many. "You can consider me a leader, because I will show you the way, but those who recognize me are not followers, but brothers and sisters by my side. Covens will be formed through bonds of friendship, respect and love, so that vampires can help one another to be strong against evil tendencies, because *that* is the future I see for our kind; creatures proud, strong and unashamed; not skulking horrors of the dark, feeding off of fear and in turn being fearful.

The blood in me is so strong. It remembers the nights of our past glory and how we fell from power to become mere shadows of the creatures we once were. It shows me visions of mistakes of the past. If we are not only to survive, but to thrive, we must take a new path."

"Tell me more of this path you envision. What will we be, if not killers?" Elric wanted to know.

"Vampires will secretly foster the human race, as guardians, shepherds protecting those less powerful than ourselves." This elicited some chuckles of disbelief, but she pressed on. "We see ourselves as superior to humans, don't we? Yet we fight and squabble among ourselves like primitive heathens. We may be more powerful than humans, but we should never forget that we were once like them. They deserve our mercy. We will feed with discretion and decorum, not as monsters or animals. The civil arrangements you have with your harems are a step in the right direction, but for the wrong reasons. They will be refined, and those vampires drinking from the populace will do so with control and stealth, sparing the lives of their donors."

Some of those before her seemed doubtful that this was manageable, but she did not have time to argue over it now or get into further specifics.

She had already gone on longer than planned. It was enough that they knew she had power and a larger plan. They may not all agree with her vision, but they were unsure enough that they would all be either afraid or unwilling to act against her in defense of Arif. Time to wrap this up. "Embrace my authority, and allow me to enlighten your existences. A change is coming for vampire kind, and I am truly honored to be The United One, a revelation of our destiny."

A dark mist flowed through the crowd to coalesce in the empty space before her. The other vampires were momentarily startled, but then recognized their coven-mate, as Kieran formed. He let the others note who he was, and then he made a deep bow to her, eliciting a gasp from the crowd. "I'll follow you."

"Traitor," a random vampire hissed from somewhere behind him.

Elric shushed them and stepped forward, closer to Kieran. "I am the senior guardsman here, and I have authority over the coven while the master is away." The words had the formal air of standard protocol. Kieran straightened and spent a moment looking Elric in the eye, before he nodded, accepting his friend's authority. "Do you formally resign," Elric asked, "accepting this woman to lead you, rather than the coven master Arif?"

"This woman, *is The United One*. Yes, I do."

Elric's gaze bore into him, steadily, betraying no hint of what Elric personally thought of the act. "You realize that in doing so, you forgo any protection that the coven has to offer. You are giving up your residence, your harem, and your rank, relinquishing command of all underlings here and abandoning your post."

One side of Kieran's mouth twisted upwards in a slight smile. "I understand the scope of my actions. I'm leaving the coven and all of its perks behind. It means nothing compared to her," he proclaimed, turning to show the crowd that he meant it. "I believe in her, and I cannot allow myself to remain here and be governed by someone who does not acknowledge her as their superior. She's The United One."

Elric quietly let Kieran's words die away, and then bowed his head in a formal gesture of acceptance. "Very well. Your ties here are broken." There were sounds of uneasiness from the crowd. Many hadn't believed he would go through with it. Now Elric allowed himself a smile. "I wish you luck."

There was silence as Kieran nodded to Elric in return and walked to stand behind Allie. She looked out over the coven, but none seemed inclined to speak further, or join them. "I leave you now, to face Arif," Alyson announced. "Think about everything I've said and spread the word.

I will return once the Coven Master Arif has sworn fealty to me...or is no more." Alyson rose into the air, Kieran swirling into mist, to rise and follow. "Until we meet again, my brothers and sisters."

"Alyson..." Elric called from the crowd, making her pause. "United One," he corrected himself. She hovered in the air, watching him and trying to read his intent, without much success. He stood silent for a second, and she wondered whether he was going to rebuke her, warn her, or wish her well. He didn't seem to mean her harm, but he was surprisingly good at hiding his emotions from her. After what seemed a silent eternity, he rose into the air as well. The other vampires of the coven had seen him do this many times, but they still reacted with astonishment over the unexpected action. "I choose to join you as well."

A collective gasp rose from the vampires around him as they stepped back to make space beneath him, keeping themselves separate in their uncertainty. "Traitors, both of you!" an anonymous voice yelled.

Elric stared down all within sight before answering the accusation. "I have served this coven faithfully for well over a hundred years. I have accepted Arif's leadership and obeyed his rules, regardless of my own personal opinions. You all have known and respected me. My reputation speaks for itself, and you can believe this is not a decision made lightly."

A vampire stepped forward from the crowd to speak, a dark-haired, pale man of about thirty or so in appearance. "That's what makes the decision all the more traitorous, made while the Master is conveniently busy elsewhere."

"Are you calling me a coward too, Tomas?" he asked, lowering himself to the ground without sacrificing a single bit of the intimidation imposed by his height. "We've been presented with this amazing discovery...The United One is among us. In light of what she has offered, I have made my choice and you can rest assured that I will be leaving immediately to inform Arif of my departure in person. Once all is settled, I will return shortly to put my house and harem in final order.

Those who have trusted my judgment these many years may want to consider leaving Arif as well. Those satisfied with his rule and the current order of things are welcome to stay, but know this: The United One is real. She is revealed before us and her blood lineage is undeniable; it gives her inherent authority over us all, as the divine matriarch of vampires. If you refuse to believe me, look into her eyes and see it for yourself. No matter how you try to deny it, your blood will know.

She speaks honestly, when she says that Arif has been presented with this truth and sought instead to defy her, and bend her will to satisfy his thirst for power. I know; I was there. I had my doubts all along in his decisions, but I obeyed him as my loyalty dictated.

However, I can keep silent no longer. Arif's attempts to control this amazing creature are nothing but misguided folly driven by greed. Do not take on his folly as your own. If you fear to join us, then do as you will, but should you assist Arif in his campaign to enslave her blood, I promise that you will meet your ends regretting the decision. The choice is yours."

Tomas answered Elric. His mark showed him to be just a bit younger than Elric, and Alyson guessed that he must also be a member of the senior guard, although she didn't recognize him. "What she talks about is fantasy, an idealistic daydream. Vampires are superior to humans. We are their natural predators now, and are meant to rule them, not harbor and protect them. They are inferior beings. Our harems serve us, not we them."

Elric narrowed his eyes. "I have spent over 150 years on this earth, and suffered oppression you've probably never even had to think twice about. I have dealt with more than my share of people who wanted me to believe I was inferior because of what I saw when I looked in the mirror, but I never had a problem with what I saw...they did. My reflection is gone now, but I never needed a mirror to tell me that I deserve to be treated with dignity, and neither does any other person on this planet, living or dead. Neither skin, sex, money, nor heartbeat can determine whether a person is worthy of respect.

We drink the blood of humans to survive, but to enslave them only betrays fear and weakness in ourselves. Remember where we came from; treat them with dignity, and we will thrive as species truly inferior to none. When we show mercy and kindness where humans have not, is when we will be able to consider ourselves as having evolved to our fullest potential."

Alyson smiled. Kieran was right; Elric was definitely a man she wanted on her side! There was complete silence as the vampires of the coven took in his words and snuck furtive glances at The United One. Alyson nodded and addressed the crowd. "Well put. Someone recently told me that if we try to dehumanize those we drink from, we'll only end up dehumanizing ourselves. I totally agree." She added a quick mental note to Elric with a smile. *I think we are going to get along just fine.*

He narrowed his eyes at her a bit. *I just hope you know what you're getting yourself into, little girl.* She wanted to be offended by the term, but he smiled and she couldn't help but smile back. He knew how powerful she was; he just didn't want to see her get too cocky.

After a respectful pause, Byron made his way forward out of the crowd. "I choose to join you," he announced clearly, for all to hear.

"And I," said another vampire, stepping forward with two more right behind him, speaking the same. The crowd was divided as a few more chose to align with Alyson, and quick comments of gossip and amazement stole over them all at each new development.

Alyson floated a few feet above them in the air, and gratefully acknowledged those few who chose to back her. Including Kieran and Elric, they had eight. Hardly an army, but it would have to do. She telepathically gave them each a quick mental update, of how she was heading to the Montauk Lighthouse to face Arif, and those who cared to support her were welcome to meet her there.

A woman stepped forward through the crowd to stand beneath Alyson, and after a moment, the vampires surrounding her were stunned as she too rose swiftly into the air, as Elric had done.

"I swear my allegiance to The United One as well," she proclaimed, among murmurs of astonishment from the others.

"Latisha," Elric whispered the name with a smile. Fresh and beautiful, as though a new blush of youth had been bestowed upon her, Latisha hovered before The United One as a vision of loveliness and grace. This beautiful woman of color, who had spent her life in Elric's service, had been reborn as a vampire, her mark uncovered to reveal that she was made as recently as last night.

She respectfully bowed her head before Alyson, and then lowered herself to land lightly on the ground. She turned and gave an elegant curtsy of respect to Elric before he took her hand into his own with a smile. "Where you go, I will follow," she told him, more for the crowd than his benefit. Surely, he'd expected as much.

"She was a human of his harem," someone informed the coven with a shocked shout. "His favorite!" A vampire stepped forward before Elric and Latisha, and turned to address the coven. "She was never brought before us in ceremony. Elric played the traitor all along, betraying the coven to turn a human without the master's blessing! That is a punishable offense!"

Elric ignored the accusation to raise Latisha's hand to his lips for a kiss, slow and respectful, before bothering to give the other vampires his attention. Finally, he looked to the one who had spoken against him. "I suppose it would be, but I'm no longer a member of this coven."

Chapter 20 - Destiny

Cain

About a mile from the Lighthouse
Montauk Point, Long Island, New York
Almost midnight

Cain paced back and forth, tightly gripping the sword, Ash-bringer, and trying to be calm and patient. To think that Felicity was suffering in the hands of that egotistical, smarmy, selfish, heartless tyrant of a vampire, while he was forced to wait out here for plans to fall into place, was simply maddening. To think that she should be so frightened and humiliated, ripped away from her life, as a penalty for opening her heart to Cain those many years ago, was disgusting and unacceptable. She was probably wishing she'd never met him.

How dare Arif make Felicity feel that perhaps her relationship with him was truly a mistake, something she should regret and feel shameful over! How dare he think to punish a good woman, in order to try to twist Cain to do his bidding! Cain was not only a vampire many years his elder, but also a hundred times the man Arif could ever hope to be, and refused to bow down to Arif's will. He refused to be forced to drag Alyson to Arif, give him her blood and damn the world to suffer whatever wretched plans he had, in order to spare Felicity any further disgrace and preserve her precious life! It took every ounce of will he had to keep from storming to the damn lighthouse and fighting his way in to her, plan and back-up be damned!

Where was Alyson? What if Mattie was very greatly injured, as Arif had hinted? Was Alyson delayed because Mattie was too wounded for her to leave him, or...heaven forbid...grief stricken that he had succumbed to his injuries? Once again, he dug out the pocket watch that he'd dredged up out of an old dresser-drawer to check the time. Eleven thirty p.m. He wished Alyson would get here already so he could lay his fears to rest, put things in motion and get this over with already.

Take it easy, I'm here.

Alyson's voice sounded in his mind along with a warm current of soothing understanding, as though she was trying to give him a spiritual hug as she suddenly appeared before him. He was startled by her sudden presence. It seemed as though she had materialized in the very spot in front of him out of thin air. She was fully clothed, and he realized that in actuality, she must have run to him, but the movement was so fast that he hadn't even seen her approach.

"Finally. Is Mattie alright?"

She looked surprised to find that he even knew there was cause for concern. "He'll be okay."

"Good." That was a relief, at least. He'd get the details later, but why hadn't she told him what was going on sooner, rather than leave him to worry?

Despite his agitation, he couldn't help but smile with relief to see her again. "You're a sight for sore eyes." She began to smile just as his left his face. "I can't believe you took off on me, while I was out cleaning up your mess...and right when I need you most!"

"I didn't know you were gonna need me! We left a note."

"Yes, I got it," he answered sarcastically. "*We need some space - TTYL.* What the hell does that even mean?"

Allie pursed her lips and tried not to smile at his impatient confusion. "It means 'talk to you later'. Sorry, I should have realized you wouldn't get that."

"It wouldn't matter if I had. It doesn't tell me anything anyway. And how much later were you planning to wait for? It's been weeks, and it's not as though you needed a telephone or anything."

"I'm sorry! I was going to contact you, but Mattie was all pouty about us never having time alone. I was waiting just a little longer, and then Zach showed up and things got kind of crazy."

"Zach...the musician you killed and left for Sindy to turn?" She visibly flinched at his recount of the situation, although she nodded at its accuracy. "You've seen him?" he asked in astonishment.

"Yeah, long story that will end with you saying *I told you so.* I'll tell you later. We were coming back to see you at your place though, even though I figured you might still be mad at me. I know I screwed up, big time. I tried to make it right and I apologized, but you said you didn't even forgive me."

Cain rolled his eyes with a sigh. "That's not what I said. I told you it would be nice if you weren't constantly having to ask me for forgiveness."

"Same thing."

"Not exactly."

Allie averted her eyes. He could tell that she wanted to know whether he actually did forgive her, but he didn't say anything. Of course, he did, but he was still hurt that she and Mattie had been hiding things from him until it blew up in their faces at the expense of everyone around them. He, Sindy, Felicity and apparently Mattie too, were all paying for Alyson's lack of judgment, even if she hadn't meant to cause problems.

Finally, she sighed and spoke quietly, although she still didn't meet his eyes. "Can we talk about this later? We kind of have stuff to do."

Stuff to do...Felicity. At just the thought of her suffering because of him, tears tried to rush to his eyes, but he blinked them back. "Yes, we do."

She laid a hand on his sword arm, a hesitant gesture to try to somehow bond with him again. "Nice piece, but you can put that thing away for now," she said quietly, with a nod towards the weapon. "Unless you've decided you want to take my head off." He let out a small huff of a laugh as he shook his head and lowered his sword arm. She was happy to see him loosen up a little. "According to what you told Arif, we're supposed to be negotiating a peaceful trade, remember?"

"I know. Holding the sword just makes me feel better. She's in there, helpless under his control, while I'm just standing here, feeling so damn incapable of rescuing her without this whole facade we've got to go through. It makes me sick. I hope you realize that no matter what happens, this evening is going to end with Arif's beheading. I will not let him survive the liberties he has taken at Felicity's expense. I won't stand for anything less than seeing him turn to dust. I should have found a way to put an end to this sooner."

"Alright, take it easy. You know trying to do anything sooner would have gotten one of you killed. Just stick to the plan. She'll be okay."

"How is she? Is she terribly frightened?"

"I don't know," Allie seemed momentarily confused, until she realized that Cain assumed they were in telepathic contact. "I can't read her right now," she explained, apologetically. "Arif seems to be blocking her from telepathy, but don't worry. The last time I was able to talk to her, she was scared, but okay. I was cut off before I could say much, but I'm sure she knows that we're doing everything we can to get her out of there."

"I don't like this plan. I'm not interested in leading a crusade or a rebellion right now, I just want to see her safe. I know we've discussed it before, but in these circumstances, exposing yourself to vampires everywhere seems like a bad idea."

"Well, I never was the shy type," she told him with a sly smile. "Anyway, it's too late for second-guessing now. As far as exposing myself...already been done, literally and completely."

Cain was taken aback as Alyson sent the image to his mind of her entrance into Arif's compound to confront his coven. She showed him how she'd flown in over the fences to find the common house, and they'd seemed to pour into the streets from everywhere to stare at her in awe.

"Oh, my word! Those wings... How on earth did you do that? I have had shape-shifting vampires residing on my property for years, and I've never seen anyone look like that!"

"And you never will. That's the point! I'm unique. Shape shifters only have a limited amount of time to take shape, so they usually have to fall back on a blueprint their blood's already familiar with, unless they're super talented and really work at it. Even then, some shifters just can't alter their form from what they know. But I'm The United One. I can stay mist for as long as I need, while I construct a plan for whatever I want my body to look like. It wasn't easy, but I think it was worth it. Pretty cool, huh?"

She continued to send him images of her display. Winged, nude and white eyes shining, she had certainly made a glorious sight. Word of that spectacle should be spreading among vampires like wildfire. "Good or bad, the plan's already in motion," she confirmed. Cain caught his breath at the vision and shook his head, marveling at her pageantry, a bit too uncomfortable to comment. "I looked *good,* didn't I?" she asked with a laugh. "Cain, are you blushing?"

"Unbelievable..." he muttered with a sigh. The girl truly seemed to have no boundaries. "I think I might have chosen a slightly more subtle approach, myself."

"Since when do I bother with being subtle? Fast and effective, that's me. Cain, you know I adore you, and we are pretty like-minded about most things, but your methods are just not my style. The passive-aggressive approach you've been working with has definitely made a change for the better, but you've been at it for centuries. You said yourself that I could get it done quicker."

"Well, I still don't like it. Why you've put so much faith in Kieran's planning is beyond me."

"Because I can read him and I know he's right," she said, flashing him a reassuring grin. "You'd have been proud of me. I think I said everything you would have. Mattie and Kieran helped me write the script. If I need to take charge to put things right; put on a show and dust a few vampires to put the fear of The United One into the rest of them, so be it."

"Dear Lord, you didn't dust anyone, did you?"

"No," she insisted, but then hesitated. "Well, I did dust Zach, but no one at the coven."

"You killed Zach?" Cain asked in disbelief.

"I had to, and it wasn't easy. He had white eyes, Cain."

Cain was shocked by the admission, but before he could ask the dozens of questions that now plagued him, Allie cut him off. "I'm just sayin'. I need to do this quick and dirty, whether you're okay with it or not, because not only is Felicity in danger, but waiting and hiding has nearly gotten Mattie killed, *twice*, and this last time was *way* too close for comfort."

She was visibly shaken by whatever had happened, enough to make Cain realize that Arif may not have been exaggerating after all. She was upset enough to make him even more anxious than he already was. "What happened?"

"Zach tried to kill Mattie. I dusted him, but Mattie was hurt." She answered with a shiver of remembrance.

"How badly?" He could see on her face, it must have been pretty bad.

"Bad...really bad. I almost lost him, Cain."

"You've healed him though? He's alright?"

She nodded with a sigh. "He will be, but this ends now. When I was human, I never really cared about the future much. I never felt responsible for anyone else. Now, I kind of feel like I'm responsible for *everyone* else. Things need to change, and I'm gonna change them. So follow the plan, or get out of the way."

"Now who needs to take it easy?" Cain asked. She was nervous beneath all of her bravado, over-compensating. He eyed her discerningly for a moment. "You can't do this without me. I am the plan."

Allie squinted at him with a scowl on her face for his irrefutable logic. "Then I'll come up with my own damn plan, and it'll probably suck, but I'm willing to try. You gonna send me in there alone?"

Of course, he was going through with it, and she had to know that. She was just being jumpy. After staring her down for a moment, Cain broke into a grin. "You remind me of my daughter."

Allie raised her eyebrows with a surprised smile. "Really?"

He wasn't sure if Alyson had even known that he'd had a daughter. They'd never spoken of her. "More than I've realized. Headstrong to a fault, my Amelia." he assessed, with a chuckle.

Allie seemed pleased by the description. "What would she do in my place, faced with Arif?"

This truly made Cain laugh. "She'd surely throw a spectacular temper-tantrum, stick out her tongue and throw rocks at him…" Allie was surprised and confused by the admission. "She was only four," Cain explained.

Allie smiled. "Oh…" Her face changed as she realized Amy must not have lived past the age. "I'm sorry. You never told me." Cain shrugged it off, not wanting to delve further while pressing matters were at hand. "Still, I like her attitude…better than yours. I am not negotiating. I can't, and I shouldn't have to. I'm not taking any more shit from anyone; not even the most powerful coven master on the coast."

Cain sighed. "Well I hope you plan to do more than throw rocks. If I can't talk you out of this, then let's at least stick with the plan."

"Alright, but never underestimate the effectiveness of a good temper-tantrum. I'm gonna consider that a solid back-up plan."

Cain shook his head with a sigh. "Fabulous," he muttered sarcastically. He stood up straighter and held his hands out towards her as though introducing her to an unseen crowd. "Ladies and gentleman, may I present the most powerful vampire in the world. Try not to make her cranky."

"Damn straight."

~~~~~~~~~~~~~~~~~~~~~~~~~~~~~

Allie hopped off the back of Cain's motorcycle as he cut the engine. He parked it against a white and red sign that read *Montauk Point Lighthouse: National Historic Site,* with museum and gift shop hours printed beneath. The lighthouse was still a bit further up the hill, but just past that point the gates were closed across the road. They would walk from here.

A cool and steady salt breeze was blowing at them over the cliff-ledge from the water. Nothing could be heard but the crashing of waves against the rocky barrier between the thin strip of beach and the grassy hillside rising steeply up to the lighthouse and buildings surrounding it. The lighthouse tower stood large and imposing, rising up out of the relative darkness, its beacon flashing brightly out over the sea to light up the night surf.

There was a large rectangular building before the actual watchtower, that must serve as the museum and gift shop advertised on the sign. The path that they were on led not only up to the building entrance, but also around to the side where Cain assumed they could gain access to the tower itself. He could just make out some figures on the top lookout landing of the tower, and there was no doubt in his mind that Arif would settle for nothing less than holding Felicity at the very top, where she was most easily guarded.

Cain took Ash-bringer from the back of the Harley, slipping the sheath through the belt at his hip. Alyson gestured to it. "What's Arif gonna think of that?"

"Probably that he regrets giving it to me," Cain answered with a wry grin. Allie raised an eyebrow. "It was a gift, and I intend to return it to him...blade first. But at the start, we'll play the charade and see what he has to say for himself. Let him think he's running the show. Try not to let him bait you; let me do the talking."

Alyson put her hands up in surrender as they began making their way up the path to the lighthouse. "Consider me meek and humble...until shit goes down, then the gloves are coming off, and he is toast," she warned.

"Believe me, I'm right there with you."

"I think we've got some back-up on the way."

"That's good, but don't rely on them too strongly. They'll only be helpful if they can get up the tower. Arif will have it guarded and we've no way of knowing if your supporters will be able to get through."

"Well, I know we'll have at least three who can make it up there to help us."

"How can you be sure?"

"Because three of them can fly," she told him with a sly grin.

Cain smiled in return. "Kieran, and...Elric?"

"And Elric's girlfriend apparently. I think her name is Latisha."

"Excellent. If you can count on Elric, I think he'll be a good ally to have," Cain agreed. "And remember, if you see the Everhearts, they are not expressly on our side." He could only assume that the men would keep to the arrangement they had planned. As far as Arif knew, both Everhearts hated all vampires bitterly, including Cain and Alyson, and would never go so far as to cooperate with them. Cain and Alyson needed to keep up that appearance.

"Ben," Alyson said quietly, as she stopped walking by his side.

"Yes, Ben or his father." Cain turned to urge her to keep walking, but then noticed that she seemed distracted.

"No...I mean, right there, Ben," Allie clarified. She was looking up the path to the lighthouse.

Cain followed her line of sight and found the tall, dark figure standing at the corner of the building. Alyson must have somehow recognized him by his mental presence. He'd positioned himself perfectly, so that the floodlights on the path shone out ahead of him, yet he was mostly hidden in shadow. He held a sword loosely by his side.

Cain glanced back at Alyson. "Oh...alright then, I guess it's show time." They continued up the path, pausing about fifteen feet from where Ben stood. The bright lights hindered their sight a bit, but Cain wasn't ready to move closer yet. "What are you doing here?" he asked the man many considered his former rival.

Ben seemed transfixed. He was staring at Allie. Cain suddenly realized that this was the first time that Ben had actually seen Alyson since acknowledging her death. He gave them respectful silence. After a moment, Ben seemed to come back to his senses and spare Cain a glance. "I'm guarding the door."

Ben's gaze was drawn back to Alyson again as though she was magnetic. She stood there, quiet and unimposing, and gave him a shy smile. "Hi Benji."

"Don't call me that." Ben spoke quietly, as though the words were an automatic response, almost without thought. "I hate it when you call me that."

Allie gave him a lopsided grin. "No you don't. Secretly, you kind of love it, because I'm the only one who ever calls you that. You just always say that, because you don't want anyone else getting ideas."

Ben seemed startled by her response. She must have read it from his mind, or then again, maybe she just knew him that well. Ben tore his gaze from her face as though deciding he'd rather deal with Cain for now. "No one gets up there but you and her," he said, throwing a quick glance up at the lighthouse tower.

Allie answered before Cain had a chance. "Who else are you expecting?"

Cain let out a disgruntled huff of breath while mentally reminding Allie that she was supposed to let him handle this, before addressing Ben. "So, you're doing Arif's dirty work now, are you?"

"I'll do whatever it takes to get my wife back...from him, or from you."

Allie actually laughed at his warning. "Ha! You might as well go wait at home Ben. You're out of your league. We'll take it from here. And if Cain didn't want to bring her home to you afterwards, there wouldn't be a damn thing you could do about it anyway."

Cain inwardly cringed. Surely, Alyson was putting on a bit of a show for Arif, who was undoubtedly privy to their conversation through Ben, if the man was acting as his guard. However, Ben didn't know Alyson's true feelings. He couldn't, or Arif would know as well.

At Allie's words, Everheart senior came around the corner behind his son. "I disagree."

Now Alyson spoke with a voice falsely chipper to go with her smile. "Hi Mr. Everheart," she said with a familiar little wave. "Long time no see."

"I could have waited longer," he responded drolly. "So, I understand you're what all this fuss is about."

"Yeah, I think you'll find I've changed since the last time I knocked on your door to see if Ben could come out and play."

"I'm not impressed."

"Want me to impress you?"

Cain gripped her arm at the elbow. "What happened to meek and humble?" he muttered to her harshly.

Bernard smiled, seeming amused by her. "Some other time. Right now, I think you should head upstairs and do whatever it is you're here for, so we can take Felicity home."

It was smart of Allie to cement Arif's belief that the Everheart's were Cain and Alyson's enemies, but baiting them was uncalled for. Cain stared her down, as he answered for them. "Yes, let's."

Bernard led the way around the building. Ben stood silently watching them follow and then walked behind them. The back of the building, which at one time served as the light-keeper's residence, was actually attached to a smaller, white structure, the oil room and communications center, that was also entry to the stairway up to the top of the lighthouse tower.

Bernard showed them through a small brick archway to the bottom of the spiraling metal stairway, and then moved aside. Apparently, the men were not joining them, but planned to guard the entrance behind them once they entered. "Take her up to the first door."

Cain began to ascend with Alyson following behind. Neither of them spoke as they climbed the spiraling stair. Ash-bringer rhythmically rapped against his hip as the tension mounted with every step, until finally Alyson paused, looking up at Cain above her. Nothing could be seen of where they were going, only the tight spiral of metal stairs above them. "Where the hell is the top? These stairs go on forever!"

A male voice startled them, answering from somewhere above. "What do you expect? It's over 110 feet high. There are 137 steps total. You're almost there." They continued their climb to see the man who had spoken standing near the top. One of Arif's vampires, whom neither of them knew, was standing on the landing where the spiraling stairs ended. He watched them approach, as he held a small, mini-crossbow pistol, armed with wooden arrows trained on Cain's chest.

"It's pretty impressive, the lighthouse, isn't it?" he asked, casually, as though he weren't pointing a deadly weapon and guarding the door to a tower which held an innocent woman prisoner for blackmail... "I'm kind of a history buff."

Cain ignored the idiot's annoying enthusiasm. Although there was a final flight of ladder-like stairs continuing up higher to another exit point, the vampire opened the first door for them to go through. Mindful of the man's weapon, and of a sign that warned *Low Headroom,* Cain ducked and went through the doorway, which led out to an observation platform that circled the tower.

They were not actually level with the lamp, but just below it. It flashed brightly over their heads, lighting the darkness. The platform was just wide enough for two people to walk side-by-side comfortably around the tower. The view was amazing, but Cain was only interested in confronting Felicity's captor and negotiating for her freedom.

He saw no one there to immediately meet them. A wrought iron railing surrounded the walkway in a decorative X design. Cain noticed that at one point in the rail, there was a section done in a circle with the date 1860 formed in the bars.

"That's actually the date they renovated," the door-man informed them, as he came out onto the walkway, closing the tower door behind him. "The actual lighthouse was built in 1796, under orders from George Washington."

Cain squinted at the man as the light flashed by overhead. "I know; I was there. Where's Felicity?"

Arif's voice answered, as he came from around the walkway up ahead. "She's up above you. Lorelei, give us a little wave, will you?" he called out.

Cain leaned over the railing, looking up to see another, outdoor walkway about ten feet over their heads, around the narrow top of the tower and windowed lamp room. As he watched, he saw Lorelei lean forward, her long blonde hair swinging out in the wind. She had her arm around Felicity, who stood next to her, staring blankly out at the ocean. As Cain watched, Lorelei took Felicity by the wrist and made her wave. "Hi sweetie!" Lorelei called down, mockingly.

"Felicity!" At the sound of her name, Felicity finally looked down at him, dazed. "Are you alright? Don't worry, we're going to get you down from there."

"Very touching, but she can't really hear you," Arif answered. "She is completely unaware of her surroundings. My lovely progeny, Lorelei, is keeping her safely in thrall until we are through with our business."

"You don't need her any longer. I brought Alyson to you as promised, now let Felicity go."

"In good time." Arif tilted his head to see Allie, standing quietly behind Cain and assessing their surroundings. "Alyson, my dear girl, I have looked forward to seeing you again."

"Don't call me girl...and I'm not your *dear* anything."

"Simply a friendly nickname to keep things civilized, such as the one you used downstairs with the young Mr. Everheart. Pity he is so disappointed by your transformation. I think you turned out splendidly."

"I'm here," she replied tightly. "What do you want?"

Arif raised a hand to make a slight motion over his shoulder. After a moment, the vampire Jin stepped up behind him with a human boy in tow. "I believe you have met Jin before... Although, of course you have no recollection of the meeting, do you?" he amended with a laugh, "Thanks to Lorelei."

Cain realized that Arif must believe that Lorelei had somehow erased the memory of the encounter from Alyson's mind. That was why she and Mattie had difficulty recounting it for him, but it was only Lorelei they didn't remember seeing. They had told Cain about Jin, and his powers. The fact that Arif did not know that, would definitely work in their favor.

"Now, I would like you to meet the young Ilker," Arif told them, as Jin moved aside to allow his charge to come shyly forward to stand by Arif; he was barely a teenager. He bowed his head to Arif and then bowed to Alyson as well.

Alyson spared Cain a confused glance and then turned back to Arif. "Charmed, I'm sure," she told them, sarcastically.

Arif smiled. "You will be changing him to become a vampire like yourself."

"The hell I will! Let's get something straight; I only came here tonight because Cain begged me to, and I knew it was the only way to get you off my back once and for all, but I am not doing anything for you...ever. What I am, is tired of you having me spied on, sending your goons after me and kidnapping my friends!"

"Then do as I ask, and I will have no further interest in you."

"No way."

"If you do not, then your friend Felicity will die."

"So, kill her," Allie said with a shrug as Cain turned to her in horror. "She's human," Alyson continued. "She's gonna die eventually anyway. It won't change anything," she told Cain callously before turning back to Arif. "You still can't force me to do what you want."

Arif raised his eyebrows in surprise, turning his attention to Cain, to see what he made of Alyson's reply. Cain stared her down grimly, as Arif commented. "Not very sentimental, is she?"

When Alyson refused to show any deference, Cain spoke in a voice quietly filled with lethal sincerity. "I will not allow Felicity to die. Not here, not now."

Allie shrugged again with a mirthless little smile. "Then I guess you'll have to kill *him*," she said with a gesture towards Arif.

Before anyone could even observe Cain's reaction to the statement, the man behind him, the history buff, raised his hand-held crossbow and fired a stake at Cain's back, at point-blank range.

Alyson turned to push him out of the way, but was too late. Cain felt the impact in his back with the force and sting of a bullet wound, but the stake clattered to the floor. Had he not been wearing his chain-mail vest, in all likelihood it would have penetrated his flesh to impale his heart from behind.

The others barely had time to understand what had happened before Cain turned in a quick, fluid motion and stabbed the man through the chest with the wooden stake he had kept concealed in his sleeve. The vampire turned to ash that blew and scattered in the wind out over the sea as it fell. His crossbow pistol dropped to the floor with a thunk, as Cain turned back to see the others.

Alyson looked confused and stricken over the sudden display of violence, and her inability to prevent it. Arif hadn't even moved. He seemed shocked, as Cain spoke. "Well, that was rude."

Arif quickly gathered his composure and smiled. "You'll have to forgive him. My men can be a bit over-protective."

Cain glanced at the last of the vampire's ashes as they scattered from around the bits of clothing and his weapon. "Consider him forgiven," Cain muttered as he stooped to pick up the crossbow pistol. He did his best to move smoothly, without obvious hindrance, although he felt like someone had buried an ice-pick in his back. "I like this," he said, admiring the weapon. "I think I'll keep it."

"Haven't I given you enough weapons?" Arif asked, with a pointed glance at Ash-bringer, sheathed at Cain's hip.

"Don't give me reason to use them and it won't be a concern."

Arif dismissed the comment with a grimace and gave his attention back to Alyson. "Young lady, you will turn the human as I have asked, or I *will* force you to. Either way, it will be done.

As you have surely just noticed, when you entered the lighthouse, your powers were stripped from you by my good man Jin. That's his specialty, negating the powers of others, a very subtle, insidious gift."

Alyson seemed to be assessing her state, and finding his words to be true; her loss of supernatural speed and agility the cause for her delayed reaction to Cain's peril. "He's right," she exclaimed to Cain in rising panic. "I can't do anything." They had known this would be the case, but she was playing along, as though it was an unexpected development.

Arif continued. "I'm not a fool. I know that were you uninhibited, you could have simply levitated yourself to wrest Felicity from Lorelei, and flown away with her before we could do a thing to stop you, even if it left Cain in a somewhat awkward position.

Surely, he would accept the danger, even though it would likely mean his true death, but luckily, he needn't play out such a scenario. He brought you here because he has faith that you will accomplish my will to save his love, whether you are amicable or not."

Cain spoke to Alyson, as though trying to soothe her fears. "Calm down. We'll just do as he asks, take Felicity and go."

"Do as he asks?" Alyson widened her eyes in supposed realization. "Cain, you knew?" she asked, as though he had betrayed her.

"It's alright."

"Like hell it is! I'm not sharing my blood; not even to save Felicity."

Arif interjected on Cain's behalf. "Listen to him. You know he cares for your safety as well as the human's. Do as I ask, and no one will come to harm. Without your powers to protect you, you are helpless. Just a little girl who is sorely out of her depth here, and I can force you to do anything I please. You will change Ilker, and then I will allow you and Cain to take Felicity and leave. I'm sure Cain will agree, that scenario is preferable to anything else that might be done here."

Alyson quickly pulled a stake of her own from her boot, and lunged forward to plunge it into Arif's chest, but Jin sprang to counter the strike before it could land with any force. He struck her wrist, and then grabbed and twisted her arm behind her in a martial arts move that caused her to drop the stake. She struggled, but was held firmly in an arm lock.

Cain was taken aback, but quickly composed himself to face Arif with a smirk. "Forgive her. I guess she's over-protective too."

Arif gave him an insincere smile in return, and then addressed Alyson with a chuckle. "Without your strength and speed, you cannot hope to harm me. Besides, I have taken a page from Cain's book this evening," Arif informed them, unbuttoning his shirt to reveal that he also wore chain-mail beneath. "I was informed of his habit of wearing such protection when first we met, and deemed it a prudent precaution to adopt for myself. Vampires as old as we are know better than to take unnecessary chances.

Now, let us ascend to the lamp room and perform what needs to be done, so that you might both go on your way."

Jin ushered the struggling Alyson ahead of him as Arif bid Cain to follow them. They circled the tower to the door. Once there, Jin released hold of Alyson's wrist and gestured for her to open the door. She simply stood there, rubbing her sore wrist. "Screw you."

The door opened from within, and another of Arif's guards was there. Apparently, he had been called from somewhere to replace the man Cain had dusted. He was waiting for her to enter and climb up to the next level as Arif answered her protest. "Climb. I am sure Cain is eager to be reunited with his beloved human." Cain gave him a dirty look, before exchanging a glance with Allie. She glared at him angrily, but entered the tower and climbed the stairs.

The door at the top of the stairs was opened for her from within by an oriental woman wearing odd, thigh-high white boots, and a pink spandex jumpsuit decorated with a large white and silver diamond stripe design. She wore a wig of long hair, white as shimmering snow, with heavy bangs. The bulk of it was piled on her head in an elaborate array of buns and knots that were accented with pink cherry blossom flowers and many long, white and pink oriental hair sticks, some with small, chained gems hanging from them. Her eyes were thickly lined dark black and ringed with heavy, spiked lashes, while her face was painted with wide striped swaths of pink and white shadow on her cheeks, beneath her eyes like war paint.

As she backed away from the door, it could be seen that her boots actually had her standing completely on tip-toe with no heel, like a ballet dancer, each foot balancing only on the sharp tip of a lethal looking spike.

Alyson stopped in the doorway, taking in the layout of the circular room. It wasn't a very large space. The lamp for the lighthouse was surprisingly unimpressive. It stood in the center, mounted on a pole about six feet high, with a circular ledge-like platform beneath it. The remainder of the space sported floor to ceiling windows, and was bare, save for a small orange lifeboat about the size of a stretcher, piled with ropes and first-aid supply packs.

There were three other male vampires in the confined space, making the room seem quite full. Alyson didn't know any of them, but Cain recognized them as vampires he'd had the displeasure of dealing with before; Joseph, Richard and Anthony. Although he'd never actually sparred with any of the men, Cain knew they harbored a dislike for him. The feeling was mutual.

Felicity and Lorelei could be seen outside, through the windows, as they stood on the upper walkway, which put them about four feet above those inside the lamp room. The upper walkway was not meant for visitors and there was no visible access point to get out to it. They must have somehow been lifted there.

Arif nodded for Alyson to continue walking. "In."

"I'm going," she told him, while sizing up the woman before her. "Who are you supposed to be, the pink Power-Ranger?"

The woman moved back a step and gracefully bent her knee in a slow, deliberate movement that looked as though she was beginning a motion of dance. Then she suddenly spun, twirling faster than eyes could follow, pivoted her body and straightened her leg in a sideways kick, so that the pointed spike of her boot was level with Alyson's chest, a mere centimeter's thrust from piercing her heart.

"I'm Cat, and I'm here to make sure everything goes as planned," she said in an accented breathy purr.

Alyson looked down at the menacing spike. Upon closer inspection, it could be seen to be made of whitewashed wood, with only the tiny, sharp tip sheathed in silver metal for walking on without overly blunting its point. Once stabbed into a vampire's chest, the length of wood would be as lethal as any stake.

Alyson reached out to brush the boot-tip aside, but found that it could not be budged. Although standing on one leg, with the other outstretched in front of her without support, appeared to be a tenuous position, for Cat, it sacrificed none of her agility or strength. She held herself firmly planted, despite Alyson's push against her boot, and smiled. After a moment, she deliberately bent her knee and lowered her leg, and then bowed with an arm outstretched for Allie to move past her inside.

Alyson was visibly rattled. Cain sincerely hoped she was trying to look more shaken than she was, for the sake of their audience. If things came down to a fight, which they surely would, Cat's power and agility couldn't be matched by anyone but Allie herself. Cat was hers to handle. But Cain had to get her powers back first...

"You still can't make me change someone against my will," she informed them bitterly, as she walked past Cat, further into the room.

Arif crossed his arms and smiled. "I don't actually need *you* to do anything. With Jin dampening your powers, I can simply use my own mental abilities to force whatever actions from your body I please, including drinking from Ilker and feeding him your blood. Cain understands this, and has wisely agreed."

"On second thought," Cain replied, "I don't think I find that acceptable at all, no matter what Jin is doing."

Arif turned to squint at Cain, skeptical that he could be in any position to dispute the plan. Cain ignored him to address the other vampire. "Jin...that's a Chinese name, isn't it? Fairly common in China, I believe. But I'm guessing that you didn't take the name until after you were turned into a vampire, did you?"

All present seemed quite confused by this line of questioning. Jin answered, after an uncertain glance at Arif for approval. "That's right."

Cain nodded, his conjecture having been confirmed. "Your power to strip others of their vampiric talents is very impressive, and I am sure that Arif is quite relieved by the fact that you will keep Alyson abated for him. What he may not have counted on, is my passing knowledge of Mandarin Chinese. I'm far from fluent, but I do know that Jin means *gold*...like the color of your eyes. Your eyes are gold, aren't they..." he asked, narrowing his own eyes as he completed the question in a menacing whisper, "same as mine?"

To prove his point, Cain shifted his eyes to reveal their vampiric hue of yellow gold, painting the other vampires in cold tones of blue and green to his vision. Cain smiled, his fangs fully distending and giving some small outlet to the malice brewing within him. "So Arif, you won't be forcing anyone to do anything, because I'll be using my own formidable talent to strip your powers from you."

Arif tried not to show alarm over the realization that his powers had now in fact deserted him. A sneer of annoyed discomfort passed over his face. "So, the prudent teacher of restraint has ventured outside the careful boundaries set for himself to discover and awaken his power; unexpected, I will admit. How many humans did you need to kill to bring your talent out of its dormancy?"

Cain glared at him in disdain. "None. I don't kill...humans."

Allie grinned as she interjected, "I gave him a sweet long drink before we got here. And I've had plenty of human blood to fuel me, with some to spare. He may not have been practicing, but I'm thinkin' he's plenty old enough to easily suppress *you*."

Arif gave her a condescending smile. "Nicely done, but it won't make much of a difference. You are still greatly outnumbered, by others you cannot suppress, and even if you could, I am quite confident that my guards can best you in physical combat. You are only one man and a petite young girl. I will have you restrained by my men. I can drain Ilker myself, then draw blood from Alyson without her cooperation, and feed it to him. Once he has been changed, and awakens as a white-eyed vampire, I will allow Cain to take Felicity to safety, and not before."

Cain stepped forward, looking more dangerous than surely any vampire present had ever remembered seeing him, and took back their attention. "I don't think I like that plan. In fact, I've come up with one of my own. What do you think would happen if while Jin was using his talent to hold Alyson at bay, I were to use my own formidable talent to strip Jin of his powers? I may be a bit new at this, but I'm older and stronger than he is by far. If it were to work, Alyson would be unfettered...and fully capable of doing whatever she pleased. That would be quite a problem for you, I'd imagine...unless Jin were able to dampen Alyson *and* shield himself from me. That sounds rather unlikely. What do you think?"

Arif didn't bother to answer. His face paled as he took a slight step back from Cain and called out, "Guards!"

Cat quickly moved to Arif's side. His most daunting vampire would be used to protect him personally; he was taking no risks. "Jin?" he asked, sounding none too hopeful that the vampire could keep Alyson at bay.

Jin worriedly shook his head no, as Cain dampened his powers and Alyson levitated herself off the ground with a wickedly gleeful grin.

"Take Ilker to safety," Arif ordered, disgusted with Jin's uselessness. He must have decided that with Cain and Jin cancelling out each other's powers, the man would serve better elsewhere. Jin quickly made for the door with Ilker in tow and descended out of view down the stairs. Cain and Allie let him go. The human was meaningless, and secretly, Cain was relieved not to have to deal with Jin. Alyson had described him as a master martial artist.

As Jin left, the man who had been guarding the top of the stairwell replaced him inside to assist Arif.

"What do you really hope to accomplish by trying to defy me?" Arif asked, mockingly. "You are still outnumbered. It is only blood. Share it and be on your way. Do you and your friends truly plan to forfeit your immortal lives just to keep it from me? What a ludicrous waste."

Alyson sneered at him while hovering as she answered. "The only thing getting wasted here, is you."

The door was flung open as Jin returned, still pulling the human boy behind him. "There's fighting in the stairwell. The exit is blocked," he explained.

Allie smiled. "Sounds like my back-up has arrived."

Arif smirked at her. "Don't be too relieved. Whatever small handful of supporters you may have collected are nothing compared to the reinforcements I can bring."

As he spoke, Cain noticed a dark mist funnel its way through the top of the door crack before it was closed again. The smoke collected itself into a cloud near the ceiling over Arif and then coalesced before him into the shape of Kieran.

Arif smiled as his trusted spy took form. "Ah, see. Perfect timing, Kieran."

Kieran gave him a devilish grin. "Yeah, I thought so." As he finished speaking, he allowed his mark to come into view. It was a strong and steady mark, showing him to be a vampire of fairly good age and strength. It was also clearly covered with the signature of The United One.

Arif's expression transformed from one of astonished disbelief, to disgusted hatred. "After all I have done for you."

"All you've done is provide well deserved payment for the unique services I've put at your disposal for the past forty-five years. I've given you unflinching loyalty and continuously carried out your orders without fail, no matter how distasteful. In return, you've discounted my opinions and used me as a guinea pig for Cat's power inhibitors and crazy torture devices. I won't say I haven't enjoyed the coven lifestyle, but you're not my maker and I don't owe you anything. If you're too stupid and greedy to recognize The United One as your superior, then I am more than happy to help rid her of you."

Cat seemed amused by his betrayal as she positioned herself in a protective stance before her master. Arif was quick to answer. "Careful... One telepathic directive from me, and Lorelei will run Felicity through with her sword," he warned.

Kieran and Cain worriedly glanced out the window, to see that Lorelei did indeed have Felicity held close, her sword at the ready. As Kieran paused, momentarily defeated, further movement at the window caught their eyes.

Elric rose up from below, levitating himself over the railing to confront the vampiress. He kept his distance, and her attention. Lorelei smiled, having the upper hand in threatening her hostage, but was suddenly shoved from behind. A woman, who could only be Latisha, had unexpectedly risen up behind her. Lorelei had been focused on Elric, not anticipating that anyone could sneak up on her position.

Lorelei stumbled into Elric's arms, but before he could take firm hold of her, she swung wildly around her, sword flashing and slicing through Latisha's side as Elric's new progeny shoved Felicity out of the way.

Latisha was badly wounded, but thanks to her new vampiric state, it wasn't lethal. Felicity struck the window and slumped to the floor in her dazed enthrallment, still incapable of taking independent action. Elric struggled to disarm Lorelei, but the vampiress was far too good a swordswoman to allow it.

Confident that whatever the outcome, Elric would keep Lorelei held sufficiently harmless, Kieran returned his focus to Arif. "I don't think so," he answered. "By the way, Elric wanted me to let you know, he's sick of your superiority shit. You're not our *master*, not anymore," he concluded, as he phased his lower half into mist once again and propelled himself forward to attack. Before he could connect with Cat or Arif, the door guard and Anthony blocked his way.

Richard and Joseph both moved aside, giving the others room to deal with Kieran as they focused on Cain. Cain looked around to see what Alyson was doing, but she seemed to have inexplicably disappeared. He couldn't look for her, he had business of his own to handle. Joseph tried to come at him with a stake, but Cain easily disarmed the vampire and pushed him to the ground as Richard attacked him from the other side. Cain grabbed at Joseph and shoved him into his partner, backing away as the two became tangled in each other for a moment, allowing Cain to back away and observe the other occupants of the room.

Cain saw that Arif's guard and Anthony were trying to fight Kieran, but the shade kept dispersing parts of his body into smoke so that their strikes couldn't land. Anthony was cursing up a storm, but was managing to avoid Kieran's retaliations, while the other guard seemed sorely out of his league in the fight. Finally, Kieran was able to wrest a stake away from the door guard and pierce his heart with it.

As the guard vampire crumbled into dust, Anthony became enraged. "You annoying little shit! First you act like the master's spoiled little pet, and then you bite the hand that feeds you? Just wait 'til I get my hands on you, you ungrateful freak!"

Kieran didn't seem worried. In fact, he became stoically confident as he fully formed himself standing before Anthony in a rare moment of stillness. "I am so sick of you," he said quietly. Anthony couldn't help but take the bait and charged for Kieran, hoping to grab the elusive vampire while calling him names. "You never shut your mouth," Kieran remarked, as he suddenly swirled into mist and unexpectedly siphoned himself right into Anthony's open mouth.

The vampire immediately shut his trap and looked alarmed, as though he had swallowed a bug. Unfortunately for him, what had gone down his throat was much bigger than any insect. Anthony's eyes went wide and then he suddenly exploded as Kieran reformed himself inside the man. Blood and gore flew everywhere, but quickly turned to dust as it struck the other vampires, the windows and floor. Kieran stood in the center of it, naked and covered in a sludge of blood turned dust as he tried to spit some of Anthony's remains out of his mouth. "I really hate doing that," he said with a shudder.

Everyone in the room was still in shock over the incident when Allie suddenly appeared, coalescing her form from the shadows behind Arif. "Neat trick," she commented to Kieran, as she gripped her hands tightly about Arif's throat and beneath his chin. She obviously planned to use her super-strength to behead him using brute force. She began to levitate off the ground with his head in her hands, but was quickly grabbed around the waist by Cat, who had the formidable strength to counter her.

"Get off me, bitch!" Allie screamed. She tried to turn only the bottom half of her body to mist, as Kieran often did, but she wasn't as experienced in such partial transformation, and her hold on Arif suffered. She was forced to let go of him and deal with Cat instead.

Joseph tried to take advantage of the distraction to rush at Cain again, but Cain instinctively raised the small crossbow he still held, and fired it at Joseph's chest. There was such little space between them, he'd hardly needed to aim, and the bolt could barely be heard leaving the bow before Joseph was struck in the heart and turned to dust.

Richard held a crossbow as well, but lowered it in favor of a small, wickedly curved sickle in his other hand as he came for Cain. Arif must have informed him that Cain was wearing chainmail. With a quick glance, Cain told Kieran to leave him and go help Alyson with Jin, Cat and Arif. Cain dropped his bow and drew Ash-bringer from its sheath, making Richard pause in healthy respect. Most likely, he knew the sword, and he had no doubt that someone of Cain's age had learned, at some point in his life, to wield it. Richard was backing away when both men heard Cat let out a chilling scream.

Rather than continue to try to fight the woman, Allie had simply grabbed her and thrown her as hard as she could towards the wall of windows; and Allie could throw ridiculously hard. Cat shrieked and smashed through the glass, as she went flying out over the railing and off the tower.

Richard was keeping his distance, trying to weigh his chances against Cain's sword, while Jin was warily circling Kieran. Allie turned back to Arif, who now only had the human boy with him. Undaunted, Arif seemed ready to meet Alyson with his usual cocky arrogance. "You may want to take this opportunity to retreat," Arif told her mockingly. "I think your assistance may be needed elsewhere."

Cain found the suggestion ludicrous, a desperate ploy, but Alyson took it more seriously and paused, distracted. "Mattie? Where are you?" She must feel him nearby through their mark. Now that she had alerted him to Mattie's presence, Cain could feel him too, though not nearly as strongly. Arif must have been telepathically informed of his arrival, but was he in danger?

Cain caught Alyson's eye, and she allowed him into her telepathic communication as Mattie responded in thought. *I'm outside with the Everhearts and a lot of really pissed-off vampires. Arif must have called for help.*

Cain could feel Allie's instant concern. *Are you okay?*

I'm fine for now. Don't worry about me.

She wasn't very reassured. *Stay out of Ben's way. I'm not sure what he's thinking about all of this. And keep your guard up around his dad too... I don't trust him.*

I'm fine, you just focus on what you're doing, Mattie reprimanded her. *Watch out for Cat. Kieran says she's nasty.*

I can handle her, Allie assured him with a chuckle.

Mattie still seemed worried. *She's just as strong and fast as you are, and she's had decades of experience. Don't be over-confident.*

It's okay, I sent her for a swim, but I'll be careful, Allie agreed dutifully. *I love you.*

I love you too.

There was brief mental silence, during which the sounds of fighting could be heard down below, mingling with the crash of ocean waves. Alyson mentally called out for him again. Cain could feel her urgent sense of desperation, as though she worried she might lose the chance to communicate with him further. *Mattie...don't get killed. I don't think I could handle that again.*

I won't if you won't, he answered.

Deal.

"Do you think I can't hear you?" Arif interjected, snidely.

Alyson looked alarmed, but Cain reassured her. "Don't listen to him. He's just trying to mess with your head."

"He's lucky I haven't taken off his," Allie answered, keeping her focus on Arif. "It doesn't matter how many coven members you call. I'm The United One; I don't take orders, I give them. In my blood swims cells from the very first vampire to ever walk the Earth. My blood remembers nights of dark glory when vampires ruled this world as gods, and it is destined to return to that divinity. You were nothing more than a tool to speed the process, a means to an end. And I'm pretty sure that at this point, the blood believes *your* usefulness has reached *its* end."

"The *blood* believes...?" Arif asked, in hesitant confusion.

"You didn't really think *you* were the mastermind behind everything that happened to make me what I am, did you? Your arrogant greed was an opportunity for the blood to move the pieces into position. It doesn't need you anymore, and quite frankly, your aspirations are annoying. The blood has been reunited in me now. This is my destiny, and I'll take it from here."

Cain felt almost the same amazed confusion as Arif did over Alyson's words, but dearly hoped she was just trying to be dramatic for the sake of the small audience of vampires left in the room.

Arif's confidence had finally begun to desert him as he assessed the chances of him, the human, Jin and Richard surviving a confrontation against The United One, backed by Kieran and Cain. "What are you planning to do?" he asked her quietly.

"You wanted my powers so badly?" she asked. "Here's one for you. Ever wanted to fly?"

Arif found himself lifting into the air. "Master!" Ilker, the young human beside him yelled, grabbing at his legs and trying to bring him back to the ground. "No!" the boy pleaded to Allie.

Cain could tell that Jin was desperately trying to dampen Alyson's powers. Cain kept his focus on Jin, concentrating to direct his newly discovered talent to keep Jin from defending his master.

Jin charged at Cain, hoping to distract him physically and break his focus, but although new to using his talent, Cain was well experienced in self-control. He allowed Jin to tackle him, only minimally defending himself, knowing that allowing Alyson to act unfettered was the key to their success.

Richard approached to try to help Jin, but Kieran appeared unexpectedly at his side and disarmed the vampire of his weapon, wresting the sickle from his hand and then swiping at him with it. Kieran managed to slice his arm pretty badly. It wasn't a debilitating wound, but it forced Richard to back off.

Meanwhile, Alyson was using her telekinesis to float Arif towards the gaping hole in the windows where Cat had crashed through. Arif spoke to her, trying to remain calm and somehow endear himself to her. "Such power you display! You are indeed queen of us all. I now recognize it to be true. Your unquestionable omnipotence is magnificent."

Alyson stepped over the broken glass and passed through the window frame, following Arif as she levitated him above the lower walkway, and then out over the edge of the railing.

Higher, and higher, she levitated him. Arif continued to speak to her as he was raised into the sky, above the crashing ocean waves that pounded the rocky shoreline. "I know that you resent my efforts, but can you blame me for desiring to harness such raw power? You are angry. Dash me upon the rocks," he suggested, eyeing the jagged outcroppings of stone far below as he was tugged at and pummeled by the increasing wind. "Drop me to my doom so that I might suffer for the anguish that I have caused you to suffer. And when I heal, I will crawl back to you, a humble and broken servant to the queen."

Allie cocked an eyebrow at him. "Drop you? I'm not going to drop you. I don't think such a crude act of clumsy violence is befitting a queen, do you?"

Arif smiled in relief. "Ah...mercy is the mark of true nobility."

Allie laughed as thunder rumbled in the air around them. "Mercy? Oh no...you *will* suffer for all you've done. I just thought I should repay you with something a little more elegant than bashing your head in." He squinted at her, wondering what she could have in mind. "Thanks for making it so easy for me."

Arif's chest seemed to be faintly glowing with the soft blue-green light of St. Elmo's Fire, his chainmail vest reacting to the eminent storm. His hair began to stand on end as a booming crack of thunder sounded and a bolt of lightning streaked through the sky. It was unerringly drawn to Arif, its closest target. Arif's face distorted in pain and surprise as the voltage flowed through him and his entire chest suddenly seemed to glow.

Cain realized that the chainmail Arif wore was acting as a conductor, attracting the electricity as lightning struck him again and again. Cain worried the metal chainmail would take the bulk of the charge, acting as a Faraday suit to divert the electricity and protect Arif himself, but as Arif was flying in the air, there was nowhere else for the electricity to flow. It raced through his form, super-heating the metal and seeking outlet to the ground. The metal of the chainmail paired with the electricity flowing within made his entire form glow bright like the sun; orange, yellow and then white.

Each link of metal became a searing brand of white-hot pain as its particles began to soften, melt and flow with the incredible heat, but already the vampire within was meeting his demise. Arif's eyes widened and suddenly pooled with blood, while at the same instant, his mouth opened as though to scream, but rather than voice, all that could be heard was a rush of air and singeing crackle as he completely exploded into dust.

Pieces of red-hot molten metal and clothing were still falling through the air towards the ground as twin feminine screams of dual hysteria erupted from Lorelei on the walkway up above, and Cat somewhere below simultaneously as they saw their master explode.

Cat could not be seen. She must still be trying to make her way back up the tower after Allie had thrown her off it. Lorelei, however, was quite clearly visible through the window from her place on the walkway where Elric had been holding her at bay and keeping her from harming Felicity. Lorelei went wild with rage. "They destroyed him! You let her destroy him! How could you?"

She began to viciously attack Elric with her sword, but luckily, the walkway behind him was clear. He was able to keep taking steps of retreat to avoid her strikes. She was stabbing at him viciously, but was too blinded by grief to be clever and couldn't make contact, no matter how she advanced on him.

The occupants of the tower watched her attempts, as Alyson re-entered through the broken window and retrieved her clothes from the floor so she could get dressed. Elric continued around the walkway above, unconcerned with Lorelei's emotional and clumsy attacks.

Cain was momentarily startled when Kieran suddenly appeared between he and Alyson. Allie, having marked the shade, was unsurprised, knowing exactly where he was. "Go check on Mattie for me, will you?" she asked him. Kieran had barely nodded before wisping into smoke and disappearing to carry out the directive.

Their gazes were drawn up to the window again as Lorelei bumped it with the hilt of her sword after another unsuccessful swing. Finally, Elric pulled a stake from his pocket and held it up, menacingly. "Don't make me use it, Lorelei."

She stopped her vengeful cries of insult and outrage, and actually laughed at him. Considering that she was armed with a sword, it did seem unlikely that he was in any position to harm her. She checked behind her, to make sure that the injured Latisha was not sneaking up on her again, but Latisha and Felicity could not be seen by her from around the bend of the lighthouse. Surely, she assumed they were both still lying motionless where they had been left. Lorelei may not be thinking quite clearly, but even she realized Elric posed no real threat to her now. She changed her stance as though taunting him to go ahead and try something.

Elric held the stake up over his shoulder to be thrown at her like a spear. It was a large stake, but still less than two feet long. It did not have the weight and heft to be thrown a distance with any real force. Even if he hit Lorelei with it, it would be lucky to break the skin, let alone pierce her heart to do her true damage. Elric was strong, but he didn't have the supernatural strength and dexterity that Cat wielded to perform such a trick.

He threw the stake, and Lorelei easily avoided it, brushing it aside with her sword while chuckling at him. He shrugged as though to say, *I tried.* Lorelei, being focused on him, did not see Latisha, high up, directly above her. As Lorelei lowered her blade, distracted, Latisha dropped on her like a stone, making the sword clatter from the vampiress's clasp.

Elric darted forward and claimed the weapon as the women wrestled. Elric held the sword ready before him as the vampiresses got to their feet. Seeing she was bested, Lorelei did the unexpected. She grabbed Latisha in a bear hug and threw her weight to carry them both over the railing. Elric rushed to see them tumbling through the air and then jumped the railing himself to go after them.

Cain could not see what happened next, as the three fell below his floor level, but realized that what Lorelei had done was not as crazy as it seemed. A fall from that height would almost certainly kill a human, but a vampire could survive it, although not pleasantly. Lorelei also knew that Latisha could fly. She wouldn't allow herself to hit the ground if she could help it, and as long as Lorelei clung tightly to her, she'd also be spared the fall. Most likely, Latisha would manage to stop their descent as they neared the ground, and then throw Lorelei off her. It would be a vicious fight between the two women, but without sword or stake, they would each probably survive the encounter.

Alyson faced the occupants of the room, addressing Jin and Richard in particular. "Are we done here?"

Richard seemed to want nothing further to do with the fight, but Jin was not backing down so easily. "And who's taking over the coven now, *you?* Just 'cause you fried Arif, you think I'm supposed to bow down to you now or something?"

Cain didn't want to waste time with displays of authority. He just wanted to go and collect Felicity so they could get out of here. He sheathed his sword, hoping to ease the tension and defuse the situation. "No one is asking anyone to bow down in submission. How about we just settle for you going on your way?"

Alyson threw him a look of annoyance. "And what if I am looking for submission? This guy thinks he's better than me?" she asked in challenge.

Cain gave her a stern look of disapproval that went totally unheeded. He couldn't leave her with him, because without Cain dampening Jin's powers, Jin could render Alyson practically helpless. She might be able to negate his power on her own if she had a jump on him, but it was risky to think she could focus to hold him powerless while also using her other talents. She was still fairly new at all of this.

Cain couldn't get to Felicity on his own. From what he could tell, Alyson would have to fly up to retrieve her. He made a face at her to back down on the bravado, but she was still resentful over her first encounter with the man, when Jin had bested her in a fight and held her down until she'd needed Mattie to come to her rescue. She wasn't letting him leave the room without acknowledging her as his superior, and that meant Cain couldn't leave yet either. She needed him, and she knew he wouldn't desert her.

Alyson approached Jin, full of new confidence and eager to meet the martial arts master in battle. "You may know more moves than I do, but I'm stronger than you now...way stronger."

Jin shook his head with a smile, as they circled each other. "Such a novice. Didn't anyone ever teach you that it's not about strength? It's about leverage."

"Yeah, I've heard that. But I don't think it applies when your opponent can lift and toss a Mack truck..."

Alyson darted forward, but Jin apparently anticipated the move she had planned and knew how to meet it. "There's more than one kind of leverage," Jin commented, cryptically, as he countered her. Her extra strength made it difficult for him, but he managed to dance out of reach with only a glancing blow hindering him. "Lorelei wants me to let you know that you'd better watch your back. She'll be coming for you," Jin informed her as he backed away from Allie, towards the door.

Lorelei must have escaped, and was in telepathic contact with him. Something about the way he'd mentioned leverage sounded suspicious. Cain tried to sort out what he could mean. Felicity had been used as leverage against them... Cain looked worriedly out the window, but Felicity was still alone up on the walkway. She had just regained consciousness, awakening from Lorelei's enthrallment when the vampiress fled.

Felicity began to rise shakily to her feet, seeming unharmed, but unsteady. She was dazed, gripping the railing to steady herself, but not knowing where she was and being alternately thrust into darkness and then blinded by the lighthouse lamp flashing at her every few moments. Her eyes couldn't adjust, and she was very confused. She was also unprotected, and Cain didn't even know how to get up to that level; it wasn't meant for visitors, and there were no stairs or ladder that he had seen. "Felicity," he called, hoping to reassure her, but with the noise of the ocean and fighting down below, she couldn't even hear him.

He quickly assessed the situation. Jin and Alyson were occupied with each other, leaving only the human boy, Ilker who cowered in the corner, and Richard, who had retreated to sit on the lifeboat and nurse his wounds.

Cain ran to meet Alyson before she tried to pursue Jin any further, but was too late. Alyson leapt forward again, kicked low and swept Jin off his feet. He scrambled out of reach but had to move further away from the door to do it. She tried to grab and get him in a hold, with speed and strength he couldn't hope to outmaneuver for long. Once she truly caught him, he was done for. He barely avoided her as Cain ran up on them. "Where's Cat?"

Alyson spared a moment to glance away from Jin, who quickly took advantage of her distraction to duck and roll out of her reach again. "I don't know," she called to Cain in irritation.

"Forget Jin. Find Cat!"

Allie was still focused on Jin, unwilling to walk away from the fight. "But..."

"I'll handle him," Cain insisted.

Jin laughed. "I don't think so, old man." Jin was a much more seasoned fighter than Cain, being a formally trained expert, but it really didn't matter, because at this point Cain had deduced that he was only stalling them anyway. He was trying to be a distraction.

Cain moved to take Jin's attention as he pleaded with The United One. "Alyson, you have to find Cat, because *you* are the only one even remotely capable of dealing with her."

A blur of pink motion outside the window drew their attention. It was Cat, just as Cain had feared. She looked damp and dangerously furious as she stood on their level, outside the window, on the opposite side of the tower from where she had been thrown. She was on the walkway below Felicity, but as they watched, she leapt straight up to land truly cat-like, on the railing. She balanced on the pointed spike-tips of her boots, like an impossible ballerina on a high wire.

Jin broke their entranced stares with a well-placed kick at Cain's chest, knocking him back and drawing Alyson's concern. As Cain returned to his feet, he glanced worriedly out the window to see that Cat had reached up to grasp the edge of the walkway above her, facing them, and was swinging herself forward and back like a gymnast. Cain, Allie and Jin were all mesmerized for a second, watching her, as she gave a last swing backward to do a handstand on the upper walkway, her back now leaning up against the upper railing. In a quick, fluid motion, she hooked her knees over the upper railing and let go with her hands to sit up and propel herself over the railing onto the upper walkway. Once Cat stood, she began purposefully moving towards the only other person up there, Felicity.

Jin chuckled as Cain's eyes widened in panic. Ignoring Cain as no real threat, Jin rushed at Alyson in a swirling flash of motion. She easily blocked the strikes he had aimed at her, but Cain rushed to pull him away from her. He was keeping her unfocused. "She's after Felicity," Cain yelled to Allie. "Go!"

Alyson realized his thinking. Jin might be a formidable fighter, but Cain could hold his own against the martial artist. There was no one capable of getting to Felicity but Allie.

Alyson extricated herself from Jin's attack. Without bothering to find the door, she simply leapt forward with a burst of speed and ducked her head, striking the lower windows in an explosion of glass, flying forward and out of the tower. In the chaos of shattering glass, Jin was able to land a solid punch to Cain's jaw, rocking him back a few steps and making his head spin for the moment.

Even as Alyson crashed through the windows, turning to rise up a level and orient herself to reach the women on the upper deck, Cain looked on in horror to see Cat spin, raising her leg before her with a swift kick to impale the spike tip of her boot forcefully into Felicity's abdomen.

"No!" The yell emerged from Cain's throat as a shocked plea of utter despair as Jin tackled him to the floor. Cain couldn't take his eyes from the window, even as Jin pummeled him with kicks and punches.

Like a sick and twisted nightmare of slow motion, Cain watched as Cat's boot stake punctured Felicity's body, and then she lifted her leg further, raising Felicity off the floor to dangle from it. Felicity screamed; a sound that felt like a stake through Cain's own heart and would unfailingly haunt his nightmares for years to come, as the woman he loved tried to push at the spike impaled through her core.

With her tremendous agility and strength, Cat gave a vicious flick of her leg, and kicked out over the railing, sending Felicity sliding off the length of the spike and flying over the ocean waves below.

Cain pushed Jin off him, a burst of terror-stricken disbelief making him seemingly impervious to the man's attacks against him, and ran to the window. Even as Felicity flew out over the railing, Cat was suddenly tackled by Alyson with a blow so hard it propelled both women through the upper windows in a cascading shower of glass, to land as a rolling tumult of screams and wrestling bodies on the floor between Cain and Jin. Alyson had been so focused on crashing out through the windows, and flying up to find and subdue Cat, Cain wasn't even sure if she understood what had happened to Felicity.

Cain's eyes wouldn't leave the window, even as he yelled to correct Alyson's mistake. "Forget her now! Get Felicity!" He frantically searched the view before him and found the splash amidst the waves where Felicity struck the surface and sank. He wouldn't let his eyes leave the spot as he tried to memorize the location in the shifting waves where Felicity had slipped beneath the water. He formulated how much time he might have to reach her, even as he refused to acknowledge that he had no way to actually get there before she was lost. No, he could not lose her like this. He hadn't preserved her life to be so senselessly thrown away. Surely, a greater destiny awaited her than this...

A figure rose into his view on the other side of the glass. Elric levitated up, passing Cain and heading up to land the upper walkway. Cain pounded on the window desperately for his attention. Elric halted his ascent to focus on Cain, as Latisha levitated into view behind him.

Cain yelled to be heard through the window and amidst the noise. "Felicity; please, you have to get her for me. She just went over the railing into the water." Cain felt a flash of relief when the man instantly turned to sweep his gaze along the shoreline, seeming eager to help.

"The water?" Elric asked skeptically. Although the spectacular view from the top of the lighthouse made it seem as though the ocean was just below, in actuality there was another small building and at least a hundred feet of pavement, steep grassy hillside and rocky shoreline before the actual water.

"About fifty feet out in the ocean, straight behind you. Cat threw her."

Elric immediately understood upon hearing Cat's name. The woman's supernatural strength could easily account for such a distance. "I'll try," he answered, ready to take off on the rescue mission.

Cain banged his flat hand on the glass once again, before Elric could leave. "She's hurt...severely."

Elric looked distressed to hear it and although he nodded understanding, Cain could tell that he thought the errand useless. Felicity would likely drown before he could find her, if she wasn't dead already.

"Just bring her back," Cain pleaded.

Elric's lover floated closer to the window and put a hand flat upon it, in a strangely calming gesture of understanding, meeting his eyes with reassurance. "Don't worry, we'll find her." Elric nodded gravely. He and Latisha knew that as long as they brought her back to him quickly, he could do something for her...even if he had to bring her back from the dead.

Cain watched them zoom out over the ocean in their search, and then faced the room once again. Jin seemed to have disappeared out the door, but Cain didn't care; let him run. He needed to get Alyson. He knew that Elric and Latisha would do what they could, but he had no idea whether Felicity was capable or cognizant enough to tread water, or if she had truly sunk beneath the surface, making her that much more difficult to find. The vampires didn't need to breathe, and could search the bottom of the ocean floor for her, if it came to that, but they'd find her quicker if Alyson could establish a telepathic link.

Unfortunately, Allie was preoccupied at the moment, tangling with Cat...and the proverbial 'cat-fight' didn't even begin to describe what was going on before him. The women were kicking, screaming, punching and whirling before him in a blur of acrobatic dervish that eyes could not follow.

Cat kicked at Allie, trying to puncture her chest, but only was rewarded with a rare moment of unbalance as The United One transformed into mist to escape the deadly strike. Cat's leg struck out into the air, her once-white boot tip still covered in Felicity's blood...

Allie reappeared behind the vampiress to take her by surprise and grab her by the hair. Cain knew Allie thought to grab the woman's decorative locks and use her incredible strength to simply pull her head from her body, but Cat's voluminous wig came off in Allie's hands.

Cat screeched at a volume and pitch Cain thought might break the remaining windows. Some black hair clung to the inside of the white wig as Alyson threw it aside in disgust. Cat's long black hair tumbled down around her shoulders, as she jumped to perch on the central lamp fixture and Allie came after her again.

Cain couldn't follow their actions further. He needed to get outside to Felicity, but as he tried to cross to the door, an arrow thunked into his shoulder with a sharp and painful stabbing sting. Ignoring the wound, his eyes followed the direction of flight to find Richard fitting a new bolt into his crossbow with a grunt of annoyance that he had aimed too high and to the right.

Cain dodged the next arrow that flew towards him, and tried to pull out the one lodged in his shoulder before charging the man. The barbed spear-like head wouldn't pull free, so he broke the shaft, holding it as a makeshift stake as he attacked Richard, aiming for his heart.

The vampire used the crossbow to block Cain's thrust and then discarded the weapon, as it would be useless in such close combat. Possibly, he had also remembered that Cain was wearing a chainmail vest. It hadn't protected his shoulder, but the vampire was unlikely to be able to pierce Cain's heart.

Cain didn't bother to try stabbing him again, but instead just pushed him aside, impatient to get past him to the door. Richard fell to the floor, but thrust a leg out, tripping Cain before he could dismiss the man. Richard's face was twisted in a grimace of anger as Cain looked back at him. "I'm trying!" the man yelled.

Cain was very confused for a moment, until he realized that Lorelei was most likely communicating with the vampire telepathically. That was why Richard had suddenly taken an interest again in fighting Cain. It was on a directive from Lorelei, whom he must consider to hold a high rank in the coven, now that Arif was gone and Elric had defected.

As Cain regained his feet, Richard stood to meet him. Richard had recovered the sickle he'd held earlier, but it was no match for Cain's fury over the delay. Richard barely had time to raise his weapon before Cain had drawn Ash-bringer from the sheath at his hip. Cain swung the blade in a strong arc that separated Richard's head from his body in one clean slice. He sped for the door before the man had even finished crumpling to ash.

Every moment was precious. Felicity was slipping away from him.

Chapter 21 - Discretion

Ben

At the base of the lighthouse
Montauk, Long Island, New York
Just a little earlier

Block, parry, block, lunge... Too far, he was over-extended and his assailant was just out of reach. Ben immediately regained his posture and backed up a step, stopping his opponent's retaliating overhead strike with a rising block. His arms shook with the force of the jolt; this guy had some serious strength behind his blade. Ben tensed his wrists and fought to counter the push, keeping control. Ben was strong too...all those hours swinging steel and pumping iron weren't for nothing!

This was the fourth vampire Ben had come up against while guarding the door. He'd been assigned to keep Cain and Allie's supporters from getting through to the lighthouse tower, but he wasn't letting Arif's reinforcements up there either. A pair of vampires had surprisingly lifted themselves from the ground to fly up the tower, but he couldn't do anything to stop them and didn't know whose side they were on anyway; how was he supposed to know who was who? From what he could tell, Cain and Allie didn't have many coming to their assistance. All of those approaching were vocally loyal to the coven. He prayed that wasn't a bad sign...

If Allie and Cain had as much combined power as they seemed to think they did, they shouldn't need help from those below. He hoped to God they weren't just boasting. As long as Ben kept most of Arif's coven down here on the ground, hopefully Allie could dust Arif's ass and they could finally bring Felicity home.

Seeing Allie again...that had been a shock no amount of preparation could steel him for. She looked different. Her hair was in a cute bob, actually long enough to touch her shoulders - longer than he had seen it in ages, but that almost made her look more human somehow. Her face...her eyes were still the same, at least while she had gazed at him anyway. She'd used her old pet name for him, but then she had taunted him with mocking jibes. In a strange way that others would probably never understand, it made her seem exactly like her old self. If she were truly different, trying to *pretend* to be the girl he'd known, wouldn't she have coddled him, spoken in terms of endearment and cajoling persuasion? She was Allie...the same lil' big sis that had always been his dearest friend, and his biggest pain in the ass.

Kieran had told him that she was going to help get Felicity back, and that she might put on a bit of a show against Ben and Bernard to do it. He'd urged Ben to trust that she was still his old friend. Seeing the way she interacted with Cain, looking into her eyes and observing her same old kick-ass attitude, he had to believe it. Allie wasn't one to take shit from anybody. Arif had wronged her and she was pissed. No matter what kind of mess things were between her and Ben, she was still Allie, she had to be, and he had to trust her. She was going to kill Arif and rescue Felicity. Ben's job was to keep everyone else down here on the ground so she had the time to do it.

After Cain and Alyson had arrived, things had been quiet for a little while, but then other vampires had begun to appear and challenge him, wanting to enter the tower as well. He and his father weren't letting anyone else up there. At first, Arif had tried to contact him mentally to give direction, but it wasn't long before the coven master became too busy to monitor what was going on down here, and then the fighting had begun in earnest.

The first three vampires Ben had faced had been fairly simple to dispatch. They were used to attacking unarmed humans, who feared their fangs and were easily overcome. Two had held mini-crossbow pistols, but Ben had managed to avoid being struck, and once he was close enough to meet them with his sword, they had all been swiftly beheaded.

Unfortunately, the guy he was fighting now carried a broadsword and knew how to use it. There were two other vampires who were true swordsman that Ben had seen come to defend their coven master, but they were both currently engaged in battle with his father. This guy was his.

Ben had almost had him, more than once. The guy was covered in blood from a deep slice in the side of his neck, but Ben hadn't managed to take his head off...yet. It was clearly evident that his opponent wasn't human; if he had been, he would have succumbed by now, if only from blood loss. The vampire must be old enough to know better than to pay much mind to wounds that weren't lethal. He had quite a few nicks and cuts on his arms and legs from Ben's offensive moves, and even a bad puncture wound in the gut, but he just kept on swinging.

Ben was bleeding too, but not nearly as badly. Like the vampire, Ben refused to pay any attention to his minor injuries. It was just some small superficial stuff that he had earned by forgetting to guard himself against 'illegal' moves. If anything, the sting of his scratches helped to remind him that this was no point match, and a poor performance would be his last. Distraction would mean death.

The vampire, on the other hand, had an arrogance about him that must have come from his supposed immortality. It was like he didn't believe he could be killed. Ben would be happy to correct the assumption. He started on the offensive again, backing the vampire towards the side of the building, hoping to make him stumble over a pile of construction materials heaped near the metal garbage pail there. The man stepped nimbly over the metal hooks and chains with distressingly unerring footing, and then pressed back at Ben, undaunted.

They both paused as the shattering of glass disrupted their concentration, accompanied by a distant scream from high up on the tower. Neither Ben nor the vampire wanted to risk glancing in the direction of the noise, allowing their opponent an opening, but Ben could see some of the commotion in his peripheral vision. A woman had been thrown from the tower. She was little more than a blur of color and sparkling glass fragments from his vantage point. All he could do was keep his mind on his own battle, and pray Felicity hadn't been wearing pink.

The vampire slashed at him with his sword, but Ben arched to avoid the strike and came back with a jab at the man's exposed left side. The vampire laughed, as though Ben had forgotten that going for bodily strikes would be useless, but Ben wasn't really trying to harm him. The move was a feint, after which he pivoted his blade to intercept the vampire's next swing, and touch his opponent with the end-tip on the hilt of his weapon rather than the point.

The vampire jerked back with a hiss over the touch, surprised to find that it had left a painful burn on his hand. Ben smiled. The pommel of his sword was adorned with the emblem of a cross; a nice touch his father had included when he'd had the sword specially made. Ben had even had it blessed by a priest a few nights ago. The minister had thought Ben's request to be sentimental and ceremonial. Ben wasn't even sure if it had been necessary, but was still very glad that he'd done it.

The vampire couldn't help but look down and observe the unexpected burn. Ben took advantage of his confused distraction to reverse his swing and bring his blade back around in a quick, sudden arc. It connected with the neck of his assailant, on the side opposite the bleeding slice from his earlier attempt, but this time, Ben had enough power behind the swing to pass through. He felt the blade connect and cut through flesh and bone before his opponent crumbled into dust.

Ben fought to control his follow-through as his victim disappeared into ash, and then breathed a sigh of relief, lowering his blade. He allowed his tensed muscles a welcome rest for a moment as he looked around, on guard against new attackers. No one else seemed near him, and he focused on his father just in time to see Bernard dispatch one of the two vampires he had been fighting. They must have both been pretty good to have lasted this long against the famed vampire hunter, even double-teaming him.

Confident that his father needed no help against the single remaining opponent, Ben regained his place guarding the door and continued to observe the surroundings as he watched the swordfight. The vampire's main advantage was that Bernard was susceptible to human exhaustion, while the vampire's only draining would be of his focus after a drawn out match. Ben knew that his dad thrived on this stuff, though. The other swordsman was good, there was no doubt, but Ben could tell his father was better. Unless there was some unforeseen trick in store, his father would be the eventual victor. The fight was moving further from the tower. Bernard would be insulted if Ben tried to assist, so he wouldn't approach unless it seemed absolutely necessary.

Motion caught his eye, from the corner of another building, just a bit apart from the lighthouse tower. Ben could see a figure there, leaning against the building, also watching the sword fight. Although it was dark, the person wasn't being very careful to stay concealed. He was standing by one of the floodlights. After a second of shocked disbelief, Ben realized that it was Mattie.

Ben stood there, having the unobserved freedom to study this vampire who used to be his best friend. He looked the same...the same as before he'd disappeared, having been captured and turned into a vampire. The same as when he'd found Ben out in the woods afterward, hunting for him, and Ben had realized the awful truth; that his friend was no longer human. He looked the same as every one of a million memories Ben had of them doing everything together; four-wheeling, shooting hoops in the driveway, fishing, exploring; the same as the yearbook photos of him on the lacrosse team and at the prom.

It was Mattie. He looked young though. That was Ben's first impression, but of course, it was only because his own perspective had changed. Almost ten years had gone by since Mattie's death, but in appearance, he was still only eighteen...no, seventeen, Ben realized. Mattie had died just before his eighteenth birthday. Wow, they'd both been so young when they had thought they were brave men, capable of going out into the night to hunt vampires.

Mattie was a handsome young man, unimposing, but strong and athletic with a friendly countenance and disarming features. He wasn't the dark, foreboding image you'd conjure up for a vampire, and it didn't look like dying had been very wearing on him. He *looked* like he should be someone's best friend.

He stood watching the swordfight between Bernard and the other vampire. At first, he was intensely focused, but after a few minutes he seemed to come to the same conclusion that Ben had; Bernard had the distinct advantage and it was only a matter of time before he took the vampire down.

Matt took his attention from the swordfight to turn and meet Ben's gaze. It shook Ben for a second; he could just tell that Mattie had known he was there all along. Ben realized that Mattie had probably been standing there observing Ben's fight as well, a few moments earlier. Ben could see Mattie struggling with indecision for a moment, before he visibly sighed and chose to come and confront Ben.

Mattie walked very slowly, his gate unsteady. Ben could tell right away that he must be injured. Maybe that's why he'd been keeping back from the action; not that Ben or his father had needed any help.

Ben kept his sword lowered, but ready. He still wasn't quite sure what to think of this vampire he used to know. What guarantee did he have that Mattie meant him no harm? He didn't know what Matt's motives were. Allie had been intentionally escorted up the tower into a trap, and Ben was here guarding the door. He'd been told that Matt understood the Everheart's secret alliance with Cain and Alyson, but Ben wasn't sure if Mattie agreed with or respected it.

Mattie stopped a few feet before him. He didn't say anything or look particularly happy to see him. If anything, he just looked tired and resigned to getting their reunion over with. Ben took a deep breath and tried to give a tentative smile. Years ago, Mattie had tried to extend the olive branch first after he'd been turned, and Ben had rejected him. This time it was Ben's turn to go first.

"Good to finally see you again." Mattie didn't offer a change in expression, so Ben continued. "So much has happened. We've been needing to talk for a while."

"Yeah," was his terse reply.

Up close, it was even more clearly evident that Mattie had barely changed. He might be a slight bit paler, but it was almost eerie how his appearance had simply halted in age. "My God, you...you still look the same."

"The same as the night you abandoned me out in the woods?"

Wow, okay...he was obviously still bitter. So much for old friends letting bygones be bygones. Mattie was usually super-forgiving and they had almost never argued throughout their entire friendship, but in Mattie's eyes, this rift was over a betrayal too large to just write-off and so easily forgive. Ben couldn't really blame him, and should have known he couldn't be that lucky.

"I didn't know what to think," Ben stammered, "what to believe. I thought you were a demon masquerading as my friend. I didn't know if it was still you," Ben explained, pleading for understanding. "I thought you were trying to trick me."

Mattie let out a huff of a laugh. "I was kidnapped, tortured, and lost everything and everyone I ever cared about. Yeah, that was some trick."

Ben exhaled, sympathy washing over him as he tried to imagine what that would have been like; something he'd tried not to dwell on in the past, almost *wanting* to believe it couldn't have been true. Why had he been so quick to believe overheard phone conversations of his father's, saying vampires were nothing but soulless demons? Why had he been so quick to believe his friend was gone? Allie hadn't given up on him...but look what that had gotten her. "You didn't lose Allie."

"No," Mattie agreed with a smile. "I didn't lose Allie, not for long. Honestly, she's all that ever really mattered anyway."

Ben couldn't dismiss the sick lump that fact brought to his throat. "And you killed her."

The words wounded Mattie, he could see it. No matter whether or not he believed what he had done was somehow good, or right, Ben could tell he was slightly ashamed to have to admit to the act. Ben watched him summon his will to defend it. "Yes, I did," Mattie confirmed with quiet resolution. "Lovingly, carefully, because she asked me to." It seemed Mattie had a lump in his throat as well.

Lovingly? Ben couldn't even try to imagine what that might have been like. She was human; a young woman with strength, spirit and a lifetime stretched out before her, and Mattie had taken that away to give her an existence of darkness, thirst and constant struggle not to allow herself to devolve into a ruthless killer. "You didn't have to. What happened to you wasn't your choice. You didn't have to do it to her."

"Yes, I did," Mattie insisted. "I love her."

"And what...you always hurt the ones you love?"

Finally, some flushed emotion rose from Mattie's quiet, resigned demeanor. "I didn't hurt her!" Such anger, passion...and as mad as he was over Ben's accusation, Ben was happy to see it. Allie deserved to have someone feel that passionately for her; he just wished she hadn't needed to give up her life to find it. "Hell," Mattie continued, "I spend most of my time hoping she won't hurt me."

"The way I did," Ben added. "Matt, you have to know that I didn't want to desert you. I thought you'd already been lost. I was young, and scared, and I thought you were a soulless demon. I didn't know if you were still my friend." He could see Mattie mulling that over, trying to put himself in Ben's shoes. "Are you?"

"Am I what? A soulless demon, or still your friend?"

Ben slumped his shoulders and lowered his eyes, wishing years ago he'd had the courage to spend some real time with his friend, back when he'd first discovered his fate, so he could have made the determination for himself. At this point, he believed it probably really was Mattie, but so much time had gone by and they each harbored such resentment, it would be hard to tell. He would just have to trust that it was him, and not a demon possessing his dead body. Allie had insisted it was really him, and she would have known the difference. But was Mattie still his friend?

After a second, Mattie spread his hands and cocked his head, inviting Ben to make his own decision. "I'm still Mattie. Does that answer your question?"

"I don't know."

"Me either."

A shout came from down the hill, in the direction of the parking lot, then another. People were coming. "Vampires," Mattie supplied for him. He must see their marks. From what could be made out of their yelling, it sounded like a group from Arif's coven were heading to the lighthouse, and a couple of others were trying to stop them.

Ben quickly looked Mattie over in assessment. "Are you hurt?"

Mattie rolled his eyes and sighed. "I can take care of myself."

That didn't really answer his question. Nice to know he wouldn't need defending, but Ben still wasn't sure if Mattie could be counted on to have his back in a fight. He'd find out soon enough.

A group of four men came into view. A quick assessment told Ben none of them carried swords. He didn't even see any of those annoying mini-crossbows. Good, he'd come very close to getting speared by arrows from a few of those earlier. This was basically just an angry mob. Ben got the feeling that Arif had called them, hopefully out of desperation. Maybe Allie actually was persevering up there.

Two more men came into view, in pursuit of the group. They caught up just before the first men reached the tower. A man with light brown hair and broad shoulders grabbed hold of the arm of the man in the lead, to spin him around. "Mick, you can't be serious. Do you think Elric left for no good reason? Trust me, Arif is finished. Let it go."

The man he spoke to looked a bit older, tall, thin and apparently not in the mood to be reasoned with. "I don't care what Elric did, and neither should you, Byron. This coven did a lot for me. When I was on the balls of my ass, they took me in. If Arif calls me, I'm there."

"You willing to get dusted over it? Because I told Elric I wouldn't let anyone up there, and I meant it."

"You think you're gonna stop me?"

Byron didn't answer, or even hesitate, before cold-clocking Mick in the side of the head. The rest dissolved into an all-out brawl, as the remainder of the group turned on Byron and the other vampire who had been trying to stop them.

The fight drifted back away from the lighthouse, down towards the lot. Ben turned to see what Matt thought of the development, but was drawn to look above his head as something else caught his attention. High in the air, next to the tower, someone was floating up off the observation walkway. It was a man, just hanging there in the air. Ben couldn't be positive, but it looked like Arif. "What the hell?"

Mattie turned to see what he was looking at, and then smiled. He walked off to the side, a bit around the tower for a better view. Ben was about to follow, when one of the vampires from the fight down the hill came rushing back to the lighthouse. Ben was pretty sure it was one of Arif's supporters and he looked mad as all get out. He was running for the tower door when Ben stepped out in front of him, sword drawn. "Where do you think you're going?"

The guy kept coming, and dodged aside barely in the nick of time to avoid the swing of Ben's sword. "Get out of my way," he grunted, as he faltered and then backed up to assess how he might get past Ben to the door.

Ben shook his head, still holding his sword out menacingly before him. "Sorry buddy. Tower's closed."

The vampire sneered at Ben, his long, sharp fangs distending, and his eyes becoming a menacingly reflective orange. "Aren't you supposed to be on our side?" he asked, baring his fangs and testing Ben again with a bold step towards the entry.

"Aren't you supposed to be in hell?" Ben made a strong swipe for the man's neck with his blade, making him stumble backwards to get out of the way. He scrambled to the side to avoid Ben's backswing, and came up against the garbage pail on the side of the building. As the vampire regained his footing, he glanced down to the pile of odds and ends littering the ground around the pail.

Ben hadn't pressed too far forward, worried to leave an opening behind him for anyone to get in the door. The vampire flashed a sinister smile and fished something out of the pile of garbage. When Ben saw what it was, he rushed forward again to threaten the man, but was forced to back off as the vampire lifted and began swinging his prize. It was a good, solid, four-foot length of chain.

This vampire must know a thing or two about weaponry. A chain is bad news for a swordsman; it can wrap around the blade, nullifying his weapon and throwing him off balance with a good tug. In swordplay, balance is everything. This seemingly inconsequential trash would actually be good defense if wielded well; and this guy evidently knew enough about it to think he was in good shape.

The chain was thin, but heavy enough to have some weight to it - a length of links similar to what you might find on a swing-set. The vampire was swiveling his wrist to make the chain swing around in a vertical, circular arc, the moon throwing glinting sparks of shine off the links. Ben tensed and readied his stance as the vampire approached, trying to chase him off from his position before the door.

Most of Ben's training had been in formal fencing, tournament style; a good base of knowledge certainly, but a far cry from defending himself against anything other than another sword. His father had been sparring with him more recently, and once the whole vampire-hunting secret had come to light, he'd thrown a few hypothetical scenarios Ben's way, with advice on dealing with certain unexpected situations. Luckily, facing off against a chain-whip had been one of them.

He paused, trying to remember what his father had told him. A chain's strength and speed came from momentum. Ben's goal was to interrupt the pattern, because without repetition the chain would have much less force behind its swing. The problem was distance. Ben had to move in quickly and stay on the aggressive, because the chain had a much farther reach than his sword, and if he hung back, his opponent would have a chance to wrap his blade and try to wrest it from him.

The vampire swung out, trying to do just that, but Ben was quick to react, swatting the chain sideways and withdrawing from it before he could become tangled. He then advanced close, swinging for the vampire's neck and forcing the man to back off, or be struck. He could tell the vampire was a little flustered to find that Ben wasn't completely unprepared, and knew enough to avoid entanglement.

The vampire retreated, his chain laying dead on the ground in front of him, vertical from where he held it at waist height. A breeze picked up, blowing the salt sea air at them, as clouds began to cover over the moon. The floodlight by the door still gave off some light, but without aid from the moon, it cast deceiving shadows as well. Ben squinted to see in the darkness, but his opponent's vision wasn't hampered at all. The vampire snickered at Ben, shaking his head with a smile. He wasn't giving up yet.

Mattie came back into view, returning after hearing the clash of sword on metal chain. He stopped at a respectful distance upon seeing Ben facing off with the vampire. Ben risked a glance at him, but still wasn't absolutely certain whose side Mattie was on; he didn't seem eager to jump in.

After noting that Mattie wasn't rushing to help, the vampire reached under his chain with his opposite hand, sweeping it up and starting the momentum of a swinging arc again. A streak of lightning flashed out over the water. It wasn't that close, but Ben still flinched from the unexpected flash. The vampire jerked forward, wanting to catch Ben off-guard, but the lightning hadn't been a strong enough distraction. Ben adjusted his position, ignoring the accompanying rumble of thunder that came after, and regained his defensive posture before the vampire could move in on him.

The vampire quickly lunged at him again, whipping the chain up over Ben's sword to try to whack him in the head. Ben ducked and swung, but still caught a good stinging knock in the ear with the end of the chain. The vampire laughed and rushed him, fangs bared, but Ben was able to raise his blade and defend himself before the vamp could grab him. It was a clumsy defense and the vampire wasn't really injured, but he backed off. Good thing, because Ben was still seeing stars from that chain whip to the head.

He looked up to see Mattie standing nearby, but he wasn't doing anything. He was just staring up at the top of the tower. "Mattie," Ben acknowledged him, and Mattie briefly made eye contact, but then turned his gaze back to the sky. "Wouldn't mind a little help here," Ben muttered. The vampire chuckled.

"I can't yet," was Mattie's odd reply. Yet? What the hell was he going to wait for? After seeing that Mattie was not interfering, the vampire pressed in on Ben again. He wrapped some of the chain up around his wrist, and then changing his swing into a vertical figure eight pattern, he moved close before Ben tauntingly. He had one leg forward to mirror Ben's stance and waited for his chance to strike again.

The unnervingly threatening whir of the chain whizzed before Ben, each over-arching downward swing coming perilously close, making him want to shrink away rather than get hit again. If he backed off, the vamp had the advantage though. He had to stay close enough to make the man wary of an unexpected strike. Tense and anxious, Ben watched his opponent, waiting for a shift in weight or stance to betray an impending strike.

Another bolt of lightning flashed, so bright and close this time, that Ben swore he could hear the air sizzle. A deafening crack of thunder sounded at practically the same instant, and then crackling and hissing noises were clearly audible. It sounded like it was coming from up near the top of the lighthouse tower. The lightning must have struck something...or someone, and from the sound of it, they were getting thoroughly fried.

Practically right behind Ben, from just around the side of the tower, a woman let out a blood-curdling scream. Ben twisted to guard against this new menace, and was surprised to see the woman in pink. She was dripping wet and running towards him from the ocean side of the tower, heading for the door in an otherworldly flash of speed. Ben automatically slashed out at her with his blade, but she did a truly acrobatic jump and spun in the air to avoid contact, sending a slight spray of seawater whipping at them from her clothing and hair. The stunt took her off course for the door, but she simply hit the brick wall of the tower, dug her nails into the mortar between the bricks and began impossibly climbing up the sheer, vertical surface.

Ben couldn't help but watch her for a second in awe as she scrambled up the wall like a spider, when he was suddenly struck on the arm by the chain from behind. He'd been standing with his sword-arm out apart from his body, his weapon still raised after slashing at the woman. It gave the other vampire a nice opportunity to wrap his chain neatly around Ben's arm. He pulled Ben in, making him stumble towards the vampire. Ben tightened his grip on his sword, desperate to at least keep his weapon, if not his balance.

The vampire used his other hand to grab Ben by the throat as soon as he was close enough. Ben's sword-arm was still tangled in chain and the vampire held it tightly close to his body, not allowing Ben to do much with his sword. He tried to stab the man in the leg or the side, anywhere he could reach, but that wouldn't do much good against a vampire, even if it hurt, and he couldn't get his arm out for a decent swing.

The vampire bared his fangs and tried to bite Ben, but Ben balled his free hand into a fist and punched the guy in the side of the head. As the vampire faltered, Ben was able to shake his arm free of the chain and get out of the vamp's hold. He staggered back, giving the vamp a good kick away from him in the process and then made a swing for the vampire's neck. The man brought up his arm, wrapped in chain, just in time to ward off the blow. Ben's blade hit the metal chain with a crash of sparks.

The vampire backed up and began swinging his chain again, eager to try to wrap up Ben's sword and take it out of the fight. Thunder rumbled overhead, making Ben flinch, his nerves frazzled. The vamp whipped the chain at him and Ben barely swatted it sideways. He took a nasty wrap across his knuckles, although he pulled away without getting entangled.

Damn katana...if he'd been using his trusty fencing foil, his hand would have been protected by the guard, but the Japanese sword didn't have much of one. Then again, his fencing foil didn't have as strong a cutting edge, being more for stabbing than slicing. This was the weapon for the job, where beheading vampires was concerned, so he was going to have to get used to it.

The vampire picked up his swing momentum again, and Ben fought to keep his grip firm, although his fingers were practically numb from the hit. He was exhausted...and in trouble. He looked to Mattie again. He was very close, close enough to lend assistance, but he seemed to be ignoring Ben's distress. This was no point match, this was life or death, and prideful as he was, Ben wasn't going to let this asshole kill him while help stood a few feet away.

"Mattie, we were friends once."

Mattie didn't even look at him, not that Ben had time to observe him closely, so Ben was surprised when Mattie actually answered him quietly, "I am helping you. I just need a minute."

Ben now realized that Mattie wasn't really ignoring the fight that danced before him. He was actually just deep in concentration, but Ben couldn't imagine what he could possibly be doing. "What for?"

Thunder cracked, making them all flinch again. The vampire used the opportunity to try another swing at Ben, but Ben managed to avoid it.

Mattie moved a little closer as another loud crack of thunder sounded directly above them. "Trust me," Mattie called to Ben over the wind. Ben didn't understand how Mattie expected to help him, but he wasn't in a position to argue. He said nothing and blocked another swing, trying not to lose concentration.

The vampire was whipping the chain over his head like a lasso now, looking for an opportunity to get in another headshot. "Drop your sword." The order came from Mattie. His opponent laughed and lashed at Ben's unguarded left side, catching Ben by surprise. He'd thought the vampire was going to keep his chain up high and barely changed his stance in time to avoid the dip in swing.

Ben spared Mattie a glance of pure disbelief. "What?" Was Mattie trying to get him killed, or what?

"Drop your sword!"

The vampire was whirling his chain like a helicopter blade, and grinning like a fiend. He was wearing Ben down, and he knew it. Ben was losing his endurance and his defense was getting slower. It wouldn't be long before the vamp had him. "Drop it, now!" Mattie yelled with urgent insistence.

In that split second, Ben decided to take a leap of faith. He let his weapon fall to the ground and stumbled back a step as his opponent came in for the kill. The man wore a vicious grin of amusement that Ben had become flustered enough to lower his defense. He whipped his chain up for a formidable blow when a blinding flash lit up the night. A bolt of lightning struck down to meet the man's chain, racing along its length to electrocute the vampire holding it.

The vampire shook with the sudden surge of deadly voltage, and briefly glowed. He then exploded into a cloud of ash with a great sizzling whoosh of heat and flying dust. The chain dropped to the ground in a heap of orange glowing metal with a soft clanking sound. Ben had been cringing, holding his breath, which he now blew out in a huff of disbelief. He stood there speechless for a moment, and then looked to Mattie in shock. "Did you do that?"

Mattie nodded, walking over to retrieve Ben's sword. He handed it back to him, twisting his wrist to offer it hilt first. Ben took it, still staring at Mattie in wonder and awe. "And I thought the only good change in you, was your new game-play skill in *Modern Warfare*."

Mattie was taken aback for a moment. "You knew that was me?"

"Allie told Felicity."

Mattie shook his head with a smile. "Girls just can't keep secrets, can they?"

Ben nodded towards the dust and chain on the ground. "Thanks for that."

Matt shrugged. "I've kicked your ass so many times on *Call of Duty*, I figured I should save it at least once in real life."

"Thanks."

"Arif's dead," Mattie announced with a nod towards the top of the tower. "Well...*more* dead. He's dust. Allie fried him."

Ben's mouth fell open in disbelief. "She can do that too?"

Matt nodded. "It's not easy. Most vampires haven't got the power, even if they have the lineage, but we're stronger than most, and we've been practicing. I couldn't draw energy from the storm until she was done with Arif though, and then it takes some work to stoke it up again. Sorry I had to make you wait."

"Sorry I doubted you. I'll remember not to tick you off in the future," he said, raising his eyebrows in respect over Mattie's power. "Although, I am planning to kick your butt next time I'm online, so I hope you're not going to be a sore loser," he added with a laugh.

Before Mattie could reply, a swirling cloud of smoke surged forward between them and coalesced into the form of a blonde young man. It was the vampire Kieran. Ben jumped back a bit in surprise over having a naked man suddenly appear in front of him. "I wish you wouldn't do that," Ben grumbled.

Kieran threw him a dismissive glance and then addressed Mattie. "Everything okay down here?"

Mattie nodded, and met Ben's gaze as he answered, "We're good." Ben hoped he meant that to encompass more than just Kieran's question.

The guys were all drawn to look up, as the sound of shrieking and cursing became audible above them, getting louder by the second. Two women were hurtling off the tower towards the ground, while wrestling in the air the whole way down. One was a black woman, the other a fair-skinned blonde who was clinging to her as the black woman tried to claw her off.

They both plummeted to the earth and all three men cringed as they expected impact...but none came. The women stopped in mid-air, floating a few feet above the ground, still fighting and screaming at one another. Finally, the blonde was thrown off to stumble and stand on solid ground, brushing herself off. Ben watched her long golden hair blowing in the ocean breeze under the moonlight, and suffered a sick shock of recognition; it was Lorelei...

Ben had seen this strikingly beautiful vampire many times out his window at night as a young child. This was the woman his father had betrayed his mother for...the woman who had ultimately caused his mother's death. He didn't know the whole story, but he knew enough to make him draw his sword. "Lorelei," he growled under his breath in hatred.

Before Ben could take a step towards the vampiress, another figure dropped from the sky; a formidably large flying black man, who began angling himself towards Lorelei before he even reached the ground. Lorelei spotted him coming after her, and began backing away as she screamed at him, panicked surely, but sounding more angry than afraid. "Elric, what did you expect me to do?"

From the look on his face, he didn't care what she said. He was enraged. She took one look at his expression and ran. Elric and the other woman followed in pursuit. Kieran grinned. "Sorry boys, gotta go. There's no way I'm missing this." He glanced down at Ben's sword with a shake of his head. "If you want a piece of her, I'm afraid you're going to have to get in line." Without further ado, Kieran promptly disappeared to follow after the others.

Mattie watched Ben re-sheath his sword. "Not gonna go after her?"

Ben grimaced but shook his head no. "If she survives the night, definitely. Right now, I have more important things to do. Anyway, I doubt she'll get far. I think my dad's down there."

"Good," Mattie spat out in disgust. "I hope he lops the bitch's head off."

Ben looked at him in mild surprise. "You know her?"

"Wish I could say I didn't," Mattie said, after a nod. His mouth twisted into a snarl of a mirthless smile. "Bet I hate her even more than you do."

Ben stared off in the direction the others had gone, although he couldn't see them any longer. "I think she killed my mom," he said quietly.

"Oh, wow. Sorry," Mattie said in quiet revelation. "I *know* she killed me."

Ben turned to his friend with sudden, unexpected insight. "I guess we'll call it a tie then." He stood there mute for a moment, thinking of how Mattie had said he'd not only been kidnapped, but tortured. He could barely imagine what that would have been like. "If she gets away, help me hunt her down?"

"You can count me in," Mattie agreed with a sneer. "Just like old times."

Suddenly, another scream cut through the night. It almost sounded like... Felicity. Both men froze for a moment. It couldn't have been Felicity. Arif was dead. A cacophony of screams and shattering glass followed from up on top of the tower, but this time it was the side truly opposite them, so they couldn't see anything, but only hear it. They waited to hear if anything, or anyone, came crashing to the ground, but the only crashing heard was of the ocean waves.

Ben began stalking towards the door to the tower. "What the hell is going on up there?" Ben knew he sounded annoyed and angry, but it was only to hold back the rising panic at the thought of something going wrong. He'd let his guard down for a moment, believing the worst was over, knowing Arif was dead. Now it should just be a matter of retrieving Felicity and going home. Why was there still so much fighting going on?

Mattie's eyes glazed over, as though he was paying attention to something Ben could not see or hear, and he looked worried enough to make Ben pause. "Bad things..." he reported quietly. "Very bad things."

Without letting him elaborate, Ben ran for the door, pulling it open to climb the tower, with Mattie close behind him. Before they could enter, someone else came rushing out. After a second, Ben remembered his name, Jin. He was from Arif's coven; they'd been briefly introduced earlier, since the vampire had clearance to come and go as he pleased.

Jin pushed Ben aside and actually knocked Mattie over as he bolted out the door and kept going, running from the tower. "Sorry ginger," he yelled to Mattie over his shoulder. "I'll have to come back and teach you a lesson some other time, when your girlfriend isn't throwing a hissy fit."

"Forget about him," Ben told Mattie worriedly, helping him up. "What's going on up there? Is Felicity okay?" Mattie seemed stiff and slow, and Ben wasn't waiting for an answer, or even for Mattie to fully get to his feet before he entered the tower and started sprinting up the circular staircase. About halfway up, he heard someone else running down the metal stairs from the top.

Mattie was having some trouble with his legs, making him a little slower climbing up behind Ben, but he yelled ahead at the sound of the footsteps above. "It's Cain." Must be nice to read marks, Ben thought in a brief bout of jealousy.

"Mattie?" Cain's voice echoed from above. "Turn around. Go down." Cain practically crashed into Ben as he came down around the turn. "Go!" he yelled impatiently. "Go, go, go!" There was no time for questions. Ben turned around and went back down. Cain was in such a frantic hurry, that

Ben didn't know whether he was chasing Jin, was keen to get to something else outside, or was being chased by someone from up above.

"What's going on? I want to go up and see Felicity!" Ben complained, as he was shuffled out the door.

"She's outside," was Cain's hurried response as he began circling the tower to get out away from the buildings towards the ocean.

"What? How'd she get outside?" Ben followed, his eyes frantically searching the area within view as Mattie tried to keep up. "Where?"

Cain hadn't even stopped, but was heading down the grassy hill towards the rocky barrier before the beach. "She's in the water."

Ben was following down the hill, trying to make sense of Cain's claim, although it seemed impossible. He glanced up towards the top of the lighthouse and its observation deck. "But she was up there!" He looked around at the ground again, at the base of the buildings. "Did she fall?" That still didn't make sense; she would have hit the pavement. How would she have ended up in the water?

"No, she was...thrown," was Cain's faltering response. He was climbing onto the rocks, looking out over the ocean.

Thrown? Panicked disbelief took over Ben's thoughts. "Oh my God, Liss!" He dropped his sword and began to climb the rocks as well, passing Cain, ready to jump into the surf.

Cain grabbed his shoulder and arm, holding him back, but Ben pulled away, practically throwing Cain off balance as he did. "Ben, don't. You'll never find her. I've already got a search party looking."

Ben was in up to his knees, trying to climb over the slime covered rocks to get deep enough to swim. At the words 'search party', he paused and followed Cain's line of sight to figure out what he could mean. How long ago could this have happened? How did he already have a search party? It was hard to see much of anything in the dark, but he was finally able to pick out three figures flying out over the water. Flying vampires, he never thought he'd be grateful to know *they* existed.

"How did this happen? Shouldn't they be looking closer to shore? Who the hell could throw that far?" Cain may have answered, but Ben couldn't hear him over the noise of the wind and the ocean. He probably couldn't process an explanation anyway. All he could do was uselessly search the water with his gaze, and imagine what it would be like to have been thrown from such a height. God...you could break bones hitting the water with that kind of force; a person could get killed...

"You were supposed to protect her! How could you let that happen?" He stared out at the ocean but could see nothing but dark water, white wave tips, and every once in a while, the dark figure of a vampire flying higher to get their bearings. "Why can't they find her? She knows how to swim."

"They'll find her," was Cain's quiet reply. He moved closer next to Ben and tapped his arm. He wanted to lend him a hand to get up out of the water to where he would have a better view from on the rocks. Ben reluctantly accepted his help to get to better footing. He would rather have rejected it, but the rocks were damn slippery, and the last thing he needed was to fall on his ass.

Mattie had taken longer to catch up to them, and now made his way down to the rocks, so he could be heard. "Allie's trying to find her by contacting her telepathically, but she's having trouble reaching her," he explained to Ben, regretfully.

Cain was squinting out over the ocean, when his eyes widened and a sudden sense of foreboding seemed to come over him. "Tell her to follow the sharks," he said with quiet dread.

"Sharks?!?" Ben repeated in horror. He stared back out at the ocean, but couldn't really see anything; Cain must have better vision. "Are you fucking kidding me?" he yelled in disbelief. As though this wasn't bad enough. "Sharks, really?"

Mattie spoke with quiet apology, "This place *was* the inspiration for *Jaws*."

Cain looked down at the rocks to gather his temper before glancing back up at Mattie. "That's not helpful."

Ben also turned to Mattie, desperate for some kind of closer contact to what was happening. "Tell her! Tell Allie to follow them and find her, *now!*"

"I did. She's trying."

"Why can't Allie just read her mind or something?" Ben demanded.

Mattie shook his head with an apologetic shrug. "She might have a concussion from hitting the water so hard."

After a moment, Cain nodded. "She's undoubtedly lost consciousness. She was injured...stabbed. She's bleeding. That's what's brought the sharks."

Ben opened his mouth but nothing came out. He felt hollow and empty inside, like he was trapped in a vacuum that had sucked out all the air. This could not be actually happening; it was too surreal. He wanted to tell them to stop talking, because everything they said just kept making the situation worse and worse, but at the same time, he wanted to demand that they tell him more. He wanted to know every detail, as though somehow that would help him see a solution to make things better in a way they couldn't think of, as though they had missed some crucial detail that meant Felicity would be fine.

He finally found the air to breathe again as his analytical mind kicked in, trying to take over during crisis and solve the problem before him rather than panic. "Where was she stabbed? Was it bad?"

"Her stomach," Cain supplied, "with a stake. It went clean through." His voice was eerily calm and filled with regret. Although Ben realized that panic would accomplish nothing, Cain's quiet demeanor pissed him off. It was like he was already steeling himself to accept that she was beyond help.

"The stomach, okay. That's...bad, but not fatal, right? Shouldn't cold salt-water help a wound?" Sure, if she hadn't then been thrown off the top of a lighthouse into the ocean amidst hungry sharks... Even Ben knew he was being overly optimistic.

"They found her!" It was Mattie. He was looking out towards the ocean, but it was almost impossible to see what was happening. He must be in telepathic contact with Allie.

"Is she okay?"

"I don't know."

"Is she breathing?"

"I don't know..."

Ben stopped questioning him. *Oh God, please let her be okay, please let her be okay, please let her be okay.* The words kept circling his head in desperate prayer. He watched Mattie's face as though a single change in expression would determine the course of the rest of his life; which was a pretty accurate observation.

"She's out of the water. Allie's bringing her back to us. She's alive," he confirmed, after a moment.

Ben almost didn't believe him, it seemed too much to hope for, considering the situation. He realized he'd been holding his breath and let it go. He squinted, straining his eyes desperately to see something over the dark ocean. He could see them now, figures flying towards them from the sea. A petite young woman carrying his wife draped slack in her arms, flanked by two other vampires. It had to be Allie carrying her, but it seemed so surreal to think that the young girl who had been his best friend could be levitating out over the ocean like that. They were flying...

Felicity wasn't moving. Had Mattie just been trying to comfort him? Could she really still be alive after her ordeal? He suddenly patted his pockets, feeling for his cell phone. He wasn't carrying it with him. "Someone call 911!" he ordered desperately.

Mattie didn't move or reply. Cain just looked at Ben quietly for a moment. "I wouldn't advise that."

Ben glared at him in disbelief. "Why not?"

"Let's see what we're dealing with first...in case we need to take special measures."

"*What?* What kind of special measures? She needs medical attention, now!"

Mattie came closer to try to calm him down. "Ben, take it easy."

"Fuck that, find me a phone!"

Allie was almost at the rocks. Cain stepped out further, looking as though he wished he could fly out to meet them. Ben pulled away from Mattie to join him, somehow strangely glad to see that flying didn't seem to be in Cain's wheelhouse.

Ben put out his arms as Allie got closer, but she veered past him to get to the grass. "Let me put her down Ben. Give her some space."

"Put her down then!" he yelled, running alongside them. "Liss...Liss, can you hear me?"

Allie went up the hill some to try to get to more level ground, and then gently laid her down on the grass. Felicity's eyes were closed, her skin wet and pale. She seemed completely unresponsive. Allie was still arranging her limbs into a comfortable position while Ben was already leaning close over her, holding her face in his hands and giving her cheeks kisses. "Liss? Liss, you're okay now. I've got you. You're going to be okay. Can you hear me?"

The other flying vampires approached Alyson, and the man spoke. "I don't think there's anything more we can do here. We're heading back to the compound before all hell breaks loose, if it hasn't already. I have to protect my harem."

Allie nodded. "Yeah, sure. Elric, Latisha, thanks so much for your help. I'll be in touch." As they left, she leaned over Ben and gently put her hands to his shoulders, trying to move him back. "Ben, she's barely even breathing, give her some room."

He looked back up to Allie with a smile. "But she *is* breathing!" he asserted in triumph.

"Uh huh," Allie agreed with a nod...but she didn't sound very hopeful about the fact. "I got her to cough up half the ocean on the way back, but she's in pretty rough shape."

"She was coughing? Was she awake then?"

Allie shook her head, regretfully.

Cain appeared on the other side of Felicity. He gazed down at her with tears in his eyes. He looked heartbroken. Ben glared at him resentfully for a moment before leaning back to inspect the rest of Felicity's body. "Where was she hurt? You said you let her get stabbed?" he asked Cain acidly.

"I didn't *let* her! I couldn't reach her, and I had to deal with the vampires trying to kill me before I could even try."

Ben was trying to assess Felicity's wound, but in the dark he couldn't even tell if the dampness of her soaked clothing was saltwater or blood. However, it was distressingly easy to find the large ragged hole that had been ripped through the garment.

Allie put a hand on his shoulder again but he shrugged her off. "Ben, as soon as I realized she'd gone over the railing, I broke out the windows and flew over the ocean after her. Arif was dead, and we thought we were in the clear. Cat took us by surprise."

Ben struggled to pull up the sari Felicity had been dressed in, trying to find her skin beneath. He finally managed to expose the wound and stifled a gasp. "Aw, Liss..." This ugly hole did not belong there, marring her beautiful body. "It's not that bad," he said quietly aloud, more for himself than the others. It was actually a fairly large and open puncture. A dark hole, about an inch long and maybe half as wide could be seen just to the side of her belly button.

Allie barely looked at the wound, she was too busy trying to see and hear things the others couldn't. "I've been trying to read her mind, but there's just nothing to read right now. She's still in there, but she's not even dreaming, it's just...dark."

"There's not that much blood," Ben remarked, optimistically. "I thought there'd be more blood. It doesn't look that bad." He turned around for confirmation from the others, only to see that Cain had moved around behind him and was looking at Felicity...with inhumanly yellow vampire eyes. He turned and shoved Cain back as hard as he could, "Get the hell away from her!"

Cain fell back on the grass, but didn't make a move to retaliate. After a second, he sat up slowly, squinting at Ben with those eerily reflective eyes. "I wasn't going to hurt her," he said with impressive calm.

"You aren't going to do *anything* to her. Get the hell out of here! Hasn't anybody called a fucking ambulance yet?" he yelled to the others.

No one spoke. Cain returned to stand over Felicity, opposite Ben. "I only wanted to look at her," he explained quietly, "with these eyes." Ben shot him a dirty look, but couldn't push him away again without standing up. He stayed kneeling by Felicity's side instead. Cain continued in a tone that was obviously an appeal to be calm and rational. "I can see the lack of heat within her, Ben. She's lost a lot of blood already. She was bleeding out in the ocean."

"They can give her a transfusion," he said, gathering her into his arms. He wasn't planning to waste any more time here with no one helping him. He got to one knee, lifting Felicity into his arms so he could stand and bring her to his car. "I'm getting her to a hospital."

Cain kept after him. "Ben, please put her down. The puncture went clear through her stomach and out her back. Then she was thrown from such a height, and nearly drowned... She'll never make it to hospital."

"You don't know that," he insisted with grim determination as he got to his feet.

Cain glanced over at Mattie and Alyson, an obvious appeal for them to intervene rather than make Cain continue to try to reason with him. They both came closer to Ben, Mattie trying to make him understand their thinking. "Ben, the nearest hospital is an hour away; trust me, I just came from there. If her stomach was punctured she's probably already in septic shock."

Ben wasn't listening. He tried to turn away from his old friend to carry Felicity up past the lighthouse to the parking lot. "What do you know? You're not a doctor; you're just some vampire super-freak."

Suddenly Alyson was standing before him, blocking his way. Her eyes were shining white, as if they were made of crushed diamonds, gathering up every last tiny sparkle of wane light they could find to reflect in the night. "Put her down," she told him, quietly.

Ben froze, and then lowered Felicity down to lie on the grass as he knelt beside her. Cain came up next to them, helping to arrange Felicity comfortably. "Thank you, Alyson. That'll do. Don't keep him in thrall. He should understand that if we allow her into the hands of humans, she'll almost certainly be lost forever. There is such a slim chance that they could help her, compared with what we can do. He should know we only want what's for the best."

Ben looked up, obviously himself again as he scowled at Cain. "For the best?" he grumbled. "And what exactly do you feel is for the best?"

Alyson answered, proposing an option to Cain before he could speak. "He can try to heal her."

Ben's head whipped around at the unexpected option. "He can do that?"

"He can try. It's one of his gifts."

Cain spoke against it, on top of her answer. "It's too great a risk. We could lose her altogether."

"You've done it before. You told me."

"Of all of my teachings, that's the story you remember? Those few I've healed weren't nearly as badly wounded, and many others that I've tried to heal died...horribly. All the dozens of times that things have gone terribly wrong, and you cling to that unlikely chance?"

Ben rose up to stand before him. "And what do *you* want to do to her? You want to take her, don't you? Make her like you, and pretend it was only *for the best.*"

At first, Cain looked formidably angry, but his temper fled the moment he looked down to see Felicity, lying there, motionless and slipping away. "I don't know," he admitted in quiet grief. "I don't know what's for the best. I've only ever tried to protect her." He took a shuddering breath for calm, gathered his resolve and spoke with steady order. "I didn't want her to get hurt, but I do know this, I will not let her truly die."

"You can't make that decision," Ben asserted. "You can't turn her. It's not what she wants."

"What's the alternative?"

Ben knelt down again to take Felicity into his arms as he looked up at Allie. "Can you save her?"

Alyson's eyes widened. "Me?"

"Yes, you. You're supposed to have *all* the gifts, right? So, if Cain could heal her, so can you."

"I don't know."

"Don't." Cain ordered with wide eyes. He looked almost horrified over the idea. "Think it through, Alyson. Her wounds are too great and she's already lost a lot of blood. It would take a terrible amount of vampire blood to heal her."

"Wait, what?" Ben asked, suddenly unsure. "How is this done? Isn't it just...magic? What do you need blood for?"

"Vampire blood repairs stuff," Mattie supplied. "That's how we're all up walking around without heartbeats. The blood repairs our bodies and makes them work. To fix Felicity, we'd have to give her blood. Cain's is especially good for that."

Ben faltered, gasping to catch his breath as his unexpected sliver of hope was suddenly torn away from him. "You can't do that. You can't put vampire blood in her."

Allie tried to make him understand her suggestion. "Not enough to turn her, just enough to heal her while she's still human."

"And how much is just enough?" Cain asked. "Do you think you know? Because I thought I knew, and those I tried to help suffered for it."

He paused as they all considered the implications of such a travesty. "Too much and she'll turn, but she won't be strong, because you won't have given her much extra. Just enough to heal her without killing her is a very delicate balance. Not enough, and she'll die. Too much and the blood itself will shut her down to try to turn her, whether there is enough to do the job well or not. She could become trapped in a state between vampire and corpse. You will *not* do that to her."

Ben felt as though he was falling into darkness, all hope ripped away, nothing left to support him. He knelt over Felicity and cried.

"This would be different!" Allie insisted.

Cain was shaking his head in despair. "Why?"

"Because you're not a telepathic empath...but I am. I'll be with you, to guide you, reading her, helping to gauge her body so she heals but doesn't change."

Ben looked up, wiping his face dry of hopeless tears. "You can do that?"

Cain answered, his voice flat. "She's never done it before."

Ben wouldn't dismiss the idea. "But *you* have. You said you've done it before and it's worked, even if there were times it didn't. There is a chance it could work, and with Allie helping you, the chances are even better. Don't give her too much. Just heal her wounds; they aren't that bad."

"She's dying Ben," Cain insisted. "I'd say that's pretty bad."

"You have to help her!" When Cain seemed unwilling to cooperate, Ben turned to Allie in desperation. "Allie, do it without him. Please, don't let him scare you out of this just so *he* can have her," Ben added with a pointed look at Cain.

Cain looked more heartsick than angry over the comment. "I'm not trying to scare her. It's only that I've actually *seen* what happens when trying to heal a mortally wounded human goes frighteningly wrong. *You* should be scared...scared for Felicity. Do you truly love her, or do you just want to win out over me?"

Alyson grabbed onto Ben before he could leap forward to try to beat the hell out of Cain. Ben wasn't sure if she had read his mind or just knew him well enough to anticipate his actions, but he was definitely astounded by the fact that Allie was able to hold him down without batting an eye. "Let go of me!" He stopped struggling and met Allie's eyes, letting her know restraint wasn't necessary. "Let go," he said again, quietly. She complied.

Ben glared at Cain, angrily. "God damn you, I won't let you turn her into a vampire just because you can't stand to let her go. You lost her a long time ago. If she wanted to give up her humanity, she could have done it any time, because I'm sure you would have been happy to rush over and take her away from me at the slightest word. She chose to stay human with me, and that's where she belongs."

Cain didn't say anything, but Allie spoke, cutting the silent tension. "I don't know if I can do it alone, Ben. I want to try to heal her, but I shouldn't do it alone. My self-control is kind of dicey, and I don't have the experience Cain does. He's the one to heal her, and if he says it's too risky, maybe we should trust his expertise."

"Fuck his expertise! I may be eloquent in a courtroom but I'm not going to mince words, trying to construct a moving speech of persuasion while you all sit around watching my wife die. Read it from my heart, Allie. I cannot lose her. You have to try to keep her human. If it doesn't work...then she'll die," he contended, swallowing over the lump in his throat, "but you have to at least try."

Cain squinted at him in angry disbelief. "Then she'll die? Do you realize that if she is not healed, if it doesn't work, we may lose our only chance of even turning her into a cognizant vampire? Partial turns do not transition well. Believe me, I know. She'll just be...gone."

"Then she'll be gone. I want her back, but if our time is cut short, then let her die with dignity and rest in peace. That's what I'd want done for me. I won't let you turn her into a vampire. Heal her or let her go."

"Maybe you're willing to let her go, but I'm not, and I won't lose her just to spare your ego. Becoming a vampire isn't the horrible transition you may think."

"Cain," Allie's voice cut through not only the air but their thoughts as well. It was steady and demanded attention. "I think I can do this. I am going to do this. I'm going to try to heal her, but I shouldn't do it alone. Will you help me?"

Cain just knelt next to Felicity, opposite Ben, without speaking. He slowly lifted his hand to caress her cheek. It took everything Ben had in him to keep from smacking the vampire's hand away, but he kept himself still and silent...until Cain slightly shook his head. Whether that meant he wouldn't help, or he was just trying to express how deeply he wished this hadn't happened, wasn't clear, but Ben wasn't waiting to find out. "Let Mattie help you," Ben suggested to Allie. "I don't want *his* blood in her anyway," he said with a nod towards Cain.

Mattie immediately declined. "I may be a super-freak," he said, quoting Ben's words from before, "but he's still stronger than me, and healing is more his thing than mine."

"Don't be stupid, Ben," Allie interjected. "I want Cain's help because his blood will give her the best chance. Mine would be good too, but I need to concentrate on reading her, and he's better at this than I am. I want her to have her best chance, don't you?"

Ben bitterly looked at Cain, leaning over his wife, and nodded. Cain didn't offer comment, so Allie continued. "But I'll do it either way."

Cain looked up to Allie but Ben blocked his view and met his gaze instead, speaking with quiet ferocity. "We're going to save her, and we don't have a lot of time. Allie is asking for your help. Give it, or get out of the way."

"Alright," Cain answered softly. "It would be a much surer thing to turn her, preserving her beautiful mind and heart as a well made vampire, but I know it wasn't her wish, so I will leave that as a last resort."

"No," Ben retorted, angrily. "No last resorts. Just heal her."

"Ben, I will heal her and do my level best to keep her human; you have my word. But if it isn't working, I'm not going to let her go. If she dies, I will have a very short window in which to turn her, and I'm not going to miss it, no matter what you want."

Allie took hold of Ben's shoulders again, in case he felt inclined to disagree. He didn't shrug her off. She was so freakishly strong; he couldn't if he tried. "I'm her husband."

Cain nodded. "Yes, you are her husband. You are bonded to her in the eyes of God and man, until death do you part, and I have always respected that. If she dies, her care is no longer for you to determine. That is my realm, and you will leave me to handle it. It won't mean that she no longer loves you. If she becomes a vampire, you can ask her yourself. But I will leave it as a last resort. I'm going to try to heal her and I ask that you trust me to do what is best. I would never hurt her... I love her."

Ben swallowed over the bitter lump in his throat. "You love her...but you also left her, and I was the one who watched her suffer from a broken heart. She was miserable, and you didn't have to deal with it, did you? I held her as she cried. I was there to help when her classes were hard. I was there to congratulate her when she graduated. I was there when she worried about starting her new job. I was there to drive her home in a frantic rush in the middle of the night when her dad went into the hospital. I was there for her on our wedding day and during the birth of our son, and I have been there for her every single day since.

You can say you love her, and I believe that you do, but I know I love her more. Felicity and I have shared hopes and dreams. We're building a life together, the kind of life I know she wants to share with me, and that you just can't give her. We have a child, and a future, so if you love her as you say you do, you will save her, and then you'll give her back to me. God damn it, you owe me that.

I may be her husband, the father of her child and her lover, but you will always be her first. I have to live with that every damn day, wondering if she wishes I were you. I'm not you. I'm a *better* man for her than you. So you save her, and then you give her back to me."

Cain just stared at him in the silence as his last words died away. The only sounds in Ben's ears were the ocean waves and his ragged breath. It suddenly occurred to him that of the five people gathered there on the hill, he was the only one breathing...him and Felicity. Her breath was so faint he had to quickly check and reassure himself, but she was indeed still alive...barely.

Cain seemed to have soaked in his words and weighed them, finding them all to be true. Damn right, it was all true. He had thought Cain might try to dispute it, but apparently, the vampire felt himself above petty arguing. He just sighed and met Ben's eyes with a slight smile. "I thought you said you weren't going to give a speech?" Ben couldn't even find anything to say to that, so Cain continued. "If you want me to try and heal her, you're going to have to get out of the way."

Chapter 22 - Clarity

Cain

At the base of the lighthouse
Montauk Point, Long Island, New York
Sometime in the dead of night

Cain watched Ben lean down to give Felicity a brief, loving kiss and hold his cheek next to hers for a moment, whispering in her ear before moving to allow Cain and Alyson to take up a place on either side of her.

Cain allowed himself a moment as well, to gaze down at her face. Her hair was a wet and matted mess beneath her head, her skin pale and damp, her eyes closed...and gazing down at her still made his heart ache to beat faster...or at all. Felicity...his sweet, kind, openhearted, clever and beautiful Felicity. Always wanting to believe the best in people; always believing in him. He had failed to protect her. She liked to tell him she didn't need protecting, but he should have protected her anyway. She needed him now...this could not be her end. One way or another, she must go on; he could not fail her.

He gathered his resolve and readied himself for the task. "Has anyone got a knife?" he asked. He could open his vein with his fangs, but a larger wound would be faster and easier to work with.

Ben went and retrieved something from the grass a few feet away. He came back and drew his sword from its sheath with a smile. "Will this do?" he asked with a smile. He looked like he would be more than happy to slice Cain open with it.

Cain squinted up at him with a smirk. "I suppose...if you know how to use it with precision. I'd like to slit my wrist, not lose my hand."

"Happy to help."

"Wait a minute," Allie commanded, putting her hands up as though the mere motion could halt time. Her eyes were closed, but Cain could almost feel the power emanating from her, as though she were spreading her mental feelers, preparing herself.

Ben was watching her, seeming worried that she could actually be able to assist Cain in any way. "What exactly are you going to do? I know you can read her mind, but she's unconscious. You said you couldn't read her right now."

"I'm not just telepathic," Allie explained. "I'm also an empath. That means I can tap into other people's feelings, emotions, sensations...pain. I've gotten pretty used to shutting everything out for the most part, because, well, you don't want to go around getting pounded with everybody else's baggage all the time, trust me. But I can focus on someone when I want to, and let their feelings in. That's how I found Felicity, out in the ocean, I felt her pain."

Ben seemed suddenly filled with sorrow at the thought; Cain knew just how he felt. "Oh God, was it bad?" Ben asked quietly.

Allie kind of shrugged, not wanting to dwell on it. "Yeah, but, that's why she's unconscious. Her mind has retreated to a state of numb unawareness. It's not on purpose, it's just sort of an automatic self-preservation tactic. Your mind tries close you off from feeling that amount of pain until you can deal with it."

"Or you don't wake up," Cain added quietly. "If we are going to wake her, then we'd better get to healing her before it's too much to handle. Can you manage this?" he asked Alyson.

She threw a glance at Mattie, who was instantly by her side to hold her hand. She looked from Mattie to Cain, and smiled. "We're a coven. Together we can handle anything."

Mattie squeezed her hand. "I wish I could do more to help."

"Are you kidding? You're an important part of this. You're my rock...my kite string. This might be a windy ride for me. Hold me down, okay?"

"You got it."

Cain was studying Felicity. As he lifted her up into his arms, Ben moved closer, protectively. Cain decided he'd better give a bit of explanation. "I'm going to bite her; not to drink, but to give her venom. It will help dull the pain. I know she's not conscious, but it should help Alyson as well." Ben didn't look happy, but he didn't say anything. It wouldn't matter if he had; Cain wasn't waiting for approval.

Even with the salt smell of the sea trying to mask her human scent, as Cain's face came close to her throat, he could inhale and decipher her aroma, slight but unique and alluring. It was a scent often visited upon him in his dreams...Felicity. He unsheathed his fangs and bit into her vein quickly. He didn't have much time, and this drink was not one he would savor, or care to remember.

She did not even flinch in his arms as he broke her skin. He gave her a powerful amount of venom, worried for her state when she came back to awareness. It was Alyson who finally spoke to stop him. "It's enough, Cain. Let's treat the problem, not just the symptom."

He disengaged from her carefully, inspecting the bite. There was barely enough blood at the site to even tempt him. "Of course. Ben?"

As her husband came closer, Cain bared his arm. He didn't bother to give any more instruction or warning. If Ben wanted to take his arm off, let him. He didn't take his eyes from Felicity. A quick, sharp sting grazed the inside of his arm from elbow to wrist. The pain was so slight, Cain wondered if the scratch was even deep enough to bleed. He looked down at it to find that it was actually very deep indeed. The sword must be quite sharp, and Ben clearly knew how to use it.

Blood began to pool at the site, emerging from the slice in his arm, and looking to drip from his skin. He held his arm face up as Allie and Mattie quickly helped to rearrange Felicity's garment, laying bare the puncture wound. Cain had healed many in his time, quite a few humans, and dozens of vampires, he could do this right; he had to. Cain forced himself to see her only as a body to be healed...a patient, not the keeper of his heart. He needed to concentrate.

He reached down with his other hand and gently pressed on her belly, just below the wound, pulling the skin down a bit to make the hole gape open as much as he could. It was awful, eliciting a few gasps from the others, although Allie's must have been more from the sensation shared through their patient than from the sight; her eyes remained closed.

Once Felicity's damaged insides were as exposed as he could make them without hurting her further, he angled his arm and began to bleed into the wound as much as he could. "Mattie?" Without further request, Mattie used his free hand to help hold the wound open so that Cain was able to do what he could to keep his own blood flowing freely.

Cain glanced at Alyson, looking for some sort of progress report, but she still never opened her eyes or physically acknowledged him. After a second, he could feel her presence within his mind. *It's working. The pain is pretty bad, but I can navigate through it; the venom is helping. I can feel the vampire blood trying to mend the ripped tissue inside her. It's weird. I can feel Felicity and be in tune with her body, but it's also almost like...like I can read the blood too. It's eager to fix her, I can feel it.*

Cain glanced at her, worriedly. *I'm not certain that's reassuring. If it can actually want anything, I'd imagine it would want not only to heal her, but to turn her as well. Do you have command over it? Can you control it?*

Now Alyson's eyes did flick open, betraying her surprise over the idea. *I don't think so. I'm only The United One because it made me be that way. I'm just the vessel. I don't command the blood, the blood wants to command me.*

Alyson focused on the wound again. She gave him careful instruction, making him privy to the intimate details of the progress of Felicity's inner injuries, and giving guidance as to what was needed, even using her own powers to try to manipulate the tissue a bit and mend things from the inside. Finally, Cain lifted his arm from the wound and spoke to Mattie. "Let's close it."

Mattie spared a glance at Allie before taking his hand from hers to help hold the puncture closed. "You okay?" She nodded. The venom had definitely helped; she could easily stand the pain, now that it had been dulled, and she could tune out any side effects from the venom that Felicity might normally feel as well.

Mattie held the wound closed as best he could, while Cain bathed the site in his blood while keeping his own wound from closing. *Alyson, you are The United One. Do not underestimate your position. Vampires walked the earth for centuries before the blood was able to reconstruct all breeds to unite in you. That's a long time to wait. How many others have the potential to make another United One? There are very few of us. Just you, Mattie, and me really.*

And Sindy, she quickly supplied.

Sindy? Alright, even so, if the blood is able to have any sort of feelings on the matter, I would think it should consider our elite group somewhat valuable, don't you think? We are asking very little of the blood really. We want it to save the life of one human. Honestly, the blood is fortunate that we don't all just plan to throw ourselves into a great fire, rather than risk loosing its power on the world. I should think it would be happy to grant us this small boon.

Do you really think it can understand things that way? Alyson asked. *Is it smart enough to negotiate, or has all of this been coincidence driven by instinct?*

Cain sighed. *It sounds as though you're speaking my lines.*

I'm not actually speaking at all, she reminded him with a smile.

See, and just a few short years ago you wouldn't have thought that possible, would you? I'm not sure what I believe about this blood within us. I've been reluctant to allow you to convince me that it could be a sentient entity, but at this point, I don't think we can afford not to consider it a possibility. You seem to have the closest connection to it, and if, by some amazing circumstance, it actually can be reasoned with, you are closer to communicating with it than anyone. I don't care if you think it is utter nonsense, it couldn't hurt. Beg it to spare her...to heal her as a human, please.

There was a moment of mental silence as Allie thought it over. *I'll try.*

"Help me roll her over."

Cain was speaking to Mattie, but Ben also quickly moved in to help. "Is it working?" Ben asked.

Before they moved her, Cain let Ben have a good view of their handiwork. Where the puncture wound had been, there was now only an indent in her skin, and a puckered and angry line of scarring, her flesh red and raw around the edges...but it was closed. "Oh my God! It's really healing!"

Cain would like to give the skin a chance to heal more, but he wanted to tend the other puncture, in her back, before going any further.

"Maybe that's enough," Ben suggested. "Maybe we should take her to the hospital now."

Cain slumped his shoulders and began to carefully roll Felicity over, forcing the others to help rather than question him further. Once she was settled, he explained. "Ben, we can't take her to hospital. They'll take blood samples, and do tests. I can't allow that. She is in our hands, and that is where she will stay."

Ben reluctantly nodded, unable to argue with the obvious success Cain had shown in healing her so far. "Okay. Just don't give her too much."

"I know. Please, move back and let me work."

Cain and Alyson worked on healing the puncture in her back, just as they'd done for the front. This wound was not as large, and they helped it well on its way to closing, but did not use any more blood than necessary. Once the inside tissue seemed mended, Cain only repaired the skin enough to protect the site, leaving it to heal further on its own, rather than fuss over the job until she was as good as new.

Allie sat back, massaging her temples for a moment and taking a few deep breaths, trying to clear her mind. "Wow, I am really drained, but it wasn't as bad as I thought it would be. The venom really helped."

"Good. Help me to roll her again and sit her up," Cain asked the men. They obliged as he explained his motive. "I'd like to get her to drink some."

Ben was quick to question him. "I don't see how that's necessary."

Cain glared at him for a moment. *I didn't ask for your opinion,* were the words that sprang to mind, but he didn't speak them.

"Cain," it was Alyson, speaking quietly to remind him to keep things calm.

"The injury was in her stomach," Cain explained to Ben, patiently. "I'd like to get her to digest some vampire blood, in the hopes that it might repair any tears in the lining."

"Oh," was Ben's soft response. "But how can she drink anything? She's unconscious. She'll just choke on it," he added, in worry.

"She doesn't really need to swallow it. Vampire blood is capable of finding its way down her throat under its own propulsion."

Alyson spoke up, hoping to overcome the fact that Ben had begun to look ill over the information. "Anyway, I can get her to swallow it. It's not a big deal."

"What do you mean?"

Allie gave a little shrug. "I can control her, just like Arif was able to. It's one of my gifts. I could make her get up and do a song and dance if I wanted to." Ben was staring at her in distasteful awe, bordering on horror. "But I won't."

Ben met her eyes for a droll moment. "Thanks for that."

The cut on Cain's arm was healing. Rather than open it again, he brought his wrist to his mouth, biting into it with his fangs, and tearing the wound so it would bleed. He then brought it to Felicity's lips as he turned her to rest over his lap, holding her in his arms.

Alyson was staring at Felicity intently. After a moment, it seemed as though consciousness stole over Felicity's form as she lay in Cain's arms. She stirred slightly and then sat up a little better.

Ben gasped, leaning closer, visibly heartened by the movement. "It's just me, Ben," Alyson reminded him gently.

Felicity's eyes never opened. Cain was glad for that, it would be too strange and heart wrenching, knowing she wasn't really behind them. As Cain brought his wrist to her lips, he could feel her mouth close over the bite and begin to suck his blood. It was odd to know that the motions were only being made at Alyson's behest, but he had to admit, it was much easier and more certain to allow her to ingest it this way.

"Don't forget to focus on her body, not just her actions," Cain reminded Alyson after a few pulls. "Only give her what she needs."

As soon as he spoke, Cain felt Felicity's body go lax in his arms. He removed his wrist from her mouth, absently wiping it on the side of his pant leg. He couldn't help but wonder whether Alyson had deemed the blood Felicity had drunk to be the proper amount, or if she had lost track of things while controlling her body, and had only stopped at Cain's reminder. Whether or not she'd been given too much would just have to remain to be seen.

Sorry if that seemed a little abrupt. I was paying attention, honest, she insisted, speaking to his unvoiced worry. *It was just that...well, I've done an awful lot tonight. My reserves are dwindling and...*

Are you alright?

I'm fine, I just...caught her scent all of a sudden and it kind of threw me.

Your thirst, of course. He could tell she was embarrassed to admit it. *You've done better than anyone has a right to expect. Don't give it another thought. Just clear your mind for a moment and put your thirst back in its place. We're almost through, and then you can hunt.*

Allie nodded. *I'll be okay. It just shook me up a little.*

Cain smiled at her and spoke for the others to hear. "Thank you, Alyson, you've done wonderfully. Why don't you step back and take a break for a moment?" Alyson rose, thankful for the dismissal and walked a bit away from them, downwind of Felicity and Ben's tempting aromas.

Cain gazed at Felicity once more, and carefully wiped a drop of blood from her lips. Then, closing his fist, he lovingly grazed the backs of his knuckles across her cheek in a soft caress. He'd barely finished the motion when suddenly Ben was hovering over him, attempting to remove Felicity from his arms. "Alright, thank you. I'll take her now."

Cain didn't even glance up to meet his eyes. He kept his gaze steady on Felicity, but loosened his grip and allowed Ben to take her.

"Now what do we do?" Ben asked.

"Now, we wait." Cain looked to Alyson standing a few paces away, finding her to be gazing at him with a mixture of appreciation and sympathy. "Can you read anything from her? Any change?"

"She's more comfortable now. The pain is almost gone. I can feel the heat spreading through her...the blood, but it isn't turning her. Not yet, anyway."

"Not at all, I hope," Ben clarified.

Allie nodded. "I tried my best; we both did. We just have to wait and see."

Were you able to communicate with the blood at all? Cain asked her, mentally.

She shrugged. *I don't even know. I tried. I didn't get any kind of response. I have no idea if it could understand me, or if it did, maybe it just didn't care.*

Cain nodded. *It was worth a try, anyway.*

Allie gave him a little smile. *Thank you, for the way you handled this. It was very big of you.*

I'm still not sure if we did the right thing. Let's hope it was worth it.

"So, how long do you think it will be, before she wakes up?" Ben asked.

Cain shook his head. "It could be hours, or days. There is really no way to tell. Every case is different. She was pretty severely injured, so I would guess it will take a while."

Ben nodded, straightening up with his wife in his arms. He was obviously planning to carry her to the car. "I'm going to take her home; make her comfortable in bed."

"We should come with you." Allie offered. "So I can let you know right away if I hear her thoughts." *Or see a change in her mark,* she added silently to Cain.

Felicity now wore Cain's mark, from when he had bitten her. He treasured feeling that connection to her again. She was marked only as a human would be, for the moment, but Alyson was right, they would need to watch that mark carefully. If the mark disappeared, they would know that she was dying, despite their efforts. If that happened...or if she began to develop a mark of her own, Cain would need to give her more blood, immediately.

"Okay," Ben agreed, allowing them all to follow him, as he walked towards the parking lot with Felicity in his arms. It was quite a long walk, but the grounds seemed deserted at this point. There was no one to be seen or heard. Ben kept a quick pace, keeping an observant eye on their surroundings and not seeming at all troubled to carry Felicity so far.

They reached Cain's motorcycle, parked next to the sign at the gate. The actual parking lot was still a bit further. Cain kicked up the stand, but didn't mount the bike. "Want to put her down?" he asked, nodding towards the seat.

Ben shook his head. "No thanks, I've got her." Cain shrugged, and walked the bike beside him as Ben continued. "I'd appreciate it if you took Sindy back while you're at the house. I doubt she's someone Felicity would like to see, first thing when she wakes up."

"Of course," Cain told him with a smile. "Thank you for looking after her."

"It's alright. She wasn't much trouble. The experience was probably good for both of us," Ben commented, as they crossed to the lot. Ben's classic yellow Mustang was there, still looking as pristine as ever. As they reached Ben's car, Cain curiously looked to Alyson, knowing she'd be hard pressed to keep herself from snooping about Ben's time with Sindy, but she didn't give him any insight over it.

Mattie opened the passenger side door for Ben, and he put Felicity down and reclined the seat. He watched her for a moment, but she didn't move. Finally, he put on her seatbelt and closed the door. Once he straightened up, Ben noticed the expressions of Cain and Alyson over his comment and added, "It's been a long time since Sindy and I actually talked. I'm somewhat proud of us. We didn't try to kill each other," he said with a laugh. The others chuckled as well, but Ben quickly cut short their mirth. "You can follow me home, but just so you know, I'm still uninviting you all from my house the minute you leave."

"Of course," Cain repeated with a grin.

Ben was walking to his side of the car, when he stopped and looked around. "Anyone heard from my father?"

Allie quickly flew up into the air, giving Ben an unexpected start. "I'll look for him," she offered, and was off in a flash. Cain looked around, but all was quiet. There were a few cars scattered in the parking lot, but Cain had no idea if any of them belonged to the vampire hunter. He noticed Alyson's orange Charger parked off to the side. Mattie must have brought it. Allie was back again before he could mention it. "Bernard's not in the immediate area."

Ben's mouth was still hanging open from seeing Alyson perform such impossible feats as if they were nothing. "You were gone for like a minute. How can you have even seen anything? He could be hiding, or lying injured somewhere."

She grinned, shaking her head against the idea. "First of all, I'm fast. I searched the whole hill, trust me." Ben raised an eyebrow, as she nodded and continued. "Second of all, he's a warm-blooded, living being. He'd have a hard time hiding from these eyes, trust me."

The others hid their smiles as Ben tried not to betray how unnerved he was when she let her eyes flash to their white brilliance for a moment to prove her point, before continuing. "If that's not enough for you, I'm an empath, remember? If he were in pain, I would feel it, even if he wasn't conscious. I suppose he could have been killed and his body hidden or thrown into the ocean, but from what I've heard, he's pretty capable of taking care of himself. So, before we jump to that conclusion, maybe you should just try giving him a call."

Ben stood stunned for a moment, before reaching into the car for his cell phone. "Okay." He turned it on to make the call, but his phone made a pinging sound before he had the chance. "He texted me: I'm hunting down Lorelei, I don't want to lose her trail. I'll be in touch. Let me know how everything works out."

Ben stood staring down at the phone for a minute. "Sure dad, go do your own thing...like you always do. Felicity may or may not be dying...or turning into a vampire. I'll let you know how it works out." As he spoke the last words, he viciously threw his phone into the back of the car.

Allie looked like she wanted to go and comfort him, but Cain could see her hesitation. She probably worried that he wouldn't want her support. After a few minutes, Mattie broke the uncomfortable silence. "We should get going, before Felicity wakes up. I brought the car," he told them, gesturing to Allie's old orange Charger across the lot. "We'll see you at the house." Mattie headed to the car, and Cain followed, walking his Harley.

Allie was turning to join them, when Ben called out to stop her. "Allie?" he gestured towards his car as he spoke. "Do you want to ride in the back? You can keep watch over Felicity while I drive...and maybe we could talk?"

Cain and Mattie turned to see what she would do. She paused, indecisive. Cain knew she was nervous to finally have this conversation, but it was what she had wanted and been waiting for. She smiled, but before she could answer, a breeze picked up, the wind at Ben's back. His scent came across the parking lot, and Cain could tell that a frighteningly strong, sharp surge of thirst washed over her.

Allie turned away, to block Ben's scent and clear her vision, which was trying to show him to her as prey. "Sorry, Ben. Not now. I'll see you at the house."

"Why not? It's like a forty-five minute ride. Felicity could wake up on the way home."

"I'm sure she'll be fine until we get there. It's been a really active night and I'm way too tapped to talk right now," she said, beginning to walk away.

"It's been way too long already, Allie. I don't want to wait any longer," he insisted, trying to follow her.

Next to Cain, Mattie lurched forward a bit, wanting to go to her and usher her away from Ben. Cain stopped him with a light hand on his arm. "Let her handle it, or Ben will think she's only under your influence. She'll be alright."

Allie met the guys at her car, her back to Ben. He still approached, from across the lot, not letting her leave without facing him. He briefly made eye contact with Cain and Mattie over her shoulder, as he got closer.

Cain sighed. "Ben, there'll be time to talk later."

"Allie, I've missed you," he told her with a voice filled with quiet regret. Alyson must mean an awful lot to him, for him to swallow his pride and continue to beseech her in front of Cain. "Mattie too," he added quietly, "but you and I..."

Alyson suddenly opened up her emotions to her little coven, as though they were too much to contain and she had to share them or burst. She quickly explained her feelings and Ben's thoughts to the others, although they probably had a good grasp of things already.

Ben's friendship with Mattie was different. Mattie had disappeared so long ago. They still needed to smooth over things, but they were guys, old buddies, and they'd work it out. Allie was special. She and Ben had clung to each other so desperately as humans, considering each other their only true family, even without blood ties. Her absence had left a huge hole in his life and his heart, even if he was at fault for it. He was worried she wouldn't forgive him for their years apart.

How could he even question her feelings? It broke her heart, but she couldn't do this right now. His trust in her as a vampire was still too fragile, and she was skirting the edge of control. She wasn't used to being close to humans often, other than those she drank from...

Just tell him the truth, Allie, Mattie advised.

"Ben, you're not listening to me," she told him, over her shoulder. *"I can't."*

He faltered in his pursuit as she turned back to face him, practically trembling with anxious distress, a look of desperate pleading in her eyes. They were still blue, though; still Allie-eyes, and he wanted to come closer. She put out a hand, motioning for him to stop. "Ben, remember those candies we used to get from the ice-cream truck, the little wax soda bottles?"

He looked at her, quizzically. "Yeah... You had to bite through the wax to suck out the sweet syrup stuff inside. I haven't thought of them in years. I always thought they were gross, but you used to love those things." He laughed with a little smile, reassured. "You really are the same Allie."

"Yeah, I am. Not really my point, though. Ben, I have had a hell of a night flying around, fighting evil and saving Felicity's life...hopefully."

"I know. I want to thank you, and tell you how sorry I am..."

She nodded, barely acknowledging his gratitude. It was more important to make her point. "I'm exhausted...and thirsty. Right now, you look like a big wax soda bottle to me. If you trap me in a car, or corner me to talk, I may not have the strength not to take a bite. I know we need to talk, but trust me, it can wait."

Ben became very alarmed as he realized the severity of her explanation. "Okay..." he said, backing up a few steps, "but if you all come to my house..."

"I think we passed a ranch on the way here. I could smell horses, lots of 'em. We'll stop, snag a few quick drinks, and be back on our way in no time."

Ben was just staring at them all, blankly. "Horses?" he finally asked.

"Don't worry," Alyson assured him. "We won't hurt them."

Ben put up his hands in surrender, backing towards his car. "Good. Thanks...but, TMI. See you at the house."

~~~~~~~~~~~~~~~~~~~~~~~~~~~~~~~~

As it turned out, Mattie had some blood stashed for them in the car. Apparently, he and Kieran had lifted some reserves from the local hospital. He clearly felt guilty over it, but Cain gave him a pat on the shoulder. "We've all done it, even me, in my earlier days...and more than once. Not some of my prouder moments, but still preferable to the alternative."

"I went for the alternative too. That's why there's any left." Cain raised an eyebrow, but didn't comment. "Don't worry, she survived," Mattie mumbled.

Alyson didn't seem surprised; she must have known. She was quick to try to comfort him over it. "Look, it got you walking again. You're almost good as new!"

Mattie just shrugged. "You guys can have the rest of the bags," he told Allie and Cain. "I'm good for now."

Cain was satisfied with that, but Alyson declined. "No thanks, I'm still gonna hit the ranch."

"But this is human!" Mattie insisted, holding up a bag.

"I know baby, but I need more than that; a lot more. Don't wait for me. I'll see you guys back at Ben's." She gave him a quick kiss and started stripping her clothes to throw in the car. Cain turned away, got on his bike and started it up. By the time he was ready to leave, Allie was flitting around above them as a large bat. She did a few loops and then sped off towards her feast.

The guys ended up catching up to Ben on the road, and following him for the whole ride. Although Ben was speeding terribly for most of the way, they all arrived without incident. They met Ben on the driveway as he was gently lifting Felicity from the car. He lifted her out and then bid Mattie to take the keys from his hand. "Open it for me? I'm not sure if Sindy's up to answering the door."

Cain came closer, closing the car door for him and observing Felicity for a moment, as she slept in Ben's arms. She looked awfully pale. "Why wouldn't Sindy be able to get the door? I thought you said you two *didn't* try to kill each other."

"We didn't. She had plenty of damage to deal with before I got anywhere near her." Ben replied, as he turned Felicity away from Cain and climbed to the porch. He showed Matt which key to use, and waited for him to open the door.

"Other than the fact that your father so gallantly clubbed her over the head, she seemed alright when I left her with you," Cain remarked, following.

"Looks can be deceiving. Don't get all protective, I took good care of her. Ask her yourself."

Mattie got the door open, and Ben carried Felicity inside. The house was quiet and seemingly empty. He was halfway to the bedroom, before he paused reluctantly, to call over his shoulder, "Come on in, both of you,"

Ben closed himself in the master bedroom with Felicity, leaving Matt and Cain to enter the house on their own. It didn't take long to ascertain that Sindy was no longer there. By the time Ben came out, Alyson had arrived. She had gotten dressed in the car out front, and was now standing on the porch in front of the doorway, waiting to be invited in.

"Any change?" Cain asked Ben of Felicity.

Ben just shook his head, no. He stood staring at Alyson for a second from the living room, and then issued the invitation to allow her entrance.

She took a look around as she came in and closed the door behind her. "Where's Christian?"

"Felicity's mom has him."

Allie nodded. "He's adorable, by the way." After a second, she smiled and added, "It still smells like baby in here. In a good way, I mean. You know, all the lotions, and powder, and stuff."

Ben was staring at her. "Please tell me that doesn't make you hungry."

"No. I'm full now, thanks," she added sarcastically. "I just miss him. I haven't gotten to see him in a while."

"You don't even like kids," he replied, flatly.

"I know, right? Go figure."

Ben couldn't seem to stop staring at her. "Come sit with Felicity. Maybe you can get through to her now."

The invitation was for Alyson, but Cain and Mattie followed them to the bedroom as well. It was a fairly large, comfortable space. Felicity lay in bed with the covers pulled up to her waist and her hands neatly folded over her chest. Ben had changed her clothes and brushed out her hair. She looked lovely, and Cain was heartened to notice that a faint blush of color had returned to her previously pale cheeks and lips. That was a good sign.

At Ben's behest, Alyson sat down on the bed next to Felicity and took her hand. She held it for a moment with her eyes closed. "Sorry...nothing yet."

Ben was obviously disappointed. He sat down on the chaise lounge near the bed. "Okay, well, she just needs a little more time, that's all." Allie nodded and tried to smile.

Cain stood next to the bed. He was lost in thought, gazing down at this precious woman who rested at the brink between life and eternity, when Mattie quietly called for his attention. "Cain?"

"What?" he answered, unable to take his eyes from Felicity.

"Why don't we go and wait outside for a while?"

Cain looked up to find everyone staring at him. Allie put her hand on his shoulder, her lightly marked touch, warm and reassuring. "Go ahead. I'll let you know if we need you."

Of course, he'd rather stay, but Ben clearly would rather he left, and Alyson presumably wanted some private time for that talk between them anyway. He followed Mattie out to pace in the living room. Finally, Mattie took him out onto the deck, so the ocean waves could fill the thought-burdened silence.

Alyson came out to find them eventually, drawing Cain's anxious gaze. She shook her head, nothing yet. Cain sighed in disappointment. "Did you and Ben have a nice chat?"

"Yeah, we're okay, I guess. He's still pretty skittish around me, though."

Mattie shrugged. "He'll get over it."

"I hope so, 'cause now it's your turn." Mattie didn't look eager to go inside. "Just go talk to him...and be nice, he's had a rough time."

Mattie turned to face her with a scowl. "He thinks *he's* had a rough time?"

Alyson just shooed him inside with an air kiss. After a few minutes of watching Cain stare out at the sea, she took his hand and headed for the gate. "Let's go walk on the beach."

"Could you read anything from her while you were in there, anything at all?" Cain asked.

"No. It's been a few hours now, Cain. If she was going to heal and stay human, wouldn't she have woken up by now?"

Cain shook his head. "No, not necessarily. It's always different. You just can't tell what will happen, until it happens."

They walked a few paces down the beach, Alyson picking up stones and shells to toss into the water as they walked. Most of them went further then could be seen. "Oh Cain, this is horrible. This is all my fault. I'm a terrible friend!"

"No you're not."

"Yes, I am. I should have known sooner. I have telepathic access to her, for Pete's sake! Why didn't I know? It should never have gotten this far."

"You can't blame yourself. With everything you've had to worry about...Arif, Sindy, then Zach and Mattie...you were trying to manage your own problems. You had no reason to believe she'd be in danger."

Alyson tossed another stone into an oncoming wave. "But she was in danger, and now look what's happened. I should have protected her!"

Cain tried to infuse his voice with supportive confidence, but it still sounded miserable and defeated in his ears. "You can't protect everyone."

"What good is having supernatural abilities, if I can't protect everyone?"

Cain chuckled. "Now you know how I feel half the time. I even said as much to her once, and you know what she told me? She said you can't always worry and be responsible for everyone. Sometimes you have to be allowed to take a break and have a life."

"She needed me, and I let her down."

"Don't you think I feel the same? But we need to keep things in perspective...have some clarity. There's another saying: you're only human."

"Except I'm *not!*"

"Yes you are...*almost,*" he teased. "You're not a Goddess Alyson, no matter what you can get others to believe. You've got amazing abilities, that's true, but that doesn't mean that you should be able to solve every problem, and right every wrong. You were born a child of this Earth just like any other, and although you have gone through some changes and been given great power, you and I both know, that at heart, you are still only human. You're not infallible, and you can't hold yourself to be. You're just doing the best you can, and that's all any of us can do."

"But *was* I doing my best, or was I just letting myself ignore things and be distracted? That's how Mattie got hurt, you know, because I didn't want to be suspicious and worry about Zach. I just wanted to assume things would be fine and have some fun, and Mattie almost died, Cain. Now the same thing is happening with Felicity. I wasn't paying attention. I mean...I think Zach was blocking my telepathy when we were together, so I couldn't check on her, but I should have realized that something was wrong. God, I was probably ignoring red flags all over the place!"

"I'm sure it wasn't as obvious as you think, or you would have picked up on it. Hindsight is 20/20."

"Maybe, but look at what happened to her, Cain. She'll never forgive me."

"Yes, she will. You know her as well as I do, and even if, God forbid, she doesn't wake up, you should still know that she forgives you."

"Don't say that! She has to wake up. She will, won't she?"

"I hope so."

"What if she turns? What if she wakes up as a vampire? Then *Ben* will never forgive me."

"Then he's not a very good friend. You realize that no matter what happens, he's going to blame me anyway, so you shouldn't worry about it. You know that we did everything we could to preserve her humanity. We took the measures we deemed necessary. What were we supposed to do, let her die? We tried to save her. There's nothing more that can be done now, but to wait and see."

"Do you think she might turn?"

"I don't know. I've been watching her mark, diligently. She hasn't so far."

Alyson stopped walking. "Do you want her to?"

Cain stopped as well, but only to give her a glance of disapproval and then continue walking down-beach. "No...because I know that's not what she wanted. If she'd wanted that, I would have done it a long time ago."

"I didn't ask what she wanted. I asked if you wanted her to..."

"It doesn't matter what I want."

She gave him a light shove. "Stop ducking the question."

Cain stopped and faced her. "What do you want me to say? You're so smart, read it from my mind then. You want me to be selfish and say that I'd like her to change? That wouldn't make things any easier, you know; it would only introduce a whole new set of problems. I want her to be happy. That is all I have ever wanted. Being with Benjamin seems to make her happy." He picked up a rock of his own to throw into the ocean, delighting in the simple, but almost violent act of taking this small stone that had spent years working its way to the shore, and then snatching it up to be brutally hurled back to the bottom of the sea with a hopeless splash. "If she awakens,"

Alyson was quick to correct him. "When," she asserted.

"When she awakens, in whatever state she finds herself, I hope that she can care for her child and be happy. We've done all that we can to try to ensure that will be the case. Now, we'll just have to wait and see, and whatever the situation, we'll deal with it. That is all one can ever do."

Allie sighed, but accepted it without further questioning. She threw one more rock towards the water and then turned around to start them walking back towards the house. "Dawn's coming."

"What?" Cain asked, stopping in alarm. "She very well had better not be. I gave her explicit instructions not to follow me. She was to wait at the house under Khalon's watch." Alyson was staring at him with curious confusion, forcing Cain to slow down and rethink the statement. "What were you talking about?"

"Dawn," she repeated in amusement. "You know...the sunrise. But now I want to know who you're talking about."

Cain waved his hand in front of his face as though shooing away a fly. "Get out of my head, I'll tell you." Allie made a face at him, and started walking again as he spoke. "She's just a youngling stray I picked up to mentor. She's been staying with me for a bit. I had to fill the house with someone, didn't I?" he added with a pointed glance. "It was far too quiet when I came home to find the place empty."

"Sorry about that. We thought you'd be with Sindy and...that Sindy might be working for Arif. We didn't want to come between you, but Mattie was afraid it wasn't safe."

"Mattie was probably right."

"We didn't know you'd be alone. Sindy never came back, huh?"

He shook his head. "She's never coming back, is she? Otherwise she would've waited here for me."

"I'm sorry, Cain. It's my fault you got involved with her to begin with. You distanced yourself from her for so long. Then I really threw her at you and pushed you into it. I thought you'd be good for each other. I could feel her wanting to let her guard down, and be honestly appreciated by someone for a change. She needed guidance and that's your thing. I know she wasn't really Miss-Right for you, but I figured she made a pretty good Miss-Right-Now. You needed to get up out of the dumps and feel good about yourself again, and that's kind of Sindy's claim to fame, making a man feel good. I hope her leaving isn't going to make you feel even worse now. Maybe I shouldn't have meddled."

"Alyson, don't over-estimate your influence on me. Do you think I haven't got desires of my own?" he asked with a smirk. "I know you were nudging, but I made my own choices. It was good for both of us, for a time. The sad part is, I'm not even sure if she should come back. Is that awful?"

"Not at all! It means you both got what you needed to move on. It's okay to move on. You don't have to feel bad about it. If she split, then that was her choice. Anyway, *Dawn* seems nice. I pulled a few snippets from your head, and she's tougher than she looks." Cain scowled at her for snooping, but Alyson ignored him and kept talking. "She's pretty too. I like her. She could be just what you need. Maybe this one will be good for you."

"No! Alyson, stop match-making!"

Alyson faltered, a look of terrible sadness coming over her for a moment. "Oh my God, you are hoping Felicity will turn, aren't you? That somehow you can be together now."

The unexpected statement struck him like a blow and almost made him break down in tears, but he held it back. He and Felicity, able to be together...that just didn't seem a realistic possibility, maybe not ever, but certainly not right now. "No. I told you... I don't know. How am I supposed to know what's best? Even if she did turn, she still has a family. I don't know what I want to hope for, I just want her to be conscious and happy. I just want to know one way or the other, so this horrible waiting can end."

Alyson pulled him in for a hug. "I know honey. It's okay. You don't have to have all the answers." After a few minutes, she let him go and gave him a smile. "You don't have to push Dawn away either, just because things are complicated."

He gave her a weary shake of his head. "You never listen to me. How many times do I have to tell you? *No.* Absolutely not, and I don't need you trying to put any more ideas into my head! I refuse to see her that way. I haven't, and I won't. Can't you read that from my heart? She's just not for me. Anyway, young vampires are in a very fragile emotional state, driven to distraction by their cravings and trying to fight their compelling urges to hunt. Something I'm sure you can empathize with."

"Oh yeah, that is something I know a little about."

"Yes, but you had the support of friends and an established, loving relationship to lean on. Most young ones feel they have been ripped from their families and cast out of society; suddenly struggling with an addiction they can scarce understand or control. They feel desperate, helpless and hopeless. I provide them sustenance, shelter and support. It puts them in a very compromised and indebted position. I would never take advantage of that! I have a very strict platonic rule when it comes to those I mentor, no exceptions."

"Sindy was an exception, wasn't she?"

"Sindy received nothing more from me than guidance and advice when I found her. It wasn't until months later, after she was well off on her own, capable and independent, that I allowed things to change direction between us…and even then, it was far too soon, a trespass on my part. But Sindy is a woman who knows what she wants. I think even she would tell you that the first night we were together, she was taking advantage of my weakened emotional state, more than I might have compromised hers."

Alyson laughed, knowing it was undoubtedly true. Cain gave her a nudge with his shoulder as they walked. "I'm not a saint, Alyson. We all make mistakes, and I count that night as one of mine. I'm just glad that in time and through future circumstance, I was able to show her that I truly do care for her.

Enough. How do you do that? You always manage to work your way into my head and my heart, laying bare truths I would never normally admit or display to another. The bottom line, is that Felicity is in her rightful place with her husband, Sindy's gone, and I am alone now. It may not have been by my own choice, but I can make peace with it."

They reached the stairs to Ben and Felicity's deck. Cain began to climb them, but Alyson chose instead to float alongside. "Show off," he muttered, before continuing the conversation. "I can be very happy and content without romance, honestly. I've spent decades mentoring others and sending them off on their own. It's much simpler than trying to navigate intimate relationships. The past few years have been very emotionally messy for me. I hate that. I just want to perform the tasks I've set for myself and be left alone."

"Left alone? What are you, a monk?"

"Ha! As though a monastery would have me."

"You know what I mean. Anyway, we are still a coven, aren't we?"

Cain gave her a reluctant smile and a nod. "If you both want to be." She and Mattie still had explaining to do, but in his heart, they were forgiven.

She grinned, happy he'd still have them. "Good, 'cause Mattie and I are going to need your help, now that this whole United One thing is out of the bag. Alone is not an option for you. You want to play abstinence boy, that's your business, but you're still gonna be getting my good vibrations buddy, whether you want them or not. I am not giving up our coven marking sessions!"

Mattie met them at the top of the stairs with a smirk. "Okay miss hot-to-trot. Want to tone it down a little?"

Cain ignored his feigned insult. "Felicity?"

"No, sorry, she's still sleeping." Cain went to sit on a deck chair while Mattie continued to reprimand his wife. "And you...don't worry, you'll get your tinglies. In the meantime, could you at least *try* to act like I keep you satisfied? Stroke a guy's ego, would you?"

She levitated over the railing and hovered behind Mattie, draping herself over his back and shoulders to kiss the side of his neck. "Oh, relax. Cain knows *you're* my super-stud. Can I help it if I have an overactive appetite?"

Ben emerged from the house. As he did, Alyson immediately stopped levitating to drop herself to the deck with a thud, and a look of repentant guilt for her teasing attitude. "You're all about appetite now, huh?" he asked in disapproval.

She shot him a strange look of apology, wrapped up in reprimand. She was sorry to have been acting jovial at a time like this, but he should know she didn't mean to offend. Making it about the fact that she was a vampire was just misplaced irritation. Cain had a feeling she might have said something to him in his mind about it, but she didn't share.

"Ben," she finally said aloud, "I'm going to have to go."

"What? You can't go anywhere. Felicity is going to wake up soon, I know it. She might need you."

"Ben, the sun is going to come up."

"I'll stay," Cain offered, quietly.

Ben looked back to her from the others, "He can stay and you can't?"

Mattie spoke up in her defense. "She can't help it, Ben. She has to sleep during the day. She hasn't got a choice. She's not like us."

"I have a guestroom. If I close all the curtains, it's nice and dark. Sindy slept in there. Would that be okay for you, or do you need something else?"

Allie had to smile at the way he said it, as though she should have to dig a hole in the ground or sleep in a coffin. "I guess that would be okay," she answered reluctantly, "as long as the guys are going to stay."

Ben looked insulted. "What, like I'm going to stake you in your sleep?"

Mattie put his arm around her. "Can't say *I'm* sure what you'd do, if Felicity dies during the day."

"She isn't going to."

"I hope not. Whatever happens, we'll be here."

~~~~~~~~~~~~~~~~~~~~~~~~~~~~~~~~

"Liss?" Ben woke with a start, calling his wife's pet name. He lay next to her on the bed, on top of the covers.

"She hasn't moved," Cain answered from the chaise lounge. He had pulled it back from the bed earlier, to the other side of the room, to escape the glow of the skylight during the day.

Ben assured himself that Felicity was breathing, but was indeed still unconscious. The skylight above proved that it was full dark outside. Ben sat up to observe Cain, obviously annoyed that the vampire had been in their bedroom as they slept. "How long have you been sitting there?"

"All day," Cain answered, unapologetically daring him to say he should have left. Ben chose not to comment. "Your father came round. He left you some food, and gives his love to you and Felicity. He lost Lorelei with the dawn, but I think he's gone back out to see if he can pick up her mark again."

"Great."

"The phone's been ringing quite a bit too. Felicity's mother left a message on the machine." Ben looked anxious until Cain quickly added. "The baby's fine."

"Thanks." Ben turned to stroke Felicity's cheek and squeeze her hand, hoping to elicit some response. "She hasn't moved all day? That's bad isn't it?" Cain was shaking his head, when Ben clarified, "Bad for me, I mean."

As though that would be good for anyone else? Cain sighed. "Ben, the whole situation is bad for everyone. She is your wife, and I know she loves you. If I were planning to try to take her from you, I would have just done it. The fact that she hasn't stirred doesn't mean anything, but that her body is not ready for her mind to come back yet, in any state. She is resting, recuperating and rebuilding. When she is ready, she will awaken. Maddening as it may be for us, we just have to wait."

"Allie should try again. It's dark enough, she should be up, right? It's been so long, maybe Felicity's closer to consciousness now, for Allie to reach her."

"Maybe," Cain acceded.

The bedroom door opened as someone gave a slight knock on it. It was Mattie. "I thought I heard talking in here. Everything okay?"

"Is Allie up?" Ben asked. "Can you send her in?"

"She's up. She's outside. She's busy, but I'll have her come in a minute."

Ben got up off the bed. "Busy doing what?"

"She's probably out hunting," Cain gently supplied for him.

"Hunting what, my neighbor's dog?" Ben asked in annoyance. He got up and went out into the living room, although Mattie tried to stop him.

"She's not hunting, we've already fed," Mattie corrected them.

"Then she should come in," Ben said over his shoulder as he reached the front door. He opened it and stood in mute shock for a moment. "Why are there a bunch of vampires on my lawn?"

"They're here to talk to Allie."

"Well, get them out of here."

"Relax, they only just got here, and they won't stay long. You don't have to invite them in or anything."

"Damn right I'm not!"

Cain came up behind them, to see what the fuss was about. There were five vampires out on the lawn, talking to Alyson; two men and three women. One was unmistakably Elric, although his back was to the house, meaning the woman by his side was most likely his recent progeny, Latisha. Kieran was with them, standing quite close to Sindy... Sindy was back. And who was the woman on the other side of Elric? Cain's eyes widened as he recognized her and pushed his way past Ben and Mattie, out the door.

"Maribeth, what are you doing here?"

She looked up at him, adopting a look of coy innocence. "Thought I'd pay you a visit." She looked around at their company with a pleased smile. "Ought'nt I have? Considering you've picked me out of the crowd as worth addressing above all others, I'd say my presence strikes you just as I'd hoped."

Cain paused just shy of the group, who had stopped talking upon his arrival. He found himself looking to Sindy, to see what she made of his approach. She looked happy to see him, and amused that Maribeth had made him lose his composure. He gathered his patience, rather than let Maribeth get the better of him. "I'm rather surprised to see all of you actually. What are you doing here?"

"Arif's coven is a mess," Maribeth confided.

"I can imagine."

"No it isn't," Kieran disputed. "Elric can lead them."

Elric smiled. "Of course I can, but they want her," he said, with a nod towards Allie.

Allie shook her head. "Well, I'm kind of busy. Tell them I want you to take care of things for me."

Elric tilted his head and crossed his arms. "I already did."

Maribeth snorted. "Did you...already? Well, aren't you the ambitious one?"

"It's my right, as second in command."

"Last I heard, you had resigned. Although I must admit, you certainly seem proper hench for the job," Maribeth added with a wink.

Allie hid her face with her hands for a moment and then put them up for attention. "Look, I can't deal with this right now. Elric, just keep things calm over there for me, please? Clearly we're going to have to make some changes."

"Clearly," he repeated, drolly. "I know what needs to be done. I've been wanting to bring that place to its full potential for years. Quite frankly, having the coven doubt my authority because they're all smitten by some white eyed, bat-winged little girl, who was only turned just shy of yesterday, is pretty insulting."

"Watch it," Kieran interjected over him.

"Your Majesty," Elric added with a facetious little bow and a sidelong glance at Kieran.

Allie accepted his bow with a smirk. "Fine. I'll just have to show them you're acting under my authority then."

"How do you plan to do that?" Elric asked, warily.

Alyson smiled, letting her eyes glaze white and her fangs distend past her parted lips. "Take a guess."

Elric spared a glance towards Latisha. "You can't bite me. I'm marked."

Allie chuckled. "I'm sure you are, you sly dog. But it looks to me like she actually *was* made just shy of yesterday. I'm the United One. You think I can't cross the mark of a newborn?"

Everyone exchanged glances, unsure of her assertion. A powerful vampire might cross the mark of a lesser vampire once it had faded a bit, but a fresh mark was very difficult to cross, if not impossible, no matter how powerful a vampire may be. Elric displayed his aura to show that Latisha's mark on him was very fresh indeed. She'd probably exchanged blood with him less than an hour ago. She was newborn, but Elric had made her strong... Cain found himself quite curious as to whether Alyson could back her claim.

Alyson had no such reservations. "Latisha, why don't you bite his wrist, honey? I'd hate to block you out and spoil your fun for later."

Latisha looked to Elric, to see what he made of the direction. He just uncrossed his arms and held one out for Latisha, while daring Alyson with his gaze to try to act on her boast.

Alyson was undaunted. As Latisha's fangs broke the skin of Elric's wrist, Alyson moved in to embrace him in a flash of speed. She was suddenly upon the huge man, her body levitating to reach his throat, her arms locked over his shoulders, around his neck. She tilted her head and sank her teeth into his vein without a moment's hesitation. Her actions elicited a gasp from the crowd, but none were as surprised as Elric. Latisha continued to drink from his arm, afraid to stop, and be shut out of his mark.

The door to the house opened and Mattie emerged from where he had been keeping Ben inside. He ran across the lawn, but Cain held up a hand to assure him that all was under control. It was only when Alyson wrapped her legs around Elric's waist, that Cain and Mattie came forward to remove her from him. Thankfully, she allowed them to disengage her without causing more of a scene.

Kieran was laughing as Elric tried to keep his feet and failed, finally collapsing to sit on the grass. Latisha knelt next to him, her arms around him as she whispered in his ear.

"You okay big guy?" Kieran asked. Elric just looked up at him with a dazed expression of disbelief. "I told you," Kieran remarked with a shrug.

Mattie looked around at the others, as Cain backed away from him, letting him hold Alyson on his own. Mattie held her protectively, but she was in fine form, if a little giddy from the experience. "Okay, got what you needed?" Mattie asked them all. "I'm taking her inside now."

Kieran lent Elric a hand, as Latisha also helped him to his feet. "Let the coven try to question that," Kieran taunted, with a grin.

Elric's mark was now covered by that of the United One. No one could doubt that he had pledged his loyalty to her, and was acting under her blessing. He gave the crowd a quick nod, making a point to address Cain specifically. "I hope Felicity is all right. Good luck. I've got business to attend to." He took Latisha's hand. "Let' go." Kieran went to speak with them for a moment before they would leave to return to *Kana Susamiş Icin Ev.*

Mattie walked Alyson inside, leaving Cain with Sindy and Maribeth. Elric was surely fit to assume the role the coven master, but Cain was more concerned that someone else might move to try to assert authority of age over the coven at this point. He studied Maribeth for a moment. "You're not going back with them, to be hanging around there, are you?"

She smiled. "I may pop in from time to time, but I don't plan to stay, if that's what you're asking. I'm happy to leave it to Elric. You know I don't like to be tied down with responsibilities."

Cain appreciated her answer, but still uneasy. "Maribeth, where's Drake?"

"Drake?" she asked with a lilt of innocence he knew was only an act. "Oh, you needn't worry about him anytime soon. I decided he wasn't worthy of my affections. What was it you called him, a bit of a git? I have to admit that you were absolutely right, darling."

Cain couldn't help but notice Sindy giving him a curious look over the term of affection. "What did you do?" he asked Maribeth.

Maribeth grinned. "Always want the details, don't you? If you must know, he was foolish enough to allow me to drink from him. I took the opportunity to drain every last drop. He's used his powers of coercion on me for the last time."

Cain knew that for a vampire as old as Drake, such an act would make him vulnerable, but it wouldn't turn him to dust. "Did you kill him?"

"Where would be the fun in that? Let him suffer. While he was defenseless, I plucked those powerful purple eyes right out of his arrogant head."

Sindy gasped. "Oh my God! You plucked his eyes out?"

Maribeth looked rather pleased with herself. "Scooped, actually, with a teaspoon."

"Ew! And he'll have to live like that? They won't grow back, will they?"

"No, but I've got them in safe keeping, in case he comes crawling back on hands and knees, and I'm feeling generous. In the meantime, he can see through reading the minds of others. He'll manage."

Sindy seemed impressed by her audacity. Cain sighed. The last thing he had ever intended to do was supply Sindy with Maribeth for a role model. "Aren't you worried he'll come after you, for revenge?"

"I'm sure he will, eventually. I'm looking forward to it, but he's more pressing matters to deal with first. I handcuffed him to a rather heavy weight, and dumped him in the ocean."

Sindy snickered and raised her eyebrows at Cain. "Wow. And I thought I was scary for an ex-girlfriend."

Maribeth chuckled and then turned to Cain. "That reminds me. Your girl Felicity is quite annoying."

"Isn't she?" Sindy agreed.

Cain saw the vampiresses through cold tones of green and blue as his fangs distended and growl infused his voice. "Don't you dare say a word against her, either of you. I am in no mood for forgiveness. She was mortally wounded last night, and I have spent the past twenty-four hours tending to her. I don't yet know if I've been successful, but I won't have you speaking ill of her regardless."

"I'm sorry for your troubles, dear," Maribeth continued, "but rude is rude."

Cain bared his fangs, but forced himself to remain in calm control. He turned his focus to Sindy, who was watching his reaction to Maribeth intently. "Sindy, would you excuse us for a moment, please? I would very much like to speak with you in private, but I need to clarify a few things for Maribeth first."

Sindy seemed to be rather taken with his display of thinly restrained ire, but nodded. She moved off to speak with Kieran as Elric and Latisha left, leaving Cain alone to deal with Maribeth.

"Maribeth, you will learn to bite your tongue or I'll rip it out, just as you've robbed Drake of his eyes. Is that understood? Because if not, honestly, I think a few years without speech might be a good experience for you."

Maribeth was obviously quite shaken, but she accepted the vicious rebuke with grace. "Well, my apologies then. I can't imagine you've ever defended *my* name with such ferocity. The girl told me that you spoke of me though."

Cain watched her for a moment, to see that she planned to heed his words of warning. "I did. I told her of my life before my change, and though it is my story to tell, you are an inextricable part of it."

"I am, aren't I?" she said with a smile. "Well, I'm curious as to what you might have said. I'd like to keep my tongue, but I must report that she did over step her place a bit," she answered with hesitant caution.

"How so?"

"Would you believe she had the gall to imply that she *knew* me," Maribeth began, flinching when Cain narrowed his eyes at the word *gall*. She dipped her head by way of apology, and continued. "She then suggested that I couldn't leave Drake without seeking your help. If you're going to talk about me, at least have the decency to paint me as the powerful, independent woman you know me to be."

"Tales could never suffice to describe your audacious fortitude. Felicity just tries to see the good in people, and wants to help everyone, even you, apparently."

"Hmmm, wonder where she gets that from?"

"She doesn't know you like I do."

"Obviously."

"If you are quite finished, I have more pressing things to attend to this evening than your sensitivities."

"Actually, there is something I was hoping you might assist me with. Did you know that I have a talent for casting the weather?"

"I did."

She raised her eyebrows with a, "Hmmm," over the fact that he'd never seen fit to tell her. "Well, I've been fostering it for a bit, nothing terribly drastic, but I can make the fog roll in when I please. It's rather moody and dramatic...it suits me. I must admit, it can be very practical on a sunny day, but according to Lorelei, I may be able to call down lightening to strike another vampire, if I've a mind to. That might prove useful if Drake slogs his way back to shore and comes sniffing around again without an appropriate apology."

"Only vampires of extraordinary power can create such a storm as you suggest. Most can't do more than call the clouds. Anyway, I'm afraid that's not my area of expertise."

"No, I suppose it wouldn't be, would it?"

"Do me a favor and keep the knowledge of powers to yourself, please."

"You know I am a lady of discretion." He couldn't help but laugh at her claim, but she continued. "I'm of the mind that power is always strongest when you keep its secrets for yourself."

"Wonderful, thank you."

"Are you sure I can't persuade you to tutor me? I've heard you've become quite a capable mentor, and after all, I did take it upon myself to teach you a thing or two in our time."

The only things she had ever truly taught him were ways in which to betray his wife. Cain fixed her with a bitter stare as he answered. "I don't think so."

She smiled, and mouthed him a small kiss. "No matter. I'll just practice it on my own then. I will learn to call the lightning...you'll see."

"Not around humans, I hope."

"Really Christian, do you think I haven't matured at all since we've parted? I wouldn't electrocute random humans just for target practice. That wouldn't be sporting at all."

"Do you still drink them?"

"Of course, I'm civilized, not stupid. Human blood is far more powerful than that of animals. Besides, why would I want to drink something that tastes like the floor of a barn?"

"Just use caution. I doubt you'll be capable, but I'm quite fond of the woodlands surrounding my home, and the last thing I need is to risk you leveling half of the state forests with lightning strikes and hurricanes."

"Never fear, darling. But is that truly your concern, or are you perhaps worried that we'll have a falling out one evening, and I'll be using the knowledge against you?"

"Maribeth, your nights of holding sway over me are long past. I've a few talents of my own, and the magic of other vampires doesn't work on me."

"Is that so? Well, fortunately not all of my powers of influence are mystical...as you well know," she reminded him with a wink.

He ignored it. "Your friend Lorelei is being hunted, by the way. You might want to stay clear of her, or you'll be losing more than your tongue."

"Really? Well, we're not very good friends, actually. Perhaps if I get bored, I might lend my services to helping hunt her. Could be fun."

Cain narrowed his eyes and shook his head. "Don't get involved, just stay out of the way. I've already spoken for your protection more than you've a right to expect...and I'm not even sure why."

"You're still fond of me, darling, admit it. It's always been plainly apparent to me."

"Or maybe I just don't want the burden of knowing I'm the oldest creature on the earth."

Maribeth squinted at him with a haughty smirk. "Don't taunt a lady with her age, it's rude." She put her hands to his shoulders, leaning in to give him an air kiss at either cheek. He allowed it, standing still and watching her with a stony stare as she backed away. "Ta."

As Maribeth moved off, Cain was distracted by the sound of feminine laughter, a chuckle throaty and seductive. Sindy was reaching up to give Kieran a playfully light tapping smack on the cheek. He didn't seem to mind, and as she took her hand away, he mouthed her a kiss.

It was hard for Cain to tell whether he was just teasing her, or if there was actually something between them. He'd like to pretend he didn't care, but it did irk him more than he'd expected. After a moment, Sindy turned and noticed him watching. She said something to Kieran, and left him to come speak to Cain. He couldn't help but notice that Kieran seemed to be waiting for her.

The sound of a car door closing came from down the road. Maribeth had just entered an expensive, sporty little foreign automobile. Her tires screeched as she sped off down the street. Sindy reached him and commented with a smile. "She's something else, huh?"

Cain looked to her, unamused. "Yes. So are you." She wasn't sure whether to be insulted or pleased by the remark. Let her take it however she'd like. "Do you have time to talk," he asked, with a glance in Kieran's direction, "or are you going to run off on me again?"

Now she was definitely insulted, not that she had a right to be if memory served. "I didn't run off on you," she asserted.

"Really? Because I seem to recall my bed being inexplicably empty for the past month, and when you finally did turn up, you were marked by someone else." Her mark from Arif would have disappeared now that he had turned to dust. Cain couldn't help but wonder if she had replaced it yet with that of another. She remained cloaked, so he couldn't tell.

"I didn't..." she began harshly, but then gave up, with a huff. "Forget it. It's just easier to believe I'm a fickle bitch, right?"

"That's not fair. I am one of the few people who never painted you that way...even when it was true."

He could see that statement break through her defenses. She shuddered and broke eye contact, trying to gather her pride, but opted instead for quiet honesty. "I know," she finally admitted. "I'm sorry, it's complicated."

"So, explain it to me!" She looked like she didn't know where to start. "Ben said you were hurt," he supplied, giving her a quick look-over to see that she seemed to be untroubled. "Are you alright?"

"I'm always alright. Good thing too, because it sounds like *she* needed you." She nodded towards the house, to indicate Felicity. "Finally turned her, huh?"

"No."

"I thought you said it was a mortal wound?"

"It was. I healed her."

Sindy looked as though she must have heard him wrong. He let the statement stand. "Why?" she finally asked. "Isn't something like this just what you've been waiting for?"

The accusation made him feel sick. He suppressed the anger bubbling up inside of him, refusing to let her turn the tables, as though he was the one dooming the relationship he and Sindy had been building. "No, it isn't. I'm not out here to talk about her. I asked about you. Why did you leave me?"

"I didn't *leave* you."

"Then where have you been?" Not that he didn't know, but she should have to explain herself.

She sighed. "Did Allie tell you about Zach?"

"Yes, eventually, although I don't know why you girls felt the need to try and concoct lies about it." She shrugged. "What you did for Alyson was very selfless. You were helping her. Why wouldn't you want me to know that?"

"Because I'm the bad influence who got her drinking in the first place."

Cain chuckled. "Did you think I didn't know that? Do you think I don't know you?" he asked more quietly. "Am I really so difficult to confide in?"

"It just sort of spiraled into a really catastrophic mess."

"I went to the motel to help you with him."

"You did?" She was genuinely surprised to hear it.

"Yes, but you'd already taken off with Arif."

"I didn't *take off* with him," she insisted. "I didn't have a choice. I wanted to stay with you."

"Don't try to tell me that you hadn't been dealing with him all along. I'm trusting...not stupid."

"I know... I was," she admitted in defeat. "I made a deal with the devil, but I tried to get out of it. I wanted to come home to you, I really did, but Arif's guys showed up and forced us into the car."

"Forced you? I thought you left me for him; went to him willingly to try to gain entrance to his coven."

"That was the plan, but it wasn't what I wanted...not anymore. I went to him years ago, after I'd left you on New Year's Eve. I felt like you didn't want me and you were shoving me off on the Crimson Coven, so I bolted. I figured if I was going to join a coven, I might as well get more out of it than living as a wolf in the woods; I can do that by myself. I went to Arif for a position of power, and keeping tabs on Allie was the way to get it.

I agreed to try to get her to go to his compound with me, but I didn't know what was going on. I'd never even heard of The United One. I didn't know Allie was anyone special, or what Arif was going to do with her. I was just looking for an easy way into *Kana Susamiş İçin Ev*.

Granted, I knew things were shady, but I had no idea there was like, large scale evil afoot. Maybe I should have guessed. Maybe it doesn't matter. I wasn't honest with you guys, and I was stuck having to screw over the only true friends I've ever had...but in the end, I didn't do it, I couldn't. The feelings I had for you...and for Allie and Mattie, they weren't an act, they were real, and I didn't want to betray them. I refused to help him, I swear. I wasn't playing you Cain."

"You refused? Arif can't have been very happy about that."

"No, and I've got the scars to prove it...until I can finally shift shape and get rid of them."

"Scars?"

She stared at him stonily for a second before adding, "I'm not going to show them off if you don't mind. You'll just have to take my word for it."

"You were really being held at Arif's compound all of this time, against your will?" Cain asked, horrified.

Sindy shrugged. "I made my bed, and I had to lay in it...even if it did turn out to be a bed of stakes...or, toothpicks actually. I'm still pulling fucking cellophane out of my skin."

"Cellophane?" he asked, thoroughly confused. Finally, he decided it didn't matter. He'd get the details later. Right now, she needed to know that he hadn't abandoned her. "I had no idea. I thought...I thought you'd chosen him over me."

"Ha! He wished! Prick even kept me chained to his bed for a while. You'd think after 200 years, a guy could learn to take 'no' for an answer."

"Oh my God! I didn't know. Sindy, I would never have allowed that to go on. I went looking for you. I followed your trail. I thought it was your choice to be there. I thought you had betrayed me and were trying to play on my sympathies. If I had known you really had been abducted, I would have come for you."

"You would have?" she actually looked as though she wasn't sure.

"Of course! I would have broken down the gates and demanded your release immediately. I wouldn't just leave you there! I love you."

She'd never let him say it before; he'd tried. He still wasn't certain if they had a future together, but there was no denying that in his heart, he did love her. She didn't give him her normal reprimand not to speak about his feelings that way. He knew she'd always stopped him because she was afraid to say it back, although he didn't know if she honestly couldn't, or just wouldn't. She looked as though she wasn't sure what to do. After a moment, she gave up trying to find the appropriate response, and kissed him.

He wasn't sure if it meant something profound to her, or just seemed to be right in the moment, but it was passionate enough that he didn't care. When the kiss finally ended, she looked up at him with a smile. "Wow...that is a kiss I am going to miss..."

She was leaving him after all. After all the time it had taken them to build something real out of the chaos of their interactions over all these years. When she hadn't been here to greet him last night, he had thought he may not see her again, and hadn't been sure how to feel about her leaving, but faced with her now, he couldn't say he wasn't disappointed. "So, stay and I'll give you another."

"It was real, you know...what I felt for you. It wasn't just an act that I was putting on, to gain your trust and get closer to Allie. What we had was real."

"I know it is," he agreed, forcing her to acknowledge that he was using the present tense. "I didn't think I could have read you that wrongly."

She smiled. "I'm not going to stay, though."

"Why? Our hearts found a good place together for a little while, didn't they? You let me in."

He worried she might become defensive about letting her guard down, but she smiled. "Remember the day that..." After a brief pause, she shook her hair, letting it momentarily mist and resolidify in a light brown color. Apparently, she had decided it was easier to show him the memory than to describe it.

He remembered the day well; how he had convinced her to allow herself to be Sindy from a different time, before the artifice of her dark and dangerous Goth persona. They had spent the whole day in bed just being two loving people without expectations, roles or worries outside the room. "How could I forget?" he asked her with a quiet smile. "That was a good day."

"That was a really good day," she agreed. "It was a little scary though." He gave her a questioning look. "It was like, only by pretending to be someone else could I let myself see who I might really be inside. It started out feeling like pretend, but after a while, I stopped trying to play a part and it was...sort of real. That was a little frightening. I wouldn't trade it though. It was a great day."

Cain gave her a reassuring nod that he understood. "It's only when we allow ourselves to be a little scared, that we leave comfort zones to stretch and grow. I didn't want you to pretend to be someone else. I just wanted you to know that you can be whoever you want to be." She gave him a grateful little nod. "So, who do you want to be?"

"Who do I want to *be*, or who do I want to be with?"

"Well, I know there was a time when you very much seemed to want me, until you actually got me, that is."

She shook her head. "I may be leaving, but I never stopped *wanting* you," she assured him, giving his body an appreciative appraisal. Her gaze finally landed to meet his own and she gave him a smirk of a smile... "Damn, I'm going to miss having you in bed! You're hot as hell," she told him accusingly.

He lowered his eyes with a little chuckle as she continued. "You're powerful, old and strong, and you know what you want to do with your life. You don't give up on your goals, no matter how hard it is. You fight for what you know is right, and you don't push other people down to get what you want. I've never met anyone like that. Who knew *I'd* find true chivalry so sexy?

I wanted you. It started simple like that, and I never suspected it was going to grow into something more. I thought your age and your strength made you a man I should be seen with, not to mention the stunning good looks," she added with a grin. "If I could be with you, maybe it'd show the world I was worth something. That was *my* goal. You were trying to save the world, but…I thought it was all about the show.

Make yourself attractive, have nice things, and show the world how great your life is, so everyone wishes they were you. My parents were all about the show, and boy did they have a good one," Sindy admitted with disgust. "Deserved an Emmy for what they put on. Mom was the happy housewife. Dad was the stand-up family man, devoted husband and doting father." Sindy gagged with a huff of disdain. "Really, she was wasted most of the time, and he…he'd better be in a special place in Hell for the things he did to me."

Cain would have pulled her in for a hug, but she wouldn't come. She wasn't finished. "I thought everyone was like that, though. Bright candy colored shell, with a dark gooey mess inside. I don't think I ever believed that anyone was really *happy*. I don't think I believed in love. So how could I love you?" She said it in a tearful whisper that was almost accusing. "It's all your fault; you made me believe in real love. You made me feel it, but I also felt what it was lacking. I know I'm not who you want me to be…and now I know what I'm missing.

You do love me. I know you do. You showed me what it is to have someone care and sacrifice for you, without resentment or regret. You wanted to make it real for me. You taught me that I deserve for it to be real. But the thing is, no matter how much you love me, I know you love *her* more." She didn't even need to glance towards the house for him to know that she meant Felicity…and he knew it was true. "So it's still a show, isn't it? You really did try, I'll give you that," she told him with a smile. "And don't think I didn't enjoy it. But we both know that as much as you might love me, I'll never be her. And as much as I love being with you, I know now, that I deserve better than to be second choice."

Cain was surprised to find tears in his eyes. What could he say? They both knew it was true. He nodded, cupping his hand to her cheek. "I was out on the grounds round my house the other night, and I came across this lovely little secluded garden. Would you know anything about that?"

She gave him a guilty grin. "I was working on it. I wanted to surprise you."

"You do surprise me...often and in many ways. I love it. The garden is beautiful, such a thoughtful gesture."

She shook her head in regret. "There just wasn't enough time."

"There are some terrible drawbacks to being a vampire, but one thing we always seem to have in plenty, is time. There's time." He wasn't necessarily talking about the garden any more, and she knew it.

"No, there isn't. Back when we first met, maybe things could have been different, but now? There isn't enough time in existence to erase the feelings you have for her. I know it's true. So no matter how long I wait, it won't be long enough." She sniffed back her impending tears and held her head a little higher. "And honestly, I've got better things to do than wait around for a guy who's never going to love me more than he loves someone else."

He gave her a nod of acceptance. He'd miss her, but he was also happy that she had finally come to feel that way about herself. "My loss then."

She smiled, tilting her shoulder back in an attitude of self-importance. "Yeah, it is."

He laughed. "Will you be okay?"

"I'll be fine." She glanced back to where Kieran was discreetly waiting for her. "In fact, someone owes me one hell of a good time."

"I see. Well, I suppose he really is more your speed. Have you marked each other yet?"

She looked at him quizzically, unsure why he should ask, or care. "No."

"Good. I'm going to have to prevent that, aren't I?"

"What? You can't tell me who to share blood with. That's part of the whole breaking up thing...it's none of your business!"

He let his eyes glaze over golden, and came closer, undaunted. "Zach had white eyes, didn't he?"

She tried to follow his line of thought, suddenly alarmed to realize where he was going with this. "Well, yeah, but..."

"You know I can't let you pass that blood to another. One is enough." He didn't give her any time to protest or make promises. She had the blood of the United One within her, and it could not be shared, at any cost. There were already enough problems to deal with, and until they could decide how they should handle things, the spread of United blood had to be contained.

He grasped her shoulders strongly and went for her throat. She struggled, but he was sure to dampen her powers so that she couldn't turn to mist to escape him. It didn't take much to subdue her. He'd broken her skin so quickly that she was marked by him before she could prevent it. Fighting him might mean getting away with a weaker mark, but the damage was already done. She decided instead to stay and enjoy it.

Good, because he was hoping to give her enough venom to last a long while. Once she escaped him, it might take some doing to find her again and renew it. It felt wonderful to embrace her, laying claim upon her again, even if she would no longer be his. He felt guilty for marking her against all others, but it had to be done. Sindy enjoyed being drunk from by her lovers...who didn't? He could not allow the blood of the United One to be transferred and possibly be passed on to create another.

Sindy swooned, cleaving to him and forcing his body to acknowledge what he would be missing in letting her go. He withdrew his fangs to take a sweet taste of her delectable blood before turning her loose. Finally, he kissed the bite at her throat and gave her freedom to stand apart, although she was rather unsteady.

He saw that Kieran had approached, and was standing a few paces away. He did not look happy. He didn't say anything though. He may not understand Cain's motive for marking her, but Cain's authority of age and power was something he was smart enough not to challenge. Cain helped Sindy into Kieran's arms, since she seemed to be having a hard time standing on her own.

"Sorry, mate," Cain told him. "You can have her body and her heart, if she decides to grace you with them, but I'm afraid her blood is mine."

Kieran didn't respond, and frankly seemed flabbergasted over the whole display, but Cain didn't wait for any more of a reaction. He just turned and left them, to make his way back up the drive to the house.

Cain re-entered to find Ben standing right in the front foyer, glaring at him. Cain closed the door behind himself. He could see Mattie and Alyson sitting sedately on the couch in the living room, but Ben didn't move to allow him any further into the house. "You do that shit right in the street? Really?"

Alyson called from the living room, "Let him in Ben."

Ben moved aside and Cain joined the others in the living room. Ben followed behind, unfinished. "Just, right out in the middle of the street? I almost expected that kind of crap from her," he said with a wave of his hand towards Allie, "but I thought you were supposed to have a little class."

"Hey!" Alyson protested.

"I have neighbors. I have to live here!"

"He's right," Cain acceded. "My apologies, but it was unavoidable."

"Whatever," Ben said, throwing his hands up. "You guys are never being invited back here...ever."

Alyson let out a gasp, making Ben turn to her. "Can you blame me?"

She shook her head with wide eyes. "It's not that, I know you were just being sarcastic." Her gasp hadn't been in response him at all. "Felicity!"

She took off for the bedroom in a streak of motion so fast, she may as well have disappeared. She was gone before the men even had a chance to decipher her meaning, but it was only a second before they all ran to follow.

Cain and Ben reached the bedroom doorway at the same time. After a brief second, Cain backed up a step to allow him to enter first. Felicity still lay in the bed, seeming unresponsive as ever. Alyson sat cross-legged, on the floor next to the bed.

Ben rushed to Felicity's side, sitting on the bed next to her. "Liss?" When there was no response, he turned to Allie. "Is she okay?" Alyson nodded, seeming to be in deep concentration. "Tell her I'm here," Ben asked, with desperate excitement. "Tell her I'm with her, and that I never gave up on her." Alyson never opened her eyes, obviously focused, and loathe to speak. "Tell her..."

"Ben, please!" Allie interrupted him. "We're not up to that yet, okay?"

"What do you mean?"

Alyson opened her eyes to focus on Ben with a sigh. "I can't just talk to her. I've got barely a glimmer here. I'm working on it. Right now, I'm dealing with basics... You know, 'Don't go into the light' type stuff. When she's up to more, I'll let you know."

Ben eyes were wide with awe and worry. "Okay, I'm sorry. Do your thing."

Mattie came in and sat down on the chaise. Cain had decided to remain in the doorway, unobtrusive, for now. Ben watched Allie and Felicity for a moment, and then left the bed to question Cain. "She has a mark from you now?"

Cain answered reluctantly. "Yes, she's marked by me."

"You can see it right?" Ben asked. Cain nodded. "What does it look like?"

Cain couldn't imagine how he could explain. He allowed himself to focus on her, lying there, motionless, Sleeping Beauty incarnate. "It looks... It looks good Ben; strong, human." Ben let out a loud sigh of relief. "I think she'll be okay."

Allie spoke, her quiet voice demanding their immediate attention. "She can feel you." She opened her eyes to stare directly at Cain, still hovering in the doorway. Ben's face showed that he distinctly had mixed feelings over the announcement, but ultimately he seemed to decide that he was happy just to hear that she could feel or react to anything.

"Cain, come in and hold her hand." Alyson couldn't help but notice the look of hurt in Ben's eyes as she made the request. "Ben, she can feel the mark. It's grounding her. I'm hoping if it's paired with the physical sensation, it might be enough to pull her out of the murkiness she's in and wake her up."

"Sure," Ben acknowledged, graciously, giving Cain a wave towards the bed. "Go ahead."

Cain entered the room, keenly aware of everyone's eyes on him, but as soon as he approached the bed and laid eyes upon Felicity once more, it was as though the others no longer existed. He sat down next to her, and after a brief pause of anticipation, he took her hand into both of his own. Her skin was soft, warm and charged with the magical sensation of their shared bond, his mark upon her, claiming her as his own. She wasn't his, not according to the world, but his blood definitely felt differently.

Felicity visibly trembled a bit at his touch. A small gasp escaped her lips and after a moment, he felt slight pressure in his hand as her fingers clasped tighter to his. An irrepressible smile spread across his face. Whether she had remained human, become a vampire, or even awakened as something in between, she was Felicity. He loved her and he would never desert her.

He had spoken truly to Ben, though. Judging by her mark, she was still human, completely. He could only hope that she had come through her ordeal without any lasting damage.

"It's working," Alyson reported for the others. "She's thinking with some clarity now. I think she's okay! She's waking up."

Ben and Mattie came closer to the bed with Alyson's words. Just as Cain felt the others begin to crowd around him, Felicity opened her eyes. With beautiful, human, hazel green eyes, she met his gaze and held it for a moment, focusing, trying to process being in the world once more.

Then, the moment passed. Ben was at her side, pressing in to see her, Mattie leaned in to determine her state and Alyson rose from the floor to be next to her as well. Cain let her fingers slip from his hand as he slipped back through the others and left them to her. He returned to his place in the doorway, satisfied just to know that she was no longer lost.

"Liss? Oh God, Liss, you're awake. I was so worried. I was out of my mind thinking I'd lost you."

"Hi," she replied meekly, in a soft whisper, to display her awareness.

Ben laughed in relief and leaned down to hold her. "Hi baby. Are you okay?" he asked, straightening up again as though afraid to hurt her.

"I think so."

"You were badly hurt but we rescued you. You gave us an awful scare, but Alyson and Cain healed you."

She was quiet for a moment, reflecting on the information. "Yes. I know they did," she said with a grateful glance at Alyson. "Where is Cain?"

Felicity couldn't see him from the bed. Everyone was in the way. Ben answered for him, before Cain could even speak. "He's here. We've all been here, watching over you. Thank God you're okay."

Cain sighed and backed out into the hall. She was overwhelmed, he was sure. Let things calm down. Let Ben fuss over her and give her his hugs and kisses. She was alright. That was all he really needed to know. There would be time for him to speak with her later if she wanted. As he'd told Sindy, time was the one thing he always seemed to have in plenty.

He went out the back, onto the deck to lean over the rail, looking out over the ocean. It really was a beautiful sight. He'd always preferred the forest to the beach, but the brisk salt air was invigorating, and the soothing sound of the ocean waves lent a serenity that could not be denied.

Cain closed his eyes, clearing his mind and letting his surroundings carry his thoughts away from worries and responsibilities. Felicity was alright, and that was knowledge to sustain him. Other anxieties and strategies for the future could wait for tomorrow. Tonight was for him to revel in relief for Felicity.

Things may not be exactly as he'd like them, but he knew that it was okay. It was good. The warm and gentle current of happiness and love he felt surrounding him was something he could hardly understand, but could not deny. He felt better than he might have imagined, even though he was going to have to leave her here with her human family; it felt right.

Cain? The telepathic thought caressed his mind like a whisper breathed against his cheek. It brought with it a shiver of delight and intimacy unlike any other... It wasn't Alyson. Cain froze, sudden realization forcing him to recognize the warm and loving sensations he'd been experiencing to be influenced from afar, not originating as feelings of his own. Again, the feminine voice spoke in his mind... *Thank you.*

It was Felicity.

Chapter 23 - Divinity

Allie

Kana Susamiş Icin Ev
Montauk, Long Island, New York
A few nights later

Mattie took his arms from their hold around Alyson's neck as they lightly touched down to land on the roof of the common house in *Kana Susamiş Icin Ev,* the coven compound formerly owned and run by the vampire Arif. Allie couldn't help but smile and nod as she read Mattie's awe over the size and scope of the place, and the mansion across the road before them.

Their approach from the air had been spotted and tracked by many of the compound's residents. After Alyson's last visit, keeping a low profile didn't seem to be an option. A crowd had gathered surrounding the building, which was why she had opted to land on the roof, as she had last time, rather than in the street. As they looked over the crowd, the vampires before them all sank to their knees and bowed their heads.

Mattie was immediately uncomfortable with the scenario. "They're bowing," he whispered incredulously. "Why are they bowing? Tell them to stop that."

Allie giggled. "Why? I kind of like it." She addressed the crowd, after Mattie gave her a look of derision and a shove. "Please, rise."

As they hesitantly raised their heads and got to their feet, Mattie spoke to them as well. "You don't have to do that. There are no masters here, remember?" He gave Allie a sidelong glance of reminder as well. "We're all brothers and sisters of the same species, even if not the same breed."

They all listened to Mattie, respectfully, as consort to The United One, but then immediately looked to Allie to see what she would say about it. She couldn't help but grin as they awaited her words with baited breath. "He's right, but I am honored by your deference, and grateful that you look to me to lead you." They seemed pleased by her response. She could tell

Mattie was trying to squash an overwhelming urge to roll his eyes. *Don't you dare,* she warned him.

"The vampire Arif refused to acknowledge my divine authority, and instead sought to control me, so he is no longer among us. As I said before, I do not seek to master you, but only to advise and guide our kind towards a proud and prosperous future. Those who deny my authority to lead are welcome to leave, but I urge you all to stay. There are changes in store for our kind, and those who accept my teachings will surely be better for it.

I have reinstated Elric as Senior Advisor here, and I thank you for accepting him. He is truly capable of acting on my behalf in matters of practical change and operation of this community. I'll be meeting with him now, to ensure all is well here. Please, carry on with your evening and rest assured that I plan to oversee the well being of all who reside here."

With that, she put her arms around Mattie and held him as they lightly jumped down to the ground. The crowd parted for them, and they walked across the street, up to the entrance of Arif's magnificent home. She could see and feel her mark upon Elric coming from somewhere within the enormous house. There was a vampire stationed as a guard just inside the door, but he immediately became flustered and bowed his head when he recognized who it was that had entered.

Allie watched him for a second with a grin. "Hi."

The vampire was clearly at a loss as to how he should address her. Finally, he gathered himself to nod to her formally. "Good evening, honored United One."

She smiled in approval, nodded her head, took Mattie by the arm and walked further inside the house. Mattie turned to her, curiously. "Don't you want to ask him to call Elric, or tell us where we should go?"

She shook her head. "Na, I can find him. He's on this level," she told him, after assessing her mark upon the man. "That way." She followed her senses until she found the door to what must have once been Arif's personal office. She didn't bother to knock, but just opened it, to find Elric consulting with a handful of others vampires within.

He must have felt her coming. He was sitting back in his chair behind an enormous desk, and although it was covered in paperwork and everyone was gathered around, no one was speaking as she and Mattie entered. Apparently, he had asked them to pause for her arrival. "Good evening," Elric greeted her. "What a lovely and unexpected surprise."

Allie smirked at him, knowing he was referring to the fact that she hadn't bothered to try to contact him for an appointment...or even knock.

"I'm sure you're really busy, but you've got a little time for us to chat, don't you?"

Before he could even answer, the other vampires immediately rose and left the room, dipping their heads and muttering things like "Please excuse us," and "Anything you need." Elric did not look thrilled, but Allie just smiled and telekinetically shut the door behind the last one. The small display of her power wasn't lost on Elric, who was taken a bit by surprise. He'd obviously never seen that trick before.

Allie went to sit in a large chair before the desk, slumping down and making herself comfortable. She looked around at the lushly appointed office as Mattie took a seat in the chair next to her. "Nice place. All moved in already, huh?" she asked Elric.

"Not exactly," he corrected her. "I'm going through his paperwork to see what needs to be put in order. We're paying off the humans who want to leave, and renegotiating terms and assignments for those who wish to stay, among other things."

"Oh. Paperwork isn't really my thing so...keep at it," she told him, with an enthusiastic thumbs up. Elric looked as though he wasn't sure whether to be annoyed or burst into laughter.

He hid his face with his hand, which he then rubbed up over his head with a sigh. "I live in the house next door. You overthrew and dusted Arif. To the victor go the spoils, so technically, this place is yours now, if you want it."

Alyson sat up straighter in shock, looking around again with wide eyes. "Mine? *If* I want it?" She met his eyes again for a moment, before adding, "I live in a trailer."

Mattie turned to her, insulted. "It's a luxury motor coach."

She met his gaze with a look of droll disbelief over his affection for the thing. "Seriously? It's cute, but it's been totally trashed by Zach, and..." she emphatically spread her hands for him to take a look around.

"Actually, I was the one who broke all the windows," Mattie corrected her quietly.

"Then you can fix 'em. I'm moving in here," she told him with a chuckle. After a second, she reassured him that she was teasing. "Look, we can keep the R.V., but you've got to admit, this place is pretty damn sweet."

Elric crossed his arms, assessing their demeanor. "You'll be staying then."

She read Mattie for a moment before answering. "Not permanently. You can run the show. Just save us a bedroom, 'kay? We'll just stop in from time to time and hang out for a while. How's that sound?"

Elric nodded with a smile. "Sounds perfect. I hope you have a few nights to spend now though. I could use your unique abilities to help with a few things."

"Like what?" Mattie asked.

Alyson interjected before Elric could answer though. "We should really be getting back to Cain." She wasn't exactly looking forward to being roped into doing any actual work right now. She just fought a bunch of vampires and brought a woman back from the brink of death! Didn't she deserve a vacation?

"You didn't bring him?" Elric asked. "I'd hoped we could talk."

"He...had to get back home. He had people waiting on him," Allie explained. Dawn and the Crimson Coven would be happy to see Cain, surely, but really, she knew he had just wanted to go home to be left alone for a while after everything.

Elric knew it too. "Well, I hope all is well with him and he'll come when he can. How is Felicity?"

"She's fine. Great, actually. We were able to heal her."

Elric nodded as Mattie changed the subject. "So, what did you need help with? You seem to have everything under control here."

"Just about, but I'm afraid there are some things I really need Alyson to handle. Arif kept a small group of children."

"Children?" Mattie asked in shock.

"To be turned. Some are only babies. The older ones have been brainwashed to forget their former identities and believe only in Arif's teachings and ideals. He was raising them to be vessels for the blood of The United One. We'd like to reintroduce them back into society, but I'm afraid we can't put them into the hands of humans as they are now."

Alyson was staring at him in dread. "Well what do you expect me to do with them?" The sudden flash of thoughts and ideas coming from Mattie was even more frightening than anything she could imagine Elric had in mind. The idea of raising children...being a father, was something that Mattie had always mourned as an opportunity snatched from him with his humanity. The thought of children unexpectedly needing him and Allie for care and guidance was very appealing to him. *Are you insane? No. I'm sorry baby, but no. I realize the idea of playing house and having a family strikes an emotional chord for you, but I have too much on my plate as it is. I'm not exactly feeling like mommy material right now...or maybe ever.*

Elric had obviously recognized that she and Mattie were having a private conference, and stayed respectfully quiet for a moment, as Mattie gazed at her in disappointment. *I guess you're right. We'll never be able to have that, will we?*

She took a second to show him that she was actually thinking about it before answering. *Look, I'm not going to say never. Maybe someday we'll be in a position where we could dedicate ourselves to caring for a child...maybe. But if that night ever comes, it will be a super long time from now, so let's not get ahead of ourselves, okay?*

Mattie smiled as Elric cleared his throat for their attention. "If I may? Alyson, you are the only telepath we have access to at the moment. We need you to work with these children; have regular sessions with each one, to try to eradicate whatever harmful directives Arif might have instilled in them, and try to help their human memories resurface. Help them to remember their names so we can get them back to their families. Help them to readjust to the idea of having a stable, normal human childhood. Police can fingerprint them and try to figure out where they go, but only you can make sure they have a chance at being emotionally stable when they get there."

Allie sighed. "I don't even like kids," she asserted, uselessly. "Why does everybody always want me to be the freakin' baby-whisperer?"

Mattie gave her a nudge and answered Elric with a smile. "She'll be happy to help."

Elric gave her a tight grin. "Great. One more thing."

"What's your other problem?" she asked with a roll of her eyes.

"The dogs."

"Dogs?" she and Mattie both asked in surprise.

"Yes, the guard dogs, Dobermans, we have quite a large pack of them."

"So?"

"They were Arif's. They had a very close bond, and they're rather upset over his demise. The only other vampire they had a good rapport with was Lorelei, and she knows better than to show her face here any time soon."

"Okay, so you'll need to retrain them. The *Dog Whisperer* actually is a real thing. You can call him."

Elric laughed. "If only it were that simple. Some of them will manage to get over it I'm sure, but the trouble is, they aren't normal dogs. Arif raised them, feeding them rations of his blood, you see. That is why they had such a strong bond. It's helped to boost their empathetic awareness and some of them have even become telepathic."

"Are you shitting me?"

Elric seemed amused by her response. "I'm afraid not. Perhaps a few sessions with them might be effective as well. Although, I worry that Katil, the nasty alpha bitch of the pack, will never get over Lorelei's absence and Arif's loss enough to be handled by anyone else. She is smart, telepathic, and can be rather vicious to those she doesn't like. We may have to put her down."

Allie was thoughtful. "A telepathic dog, huh?" She gave Mattie a curious glance. *I am definitely not ready for motherhood, but a dog, I think we can handle. What do you say?*

A nasty telepathic dog? Bad enough I have you snapping at me when you don't get your way. When I said I'd like to start a family, adopting a vicious bitch wasn't exactly what I had in mind.

Allie tried to reason with him over it. *I'll bet she's not really vicious. Maybe she's just misunderstood. She's smart and gifted. She probably just doesn't have patience for stupid people.*

Great, she sounds just like you...just what I need. Mattie sighed. "I guess we can meet her," he told Elric. "Maybe we'll be able to take her off your hands." Both Elric and Allie grinned at the tentative offer.

"Wonderful, I really appreciate your help," Elric told them.

So, just as Allie had feared, they were roped into staying for a while. Not that she was at all unhappy with the accommodations, but she hated not feeling free to leave. Mattie, however, had impressed upon her that they could not, in good conscience, go back to see Cain until everything could be sorted out with the children. It may take a while, but he would not be content to take a break from responsibility until each child was placed safely into the hands of human authorities; another aspect of the situation that Alyson was going to have to handle. She was going to have to come up with a good story, and brainwash the cops into believing it, when she suddenly dumped a bunch of long missing children into their laps.

There were plenty of details to be arranged, but for now, Elric suggested they go and take a tour of the kennels. As they left the mansion, Allie and Mattie couldn't help but be very surprised to see a familiar pair walking up the roads towards them.

Sindy and Kieran were approaching, but hadn't seen them. They paused at a bench on the side of the path. Alyson convinced Mattie to stay back and let her eavesdrop before encountering them. "Just for a minute," Sindy was saying, to Kieran's apparent annoyance. "You'll have to forgive me if I'm having an anxiety attack," she told him, snidely. "Don't forget that I spent the past month trying to figure out how to escape this place. I can't believe you are dragging me back here."

"I told you, Elric has reinstated me and I want to check in at my house. I have to make sure they haven't been giving my stuff away and auctioning off my harem."

"We're here for your harem?" she asked in disbelief.

"Well, yeah. I went through a lot of trouble to establish a routine with those girls. I don't want to have to start from scratch."

Sindy was squinting at him in disbelief. "You can't be serious! Do you really think Allie is going to let that kind of thing continue to go on around here?"

"She'd have a hell of a time trying to stop it. As long as no one is being tortured and killed, I don't think Allie gives a shit what we do. She's got bigger things to worry about. Besides, this place actually has a very elegant, respectable and resourceful feeding system going on here. I'm sure the reform cellar will be abolished, but other than that, it only needs minor refinement, don't you think?"

"Well...yeah, I've always thought so, but... Sorry, I'm not used to being one of the good guys. I don't really know what I'm supposed to condemn or condone. It's kind of confusing new territory."

He laughed at her, shaking his head. "You don't have to be a good guy...or a bad guy. Why don't you just be yourself and see what happens?"

She chuckled. "That seems to be the theme people are pushing at me lately. I don't know if that's going to work for me though. I have a feeling that being myself is bound to put me on the dark side."

"You may get a little murky sometimes, but baby, I've seen dark, and you ain't it. You're allowed to have some fun, and believe me, I can show you fun," he added with a wink. "You can keep your humans too, if you want 'em. Brett and Val, right? You can even pick out a few more to keep things even. I don't mind."

For all the outrage she had been trying to portray a moment ago, Allie could tell that Sindy was suddenly finding the idea a bit more appealing. "Okay, I'm interested, but what are we going to do with them all? I am not movin' in here, even without Arif. I think I've had my fill for now. I don't like to be tied down."

"That's not what I've heard," Kieran said with a smirk. "Don't tell me Arif has spoiled bondage for you. That would be a shame."

She humored him with a coy smile, and went on without addressing the comment. "I was thinking we'd hit the road. You told me we could travel."

"Sure we can, what's the problem? I'll set our humans up all comfy cozy, and we'll go do whatever you want. That way, they'll be here safely marked, ready and waiting for us whenever we're in the mood for some company."

"Set them up how? Do you have any idea what it'd cost to take care of a dozen people indefinitely? I don't know how this place'll float without Arif footing the bill, but I certainly can't afford to be anybody's sugar-mama!"

"Relax," he told her with a laugh. "I've got you covered."

"And where are you going to get the money from? Steal it? Won't that take an annoying amount of ongoing time and effort?"

"First of all, you'd be surprised what I could pull in with one heist. I don't waste my time with petty stuff. I know what I'm doing. Second of all, I haven't even bothered to steal for the money in years. I only take stuff I actually want. Arif has been paying me a nice salary since 1969, for Pete's sake."

"Okay, but that ride is over. You can't have that much in the bank. Didn't you spend what he gave you?"

"On what? He already set me up with a mansion full of hotties that *he* supported. What did I need money for? Fancy clothes? As a shifter, you know clothes are really just a pain in the ass. I spend half my time as a freakin' ghost, what do I need clothing for? Fancy cars? I can dig it, but what do I need a car for, when I can fly? If I feel like taking a spin in a sweet machine for a spell, I just borrow someone else's. I'm a master thief, remember? What do I need to buy that I can't just take? Money doesn't mean anything to me anymore. I have access to anything I can think of with just a snap of my fingers and a puff of smoke. What more could I possibly want that I don't already have?"

Sindy shrugged, and then came up with the answer. "Something fun to do?"

Kieran gave her a broad grin. "Exactly, and I have a feeling that you my dear, are going to be very fun to do."

She looked him over for a moment and then stood from the bench with a sly smile. "We'll see."

As Alyson took Mattie by the arm and came closer to the pair, Kieran became aware of her approach. He smiled and gave her a gentlemanly bow. "My liege. I knew I was feeling the enjoyable sensations of your divine proximity."

Mattie shook his head as Alyson allowed Kieran to take her hand for a brief kiss. "You are really going to have to stop this subservient shit. It makes me nauseous," Mattie told him.

Sindy raised her hand with a scowl. "I'll second that."

Kieran stood and released Allie's hand, unapologetic. "She is The United One. Maybe you all think it's a big joke, but I show respect where respect is due. And you, my divine royal highness, have earned my utmost respect." He looked around to see Mattie and Sindy both looking at him as though he was being ridiculous. "Come on, you guys have to admit, she is fucking amazing, isn't she?"

Mattie grinned. "Oh, she is amazing alright. There is definitely something incredibly sexy about a strong woman in control. When that woman is Alyson, it can also be damn scary."

Kieran grinned. "All hail the Queen."

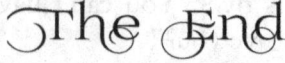

The End

~~~~~~~~~~~~~~~~~~~~~~~~~~~~~~~

PLEASE LOOK FOR FUTURE ADVENTURES

IN

ALMOST HUMAN

THE THIRD TRILOGY

~~~~~~~~~~~~~~~~~~~~~~~~~~~~~~~

If you enjoyed this book, please take a moment to leave a review online,
on your favorite book review website!

You can join author/reader discussions about the series,
and get updates on upcoming book releases for this series
on the author's web site at: www.MelanieNowak.com

www.ingramcontent.com/pod-product-compliance
Lightning Source LLC
Chambersburg PA
CBHW010252030726
47497CB00010BA/3182